A century before the term "crossover" became a buzzword in popular culture, Edgar Rice Burroughs created the first expansive, fully cohesive literary universe. Coexisting in this vast cosmos was a pantheon of immortal heroes and heroines—Tarzan of the Apes™, Jane Porter®, John Carter®, Dejah Thoris®, Carson Napier™, and David Innes™ being only the best known among them. In Burroughs' 80-plus novels, their epic adventures transported them to the strange and exotic worlds of Barsoom®, Amtor™, Pellucidar®, Caspak™, and Va-nah™, as well as the lost civilizations of Earth and even realms beyond the farthest star. Now the Edgar Rice Burroughs Universe expands in both new definitive editions of Burroughs' classic works and an adventure-filled series of canonical novels written by today's talented authors!

EDGAR RICE BURROUGHS UNIVERSE™

COSMIC EPICS

THE SEMINAL WORKS OF EDGAR RICE BURROUGHS

EDGAR RICE BURROUGHS UNIVERSE™

The Edgar Rice Burroughs Universe is the interconnected and cohesive literary cosmos created by the Master of Adventure and continued in new canonical works authorized by Edgar Rice Burroughs, Inc., the corporation based in Tarzana, California, that was founded by Burroughs in 1923. Unravel the mysteries and explore the wonders of the Edgar Rice Burroughs Universe alongside the pantheon of heroes and heroines that inhabit it in both classic tales of adventure penned by Burroughs and brand-new epics from today's talented authors.

TARZAN® SERIES
Tarzan of the Apes
The Return of Tarzan
The Beasts of Tarzan
The Son of Tarzan
Tarzan and the Jewels of Opar
Jungle Tales of Tarzan
Tarzan the Untamed
Tarzan the Terrible
Tarzan and the Golden Lion
Tarzan and the Ant Men
Tarzan, Lord of the Jungle
Tarzan and the Lost Empire
Tarzan at the Earth's Core
Tarzan the Invincible
Tarzan Triumphant
Tarzan and the City of Gold
Tarzan and the Lion Man
Tarzan and the Leopard Men
Tarzan's Quest
Tarzan and the Forbidden City
Tarzan the Magnificent
Tarzan and "The Foreign Legion"
Tarzan and the Madman
Tarzan and the Castaways
Tarzan and the Tarzan Twins
Tarzan: The Lost Adventure (with Joe R. Lansdale)

BARSOOM® SERIES
A Princess of Mars
The Gods of Mars
The Warlord of Mars
Thuvia, Maid of Mars
The Chessmen of Mars
The Master Mind of Mars
A Fighting Man of Mars
Swords of Mars
Synthetic Men of Mars
Llana of Gathol
John Carter of Mars

PELLUCIDAR® SERIES
At the Earth's Core
Pellucidar
Tanar of Pellucidar
Tarzan at the Earth's Core
Back to the Stone Age
Land of Terror
Savage Pellucidar

AMTOR™ SERIES
Pirates of Venus
Lost on Venus
Carson of Venus
Escape on Venus
The Wizard of Venus

ERBUniverse.com

ERB UNIVERSE™

SWORDS OF ETERNITY SUPER-ARC

Carson of Venus: The Edge of All Worlds
by Matt Betts

Tarzan: Battle for Pellucidar
by Win Scott Eckert

John Carter of Mars: Gods of the Forgotten
by Geary Gravel

Victory Harben: Fires of Halos
by Christopher Paul Carey

THE DEAD MOON SUPER-ARC

*Korak at the Earth's Core**
by Win Scott Eckert

* Releasing 2023

OTHER ERB UNIVERSE BOOKS

Savage Epics: The Seminal Works of Edgar Rice Burroughs (Tarzan of the Apes, At the Earth's Core, and *The Land That Time Forgot)*
by Edgar Rice Burroughs

A Princess of Mars: Shadow of the Assassins**
by Ann Tonsor Zeddies

Tarzan and the Forest of Stone
by Jeffrey J. Mariotte

** Releasing 2024

Mahars of Pellucidar
by John Eric Holmes

Red Axe of Pellucidar
by John Eric Holmes

Tarzan and the Forest of Stone
by Jeffrey J. Mariotte

Tarzan and the Dark Heart of Time
by Philip José Farmer

Tarzan and the Valley of Gold
by Fritz Leiber

EDGAR RICE BURROUGHS UNIVERSE™

COSMIC EPICS

THE SEMINAL WORKS OF EDGAR RICE BURROUGHS

A **PRINCESS** OF **MARS**®

THE **MOON MAID**™

PIRATES OF **VENUS**

Illustrations by
RICHARD HESCOX, J. ALLEN ST. JOHN, FRANK SCHOONOVER,
MICHAEL WHELAN, AND MIKE WOLFER

EDGAR RICE BURROUGHS, INC.
100
1923   2023
YEARS
TARZANA, CALIFORNIA

EDGAR RICE BURROUGHS, Inc.

Publishers

TARZANA   CALIFORNIA

COSMIC EPICS:
THE SEMINAL WORKS OF EDGAR RICE BURROUGHS

Special thanks to Kathleen Bonnaud, John Burroughs, Christopher Paul Carey,
Steven K. Dowd, Win Scott Eckert, Janet Mann, Garyn G. Roberts,
James Sullos, Jess Terrell, Cathy Wilbanks, Charlotte Wilbanks, Mike Wolfer,
and Bill Wormstedt for their valuable assistance in producing this book.

Garyn G. Roberts would like to extend his heartfelt thanks to Jim Sullos, Cathy Wilbanks,
Christopher Paul Carey, and the Edgar Rice Burroughs family and corporation for allowing
his modest contribution to their definitive volumes of the work of Edgar Rice Burroughs.

First standard hardcover edition

Published by Edgar Rice Burroughs, Inc.
Tarzana, California
EdgarRiceBurroughs.com

ISBN-13: 978-1-945462-54-2

- 9 8 7 6 5 4 3 2 1 -

To Steven K. Dowd,
for the generous support he has provided for both
this book and the legacy of Edgar Rice Burroughs.

CONTENTS

PREFACE
AN INTERCONNECTED COSMOS
CHRISTOPHER PAUL CAREY

T HE THREE NOVELS COLLECTED IN THIS BOOK are mystical portals that can transport you, the reader, to the Edgar Rice Burroughs Universe. Much like John Carter stretching up his arms to the heavens and willing himself to the Red Planet in the foreword to *A Princess of Mars*, picking up this book and reading the stories contained herein will sweep you away to the fantastical worlds of Barsoom (Mars), Va-nah (the Moon's hollow interior), and Amtor (Venus). Thus it has been for decades now, with successive generations of readers translocated to weird and wondrous worlds that, in some ways, seem more real than life itself, all thanks to the timeless storytelling ability of Edgar Rice Burroughs, the Master of Adventure.

If you are new to Burroughs, you might not realize that my reference to his "universe" is not just a vague allusion to his literary opus; the author deliberately interconnected his characters, worlds, and storylines in an intricate web, setting them in shared continuity and establishing a cosmos of crossovers populated by daring heroes and heroines and maleficent villains long before the Marvel or DC Universes were even the faintest idea in anyone's head. As early as 1913, Edgar Rice Burroughs began crossing over characters between his various storylines, such as when Tarzan cameos in the novel *The Eternal Lover* (aka *The Eternal Savage*), and brother and sister Barney and Victoria Custer make appearances in both *The Mad King* and *The Eternal Lover*. Such crossovers kicked into high gear in 1922, when Burroughs made the curious and compelling decision to tie in his Barsoom series with his then-future timeline of *The Moon Maid*. But things didn't stop there. In *Tanar of Pellucidar* (1929), a character named Jason Gridley invents a unique type of radio set that can penetrate the Earth's crust and permits communication with the inner world of Pellucidar. This discovery prompts Jason Gridley to find a patron in the wealthy Lord Greystoke, and in *Tarzan at the Earth's Core* (1930) we find Jason accompanying the Lord of the Jungle as he leads an airship expedition through the north polar opening to the inner world. Then, in *A Fighting Man of Mars* (1930), Edgar Rice Burroughs himself, operating Jason's transmitter-receiver apparatus while the handsome radio bug is off adventuring with Tarzan in the hollow Earth, discovers that the "Gridley Wave" can also cross the cold void of space to distant worlds, and thereby makes contact with the inhabitants of Mars. And, as you will soon read in *Pirates of Venus* (1932), Jason Gridley returns to the outer crust and is visiting Burroughs in his office in Tarzana, California, just prior to Carson Napier's first meeting with the great author to discuss his plans to leave our planet in an immense rocket ship.

It is true that some other earlier authors, such as H. Rider Haggard and Jules Verne, partook in literary crossovers involving their own works and characters, but none did so on such a grand scale until Edgar Rice Burroughs came along and showed how artfully it could be accomplished. Ultimately, Burroughs interconnected five of his six major fantastical series—Tarzan, Barsoom, Pellucidar, Amtor, and Va-nah—the sole exception being the Caspak (or Land That Time Forgot) trilogy. Even there, however, he subtly placed the three novels in his larger continuity by explaining that he found the manuscript detailing the events of *The Land That Time Forgot* in an old thermos bottle floating in the frigid waters off the coast of Greenland; he was merely the story's "editor," just as he was when he conveyed the remarkable accounts of his other five series.

Like any good mythmaker, Edgar Rice Burroughs wants us to believe his tales are real. And it is a testament to his storytelling abilities that, even in this often cynical age of "fake news," phishing schemes, and social media phoniness, he succeeds so wonderfully. I remember my twelve-year-old self standing out in the cold air of a spring night and stretching up my arms toward the Red Planet in the star-speckled heavens above, believing I could transport myself to Mars just as John Carter did. There I would find myself on a world of romance and adventure, where I might live up to my utmost potential and discover my destiny. Even now, despite having seen the many breathtaking images of a dead, barren world beamed back to Earth by NASA's Mars rovers, I sometimes wonder if there might be a way to make the leap to that (to quote the poet E. E. Cummings) "hell of a good universe next door." Of course, you hold the answer right now in your hands in the form of this very book, as it contains the first installments in three of Burroughs' major science fiction series. The same might be said of its companion volume, *Savage Epics*, which collects the first novels in Burroughs' series of primordial adventure: *Tarzan of the Apes*, *At the Earth's Core*, and *The Land That Time Forgot*. Whichever portal you end up taking into the Edgar Rice Burroughs Universe, rest assured that you will soon leave the troubles and stresses of this world behind as you embark on an unforgettable and rewarding journey into exotic realms of romance and adventure.

Christopher Paul Carey
Tarzana, California
May 2023

CHRISTOPHER PAUL CAREY *is the Director of Publishing and Creative Director of the ERB Universe at Edgar Rice Burroughs, Inc. He is the author of the ERB Universe novel* Victory Harben: Fires of Halos *as well as* Swords Against the Moon Men, *an authorized sequel to Edgar Rice Burroughs' classic science fantasy novel* The Moon Maid. *He has scripted several comic books set in Mr. Burroughs' worlds, including* Pellucidar: Across Savage Seas, Pellucidar: Dark of the Sun, *and* Carson of Venus: The Flames Beyond. *He holds a master's degree in Writing Popular Fiction from Seton Hill University, and has edited more than ninety novels, anthologies, and collections for a variety of publishers. He lives in Southern California.*

INTRODUCTION
ERB AND THE COSMIC EPIC
GARYN G. ROBERTS, PH.D.

HUNDREDS, IF NOT THOUSANDS, of biographers, analysts, critics, celebrants/fans, literary historians, and experts—with a diverse range of backgrounds and perspectives—have "weighed in" regarding the life and works of Edgar Rice Burroughs (September 1, 1875–March 19, 1950) since he debuted on the popular pulpwood pages (alliteration intended) just a couple of years prior to the United States' entry into World War I. The cumulative body of written and otherwise recorded material generated by this multifaceted group has often been fascinating and informative.

My humble observations and perspectives found in this introduction are just that—observations and perspectives. These are based on my cultural and literary heritage and personal experience with the biography and works of Edgar Rice Burroughs for more than 50 years. Very modestly, I hope my ideas shared here might in some minor way review, bring together, and expand upon what has been written and recorded about the life and career of the master for more than 110 years.

While each of the mindsets (worldviews, paradigms) of Burroughs' legions of followers (many millions in number) is to a degree unique, insightful and sometimes inaccurate, five of my personal favorites of this group begin with Sam Moskowitz (1920–97), premier science fiction historian who worked closely with the likes of none other than eminent editor and magazine publisher Hugo Gernsback (1884–1967). Moskowitz is the author of many definitive and landmark studies of the genre including *Under the Moons of Mars: A History and Anthology of "The Scientific Romance" in the Munsey Magazines, 1912–1920* (New York: Holt, Rinehart,

Winston, 1970). And then there are Irwin Porges (1909–1998), author of *Edgar Rice Burroughs: The Man Who Created Tarzan* (Provo, UT: Brigham Young University, 1975); Richard A. Lupoff (1935–2020), prolific and talented fantasy and science fiction writer and historian, and author of *Edgar Rice Burroughs: Master of Adventure* (New York: Ace Books, 1965, revised 1968 and 1975); Robert B. Zeuschner, Ph.D., author of the definitive *Edgar Rice Burroughs: The Bibliography* (Tarzana, CA: Edgar Rice Burroughs, Inc., 2016); and B. J. Lukes, compiler of *Edgar Rice Burroughs: The Descriptive Bibliography of the Grosset & Dunlap Reprints* (Tarzana, CA: Edgar Rice Burroughs, Inc., 2017).

DIME NOVELS AND STORY PAPERS. Literally billions of "dime" (and sometimes "half-dime") novels and similar story papers were printed and sold in the United States during the second half of the nineteenth century and first two decades of the twentieth—roughly from the start of the Civil War until the end of World War I. Genres and formulas of fiction abounded in dime novels; some emerged anew, several flourished. In the 1860s and '70s, frontier stories—which in a pseudo-factual and highly embellished fictional fashion chronicled European Americans' expansion westward—were dime novel staples. In the 1880s and '90s—along with frontier stories—tales of mystery, crime, and its detection were all the rage in dime novels. For the first time in American history, a mass audience was targeted for a relatively inexpensive entertainment form (other than newspapers) that was physically accessible to a large portion of the total populous.

The term "story papers" is a very accurate description of dime novels. The earliest dime novels, and majority of dime novels, were printed in a very similar fashion to newspapers of the day. (A digest dime novel format appeared in the late 1800s and early 1900s.) Dime novels were roughly 9 inches wide and 12 inches tall (somewhat larger in surface size than our standard copy paper today, which is 8 ½ by 11 inches). Text was set in two or three columns per page. Small font sizes of 9 or 10 point were common. Titles of stories resembled those of articles commonly found in broadsheet newspapers of the day. These titles attracted readers to the stories. Authors of dime novels frequently had their beginnings in journalism. The writing styles employed in dime novel stories, like those in newspapers, were filled with intense action and colorful, clipped wording. Chapters were short and usually featured cliffhanger endings.

Dime novels were often issued as part of "Libraries," a marketing device that encouraged subscriptions so that readers would not miss a single, often weekly, issue. This marketing strategy helped insure a degree of market share for dime novel publishers. The dime novel was a sensual medium that appealed to a variety of emotions—base and moral alike.

As can be anticipated, a variety of causes contributed to the decline of the dime novel. Ultimately, America's first popular entertainment medium died as it was born—slowly, over a span of years. The descent began about the turn of the century and continued for another twenty years. Story formulas simply wore out. Convention overshadowed invention. Dime novel publishers had measured profits by the fraction of cent and cent per copy—mass production of a form with low profit margins was necessary to sustain market success. When the United States Postal Service increased the postage on dime novels and similar periodicals sent through the mails in 1912, the increased postage of one or two cents per issue was enough to destroy the profitability that had been inherent in dime novels for years.

There were other contributors to the downfall of the dime novel. Almost from the start, individuals emerged who condemned the content inherent in dime novel storylines. These "moralists" usually arose from the ranks of clergy and "ivory tower" educators. (Some things never change. Consider the contemporary ravaging of libraries by individuals and groups that seek to edit content.) The reality was that the dime novel industry monitored itself better than any outside group could. Publishers were well aware that consuming readers could not be offended *en masse* if they, the publishers, wished to retain market share.

Perhaps the most important reason dime novels were so important was that formal education and books were designed for the wealthy elite, a very small percentage of the total United States population. Most people in American prior to the Civil War were functionally illiterate. Most books were comparatively very expensive to purchase and were published in relatively small press runs. It was not the common experience that one could have physical access to and read expensive, hard-to-find books.

When story formulas wore out and relevant postal rates increased circa 1912, changes were needed for the survival of popular literature—championed by dime novels in the United States. These changes came in two forms. First, the traditional format of the dime novel radically changed; and second, for publishers, rather radical adjustments were necessary in marketing and distribution systems. With the notable exception of Street & Smith, most dime novel publishers did not successfully make the transition from dime novels to what would be called "pulpwood magazines" or "pulps."

The transition from dime novels to pulps occurred in about a twenty-year time frame, from the mid 1890s until the mid 1910s. Publishing mogul Frank A. Munsey (1854–1925) created the template, the boiler-plate, for the pulps in the October 1912 issue of his company's *The Argosy*.

"Pulps" were named for the coarse pulpwood paper upon which they were printed. The term "pulp fiction" ultimately became a kind of pe-jorative, equating stories and features found in pulps with the cheap, low-grade, acid-ridden paper upon which they were printed. Pulps were designed to be ephemera, fleeting, and for the short term. Few of that day realized that some of the most important revered fiction of the twentieth century debuted in the pulps. Pulp magazines were physi-cally quite different from their story paper predecessors. In surface size, pulps measured roughly 7 ½ x 9 ½ inches, and they were roughly ½ inch thick, usually running 128 pages, more or less, in length. Dime novels typically averaged 32 pages or less. Pulps also showcased a range of different fictional and nonfictional features including short stories, serials, letter columns, poems, novellas and novelettes, novels and ad-vertising. Advertising was, of course, another important means for pulp publishers to generate income and profitability. Dime novels had tradi-tionally featured "one novel," and no advertising. By making the pulp magazine significantly distinct from old dime novels, the legend goes that pulps were able to get around the postal increase targeted at novels being sent (often by railroad cars) through the mail system.

With a unique physical design and adjusting to new postal regula-tions, pulp magazines were on their way. In addition, garishly colored paintings graced pulp covers. During the last few years of the nineteenth and first years of the twentieth centuries, the science and techniques of the "four-color process" of separating and combining colors on inexpensively produced paper advanced and became increasingly viable. This explains the emergence of splashy Sunday newspaper comic strip sections generated by the Hearst, Chicago Tribune–New York News, and other syndicates. This advancement also made color covers on pulp magazines possible.

Perhaps most importantly, pulp magazines—unlike dime novels—moved away from a reliance on the postal system for distribution. Pulp magazines—most often published in New York City (the publishing center of the world for centuries) and large metropolitan areas—relied on "DIRECT" or newsstand sales for dissemination. The increasingly larger urban populations at the turn of the last century made direct sales fiscally viable.

Extensive studies on the dime novel and the pulp magazine, and the overlap of the two, relate this publishing history much more effectively than this author's brief missive on these subjects here. Top dime novel scholars include E. F. Bleiler, Richard Bleiler, Charles Bragin, Edward T. LeBlanc, and J. Randolph Cox. There have historically been, and continue to be, a range of really talented pulp magazine scholars and authorities.

It was at this juncture between dime novels and pulp magazines that Edgar Rice Burroughs debuted in an all-out apocalypse for the old order that single-handedly changed the future of popular literature.

A real-life adventurer and dauntless entrepreneur, Edgar Rice Burroughs first appeared as a popular author in the twilight of the dime novel era and the dawn of the pulp magazine. Burroughs is best remembered for his archetypal jungle hero, Tarzan, who first appeared in 1912. But he was ultimately responsible for other enduring fantasies and science fiction, including his Mars space opera series that began with the serial novel *Under the Moons of Mars*. (This novel was later retitled *A Princess of Mars* when A. C. McClurg & Co. [Chicago] published the story in hardcover form.) *Under the Moons of Mars* was an important bridge between nineteenth-century scientific romance and early twentieth-century space opera (Westerns set in outer space, such as, years later, *Star Wars* [1977]), and between dime novels and pulp magazines.

The list and varieties of genre fiction to which Edgar Rice Burroughs contributed is extensive. These include lost world fantasies, tales of the Stone Age, medieval adventures, Westerns, scientific romances, space opera, jungle adventures, mysteries, and more. His predecessors and contemporaries were and are part of literary history; his followers were and are numerous, and heavily indebted to him.

Predecessors to Edgar Rice Burroughs in the area of "cosmic epics" include, most notably, Jules Verne (1828–1905), Edward Page Mitchell (1852–1927), and H. G. Wells (1866–1946). There were two very popular adolescent series that were predecessors and contemporaries of Burroughs' cosmic epics. These were the Frank Reade, Jr. dime novels (as by "Noname") begun in 1892 which featured the exploits of the title character, a young inventor. Adventures of Frank Reade, Jr. were followed by the Stratemeyer syndicate's hardcover Tom Swift series begun in 1910. (The Tom Swift stories [as by "Victor Appleton"] were, at least initially, highly derivative of the Frank Reade dime novels.)

Contemporaries and followers of Edgar Rice Burroughs' cosmic epics included J. U. Giesy (1877–1947), Charles B. Stillson (1880–1932), A. Merritt (1884–1943), Frances Stevens (pseudonym for Gertrude Barrows Bennett, 1884–1948), Austin Hall (1885–1933) and Homer Eon Flint (1888–1924), Ray Cummings (1887–1957), E. E. "Doc" Smith (1890–1965), Otis Albert Kline (1891–1946), Murray Leinster (pseudonym for Will F. Jenkins, 1896–1975), Edmond Hamilton (1904–77), Fritz Leiber, Jr. (1910–92), C. L. Moore (1911-87), Henry Kuttner (1915–58), Leigh Brackett (1915–78), Ray Bradbury (1920–2012), and most recently, a range of critically acclaimed and popular authors.

Along with Edmond Hamilton and E. E. "Doc" Smith, Dr. John "Jack" Williamson (1908–2006) was one of the greatest practitioners and champions of space opera. Williamson's Legion of Space series (*Legion of Space*, 1934, 1947; *The Cometeers*, 1936, 1939, 1950; *One Against the Legion*, 1939; *The Legion of Time*, 1952; and *The Queen of the Legion*, 1983) has been cited by George Lucas (1944–) as a primary influence on the Star Wars movies. Edgar Rice Burroughs' cosmic epics, begun in *A Princess of Mars*, set the stage for all that followed in this regard. (Dr. Williamson wrote the foreword to my award-winning anthology, *The Prentice Hall Anthology of Science Fiction and Fantasy*, 2001.)

And *A Princess of Mars* influenced so many other storytellers to follow. For example, some pulp authorities and scholars suggest that H. P. Lovecraft's (1890–1937) "The Dream-Quest of Unknown Kadath" (written circa 1926-7, published posthumously by August Derleth's [1909–71] Arkham House in 1943) owes a great deal to this masterpiece by Edgar Rice Burroughs. There are other Lovecraftian dream quests that may indeed owe at least partial credit to Burroughs.

Tremendously influenced by Edgar Rice Burroughs' cosmic epic storylines, settings, character types, and more, many hundreds of newspaper comic pages featured what would become incredibly popular cosmic epic comic strip series. There were several, but the most famous include Phillip Francis Nowlan's (1888–1940) and Dick Calkins' (1894–1964) *Buck Rogers* (1929–67). *Buck Rogers* actually began as an *Amazing Stories* (August 1928) pulp magazine prose story. And then there was, of course, Alex Raymond's (1909–56) *Flash Gordon* (1934–2003).

Pulp magazines that featured Burroughs' types of scientific romance and space opera included *Weird Tales* (1923–54, and several later reincarnations); *Amazing Stories* (1926–2021), and other Hugo Gernsback publications; *Astounding Stories* (*of Super-Science*) (begun in 1930, and continued for decades under various titles including *Analog Science Fiction and Fact*); (*Thrilling*) *Wonder Stories* (1929–55); and *Planet Stories* (1939–55).

The first of Edgar Rice Burroughs' "Barsoom" or Mars series is:

A Princess of Mars (first published as a six-part serial in Munsey's *The All-Story*, February, March, April May, June, July, 1912, as *Under the Moons of Mars* as by "Norman Bean"). The "*Norman* Bean" byline was supposed to read "*Normal* Bean," but this was intentionally or unintentionally revised by an editor. Under the name "Normal Bean," Edgar Rice Burroughs was trying to indicate that, despite his wild story to follow, he was a rational person. McClurg publishers of Chicago published the first edition hardcover of *A Princess of Mars* in 1917.*

The Barsoom series includes:

2. *The Gods of Mars* (*The All-Story* serial, January to May 1913; McClurg hardcover, 1918);

3. *The Warlord of Mars* (*The All-Story* serial, December 1913 to March 1914; McClurg hardcover, 1919);

---

* Important to note here is that Frank A. Munsey would often alter the titles of his periodicals over time. For example, *The All-Story* morphed into *All-Story Weekly* and *Argosy* into *Argosy All-Story*. I believe that these title changes are accounted for correctly in my writing here, but the definitive authority on this topic and related Edgar Rice Burroughs stories in Munsey periodicals is Robert B. Zeuschner.

4. *Thuvia, Maid of Mars* (*All-Story Weekly* serial, April 8, 15, 22, 1916; McClurg hardcover, 1920);

5. *The Chessmen of Mars* (*Argosy All-Story Weekly* serial, February 18 and 25, March 4, 11, 18 and 25, 1922; McClurg hardcover, 1922);

6. *The Mastermind of Mars* (*Amazing Stories Annual* #1, July 1927; McClurg hardcover, 1928);

7. *A Fighting Man of Mars* (*The Blue Book Magazine* serial, April to September 1930; Metropolitan hardcover, 1931);

8. *Swords of Mars* (*The Blue Book Magazine* serial, November 1934 to April 1935; Edgar Rice Burroughs, Inc., hardcover, 1936);

9. *Synthetic Men of Mars* (*Argosy Weekly* serial, January 7, 14, 21, and 28, February 4 and 11, 1939; Edgar Rice Burroughs, Inc., hardcover, 1940);

10. *Llana of Gathol* ("The City of Mummies" [*Amazing Stories*, March 1941] retitled "The Ancient Dead" for the hardcover; "The Black Pirates of Barsoom" [*Amazing Stories*, June 1941]; "Yellow Men of Mars" [*Amazing Stories*, August 1941], retitled "Escape on Mars" for the hardcover; and "Invisible Men of Mars" [*Amazing Stories*, October 1941]; Edgar Rice Burroughs, Inc., hardcover, 1948); and

11. *John Carter of Mars* ("John Carter and the Giant of Mars" by John Coleman Burroughs under the byline "Edgar Rice Burroughs"— *Amazing Stories*, January 1941—this is an expanded version of the Whitman Better Little Book, *John Carter of Mars*, 1940; "Skeleton Men of Jupiter," *Amazing Stories*, February 1943; collected and published posthumously in hardcover by Canaveral Press in 1964).

The saga of John Carter—the hero of the early installments of the Barsoom series—reads very much like a Western in outer space, or what would later be deemed "space opera." Carter is a Confederate veteran of the Great War Between the States. Early in the story, he is in Arizona prospecting for gold. At one point, fleeing from Apache Indians, he hides in a cave. From there, he is mysteriously transported to Mars. Upon arriving on Mars (called "Barsoom" by its inhabitants) Carter finds that he has greatly increased strength, agility and speed due to the much less intense Martian gravity and related environment. Soon he meets both green (the six-appendaged Tharks) and red Martians, the latter being human-like. Carter meets, rescues, and falls for the beautiful female love interest of the story—Dejah Thoris, Princess of Helium, herself a red Martian. (Now, consider the parallels between the beautiful, strong Dejah Thoris and Buck Roger's Wilma Deering and Flash Gordon's Dale Arden to follow.)

A Princess of Mars, as an epic cosmic, interplanetary planetary saga, relies heavily on the romanticism found in "Western" dime novels. John Carter, the Western hero, has all the regalia and encounters found in the fantasized American western frontier. The hero is on an ongoing adventure or journey. Carter, like the reader, does not know exactly where this journey will take him. He interacts both positively and negatively with the varied native peoples he finds on Barsoom. And, John Carter has a love interest in Dejah Thoris. Fast action and short chapters with cliffhanger endings compel us through Edgar Rice Burroughs' tale. John Carter, himself, has traits of the classical frontier hero—he is strong, handsome, a quick thinker. He epitomizes justice and drive to do what he believes is right, and he treasures friendship and love.

The setting Carter finds himself in is very much James Fenimore Cooper and dime novelesque. Barsoom is both beautiful and arid; it is vast and full of natural resources, and it is dangerous and life-threatening. Only the Western hero can survive in such a place.

Without apology, Burroughs' saga is pure escapism, and yet so much more in terms of nineteenth- and early twentieth-century stereotypes (race, gender, class), political situations, and themes. But perhaps most importantly what happens in this archetypal story is that Burroughs single-handedly rescues the worn-out formulas of nineteenth-century story lines and launches the era of the pulp magazine. *A Princess of Mars* is more inventive and creative than any story that preceded it. The colors, the architecture, the world building, the use of language, the inventive story characters, and the speculation in which the author engages are wonderfully captivating to his readers, in 1912 and today more than a century later.

So much to consider, so many followers and imitators and aficionados. The very first time I watched Marty McFly (Michael J. Fox) in his time-traveling DeLorean go back to the Wild West of 1885 to rescue "Doc" Emmett Brown (Christopher Lloyd) in *Back to the Future III* (Robert

Zemeckis, director,1990), I saw an immediate and obvious parallel to John Carter's first arrival on Mars. Next time you watch this movie, see what you think.

Edgar Rice Burroughs' *The Moon Maid* was first published as a five-part serial in Munsey's *Argosy All-Story*, May 5, 12, 19, 26, and June 2, 1923. This was followed by two sequels:

2. *The Moon Men* (first published as a four-part serial in *Argosy All-Story Weekly*, February 21 and 28, and March 7 and 14, 1925); and

3. "The Red Hawk" (first published as a three-part serial in *Argosy All-Story Weekly*, September 5, 12 and 19, 1925). All three cosmic epics were first collected together in the 1926 McClurg hardcover.

While still very firmly entrenched in fading dime novel tradition, *The Moon Maid* became a mainstay, a template for scientifiction, scientific romance, and space opera that would emerge and flourish in 1920s pulp magazines.

Julian, the captain of the spaceship from Earth and hero of *The Moon Maid*, is forced to radically alter his mission and land on the Moon. His vindictive and destructive second-in-command, Orthis, makes this necessary when he sabotages the ship's engines. (Does this sound like the origin story, the first episodes, of Irwin Allen's television series, *Lost in Space*, when stowaway Dr. Zachary Smith subverts the Robinson's trip to Jupiter? I think very much so.) Julian and his team discover that the Moon is hollow and find warring factions inside. Julian falls in love with Moon princess Nah-ee-lah much in the fashion John Carter falls for Dejah Thoris in *A Princess of Mars*. The story is filled with complications and plot twists, a love story, and nonstop action (as we would expect from a dime novel descendant). The hollow world theme and setting is one that Edgar Rice Burroughs would revisit on several occasions (see my introduction in *Savage Epics: The Seminal Works of Edgar Rice Burroughs*, Tarzana, CA: Edgar Rice Burroughs, Inc., 2023).

The tale of Captain Julian, his crew, and his spaceship successfully landing humans on the Moon for the first time is, of course, science fantasy. In reality, the United States of America first successfully landed men on the Moon on July 20, 1969. Neil Armstrong and Buzz Aldrin walked on the Moon while Michael Collins orbited around it waiting for their return.

Pirates of Venus was first published as a six-part serial in Munsey's *Argosy Weekly*, September 17, 24; October 1, 8, 15, 22, 1932. The first of four novels and one novella of what would be deemed Edgar Rice Burroughs' "Amtor" or Venus series, *Pirates of Venus* introduces Carson Napier, who heads for Mars but instead crash lands on Venus.

Subsequent Amtor stories include:

2. *Lost on Venus* (first published as a seven-part serial in *Argosy Weekly*, March 4, 11, 18, 25, and April 1, 8, and 15, 1933; Edgar Rice Burroughs, Inc., hardcover, 1935);

3. *Carson of Venus* (first published as a six-part serial in *Argosy Weekly*, January 8, 15, 22, 29, and February 5 and 12, 1938; Edgar Rice Burroughs, Inc., hardcover, 1939);

4. *Escape on Venus* (first published in *Fantastic Adventures* as "Slaves of the Fish Men [March 1941], "Goddess of Fire" [July 1941], "The Living Dead" [November 1941], and "War on Venus" [March 1942]; Edgar Rice Burroughs, Inc., hardcover, 1946); and

5. "The Wizard of Venus" (novella written in 1941, and first published posthumously in 1964 in the Canaveral Press hardcover collection, *Tales of Three Planets*).

The dime novel/pulp magazine connection continues in Edgar Rice Burroughs' Amtor series. (In Burroughs' universe, "Amtor" is to Barsoom as Venus is to Mars—"Amtor" is what those inhabiting Venus call their home planet.)

Pirates of Venus begins when Edgar Rice Burroughs meets with Jason Gridley and gets an update regarding an expedition to Pellucidar (another Burroughs series that at one point includes Tarzan and others). Edgar Rice Burroughs' Pellucidar series is a whole other landmark of scientific romance (see *Savage Epics: The Seminal Works of Edgar Rice Burroughs*). Soon thereafter, Burroughs witnesses a ghostly apparition, which turns out to be a test by Carson Napier, soon to become the hero of the story. Napier wishes to determine whether he can communicate telepathically with Burroughs and thereby relate his intended future adventures in outer space to a subject back on Earth. The ensuing storyline of *Pirates of Venus* is, for lack of a more professional word, wonderful. Burroughs' narrative here, though connected to some of his other works in terms of themes, settings, and character types, is unique. So many colorful details. So enthralling for the reader. So much fun.

Once again we enjoy the best of dime novel tradition in this story, and yet this is now clearly an Edgar Rice Burroughs pulp magazine story. Carson Napier heads for Mars in his rocket ship, but a miscalculation sends him to Venus. High-paced adventure and action, exotic creatures, and beautiful women populate Amtor. The temptation here is relate more of the plot synopses, but that is better left, perhaps, to you the reader. Unashamedly, I can passionately tell you that the Venus stories are excellent. The late Richard Lupoff has been quoted as saying that he believed that the Moon Maid series may be some of Edgar Rice Burroughs' finest work—of course, Burroughs produced so many landmark tales. For me, along with the Mars and Moon stories, the Venus stories are some of my very favorite. In *Pirates of Venus*, Edgar Rice Burroughs showcases his vast cultural and literary background, and he arrives not only as a master author of the pulps, but a master storyteller of the twentieth century.

Edgar Rice Burroughs' cosmic epics, savage epics, and other storylines, character types, and settings have, of course, appeared in innumerable volumes (hardcover, paperback, periodical) and translations worldwide. And, they have been adapted for a range of popular media including motion pictures (silent and sound), radio drama, television programming, comic books, graphic novels, animation, audiobooks, online presentations and more. While these volumes and adaptations are not our focus here, these are indeed worth investigating.

The importance of Edgar Rice Burroughs' contribution to the bridge between dime novels and pulp magazines—and to the wonderful positive apocalypse of popular literature in the early days of the twentieth century—cannot be overappreciated. Burroughs is responsible for so many specific and general contributions to world popular culture. And yet, his single-most important achievement may well be his revitalization of popular literature (and literacy) for humanity. Overstated? Not even close. Edgar Rice Burroughs' bridging the gap between declining dime novels and burgeoning pulp magazines set the stage for our storytelling and reading for more than a century since.

GARYN G. ROBERTS, PH.D., *is a multi-awarded college and university professor, and author. Among his longtime interests and pursuits is the history of the pulp magazine (1896–1960). Roberts was presented with the Munsey Award in 2013 for his work in this field. He has authored, edited, and appeared in many hundreds of books and periodicals worldwide.*

As a young boy of about eight in the late 1960s, he read his first Edgar Rice Burroughs books and was hooked for life. ERB's A Princess of Mars *has long been one of his all-time favorite books, and it is included in his award-winning anthology,* The Prentice Hall Anthology of Science Fiction and Fantasy. *The list of other Edgar Rice Burroughs tales he treasures and owns in first edition, original pulp magazine, and other states is too numerous to detail.*

With my back against the golden throne, I fought once again for Dejah Thoris.

Contents

TO MY SON
JACK

FOREWORD

TO THE READER OF THIS WORK:

In submitting Captain Carter's strange manuscript to you in book form, I believe that a few words relative to this remarkable personality will be of interest.

My first recollection of Captain Carter is of the few months he spent at my father's home in Virginia, just prior to the opening of the civil war. I was then a child of but five years, yet I well remember the tall, dark, smooth-faced, athletic man whom I called Uncle Jack.

He seemed always to be laughing; and he entered into the sports of the children with the same hearty good fellowship he displayed toward those pastimes in which the men and women of his own age indulged; or he would sit for an hour at a time entertaining my old grandmother with stories of his strange, wild life in all parts of the world. We all loved him, and our servants fairly worshipped the ground he trod.

He was a splendid specimen of manhood, standing a good two inches over six feet, broad of shoulder and narrow of hip, with the carriage of the trained fighting man. His features were regular and clear cut, his hair black and closely cropped, while his eyes were of a steel gray, reflecting a strong and loyal character, filled with fire and initiative. His manners were perfect, and his courtliness was that of a typical southern gentleman of the highest type.

His horsemanship, especially after hounds, was a marvel and delight even in that country of magnificent horsemen. I have often heard my father caution him against his wild recklessness, but he would only laugh, and say that the tumble that killed him would be from the back of a horse yet unfoaled.

When the war broke out he left us, nor did I see him again for some fifteen or sixteen years. When he returned it was without warning, and I was much surprised to note that he had not aged apparently a moment, nor had he changed in any other outward way. He was, when others were with him, the same genial, happy fellow we had known of old, but when he thought himself alone I have seen him sit for hours gazing off into space, his face set in a look of wistful longing and hopeless misery; and at

night he would sit thus looking up into the heavens, at what I did not know until I read his manuscript years afterward.

He told us that he had been prospecting and mining in Arizona part of the time since the war; and that he had been very successful was evidenced by the unlimited amount of money with which he was supplied. As to the details of his life during these years he was very reticent, in fact he would not talk of them at all.

He remained with us for about a year and then went to New York, where he purchased a little place on the Hudson, where I visited him once a year on the occasions of my trips to the New York market—my father and I owning and operating a string of general stores throughout Virginia at that time. Captain Carter had a small but beautiful cottage, situated on a bluff overlooking the river, and during one of my last visits, in the winter of 1885, I observed he was much occupied in writing, I presume now, upon this manuscript.

He told me at this time that if anything should happen to him he wished me to take charge of his estate, and he gave me a key to a compartment in the safe which stood in his study, telling me I would find his will there and some personal instructions which he had me pledge myself to carry out with absolute fidelity.

After I had retired for the night I have seen him from my window standing in the moonlight on the brink of the bluff overlooking the Hudson with his arms stretched out to the heavens as though in appeal. I thought at the time that he was praying, although I never had understood that he was in the strict sense of the term a religious man.

Several months after I had returned home from my last visit, the first of March, 1886, I think, I received a telegram from him asking me to come to him at once. I had always been his favorite among the younger generation of Carters and so I hastened to comply with his demand.

I arrived at the little station, about a mile from his grounds, on the morning of March 4, 1886, and when I asked the livery man to drive me out to Captain Carter's he replied that if I was a friend of the Captain's he had some very bad news for me; the Captain had been found dead shortly after daylight that very morning by the watchman attached to an adjoining property.

For some reason this news did not surprise me, but I hurried out to his place as quickly as possible, so that I could take charge of the body and of his affairs.

I found the watchman who had discovered him, together with the local police chief and several townspeople, assembled in his little study. The watchman related the few details connected with the finding of the body, which he said had been still warm when he came upon it. It lay, he said, stretched full length in the snow with the arms outstretched above the head toward the edge of the bluff, and when he showed me the spot it flashed upon me that it was the identical one where I had seen him on those other nights, with his arms raised in supplication to the skies.

There were no marks of violence on the body, and with the aid of a local physician the coroner's jury quickly reached a decision of death from heart failure. Left alone in the study, I opened the safe and withdrew the contents of the drawer in which he had told me I would find my instructions. They were in part peculiar indeed, but I have followed them to each last detail as faithfully as I was able.

He directed that I remove his body to Virginia without embalming, and that he be laid in an open coffin within a tomb which he previously had had constructed and which, as I later learned, was well ventilated. The instructions impressed upon me that I must personally see that this was carried out just as he directed, even in secrecy if necessary.

His property was left in such a way that I was to receive the entire income for twenty-five years, when the principal was to become mine. His further instructions related to this manuscript which I was to retain sealed and unread, just as I found it, for eleven years; nor was I to divulge its contents until twenty-one years after his death.

A strange feature about the tomb, where his body still lies, is that the massive door is equipped with a single, huge gold-plated spring lock which can be opened *only from the inside.*

Yours very sincerely,

Edgar Rice Burroughs.

CHAPTER ONE
ON THE ARIZONA HILLS

I AM A VERY OLD MAN; how old I do not know. Possibly I am a hundred, possibly more; but I cannot tell because I have never aged as other men, nor do I remember any childhood. So far as I can recollect I have always been a man, a man of about thirty. I appear today as I did forty years and more ago, and yet I feel that I cannot go on living forever; that some day I shall die the real death from which there is no resurrection. I do not know why I should fear death, I who have died twice and am still alive; but yet I have the same horror of it as you who have never died, and it is because of this terror of death, I believe, that I am so convinced of my mortality.

And because of this conviction I have determined to write down the story of the interesting periods of my life and of my death. I cannot explain the phenomena; I can only set down here in the words of an ordinary soldier of fortune a chronicle of the strange events that befell me during the ten years that my dead body lay undiscovered in an Arizona cave.

I have never told this story, nor shall mortal man see this manuscript until after I have passed over for eternity. I know that the average human mind will not believe what it cannot grasp, and so I do not purpose being pilloried by the public, the pulpit, and the press, and held up as a colossal liar when I am but telling the simple truths which some day science will substantiate. Possibly the suggestions which I gained upon Mars, and the knowledge which I can set down in this chronicle, will aid in an earlier understanding of the mysteries of our sister planet; mysteries to you, but no longer mysteries to me.

My name is John Carter; I am better known as Captain Jack Carter of Virginia. At the close of the Civil War I found myself possessed of several hundred thousand dollars (Confederate) and a captain's commission in the cavalry arm of an army which no longer existed; the servant of a state which had vanished with the hopes of the South. Masterless, penniless, and with my only means of livelihood, fighting, gone, I determined to work my way to the southwest and attempt to retrieve my fallen fortunes in a search for gold.

I spent nearly a year prospecting in company with another Confederate officer, Captain James K. Powell of Richmond. We were extremely fortunate, for late in the winter of 1865, after many hardships and privations, we located the most remarkable gold-bearing quartz vein that our wildest dreams had ever pictured. Powell, who was a mining engineer by education, stated that we had uncovered over a million dollars' worth of ore in a trifle over three months.

As our equipment was crude in the extreme we decided that one of us must return to civilization, purchase the necessary machinery and return with a sufficient force of men properly to work the mine.

As Powell was familiar with the country, as well as with the mechanical requirements of mining we determined that it would be best for him to make the trip. It was agreed that I was to hold down our claim against the remote possibility of its being jumped by some wandering prospector.

On March 3, 1866, Powell and I packed his provisions on two of our burros, and bidding me good-bye he mounted his horse, and started down the mountainside toward the valley, across which led the first stage of his journey.

The morning of Powell's departure was, like nearly all Arizona mornings, clear and beautiful; I could see him and his little pack animals picking their way down the mountainside toward the valley, and all during the morning I would catch occasional glimpses of them as they topped a hogback or came out upon a level plateau. My last sight of Powell was about three in the afternoon as he entered the shadows of the range on the opposite side of the valley.

Some half hour later I happened to glance casually across the valley and was much surprised to note three little dots in about the same place I had last seen my friend and his two pack animals. I am not given to needless worrying, but the more I tried to convince myself that all was well with Powell, and that the dots I had seen on his trail were antelope or wild horses, the less I was able to assure myself.

Since we had entered the territory we had not seen a hostile Indian, and we had, therefore, become careless in the extreme, and were wont to ridicule the stories we had heard of the great numbers of these vicious marauders that were supposed to haunt the trails, taking their toll in lives and torture of every white party which fell into their merciless clutches.

Powell, I knew, was well armed and, further, an experienced Indian fighter; but I too had lived and fought for years among the Sioux in the North, and I knew that his chances were small against a party of cunning trailing Apaches. Finally I could endure the suspense no longer, and, arming myself with my two Colt revolvers and a carbine, I strapped two belts of cartridges about me and catching my saddle horse, started down the trail taken by Powell in the morning.

As soon as I reached comparatively level ground I urged my mount into a canter and continued this, where the going permitted, until, close upon dusk, I discovered the point where other tracks joined those of Powell. They were the tracks of unshod ponies, three of them, and the ponies had been galloping.

I followed rapidly until, darkness shutting down, I was forced to await the rising of the moon, and given an opportunity to speculate on the question of the wisdom of my chase. Possibly I had conjured up impossible dangers, like some nervous old housewife, and when I should catch up with Powell would get a good laugh for my pains. However, I am not prone to sensitiveness, and the following of a sense of duty, wherever it may lead, has always been a kind of fetish with me throughout my life; which may account for the honors bestowed upon me by three republics and the decorations and friendships of an old and powerful emperor and several lesser kings, in whose service my sword has been red many a time.

About nine o'clock the moon was sufficiently bright for me to proceed on my way and I had no difficulty in following the trail at a fast walk, and in some places at a brisk trot until, about midnight, I reached the water hole where Powell had expected to camp. I came upon the spot unexpectedly, finding it entirely deserted, with no signs of having been recently occupied as a camp.

I was interested to note that the tracks of the pursuing horsemen, for such I was now convinced they must be, continued after Powell with only a brief stop at the hole for water; and always at the same rate of speed as his.

I was positive now that the trailers were Apaches and that they wished to capture Powell alive for the fiendish pleasure of the torture, so I urged my horse onward at a most dangerous pace, hoping against hope that I would catch up with them before they attacked him.

Further speculation was suddenly cut short by the faint report of two shots far ahead of me. I knew that Powell would need me now if ever, and I instantly urged my horse to his topmost speed up the narrow and difficult mountain trail.

I had forged ahead for perhaps a mile or more without hearing further sounds, when the trail suddenly debouched onto a small, open plateau near the summit of the pass. I had passed through a narrow, overhanging gorge just before entering suddenly upon this table land, and the sight which met my eyes filled me with consternation and dismay.

The little stretch of level land was white with Indian tepees, and there were probably half a thousand red warriors clustered around some object near the center of the camp. Their attention was so wholly riveted to this point of interest that they did not notice me, and I easily could have turned back into the dark recesses of the gorge and made my escape with perfect safety. The fact, however, that this thought did not occur to me until the following day removes any possible right to a claim to heroism to which the narration of this episode might possibly otherwise entitle me.

I do not believe that I am made of the stuff which constitutes heroes, because, in all of the hundreds of instances that my voluntary acts have placed me face to face with death, I cannot recall a single one where any alternative step to that I took occurred to me until many hours later. My mind is evidently so constituted that I am subconsciously forced into the path of duty without recourse to tiresome mental processes. However that may be, I have never regretted that cowardice is not optional with me.

In this instance I was, of course, positive that Powell was the center of attraction, but whether I thought or acted first I do not know, but within an instant from the moment the scene broke upon my view I had whipped out my revolvers and was charging down upon the entire army of warriors, shooting rapidly, and whooping at the top of my lungs. Single handed, I could not have pursued better tactics, for the red men, convinced by sudden surprise that not less than a regiment of regulars was upon them, turned and fled in every direction for their bows, arrows, and rifles.

The view which their hurried routing disclosed filled me with apprehension and with rage. Under the clear rays of the Arizona moon lay Powell, his body fairly bristling with the hostile arrows of the braves. That he was already dead I could not but be convinced, and yet I would have saved his body from mutilation at the hands of the Apaches as quickly as I would have saved the man himself from death.

Riding close to him I reached down from the saddle, and grasping his cartridge belt drew him up across the withers of my mount. A backward glance convinced me that to return by the way I had come would be more hazardous than to continue across the plateau, so, putting spurs to my poor beast, I made a dash for the opening to the pass which I could distinguish on the far side of the table land.

The Indians had by this time discovered that I was alone and I was pursued with imprecations, arrows, and rifle balls. The fact that it is difficult to aim anything but imprecations accurately by moonlight, that they were upset by the sudden and unexpected manner of my advent, and that I was a rather rapidly moving target saved me from the various deadly projectiles of the enemy and permitted me to reach the shadows of the surrounding peaks before an orderly pursuit could be organized.

My horse was traveling practically unguided as I knew that I had probably less knowledge of the exact location of the trail to the pass than he, and thus it happened that he entered a defile which led to the summit of the range and not to the pass which I had hoped would carry me to the valley and to safety. It is probable, however, that to this fact I owe my life and the remarkable experiences and adventures which befell me during the following ten years.

My first knowledge that I was on the wrong trail came when I heard the yells of the pursuing warriors suddenly grow fainter and fainter far off to my left.

I knew then that they had passed to the left of the jagged rock formation at the edge of the plateau, to the right of which my horse had borne me and the body of Powell.

I drew rein on a little level promontory overlooking the trail below and to my left, and saw the party of pursuing warriors disappearing around the point of a neighboring peak.

I knew the Indians would soon discover that they were on the wrong trail and that the search for me would be renewed in the right direction as soon as they located my tracks.

I had gone but a short distance further when what seemed to be an excellent trail opened up around the face of a high cliff. The trail was level and quite broad and led upward and in the general direction I wished to go. The cliff arose for several hundred feet on my right, and on my left was an equal and nearly perpendicular drop to the bottom of a rocky ravine.

I had followed this trail for perhaps a hundred yards when a sharp turn to the right brought me to the mouth of a large cave. The opening was about four feet in height and three to four feet wide, and at this opening the trail ended.

It was now morning, and, with the customary lack of dawn which is a startling characteristic of Arizona, it had become daylight almost without warning.

Dismounting, I laid Powell upon the ground, but the most painstaking examination failed to reveal the faintest spark of life. I forced water from my canteen between his dead lips, bathed his face and rubbed his hands, working over him continuously for the better part of an hour in the face of the fact that I knew him to be dead.

I was very fond of Powell; he was thoroughly a man in every respect; a polished southern gentleman; a staunch and true friend; and it was with a feeling of the deepest grief that I finally gave up my crude endeavors at resuscitation.

Leaving Powell's body where it lay on the ledge I crept into the cave to reconnoiter. I found a large chamber, possibly a hundred feet in diameter and thirty or forty feet in height; a smooth and well-worn floor, and many other evidences that the cave had, at some remote period, been inhabited. The back of the cave was so lost in dense shadow that I could not distinguish whether there were openings into other apartments or not.

As I was continuing my examination I commenced to feel a pleasant drowsiness creeping over me which I attributed to the fatigue of my long and strenuous ride, and the reaction from the excitement of the fight and the pursuit. I felt comparatively safe in my present location as I knew that one man could defend the trail to the cave against an army.

I soon became so drowsy that I could scarcely resist the strong desire to throw myself on the floor of the cave for a few moments' rest, but I knew that this would never do, as it would mean certain death at the hands of my red friends, who might be upon me at any moment. With an effort I started toward the opening of the cave only to reel drunkenly against a side wall, and from there slip prone upon the floor.

CHAPTER TWO
THE ESCAPE OF THE DEAD

ASENSE OF DELICIOUS DREAMINESS overcame me, my muscles relaxed, and I was on the point of giving away to my desire to sleep when the sound of approaching horses reached my ears. I attempted to spring to my feet but was horrified to discover that my muscles refused to respond to my will. I was now thoroughly awake, but as unable to move a muscle as though turned to stone. It was then, for the first time, that I noticed a slight vapor filling the cave. It was extremely tenuous and only noticeable against the opening which led to daylight. There also came to my nostrils a faintly pungent odor, and I could only assume that I had been overcome by some poisonous gas, but why I should retain my mental faculties and yet be unable to move I could not fathom.

I lay facing the opening of the cave and where I could see the short stretch of trail which lay between the cave and the turn of the cliff around which the trail led. The noise of the approaching horses had ceased, and I judged the Indians were creeping stealthily upon me along the little ledge which led to my living tomb. I remember that I hoped they would make short work of me as I did not particularly relish the thought of the innumerable things they might do to me if the spirit prompted them.

I had not long to wait before a stealthy sound apprised me of their nearness, and then a war-bonneted, paint-streaked face was thrust cautiously around the shoulder of the cliff, and savage eyes looked into mine. That he could see me in the dim light of the cave I was sure for the early morning sun was falling full upon me through the opening.

The fellow, instead of approaching, merely stood and stared; his eyes bulging and his jaw dropped. And then another savage face appeared, and a third and fourth and fifth craning their necks over the shoulders of their fellows whom they could not pass upon the narrow ledge. Each face was the picture of awe and fear, but for what reason I did not know, nor did I learn until ten years later. That there were still other braves behind those who regarded me was apparent from the fact that the leaders passed back whispered word to those behind them.

Suddenly a low but distinct moaning sound issued from the recesses of the cave behind me, and, as it reached the ears of the Indians, they turned and fled in terror, panic stricken. So frantic were their efforts to escape from the unseen thing behind me that one of the braves was hurled headlong from the cliff to the rocks below. Their wild cries echoed in the canyon for a short time, and then all was still once more.

The sound which had frightened them was not repeated, but it had been sufficient as it was to start me speculating on the possible horror which lurked in the shadows at my back. Fear is a relative term and so I can only measure my feelings at that time by what I had experienced in previous positions of danger and by those I have passed through since; but I can say without shame that if the sensations I endured during the next few minutes were fear, then may God help the coward, for cowardice is of a surety its own punishment.

To be held paralyzed, with one's back toward some horrible and unknown danger from the very sound of which the ferocious Apache warriors turn in wild stampede, as a flock of sheep would madly flee from a pack of wolves, seems to me the last word in fearsome predicaments for a man who had ever been used to fighting for his life with all the energy of a powerful physique.

Several times I thought I heard faint sounds behind me as of somebody moving cautiously, but eventually even these ceased, and I was left to the contemplation of my position without interruption. I could but vaguely conjecture the cause of my paralysis, and my only hope lay in that it might pass off as suddenly as it had fallen upon me.

Late in the afternoon my horse, which had been standing with dragging rein before the cave, started slowly down the trail, evidently in search of food and water, and I was left alone with my mysterious unknown companion and the dead body of my friend, which lay just within my range of vision upon the ledge where I had placed it in the early morning.

From then until possibly midnight all was silence, the silence of the dead; then, suddenly, the awful moan of the morning broke upon my startled ears, and there came again from the black shadows the sound of a moving thing, and a faint rustling as of dead leaves. The shock to my already overstrained nervous system was terrible in the extreme, and with a superhuman effort I strove to break my awful bonds. It was an effort of the mind, of the will, of the nerves; not muscular, for I could not move even so much as my little finger, but none the less mighty for all that.

And then something gave, there was a momentary feeling of nausea, a sharp click as of the snapping of a steel wire, and I stood with my back against the wall of the cave facing my unknown foe.

And then the moonlight flooded the cave, and there before me lay my own body as it had been lying all these hours, with the eyes staring toward the open ledge and the hands resting limply upon the ground. I looked first at my lifeless clay there upon the floor of the cave and then down at myself in utter bewilderment; for there.I lay clothed, and yet here I stood but naked as at the minute of my birth.

The transition had been so sudden and so unexpected that it left me for a moment forgetful of aught else than my strange metamorphosis. My first thought was, is this then death! Have I indeed passed over forever into that other life! But I could not well believe this, as I could feel my heart pounding against my ribs from the exertion of my efforts to release myself from the anaesthesis which had held me. My breath was coming in quick, short gasps, cold sweat stood out from every pore of my body, and the ancient experiment of pinching revealed the fact that I was anything other than a wraith.

Again was I suddenly recalled to my immediate surroundings by a repetition of the weird moan from the depths of the cave. Naked and unarmed as I was, I had no desire to face the unseen thing which menaced me.

My revolvers were strapped to my lifeless body which, for some unfathomable reason, I could not bring myself to touch. My carbine was in its boot, strapped to my saddle, and as my horse had wandered off I was left without means of defense. My only alternative seemed to lie in flight and my decision was crystallized by a recurrence of the rustling sound from the thing which now seemed, in the darkness of the cave and to my distorted imagination, to be creeping stealthily upon me.

Unable longer to resist the temptation to escape this horrible place I leaped quickly through the opening into the starlight of a clear Arizona night. The crisp, fresh mountain air outside the cave acted as an immediate tonic and I felt new life and new courage coursing through me. Pausing upon the brink of the ledge I upbraided myself for what now seemed to me wholly unwarranted apprehension. I reasoned with myself that I had lain helpless for many hours within the cave, yet nothing had molested me, and my better judgment, when permitted the direction of clear and logical reasoning, convinced me that the noises I had heard must have resulted from purely natural and harmless causes; probably the conformation of the cave was such that a slight breeze had caused the sounds I heard.

I decided to investigate, but first I lifted my head to fill my lungs with the pure, invigorating night air of the mountains. As I did so I saw stretching far below me the beautiful vista of rocky gorge, and level, cacti-studded flat, wrought by the moonlight into a miracle of soft splendor and wondrous enchantment.

Few western wonders are more inspiring than the beauties of an Arizona moonlit landscape; the silvered mountains in the distance, the strange lights and shadows upon hogback and arroyo, and the grotesque details of the stiff, yet beautiful cacti form a picture at once enchanting and inspiring; as though one were catching for the first time a glimpse of some dead and forgotten world, so different is it from the aspect of any other spot upon our Earth.

As I stood thus meditating, I turned my gaze from the landscape to the heavens where the myriad stars formed a gorgeous and fitting canopy for the wonders of the earthly scene. My attention was quickly riveted by a large red star close to the distant horizon. As I gazed upon it I felt a spell of overpowering fascination—it was Mars, the god of war, and for me, the fighting man, it had always held the power of irresistible enchantment. As I gazed at it on that far-gone night it seemed to call across the unthinkable void, to lure me to it, to draw me as the lodestone attracts a particle of iron.

My longing was beyond the power of opposition; I closed my eyes, stretched out my arms toward the god of my vocation and felt myself drawn with the suddenness of thought through the trackless immensity of space. There was an instant of extreme cold and utter darkness.

CHAPTER THREE
MY ADVENT ON MARS

I OPENED MY EYES upon a strange and weird landscape. I knew that I was on Mars; not once did I question either my sanity or my wakefulness. I was not asleep, no need for pinching here; my inner consciousness told me as plainly that I was upon Mars as your conscious mind tells you that you are upon Earth. You do not question the fact; neither did I.

I found myself lying prone upon a bed of yellowish, mosslike vegetation which stretched around me in all directions for interminable miles. I seemed to be lying in a deep, circular basin, along the outer verge of which I could distinguish the irregularities of low hills.

It was midday, the sun was shining full upon me and the heat of it was rather intense upon my naked body, yet no greater than would have been true under similar conditions on an Arizona desert. Here and there were slight outcroppings of quartz-bearing rock which glistened in the sunlight; and a little to my left, perhaps a hundred yards, appeared a low, walled enclosure about four feet in height. No water, and no other vegetation than the moss was in evidence, and as I was somewhat thirsty I determined to do a little exploring.

Springing to my feet I received my first Martian surprise, for the effort, which on Earth would have brought me standing upright, carried me into the Martian air to the height of about three yards. I alighted softly upon the ground, however, without appreciable shock or jar. Now commenced a series of evolutions which even then seemed ludicrous in the extreme. I found that I must learn to walk all over again, as the muscular exertion which carried me easily and safely upon Earth played strange antics with me upon Mars.

Instead of progressing in a sane and dignified manner, my attempts to walk resulted in a variety of hops which took me clear of the ground a couple of feet at each step and landed me sprawling upon my face or back at the end of each second or third hop. My muscles, perfectly attuned and accustomed to the force of gravity on Earth, played the mischief with me in attempting for the first time to cope with the lesser gravitation and lower air pressure on Mars.

I was determined, however, to explore the low structure which was the only evidence of habitation in sight, and so I hit upon the unique plan of reverting to first principles in locomotion, creeping. I did fairly well at this and in a few moments had reached the low, encircling wall of the enclosure.

There appeared to be no doors or windows upon the side nearest me, but as the wall was but about four feet high I cautiously gained my feet and peered over the top upon the strangest sight it had ever been given me to see.

The roof of the enclosure was of solid glass about four or five inches in thickness, and beneath this were several hundred large eggs, perfectly round and snowy white. The eggs were nearly uniform in size being about two and one-half feet in diameter.

Five or six had already hatched and the grotesque caricatures which sat blinking in the sunlight were enough to cause me to doubt my sanity. They seemed mostly head, with little scrawny bodies, long necks and six legs, or, as I afterward learned, two legs and two arms, with an intermediary pair of limbs which could be used at will either as arms or legs. Their eyes were set at the extreme sides of their heads a trifle above the center and protruded in such a manner that they could be directed either forward or back and also independently of each other, thus permitting this queer animal to look in any direction, or in two directions at once, without the necessity of turning the head.

The ears, which were slightly above the eyes and closer together, were small, cup-shaped antennae, protruding not more than an inch on these young specimens. Their noses were but longitudinal slits in the center of their faces, midway between their mouths and ears.

There was no hair on their bodies, which were of a very light yellowish-green color. In the adults, as I was to learn quite soon, this color deepens to an olive green and is darker in the male than in the female. Further, the heads of the adults are not so out of proportion to their bodies as in the case of the young.

The iris of the eyes is blood red, as in albinos, while the pupil is dark. The eyeball itself is very white, as are the teeth. These latter add a most ferocious appearance to an otherwise fearsome and terrible countenance, as the lower tusks curve upward to sharp points which end about where the eyes of earthly human beings are located. The whiteness of the teeth is not that of ivory, but of the snowiest and most gleaming of china. Against the dark background of their olive skins their tusks stand out in a most striking manner, making these weapons present a singularly for-midable appearance.

Most of these details I noted later, for I was given but little time to speculate on the wonders of my new discovery. I had seen that the eggs were in the process of hatching, and as I stood watching the hideous little monsters break from their shells I failed to note the approach of a score of full-grown Martians from behind me.

Coming, as they did, over the soft and soundless moss, which covers practically the entire surface of Mars with the exception of the frozen areas at the poles and the scattered cultivated districts, they might have captured me easily, but their intentions were far more sinister. It was the rattling of the accouterments of the foremost warrior which warned me.

On such a little thing my life hung that I often marvel that I escaped so easily. Had not the rifle of the leader of the party swung from its fastenings beside his saddle in such a way as to strike against the butt of his great metal shod spear I should have snuffed out without ever knowing that death was near me. But the little sound caused me to turn, and there upon me, not ten feet from my breast, was the point of that huge spear, a spear forty feet long, tipped with gleaming metal, and held low at the side of a mounted replica of the little devils I had been watching.

But how puny and harmless they now looked beside this huge and terrific incarnation of hate, of vengeance and of death. The man himself, for such I may call him, was fully fifteen feet in height and, on Earth, would have weighed some four hundred pounds. He sat his mount as we sit a horse, grasping the animal's barrel with his lower limbs, while the hands of his two right arms held his immense spear low at the side of his mount; his two left arms were outstretched laterally to help preserve his balance, the thing he rode having neither bridle or reins of any description for guidance.

And his mount! How can earthly words describe it! It towered ten feet at the shoulder; had four legs on either side; a broad flat tail, larger at the tip than at the root, and which it held straight out behind while running; a gaping mouth which split its head from its snout to its long, massive neck.

Like its master, it was entirely devoid of hair, but was of a dark slate color and exceeding smooth and glossy. Its belly was white, and its legs shaded from the slate of its shoulders and hips to a vivid yellow at the feet. The feet themselves were heavily padded and nailless, which fact had also contributed to the noiselessness of their approach, and, in common with a multiplicity of legs, is a characteristic feature of the fauna of Mars. The highest type of man and one other animal, the only mammal existing on Mars, alone have well-formed nails, and there are absolutely no hoofed animals in existence there.

Behind this first charging demon trailed nineteen others, similar in all respects, but, as I learned later, bearing individual characteristics peculiar to themselves; precisely as no two of us are identical although we are all cast in a similar mold. This picture, or rather materialized nightmare, which I have described at length, made but one terrible and swift impression on me as I turned to meet it.

Unarmed and naked as I was, the first law of nature manifested itself in the only possible solution of my immediate problem, and that was to get out of the vicinity of the point of the charging spear. Consequently I gave a very earthly and at the same time superhuman leap to reach the top of the Martian incubator, for such I had determined it must be.

My effort was crowned with a success which appalled me no less than it seemed to surprise the Martian warriors, for it carried me fully thirty feet into the air and landed me a hundred feet from my pursuers and on the opposite side of the enclosure.

I alighted upon the soft moss easily and without mishap, and turning saw my enemies lined up along the further wall. Some were surveying me with expressions which I afterward discovered marked extreme astonishment, and the others were evidently satisfying themselves that I had not molested their young.

They were conversing together in low tones, and gesticulating and pointing toward me. Their discovery that I had not harmed the little Martians, and that I was unarmed, must have caused them to look upon me with less ferocity; but, as I was to learn later, the thing which weighed most in my favor was my exhibition of hurdling.

While the Martians are immense, their bones are very large and they are muscled only in proportion to the gravitation which they must overcome. The result is that they are infinitely less agile and less powerful, in proportion to their weight, than an Earth man, and I doubt that were one of them suddenly to be transported to Earth he could lift his own weight from the ground; in fact, I am convinced that he could not do so.

My feat then was as marvelous upon Mars as it would have been upon Earth, and from desiring to annihilate me they suddenly looked upon me as a wonderful discovery to be captured and exhibited among their fellows.

The respite my unexpected agility had given me permitted me to formulate plans for the immediate future and to note more closely the appearance of the warriors, for I could not disassociate these people in my mind from those other warriors who, only the day before, had been pursuing me.

I noted that each was armed with several other weapons in addition to the huge spear which I have described. The weapon which caused me to decide against an attempt at escape by flight was what was evidently a rifle of some description, and which I felt, for some reason, they were peculiarly efficient in handling.

These rifles were of a white metal stocked with wood, which I learned later was a very light and intensely hard growth much prized on Mars, and entirely unknown to us denizens of Earth. The metal of the barrel is an alloy composed principally of aluminum and steel which they have learned to temper to a hardness far exceeding that of the steel with which we are familiar. The weight of these rifles is comparatively little, and with the small caliber, explosive, radium projectiles which they use, and the great length of the barrel, they are deadly in the extreme and at ranges which would be unthinkable on Earth. The theoretic effective radius of this rifle is three hundred miles, but the best they can do in actual service when equipped with their wireless finders and sighters is but a trifle over two hundred miles.

This is quite far enough to imbue me with great respect for the Martian firearm, and some telepathic force must have warned me against an attempt to escape in broad daylight from under the muzzles of twenty of these death-dealing machines.

The Martians, after conversing for a short time, turned and rode away in the direction from which they had come, leaving one of their number alone by the enclosure. When they had covered perhaps two hundred yards they halted, and turning their mounts toward us sat watching the warrior by the enclosure.

He was the one whose spear had so nearly transfixed me, and was evidently the leader of the band, as I had noted that they seemed to have moved to their present position at his direction. When his force had come to a halt he dismounted, threw down his spear and small arms, and came around the end of the incubator toward me, entirely unarmed and as naked as I, except for the ornaments strapped upon his head, limbs, and breast.

When he was within about fifty feet of me he unclasped an enormous metal armlet, and holding it toward me in the open palm of his hand, addressed me in a clear, resonant voice, but in a language, it is needless to say, I could not understand. He then stopped as though waiting for my reply, pricking up his antennae-like ears and cocking his strange looking eyes still further toward me.

As the silence became painful I concluded to hazard a little conversation on my own part, as I had guessed that he was making overtures of peace.

The throwing down of his weapons and the withdrawing of his troop before his advance toward me would have signified a peaceful mission anywhere on Earth, so why not, then, on Mars!

Placing my hand over my heart I bowed low to the Martian and explained to him that while I did not understand his language, his actions spoke for the peace and friendship that at the present moment were most dear to my heart. Of course I might have been a babbling brook for all the intelligence my speech carried to him, but he understood the action with which I immediately followed my words.

Stretching my hand toward him, I advanced and took the armlet from his open palm, clasping it about my arm above the elbow; smiled at him and stood waiting. His wide mouth spread into an answering smile, and locking one of his intermediary arms in mine we turned and walked back toward his mount. At the same time he motioned his followers to advance. They started toward us on a wild run, but were checked by a signal from him. Evidently he feared that were I to be really frightened again I might jump entirely out of the landscape.

He exchanged a few words with his men, motioned to me that I would ride behind one of them, and then mounted his own animal. The fellow designated reached down two or three hands and lifted me up behind him on the glossy back of his mount, where I hung on as best I could by the belts and straps which held the Martian's weapons and ornaments.

The entire cavalcade then turned and galloped away toward the range of hills in the distance.

CHAPTER FOUR
A PRISONER

WE HAD GONE PERHAPS TEN MILES when the ground began to rise very rapidly. We were, as I was later to learn, nearing the edge of one of Mars' long dead seas, in the bottom of which my encounter with the Martians had taken place.

In a short time we gained the foot of the mountains, and after traversing a narrow gorge came to an open valley, at the far extremity of which was a low tableland upon which I beheld an enormous city. Toward this we galloped, entering it by what appeared to be a ruined roadway leading out from the city, but only to the edge of the tableland, where it ended abruptly in a flight of broad steps.

Upon closer observation I saw as we passed them that the buildings were deserted, and while not greatly decayed had the appearance of not having been tenanted for years, possibly for ages. Toward the center of the city was a large plaza, and upon this and in the buildings immediately surrounding it were camped some nine or ten hundred creatures of the same breed as my captors, for such I now considered them despite the suave manner in which I had been trapped.

With the exception of their ornaments all were naked. The women varied in appearance but little from the men, except that their tusks were much larger in proportion to their height, in some instances curving nearly to their high-set ears. Their bodies were smaller and lighter in color, and their fingers and toes bore the rudiments of nails, which were entirely lacking among the males. The adult females ranged in height from ten to twelve feet.

The children were light in color, even lighter than the women, and all looked precisely alike to me, except that some were taller than others; older, I presumed.

I saw no signs of extreme age among them, nor is there any appreciable difference in their appearance from the age of maturity, about forty, until, at about the age of one thousand years, they go voluntarily upon their last strange pilgrimage down the river Iss, which leads no living Martian knows whither and from whose bosom no Martian has ever returned, or would be allowed to live did he return after once embarking upon its cold, dark waters.

Only about one Martian in a thousand dies of sickness or disease, and possibly about twenty take the voluntary pilgrimage. The other nine hundred and seventy-nine die violent deaths in duels, in hunting, in avia-tion, and in war; but perhaps by far the greatest death loss comes during the age of childhood, when vast numbers of the little Martians fall victims to the great white apes of Mars.

The average life expectancy of a Martian after the age of maturity is about three hundred years, but would be nearer the one-thousand mark were it not for the various means leading to violent death. Owing to the waning resources of the planet it evidently became necessary to counteract the increasing longevity which their remarkable skill in therapeutics and surgery produced, and so human life has come to be considered but lightly on Mars, as is evidenced by their dangerous sports and the almost continual warfare between the various communities.

There are other and natural causes tending toward a diminution of population, but nothing contributes so greatly to this end as the fact that no male or female Martian is ever voluntarily without a weapon of destruction.

As we neared the plaza and my presence was discovered we were immediately surrounded by hundreds of the creatures who seemed anxious to pluck me from my seat behind my guard. A word from the leader of the party stilled their clamor, and we proceeded at a trot across the plaza to the entrance of as magnificent an edifice as mortal eye has rested upon.

The building was low, but covered an enormous area. It was constructed of gleaming white marble inlaid with gold and brilliant stones which sparkled and scintillated in the sunlight. The main entrance was some hundred feet in width and projected from the building proper to form a huge canopy above the entrance hall. There was no stairway, but a gentle incline to the first floor of the building opened into an enormous chamber encircled by galleries.

On the floor of this chamber, which was dotted with highly carved wooden desks and chairs, were assembled about forty or fifty male Martians around the steps of a rostrum. On the platform proper squatted an enormous warrior heavily loaded with metal ornaments, gay-colored feathers and beautifully wrought leather trappings ingeniously set with precious stones. From his shoulders depended a short cape of white fur lined with brilliant scarlet silk.

What struck me as most remarkable about this assemblage and the hall in which they were congregated was the fact that the creatures were entirely out of proportion to the desks, chairs, and other furnishings; these being of a size adapted to human beings such as I, whereas the great bulks of the Martians could scarcely have squeezed into the chairs, nor was there room beneath the desks for their long legs. Evidently, then, there were other denizens on Mars than the wild and grotesque creatures into whose hands I had fallen, but the evidences of extreme antiquity which showed all around me indicated that these buildings might have belonged to some long extinct and forgotten race in the dim antiquity of Mars.

Our party had halted at the entrance to the building, and at a sign from the leader I had been lowered to the ground. Again locking his arm in mine, we had proceeded into the audience chamber. There were few formalities observed in approaching the Martian chieftain. My captor merely strode up to the rostrum, the others making way for him as he advanced. The chieftain rose to his feet and uttered the name of my escort who, in turn, halted and repeated the name of the ruler followed by his title.

At the time, this ceremony and the words they uttered meant nothing to me, but later I came to know that this was the customary greeting between green Martians. Had the men been strangers, and therefore unable to exchange names, they would have silently exchanged ornaments, had their missions been peaceful—otherwise they would have exchanged shots, or have fought out their introduction with some other of their various weapons.

My captor, whose name was Tars Tarkas, was virtually the vice-chieftain of the community, and a man of great ability as a statesman and warrior. He evidently explained briefly the incidents connected with his expedition, including my capture, and when he had concluded the chieftain addressed me at some length.

I replied in our good old English tongue merely to convince him that neither of us could understand the other; but I noticed that when I smiled slightly on concluding, he did likewise. This fact, and the similar occurrence during my first talk with Tars Tarkas, convinced me that we had at least something in common; the ability to smile, therefore to laugh; denoting a sense of humor. But I was to learn that the Martian smile is merely perfunctory, and that the Martian laugh is a thing to cause strong men to blanch in horror.

The ideas of humor among the green men of Mars are widely at variance with our conceptions of incitants to merriment. The death agonies of a fellow being are, to these strange creatures, provocative of the wildest hilarity, while their chief form of commonest amusement is to inflict death on their prisoners of war in various ingenious and horrible ways.

The assembled warriors and chieftains examined me closely, feeling my muscles and the texture of my skin. The principal chieftain then evidently signified a desire to see me perform, and, motioning me to follow, he started with Tars Tarkas for the open plaza.

Now, I had made no attempt to walk, since my first signal failure, except while tightly grasping Tars Tarkas' arm, and so now I went skipping and flitting about among the desks and chairs like some monstrous grasshopper. After bruising myself severely, much to the amusement of the Martians, I again had recourse to creeping, but this did not suit them and I was roughly jerked to my feet by a towering fellow who had laughed most heartily at my misfortunes.

As he banged me down upon my feet his face was bent close to mine and I did the only thing a gentleman might do under the circumstances of brutality, boorishness, and lack of consideration for a stranger's rights; I swung my fist squarely to his jaw and he went down like a felled ox. As he sunk to the floor I wheeled around with my back toward the nearest desk, expecting to be overwhelmed by the vengeance of his fellows, but determined to give them as good a battle as the unequal odds would permit before I gave up my life.

My fears were groundless, however, as the other Martians, at first struck dumb with wonderment, finally broke into wild peals of laughter and applause. I did not recognize the applause as such, but later, when I had become acquainted with their customs, I learned that I had won what they seldom accord, a manifestation of approbation.

The fellow whom I had struck lay where he had fallen, nor did any of his mates approach him. Tars Tarkas advanced toward me, holding out one of his arms, and we thus proceeded to the plaza without further mishap. I did not, of course, know the reason for which we had come to the open, but I was not long in being enlightened. They first repeated the word "sak" a number of times, and then Tars Tarkas made several jumps, repeating the same word before each leap; then, turning to me, he said, "sak!" I saw what they were after, and gathering myself together I "sakked" with such marvelous success that I cleared a good hundred and fifty feet; nor did I, this time, lose my equilibrium, but landed squarely upon my feet without falling. I then returned by easy jumps of twenty-five or thirty feet to the little group of warriors.

My exhibition had been witnessed by several hundred lesser Martians, and they immediately broke into demands for a repetition, which the chieftain then ordered me to make; but I was both hungry and thirsty, and determined on the spot that my only method of salvation was to demand the consideration from these creatures which they evidently would not voluntarily accord. I therefore ignored the repeated commands to "sak," and each time they were made I motioned to my mouth and rubbed my stomach.

Tars Tarkas and the chief exchanged a few words, and the former, calling to a young female among the throng, gave her some instructions and motioned me to accompany her. I grasped her proffered arm and together we crossed the plaza toward a large building on the far side.

My fair companion was about eight feet tall, having just arrived at maturity, but not yet to her full height. She was of a light olive-green color, with a smooth, glossy hide. Her name, as I afterward learned, was Sola, and she belonged to the retinue of Tars Tarkas. She conducted me to a spacious chamber in one of the buildings fronting on the plaza, and which, from the litter of silks and furs upon the floor, I took to be the sleeping quarters of several of the natives.

The room was well lighted by a number of large windows and was beautifully decorated with mural paintings and mosaics, but upon all there seemed to rest that indefinable touch of the finger of antiquity which convinced me that the architects and builders of these wondrous creations had nothing in common with the crude half-brutes which now occupied them.

Sola motioned me to be seated upon a pile of silks near the center of the room, and, turning, made a peculiar hissing sound, as though signaling to someone in an adjoining room. In response to her call I obtained my first sight of a new Martian wonder. It waddled in on its ten short legs, and squatted down before the girl like an obedient puppy. The thing was about the size of a Shetland pony, but its head bore a slight resemblance to that of a frog, except that the jaws were equipped with three rows of long, sharp tusks.

CHAPTER FIVE
I ELUDE MY WATCHDOG

SOLA STARED INTO THE BRUTE'S wicked-looking eyes, muttered a word or two of command, pointed to me, and left the chamber. I could not but wonder what this ferocious-looking monstrosity might do when left alone in such close proximity to such a relatively tender morsel of meat; but my fears were groundless, as the beast, after surveying me intently for a moment, crossed the room to the only exit which led to the street, and lay down full length across the threshold.

This was my first experience with a Martian watchdog, but it was destined not to be my last, for this fellow guarded me carefully during the time I remained a captive among these green men; twice saving my life, and never voluntarily being away from me a moment.

While Sola was away I took occasion to examine more minutely the room in which I found myself captive. The mural painting depicted scenes of rare and wonderful beauty: mountains, rivers, lake, ocean, meadow, trees and flowers, winding roadways, sun-kissed gardens—scenes which might have portrayed earthly views but for the different colorings of the vegetation. The work had evidently been wrought by a master hand, so subtle the atmosphere, so perfect the technique; yet nowhere was there a representation of a living animal, either human or brute, by which I could guess at the likeness of these other and perhaps extinct denizens of Mars.

While I was allowing my fancy to run riot in wild conjecture on the possible explanation of the strange anomalies which I had so far met with on Mars, Sola returned bearing both food and drink. These she placed on the floor beside me, and seating herself a short ways off regarded me intently. The food consisted of about a pound of some solid substance of the consistency of cheese and almost tasteless, while the liquid was apparently milk from some animal. It was not unpleasant to the taste, though slightly acid, and I learned in a short time to prize it very highly. It came, as I later discovered, not from an animal, as there is only one mammal on Mars and that one very rare indeed, but from a large plant which grows practically without water, but seems to distill its plentiful supply of milk from the products of the soil, the moisture of the air, and the rays of the sun. A single plant of this species will give eight or ten quarts of milk per day.

After I had eaten I was greatly invigorated, but feeling the need of rest I stretched out upon the silks and was soon asleep. I must have slept several hours, as it was dark when I awoke, and I was very cold. I noticed that someone had thrown a fur over me, but it had become partially dislodged and in the darkness I could not see to replace it. Suddenly a hand reached out and pulled the fur over me, shortly afterward adding another to my covering.

I presumed that my watchful guardian was Sola, nor was I wrong. This girl alone, among all the green Martians with whom I came in contact, disclosed characteristics of sympathy, kindliness, and affection; her ministrations to my bodily wants were unfailing, and her solicitous care saved me from much suffering and many hardships.

As I was to learn, the Martian nights are extremely cold, and as there is practically no twilight or dawn, the changes in temperature are sudden and most uncomfortable, as are the transitions from brilliant daylight to darkness. The nights are either brilliantly illumined or very dark, for if neither of the two moons of Mars happen to be in the sky almost total darkness results, since the lack of atmosphere, or, rather, the very thin atmosphere, fails to diffuse the starlight to any great extent; on the other hand, if both of the moons are in the heavens at night the surface of the ground is brightly illuminated.

Both of Mars' moons are vastly nearer her than is our moon to Earth; the nearer moon being but about five thousand miles distant, while the further is but little more than fourteen thousand miles away, against the nearly one-quarter million miles which separate us from our moon. The nearer moon of Mars makes a complete revolution around the planet in a little over seven and one-half hours, so that she may be seen hurtling through the sky like some huge meteor two or three times each night, revealing all her phases during each transit of the heavens.

The further moon revolves about Mars in something over thirty and one-quarter hours, and with her sister satellite makes a nocturnal Martian scene one of splendid and weird grandeur. And it is well that nature has so graciously and abundantly lighted the Martian night, for the green men of Mars, being a nomadic race without high intellectual development, have but crude means for artificial lighting; depending principally upon torches, a kind of candle, and a peculiar oil lamp which generates a gas and burns without a wick.

This last device produces an intensely brilliant far-reaching white light, but as the natural oil which it requires can only be obtained by mining in one of several widely separated and remote localities it is seldom used by these creatures whose only thought is for today, and whose hatred for manual labor has kept them in a semi-barbaric state for countless ages.

After Sola had replenished my coverings I again slept, nor did I awaken until daylight. The other occupants of the room, five in number, were all females, and they were still sleeping, piled high with a motley array of silks and furs. Across the threshold lay stretched the sleepless guardian brute, just as I had last seen him on the preceding day; apparently he had not moved a muscle; his eyes were fairly glued upon me, and I fell to wondering just what might befall me should I endeavor to escape.

I have ever been prone to seek adventure and to investigate and experiment where wiser men would have left well enough alone. It therefore now occurred to me that the surest way of learning the exact attitude of this beast toward me would be to attempt to leave the room. I felt fairly secure in my belief that I could escape him should he pursue me once I was outside the building, for I had begun to take great pride in my ability as a jumper. Furthermore, I could see from the shortness of his legs that the brute himself was no jumper and probably no runner.

Slowly and carefully, therefore, I gained my feet, only to see that my watcher did the same; cautiously I advanced toward him, finding that by moving with a shuffling gait I could retain my balance as well as make reasonably rapid progress. As I neared the brute he backed cautiously away from me, and when I had reached the open he moved to one side to let me pass. He then fell in behind me and followed about ten paces in my rear as I made my way along the deserted street.

Evidently his mission was to protect me only, I thought, but when we reached the edge of the city he suddenly sprang before me, uttering strange sounds and baring his ugly and ferocious tusks. Thinking to have some amusement at his expense, I rushed toward him, and when almost upon him sprang into the air, alighting far beyond him and away from the city. He wheeled instantly and charged me with the most appalling speed I had ever beheld. I had thought his short legs a bar to swiftness, but had he been coursing with greyhounds the latter would have appeared as though asleep on a door mat. As I was to learn, this is the fleetest animal on Mars, and owing to its intelligence, loyalty, and ferocity is used in hunting, in war, and as the protector of the Martian man.

I quickly saw that I would have difficulty in escaping the fangs of the beast on a straightaway course, and so I met his charge by doubling in my tracks and leaping over him as he was almost upon me. This maneuver gave me a considerable advantage, and I was able to reach the city quite a bit ahead of him, and as he came tearing after me I jumped for a window about thirty feet from the ground in the face of one of the buildings overlooking the valley.

Grasping the sill I pulled myself up to a sitting posture without looking into the building, and gazed down at the baffled animal beneath me. My exultation was short lived, however, for scarcely had I gained a secure seat upon the sill than a huge hand grasped me by the neck from behind and dragged me violently into the room. Here I was thrown upon my back, and beheld standing over me a colossal apelike creature, white and hairless except for an enormous shock of bristly hair upon its head.

CHAPTER SIX
A Fight that Won Friends

THE THING, WHICH MORE NEARLY RESEMBLED our earthly men than it did the Martians I had seen, held me pinioned to the ground with one huge foot, while it jabbered and gesticulated at some answering creature behind me. This other, which was evidently its mate, soon came toward us, bearing a mighty stone cudgel with which it evidently intended to brain me.

The creatures were about ten or fifteen feet tall, standing erect, and had, like the green Martians, an intermediary set of arms or legs, midway between their upper and lower limbs. Their eyes were close together and non-protruding; their ears were high set, but more laterally located than those of the Martians, while their snouts and teeth were strikingly like those of our African gorilla. Altogether they were not unlovely when viewed in comparison with the green Martians.

The cudgel was swinging in the arc which ended upon my upturned face when a bolt of myriad-legged horror hurled itself through the doorway full upon the breast of my executioner. With a shriek of fear the ape which held me leaped through the open window, but its mate closed in a terrific death struggle with my preserver, which was nothing less than my faithful watch-thing; I cannot bring myself to call so hideous a creature a dog.

As quickly as possible I gained my feet and backing against the wall I witnessed such a battle as it is vouchsafed few beings to see. The strength, agility, and blind ferocity of these two creatures is approached by nothing known to earthly man. My beast had an advantage in his first hold, having sunk his mighty fangs far into the breast of his adversary; but the great arms and paws of the ape, backed by muscles far transcending those of the Martian men I had seen, had locked the throat of my guardian and slowly were choking out his life, and bending back his head and neck upon his body, where I momentarily expected the former to fall limp at the end of a broken neck.

In accomplishing this the ape was tearing away the entire front of its breast, which was held in the viselike grip of the powerful jaws. Back and forth upon the floor they rolled, neither one emitting a sound of fear or pain. Presently I saw the great eyes of my beast bulging completely from their sockets and blood flowing from its nostrils. That he was weakening perceptibly was evident, but so also was the ape, whose struggles were growing momentarily less.

Suddenly I came to myself and, with that strange instinct which seems ever to prompt me to my duty, I seized the cudgel, which had fallen to the floor at the commencement of the battle, and swinging it with all the power of my earthly arms I crashed it full upon the head of the ape, crushing his skull as though it had been an egg shell.

Scarcely had the blow descended when I was confronted with a new danger. The ape's mate, recovered from its first shock of terror, had returned to the scene of the encounter by way of the interior of the building. I glimpsed him just before he reached the doorway and the sight of him, now roaring as he perceived his lifeless fellow stretched upon the floor, and frothing at the mouth, in the extremity of his rage, filled me, I must confess, with dire forebodings.

I am ever willing to stand and fight when the odds are not too overwhelmingly against me, but in this instance I perceived neither glory nor profit in pitting my relatively puny strength against the iron muscles and brutal ferocity of this enraged denizen of an unknown world; in fact, the only outcome of such an encounter, so far as I might be concerned, seemed sudden death.

I was standing near the window and I knew that once in the street I might gain the plaza and safety before the creature could overtake me; at least there was a chance for safety in flight, against almost certain death should I remain and fight however desperately.

It is true I held the cudgel, but what could I do with it against his four great arms? Even should I break one of them with my first blow, for I figured that he would attempt to ward off the cudgel, he could reach out and annihilate me with the others before I could recover for a second attack.

In the instant that these thoughts passed through my mind I had turned to make for the window, but my eyes alighting on the form of my erstwhile guardian threw all thoughts of flight to the four winds. He lay gasping upon the floor of the chamber, his great eyes fastened upon me in what seemed a pitiful appeal for protection. I could not withstand that look, nor could I, on second thought, have deserted my rescuer without giving as good an account of myself in his behalf as he had in mine.

Without more ado, therefore, I turned to meet the charge of the infuriated bull ape. He was now too close upon me for the cudgel to prove of any effective assistance, so I merely threw it as heavily as I could at his advancing bulk. It struck him just below the knees, eliciting a howl of pain and rage, and so throwing him off his balance that he lunged full upon me with arms wide stretched to ease his fall.

Again, as on the preceding day, I had recourse to earthly tactics, and swinging my right fist full upon the point of his chin I followed it with a smashing left to the pit of his stomach. The effect was marvelous, for, as I lightly side-stepped, after delivering the second blow, he reeled and fell upon the floor doubled up with pain and gasping for wind. Leaping over his prostrate body, I seized the cudgel and finished the monster before he could regain his feet.

As I delivered the blow a low laugh rang out behind me, and, turning, I beheld Tars Tarkas, Sola, and three or four warriors standing in the doorway of the chamber. As my eyes met theirs I was, for the second time, the recipient of their zealously guarded applause.

My absence had been noted by Sola on her awakening, and she had quickly informed Tars Tarkas, who had set out immediately with a handful of warriors to search for me. As they had approached the limits of the city they had witnessed the actions of the bull ape as he bolted into the building, frothing with rage.

They had followed immediately behind him, thinking it barely possible that his actions might prove a clue to my whereabouts, and had witnessed my short but decisive battle with him. This encounter, together with my set-to with the Martian warrior on the previous day and my feats of jumping placed me upon a high pinnacle in their regard. Evidently devoid of all the finer sentiments of friendship, love, or affection, these people fairly worship physical prowess and bravery, and nothing is too good for the object of their adoration as long as he maintains his position by repeated examples of his skill, strength, and courage.

Sola, who had accompanied the searching party of her own volition, was the only one of the Martians whose face had not been twisted in laughter as I battled for my life. She, on the contrary, was sober with apparent solicitude and, as soon as I had finished the monster, rushed to me and carefully examined my body for possible wounds or injuries. Satisfying herself that I had come off unscathed she smiled quietly, and, taking my hand, started toward the door of the chamber.

Tars Tarkas and the other warriors had entered and were standing over the now rapidly reviving brute which had saved my life, and whose life I, in turn, had rescued. They seemed to be deep in argument, and finally one of them addressed me, but remembering my ignorance of his language turned back to Tars Tarkas, who, with a word and gesture, gave some command to the fellow and turned to follow us from the room.

There seemed something menacing in their attitude toward my beast, and I hesitated to leave until I had learned the outcome. It was well I did so, for the warrior drew an evil-looking pistol from its holster and was on the point of putting an end to the creature when I sprang forward and struck up his arm. The bullet striking the wooden casing of the window exploded, blowing a hole completely through the wood and masonry.

I then knelt down beside the fearsome looking thing, and raising it to its feet motioned for it to follow me. The looks of surprise which my actions elicited from the Martians were ludicrous; they could not understand, except in a feeble and childish way, such attributes as gratitude and compassion. The warrior whose gun I had struck up looked inquiringly at Tars Tarkas, but the latter signed that I be left to my own devices, and so we returned to the plaza with my great beast following close at heel, and Sola grasping me tightly by the arm.

I had at least two friends on Mars; a young woman who watched over me with motherly solicitude, and a dumb brute which, as I later came to know, held in its poor ugly carcass more love, more loyalty, more gratitude than could have been found in the entire five million green Martians who rove the deserted cities and dead sea bottoms of Mars.

CHAPTER SEVEN
CHILD-RAISING ON MARS

AFTER A BREAKFAST, which was an exact replica of the meal of the preceding day and an index of practically every meal which followed while I was with the green men of Mars, Sola escorted me to the plaza, where I found the entire community engaged in watching or helping at the harnessing of huge mastodonian animals to great three-wheeled chariots. There were about two hundred and fifty of these vehicles, each drawn by a single animal, any one of which, from their appearance, might easily have drawn the entire wagon train when fully loaded.

The chariots themselves were large, commodious, and gorgeously decorated. In each was seated a female Martian loaded with ornaments of metal, with jewels and silks and furs, and upon the back of each of the beasts which drew the chariots was perched a young Martian driver. Like the animals upon which the warriors were mounted, the heavier draft animals wore neither bit nor bridle, but were guided entirely by telepathic means.

This power is wonderfully developed in all Martians, and accounts largely for the simplicity of their language and the relatively few spoken words exchanged even in long conversations. It is the universal language of Mars, through the medium of which the higher and lower animals of this world of paradoxes are able to communicate to a greater or less extent, depending upon the intellectual sphere of the species and the development of the individual.

As the cavalcade took up the line of march in single file, Sola dragged me into an empty chariot and we proceeded with the procession toward the point by which I had entered the city the day before. At the head of the caravan rode some two hundred warriors, five abreast, and a like number brought up the rear, while twenty-five or thirty outriders flanked us on either side.

Everyone but myself—men, women, and children— were heavily armed, and at the tail of each chariot trotted a Martian hound, my own beast following closely behind ours; in fact, the faithful creature never left me voluntarily during the entire ten years I spent on Mars. Our way led out across the little valley before the city, through the hills, and down into the dead sea bottom which I had traversed on my journey from the incubator to the plaza. The incubator, as it proved, was the terminal point of our journey this day, and, as the entire cavalcade broke into a mad gallop as soon as we reached the level expanse of sea bottom, we were soon within sight of our goal.

On reaching it the chariots were parked with military precision on the four sides of the enclosure, and half a score of warriors, headed by the enormous chieftain, and including Tars Tarkas and several other lesser chiefs, dismounted and advanced toward it. I could see Tars Tarkas explaining something to the principal chieftain, whose name, by the way, was, as nearly as I can translate it into English, Lorquas Ptomel, Jed; jed being his title.

I was soon apprised of the subject of their conversation, as, calling to Sola, Tars Tarkas signed for her to send me to him. I had by this time mastered the intricacies of walking under Martian conditions, and quickly responding to his command I advanced to the side of the incubator where the warriors stood.

As I reached their side a glance showed me that all but a very few eggs had hatched, the incubator being fairly alive with the hideous little devils. They ranged in height from three to four feet, and were moving restlessly about the enclosure as though searching for food.

As I came to a halt before him, Tars Tarkas pointed over the incubator and said, "sak." I saw that he wanted me to repeat my performance of yesterday for the edification of Lorquas Ptomel, and, as I must confess that my prowess gave me no little satisfaction, I responded quickly, leaping entirely over the parked chariots on the far side of the incubator. As I returned, Lorquas Ptomel grunted something at me, and turning to his warriors gave a few words of command relative to the incubator. They paid no further attention to me and I was thus permitted to remain close and watch their operations, which consisted in breaking an opening in the wall of the incubator large enough to permit of the exit of the young Martians.

On either side of this opening the women and the younger Martians, both male and female, formed two solid walls leading out through the chariots and quite away into the plain beyond. Between these walls the little Martians scampered, wild as deer; being permitted to run the full length of the aisle, where they were captured one at a time by the women and older children; the last in the line capturing the first little one to reach the end of the gauntlet, her opposite in the line capturing the second, and so on until all the little fellows had left the enclosure and been appropriated by some youth or female. As the women caught the young they fell out of line and returned to their respective chariots, while those who fell into the hands of the young men were later turned over to some of the women.

I saw that the ceremony, if it could be dignified by such a name, was over, and seeking out Sola I found her in our chariot with a hideous little creature held tightly in her arms.

The work of rearing young, green Martians consists solely in teaching them to talk, and to use the weapons of warfare with which they are loaded down from the very first year of their lives. Coming from eggs in which they have lain for five years, the period of incubation, they step forth into the world perfectly developed except in size. Entirely unknown to their own mothers, who, in turn, would have difficulty in pointing out the fathers with any degree of accuracy, they are the common children of the community, and their education devolves upon the females who chance to capture them as they leave the incubator.

Their foster mothers may not even have had an egg in the incubator, as was the case with Sola, who had not commenced to lay, until less than a year before she became the mother of another woman's offspring. But this counts for little among the green Martians, as parental and filial love is as unknown to them as it is common among us. I believe this horrible system which has been carried on for ages is the direct cause of the loss of all the finer feelings and higher humanitarian instincts among these poor creatures. From birth they know no father or mother love, they know not the meaning of the word home; they are taught that they are only suffered to live until they can demonstrate by their physique and ferocity that they are fit to live. Should they prove deformed or defective in any way they are promptly shot; nor do they see a tear shed for a single one of the many cruel hardships they pass through from earliest infancy.

I do not mean that the adult Martians are unnecessarily or intentionally cruel to the young, but theirs is a hard and pitiless struggle for existence upon a dying planet, the natural resources of which have dwindled to a point where the support of each additional life means an added tax upon the community into which it is thrown.

By careful selection they rear only the hardiest specimens of each species, and with almost supernatural foresight they regulate the birth rate to merely offset the loss by death. Each adult Martian female brings forth about thirteen eggs each year, and those which meet the size, weight, and specific gravity tests are hidden in the recesses of some subterranean vault where the temperature is too low for incubation. Every year these eggs are carefully examined by a council of twenty chieftains, and all but about one hundred of the most perfect are destroyed out of each yearly supply. At the end of five years about five hundred almost perfect eggs have been chosen from the thousands brought forth. These are then placed in the almost airtight incubators to be hatched by the sun's rays after a period of another five years. The hatching which we had witnessed today was a fairly representative event of its kind, all but about one percent of the eggs hatching in two days. If the remaining eggs ever hatched we knew nothing of the fate of the little Martians. They were not wanted, as their offspring might inherit and transmit the tendency to prolonged incubation, and thus upset the system which has maintained for ages and which permits the adult Martians to figure the proper time for return to the incubators, almost to an hour.

The incubators are built in remote fastnesses, where there is little or no likelihood of their being discovered by other tribes. The result of such a catastrophe would mean no children in the community for another five years. I was later to witness the results of the discovery of an alien incubator.

The community of which the green Martians with whom my lot was cast formed a part was composed of some thirty thousand souls. They roamed an enormous tract of arid and semiarid land between forty and eighty degrees south latitude, and bounded on the east and west by two large fertile tracts. Their headquarters lay in the southwest corner of this district, near the crossing of two of the so-called Martian canals.

As the incubator had been placed far north of their own territory in a supposedly uninhabited and unfrequented, area, we had before us a tremendous journey, concerning which I, of course, knew nothing.

After our return to the dead city I passed several days in comparative idleness. On the day following our return all the warriors had ridden forth early in the morning and had not returned until just before darkness fell. As I later learned, they had been to the subterranean vaults in which the eggs were kept and had transported them to the incubator, which they had then walled up for another five years, and which, in all probability, would not be visited again during that period.

The vaults which hid the eggs until they were ready for the incubator were located many miles south of the incubator, and would be visited yearly by the council of twenty chieftains. Why they did not arrange to build their vaults and incubators nearer home has always been a mystery to me, and, like many other Martian mysteries, unsolved and unsolvable by earthly reasoning and customs.

Sola's duties were now doubled, as she was compelled to care for the young Martian as well as for me, but neither one of us required much attention, and as we were both about equally advanced in Martian education, Sola took it upon herself to train us together.

Her prize consisted in a male about four feet tall, very strong and physically perfect; also, he learned quickly, and we had considerable amusement, at least I did, over the keen rivalry we displayed. The Martian language, as I have said, is extremely simple, and in a week I could make all my wants known and understand nearly everything that was said to me. Likewise, under Sola's tutelage, I developed my telepathic powers so that I shortly could sense practically everything that went on around me.

What surprised Sola most in me was that while I could catch telepathic messages easily from others, and often when they were not intended for me, no one could read a jot from my mind under any circumstances. At first this vexed me, but later I was very glad of it, as it gave me an undoubted advantage over the Martians.

CHAPTER EIGHT
A Fair Captive from the Sky

THE THIRD DAY AFTER THE INCUBATOR CEREMONY we set forth toward home, but scarcely had the head of the procession debouched into the open ground before the city than orders were given for an immediate and hasty return. As though trained for years in this particular evolution, the green Martians melted like mist into the spacious doorways of the nearby buildings, until, in less than three minutes, the entire cavalcade of chariots, mastodons and mounted warriors was nowhere to be seen.

Sola and I had entered a building upon the front of the city, in fact, the same one in which I had had my encounter with the apes, and, wishing to see what had caused the sudden retreat, I mounted to an upper floor and peered from the window out over the valley and the hills beyond; and there I saw the cause of their sudden scurrying to cover. A huge craft, long, low, and gray painted, swung slowly over the crest of the nearest hill. Following it came another, and another, and another, until twenty of them, swinging low above the ground, sailed slowly and majestically toward us.

Each carried a strange banner swung from stem to stem above the upper works, and upon the prow of each was painted some odd device that gleamed in the sunlight and showed plainly even at the distance at which we were from the vessels. I could see figures crowding the forward decks and upper works of the air craft. Whether they had discovered us or simply were looking at the deserted city I could not say, but in any event they received a rude reception, for suddenly and without warning the green Martian warriors fired a terrific volley from the windows of the buildings facing the little valley across which the great ships were so peacefully advancing.

Instantly the scene changed as by magic; the foremost vessel swung broadside toward us, and bringing her guns into play returned our fire, at the same time moving parallel to our front for a short distance and then turning back with the evident intention of completing a great circle which would bring her up to position once more opposite our firing line; the other vessels followed in her wake, each one opening upon us as she swung into position. Our own fire never diminished, and I doubt if twenty-five per cent of our shots went wild. It had never been given me to see such deadly accuracy of aim, and it seemed as though a little figure on one of the craft dropped at the explosion of each bullet, while the banners and upper works dissolved in spurts of flame as the irresistible projectiles of our warriors mowed through them.

The fire from the vessels was most ineffectual, owing, as I afterward learned, to the unexpected suddenness of the first volley, which caught the ship's crews entirely unprepared and the sighting apparatus of the guns unprotected from the deadly aim of our warriors.

It seems that each green warrior has certain objective points for his fire under relatively identical circumstances of warfare. For example, a proportion of them, always the best marksmen, direct their fire entirely upon the wireless finding and sighting apparatus of the big guns of an attacking naval force; another detail attends to the smaller guns in the same way; others pick off the gunners; still others the officers; while certain other quotas concentrate their attention upon the other members of the crew, upon the upper works, and upon the steering gear and propellers.

Twenty minutes after the first volley the great fleet swung trailing off in the direction from which it had first appeared. Several of the craft were limping perceptibly, and seemed but barely under the control of their depleted crews. Their fire had ceased entirely and all their energies seemed focused upon escape. Our warriors then rushed up to the roofs of the buildings which we occupied and followed the retreating armada with a continuous fusillade of deadly fire.

One by one, however, the ships managed to dip below the crests of the outlying hills until only one barely moving craft was in sight. This had received the brunt of our fire and seemed to be entirely unmanned, as not a moving figure was visible upon her decks. Slowly she swung from her course, circling back toward us in an erratic and pitiful manner. Instantly the warriors ceased firing, for it was quite apparent that the vessel was entirely helpless, and, far from being in a position to inflict harm upon us, she could not even control herself sufficiently to escape.

As she neared the city the warriors rushed out upon the plain to meet her, but it was evident that she still was too high for them to hope to reach her decks. From my vantage point in the window I could see the bodies of her crew strewn about, although I could not make out what manner of creatures they might be. Not a sign of life was manifest upon her as she drifted slowly with the light breeze in a southeasterly direction.

She was drifting some fifty feet above the ground, followed by all but some hundred of the warriors who had been ordered back to the roofs to cover the possibility of a return of the fleet, or of reinforcements. It soon became evident that she would strike the face of the buildings about a mile south of our position, and as I watched the progress of the chase I saw a number of warriors gallop ahead, dismount and enter the building she seemed destined to touch.

As the craft neared the building, and just before she struck, the Martian warriors swarmed upon her from the windows, and with their great spears eased the shock of the collision, and in a few moments they had thrown out grappling hooks and the big boat was being hauled to ground by their fellows below.

After making her fast, they swarmed the sides and searched the vessel from stem to stern. I could see them examining the dead sailors, evidently for signs of life, and presently a party of them appeared from below dragging a little figure among them. The creature was considerably less than half as tall as the green Martian warriors, and from my balcony I could see that it walked erect upon two legs and surmised that it was some new and strange Martian monstrosity with which I had not as yet become acquainted.

They removed their prisoner to the ground and then commenced a systematic rifling of the vessel. This operation required several hours, during which time a number of the chariots were requisitioned to transport the loot, which consisted in arms, ammunition, silks, furs, jewels, strangely carved stone vessels, and a quantity of solid foods and liquids, including many casks of water, the first I had seen since my advent upon Mars.

After the last load had been removed the warriors made lines fast to the craft and towed her far out into the valley in a southwesterly direction. A few of them then boarded her and were busily engaged in what appeared, from my distant position, as the emptying of the contents of various carboys upon the dead bodies of the sailors and over the decks and works of the vessel.

This operation concluded, they hastily clambered over her sides, sliding down the guy ropes to the ground. The last warrior to leave the deck turned and threw something back upon the vessel, waiting an instant to note the outcome of his act. As a faint spurt of flame rose from the point where the missile struck he swung over the side and was quickly upon the ground. Scarcely had he alighted than the guy ropes were simultaneously released, and the great warship, lightened by the removal of the loot, soared majestically into the air, her decks and upper works a mass of roaring flames.

Slowly she drifted to the southeast, rising higher and higher as the flames ate away her wooden parts and diminished the weight upon her. Ascending to the roof of the building I watched her for hours, until finally she was lost in the dim vistas of the distance. The sight was awe-inspiring in the extreme as one contemplated this mighty floating funeral pyre, drifting unguided and unmanned through the lonely wastes of the Martian heavens; a derelict of death and destruction, typifying the life story of these strange and ferocious creatures into whose unfriendly hands fate had carried it.

Much depressed, and, to me, unaccountably so, I slowly descended to the street. The scene I had witnessed seemed to mark the defeat and annihilation of the forces of a kindred people, rather than the routing by our green warriors of a horde of similar, though unfriendly, creatures. I could not fathom the seeming hallucination, nor could I free myself from it; but somewhere in the innermost recesses of my soul I felt a strange yearning toward these unknown foemen, and a mighty hope surged through me that the fleet would return and demand a reckoning from the green warriors who had so ruthlessly and wantonly attacked it.

Close at my heel, in his now accustomed place, followed Woola, the hound, and as I emerged upon the street Sola rushed up to me as though I had been the object of some search on her part. The cavalcade was returning to the plaza, the homeward march having been given up for that day; nor, in fact, was it recommenced for more than a week, owing to the fear of a return attack by the air craft.

Lorquas Ptomel was too astute an old warrior to be caught upon the open plains with a caravan of chariots and children, and so we remained at the deserted city until the danger seemed passed.

As Sola and I entered the plaza a sight met my eyes which filled my whole being with a great surge of mingled hope, fear, exultation, and depression, and yet most dominant was a subtle sense of relief and happiness; for just as we neared the throng of Martians I caught a glimpse of the prisoner from the battle craft who was being roughly dragged into a nearby building by a couple of green Martian females.

And the sight which met my eyes was that of a slender, girlish figure, similar in every detail to the earthly women of my past life. She did not see me at first, but just as she was disappearing through the portal of the building which was to be her prison she turned, and her eyes met mine. Her face was oval and beautiful in the extreme, her every feature was finely chiseled and exquisite, her eyes large and lustrous and her head surmounted by a mass of coal black, waving hair, caught loosely into a strange yet becoming coiffure. Her skin was of a light reddish copper color, against which the crimson glow of her cheeks and the ruby of her beautifully molded lips shone with a strangely enhancing effect.

She was as destitute of clothes as the green Martians who accompanied her; indeed, save for her highly wrought ornaments she was entirely naked, nor could any apparel have enhanced the beauty of her perfect and symmetrical figure.

As her gaze rested on me her eyes opened wide in astonishment, and she made a little sign with her free hand; a sign which I did not, of course, understand. Just a moment we gazed upon each other, and then the look of hope and renewed courage which had glorified her face as she discovered me, faded into one of utter dejection, mingled with loathing and contempt. I realized I had not answered her signal, and ignorant as I was of Martian customs, I intuitively felt that she had made an appeal for succor and protection which my unfortunate ignorance had prevented me from answering. And then she was dragged out of my sight into the depths of the deserted edifice.

CHAPTER NINE
I LEARN THE LANGUAGE

A S I CAME BACK TO MYSELF I glanced at Sola, who had witnessed this encounter and I was surprised to note a strange expression upon her usually expressionless countenance. What her thoughts were I did not know, for as yet I had learned but little of the Martian tongue; enough only to suffice for my daily needs.

As I reached the doorway of our building a strange surprise awaited me. A warrior approached bearing the arms, ornaments, and full accouterments of his kind. These he presented to me with a few unintelligible words, and a bearing at once respectful and menacing.

Later, Sola, with the aid of several of the other women, remodeled the trappings to fit my lesser proportions, and after they completed the work I went about garbed in all the panoply of war.

From then on Sola instructed me in the mysteries of the various weapons, and with the Martian young I spent several hours each day practicing upon the plaza. I was not yet proficient with all the weapons, but my great familiarity with similar earthly weapons made me an unusually apt pupil, and I progressed in a very satisfactory manner.

The training of myself and the young Martians was conducted solely by the women, who not only attend to the education of the young in the arts of individual defense and offense, but are also the artisans who produce every manufactured article wrought by the green Martians. They make the powder, the cartridges, the firearms; in fact everything of value is produced by the females. In time of actual warfare they form a part of the reserves, and when the necessity arises fight with even greater intelligence and ferocity than the men.

The men are trained in the higher branches of the art of war; in strategy and the maneuvering of large bodies of troops. They make the laws as they are needed; a new law for each emergency. They are unfettered by precedent in the administration of justice. Customs have been handed down by ages of repetition, but the punishment for ignoring a custom is a matter for individual treatment by a jury of the culprit's peers, and I may say that justice seldom misses fire, but seems rather to rule in inverse ratio to the ascendency of law. In one respect at least the Martians are a happy people; they have no lawyers.

I did not see the prisoner again for several days subsequent to our first encounter, and then only to catch a fleeting glimpse of her as she was being conducted to the great audience chamber where I had had my first meeting with Lorquas Ptomel. I could not but note the unnecessary harshness and brutality with which her guards treated her; so different from the almost maternal kindliness which Sola manifested toward me, and the respectful attitude of the few green Martians who took the trouble to notice me at all.

I had observed on the two occasions when I had seen her that the prisoner exchanged words with her guards, and this convinced me that they spoke, or at least could make themselves understood by a common language. With this added incentive I nearly drove Sola distracted by my importunities to hasten on my education, and within a few more days I had mastered the Martian tongue sufficiently well to enable me to carry on a passable conversation and to fully understand practically all that I heard.

At this time our sleeping quarters were occupied by three or four females and a couple of the recently hatched young, beside Sola and her youthful ward, myself, and Woola the hound. After they had retired for the night it was customary for the adults to carry on a desultory conversation for a short time before lapsing into sleep, and now that I could understand their language I was always a keen listener, although I never proffered any remarks myself.

On the night following the prisoner's visit to the audience chamber the conversation finally fell upon this subject, and I was all ears on the instant. I had feared to question Sola relative to the beautiful captive, as I could not but recall the strange expression I had noted upon her face after my first encounter with the prisoner. That it denoted jealousy I could not say, and yet, judging all things by mundane standards as I still did, I felt it safer to affect indifference in the matter until I learned more surely Sola's attitude toward the object of my solicitude.

Sarkoja, one of the older women who shared our domicile, had been present at the audience as one of the captive's guards, and it was toward her the questioners turned.

"When," asked one of the women, "will we enjoy the death throes of the red one? or does Lorquas Ptomel, Jed, intend holding her for ransom?"

"They have decided to carry her with us back to Thark, and exhibit her last agonies at the great games before Tal Hajus," replied Sarkoja.

"What will be the manner of her going out?" inquired Sola. "She is very small and very beautiful; I had hoped that they would hold her for ransom."

Sarkoja and the other women grunted angrily at this evidence of weakness on the part of Sola.

"It is sad, Sola, that you were not born a million years ago," snapped Sarkoja, "when all the hollows of the land were filled with water, and the peoples were as soft as the stuff they sailed upon. In our day we have progressed to a point where such sentiments mark weakness and atavism. It will not be well for you to permit Tars Tarkas to learn that you hold such degenerate sentiments, as I doubt that he would care to entrust such as you with the grave responsibilities of maternity."

"I see nothing wrong with my expression of interest in this red woman," retorted Sola. "She has never harmed us, nor would she should we have fallen into her hands. It is only the men of her kind who war upon us, and I have ever thought that their attitude toward us is but the reflection of ours toward them. They live at peace with all their fellows, except when duty calls upon them to make war, while we are at peace with none; forever warring among our own kind as well as upon the red men, and even in our own communities the individuals fight amongst themselves. Oh, it is one continual, awful period of bloodshed from the time we break the shell until we gladly embrace the bosom of the river of mystery, the dark and ancient Iss which carries us to an unknown, but at least no more frightful and terrible existence! Fortunate indeed is he who meets his end in an early death. Say what you please to Tars Tarkas, he can mete out no worse fate to me than a continuation of the horrible existence we are forced to lead in this life."

This wild outbreak on the part of Sola so greatly surprised and shocked the other women, that, after a few words of general reprimand, they all lapsed into silence and were soon asleep. One thing the episode had accomplished was to assure me of Sola's friendliness toward the poor girl, and also to convince me that I had been extremely fortunate in falling into her hands rather than those of some of the other females. I knew that she was fond of me, and now that I had discovered that she hated cruelty and barbarity I was confident that I could depend upon her to aid me and the girl captive to escape, provided of course that such a thing was within the range of possibilities.

I did not even know that there were any better conditions to escape to, but I was more than willing to take my chances among people fashioned after my own mold rather than to remain longer among the hideous and bloodthirsty green men of Mars. But where to go, and how, was as much of a puzzle to me as the age-old search for the spring of eternal life has been to earthly men since the beginning of time.

I decided that at the first opportunity I would take Sola into my confidence and openly ask her to aid me, and with this resolution strong upon me I turned among my silks and furs and slept the dreamless and refreshing sleep of Mars.

CHAPTER TEN
CHAMPION AND CHIEF

EARLY THE NEXT MORNING I was astir. Considerable freedom was allowed me, as Sola had informed me that so long as I did not attempt to leave the city I was free to go and come as I pleased. She had warned me, however, against venturing forth unarmed, as this city, like all other deserted metropolises of an ancient Martian civilization, was peopled by the great white apes of my second day's adventure.

In advising me that I must not leave the boundaries of the city Sola had explained that Woola would prevent this anyway should I attempt it, and she warned me most urgently not to arouse his fierce nature by ignoring his warnings should I venture too close to the forbidden territory. His nature was such, she said, that he would bring me back into the city dead or alive should I persist in opposing him; "preferably dead," she added.

On this morning I had chosen a new street to explore when suddenly I found myself at the limits of the city. Before me were low hills pierced by narrow and inviting ravines. I longed to explore the country before me, and, like the pioneer stock from which I sprang, to view what the landscape beyond the encircling hills might disclose from the summits which shut out my view.

It also occurred to me that this would prove an excellent opportunity to test the qualities of Woola. I was convinced that the brute loved me; I had seen more evidences of affection in him than in any other Martian animal, man or beast, and I was sure that gratitude for the acts that had twice saved his life would more than outweigh his loyalty to the duty imposed upon him by cruel and loveless masters.

As I approached the boundary line Woola ran anxiously before me, and thrust his body against my legs. His expression was pleading rather than ferocious, nor did he bare his great tusks or utter his fearful guttural warnings. Denied the friendship and companionship of my kind, I had developed considerable affection for Woola and Sola, for the normal earthly man must have some outlet for his natural affections, and so I decided upon an appeal to a like instinct in this great brute, sure that I would not be disappointed.

I had never petted nor fondled him, but now I sat upon the ground and putting my arms around his heavy neck I stroked and coaxed him, talking in my newly acquired Martian tongue as I would have to my hound at home, as I would have talked to any other friend among the lower animals. His response to my manifestation of affection was remarkable to a degree; he stretched his great mouth to its full width, baring the entire expanse of his upper rows of tusks and wrinkling his snout until his great eyes were almost hidden by the folds of flesh. If you have ever seen a collie smile you may have some idea of Woola's facial distortion.

He threw himself upon his back and fairly wallowed at my feet; jumped up and sprang upon me, rolling me upon the ground by his great weight; then wriggling and squirming around me like a playful puppy presenting its back for the petting it craves. I could not resist the ludicrousness of the spectacle, and holding my sides I rocked back and forth in the first laughter which had passed my lips in many days; the first, in fact, since the morning Powell had left camp when his horse, long unused, had precipitately and unexpectedly bucked him off headforemost into a pot of frijoles.

My laughter frightened Woola, his antics ceased and he crawled pitifully toward me, poking his ugly head far into my lap; and then I remembered what laughter signified on Mars—torture, suffering, death. Quieting myself, I rubbed the poor old fellow's head and back, talked to him for a few minutes, and then in an authoritative tone commanded him to follow me, and arising started for the hills.

There was no further question of authority between us; Woola was my devoted slave from that moment hence, and I his only and undisputed master. My walk to the hills occupied but a few minutes, and I found nothing of particular interest to reward me. Numerous brilliantly colored and strangely formed wildflowers dotted the ravines and from the summit of the first hill I saw still other hills stretching off toward the north, and rising, one range above another, until lost in mountains of quite respectable dimensions; though I afterward found that only a few peaks on all Mars exceed four thousand feet in height; the suggestion of magnitude was merely relative.

My morning's walk had been large with importance to me for it had resulted in a perfect understanding with Woola, upon whom Tars Tarkas relied for my safe keeping. I now knew that while theoretically a prisoner I was virtually free, and I hastened to regain the city limits before the defection of Woola could be discovered by his erstwhile masters. The adventure decided me never again to leave the limits of my prescribed stamping grounds until I was ready to venture forth for good and all, as it would certainly result in a curtailment of my liberties, as well as the probable death of Woola, were we to be discovered.

On regaining the plaza I had my third glimpse of the captive girl. She was standing with her guards before the entrance to the audience chamber, and as I approached she gave me one haughty glance and turned her back full upon me. The act was so womanly, so earthly womanly, that though it stung my pride it also warmed my heart with a feeling of companionship; it was good to know that someone else on Mars beside myself had human instincts of a civilized order, even though the manifestation of them was so painful and mortifying.

Had a green Martian woman desired to show dislike or contempt she would, in all likelihood, have done it with a sword thrust or a movement of her trigger finger; but as their sentiments are mostly atrophied it would have required a serious injury to have aroused such passions in them. Sola, let me add, was an exception; I never saw her perform a cruel or uncouth act, or fail in uniform kindliness and good nature. She was indeed, as her fellow Martian had said of her, an atavism; a dear and precious reversion to a former type of loved and loving ancestor.

Seeing that the prisoner seemed the center of attraction I halted to view the proceedings. I had not long to wait for presently Lorquas Ptomel and his retinue of chieftains approached the building and, signing the guards to follow with the prisoner, entered the audience chamber. Realizing that I was a somewhat favored character, and also convinced that the warriors did not know of my proficiency in their language, as I had pled with Sola to keep this a secret on the grounds that I did not wish to be forced to talk with the men until I had perfectly mastered the Martian tongue, I chanced an attempt to enter the audience chamber and listen to the proceedings.

The council squatted upon the steps of the rostrum, while below them stood the prisoner and her two guards. I saw that one of the women was Sarkoja, and thus understood how she had been present at the hearing of the preceding day, the results of which she had reported to the occupants of our dormitory last night. Her attitude toward the captive was most harsh and brutal. When she held her, she sunk her rudimentary nails into the poor girl's flesh, or twisted her arm in a most painful manner. When it was necessary to move from one spot to another she either jerked her roughly, or pushed her headlong before her. She seemed to be venting upon this poor defenseless creature all the hatred, cruelty, ferocity, and spite of her nine hundred years, backed by unguessable ages of fierce and brutal ancestors.

The other woman was less cruel because she was entirely indifferent; if the prisoner had been left to her alone and fortunately she was at night, she would have received no harsh treatment, nor, by the same token would she have received any attention at all.

As Lorquas Ptomel raised his eyes to address the prisoner they fell on me and he turned to Tars Tarkas with a word, and gesture of impatience. Tars Tarkas made some reply which I could not catch, but which caused Lorquas Ptomel to smile; after which they paid no further attention to me.

"What is your name?" asked Lorquas Ptomel, addressing the prisoner.

"Dejah Thoris, daughter of Mors Kajak of Helium."

"And the nature of your expedition?" He continued.

"It was a purely scientific research party sent out by my father's father, the Jeddak of Helium, to rechart the air currents, and to take atmospheric density tests," replied the fair prisoner, in a low, well-modulated voice.

"We were unprepared for battle," she continued, "as we were on a peaceful mission, as our banners and the colors of our craft denoted. The work we were doing was as much in your interests as in ours, for you know full well that were it not for our labors and the fruits of our scientific operations there would not be enough air or water on Mars to support a single human life. For ages we have maintained the air and water supply at practically the same point without an appreciable loss, and we have done this in the face of the brutal and ignorant interference of you green men.

"Why, oh, why will you not learn to live in amity with your fellows, must you ever go on down the ages to your final extinction but little above the plane of the dumb brutes that serve you! A people without written language, without art, without homes, without love; the victims of eons of the horrible community idea. Owning everything in common, even to your women and children, has resulted in your owning nothing in common. You hate each other as you hate all else except yourselves. Come back to the ways of our common ancestors, come back to the light of kindliness and fellowship. The way is open to you, you will find the hands of the red men stretched out to aid you. Together we may do still more to regenerate our dying planet. The granddaughter of the greatest and mightiest of the red jeddaks has asked you. Will you come?"

Lorquas Ptomel and the warriors sat looking silently and intently at the young woman for several moments after she had ceased speaking. What was passing in their minds no man may know, but that they were moved I truly believe, and if one man high among them had been strong enough to rise above custom, that moment would have marked a new and mighty era for Mars.

I saw Tars Tarkas rise to speak and on his face was such an expression as I had never seen upon the countenance of a green Martian warrior.

He bespoke an inward and mighty battle with self, with heredity, with age-old custom, and as he opened his mouth to speak, a look almost of benignity, of kindliness, momentarily lighted up his fierce and terrible countenance.

What words of moment were to have fallen from his lips were never spoken, as just then a young warrior, evidently sensing the trend of thought among the older men, leaped down from the steps of the rostrum, and striking the frail captive a powerful blow across the face, which felled her to the floor, placed his foot upon her prostrate form and turning toward the assembled council broke into peals of horrid, mirthless laughter.

For an instant I thought Tars Tarkas would strike him dead, nor did the aspect of Lorquas Ptomel augur any too favorably for the brute, but the mood passed, their old selves reasserted their ascendency, and they smiled. It was portentous however that they did not laugh aloud, for the brute's act constituted a sidesplitting witticism according to the ethics which rule green Martian humor.

That I have taken moments to write down a part of what occurred as that blow fell does not signify that I remained inactive for any such length of time. I think I must have sensed something of what was coming, for I realize now that I was crouched as for a spring as I saw the blow aimed at her beautiful, upturned, pleading face, and ere the hand descended I was halfway across the hall.

Scarcely had his hideous laugh rang out but once, when I was upon him. The brute was twelve feet in height and armed to the teeth, but I believe that I could have accounted for the whole roomful in the terrific intensity of my rage. Springing upward, I struck him full in the face as he turned at my warning cry and then as he drew his short-sword I drew mine and sprang up again upon his breast, hooking one leg over the butt of his pistol and grasping one of his huge tusks with my left hand while I delivered blow after blow upon his enormous chest.

He could not use his short-sword to advantage because I was too close to him, nor could he draw his pistol, which he attempted to do in direct opposition to Martian custom which says that you may not fight a fellow warrior in private combat with any other than the weapon with which you are attacked. In fact he could do nothing but make a wild and futile attempt to dislodge me. With all his immense bulk he was little if any stronger than I, and it was but the matter of a moment or two before he sank, bleeding and lifeless, to the floor.

Dejah Thoris had raised herself upon one elbow and was watching the battle with wide, staring eyes. When I had regained my feet I raised her in my arms and bore her to one of the benches at the side of the room.

Again no Martian interfered with me, and tearing a piece of silk from my cape I endeavored to staunch the flow of blood from her nostrils. I was soon successful as her injuries amounted to little more than an ordinary nosebleed, and when she could speak she placed her hand upon my arm and looking up into my eyes, said:

"Why did you do it? You who refused me even friendly recognition in the first hour of my peril! And now you risk your life and kill one of your companions for my sake. I cannot understand. What strange manner of man are you, that you consort with the green men, though your form is that of my race, while your color is little darker than that of the white ape? Tell me, are you human, or are you more than human?"

"It is a strange tale," I replied, "too long to attempt to tell you now, and one which I so much doubt the credibility of myself that I fear to hope that others will believe it. Suffice it, for the present, that I am your friend, and, so far as our captors will permit, your protector and your servant."

"Then you too are a prisoner? But why, then, those arms and the regalia of a Tharkian chieftain? What is your name? Where your country?"

"Yes, Dejah Thoris, I too am a prisoner; my name is John Carter, and I claim Virginia, one of the United States of America, Earth, as my home; but why I am permitted to wear arms I do not know, nor was I aware that my regalia was that of a chieftain."

We were interrupted at this juncture by the approach of one of the warriors, bearing arms, accouterments and ornaments, and in a flash one of her questions was answered and a puzzle cleared up for me. I saw that the body of my dead antagonist had been stripped, and I read in the menacing yet respectful attitude of the warrior who had brought me these trophies of the kill the same demeanor as that evinced by the other who had brought me my original equipment, and now for the first time I realized that my blow, on the occasion of my first battle in the audience chamber had resulted in the death of my adversary.

The reason for the whole attitude displayed toward me was now apparent; I had won my spurs, so to speak, and in the crude justice, which always marks Martian dealings, and which, among other things, has caused me to call her the planet of paradoxes, I was accorded the honors due a conqueror; the trappings and the position of the man I killed. In truth, I was a Martian chieftain, and this I learned later was the cause of my great freedom and my toleration in the audience chamber.

As I had turned to receive the dead warrior's chattels I had noticed that Tars Tarkas and several others had pushed forward toward us, and the eyes of the former rested upon me in a most quizzical manner. Finally he addressed me:

"You speak the tongue of Barsoom quite readily for one who was deaf and dumb to us a few short days ago. Where did you learn it, John Carter?"

"You, yourself, are responsible, Tars Tarkas," I replied, "in that you furnished me with an instructress of remarkable ability; I have to thank Sola for my learning."

"She has done well," he answered, "but your education in other respects needs considerable polish. Do you know what your unprecedented temerity would have cost you had you failed to kill either of the two chieftains whose metal you now wear?"

"I presume that that one whom I had failed to kill, would have killed me," I answered, smiling.

"No, you are wrong. Only in the last extremity of self-defense would a Martian warrior kill a prisoner; we like to save them for other purposes," and his face bespoke possibilities that were not pleasant to dwell upon.

"But one thing can save you now," he continued. "Should you, in recognition of your remarkable valor, ferocity, and prowess, be considered by Tal Hajus as worthy of his service you may be taken into the community and become a full-fledged Tharkian. Until we reach the headquarters of Tal Hajus it is the will of Lorquas Ptomel that you be accorded the respect your acts have earned you. You will be treated by us as a Tharkian chieftain, but you must not forget that every chief who ranks you is responsible for your safe delivery to our mighty and most ferocious ruler. I am done."

"I hear you, Tars Tarkas," I answered. "As you know I am not of Barsoom; your ways are not my ways, and I can only act in the future as I have in the past, in accordance with the dictates of my conscience and guided by the standards of mine own people. If you will leave me alone I will go in peace, but if not, let the individual Barsoomians with whom I must deal either respect my rights as a stranger among you, or take whatever consequences may befall. Of one thing let us be sure, whatever may be your ultimate intentions toward this unfortunate young woman, whoever would offer her injury or insult in the future must figure on making a full accounting to me. I understand that you belittle all sentiments of generosity and kindliness, but I do not, and I can convince your most doughty warrior that these characteristics are not incompatible with an ability to fight."

Ordinarily I am not given to long speeches, nor ever before had I descended to bombast, but I had guessed at the keynote which would strike an answering chord in the breasts of the green Martians, nor was I wrong, for my harangue evidently deeply impressed them, and their attitude toward me thereafter was still further respectful.

Tars Tarkas himself seemed pleased with my reply, but his only comment was more or less enigmatical—"And I think I know Tal Hajus, Jeddak of Thark."

I now turned my attention to Dejah Thoris, and assisting her to her feet I turned with her toward the exit, ignoring her hovering guardian harpies as well as the inquiring glances of the chieftains. Was I not now a chieftain also! Well, then, I would assume the responsibilities of one. They did not molest us, and so Dejah Thoris, Princess of Helium, and John Carter, gentleman of Virginia, followed by the faithful Woola, passed through utter silence from the audience chamber of Lorquas Ptomel, Jed among the Tharks of Barsoom.

CHAPTER ELEVEN
WITH DEJAH THORIS

AS WE REACHED THE OPEN the two female guards who had been detailed to watch over Dejah Thoris hurried up and made as though to assume custody of her once more. The poor child shrank against me and I felt her two little hands fold tightly over my arm. Waving the women away, I informed them that Sola would attend the captive hereafter, and I further warned Sarkoja that any more of her cruel attentions bestowed upon Dejah Thoris would result in Sarkoja's sudden and painful demise.

My threat was unfortunate and resulted in more harm than good to Dejah Thoris, for, as I learned later, men do not kill women upon Mars, nor women, men. So Sarkoja merely gave us an ugly look and departed to hatch up deviltries against us.

I soon found Sola and explained to her that I wished her to guard Dejah

Thoris as she had guarded me; that I wished her to find other quarters where they would not be molested by Sarkoja, and I finally informed her that I myself would take up my quarters among the men.

Sola glanced at the accouterments which were carried in my hand and slung across my shoulder.

"You are a great chieftain now, John Carter," she said, "and I must do your bidding, though indeed I am glad to do it under any circumstances. The man whose metal you carry was young, but he was a great warrior, and had by his promotions and kills won his way close to the rank of Tars Tarkas, who, as you know, is second to Lorquas Ptomel only. You are eleventh, there are but ten chieftains in this community who rank you in prowess."

"And if I should kill Lorquas Ptomel?" I asked.

"You would be first, John Carter; but you may only win that honor by the will of the entire council that Lorquas Ptomel meet you in combat, or should he attack you, you may kill him in self-defense, and thus win first place."

I laughed, and changed the subject. I had no particular desire to kill Lorquas Ptomel, and less to be a jed among the Tharks.

I accompanied Sola and Dejah Thoris in a search for new quarters, which we found in a building nearer the audience chamber and of far more pretentious architecture than our former habitation. We also found in this building real sleeping apartments with ancient beds of highly wrought metal swinging from enormous gold chains depending from the marble ceilings. The decoration of the walls was most elaborate, and, unlike the frescoes in the other buildings I had examined, portrayed many human figures in the compositions. These were of people like myself, and of a much lighter color than Dejah Thoris. They were clad in graceful, flowing robes, highly ornamented with metal and jewels, and their luxuriant hair was of a beautiful golden and reddish bronze. The men were beardless and only a few wore arms. The scenes depicted for the most part, a fair-skinned, fair-haired people at play.

Dejah Thoris clasped her hands with an exclamation of rapture as she gazed upon these magnificent works of art, wrought by a people long extinct; while Sola, on the other hand, apparently did not see them.

We decided to use this room, on the second floor and overlooking the plaza, for Dejah Thoris and Sola, and another room adjoining and in the rear for the cooking and supplies. I then dispatched Sola to bring the bedding and such food and utensils as she might need, telling her that I would guard Dejah Thoris until her return.

As Sola departed Dejah Thoris turned to me with a faint smile.

"And whereto, then, would your prisoner escape should you leave her, unless it was to follow you and crave your protection, and ask your pardon for the cruel thoughts she has harbored against you these past few days?"

"You are right," I answered, "there is no escape for either of us unless we go together."

"I heard your challenge to the creature you call Tars Tarkas, and I think I understand your position among these people, but what I cannot fathom is your statement that you are not of Barsoom.

"In the name of my first ancestor, then," she continued, "where may you be from? You are like unto my people, and yet so unlike. You speak my language, and yet I heard you tell Tars Tarkas that you had but learned it recently. All Barsoomians speak the same tongue from the ice-clad south to the ice-clad north, though their written languages differ. Only in the valley Dor, where the river Iss empties into the lost sea of Korus, is there supposed to be a different language spoken, and, except in the legends of our ancestors, there is no record of a Barsoomian returning up the river Iss, from the shores of Korus in the valley of Dor. Do not tell me that you have thus returned! They would kill you horribly anywhere upon the surface of Barsoom if that were true; tell me it is not!"

Her eyes were filled with a strange, weird light; her voice was pleading, and her little hands, reached up upon my breast, were pressed against me as though to wring a denial from my very heart.

"I do not know your customs, Dejah Thoris, but in my own Virginia a gentleman does not lie to save himself; I am not of Dor; I have never seen the mysterious Iss; the lost sea of Korus is still lost, so far as I am concerned. Do you believe me?"

And then it struck me suddenly that I was very anxious that she should believe me. It was not that I feared the results which would follow a general belief that I had returned from the Barsoomian heaven or hell, or whatever it was. Why was it, then! Why should I care what she thought? I looked down at her; her beautiful face upturned, and her wonderful eyes opening up the very depth of her soul; and as my eyes met hers I knew why, and—I shuddered.

A similar wave of feeling seemed to stir her; she drew away from me with a sigh, and with her earnest, beautiful face turned up to mine, she whispered: "I believe you, John Carter; I do not know what a 'gentleman' is, nor have I ever heard before of Virginia; but on Barsoom no man lies; if he does not wish to speak the truth he is silent. Where is this Virginia, your country, John Carter?" she asked, and it seemed that this fair name of my fair land had never sounded more beautiful than as it fell from those perfect lips on that far gone day.

"I am of another world," I answered, "the great planet Earth, which revolves about our common sun and next within the orbit of your Barsoom, which we know as Mars. How I came here I cannot tell you, for I do not know; but here I am, and since my presence has permitted me to serve Dejah Thoris I am glad that I am here."

She gazed at me with troubled eyes, long and questioningly. That it was difficult to believe my statement I well knew, nor could I hope that she would do so however much I craved her confidence and respect. I would much rather not have told her anything of my antecedents, but no man could look into the depth of those eyes and refuse her slightest behest.

Finally she smiled, and, rising, said: "I shall have to believe even though I cannot understand. I can readily perceive that you are not of the Barsoom of today; you are like us, yet different— but why should I trouble my poor head with such a problem, when my heart tells me that I believe because I wish to believe!"

It was good logic, good, earthly, feminine logic, and if it satisfied her I certainly could pick no flaws in it. As a matter of fact it was about the only kind of logic that could be brought to bear upon my problem. We fell into a general conversation then, asking and answering many questions on each side. She was curious to learn of the customs of my people and displayed a remarkable knowledge of events on Earth. When I questioned her closely on this seeming familiarity with earthly things she laughed, and cried out: "Why every schoolboy on Barsoom knows the geography, and much concerning the fauna and flora, as well as the history of your planet fully as well as of his own. Can we not see everything which takes place upon Earth, as you call it; is it not hanging there in the heavens in plain sight?"

This baffled me, I must confess, fully as much as my statements had confounded her; and I told her so. She then explained in general the instruments her people had used and been perfecting for ages, which permit them to throw upon a screen a perfect image of what is transpiring upon any planet and upon many of the stars. These pictures are so perfect in detail that, when photographed and enlarged, objects no greater than a blade of grass may be distinctly recognized. I afterward, in Helium, saw many of these pictures, as well as the instruments which produced them.

"If, then, you are so familiar with earthly things," I asked, "why is it that you do not recognize me as identical with the inhabitants of that planet?"

She smiled again as one might in bored indulgence of a questioning child.

"Because, John Carter," she replied, "nearly every planet and star having atmospheric conditions at all approaching those of Barsoom, shows forms of animal life almost identical with you and me; and, further, Earth men, almost without exception, cover their bodies with strange, unsightly pieces of cloth, and their heads with hideous contraptions the purpose of which we have been unable to conceive; while you, when found by the Tharkian warriors, were entirely undisfigured and unadorned.

"The fact that you wore no ornaments is a strong proof of your un-Barsoomian origin, while the absence of grotesque coverings might cause a doubt as to your earthliness."

I then narrated the details of my departure from the Earth, explaining that my body there lay fully clothed in all the, to her, strange garments of mundane dwellers. At this point Sola returned with our meager belongings and her young Martian protege, who, of course, would have to share the quarters with them.

Sola asked us if we had had a visitor during her absence, and seemed much surprised when we answered in the negative. It seemed that as she had mounted the approach to the upper floors where our quarters were located, she had met Sarkoja descending. We decided that she must have been eavesdropping, but as we could recall nothing of importance that had passed between us we dismissed the matter as of little consequence, merely promising ourselves to be warned to the utmost caution in the future.

Dejah Thoris and I then fell to examining the architecture and decorations of the beautiful chambers of the building we were occupying. She told me that these people had presumably flourished over a hundred thousand years before. They were the early progenitors of her race, but had mixed with the other great race of early Martians, who were very dark, almost black, and also with the reddish yellow race which had flourished at the same time.

These three great divisions of the higher Martians had been forced into a mighty alliance as the drying up of the Martian seas had compelled them to seek the comparatively few and always diminishing fertile areas, and to defend themselves, under new conditions of life, against the wild hordes of green men.

Ages of close relationship and intermarrying had resulted in the race of red men, of which Dejah Thoris was a fair and beautiful daughter. During the ages of hardships and incessant warring between their own various races, as well as with the green men, and before they had fitted themselves to the changed conditions, much of the high civilization and many of the arts of the fair-haired Martians had become lost; but the red race of today has reached a point where it feels that it has made up in new discoveries and in a more practical civilization for all that lies irretrievably buried with the ancient Barsoomians, beneath the countless intervening ages.

These ancient Martians had been a highly cultivated and literary race, but during the vicissitudes of those trying centuries of readjustment to new conditions, not only did their advancement and production cease entirely, but practically all their archives, records, and literature were lost.

Dejah Thoris related many interesting facts and legends concerning this lost race of noble and kindly people. She said that the city in which we were camping was supposed to have been a center of commerce and culture known as Korad. It had been built upon a beautiful, natural harbor, landlocked by magnificent hills. The little valley on the west front of the city, she explained, was all that remained of the harbor, while the pass through the hills to the old sea bottom had been the channel through which the shipping passed up to the city's gates.

The shores of the ancient seas were dotted with just such cities, and lesser ones, in diminishing numbers, were to be found converging toward the center of the oceans, as the people had found it necessary to follow the receding waters until necessity had forced upon them their ultimate salvation, the so-called Martian canals.

We had been so engrossed in exploration of the building and in our conversation that it was late in the afternoon before we realized it. We were brought back to a realization of our present conditions by a messenger bearing a summons from Lorquas Ptomel directing me to appear before him forthwith. Bidding Dejah Thoris and Sola farewell, and commanding Woola to remain on guard, I hastened to the audience chamber, where I found Lorquas Ptomel and Tars Tarkas seated upon the rostrum.

CHAPTER TWELVE
A PRISONER WITH POWER

AS I ENTERED AND SALUTED, Lorquas Ptomel signaled me to advance, and, fixing his great, hideous eyes upon me, addressed me thus:

"You have been with us a few days, yet during that time you have by your prowess won a high position among us. Be that as it may, you are not one of us; you owe us no allegiance.

"Your position is a peculiar one," he continued; "you are a prisoner and yet you give commands which must be obeyed; you are an alien and yet you are a Tharkian chieftain; you are a midget and yet you can kill a mighty warrior with one blow of your fist. And now you are reported to have been plotting to escape with another prisoner of another race; a prisoner who, from her own admission, half believes you are returned from the valley of Dor. Either one of these accusations, if proved, would be sufficient grounds for your execution, but we are a just people and you shall have a trial on our return to Thark, if Tal Hajus so commands.

"But," he continued, in his fierce guttural tones, "if you run off with the red girl it is I who shall have to account to Tal Hajus; it is I who shall have to face Tars Tarkas, and either demonstrate my right to command, or the metal from my dead carcass will go to a better man, for such is the custom of the Tharks.

"I have no quarrel with Tars Tarkas; together we rule supreme the greatest of the lesser communities among the green men; we do not wish to fight between ourselves; and so if you were dead, John Carter, I should be glad. Under two conditions only, however, may you be killed by us without orders from Tal Hajus; in personal combat in self-defense, should you attack one of us, or were you apprehended in an attempt to escape.

"As a matter of justice I must warn you that we only await one of these two excuses for ridding ourselves of so great a responsibility. The safe delivery of the red girl to Tal Hajus is of the greatest importance. Not in a thousand years have the Tharks made such a capture; she is the grand-daughter of the greatest of the red jeddaks, who is also our bitterest enemy. I have spoken. The red girl told us that we were without the softer sentiments of humanity, but we are a just and truthful race. You may go."

Turning, I left the audience chamber. So this was the beginning of Sarkoja's persecution! I knew that none other could be responsible for this report which had reached the ears of Lorquas Ptomel so quickly, and now I recalled those portions of our conversation which had touched upon escape and upon my origin.

Sarkoja was at this time Tars Tarkas' oldest and most trusted female. As such she was a mighty power behind the throne, for no warrior had the confidence of Lorquas Ptomel to such an extent as did his ablest lieutenant, Tars Tarkas.

However, instead of putting thoughts of possible escape from my mind, my audience with Lorquas Ptomel only served to center my every faculty on this subject. Now, more than before, the absolute necessity for escape, in so far as Dejah Thoris was concerned, was impressed upon me, for I was convinced that some horrible fate awaited her at the headquarters of Tal Hajus.

As described by Sola, this monster was the exaggerated personification of all the ages of cruelty, ferocity, and brutality from which he had descended. Cold, cunning, calculating; he was, also, in marked contrast to most of his fellows, a slave to that brute passion which the waning demands for procreation upon their dying planet has almost stilled in the Martian breast.

The thought that the divine Dejah Thoris might fall into the clutches of such an abysmal atavism started the cold sweat upon me. Far better that we save friendly bullets for ourselves at the last moment, as did those brave frontier women of my lost land, who took their own lives rather than fall into the hands of the Indian braves.

As I wandered about the plaza lost in my gloomy forebodings Tars Tarkas approached me on his way from the audience chamber. His demeanor toward me was unchanged, and he greeted me as though we had not just parted a few moments before.

"Where are your quarters, John Carter?" he asked.

"I have selected none," I replied. "It seemed best that I quartered either by myself or among the other warriors, and I was awaiting an opportunity to ask your advice. As you know," and I smiled, "I am not yet familiar with all the customs of the Tharks."

"Come with me," he directed, and together we moved off across the plaza to a building which I was glad to see adjoined that occupied by Sola and her charges.

"My quarters are on the first floor of this building," he said, "and the second floor also is fully occupied by warriors, but the third floor and the floors above are vacant; you may take your choice of these.

"I understand," he continued, "that you have given up your woman to the red prisoner. Well, as you have said, your ways are not our ways, but you can fight well enough to do about as you please, and so, if you wish to give your woman to a captive, it is your own affair; but as a chieftain you should have those to serve you, and in accordance with our customs you may select any or all the females from the retinues of the chieftains whose metal you now wear."

I thanked him, but assured him that I could get along very nicely without assistance except in the matter of preparing food, and so he promised to send women to me for this purpose and also for the care of my arms and the manufacture of my ammunition, which he said would be necessary. I suggested that they might also bring some of the sleeping silks and furs which belonged to me as spoils of combat, for the nights were cold and I had none of my own.

He promised to do so, and departed. Left alone, I ascended the winding corridor to the upper floors in search of suitable quarters. The beauties of the other buildings were repeated in this, and, as usual, I was soon lost in a tour of investigation and discovery.

I finally chose a front room on the third floor, because this brought me nearer to Dejah Thoris, whose apartment was on the second floor of the adjoining building, and it flashed upon me that I could rig up some means of communication whereby she might signal me in case she needed either my services or my protection.

Adjoining my sleeping apartment were baths, dressing rooms, and other sleeping and living apartments, in all some ten rooms on this floor. The windows of the back rooms overlooked an enormous court, which formed the center of the square made by the buildings which faced the four contiguous streets, and which was now given over to the quartering of the various animals belonging to the warriors occupying the adjoining buildings.

While the court was entirely overgrown with the yellow, mosslike vegetation which blankets practically the entire surface of Mars, yet numerous fountains, statuary, benches, and pergola-like contraptions bore witness to the beauty which the court must have presented in bygone times, when graced by the fair-haired, laughing people whom stern and unalterable cosmic laws had driven not only from their homes, but from all except the vague legends of their descendants.

One could easily picture the gorgeous foliage of the luxuriant Martian vegetation which once filled this scene with life and color; the graceful figures of the beautiful women, the straight and handsome men; the happy frolicking children—all sunlight, happiness and peace. It was difficult to realize that they had gone; down through ages of darkness, cruelty, and ignorance, until their hereditary instincts of culture and humanitarianism had risen ascendant once more in the final composite race which now is dominant upon Mars.

My thoughts were cut short by the advent of several young females bearing loads of weapons, silks, furs, jewels, cooking utensils, and casks of food and drink, including considerable loot from the air craft. All this, it seemed, had been the property of the two chieftains I had slain, and now, by the customs of the Tharks, it had become mine. At my direction they placed the stuff in one of the back rooms, and then departed, only to return with a second load, which they advised me constituted the balance of my goods. On the second trip they were accompanied by ten or fifteen other women and youths, who, it seemed, formed the retinues of the two chieftains.

They were not their families, nor their wives, nor their servants; the relationship was peculiar, and so unlike anything known to us that it is most difficult to describe. All property among the green Martians is owned in common by the community, except the personal weapons, ornaments and sleeping silks and furs of the individuals. These alone can one claim undisputed right to, nor may he accumulate more of these than are required for his actual needs. The surplus he holds merely as custodian, and it is passed on to the younger members of the community as necessity demands.

The women and children of a man's retinue may be likened to a military unit for which he is responsible in various ways, as in matters of instruction, discipline, sustenance, and the exigencies of their continual roamings and their unending strife with other communities and with the red Martians.

His women are in no sense wives. The green Martians use no word corresponding in meaning with this earthly word. Their mating is a matter of community interest solely, and is directed without reference to natural selection. The council of chieftains of each community control the matter as surely as the owner of a Kentucky racing stud directs the scientific breeding of his stock for the improvement of the whole.

In theory it may sound well, as is often the case with theories, but the results of ages of this unnatural practice, coupled with the community interest in the offspring being held paramount to that of the mother, is shown in the cold, cruel creatures, and their gloomy, loveless, mirthless existence.

It is true that the green Martians are absolutely virtuous, both men and women, with the exception of such degenerates as Tal Hajus; but better far a finer balance of human characteristics even at the expense of a slight and occasional loss of chastity.

Finding that I must assume responsibility for these creatures, whether I would or not, I made the best of it and directed them to find quarters on the upper floors, leaving the third floor to me. One of the girls I charged with the duties of my simple cuisine, and directed the others to take up the various activities which had formerly constituted their vocations. Thereafter I saw little of them, nor did I care to.

CHAPTER THIRTEEN
LOVE-MAKING ON MARS

FOLLOWING THE BATTLE with the air ships, the community remained within the city for several days, abandoning the homeward march until they could feel reasonably assured that the ships would not return; for to be caught on the open plains with a cavalcade of chariots and children was far from the desire of even so warlike a people as the green Martians.

During our period of inactivity, Tars Tarkas had instructed me in many of the customs and arts of war familiar to the Tharks, including lessons in riding and guiding the great beasts which bore the warriors. These creatures, which are known as thoats, are as dangerous and vicious as their masters, but when once subdued are sufficiently tractable for the purposes of the green Martians.

Two of these animals had fallen to me from the warriors whose metal I wore, and in a short time I could handle them quite as well as the native warriors. The method was not at all complicated.

If the thoats did not respond with sufficient celerity to the telepathic instructions of their riders they were dealt a terrific blow between the ears with the butt of a pistol, and if they showed fight this treatment was continued until the brutes either were subdued, or had unseated their riders.

In the latter case it became a life and death struggle between the man and the beast. If the former were quick enough with his pistol he might live to ride again, though upon some other beast; if not, his torn and mangled body was gathered up by his women and burned in accordance with Tharkian custom.

My experience with Woola determined me to attempt the experiment of kindness in my treatment of my thoats. First I taught them that they could not unseat me, and even rapped them sharply between the ears to impress upon them my authority and mastery. Then, by degrees, I won their confidence in much the same manner as I had adopted count-less times with my many mundane mounts. I was ever a good hand with animals, and by inclination, as well as because it brought more lasting and satisfactory results, I was always kind and humane in my dealings with the lower orders. I could take a human life, if neces-sary, with far less compunction than that of a poor, unreasoning, irre-sponsible brute.

In the course of a few days my thoats were the wonder of the entire community. They would follow me like dogs, rubbing their great snouts against my body in awkward evidence of affection, and respond to my every command with an alacrity and docility which caused the Martian warriors to ascribe to me the possession of some earthly power unknown on Mars.

"How have you bewitched them?" asked Tars Tarkas one afternoon, when he had seen me run my arm far between the great jaws of one of my thoats which had wedged a piece of stone between two of his teeth while feeding upon the mosslike vegetation within our courtyard.

"By kindness," I replied. "You see, Tars Tarkas, the softer sentiments have their value, even to a warrior. In the height of battle as well as upon the march I know that my thoats will obey my every command, and therefore my fighting efficiency is enhanced, and I am a better warrior for the reason that I am a kind master. Your other warriors would find it to the advantage of themselves as well as of the community to adopt my methods in this respect. Only a few days since you, yourself, told me that these great brutes, by the uncertainty of their tempers, often were the means of turning victory into defeat, since, at a crucial moment, they might elect to unseat and rend their riders."

"Show me how you accomplish these results," was Tars Tarkas' only rejoinder.

And so I explained as carefully as I could the entire method of training I had adopted with my beasts, and later he had me repeat it before Lorquas Ptomel and the assembled warriors. That moment marked the beginning of a new existence for the poor thoats, and before I left the community of Lorquas Ptomel I had the satisfaction of observing a regiment of as tractable and docile mounts as one might care to see. The effect on the precision and celerity of the military movements was so remarkable that Lorquas Ptomel presented me with a massive anklet of gold from his own leg, as a sign of his appreciation of my service to the horde.

On the seventh day following the battle with the air craft we again took up the march toward Thark, all probability of another attack being deemed remote by Lorquas Ptomel.

During the days just preceding our departure I had seen but little of Dejah Thoris, as I had been kept very busy by Tars Tarkas with my lessons in the art of Martian warfare, as well as in the training of my thoats. The few times I had visited her quarters she had been absent, walking upon the streets with Sola, or investigating the buildings in the near vicinity of the Plaza. I had warned them against venturing far from the plaza for fear of the great white apes, whose ferocity I was only too well acquainted with. However, since Woola accompanied them on all their excursions, and as Sola was well armed, there was comparatively little cause for fear.

On the evening before our departure I saw them approaching along one of the great avenues which lead into the plaza from the east. I advanced to meet them, and telling Sola that I would take the responsibility for Dejah Thoris' safe keeping, I directed her to return to her quarters on some trivial errand. I liked and trusted Sola, but for some reason I desired to be alone with Dejah Thoris, who represented to me all that I had left behind upon Earth in agreeable and congenial companionship. There seemed bonds of mutual interest between us as powerful as though we had been born under the same roof rather than upon different planets, hurtling through space some forty-eight million miles apart.

That she shared my sentiments in this respect I was positive, for on my approach the look of pitiful hopelessness left her sweet countenance to be replaced by a smile of joyful welcome, as she placed her little right hand upon my left shoulder in true red Martian salute.

"Sarkoja told Sola that you had become a true Thark," she said, "and that I would now see no more of you than of any of the other warriors."

"Sarkoja is a liar of the first magnitude," I replied, "notwithstanding the proud claim of the Tharks to absolute verity."

Dejah Thoris laughed.

"I knew that even though you became a member of the community you would not cease to be my friend; 'A warrior may change his metal, but not his heart,' as the saying is upon Barsoom.

"I think they have been trying to keep us apart," she continued, "for whenever you have been off duty one of the older women of Tars Tarkas retinue has always arranged to trump up some excuse to get Sola and me out of sight. They have had me down in the pits below the buildings helping them mix their awful radium powder, and make their terrible projectiles. You know that these have to be manufactured by artificial light, as exposure to sunlight always results in an explosion. You have noticed that their bullets explode when they strike an object? Well, the opaque, outer coating is broken by the impact, exposing a glass cylinder, almost solid, in the forward end of which is a minute particle of radium powder. The moment the sunlight, even though diffused, strikes this powder it explodes with a violence which nothing can withstand. If you ever witness a night battle you will note the absence of these explosions, while the morning following the battle will be filled at sunrise with the sharp detonations of exploding missiles fired the preceding night. As a rule, however, non-exploding projectiles are used at night."*

While I was much interested in Dejah Thoris' explanation of this wonderful adjunct to Martian warfare, I was more concerned by the

---

* I have used the word radium in describing this powder because in the light of recent discoveries on Earth I believe it to be a mixture of which radium is the base. In Captain Carter's manuscript it is mentioned always by the name used in the written language of Helium and is spelled in hieroglyphics which it would be difficult and useless to reproduce.

immediate problem of their treatment of her. That they were keeping her away from me was not a matter for surprise, but that they should subject her to dangerous and arduous labor filled me with rage.

"Have they ever subjected you to cruelty and ignominy, Dejah Thoris?" I asked, feeling the hot blood of my fighting ancestors leap in my veins as I awaited her reply.

"Only in little ways, John Carter," she answered. "Nothing that can harm me outside my pride. They know that I am the daughter of ten thousand jeddaks, that I trace my ancestry straight back without a break to the builder of the first great waterway, and they, who do not even know their own mothers, are jealous of me. At heart they hate their horrid fates, and so wreak their poor spite on me who stands for everything they have not, and for all they most crave and never can attain. Let us pity them, my chieftain, for even though we die at their hands we can afford them pity, since we are greater than they and they know it."

Had I known the significance of those words "my chieftain," as applied by a red Martian woman to a man, I should have had the surprise of my life, but I did not know at that time, nor for many months thereafter. Yes, I still had much to learn upon Barsoom.

"I presume it is the better part of wisdom that we bow to our fate with as good grace as possible, Dejah Thoris; but I hope, nevertheless, that I may be present the next time that any Martian, green, red, pink, or violet, has the temerity to even so much as frown on you, my princess."

Dejah Thoris caught her breath at my last words, and gazed upon me with dilated eyes and quickening breath, and then, with an odd little laugh, which brought roguish dimples to the corners of her mouth, she shook her head and cried: "What a child! A great warrior and yet a stumbling little child."

"What have I done now?" I asked, in sore perplexity.

"Some day you shall know, John Carter, if we live; but I may not tell you. And I, the daughter of Mors Kajak, son of Tardos Mors, have listened without anger," she soliloquized in conclusion.

Then she broke out again into one of her gay, happy, laughing moods; joking with me on my prowess as a Thark warrior as contrasted with my soft heart and natural kindliness.

"I presume that should you accidentally wound an enemy you would take him home and nurse him back to health," she laughed.

"That is precisely what we do on Earth," I answered. "At least among civilized men."

This made her laugh again. She could not understand it, for, with all her tenderness and womanly sweetness, she was still a Martian, and to a Martian the only good enemy is a dead enemy; for every dead foeman means so much more to divide between those who live.

I was very curious to know what I had said or done to cause her so much perturbation a moment before and so I continued to importune her to enlighten me.

"No," she exclaimed, "it is enough that you have said it and that I have listened. And when you learn, John Carter, and if I be dead, as likely enough I shall be ere the further moon has circled Barsoom another twelve times, remember that I listened and that I—smiled."

It was all Greek to me, but the more I begged her to explain the more positive became her denials of my request, and, so, in very hopelessness, I desisted.

Day had now given away to night and as we wandered along the great avenue lighted by the two moons of Barsoom, and with Earth looking down upon us out of her luminous green eye, it seemed that we were alone in the universe, and I, at least, was content that it should be so.

The chill of the Martian night was upon us, and removing my silks I threw them across the shoulders of Dejah Thoris. As my arm rested for an instant upon her I felt a thrill pass through every fiber of my being such as contact with no other mortal had even produced; and it seemed to me that she had leaned slightly toward me, but of that I was not sure. Only I knew that as my arm rested there across her shoulders longer than the act of adjusting the silk required she did not draw away, nor did she speak. And so, in silence, we walked the surface of a dying world, but in the breast of one of us at least had been born that which is ever oldest, yet ever new.

I loved Dejah Thoris. The touch of my arm upon her naked shoulder had spoken to me in words I could not mistake, and I knew that I had loved her since the first moment that my eyes had met hers that first time in the plaza of the dead city of Korad.

CHAPTER FOURTEEN
A DUEL TO THE DEATH

MY FIRST IMPULSE was to tell her of my love, and then I thought of the helplessness of her position wherein I alone could lighten the burdens of her captivity, and protect her in my poor way against the thousands of hereditary enemies she must face upon our arrival at Thark. I could not chance causing her additional pain or sorrow by declaring a love which, in all probability she did not return. Should I be so indiscreet, her position would be even more unbearable than now, and the thought that she might feel that I was taking advantage of her helplessness, to influence her decision was the final argument which sealed my lips.

"Why are you so quiet, Dejah Thoris?" I asked. "Possibly you would rather return to Sola and your quarters."

"No," she murmured, "I am happy here. I do not know why it is that I should always be happy and contented when you, John Carter, a stranger, are with me; yet at such times it seems that I am safe and that, with you, I shall soon return to my father's court and feel his strong arms about me and my mother's tears and kisses on my cheek."

"Do people kiss, then, upon Barsoom?" I asked, when she had explained the word she used, in answer to my inquiry as to its meaning.

"Parents, brothers, and sisters, yes; and," she added in a low, thoughtful tone, "lovers."

"And you, Dejah Thoris, have parents and brothers and sisters?"

"Yes."

"And a—lover?"

She was silent, nor could I venture to repeat the question.

"The man of Barsoom," she finally ventured, "does not ask personal questions of women, except his mother, and the woman he has fought for and won."

"But I have fought—" I started, and then I wished my tongue had been cut from my mouth; for she turned even as I caught myself and ceased, and drawing my silks from her shoulder she held them out to me, and without a word, and with head held high, she moved with the carriage of the queen she was toward the plaza and the doorway of her quarters.

74

I did not attempt to follow her, other than to see that she reached the building in safety, but, directing Woola to accompany her, I turned disconsolately and entered my own house. I sat for hours cross-legged, and cross-tempered, upon my silks meditating upon the queer freaks chance plays upon us poor devils of mortals.

So this was love! I had escaped it for all the years I had roamed the five continents and their encircling seas; in spite of beautiful women and urging opportunity; in spite of a half-desire for love and a constant search for my ideal, it had remained for me to fall furiously and hopelessly in love with a creature from another world, of a species similar possibly, yet not identical with mine. A woman who was hatched from an egg, and whose span of life might cover a thousand years; whose people had strange customs and ideas; a woman whose hopes, whose pleasures, whose standards of virtue and of right and wrong might vary as greatly from mine as did those of the green Martians.

Yes, I was a fool, but I was in love, and though I was suffering the greatest misery I had ever known I would not have had it otherwise for all the riches of Barsoom. Such is love, and such are lovers wherever love is known.

To me, Dejah Thoris was all that was perfect; all that was virtuous and beautiful and noble and good. I believed that from the bottom of my heart, from the depth of my soul on that night in Korad as I sat cross-legged upon my silks while the nearer moon of Barsoom raced through the western sky toward the horizon, and lighted up the gold and marble, and jeweled mosaics of my world-old chamber, and I believe it today as I sit at my desk in the little study overlooking the Hudson. Twenty years have intervened; for ten of them I lived and fought for Dejah Thoris and her people, and for ten I have lived upon her memory.

The morning of our departure for Thark dawned clear and hot, as do all Martian mornings except for the six weeks when the snow melts at the poles.

I sought out Dejah Thoris in the throng of departing chariots, but she turned her shoulder to me, and I could see the red blood mount to her cheek. With the foolish inconsistency of love I held my peace when I might have plead ignorance of the nature of my offense, or at least the gravity of it, and so have effected, at worst, a half conciliation.

My duty dictated that I must see that she was comfortable, and so I glanced into her chariot and rearranged her silks and furs. In doing so I noted with horror that she was heavily chained by one ankle to the side of the vehicle.

"What does this mean?" I cried, turning to Sola.

"Sarkoja thought it best," she answered, her face betokening her disapproval of the procedure.

Examining the manacles I saw that they fastened with a massive spring lock.

"Where is the key, Sola? Let me have it."

"Sarkoja wears it, John Carter," she answered.

I turned without further word and sought out Tars Tarkas, to whom I vehemently objected to the unnecessary humiliations and cruelties, as they seemed to my lover's eyes, that were being heaped upon Dejah Thoris.

"John Carter," he answered, "if ever you and Dejah Thoris escape the Tharks it will be upon this journey. We know that you will not go without her. You have shown yourself a mighty fighter, and we do not wish to manacle you, so we hold you both in the easiest way that will yet ensure security. I have spoken."

I saw the strength of his reasoning at a flash, and knew that it were futile to appeal from his decision, but I asked that the key be taken from Sarkoja and that she be directed to leave the prisoner alone in future.

"This much, Tars Tarkas, you may do for me in return for the friendship that, I must confess, I feel for you."

"Friendship?" he replied. "There is no such thing, John Carter; but have your will. I shall direct that Sarkoja cease to annoy the girl, and I myself will take the custody of the key."

"Unless you wish me to assume the responsibility," I said, smiling.

He looked at me long and earnestly before he spoke.

"Were you to give me your word that neither you nor Dejah Thoris would attempt to escape until after we have safely reached the court of Tal Hajus you might have the key and throw the chains into the river Iss."

"It were better that you held the key, Tars Tarkas," I replied.

He smiled, and said no more, but that night as we were making camp I saw him unfasten Dejah Thoris' fetters himself.

With all his cruel ferocity and coldness there was an undercurrent of something in Tars Tarkas which he seemed ever battling to subdue. Could it be a vestige of some human instinct come back from an ancient forbear to haunt him with the horror of his people's ways!

As I was approaching Dejah Thoris' chariot I passed Sarkoja, and the black, venomous look she accorded me was the sweetest balm I had felt for many hours. Lord, how she hated me! It bristled from her so palpably that one might almost have cut it with a sword.

A few moments later I saw her deep in conversation with a warrior named Zad; a big, hulking, powerful brute, but one who had never made a kill among his own chieftains, and so was still an *o mad*, or man with one name; he could win a second name only with the metal of some chieftain. It was this custom which entitled me to the names of either of the chieftains I had killed; in fact, some of the warriors addressed me as Dotar Sojat, a combination of the surnames of the two warrior chieftains whose metal I had taken, or, in other words, whom I had slain in fair fight.

As Sarkoja talked with Zad he cast occasional glances in my direction, while she seemed to be urging him very strongly to some action. I paid little attention to it at the time, but the next day I had good reason to recall the circumstances, and at the same time gain a slight insight into the depths of Sarkoja's hatred and the lengths to which she was capable of going to wreak her horrid vengeance on me.

Dejah Thoris would have none of me again on this evening, and though I spoke her name she neither replied, nor conceded by so much as the flutter of an eyelid that she realized my existence. In my extremity I did what most other lovers would have done; I sought word from her through an intimate. In this instance it was Sola whom I intercepted in another part of camp.

"What is the matter with Dejah Thoris?" I blurted out at her. "Why will she not speak to me?"

Sola seemed puzzled herself, as though such strange actions on the part of two humans were quite beyond her, as indeed they were, poor child.

"She says you have angered her, and that is all she will say, except that she is the daughter of a jed and the granddaughter of a jeddak and she has been humiliated by a creature who could not polish the teeth of her grandmother's sorak."

I pondered over this report for some time, finally asking, "What might a sorak be, Sola?"

"A little animal about as big as my hand, which the red Martian women keep to play with," explained Sola.

Not fit to polish the teeth of her grandmother's cat! I must rank pretty low in the consideration of Dejah Thoris, I thought; but I could not help laughing at the strange figure of speech, so homely and in this respect so earthly. It made me homesick, for it sounded very much like "not fit to polish her shoes." And then commenced a train of thought quite new to me. I began to wonder what my people at home were doing. I had not seen them for years. There was a family of Carters in Virginia who claimed close relationship with me; I was supposed to be a great-uncle, or something of the kind equally foolish. I could pass anywhere for twenty-five to thirty years of age, and to be a great-uncle always seemed the height of incongruity, for my thoughts and feelings were those of a boy. There were two little kiddies in the Carter family whom I had loved and who had thought there was no one on Earth like Uncle Jack; I could see them just as plainly, as I stood there under the moonlit skies of Barsoom, and I longed for them as I had never longed for any mortals before. By nature a wanderer, I had never known the true meaning of the word home, but the great hall of the Carters had always stood for all that the word did mean to me, and now my heart turned toward it from the cold and unfriendly peoples I had been thrown amongst. For did not even Dejah Thoris despise me! I was a low creature, so low in fact that I was not even fit to polish the teeth of her grandmother's cat; and then my saving sense of humor came to my rescue, and laughing I turned into my silks and furs and slept upon the moon-haunted ground the sleep of a tired and healthy fighting man.

We broke camp the next day at an early hour and marched with only a single halt until just before dark. Two incidents broke the tediousness of the march. About noon we espied far to our right what was evidently an incubator, and Lorquas Ptomel directed Tars Tarkas to investigate it. The latter took a dozen warriors, including myself, and we raced across the velvety carpeting of moss to the little enclosure.

It was indeed an incubator, but the eggs were very small in comparison with those I had seen hatching in ours at the time of my arrival on Mars.

Tars Tarkas dismounted and examined the inclosure minutely, finally announcing that it belonged to the green men of Warhoon and that the cement was scarcely dry where it had been walled up.

"They cannot be a day's march ahead of us," he exclaimed, the light of battle leaping to his fierce face.

The work at the incubator was short indeed. The warriors tore open the entrance and a couple of them, crawling in, soon demolished all the eggs with their short-swords. Then remounting we dashed back to join the cavalcade. During the ride I took occasion to ask Tars Tarkas if these Warhoons whose eggs we had destroyed were a smaller people than his Tharks.

"I noticed that their eggs were so much smaller than those I saw hatching in your incubator," I added.

He explained that the eggs had just been placed there; but, like all green Martian eggs, they would grow during the five-year period of incubation until they obtained the size of those I had seen hatching on the day of my arrival on Barsoom. This was indeed an interesting piece of information, for it had always seemed remarkable to me that the green Martian women, large as they were, could bring forth such enormous eggs as I had seen the four-foot infants emerging from. As a matter of fact, the new-laid egg is but little larger than an ordinary goose egg, and as it does not commence to grow until subjected to the light of the sun the chieftains have little difficulty in transporting several hundreds of them at one time from the storage vaults to the incubators.

Shortly after the incident of the Warhoon eggs we halted to rest the animals, and it was during this halt that the second of the day's interesting episodes occurred. I was engaged in changing my riding cloths from one of my thoats to the other, for I divided the day's work between them, when Zad approached me, and without a word struck my animal a terrific blow with his long-sword.

I did not need a manual of green Martian etiquette to know what reply to make, for, in fact, I was so wild with anger that I could scarcely refrain from drawing my pistol and shooting him down for the brute he was; but he stood waiting with drawn long-sword, and my only choice was to draw my own and meet him in fair fight with his choice of weapons or a lesser one.

This latter alternative is always permissible, therefore I could have used my short-sword, my dagger, my hatchet, or my fists had I wished, and been entirely within my rights, but I could not use fire arms or a spear while he held only his long-sword.

I chose the same weapon he had drawn because I knew he prided himself upon his ability with it, and I wished, if I worsted him at all, to do it with his own weapon. The fight that followed was a long one and delayed the resumption of the march for an hour. The entire community surrounded us, leaving a clear space about one hundred feet in diameter for our battle.

Zad first attempted to rush me down as a bull might a wolf, but I was much too quick for him, and each time I sidestepped his rushes he would go lunging past me, only to receive a nick from my sword upon his arm or back. He was soon streaming blood from a half dozen minor wounds, but I could not obtain an opening to deliver an effective thrust. Then he changed his tactics, and fighting warily and with extreme dexterity, he tried to do by science what he was unable to do by brute strength. I must admit that he was a magnificent swordsman, and had it not been for my greater endurance and the remarkable agility the lesser gravitation of Mars lent me I might not have been able to put up the creditable fight I did against him.

We circled for some time without doing much damage on either side; the long, straight, needlelike swords flashing in the sunlight, and ringing out upon the stillness as they crashed together with each effective parry. Finally Zad, realizing that he was tiring more than I, evidently decided to close in and end the battle in a final blaze of glory for himself; just as he rushed me a blinding flash of light struck full in my eyes, so that I could not see his approach and could only leap blindly to one side in an effort to escape the mighty blade that it seemed I could already feel in my vitals. I was only partially successful, as a sharp pain in my left shoulder attested, but in the sweep of my glance as I sought to again locate my adversary, a sight met my astonished gaze which paid me well for the wound the temporary blindness had caused me. There, upon Dejah Thoris' chariot stood three figures, for the purpose evidently of witnessing the encounter above the heads of the intervening Tharks. There were Dejah Thoris, Sola, and Sarkoja, and as my fleeting glance swept over them a little tableau was presented which will stand graven in my memory to the day of my death.

As I looked, Dejah Thoris turned upon Sarkoja with the fury of a young tigress and struck something from her upraised hand; something which flashed in the sunlight as it spun to the ground. Then I knew what had blinded me at that crucial moment of the fight, and how Sarkoja had found a way to kill me without herself delivering the final thrust. Another thing I saw, too, which almost lost my life for me then and there, for it took my mind for the fraction of an instant entirely from my antagonist; for, as Dejah Thoris struck the tiny mirror from her hand, Sarkoja, her face livid with hatred and baffled rage, whipped out her dagger and aimed a terrific blow at Dejah Thoris; and then Sola, our dear and faithful Sola, sprang between them; the last I saw was the great knife descending upon her shielding breast.

My enemy had recovered from his thrust and was making it extremely interesting for me, so I reluctantly gave my attention to the work in hand, but my mind was not upon the battle.

We rushed each other furiously time after time, 'til suddenly, feeling the sharp point of his sword at my breast in a thrust I could neither parry nor escape, I threw myself upon him with outstretched sword and with all the weight of my body, determined that I would not die alone if I could prevent it. I felt the steel tear into my chest, all went black before me, my head whirled in dizziness, and I felt my knees giving beneath me.

CHAPTER FIFTEEN
SOLA TELLS ME HER STORY

WHEN CONSCIOUSNESS RETURNED, and, as I soon learned, I was down but a moment, I sprang quickly to my feet searching for my sword, and there I found it, buried to the hilt in the green breast of Zad, who lay stone dead upon the ochre moss of the ancient sea bottom. As I regained my full senses I found his weapon piercing my left breast, but only through the flesh and muscles which cover my ribs, entering near the center of my chest and coming out below the shoulder. As I had lunged I had turned so that his sword merely passed beneath the muscles, inflicting a painful but not dangerous wound.

Removing the blade from my body I also regained my own, and turning my back upon his ugly carcass, I moved, sick, sore, and disgusted, toward the chariots which bore my retinue and my belongings. A murmur of Martian applause greeted me, but I cared not for it.

Bleeding and weak I reached my women, who, accustomed to such happenings, dressed my wounds, applying the wonderful healing and remedial agents which make only the most instantaneous of death blows fatal. Give a Martian woman a chance and death must take a back seat. They soon had me patched up so that, except for weakness from loss of blood and a little soreness around the wound, I suffered no great distress from this thrust which, under earthly treatment, undoubtedly would have put me flat on my back for days.

As soon as they were through with me I hastened to the chariot of Dejah Thoris, where I found my poor Sola with her chest swathed in bandages, but apparently little the worse for her encounter with Sarkoja, whose dagger it seemed had struck the edge of one of Sola's metal breast ornaments and, thus deflected, had inflicted but a slight flesh wound.

As I approached I found Dejah Thoris lying prone upon her silks and furs, her lithe form wracked with sobs. She did not notice my presence, nor did she hear me speaking with Sola, who was standing a short distance from the vehicle.

"Is she injured?" I asked of Sola, indicating Dejah Thoris by an inclination of my head.

"No," she answered, "she thinks that you are dead."

"And that her grandmother's cat may now have no one to polish its teeth?" I queried, smiling.

"I think you wrong her, John Carter," said Sola. "I do not understand either her ways or yours, but I am sure the granddaughter of ten thousand jeddaks would never grieve like this over the death of one she considered beneath her, or indeed over any who held but the highest claim upon her affections. They are a proud race, but they are just, as are all Barsoomians, and you must have hurt or wronged her grievously that she will not admit your existence living, though she mourns you dead.

"Tears are a strange sight upon Barsoom," she continued, "and so it is difficult for me to interpret them. I have seen but two people weep in all my life, other than Dejah Thoris; one wept from sorrow, the other from baffled rage. The first was my mother, years ago before they killed her; the other was Sarkoja, when they dragged her from me today."

"Your mother!" I exclaimed, "but, Sola, you could not have known your mother, child."

"But I did. And my father also," she added. "If you would like to hear the strange and un-Barsoomian story come to the chariot tonight, John Carter, and I will tell you that of which I have never spoken in all my life before. And now the signal has been given to resume the march, you must go."

"I will come tonight, Sola," I promised. "Be sure to tell Dejah Thoris I am alive and well. I shall not force myself upon her, and be sure that you do not let her know I saw her tears. If she would speak with me I but await her command." Sola mounted the chariot, which was swinging into its place in line, and I hastened to my waiting thoat and galloped to my station beside Tars Tarkas at the rear of the column.

We made a most imposing and awe-inspiring spectacle as we strung out across the yellow landscape; the two hundred and fifty ornate and brightly colored chariots, preceded by an advance guard of some two hundred mounted warriors and chieftains riding five abreast and one hundred yards apart, and followed by a like number in the same formation, with a score or more of flankers on either side; the fifty extra mastodons, or heavy draught animals, known as zitidars, and the five or six hundred extra thoats of the warriors running loose within the hollow square formed by the surrounding warriors. The gleaming metal and jewels of the gorgeous ornaments of the men and women, duplicated in the trappings of the zitidars and thoats, and interspersed with the flashing colors of magnificent silks and furs and feathers, lent a barbaric splendor to the caravan which would have turned an East Indian potentate green with envy.

The enormous broad tires of the chariots and the padded feet of the animals brought forth no sound from the moss-covered sea bottom; and so we moved in utter silence, like some huge phantasmagoria, except when the stillness was broken by the guttural growling of a goaded zitidar, or the squealing of fighting thoats. The green Martians converse but little, and then usually in monosyllables, low and like the faint rumbling of distant thunder.

We traversed a trackless waste of moss which, bending to the pressure of broad tire or padded foot, rose up again behind us, leaving no sign that we had passed. We might indeed have been the wraiths of the departed dead upon the dead sea of that dying planet for all the sound or sign we made in passing. It was the first march of a large body of men and animals I had ever witnessed which raised no dust and left no spoor; for there is no dust upon Mars except in the cultivated districts during the winter months, and even then the absence of high winds renders it almost unnoticeable.

We camped that night at the foot of the hills we had been approaching for two days and which marked the southern boundary of this particular sea. Our animals had been two days without drink, nor had they had water for nearly two months, not since shortly after leaving Thark; but, as Tars Tarkas explained to me, they require but little and can live almost indefinitely upon the moss which covers Barsoom, and which, he told me, holds in its tiny stems sufficient moisture to meet the limited demands of the animals.

After partaking of my evening meal of cheeselike food and vegetable milk I sought out Sola, whom I found working by the light of a torch upon some of Tars Tarkas' trappings. She looked up at my approach, her face lighting with pleasure and with welcome.

"I am glad you came," she said; "Dejah Thoris sleeps and I am lonely. Mine own people do not care for me, John Carter; I am too unlike them. It is a sad fate, since I must live my life amongst them, and I often wish that I were a true green Martian woman, without love and without hope; but I have known love and so I am lost.

"I promised to tell you my story, or rather the story of my parents. From what I have learned of you and the ways of your people I am sure that the tale will not seem strange to you, but among green Martians it has no parallel within the memory of the oldest living Thark, nor do our legends hold many similar tales.

"My mother was rather small, in fact too small to be allowed the responsibilities of maternity, as our chieftains breed principally for size. She was also less cold and cruel than most green Martian women, and caring little for their society, she often roamed the deserted avenues of Thark alone, or went and sat among the wildflowers that deck the nearby hills, thinking thoughts and wishing wishes which I believe I alone among Tharkian women today may understand, for am I not the child of my mother?

"And there among the hills she met a young warrior, whose duty it was to guard the feeding zitidars and thoats and see that they roamed not beyond the hills. They spoke at first only of such things as interest a community of Tharks, but gradually, as they came to meet more often, and, as was now quite evident to both, no longer by chance, they talked about themselves, their likes, their ambitions and their hopes. She trusted him and told him of the awful repugnance she felt for the cruelties of their kind, for the hideous, loveless lives they must ever lead, and then she waited for the storm of denunciation to break from his cold, hard lips; but instead he took her in his arms and kissed her.

"They kept their love a secret for six long years. She, my mother, was of the retinue of the great Tal Hajus, while her lover was a simple warrior, wearing only his own metal. Had their defection from the traditions of the Tharks been discovered both would have paid the penalty in the great arena before Tal Hajus and the assembled hordes.

"The egg from which I came was hidden beneath a great glass vessel upon the highest and most inaccessible of the partially ruined towers of ancient Thark. Once each year my mother visited it for the five long years it lay there in the process of incubation. She dared not come oftener, for in the mighty guilt of her conscience she feared that her every move was watched. During this period my father gained great distinction as a warrior and had taken the metal from several chieftains. His love for my mother had never diminished, and his one ambition in life was to reach a point where he might wrest the metal from Tal Hajus himself, and thus, as ruler of the Tharks, be free to claim her as his own, as well as, by the might of his power, protect the child which otherwise would be quickly dispatched should the truth become known.

"It was a wild dream, that of wresting the metal from Tal Hajus in five short years, but his advance was rapid, and he soon stood high in the councils of Thark. But one day the chance was lost forever, in so far as it could come in time to save his loved ones, for he was ordered away upon a long expedition to the ice-clad south, to make war upon the natives there and despoil them of their furs, for such is the manner of the green Barsoomian; he does not labor for what he can wrest in battle from others.

"He was gone for four years, and when he returned all had been over for three; for about a year after his departure, and shortly before the time for the return of an expedition which had gone forth to fetch the fruits of a community incubator, the egg had hatched. Thereafter my mother continued to keep me in the old tower, visiting me nightly and lavishing upon me the love the community life would have robbed us both of. She hoped, upon the return of the expedition from the incubator, to mix me with the other young assigned to the quarters of Tal Hajus, and thus escape the fate which would surely follow discovery of her sin against the ancient traditions of the green men.

"She taught me rapidly the language and customs of my kind, and one night she told me the story I have told to you up to this point, impressing upon me the necessity for absolute secrecy and the great caution I must exercise after she had placed me with the other young Tharks to permit no one to guess that I was further advanced in education than they, nor by any sign to divulge in the presence of others my affection for her, or my knowledge of my parentage; and then drawing me close to her she whispered in my ear the name of my father.

"And then a light flashed out upon the darkness of the tower chamber, and there stood Sarkoja, her gleaming, baleful eyes fixed in a frenzy of loathing and contempt upon my mother. The torrent of hatred and abuse she poured out upon her turned my young heart cold in terror. That she had heard the entire story was apparent, and that she had suspected something wrong from my mother's long nightly absences from her quarters accounted for her presence there on that fateful night.

"One thing she had not heard, nor did she know, the whispered name of my father. This was apparent from her repeated demands upon my mother to disclose the name of her partner in sin, but no amount of abuse or threats could wring this from her, and to save me from needless torture she lied, for she told Sarkoja that she alone knew nor would she even tell her child.

"With final imprecations, Sarkoja hastened away to Tal Hajus to report her discovery, and while she was gone my mother, wrapping me in the silks and furs of her night coverings, so that I was scarcely noticeable, descended to the streets and ran wildly away toward the outskirts of the city, in the direction which led to the far south, out toward the man whose protection she might not claim, but on whose face she wished to look once more before she died.

"As we neared the city's southern extremity a sound came to us from across the mossy flat, from the direction of the only pass through the hills which led to the gates, the pass by which caravans from either north or south or east or west would enter the city. The sounds we heard were the squealing of thoats and the grumbling of zitidars, with the occasional clank of arms which announced the approach of a body of warriors. The thought uppermost in her mind was that it was my father returned from his expedition, but the cunning of the Thark held her from headlong and precipitate flight to greet him.

"Retreating into the shadows of a doorway she awaited the coming of the cavalcade which shortly entered the avenue, breaking its formation and thronging the thoroughfare from wall to wall. As the head of the procession passed us the lesser moon swung clear of the overhanging roofs and lit up the scene with all the brilliancy of her wondrous light. My mother shrank further back into the friendly shadows, and from her hiding place saw that the expedition was not that of my father, but the returning caravan bearing the young Tharks. Instantly her plan was formed, and as a great chariot swung close to our hiding place she slipped stealthily in upon the trailing tail board, crouching low in the shadow of the high side, straining me to her bosom in a frenzy of love.

"She knew, what I did not, that never again after that night would she hold me to her breast, nor was it likely we would ever look upon each other's face again. In the confusion of the plaza she mixed me with the other children, whose guardians during the journey were now free to re-linquish their responsibility. We were herded together into a great room, fed by women who had not accompanied the expedition, and the next day we were parceled out among the retinues of the chieftains.

"I never saw my mother after that night. She was imprisoned by Tal Hajus, and every effort, including the most horrible and shameful torture, was brought to bear upon her to wring from her lips the name of my father; but she remained steadfast and loyal, dying at last amidst the laughter of Tal Hajus and his chieftains during some awful torture she was undergoing.

"I learned afterward that she told them that she had killed me to save me from a like fate at their hands, and that she had thrown my body to the white apes. Sarkoja alone disbelieved her, and I feel to this day that she suspects my true origin, but does not dare expose me, at the present, at all events, because she also guesses, I am sure, the identity of my father.

"When he returned from his expedition and learned the story of my mother's fate I was present as Tal Hajus told him; but never by the quiver of a muscle did he betray the slightest emotion; only he did not laugh as Tal Hajus gleefully described her death struggles. From that moment on he was the crudest of the cruel, and I am awaiting the day when he shall win the goal of his ambition, and feel the carcass of Tal Hajus beneath his foot, for I am as sure that he but waits the opportunity to wreak a terrible vengeance, and that his great love is as strong in his breast as when it first transfigured him nearly forty years ago, as I am that we sit here upon the edge of a world-old ocean while sensible people sleep, John Carter."

"And your father, Sola, is he with us now?" I asked.

"Yes," she replied, "but he does not know me for what I am, nor does he know who betrayed my mother to Tal Hajus. I alone know my father's name, and only I and Tal Hajus and Sarkoja know that it was she who carried the tale that brought death and torture upon her he loved."

We sat silent for a few moments, she wrapped in the gloomy thoughts of her terrible past, and I in pity for the poor creatures whom the heartless, senseless customs of their race had doomed to loveless lives of cruelty and of hate. Presently she spoke.

"John Carter, if ever a real man walked the cold, dead bosom of Barsoom you are one. I know that I can trust you, and because the knowledge may some day help you or him or Dejah Thoris or myself, I am going to tell you the name of my father, nor place any restrictions or conditions upon your tongue. When the time comes, speak the truth if it seems best to you. I trust you because I know that you are not cursed with the terrible trait of absolute and unswerving truthfulness, that you could lie like one of your own Virginia gentlemen if a lie would save others from sorrow or suffering. My father's name is Tars Tarkas."

CHAPTER SIXTEEN
WE PLAN ESCAPE

THE REMAINDER OF OUR JOURNEY to Thark was uneventful. We were twenty days upon the road, crossing two sea bottoms and passing through or around a number of ruined cities, mostly smaller than Korad. Twice we crossed the famous Martian waterways, or canals, so-called by our earthly astronomers. When we approached these points a warrior would be sent far ahead with a powerful field glass, and if no great body of red Martian troops was in sight we would advance as close as possible without chance of being seen and then camp until dark, when we would slowly approach the cultivated tract, and, locating one of the numerous, broad highways which cross these areas at regular intervals, creep silently and stealthily across to the arid lands upon the other side. It required five hours to make one of these crossings without a single halt, and the other consumed the entire night, so that we were just leaving the confines of the high-walled fields when the sun broke out upon us.

Crossing in the darkness, as we did, I was unable to see but little, except as the nearer moon, in her wild and ceaseless hurtling through the Barsoomian heavens, lit up little patches of the landscape from time to time, disclosing walled fields and low, rambling buildings, presenting much the appearance of earthly farms. There were many trees, methodically arranged, and some of them were of enormous height; there were animals in some of the enclosures, and they announced their presence by terrified squealings and snortings as they scented our queer, wild beasts and wilder human beings.

Only once did I perceive a human being, and that was at the intersection of our crossroad with the wide, white turnpike which cuts each cultivated district longitudinally at its exact center. The fellow must have been sleeping beside the road, for, as I came abreast of him, he raised upon one elbow and after a single glance at the approaching caravan leaped shrieking to his feet and fled madly down the road, scaling a nearby wall with the agility of a scared cat. The Tharks paid him not the slightest attention; they were not out upon the warpath, and the only sign that I had that they had seen him was a quickening of the pace of the caravan as we hastened toward the bordering desert which marked our entrance into the realm of Tal Hajus.

Not once did I have speech with Dejah Thoris, as she sent no word to me that I would be welcome at her chariot, and my foolish pride kept me from making any advances. I verily believe that a man's way with women is in inverse ratio to his prowess among men. The weakling and the saphead have often great ability to charm the fair sex, while the fighting man who can face a thousand real dangers unafraid, sits hiding in the shadows like some frightened child.

Just thirty days after my advent upon Barsoom we entered the ancient city of Thark, from whose long-forgotten people this horde of green men have stolen even their name. The hordes of Thark number some thirty thousand souls, and are divided into twenty-five communities. Each community has its own jed and lesser chieftains, but all are under the rule of Tal Hajus, Jeddak of Thark. Five communities make their headquarters at the city of Thark, and the balance are scattered among other deserted cities of ancient Mars throughout the district claimed by Tal Hajus.

We made our entry into the great central plaza early in the afternoon. There were no enthusiastic friendly greetings for the returned expedition. Those who chanced to be in sight spoke the names of warriors or women with whom they came in direct contact, in the formal greeting of their kind, but when it was discovered that they brought two captives a greater interest was aroused, and Dejah Thoris and I were the centers of inquiring groups.

We were soon assigned to new quarters, and the balance of the day was devoted to settling ourselves to the changed conditions. My home now was upon an avenue leading into the plaza from the south, the main artery down which we had marched from the gates of the city. I was at the far end of the square and had an entire building to myself. The same grandeur of architecture which was so noticeable a characteristic of Korad was in evidence here, only, if that were possible, on a larger and richer scale. My quarters would have been suitable for housing the greatest of earthly emperors, but to these queer creatures nothing about a building appealed to them but its size and the enormity of its chambers; the larger the building, the more desirable; and so Tal Hajus occupied what must have been an enormous public building, the largest in the city, but entirely unfitted for residence purposes; the next largest was reserved for Lorquas Ptomel, the next for the jed of a lesser rank, and so on to the bottom of the list of five jeds. The warriors occupied the buildings with the chieftains to whose retinues they belonged; or, if they preferred, sought shelter among any of the thousands of untenanted buildings in their own quarter of town; each community being assigned a certain section of the city. The selection of building had to be made in accordance with these divisions, except in so far as the jeds were concerned, they all occupying edifices which fronted upon the plaza.

When I had finally put my house in order, or rather seen that it had been done, it was nearing sunset, and I hastened out with the intention of locating Sola and her charges, as I had determined upon having speech with Dejah Thoris and trying to impress on her the necessity of our at least patching up a truce until I could find some way of aiding her to escape. I searched in vain until the upper rim of the great red sun was just disappearing behind the horizon and then I spied the ugly head of Woola peering from a second-story window on the opposite side of the very street where I was quartered but nearer the plaza.

Without waiting for a further invitation I bolted up the winding runway which led to the second floor, and entering a great chamber at the front of the building was greeted by the frenzied Woola, who threw his great carcass upon me, nearly hurling me to the floor; the poor old fellow was so glad to see me that I thought he would devour me, his head split from ear to ear, showing his three rows of tusks in his hobgoblin smile.

Quieting him with a word of command and a caress, I looked hurriedly through the approaching gloom for a sign of Dejah Thoris, and then, not seeing her, I called her name. There was an answering murmur from the far corner of the apartment, and with a couple of quick strides I was standing beside her where she crouched among the furs and silks upon an ancient carved wooden seat. As I waited she rose to her full height and looking me straight in the eye said:

"What would Dotar Sojat, Thark, of Dejah Thoris his captive?"

"Dejah Thoris, I do not know how I have angered you. It was furtherest from my desire to hurt or offend you, whom I had hoped to protect and comfort. Have none of me if it is your will, but that you must aid me in effecting your escape, if such a thing be possible, is not my request, but my command. When you are safe once more at your father's court you may do with me as you please, but from now on until that day I am your master, and you must obey and aid me." She looked at me long and earnestly and I thought that she was softening toward me.

"I understand your words, Dotar Sojat," she replied, "but you I do not understand. You are a queer mixture of child and man, of brute and noble. I only wish that I might read your heart."

"Look down at your feet, Dejah Thoris; it lies there now where it has lain since that other night at Korad, and where it will ever lie beating alone for you until death stills it forever."

She took a little step toward me, her beautiful hands outstretched in a strange, groping gesture.

"What do you mean, John Carter?" she whispered. "What are you saying to me?"

"I am saying what I had promised myself that I would not say to you, at least until you were no longer a captive among the green men; what from your attitude toward me for the past twenty days I had thought never to say to you; I am saying, Dejah Thoris, that I am yours, body and soul, to serve you, to fight for you, and to die for you. Only one thing I ask of you in return, and that is that you make no sign, either of condemnation or of approbation of my words until you are safe among your own people, and that whatever sentiments you harbor toward me they be not influenced or colored by gratitude; whatever I may do to serve you will be prompted solely from selfish motives, since it gives me more pleasure to serve you than not."

"I will respect your wishes, John Carter, because I understand the motives which prompt them, and I accept your service no more willingly than I bow to your authority; your word shall be my law. I have twice wronged you in my thoughts and again I ask your forgiveness."

Further conversation of a personal nature was prevented by the entrance of Sola, who was much agitated and wholly unlike her usual calm and possessed self.

"That horrible Sarkoja has been before Tal Hajus," she cried, "and from what I heard upon the plaza there is little hope for either of you."

"What do they say?" inquired Dejah Thoris.

"That you will be thrown to the wild calots [dogs] in the great arena as soon as the hordes have assembled for the yearly games."

"Sola," I said, "you are a Thark, but you hate and loathe the customs of your people as much as we do. Will you not accompany us in one supreme effort to escape? I am sure that Dejah Thoris can offer you a home and protection among her people, and your fate can be no worse among them than it must ever be here."

"Yes," cried Dejah Thoris, "come with us, Sola, you will be better off among the red men of Helium than you are here, and I can promise you not only a home with us, but the love and affection your nature craves and which must always be denied you by the customs of your own race. Come with us, Sola; we might go without you, but your fate would be terrible if they thought you had connived to aid us. I know that even that fear would not tempt you to interfere in our escape, but we want you with us, we want you to come to a land of sunshine and happiness, amongst a people who know the meaning of love, of sympathy, and of gratitude. Say that you will, Sola; tell me that you will."

"The great waterway which leads to Helium is but fifty miles to the south," murmured Sola, half to herself; "a swift thoat might make it in three hours; and then to Helium it is five hundred miles, most of the way through thinly settled districts. They would know and they would follow us. We might hide among the great trees for a time, but the chances are small indeed for escape. They would follow us to the very gates of Helium, and they would take toll of life at every step; you do not know them."

"Is there no other way we might reach Helium?" I asked. "Can you not draw me a rough map of the country we must traverse, Dejah Thoris?"

"Yes," she replied, and taking a great diamond from her hair she drew upon the marble floor the first map of Barsoomian territory I had ever seen. It was crisscrossed in every direction with long straight lines, sometimes running parallel and sometimes converging toward some great circle. The lines, she said, were waterways; the circles, cities; and one far to the northwest of us she pointed out as Helium. There were other cities closer, but she said she feared to enter many of them, as they were not all friendly toward Helium.

Finally, after studying the map carefully in the moonlight which now flooded the room, I pointed out a waterway far to the north of us which also seemed to lead to Helium.

"Does not this pierce your grandfather's territory?" I asked.

"Yes," she answered, "but it is two hundred miles north of us; it is one of the waterways we crossed on the trip to Thark."

"They would never suspect that we would try for that distant waterway," I answered, "and that is why I think that it is the best route for our escape."

Sola agreed with me, and it was decided that we should leave Thark this same night; just as quickly, in fact, as I could find and saddle my thoats. Sola was to ride one and Dejah Thoris and I the other; each of us carrying sufficient food and drink to last us for two days, since the animals could not be urged too rapidly for so long a distance.

I directed Sola to proceed with Dejah Thoris along one of the less frequented avenues to the southern boundary of the city, where I would overtake them with the thoats as quickly as possible; then, leaving them to gather what food, silks, and furs we were to need, I slipped quietly to the rear of the first floor, and entered the courtyard, where our animals were moving restlessly about, as was their habit, before settling down for the night.

In the shadows of the buildings and out beneath the radiance of the Martian moons moved the great herd of thoats and zitidars, the latter grunting their low gutturals and the former occasionally emitting the sharp squeal which denotes the almost habitual state of rage in which these creatures passed their existence. They were quieter now, owing to the absence of man, but as they scented me they became more restless and their hideous noise increased. It was risky business, this entering a paddock of thoats alone and at night; first, because their increasing noisiness might warn the nearby warriors that something was amiss, and also because for the slightest cause, or for no cause at all some great bull thoat might take it upon himself to lead a charge upon me.

Having no desire to awaken their nasty tempers upon such a night as this, where so much depended upon secrecy and dispatch, I hugged the shadows of the buildings, ready at an instant's warning to leap into the safety of a nearby door or window. Thus I moved silently to the great gates which opened upon the street at the back of the court, and as I neared the exit I called softly to my two animals. How I thanked the kind providence which had given me the foresight to win the love and confidence of these wild dumb brutes, for presently from the far side of the court I saw two huge bulks forcing their way toward me through the surging mountains of flesh.

They came quite close to me, rubbing their muzzles against my body and nosing for the bits of food it was always my practice to reward them with. Opening the gates I ordered the two great beasts to pass out, and then slipping quietly after them I closed the portals behind me.

I did not saddle or mount the animals there, but instead walked quietly in the shadows of the buildings toward an unfrequented avenue which led toward the point I had arranged to meet Dejah Thoris and Sola. With the noiselessness of disembodied spirits we moved stealthily along the deserted streets, but not until we were within sight of the plain beyond the city did I commence to breathe freely. I was sure that Sola and Dejah Thoris would find no difficulty in reaching our rendezvous undetected, but with my great thoats I was not so sure for myself, as it was quite unusual for warriors to leave the city after dark; in fact there was no place for them to go within any but a long ride.

I reached the appointed meeting place safely, but as Dejah Thoris and Sola were not there I led my animals into the entrance hall of one of the large buildings. Presuming that one of the other women of the same household may have come in to speak to Sola, and so delayed their departure, I did not feel any undue apprehension until nearly an hour had passed without a sign of them, and by the time another half hour had crawled away I was becoming filled with grave anxiety. Then there broke upon the stillness of the night the sound of an approaching party, which, from the noise, I know could be no fugitives creeping stealthily toward liberty. Soon the party was near me, and from the black shadows of my entrance way I perceived a score of mounted warriors, who, in passing, dropped a dozen words that fetched my heart clean into the top of my head.

"He would likely have arranged to meet them just without the city, and so—" I heard no more, they had passed on; but it was enough. Our plan had been discovered, and the chances for escape from now on to the fearful end would be small indeed. My one hope now was to return undetected to the quarters of Dejah Thoris and learn what fate had overtaken her, but how: to do it with these great monstrous thoats upon my hands, now that the city probably was aroused by the knowledge of my escape was a problem of no mean proportions.

Suddenly an idea occurred to me, and acting on my knowledge of the construction of the buildings of these ancient Martian cities with a hollow court within the center of each square, I groped my way blindly through the dark chambers, calling the great thoats after me. They had difficulty in negotiating some of the doorways, but as the buildings fronting the city's principal exposures were all designed upon a magnificent scale, they were able to wriggle through without sticking fast; and thus we finally made the inner court where I found, as I had expected, the usual carpet of mosslike vegetation which would prove their food and drink until I could return them to their own enclosure. That they would be as quiet and contented here as elsewhere I was confident, nor was there but the remotest possibility that they would be discovered, as the green men had no great desire to enter these outlying buildings, which were frequented by the only thing, I believe, which caused them the sensation of fear—the great white apes of Barsoom.

Removing the saddle trappings, I hid them just within the rear doorway of the building through which we had entered the court, and, turning the beasts loose, quickly made my way across the court to the rear of the buildings upon the further side, and thence to the avenue beyond. Waiting in the doorway of the building until I was assured that no one was approaching, I hurried across to the opposite side and through the first doorway to the court beyond; thus, crossing through court after court with only the slight chance of detection which the necessary crossing of the avenues entailed, I made my way in safety to the courtyard in the rear of Dejah Thoris' quarters.

Here, of course, I found the beasts of the warriors who quartered in the adjacent buildings, and the warriors themselves I might expect to meet within if I entered; but, fortunately for me, I had another and safer method of reaching the upper story where Dejah Thoris should be found, and, after first determining as nearly as possible which of the buildings she occupied, for I had never observed them before from the court side, I took advantage of my relatively great strength and agility and sprang upward until I grasped the sill of a second-story window which I thought to be in the rear of her apartment. Drawing myself inside the room I moved stealthily toward the front of the building, and not until I had quite reached the doorway of her room was I made aware by voices that it was occupied.

I did not rush headlong in, but listened without to assure myself that it was Dejah Thoris and that it was safe to venture within. It was well indeed that I took this precaution, for the conversation I heard was in the low gutturals of men, and the words which finally came to me proved a most timely warning. The speaker was a chieftain and he was giving orders to four of his warriors.

"And when he returns to this chamber," he was saying, "as he surely will when he finds she does not meet him at the city's edge, you four are to spring upon him and disarm him. It will require the combined strength of all of you to do it if the reports they bring back from Korad are correct. When you have him fast bound bear him to the vaults beneath the jeddak's quarters and chain him securely where he may be found when Tal Hajus wishes him. Allow him to speak with none, nor permit any other to enter this apartment before he comes. There will be no danger of the girl returning, for by this time she is safe in the arms of Tal Hajus, and may all her ancestors have pity upon her, for Tal Hajus will have none; the great Sarkoja has done a noble night's work. I go, and if you fail to capture him when he comes, I commend your carcasses to the cold bosom of Iss."

CHAPTER SEVENTEEN
A COSTLY RECAPTURE

AS THE SPEAKER CEASED he turned to leave the apartment by the door where I was standing, but I needed to wait no longer; I had heard enough to fill my soul with dread, and stealing quietly away I returned to the courtyard by the way I had come. My plan of action was formed upon the instant, and crossing the square and the bordering avenue upon the opposite side I soon stood within the courtyard of Tal Hajus.

The brilliantly lighted apartments of the first floor told me where first to seek, and advancing to the windows I peered within. I soon discovered that my approach was not to be the easy thing I had hoped, for the rear rooms bordering the court were filled with warriors and women. I then glanced up at the stories above, discovering that the third was apparently unlighted, and so decided to make my entrance to the building from that point. It was the work of but a moment for me to reach the windows above, and soon I had drawn myself within the sheltering shadows of the unlighted third floor.

Fortunately the room I had selected was untenanted, and creeping noiselessly to the corridor beyond I discovered a light in the apartments ahead of me. Reaching what appeared to be a doorway I discovered that it was but an opening upon an immense inner chamber which towered from the first floor, two stories below me, to the domelike roof of the building, high above my head. The floor of this great circular hall was thronged with chieftains, warriors and women, and at one end was a great raised platform upon which squatted the most hideous beast I had ever put my eyes upon. He had all the cold, hard, cruel, terrible features of the green warriors, but accentuated and debased by the animal passions to which he had given himself over for many years. There was not a mark of dignity or pride upon his bestial countenance, while his enormous bulk spread itself out upon the platform where he squatted like some huge devil fish, his six limbs accentuating the similarity in a horrible and startling manner.

But the sight that froze me with apprehension was that of Dejah Thoris and Sola standing there before him, and the fiendish leer of him as he let his great protruding eyes gloat upon the lines of her beautiful figure. She was speaking, but I could not hear what she said, nor could I make out the low grumbling of his reply. She stood there erect before him, her head high held, and even at the distance I was from them I could read the scorn and disgust upon her face as she let her haughty glance rest without sign of fear upon him. She was indeed the proud daughter of a thousand jeddaks, every inch of her dear, precious little body; so small, so frail beside the towering warriors around her, but in her majesty dwarfing them into insignificance; she was the mightiest figure among them and I verily believe that they felt it.

Presently Tal Hajus made a sign that the chamber be cleared, and that the prisoners be left alone before him. Slowly the chieftains, the warriors and the women melted away into the shadows of the surrounding chambers, and Dejah Thoris and Sola stood alone before the jeddak of the Tharks.

One chieftain alone had hesitated before departing; I saw him standing in the shadows of a mighty column, his fingers nervously toying with the hilt of his great-sword and his cruel eyes bent in implacable hatred upon Tal Hajus. It was Tars Tarkas, and I could read his thoughts as they were an open book for the undisguised loathing upon his face. He was thinking of that other woman who, forty years ago, had stood before this beast, and could I have spoken a word into his ear at that moment the reign of Tal Hajus would have been over; but finally he also strode from the room, not knowing that he left his own daughter at the mercy of the creature he most loathed.

Tal Hajus arose, and I, half fearing, half anticipating his intentions, hurried to the winding runway which led to the floors below. No one was near to intercept me, and I reached the main floor of the chamber unob-served, taking my station in the shadow of the same column that Tars Tarkas had but just deserted. As I reached the floor Tal Hajus was speaking.

"Princess of Helium, I might wring a mighty ransom from your people would I but return you to them unharmed, but a thousand times rather would I watch that beautiful face writhe in the agony of torture; it shall be long drawn out, that I promise you; ten days of pleasure were all too short to show the love I harbor for your race. The terrors of your death shall haunt the slumbers of the red men through all the ages to come; they will shudder in the shadows of the night as their fathers tell them of the awful vengeance of the green men; of the power and might and hate and cruelty of Tal Hajus. But before the torture you shall be mine for one short hour, and word of that too shall go forth to Tardos Mors, Jeddak of Helium, your grandfather, that he may grovel upon the ground in the agony of his sorrow. Tomorrow the torture will commence; tonight thou art Tal Hajus'; come!"

He sprang down from the platform and grasped her roughly by the arm, but scarcely had he touched her than I leaped between them. My short-sword, sharp and gleaming was in my right hand; I could have plunged it into his putrid heart before he realized that I was upon him; but as I raised my arm to strike I thought of Tars Tarkas, and, with all my rage, with all my hatred, I could not rob him of that sweet moment for which he had lived and hoped all these long, weary years, and so, instead, I swung my good right fist full upon the point of his jaw. Without a sound he slipped to the floor as one dead.

In the same deathly silence I grasped Dejah Thoris by the hand, and motioning to Sola to follow we sped noiselessly from the chamber and to the floor above. Unseen we reached a rear window and with the straps and leather of my trappings I lowered, first Sola and then Dejah Thoris to the ground below. Dropping lightly after them I drew them rapidly around the court in the shadows of the buildings, and thus we returned over the same course I had so recently followed from the distant boundary of the city.

We finally came upon my thoats in the courtyard where I had left them, and placing the trappings upon them we hastened through the building to the avenue beyond. Mounting, Sola upon one beast, and Dejah Thoris behind me upon the other, we rode from the city of Thark through the hills to the south.

Instead of circling back around the city to the northwest and toward the nearest waterway which lay so short a distance from us, we turned to the northeast and struck out upon the mossy waste across which, for two hundred dangerous and weary miles, lay another main artery leading to Helium.

No word was spoken until we had left the city far behind, but I could hear the quiet sobbing of Dejah Thoris as she clung to me with her dear head resting against my shoulder.

"If we make it, my chieftain, the debt of Helium will be a mighty one; greater than she can ever pay you; and should we not make it," she continued, "the debt is no less, though Helium will never know, for you have saved the last of our line from worse than death."

I did not answer, but instead reached to my side and pressed the little fingers of her I loved where they clung to me for support, and then, in unbroken silence, we sped over the yellow, moonlit moss; each of us occupied with his own thoughts. For my part I could not be other than joyful had I tried, with Dejah Thoris' warm body pressed close to mine, and with all our unpassed danger my heart was singing as gaily as though we were already entering the gates of Helium.

Our earlier plans had been so sadly upset that we now found ourselves without food or drink, and I alone was armed. We therefore urged our beasts to a speed that must tell on them sorely before we could hope to sight the ending of the first stage of our journey.

We rode all night and all the following day with only a few short rests. On the second night both we and our animals were completely fagged, and so we lay down upon the moss and slept for some five or six hours, taking up the journey once more before daylight. All the following day we rode, and when, late in the afternoon we had sighted no distant trees, the mark of the great waterways throughout all Barsoom, the terrible truth flashed upon us—we were lost.

Evidently we had circled, but which way it was difficult to say, nor did it seem possible with the sun to guide us by day and the moons and stars by night. At any rate no waterway was in sight, and the entire party was almost ready to drop from hunger, thirst and fatigue. Far ahead of us and a trifle to the right we could distinguish the outlines of low mountains. These we decided to attempt to reach in the hope that from some ridge we might discern the missing waterway. Night fell upon us before we reached our goal, and, almost fainting from weariness and weakness, we lay down and slept.

I was awakened early in the morning by some huge body pressing close to mine, and opening my eyes with a start I beheld my blessed old Woola snuggling close to me; the faithful brute had followed us across that trackless waste to share our fate, whatever it might be. Putting my arms about his neck I pressed my cheek close to his, nor am I ashamed that I did it, nor of the tears that came to my eyes as I thought of his love for me. Shortly after this Dejah Thoris and Sola awakened, and it was decided that we push on at once in an effort to gain the hills.

We had gone scarcely a mile when I noticed that my thoat was commencing to stumble and stagger in a most pitiful manner, although we had not attempted to force them out of a walk since about noon of the preceding day. Suddenly he lurched wildly to one side and pitched violently to the ground. Dejah Thoris and I were thrown clear of him and fell upon the soft moss with scarcely a jar; but the poor beast was in a pitiable condition, not even being able to rise, although relieved of our weight. Sola told me that the coolness of the night, when it fell, together with the rest would doubtless revive him, and so I decided not to kill him, as was my first intention, as I had thought it cruel to leave him alone there to die of hunger and thirst. Relieving him of his trappings, which I flung down beside him, we left the poor fellow to his fate, and pushed on with the one thoat as best we could. Sola and I walked, making Dejah Thoris ride, much against her will. In this way we had progressed to within about a mile of the hills we were endeavoring to reach when Dejah Thoris, from her point of vantage upon the thoat, cried out that she saw a great party of mounted men filing down from a pass in the hills several miles away. Sola and I both looked in the direction she indicated, and there, plainly discernible, were several hundred mounted warriors. They seemed to be headed in a southwesterly direction, which would take them away from us.

They doubtless were Thark warriors who had been sent out to capture us, and we breathed a great sigh of relief that they were traveling in the opposite direction. Quickly lifting Dejah Thoris from the thoat, I commanded the animal to lie down and we three then did the same, presenting as small an object as possible for fear of attracting the attention of the warriors toward us.

We could see them as they filed out of the pass, just for an instant, before they were lost to view behind a friendly ridge; to us a most providential ridge; since, had they been in view for any great length of time, they scarcely could have failed to discover us. As what proved to be the last warrior came into view from the pass, he halted and, to our consternation, threw his small but powerful fieldglass to his eye and scanned the sea bottom in all directions. Evidently he was a chieftain, for in certain marching formations among the green men a chieftain brings up at the extreme rear of the column. As his glass swung toward us our hearts stopped in our breasts, and I could feel the cold sweat start from every pore in my body.

Presently it swung full upon us and—stopped. The tension on our nerves was near the breaking point, and I doubt if any of us breathed for the few moments he held us covered by his glass; and then he lowered it and we could see him shout a command to the warriors who had passed from our sight behind the ridge. He did not wait for them to join him, however, instead he wheeled his thoat and came tearing madly in our direction.

There was but one slight chance and that we must take quickly. Raising my strange Martian rifle to my shoulder I sighted and touched the button which controlled the trigger; there was a sharp explosion as the missile reached its goal, and the charging chieftain pitched backward from his flying mount.

Springing to my feet I urged the thoat to rise, and directed Sola to take Dejah Thoris with her upon him and make a mighty effort to reach the hills before the green warriors were upon us. I knew that in the ravines and gullies they might find a temporary hiding place, and even though they died there of hunger and thirst it would be better so than that they fell into the hands of the Tharks. Forcing my two revolvers upon them as a slight means of protection, and, as a last resort, as an escape for themselves from the horrid death which recapture would surely mean, I lifted Dejah Thoris in my arms and placed her upon the thoat behind Sola, who had already mounted at my command.

"Good-bye, my princess," I whispered, "we may meet in Helium yet. I have escaped from worse plights than this," and I tried to smile as I lied.

"What," she cried, "are you not coming with us?"

"How may I, Dejah Thoris? Someone must hold these fellows off for a while, and I can better escape them alone than could the three of us together."

She sprang quickly from the thoat and, throwing her dear arms about my neck, turned to Sola, saying with quiet dignity: "Fly, Sola! Dejah Thoris remains to die with the man she loves."

Those words are engraved upon my heart. Ah, gladly would I give up my life a thousand times could I only hear them once again; but I could not then give even a second to the rapture of her sweet embrace, and pressing my lips to hers for the first time, I picked her up bodily and tossed her to her seat behind Sola again, commanding the latter in peremptory tones to hold her there by force, and then, slapping the thoat upon the flank, I saw them borne away; Dejah Thoris struggling to the last to free herself from Sola's grasp.

Turning, I beheld the green warriors mounting the ridge and looking for their chieftain. In a moment they saw him, and then me; but scarcely had they discovered me than I commenced firing, lying flat upon my belly in the moss. I had an even hundred rounds in the magazine of my rifle, and another hundred in the belt at my back, and I kept up a continuous stream of fire until I saw all of the warriors who had been first to return from behind the ridge either dead or scurrying to cover.

My respite was short-lived, however, for soon the entire party, numbering some thousand men, came charging into view, racing madly toward me. I fired until my rifle was empty and they were almost upon me, and then a glance showing me that Dejah Thoris and Sola had disappeared among the hills, I sprang up, throwing down my useless gun, and started away in the direction opposite to that taken by Sola and her charge.

If ever Martians had an exhibition of jumping, it was granted those astonished warriors on that day long years ago, but while it led them away from Dejah Thoris it did not distract their attention from endeavoring to capture me.

They raced wildly after me until, finally, my foot struck a projecting piece of quartz, and down I went sprawling upon the moss. As I looked up they were upon me, and although I drew my long-sword in an attempt to sell my life as dearly as possible, it was soon over. I reeled beneath their blows which fell upon me in perfect torrents; my head swam; all was black, and I went down beneath them to oblivion.

CHAPTER EIGHTEEN
CHAINED IN WARHOON

IT MUST HAVE BEEN SEVERAL HOURS before I regained consciousness and I well remember the feeling of surprise which swept over me as I realized that I was not dead.

I was lying among a pile of sleeping silks and furs in the corner of a small room in which were several green warriors, and bending over me was an ancient and ugly female.

As I opened my eyes she turned to one of the warriors, saying, "He will live, O, Jed."

"'Tis well," replied the one so addressed, rising and approaching my couch, "he should render rare sport for the great games."

And now as my eyes fell upon him, I saw that he was no Thark, for his ornaments and metal were not of that horde. He was a huge fellow, terribly scarred about the face and chest, and with one broken tusk and a missing ear. Strapped on either breast were human skulls and depending from these a number of dried human hands.

His reference to the great games of which I had heard so much while among the Tharks convinced me that I had but jumped from purgatory into gehenna.

After a few more words with the female, during which she assured him that I was now fully fit to travel, the jed ordered that we mount and ride after the main column.

I was strapped securely to as wild and unmanageable a thoat as I had ever seen, and, with a mounted warrior on either side to prevent the beast from bolting, we rode forth at a furious pace in pursuit of the column. My wounds gave me but little pain, so wonderfully and rapidly had the applications and injections of the female exercised their therapeutic powers, and so deftly had she bound and plastered the injuries.

Just before dark we reached the main body of troops shortly after they had made camp for the night. I was immediately taken before the leader, who proved to be the jeddak of the hordes of Warhoon.

Like the jed who had brought me, he was frightfully scarred, and also decorated with the breastplate of human skulls and dried dead hands which seemed to mark all the greater warriors among the Warhoons, as well as to indicate their awful ferocity, which greatly transcends even that of the Tharks.

The jeddak, Bar Comas, who was comparatively young, was the object of the fierce and jealous hatred of his old lieutenant, Dak Kova, the jed who had captured me, and I could not but note the almost studied efforts which the latter made to affront his superior.

He entirely omitted the usual formal salutation as we entered the presence of the jeddak, and as he pushed me roughly before the ruler he exclaimed in a loud and menacing voice, "I have brought a strange creature wearing the metal of a Thark whom it is my pleasure to have battle with a wild thoat at the great games."

"He will die as Bar Comas, your jeddak, sees fit, if at all," replied the young ruler, with emphasis and dignity.

"If at all?" roared Dak Kova. "By the dead hands at my throat but he shall die, Bar Comas. No maudlin weakness on your part shall save him. O, would that Warhoon were ruled by a real jeddak rather than by a water-hearted weakling from whom even old Dak Kova could tear the metal with his bare hands!"

Bar Comas eyed the defiant and insubordinate chieftain for an instant, his expression one of haughty, fearless contempt and hate, and then without drawing a weapon and without uttering a word he hurled himself at the throat of his defamer.

I never before had seen two green Martian warriors battle with nature's weapons and the exhibition of animal ferocity which ensued was as fearful a thing as the most disordered imagination could picture. They tore at each other's eyes and ears with their hands and with their gleaming tusks repeatedly slashed and gored until both were cut fairly to ribbons from head to foot.

Bar Comas had much the better of the battle as he was stronger, quicker and more intelligent. It soon seemed that the encounter was done saving only the final death thrust when Bar Comas slipped in breaking away from a clinch. It was the one little opening that Dak Kova needed, and hurling himself at the body of his adversary he buried his single mighty tusk in Bar Comas' groin and with a last powerful effort ripped the young jeddak wide open the full length of his body, the great tusk finally wedging in the bones of Bar Comas' jaw. Victor and vanquished rolled limp and lifeless upon the moss, a huge mass of torn and bloody flesh.

Bar Comas was stone dead, and only the most herculean efforts on the part of Dak Kova's females saved him from the fate he deserved. Three days later he walked without assistance to the body of Bar Comas which, by custom, had not been moved from where it fell, and placing his foot upon the neck of his erstwhile ruler he assumed the title of Jeddak of Warhoon.

The dead jeddak's hands and head were removed to be added to the ornaments of his conqueror, and then his women cremated what remained, amid wild and terrible laughter.

The injuries to Dak Kova had delayed the march so greatly that it was decided to give up the expedition, which was a raid upon a small Thark community in retaliation for the destruction of the incubator, until after the great games, and the entire body of warriors, ten thousand in number, turned back toward Warhoon.

My introduction to these cruel and bloodthirsty people was but an index to the scenes I witnessed almost daily while with them. They are a smaller horde than the Tharks but much more ferocious. Not a day passed but that some members of the various Warhoon communities met in deadly combat. I have seen as high as eight mortal duels within a single day.

We reached the city of Warhoon after some three days march and I was immediately cast into a dungeon and heavily chained to the floor and walls. Food was brought me at intervals but owing to the utter darkness of the place I do not know whether I lay there days, or weeks, or months. It was the most horrible experience of all my life and that my mind did not give way to the terrors of that inky blackness has been a wonder to me ever since. The place was filled with creeping, crawling things; cold, sinuous bodies passed over me when I lay down, and in the darkness I occasionally caught glimpses of gleaming, fiery eyes, fixed in horrible intentness upon me. No sound reached me from the world above and no word would my jailer vouchsafe when my food was brought to me, although I at first bombarded him with questions.

Finally all the hatred and maniacal loathing for these awful creatures who had placed me in this horrible place was centered by my tottering reason upon this single emissary who represented to me the entire horde of Warhoons.

I had noticed that he always advanced with his dim torch to where he could place the food within my reach and as he stooped to place it upon the floor his head was about on a level with my breast. So, with the cunning of a madman, I backed into the far corner of my cell when next I heard him approaching and gathering a little slack of the great chain which held me in my hand I waited his coming, crouching like some beast of prey. As he stooped to place my food upon the ground I swung the chain above my head and crashed the links with all my strength upon his skull. Without a sound he slipped to the floor, stone dead.

Laughing and chattering like the idiot I was fast becoming I fell upon his prostrate form my fingers feeling for his dead throat. Presently they came in contact with a small chain at the end of which dangled a number of keys. The touch of my fingers on these keys brought back my reason with the suddenness of thought. No longer was I a jibbering idiot, but a sane, reasoning man with the means of escape within my very hands.

As I was groping to remove the chain from about my victim's neck I glanced up into the darkness to see six pairs of gleaming eyes fixed, unwinking, upon me. Slowly they approached and slowly I shrank back from the awful horror of them. Back into my comer I crouched holding my hands, palms out, before me, and stealthily on came the awful eyes until they reached the dead body at my feet. Then slowly they retreated but this time with a strange grating sound and finally they disappeared in some black and distant recess of my dungeon.

CHAPTER NINETEEN
BATTLING IN THE ARENA

LOWLY I REGAINED MY COMPOSURE and finally essayed again to attempt to remove the keys from the dead body of my former jailer. But as I reached out into the darkness to locate it I found to my horror that it was gone. Then the truth flashed on me; the owners of those gleaming eyes had dragged my prize away from me to be devoured in their neighboring lair; as they had been waiting for days, for weeks, for months, through all this awful eternity of my imprisonment to drag my dead carcass to their feast.

For two days no food was brought me, but then a new messenger appeared and my incarceration went on as before, but not again did I allow my reason to be submerged by the horror of my position.

Shortly after this episode another prisoner was brought in and chained near me. By the dim torchlight I saw that he was a red Martian and I could scarcely await the departure of his guards to address him. As their retreating footsteps died away in the distance, I called out softly the Martian word of greeting, kaor.

"Who are you who speaks out of the darkness?" he answered.

"John Carter, a friend of the red men of Helium."

"I am of Helium," he said, "but I do not recall your name."

And then I told him my story as I have written it here, omitting only any reference to my love for Dejah Thoris. He was much excited by the news of Helium's princess and seemed quite positive that she and Sola could easily have reached a point of safety from where they left me. He said that he knew the place well because the defile through which the Warhoon warriors had passed when they discovered us was the only one ever used by them when marching to the south.

"Dejah Thoris and Sola entered the hills not five miles from a great waterway and are now probably quite safe," he assured me.

My fellow prisoner was Kantos Kan, a padwar (lieutenant) in the navy of Helium. He had been a member of the ill-fated expedition which had fallen into the hands of the Tharks at the time of Dejah Thoris' capture, and he briefly related the events which followed the defeat of the battleships.

Badly injured and only partially manned they had limped slowly toward Helium, but while passing near the city of Zodanga, the capital of Helium's hereditary enemies among the red men of Barsoom, they had been attacked by a great body of war vessels and all but the craft to which Kantos Kan belonged were either destroyed or captured. His vessel was chased for days by three of the Zodangan war ships but finally escaped during the darkness of a moonless night.

Thirty days after the capture of Dejah Thoris, or about the time of our coming to Thark, his vessel had reached Helium with about ten survivors of the original crew of seven hundred officers and men. Immediately seven great fleets, each of one hundred mighty war ships, had been dispatched to search for Dejah Thoris, and from these vessels two thousand smaller craft had been kept out continuously in futile search for the missing princess.

Two green Martian communities had been wiped off the face of Barsoom by the avenging fleets, but no trace of Dejah Thoris had been found. They had been searching among the northern hordes, and only within the past few days had they extended their quest to the south.

Kantos Kan had been detailed to one of the small one-man fliers and had had the misfortune to be discovered by the Warhoons while exploring their city. The bravery and daring of the man won my greatest respect and admiration. Alone he had landed at the city's boundary and on foot had penetrated to the buildings surrounding the plaza. For two days and nights he had explored their quarters and their dungeons in search of his beloved princess only to fall into the hands of a party of Warhoons as he was about to leave, after assuring himself that Dejah Thoris was not a captive there.

During the period of our incarceration Kantos Kan and I became well acquainted, and formed a warm personal friendship. A few days only elapsed, however, before we were dragged forth from our dungeon for the great games. We were conducted early one morning to an enormous amphitheater, which instead of having been built upon the surface of the ground was excavated below the surface. It had partially filled with debris so that how large it had originally been was difficult to say. In its present condition it held the entire twenty thousand Warhoons of the assembled hordes.

The arena was immense but extremely uneven and unkempt. Around it the Warhoons had piled building stone from some of the ruined edifices of the ancient city to prevent the animals and the captives from escaping into the audience, and at each end had been constructed cages to hold them until their turns came to meet some horrible death upon the arena.

Kantos Kan and I were confined together in one of the cages. In the others were wild calots, thoats, mad zitidars, green warriors, and women of other hordes, and many strange and ferocious wild beasts of Barsoom which I had never before seen. The din of their roaring, growling and squealing was deafening and the formidable appearance of any one of them was enough to make the stoutest heart feel grave forebodings.

Kantos Kan explained to me that at the end of the day one of these prisoners would gain freedom and the others would lie dead about the arena. The winners in the various contests of the day would be pitted against each other until only two remained alive; the victor in the last encounter being set free, whether animal or man. The following morning the cages would be filled with a new consignment of victims, and so on throughout the ten days of the games.

Shortly after we had been caged the amphitheater began to fill and within an hour every available part of the seating space was occupied. Dak Kova, with his jeds and chieftains, sat at the center of one side of the arena upon a large raised platform.

At a signal from Dak Kova the doors of two cages were thrown open and a dozen green Martian females were driven to the center of the arena. Each was given a dagger and then, at the far end, a pack of twelve calots, or wild dogs were loosed upon them.

As the brutes, growling and foaming, rushed upon the almost defenseless women I turned my head that I might not see the horrid sight. The yells and laughter of the green horde bore witness to the excellent quality of the sport and when I turned back to the arena, as Kantos Kan told me it was over, I saw three victorious calots, snarling and growling over the bodies of their prey. The women had given a good account of themselves.

Next a mad zitidar was loosed among the remaining dogs, and so it went throughout the long, hot, horrible day.

During the day I was pitted against first men and then beasts, but as I was armed with a long-sword and always outclassed my adversary in agility and generally in strength as well, it proved but child's play to me. Time and time again I won the applause of the bloodthirsty multitude, and toward the end there were cries that I be taken from the arena and be made a member of the hordes of Warhoon.

Finally there were but three of us left, a great green warrior of some far northern horde, Kantos Kan, and myself. The other two were to battle and then I to fight the conqueror for the liberty which was accorded the final winner.

Kantos Kan had fought several times during the day and like myself had always proven victorious, but occasionally by the smallest of margins, especially when pitted against the green warriors. I had little hope that he could best his giant adversary who had mowed down all before him during the day. The fellow towered nearly sixteen feet in height, while Kantos Kan was some inches under six feet. As they advanced to meet one another I saw for the first time a trick of Martian swordsmanship which centered Kantos Kan's every hope of victory and life on one cast of the dice, for, as he came to within about twenty feet of the huge fellow he threw his sword arm far behind him over his shoulder and with a mighty sweep hurled his weapon point foremost at the green warrior. It flew true as an arrow and piercing the poor devil's heart laid him dead upon the arena.

Kantos Kan and I were now pitted against each other but as we approached to the encounter I whispered to him to prolong the battle until nearly dark in the hope that we might find some means of escape. The horde evidently guessed that we had no hearts to fight each other and so they howled in rage as neither of us placed a fatal thrust. Just as I saw the sudden coming of dark I whispered to Kantos Kan to thrust his sword between my left arm and my body. As he did so I staggered back clasping the sword tightly with my arm and thus fell to the ground with his weapon apparently protruding from my chest. Kantos Kan perceived my coup and stepping quickly to my side he placed his foot upon my neck and withdrawing his sword from my body gave me the final death blow through the neck which is supposed to sever the jugular vein, but in this instance the cold blade slipped harmlessly into the sand of the arena. In the darkness which had now fallen none could tell but that he had really finished me. I whispered to him to go and claim his freedom and then look for me in the hills east of the city, and so he left me.

When the amphitheater had cleared I crept stealthily to the top and as the great excavation lay far from the plaza and in an untenanted portion of the great dead city I had little trouble in reaching the hills beyond.

CHAPTER TWENTY
IN THE ATMOSPHERE FACTORY

FOR TWO DAYS I WAITED THERE for Kantos Kan, but as he did not come I started off on foot in a northwesterly direction toward a point where he had told me lay the nearest waterway. My only food consisted of vegetable milk from the plants which gave so bounteously of this priceless fluid.

Through two long weeks I wandered, stumbling through the nights guided only by the stars and hiding during the days behind some protruding rock or among the occasional hills I traversed. Several times I was attacked by wild beasts; strange, uncouth monstrosities that leaped upon me in the dark, so that I had ever to grasp my long-sword in my hand that I might be ready for them. Usually my strange, newly acquired telepathic power warned me in ample time, but once I was down with vicious fangs at my jugular and a hairy face pressed close to mine before I knew that I was even threatened.

What manner of thing was upon me I did not know, but that it was large and heavy and many-legged I could feel. My hands were at its throat before the fangs had a chance to bury themselves in my neck, and slowly I forced the hairy face from me and closed my fingers, viselike, upon its windpipe.

Without sound we lay there, the beast exerting every effort to reach me with those awful fangs, and I straining to maintain my grip and choke the life from it as I kept it from my throat. Slowly my arms gave to the unequal struggle, and inch by inch the burning eyes and gleaming tusks of my antagonist crept toward me, until, as the hairy face touched mine again, I realized that all was over. And then a living mass of destruction sprang from the surrounding darkness full upon the creature that held me pinioned to the ground. The two rolled growling upon the moss, tearing and rending one another in a frightful manner, but it was soon over and my preserver stood with lowered head above the throat of the dead thing which would have killed me.

The nearer moon, hurtling suddenly above the horizon and lighting up the Barsoomian scene, showed me that my preserver was Woola, but from whence he had come, or how found me, I was at a loss to know. That I was glad of his companionship it is needless to say, but my pleasure at seeing him was tempered by anxiety as to the reason of his leaving Dejah Thoris. Only her death I felt sure, could account for his absence from her, so faithful I knew him to be to my commands.

By the light of the now brilliant moons I saw that he was but a shadow of his former self, and as he turned from my caress and commenced greedily to devour the dead carcass at my feet I realized that the poor fellow was more than half starved. I, myself, was in but little better plight but I could not bring myself to eat the uncooked flesh and I had no means of making a fire. When Woola had finished his meal I again took up my weary and seemingly endless wandering in quest of the elusive waterway.

At daybreak of the fifteenth day of my search I was overjoyed to see the high trees that denoted the object of my search. About noon I dragged myself wearily to the portals of a huge building which covered perhaps four square miles and towered two hundred feet in the air. It showed no aperture in the mighty walls other than the tiny door at which I sank exhausted, nor was there any sign of life about it.

I could find no bell or other method of making my presence known to the inmates of the place, unless a small round hole in the wall near the door was for that purpose. It was of about the bigness of a lead pencil and thinking that it might be in the nature of a speaking tube I put my mouth to it and was about to call into it when a voice issued from it asking me whom I might be, where from, and the nature of my errand.

I explained that I had escaped from the Warhoons and was dying of starvation and exhaustion.

"You wear the metal of a green warrior and are followed by a calot, yet you are of the figure of a red man. In color you are neither green nor red. In the name of the ninth day, what manner of creature are you?"

"I am a friend of the red men of Barsoom and I am starving. In the name of humanity open to us," I replied.

Presently the door commenced to recede before me until it had sunk into the wall fifty feet, then it stopped and slid easily to the left, exposing a short, narrow corridor of concrete, at the further end of which was another door, similar in every respect to the one I had just passed. No one was in sight, yet immediately we passed the first door it slid gently into place behind us and receded rapidly to its original position in the front wall of the building. As the door had slipped aside I had noted its great thickness, fully twenty feet, and as it reached its place once more after closing behind us, great cylinders of steel had dropped from the ceiling behind it and fitted their lower ends into apertures countersunk in the floor.

A second and a third door receded before me and slipped to one side as the first, before I reached a large inner chamber where I found food and drink set out upon a great stone table. A voice directed me to satisfy my hunger and to feed my calot, and while I was thus engaged my invisible host put me through a severe and searching cross-examination.

"Your statements are most remarkable," said the voice, on concluding its questioning, "but you are evidently speaking the truth, and it is equally evident that you are not of Barsoom. I can tell that by the conformation of your brain and the strange location of your internal organs and the shape and size of your heart."

"Can you see through me?" I exclaimed.

"Yes, I can see all but your thoughts, and were you a Barsoomian I could read those."

Then a door opened at the far side of the chamber and a strange, dried up, little mummy of a man came toward me. He wore but a single article of clothing or adornment, a small collar of gold from which depended upon his chest a great ornament as large as a dinner plate set solid with huge diamonds, except for the exact center which was occupied by a strange stone, an inch in diameter, that scintillated nine different and distinct rays; the seven colors of our earthly prism and two beautiful rays which, to me, were new and nameless. I cannot describe them any more than you could describe red to a blind man. I only know that they were beautiful in the extreme.

The old man sat and talked with me for hours, and the strangest part of our intercourse was that I could read his every thought while he could not fathom an iota from my mind unless I spoke.

I did not apprise him of my ability to sense his mental operations, and thus I learned a great deal which proved of immense value to me later and which I would never have known had he suspected my strange power, for the Martians have such perfect control of their mental machinery that they are able to direct their thoughts with absolute precision.

The building in which I found myself contained the machinery which produces that artificial atmosphere which sustains life on Mars. The secret of the entire process hinges on the use of the ninth ray, one of the beautiful scintillations which I had noted emanating from the great stone in my host's diadem.

This ray is separated from the other rays of the sun by means of finely adjusted instruments placed upon the roof of the huge building, three-quarters of which is used for reservoirs in which the ninth ray is stored. This product is then treated electrically, or rather certain proportions of refined electric vibrations are incorporated with it, and the result is then pumped to the five principal air centers of the planet where, as it is released, contact with the ether of space transforms it into atmosphere.

There is always sufficient reserve of the ninth ray stored in the great building to maintain the present Martian atmosphere for a thousand years, and the only fear, as my new friend told me, was that some accident might befall the pumping apparatus.

He led me to an inner chamber where I beheld a battery of twenty radium pumps any one of which was equal to the task of furnishing all Mars with the atmosphere compound. For eight hundred years, he told me, he had watched these pumps which are used alternately a day each at a stretch, or a little over twenty-four and one-half Earth hours. He has one assistant who divides the watch with him. Half a Martian year, about three hundred and forty-four of our days, each of these men spend alone in this huge, isolated plant.

Every red Martian is taught during earliest childhood the principles of the manufacture of atmosphere, but only two at one time ever hold the secret of ingress to the great building, which, built as it is with walls a hundred and fifty feet thick, is absolutely unassailable, even the roof being guarded from assault by air craft by a glass covering five feet thick.

The only fear they entertain of attack is from the green Martians or

some demented red man, as all Barsoomians realize that the very existence
of every form of life on Mars is dependent upon the uninterrupted working
of this plant.

One curious fact I discovered as I watched his thoughts was that the
outer doors are manipulated by telepathic means. The locks are so finely
adjusted that the doors are released by the action of a certain combination
of thought waves. To experiment with my newfound toy I thought to
surprise him into revealing this combination and so I asked him in a casual
manner how he had managed to unlock the massive doors for me from
the inner chambers of the building. As quick as a flash there leaped to his
mind nine Martian sounds, but as quickly faded as he answered that this
was a secret he must not divulge.

From then on his manner toward me changed as though he feared that
he had been surprised into divulging his great secret, and I read suspicion
and fear in his looks and thoughts, though his words were still fair.

Before I retired for the night he promised to give me a letter to a nearby
agricultural officer who would help me on my way to Zodanga, which he
said, was the nearest Martian city.

"But be sure that you do not let them know you are bound for Helium
as they are at war with that country. My assistant and I are of no country,
we belong to all Barsoom and this talisman which we wear protects us in
all lands, even among the green men—though we do not trust ourselves
to their hands if we can avoid it," he added.

"And. so good night, my friend," he continued, "may you have a long
and restful sleep—yes, a long sleep."

And though he smiled pleasantly I saw in his thoughts the wish that
he had never admitted me, and then a picture of him standing over me in
the night, and the swift thrust of a long dagger and the half formed words,
"I am sorry, but it is for the best good of Barsoom."

As he closed the door of my chamber behind him his thoughts were
cut off from me as was the sight of him, which seemed strange to me in
my little knowledge of thought transference.

What was I to do? How could I escape through these mighty walls?
Easily could I kill him now that I was warned, but once he was dead I
could no more escape, and with the stopping of the machinery of the great
plant I should die with all the other inhabitants of the planet—all, even
Dejah Thoris were she not already dead. For the others I did not give the

snap of my finger, but the thought of Dejah Thoris drove from my mind all desire to kill my mistaken host.

Cautiously I opened the door of my apartment and, followed by Woola, sought the inner of the great doors. A wild scheme had come to me; I would attempt to force the great locks by the nine thought waves I had read in my host's mind.

Creeping stealthily through corridor after corridor and down winding runways which turned hither and thither I finally reached the great hall in which I had broken my long fast that morning. Nowhere had I seen my host, nor did I know where he kept himself by night.

I was on the point of stepping boldly out into the room when a slight noise behind me warned me back into the shadows of a recess in the corridor. Dragging Woola after me I crouched low in the darkness.

Presently the old man passed close by me, and as he entered the dimly lighted chamber which I had been about to pass through I saw that he held a long thin dagger in his hand and that he was sharpening it upon a stone. In his mind was the decision to inspect the radium pumps, which would take about thirty minutes, and then return to my bed chamber and finish me.

As he passed through the great hall and disappeared down the runway which led to the pump room, I stole stealthily from my hiding place and crossed to the great door, the inner of the three which stood between me and liberty.

Concentrating my mind upon the massive lock I hurled the nine thought waves against it. In breathless expectancy I waited, when finally the great door moved softly toward me and slid quietly to one side. One after the other the remaining mighty portals opened at my command and Woola and I stepped forth into the darkness, free, but little better off than we had been before, other than that we had full stomachs.

Hastening away from the shadows of the formidable pile I made for the first crossroad, intending to strike the central turnpike as quickly as possible. This I reached about morning and entering the first enclosure I came to I searched for some evidences of a habitation.

There were low rambling buildings of concrete barred with heavy impassable doors, and no amount of hammering and hallooing brought any response. Weary and exhausted from sleeplessness I threw myself upon the ground commanding Woola to stand guard.

Sometime later I was awakened by his frightful growlings and opened my eyes to see three red Martians standing a short distance from us and covering me with their rifles.

"I am unarmed and no enemy," I hastened to explain. "I have been a prisoner among the green men and am on my way to Zodanga. All I ask is food and rest for myself and my calot and the proper directions for reaching my destination."

They lowered their rifles and advanced pleasantly toward me placing their right hands upon my left shoulder, after the manner of their custom of salute, and asking me many questions about myself and my wanderings. They then took me to the house of one of them which was only a short distance away.

The buildings I had been hammering at in the early morning were occupied only by stock and farm produce, the house proper standing among a grove of enormous trees, and, like all red-Martian homes, had been raised at night some forty or fifty feet from the ground on a large round metal shaft which slid up or down within a sleeve sunk in the ground, and was operated by a tiny radium engine in the entrance hall of the building. Instead of bothering with bolts and bars for their dwellings, the red Martians simply run them up out of harm's way during the night. They also have private means for lowering or raising them from the ground without if they wish to go away and leave them.

These brothers, with their wives and children, occupied three similar houses on this farm. They did no work themselves, being government officers in charge. The labor was performed by convicts, prisoners of war, delinquent debtors and confirmed bachelors who were too poor to pay the high celibate tax which all red-Martian governments impose.

They were the personification of cordiality and hospitality and I spent several days with them, resting and recuperating from my long and arduous experiences.

When they had heard my story—I omitted all reference to Dejah Thoris and the old man of the atmosphere plant—they advised me to color my body to more nearly resemble their own race and then attempt to find employment in Zodanga, either in the army or the navy.

"The chances are small that your tale will be believed until after you have proven your trustworthiness and won friends among the higher nobles of the court. This you can most easily do through military service, as we are a warlike people on Barsoom," explained one of them, "and save our richest favors for the fighting man."

When I was ready to depart they furnished me with a small domestic bull thoat, such as is used for saddle purposes by all red Martians. The animal is about the size of a horse and quite gentle, but in color and shape an exact replica of his huge and fierce cousin of the wilds.

The brothers had supplied me with a reddish oil with which I anointed my entire body and one of them cut my hair, which had grown quite long, in the prevailing fashion of the time, square at the back and banged in front, so that I could have passed anywhere upon Barsoom as a full-fledged red Martian. My metal and ornaments were also renewed in the style of a Zodangan gentleman, attached to the house of Ptor, which was the family name of my benefactors.

They filled a little sack at my side with Zodangan money. The medium of exchange upon Mars is not dissimilar from our own except that the coins are oval. Paper money is issued by individuals as they require it and redeemed twice yearly. If a man issues more than he can redeem, the government pays his creditors in full and the debtor works out the amount upon the farms or in mines, which are all owned by the government. This suits everybody except the debtor as it has been a difficult thing to obtain sufficient voluntary labor to work the great isolated farmlands of Mars, stretching as they do like narrow ribbons from pole to pole, through wild stretches peopled by wild animals and wilder men.

When I mentioned my inability to repay them for their kindness to me they assured me that I would have ample opportunity if I lived long upon Barsoom, and bidding me farewell they watched me until I was out of sight upon the broad white turnpike.

CHAPTER TWENTY-ONE
AN AIR SCOUT FOR ZODANGA

A S I PROCEEDED ON MY JOURNEY toward Zodanga, many strange and interesting sights arrested my attention, and at the several farmhouses where I stopped I learned a number of new and instructive things concerning the methods and manners of Barsoom.

The water which supplies the farms of Mars is collected in immense underground reservoirs at either pole from the melting ice caps, and pumped through long conduits to the various populated centers. Along either side of these conduits, and extending their entire length, lie the cultivated districts. These are divided into tracts of about the same size, each tract being under the supervision of one or more government officers.

Instead of flooding the surface of the fields, and thus wasting immense quantities of water by evaporation, the precious liquid is carried underground through a vast network of small pipes directly to the roots of the vegetation. The crops upon Mars are always uniform, for there are no droughts, no rains, no high winds, and no insects, or destroying birds.

On this trip I tasted the first meat I had eaten since leaving Earth— large, juicy steaks and chops from the well-fed domestic animals of the farms. Also I enjoyed luscious fruits and vegetables, but not a single article of food which was exactly similar to anything on Earth. Every plant and flower and vegetable and animal has been so refined by ages of careful, scientific cultivation and breeding that the like of them on Earth dwindled into pale, gray, characterless nothingness by comparison.

At a second stop I met some highly cultivated people of the noble class and while in conversation we chanced to speak of Helium. One of the older men had been there on a diplomatic mission several years before and spoke with regret of the conditions which seemed destined ever to keep these two countries at war.

"Helium," he said, "rightly boasts the most beautiful women of Barsoom, and of all her treasures the wondrous daughter of Mors Kajak, Dejah Thoris, is the most exquisite flower.

"Why," he added, "the people really worship the ground she walks upon and since her loss on that ill-starred expedition all Helium has been draped in mourning.

"That our ruler should have attacked the disabled fleet as it was returning to Helium was but another of his awful blunders which I fear will sooner or later compel Zodanga to elevate a wiser man to his place.

"Even now, though our victorious armies are surrounding Helium, the people of Zodanga are voicing their displeasure, for the war is not a popular one, since it is not based on right or justice. Our forces took advantage of the absence of the principal fleet of Helium on their search for the princess, and so we have been able easily to reduce the city to a sorry plight. It is said she will fall within the next few passages of the further moon."

"And what, think you, may have been the fate of the princess, Dejah Thoris?" I asked as casually as possible.

"She is dead," he answered. "This much was learned from a green warrior recently captured by our forces in the south. She escaped from the hordes of Thark with a strange creature of another world, only to fall into the hands of the Warhoons. Their thoats were found wandering upon the sea bottom and evidences of a bloody conflict were discovered nearby."

While this information was in no way reassuring, neither was it at all conclusive proof of the death of Dejah Thoris, and so I determined to make every effort possible to reach Helium as quickly as I could and carry to Tardos Mors such news of his granddaughter's possible whereabouts as lay in my power.

Ten days after leaving the three Ptor brothers I arrived at Zodanga. From the moment that I had come in contact with the red inhabitants of Mars I had noticed that Woola drew a great amount of unwelcome attention to me, since the huge brute belonged to a species which is never domesticated by the red men. Were one to stroll down Broadway with a Numidian lion at his heels the effect would be somewhat similar to that which I should have produced had I entered Zodanga with Woola.

The very thought of parting with the faithful fellow caused me so great regret and genuine sorrow that I put it off until just before we arrived at the city's gates; but then, finally, it became imperative that we separate. Had nothing further than my own safety or pleasure been at stake no argument could have prevailed upon me to turn away the one creature upon Barsoom that had never failed in a demonstration of affection and loyalty; but as I would willingly have offered my life in the service of her in search of whom I was about to challenge the unknown dangers of this, to me, mysterious city, I could not permit even Woola's life to threaten the success of my venture, much less his momentary happiness, for I doubted not he soon would forget me. And so I bade the poor beast an affectionate farewell, promising him, however, that if I came through my adventure in safety that in some way I should find the means to search him out.

He seemed to understand me fully, and when I pointed back in the direction of Thark he turned sorrowfully away, nor could I bear to watch him go; but resolutely set my face toward Zodanga and with a touch of heartsickness approached her frowning walls.

The letter I bore from them gained me immediate entrance to the vast, walled city. It was still very early in the morning and the streets were practically deserted. The residences, raised high upon their metal columns, resembled huge rookeries, while the uprights themselves presented the appearance of steel tree trunks. The shops as a rule were not raised from the ground nor were their doors bolted or barred, since thievery is practically unknown upon Barsoom. Assassination is the ever-present fear of all Barsoomians, and for this reason alone their homes are raised high above the ground at night, or in times of danger.

The Ptor brothers had given me explicit directions for reaching the point of the city where I could find living accommodations and be near the offices of the government agents to whom they had given me letters. My way led to the central square or plaza, which is a characteristic of all Martian cities.

The plaza of Zodanga covers a square mile and is bounded by the palaces of the jeddak, the jeds, and other members of the royalty and nobility of Zodanga, as well as by the principal public buildings, cafes, and shops.

As I was crossing the great square lost in wonder and admiration of the magnificent architecture and the gorgeous scarlet vegetation which carpeted the broad lawns I discovered a red Martian walking briskly toward me from one of the avenues. He paid not the slightest, attention to me, but as he came abreast I recognized him, and turning I placed my hand upon his shoulder, calling out:

"Kaor, Kantos Kan!"

Like lightning he wheeled and before I could so much as lower my hand the point of his long-sword was at my breast.

"Who are you?" he growled, and then as a backward leap carried me fifty feet from his sword he dropped the point to the ground and exclaimed, laughing,

"I do not need a better reply, there is but one man upon all Barsoom who can bounce about like a rubber ball. By the mother of the further moon, John Carter, how came you here, and have you become a Darseen that you can change your color at will?

"You gave me a bad half minute my friend," he continued, after I had briefly outlined my adventures since parting with him in the arena at Warhoon. "Were my name and city known to the Zodangans I would shortly be sitting on the banks of the lost sea of Korus with my revered and departed ancestors. I am here in the interests of Tardos Mors, Jeddak of Helium, to discover the whereabouts of Dejah Thoris, our princess. Sab Than, prince of Zodanga, has her hidden in the city and has fallen madly in love with her. His father, Than Kosis, Jeddak of Zodanga, has made her voluntary marriage to his son the price of peace between our countries, but Tardos Mors will not accede to the demands and has sent word that he and his people would rather look upon the dead face of their princess than see her wed to any than her own choice, and that personally he would prefer being engulfed in the ashes of a lost and burning Helium to joining the metal of his house with that of Than Kosis. His reply was the deadliest affront he could have put upon Than Kosis and the Zodangans, but his people love him the more for it and his strength in Helium is greater today than ever.

"I have been here three days," continued Kantos Kan, "but I have not yet found where Dejah Thoris is imprisoned. Today I join the Zodangan navy as an air scout and I hope in this way to win the confidence of Sab Than, the prince, who is commander of this division of the navy, and thus learn the whereabouts of Dejah Thoris. I am glad that you are here, John Carter, for I know your loyalty to my princess and two of us working together should be able to accomplish much."

The plaza was now commencing to fill with people going and coming upon the daily activities of their duties. The shops were opening and the cafes filling with early morning patrons. Kantos Kan led me to one of these gorgeous eating places where we were served entirely by mechanical apparatus. No hand touched the food from the time it entered the building in its raw state until it emerged hot and delicious upon the tables before the guests, in response to the touching of tiny buttons to indicate their desires.

After our meal, Kantos Kan took me with him to the headquarters of the air-scout squadron and introducing me to his superior asked that I be enrolled as a member of the corps. In accordance with custom an examination was necessary, but Kantos Kan had told me to have no fear on this score as he would attend to that part of the matter. He accomplished this by taking my order for examination to the examining officer and representing himself as John Carter.

"This ruse will be discovered later," he cheerfully explained, "when they check up my weights, measurements, and other personal identification data, but it will be several months before this is done and our mission should be accomplished or have failed long before that time."

The next few days were spent by Kantos Kan in teaching me the intricacies of flying and of repairing the dainty little contrivances which the Martians use for this purpose. The body of the one-man air craft is about sixteen feet long, two feet wide and three inches thick, tapering to a point at each end. The driver sits on top of this plane upon a seat constructed over the small, noiseless radium engine which propels it. The medium of buoyancy is contained within the thin metal walls of the body and consists of the eighth Barsoomian ray, or ray of propulsion, as it may be termed in view of its properties.

This ray, like the ninth ray, is unknown on Earth, but the Martians have discovered that it is an inherent property of all light no matter from what source it emanates. They have learned that it is the solar eighth ray which propels the light of the sun to the various planets, and that it is the individual eighth ray of each planet which "reflects," or propels the light thus obtained out into space once more. The solar eighth ray would be absorbed by the surface of Barsoom, but the Barsoomian eighth ray, which tends to propel light from Mars into space, is constantly streaming out from the planet constituting a force of repulsion of gravity which when confined is able to lift enormous weights from the surface of the ground.

It is this ray which has enabled them to so perfect aviation that battle ships far outweighing anything known upon Earth sail as gracefully and lightly through the thin air of Barsoom as a toy balloon in the heavy atmosphere of Earth.

During the early years of the discovery of this ray many strange accidents occurred before the Martians learned to measure and control the wonderful power they had found. In one instance, some nine hundred years before, the first great battleship to be built with eighth ray reservoirs was stored with too great a quantity of the rays and she had sailed up from Helium with five hundred officers and men, never to return.

Her power of repulsion for the planet was so great that it had carried her far into space, where she can be seen today, by the aid of powerful telescopes, hurtling through the heavens ten thousand miles from Mars; a tiny satellite that will thus encircle Barsoom to the end of time.

The fourth day after my arrival at Zodanga I made my first flight, and as a result of it I won a promotion which included quarters in the palace of Than Kosis.

As I rose above the city I circled several times, as I had seen Kantos

Kan do, and then throwing my engine into top speed I raced at terrific velocity toward the south, following one of the great waterways which enter Zodanga from that direction.

I had traversed perhaps two hundred miles in a little less than an hour when I descried far below me a party of three green warriors racing madly toward a small figure on foot which seemed to be trying to reach the confines of one of the walled fields.

Dropping my machine rapidly toward them, and circling to the rear of the warriors, I soon saw that the object of their pursuit was a red Martian wearing the metal of the scout squadron to which I was attached. A short distance away lay his tiny flier, surrounded by the tools with which he had evidently been occupied in repairing some damage when surprised by the green warriors.

They were now almost upon him; their flying mounts charging down on the relatively puny figure at terrific speed, while the warriors leaned low to the right, with their great metal-shod spears. Each seemed striving to be the first to impale the poor Zodangan and in another moment his fate would have been sealed had it not been for my timely arrival.

Driving my fleet air craft at high speed directly behind the warriors I soon overtook them and without diminishing my speed I rammed the prow of my little flier between the shoulders of the nearest. The impact sufficient to have torn through inches of solid steel, hurled the fellow's headless body into the air over the head of his thoat, where it fell sprawling upon the moss. The mounts of the other two warriors turned squealing in terror, and bolted in opposite directions.

Reducing my speed I circled and came to the ground at the feet of the astonished Zodangan. He was warm in his thanks for my timely aid and promised that my day's work would bring the reward it merited, for it was none other than a cousin of the jeddak of Zodanga whose life I had saved.

We wasted no time in talk as we knew that the warriors would surely return as soon as they had gained control of their mounts. Hastening to his damaged machine we were bending every effort to finish the needed repairs and had almost completed them when we saw the two green monsters returning at top speed from opposite sides of us. When they had approached within a hundred yards their thoats again became unmanageable and absolutely refused to advance further toward the air craft which had frightened them.

The warriors finally dismounted and hobbling their animals advanced toward us on foot with drawn long-swords. I advanced to meet the larger, telling the Zodangan to do the best he could with the other. Finishing my man with almost no effort, as had now from much practice become habitual with me, I hastened to return to my new acquaintance whom I found indeed in desperate straits.

He was wounded and down with the huge foot of his antagonist upon his throat and the great long-sword raised to deal the final thrust. With a bound I cleared the fifty feet intervening between us, and with outstretched point drove my sword completely through the body of the green warrior. His sword fell, harmless, to the ground and he sank limply upon the prostrate form of the Zodangan.

A cursory examination of the latter revealed no mortal injuries and after a brief rest he asserted that he felt fit to attempt the return voyage. He would have to pilot his own craft, however, as these frail vessels are not intended to convey but a single person.

Quickly completing the repairs we rose together into the still, cloudless Martian sky, and at great speed and without further mishap returned to Zodanga.

As we neared the city we discovered a mighty concourse of civilians and troops assembled upon the plain before the city. The sky was black with naval vessels and private and public pleasure craft, flying long streamers of gay-colored silks, and banners and flags of odd and picturesque design.

My companion signaled that I slow down, and running his machine close beside mine suggested that we approach and watch the ceremony, which, he said, was for the purpose of conferring honors on individual officers and men for bravery and other distinguished service. He then unfurled a little ensign which denoted that his craft bore a member of the royal family of Zodanga, and together we made our way through the maze of low-lying air vessels until we hung directly over the jeddak of Zodanga and his staff. All were mounted upon the small domestic bull thoats of the red Martians, and their trappings and ornamentation bore such a quantity of gorgeously colored feathers that I could not but be struck with the startling resemblance the concourse bore to a band of the red Indians of my own Earth.

One of the staff called the attention of Than Kosis to the presence of my companion above them and the ruler motioned for him to descend.

As they waited for the troops to move into position facing the jeddak the two talked earnestly together, the jeddak and his staff occasionally glancing up at me. I could not hear their conversation and presently it ceased and all dismounted, as the last body of troops had wheeled into position before their emperor. A member of the staff advanced toward the troops, and calling the name of a soldier commanded him to advance. The officer then recited the nature of the heroic act which had won the approval of the jeddak, and the latter advanced and placed a metal ornament upon the left arm of the lucky man.

Ten men had been so decorated when the aid called out, "John Carter, air scout!"

Never in my life had I been so surprised, but the habit of military discipline is strong within me, and I dropped my little machine lightly to the ground and advanced on foot as I had seen the others do. As I halted before the officer, he addressed me in a voice audible to the entire assemblage of troops and spectators.

"In recognition, John Carter," he said, "of your remarkable courage and skill in defending the person of the cousin of the jeddak Than Kosis and, single-handed, vanquishing three green warriors, it is the pleasure of our jeddak to confer on you the mark of his esteem."

Than Kosis then advanced toward me and placing an ornament upon me, said:

"My cousin has narrated the details of your wonderful achievement, which seems little short of miraculous, and if you can so well defend a cousin of the jeddak how much better could you defend the person of the jeddak himself. You are therefore appointed a padwar of The Guards and will be quartered in my palace hereafter."

I thanked him, and at his direction joined the members of his staff. After the ceremony I returned my machine to its quarters on the roof of the barracks of the air-scout squadron, and with an orderly from the palace to guide me I reported to the officer in charge of the palace.

CHAPTER TWENTY-TWO
I FIND DEJAH

THE MAJORDOMO TO WHOM I REPORTED had been given instructions to station me near the person of the jeddak, who, in time of war, is always in great danger of assassination, as the rule that all is fair in war seems to constitute the entire ethics of Martian conflict.

He therefore escorted me immediately to the apartment in which Than Kosis then was. The ruler was engaged in conversation with his son, Sab Than, and several courtiers of his household, and did not perceive my entrance.

The walls of the apartment were completely hung with splendid tapestries which hid any windows or doors which may have pierced them. The room was lighted by imprisoned rays of sunshine held between the ceiling proper and what appeared to be a ground glass false ceiling a few inches below.

My guide drew aside one of the tapestries, disclosing a passage which encircled the room, between the hangings and the walls of the chamber. Within this passage I was to remain, he said, so long as Than Kosis was in the apartment. When he left I was to follow. My only duty was to guard the ruler and keep out of sight as much as possible. I would be relieved after a period of four hours. The majordomo then left me.

The tapestries were of a strange weaving which gave the appearance of heavy solidity from one side, but from my hiding place I could perceive all that took place within the room as readily as though there had been no curtain intervening.

Scarcely had I gained my post than the tapestry at the opposite end of the chamber separated and four soldiers of The Guard entered, surrounding a female figure. As they approached Than Kosis the soldiers fell to either side and there standing before the jeddak and not ten feet from me, her beautiful face radiant with smiles, was Dejah Thoris.

Sab Than, Prince of Zodanga, advanced to meet her, and hand in hand they approached close to the jeddak. Than Kosis looked up in surprise, and, rising, saluted her.

"To what strange freak do I owe this visit from the Princess of Helium, who, two days ago, with rare consideration for my pride, assured me that she would prefer Tal Hajus, the green Thark, to my son?"

Dejah Thoris only smiled the more and with the roguish dimples playing at the corners of her mouth she made answer:

"From the beginning of time upon Barsoom it has been the prerogative of woman to change her mind as she listed and to dissemble in matters concerning her heart. That you will forgive, Than Kosis, as has your son. Two days ago I was not sure of his love for me, but now I am, and I have come to beg of you to forget my rash words and to accept the assurance of the Princess of Helium that when the time comes she will wed Sab Than, Prince of Zodanga."

"I am glad that you have so decided," replied Than Kosis. "It is far from my desire to push war further against the people of Helium, and, your promise shall be recorded and a proclamation to my people issued forthwith."

"It were better, Than Kosis," interrupted Dejah Thoris, "that the proclamation wait the ending of this war. It would look strange indeed to my people and to yours were the Princess of Helium to give herself to her country's enemy in the midst of hostilities."

"Cannot the war be ended at once?" spoke Sab Than. "It requires but the word of Than Kosis to bring peace. Say it my father, say the word that will hasten my happiness, and end this unpopular strife."

"We shall see," replied Than Kosis, "how the people of Helium take to peace. I shall at least offer it to them."

Dejah Thoris, after a few words, turned and left the apartment, still followed by her guards.

Thus was the edifice of my brief dream of happiness dashed, broken, to the ground of reality. The woman for whom I had offered my life, and from whose lips I had so recently heard a declaration of love for me, had lightly forgotten my very existence and smilingly given herself to the son of her people's most hated enemy.

Although I had heard it with my own ears I could not believe it. I must search out her apartments and force her to repeat the cruel truth to me alone before I would be convinced, and so I deserted my post and hastened through the passage behind the tapestries toward the door by which she had left the chamber. Slipping quietly through this opening I discovered a maze of winding corridors, branching and turning in every direction.

Running rapidly down first one and then another of them I soon became hopelessly lost and was standing panting against a side wall when I heard voices near me. Apparently they were coming from the opposite side of the partition against which I leaned and presently I made out the tones of Dejah Thoris. I could not hear the words but I knew that I could not possibly be mistaken in the voice.

Moving on a few steps I discovered another passageway at the end of which lay a door. Walking boldly forward I pushed into the room only to find myself in a small antechamber in which were the four guards who had accompanied her. One of them instantly arose and accosted me, asking the nature of my business.

"I am from Than Kosis," I replied, "and wish to speak privately with Dejah Thoris, Princess of Helium."

"And your order?" asked the fellow.

I did not know what he meant, but replied that I was a member of The Guard, and without waiting for a reply from him I strode toward the opposite door of the antechamber, behind which I could hear Dejah Thoris conversing.

But my entrance was not to be so easily accomplished. The guardsman stepped before me, saying,

"No one comes from Than Kosis without carrying an order or the password. You must give me one or the other before you may pass."

"The only order I require, my friend, to enter where I will, hangs at my side," I answered, tapping my long-sword; "will you let me pass in peace or no?"

For reply he whipped out his own sword, calling to the others to join him, and thus the four stood, with drawn weapons, barring my further progress.

"You are not here by the order of Than Kosis," cried the one who had first addressed me, "and not only shall you not enter the apartments of the Princess of Helium but you shall go back to Than Kosis under guard to explain this unwarranted temerity. Throw down your sword; you cannot hope to overcome four of us," he added with a grim smile.

My reply was a quick thrust which left me but three antagonists and I can assure you that they were worthy of my metal. They had me backed against the wall in no time, fighting for my life. Slowly I worked my way to a corner of the room where I could force them to come at me only one at a time, and thus we fought upward of twenty minutes; the clanging of steel on steel producing a veritable bedlam in the little room.

The noise had brought Dejah Thoris to the door of her apartment, and there she stood throughout the conflict with Sola at her back peering over her shoulder. Her face was set and emotionless and I knew that she did not recognize me, nor did Sola.

Finally a lucky cut brought down a second guardsman and then, with only two opposing me, I changed my tactics and rushed them down after the fashion of my fighting that had won me many a victory. The third fell within ten seconds after the second, and the last lay dead upon the bloody floor a few moments later. They were brave men and noble fighters, and it grieved me that I had been forced to kill them, but I would have willingly depopulated all Barsoom could I have reached the side of my Dejah Thoris in no other way.

Sheathing my bloody blade I advanced toward my Martian Princess, who still stood mutely gazing at me without sign of recognition.

"Who are you, Zodangan?" she whispered. "Another enemy to harass me in my misery?"

"I am a friend," I answered, "a once cherished friend."

"No friend of Helium's princess wears that metal," she replied, "and yet the voice! I have heard it before; it is not—it cannot be—no, for he is dead."

"It is, though, my princess, none other than John Carter," I said. "Do you not recognize, even through paint and strange metal, the heart of your chieftain?"

As I came close to her she swayed toward me with outstretched hands, but as I reached to take her in my arms she drew back with a shudder and a little moan of misery.

"Too late, too late," she grieved. "O my chieftain that was, and whom I thought dead, had you but returned one little hour before—but now it is too late, too late."

"What do you mean, Dejah Thoris?" I cried. "That you would not have promised yourself to the Zodangan prince had you known that I lived?"

"Think you, John Carter, that I would give my heart to you yesterday and today to another? I thought that it lay buried with your ashes in the pits of Warhoon, and so today I have promised my body to another to save my people from the curse of a victorious Zodangan army."

"But I am not dead, my princess. I have come to claim you, and all Zodanga cannot prevent it."

"It is too late, John Carter, my promise is given, and on Barsoom that is final. The ceremonies which follow later are but meaningless formalities. They make the fact of marriage no more certain than does the funeral cortege of a jeddak again place the seal of death upon him. I am as good as married, John Carter. No longer may you call me your princess. No longer are you my chieftain."

"I know but little of your customs here upon Barsoom, Dejah Thoris, but I do know that I love you, and if you meant the last words you spoke to me that day as the hordes of Warhoon were charging down upon us, no other man shall ever claim you as his bride. You meant them then, my princess, and you mean them still! Say that it is true."

"I meant them, John Carter," she whispered. "I cannot repeat them now for I have given myself to another. Ah, if you had only known our ways, my friend," she continued, half to herself, "the promise would have been yours long months ago, and you could have claimed me before all others. It might have meant the fall of Helium, but I would have given my empire for my Tharkian chief."

Then aloud she said: "Do you remember the night when you offended me? You called me your princess without having asked my hand of me, and then you boasted that you had fought for me. You did not know, and I should not have been offended; I see that now. But there was no one to tell you, what I could not, that upon Barsoom there are two kinds of women in the cities of the red men. The one they fight for that they may ask them in marriage; the other kind they fight for also, but never ask their hands. When a man has won a woman he may address her as his princess, or in any of the several terms which signify possession. You had fought for me, but had never asked me in marriage, and so when you called me your princess, you see," she faltered, "I was hurt, but even then, John Carter, I did not repulse you, as I should have done, until you made it doubly worse by taunting me with having won me through combat."

"I do not need ask your forgiveness now, Dejah Thoris," I cried. "You must know that my fault was of ignorance of your Barsoomian customs. What I failed to do, through implicit belief that my petition would be presumptuous and unwelcome, I do now, Dejah Thoris; I ask you to be my wife, and by all the Virginian fighting blood that flows in my veins you shall be."

"No, John Carter, it is useless," she cried, hopelessly, "I may never be yours while Sab Than lives."

"You have sealed his death warrant, my princess—Sab Than dies."

"Nor that either," she hastened to explain. "I may not wed the man who slays my husband, even in self-defense. It is custom. We are ruled by custom upon Barsoom. It is useless, my friend. You must bear the sorrow with me. That at least we may share in common. That, and the memory of the brief days among the Tharks. You must go now, nor ever see me again. Good-bye, my chieftain that was."

Disheartened and dejected, I withdrew from the room, but I was not entirely discouraged, nor would I admit that Dejah Thoris was lost to me until the ceremony had actually been performed.

As I wandered along the corridors, I was as absolutely lost in the mazes of winding passageways as I had been before I discovered Dejah Thoris' apartments.

I knew that my only hope lay in escape from the city of Zodanga, for the matter of the four dead guardsmen would have to be explained, and as I could never reach my original post without a guide, suspicion would surely rest on me so soon as I was discovered wandering aimlessly through the palace.

Presently I came upon a spiral runway leading to a lower floor, and this I followed downward for several stories until I reached the doorway of a large apartment in which were a number of guardsmen. The walls of this room were hung with transparent tapestries behind which I secreted myself without being apprehended.

The conversation of the guardsmen was general, and awakened no interest in me until an officer entered the room and ordered four of the men to relieve the detail who were guarding the Princess of Helium. Now, I knew, my troubles would commence in earnest and indeed they were upon me all too soon, for it seemed that the squad had scarcely left the guardroom before one of their number burst in again breathlessly, crying that they had found their four comrades butchered in the antechamber.

In a moment the entire palace was alive with people. Guardsmen, officers, courtiers, servants, and slaves ran helter-skelter through the corridors and apartments carrying messages and orders, and searching for signs of the assassin.

This was my opportunity and slim as it appeared I grasped it, for as a number of soldiers came hurrying past my hiding place I fell in behind them and followed through the mazes of the palace until, in passing through a great hall, I saw the blessed light of day coming in through a series of larger windows.

Here I left my guides, and, slipping to the nearest window, sought for an avenue of escape. The windows opened upon a great balcony which overlooked one of the broad avenues of Zodanga. The ground was about thirty feet below, and at a like distance from the building was a wall fully twenty feet high, constructed of polished glass about a foot in thickness. To a red Martian escape by this path would have appeared impossible, but to me, with my earthly strength and agility, it seemed already accomplished. My only fear was in being detected before darkness fell, for I could not make the leap in broad daylight while the court below and the avenue beyond were crowded with Zodangans.

Accordingly I searched for a hiding place and finally found one by accident, inside a huge hanging ornament which swung from the ceiling of the hall, and about ten feet from the floor. Into the capacious bowl-like vase I sprang with ease, and scarcely had I settled down within it than I heard a number of people enter the apartment. The group stopped beneath my hiding place and I could plainly overhear their every word.

"It is the work of Heliumites," said one of the men.

"Yes, O Jeddak, but how had they access to the palace? I could believe that even with the diligent care of your guardsmen a single enemy might reach the inner chambers, but how a force of six or eight fighting men could have done so unobserved is beyond me. We shall soon know, however, for here comes the royal psychologist."

Another man now joined the group, and, after making his formal greetings to his ruler, said:

"O mighty Jeddak, it is a strange tale I read in the dead minds of your faithful guardsmen. They were felled not by a number of fighting men, but by a single opponent."

He paused to let the full weight of this announcement impress his hearers, and that his statement was scarcely credited was evidenced by the impatient exclamation of incredulity which escaped the lips of Than Kosis.

"What manner of weird tale are you bringing me, Notan?" he cried.

"It is the truth, my Jeddak," replied the psychologist. "In fact the impressions were strongly marked on the brain of each of the four guardsmen. Their antagonist was a very tall man, wearing the metal of one of your own guardsmen, and his fighting ability was little short of marvelous for he fought fair against the entire four and vanquished them by his surpassing skill and superhuman strength and endurance. Though he wore the metal of Zodanga, my Jeddak, such a man was never seen before in this or any other country upon Barsoom.

"The mind of the Princess of Helium whom I have examined and questioned was a blank to me, she has perfect control, and I could not read one iota of it. She said that she witnessed a portion of the encounter, and that when she looked there was but one man engaged with the guardsmen; a man whom she did not recognize as ever having seen."

"Where is my erstwhile savior?" spoke another of the party, and I recognized the voice of the cousin of Than Kosis, whom I had rescued from the green warriors. "By the metal of my first ancestor," he went on, "but the description fits him to perfection, especially as to his fighting ability."

"Where is this man?" cried Than Kosis. "Have him brought to me at once. What know you of him, cousin? It seemed strange to me now that I think upon it that there should have been such a fighting man in Zodanga, of whose name, even, we were ignorant before today. And his name too, John Carter, who ever heard of such a name upon Barsoom!"

Word was soon brought that I was nowhere to be found, either in the palace or at my former quarters in the barracks of the air-scout squadron. Kantos Kan, they had found and questioned, but he knew nothing of my whereabouts, and as to my past, he had told them he knew as little, since he had but recently met me during our captivity among the Warhoons.

"Keep your eyes on this other one," commanded Than Kosis. "He also is a stranger and likely as not they both hail from Helium, and where one is we shall sooner or later find the other. Quadruple the air patrol, and let every man who leaves the city by air or ground be subjected to the closest scrutiny."

Another messenger now entered with word that I was still within the palace walls.

"The likeness of every person who has entered or left the palace grounds today has been carefully examined," concluded the fellow, "and not one approaches the likeness of this new padwar of the guards, other than that which was recorded of him at the time he entered."

"Then we will have him shortly," commented Than Kosis contentedly, "and in the meanwhile we will repair to the apartments of the Princess of Helium and question her in regard to the affair. She may know more than she cared to divulge to you, Notan. Come."

They left the hall, and, as darkness had fallen without, I slipped lightly from my hiding place and hastened to the balcony. Few were in sight, and choosing a moment when none seemed near I sprang quickly to the top of the glass wall and from there to the avenue beyond the palace grounds.

CHAPTER TWENTY-THREE
LOST IN THE SKY

WITHOUT EFFORT AT CONCEALMENT I hastened to the vicinity of our quarters, where I felt sure I should find Kantos Kan. As I neared the building I became more careful, as I judged, and rightly, that the place would be guarded. Several men in civilian metal loitered near the front entrance and in the rear were others. My only means of reaching, unseen, the upper story where our apartments were situated was through an adjoining building, and after considerable maneuvering I managed to attain the roof of a shop several doors away.

Leaping from roof to roof, I soon reached an open window in the building where I hoped to find the Heliumite, and in another moment I stood in the room before him. He was alone and showed no surprise at my coming, saying he had expected me much earlier, as my tour of duty must have ended some time since.

I saw that he knew nothing of the events of the day at the palace, and when I had enlightened him he was all excitement. The news that Dejah Thoris had promised her hand to Sab Than filled him with dismay.

"It cannot be," he exclaimed. "It is impossible! Why no man in all Helium but would prefer death to the selling of our loved princess to the ruling house of Zodanga. She must have lost her mind to have assented to such an atrocious bargain. You, who do not know how we of Helium love the members of our ruling house, cannot appreciate the horror with which I contemplate such an unholy alliance.

"What can be done, John Carter?" he continued. "You are a resourceful man. Can you not think of some way to save Helium from this disgrace?"

"If I can come within sword's reach of Sab Than," I answered, "I can solve the difficulty in so far as Helium is concerned, but for personal reasons I would prefer that another struck the blow that frees Dejah Thoris."

Kantos Kan eyed me narrowly before he spoke.

"You love her!" he said. "Does she know it?"

"She knows it, Kantos Kan, and repulses me only because she is promised to Sab Than."

The splendid fellow sprang to his feet, and grasping me by the shoulder raised his sword on high, exclaiming:

"And had the choice been left to me I could not have chosen a more fitting mate for the first princess of Barsoom. Here is my hand upon your shoulder, John Carter, and my word that Sab Than shall go out at the point of my sword for the sake of my love for Helium, for Dejah Thoris, and for you. This very night I shall try to reach his quarters in the palace."

"How?" I asked. "You are strongly guarded and a quadruple force patrols the sky."

He bent his head in thought a moment, then raised it with an air of confidence.

"I only need to pass these guards and I can do it," he said at last. "I know a secret entrance to the palace through the pinnacle of the highest tower. I fell upon it by chance one day as I was passing above the palace on patrol duty. In this work it is required that we investigate any unusual occurrence we may witness, and a face peering from the pinnacle of the high tower of the palace was, to me, most unusual. I therefore drew near and discovered that the possessor of the peering face was none other than Sab Than. He was slightly put out at being detected and commanded me to keep the matter to myself, explaining that the passage from the tower led directly to his apartments, and was known only to him. If I can reach the roof of the barracks and get my machine I can be in Sab Than's quarters in five minutes; but how am I to escape from this building, guarded as you say it is?"

"How well are the machine sheds at the barracks guarded?" I asked.

"There is usually but one man on duty there at night upon the roof."

"Go to the roof of this building, Kantos Kan, and wait me there."

Without stopping to explain my plans I retraced my way to the street and hastened to the barracks. I did not dare to enter the building, filled as it was with members of the air-scout squadron, who, in common with all Zodanga, were on the lookout for me.

The building was an enormous one, rearing its lofty head fully a thousand feet into the air. But few buildings in Zodanga were higher than these barracks, though several topped it by a few hundred feet; the docks of the great battleships of the line standing some fifteen hundred feet from the ground, while the freight and passenger stations of the merchant squadrons rose nearly as high.

It was a long climb up the face of the building, and one fraught with much danger, but there was no other way, and so I essayed the task. The fact that Barsoomian architecture is extremely ornate made the feat much simpler than I had anticipated, since I found ornamental ledges and projections which fairly formed a perfect ladder for me all the way to the eaves of the building. Here I met my first real obstacle. The eaves projected nearly twenty feet from the wall to which I clung, and though I encircled the great building I could find no opening through them.

The top floor was alight, and filled with soldiers engaged in the pastimes of their kind; I could not, therefore, reach the roof through the building.

There was one slight, desperate chance, and that I decided I must take—it was for Dejah Thoris, and no man has lived who would not risk a thousand deaths for such as she.

Clinging to the wall with my feet and one hand, I unloosened one of the long leather straps of my trappings at the end of which dangled a great hook by which air sailors are hung to the sides and bottoms of their craft for various purposes of repair, and by means of which landing parties are lowered to the ground from the battleships.

I swung this hook cautiously to the roof several times before it finally found lodgment; gently I pulled on it to strengthen its hold, but whether it would bear the weight of my body I did not know. It might be barely caught upon the very outer verge of the roof, so that as my body swung out at the end of the strap it would slip off and launch me to the pavement a thousand feet below.

An instant I hesitated, and then, releasing my grasp upon the supporting ornament, I swung out into space at the end of the strap. Far below me lay the brilliantly lighted streets, the hard pavements, and death. There was a little jerk at the top of the supporting eaves, and a nasty slipping, grating sound which turned me cold with apprehension; then the hook caught and I was safe.

Clambering quickly aloft I grasped the edge of the eaves and drew myself to the surface of the roof above. As I gained my feet I was confronted by the sentry on duty, into the muzzle of whose revolver I found myself looking.

"Who are you and whence came you?" he cried.

"I am an air scout, friend, and very near a dead one, for just by the merest chance I escaped falling to the avenue below," I replied.

"But how came you upon the roof, man? No one has landed or come up from the building for the past hour. Quick, explain yourself, or I call the guard."

"Look you here, sentry, and you shall see how I came and how close a shave I had to not coming at all," I answered, turning toward the edge of the roof, where, twenty feet below, at the end of my strap, hung all my weapons.

The fellow, acting on impulse of curiosity, stepped to my side and to his undoing, for as he leaned to peer over the eaves I grasped him by his throat and his pistol arm and threw him heavily to the roof. The weapon dropped from his grasp, and my fingers choked off his attempted cry for assistance. I gagged and bound him and then hung him over the edge of the roof as I myself had hung a few moments before. I knew it would be morning before he would be discovered, and I needed all the time that I could gain.

Donning my trappings and weapons I hastened to the sheds, and soon had out both my machine and Kantos Kan's. Making his fast behind mine I started my engine, and skimming over the edge of the roof I dove down into the streets of the city far below the plane usually occupied by the air patrol. In less than a minute I was settling safely upon the roof of our apartment beside the astonished Kantos Kan.

I lost no time in explanations, but plunged immediately into a discussion of our plans for the immediate future. It was decided that I was to try to make Helium while Kantos Kan was to enter the palace and dispatch Sab Than. If successful he was then to follow me. He set my compass for me, a clever little device which will remain steadfastly fixed upon any given point on the surface of Barsoom, and bidding each other farewell we rose together and sped in the direction of the palace which lay in the route which I must take to reach Helium.

As we neared the high tower a patrol shot down from above, throwing its piercing searchlight full upon my craft, and a voice roared out a command to halt, following with a shot as I paid no attention to his hail. Kantos Kan dropped quickly into the darkness, while I rose steadily and at terrific speed raced through the Martian sky followed by a dozen of the air-scout craft which had joined the pursuit, and later by a swift cruiser carrying a hundred men and a battery of rapid-fire guns. By twisting and turning my little machine, now rising and now falling, I managed to elude their searchlights most of the time, but I was also losing ground by these tactics, and so I decided to hazard everything on a straightaway course and leave the result to fate and the speed of my machine.

Kantos Kan had shown me a trick of gearing, which is known only to the navy of Helium, that greatly increased the speed of our machines, so that I felt sure I could distance my pursuers if I could dodge their projectiles for a few moments.

As I sped through the air the screeching of the bullets around me convinced me that only by a miracle could I escape, but the die was cast, and throwing on full speed I raced a straight course toward Helium. Gradually I left my pursuers further and further behind, and I was just congratulating myself on my lucky escape, when a well-directed shot from the cruiser exploded at the prow of my little craft. The concussion nearly capsized her, and with a sickening plunge she hurtled downward through the dark night.

How far I fell before I regained control of the plane I do not know, but I must have been very close to the ground when I started to rise again, as I plainly heard the squealing of animals below me. Rising again I scanned the heavens for my pursuers, and finally making out their lights far behind me, saw that they were landing, evidently in search of me.

Not until their lights were no longer discernible did I venture to flash my little lamp upon my compass, and then I found to my consternation that a fragment of the projectile had utterly destroyed my only guide, as well as my speedometer. It was true I could follow the stars in the general direction of Helium, but without knowing the exact location of the city or the speed at which I was traveling my chances for finding it were slim.

Helium lies a thousand miles southwest of Zodanga, and with my compass intact I should have made the trip, barring accidents, in between four and five hours. As it turned out, however, morning found me speeding over a vast expanse of dead sea bottom after nearly six hours of continuous flight at high speed. Presently a great city showed below me, but it was not Helium, as that alone of all Barsoomian metropolises consists in two immense circular walled cities about seventy-five miles apart and would have been easily distinguishable from the altitude at which I was flying.

Believing that I had come too far to the north and west, I turned back in a southeasterly direction, passing during the forenoon several other large cities, but none resembling the description which Kantos Kan had given me of Helium. In addition to the twin-city formation of Helium, another distinguishing feature is the two immense towers, one of vivid scarlet rising nearly a mile into the air from the center of one of the cities, while the other, of bright yellow and of the same height, marks her sister.

CHAPTER TWENTY-FOUR
TARS TARKAS FINDS A FRIEND

ABOUT NOON I PASSED LOW over a great dead city of ancient Mars, and as I skimmed out across the plain beyond I came full upon several thousand green warriors engaged in a terrific battle. Scarcely had I seen them than a volley of shots was directed at me, and with the almost unfailing accuracy of their aim my little craft was instantly a ruined wreck, sinking erratically to the ground.

I fell almost directly in the center of the fierce combat, among warriors who had not seen my approach so busily were they engaged in life and death struggles. The men were fighting on foot with long-swords, while an occasional shot from a sharpshooter on the outskirts of the conflict would bring down a warrior who might for an instant separate himself from the entangled mass.

As my machine sank among them I realized that it was fight or die, with good chances of dying in any event, and so I struck the ground with drawn long-sword ready to defend myself as I could.

I fell beside a huge monster who was engaged with three antagonists, and as I glanced at his fierce face, filled with the light of battle, I recognized

Tars Tarkas the Thark. He did not see me, as I was a trifle behind him, and just then the three warriors opposing him, and whom I recognized as Warhoons, charged simultaneously. The mighty fellow made quick work of one of them, but in stepping back for another thrust he fell over a dead body behind him and was down and at the mercy of his foes in an instant. Quick as lightning they were upon him, and Tars Tarkas would have been gathered to his fathers in short order had I not sprung before his prostrate form and engaged his adversaries. I had accounted for one of them when the mighty Thark regained his feet and quickly settled the other.

He gave me one look, and a slight smile touched his grim lips as, touching my shoulder, he said, "I would scarcely recognize you, John Carter, but there is no other mortal upon Barsoom who would have done what you have for me. I think I have learned that there is such a thing as friendship, my friend."

He said no more, nor was there opportunity, for the Warhoons were closing in about us, and together we fought, shoulder to shoulder, during all that long, hot afternoon, until the tide of battle turned and the remnant of the fierce Warhoon horde fell back upon their thoats, and fled into the gathering darkness.

Ten thousand men had been engaged in that titanic struggle, and upon the field of battle lay three thousand dead. Neither side asked or gave quarter, nor did they attempt to take prisoners.

On our return to the city after the battle we had gone directly to Tars Tarkas' quarters, where I was left alone while the chieftain attended the customary council which immediately follows an engagement.

As I sat awaiting the return of the green warrior I heard something move in an adjoining apartment, and as I glanced up there rushed suddenly upon me a huge and hideous creature which bore me backward upon the pile of silks and furs upon which I had been reclining. It was Woola—faithful, loving Woola. He had found his way back to Thark and, as Tars Tarkas later told me, had gone immediately to my former quarters where he had taken up his pathetic and seemingly hopeless watch for my return.

"Tal Hajus knows that you are here, John Carter," said Tars Tarkas, on his return from the jeddak's quarters; "Sarkoja saw and recognized you as we were returning. Tal Hajus has ordered me to bring you before him tonight. I have ten thoats, John Carter; you may take your choice from among them, and I will accompany you to the nearest waterway that leads to Helium. Tars Tarkas may be a cruel green warrior, but he can be a friend as well. Come, we must start."

"And when you return, Tars Tarkas?" I asked.

"The wild calots, possibly, or worse," he replied. "Unless I should chance to have the opportunity I have so long waited of battling with Tal Hajus."

"We will stay, Tars Tarkas, and see Tal Hajus tonight. You shall not sacrifice yourself, and it may be that tonight you can have the chance you wait."

He objected strenuously, saying that Tal Hajus often flew into wild fits of passion at the mere thought of the blow I had dealt him, and that if ever he laid his hands upon me I would be subjected to the most horrible tortures.

While we were eating I repeated to Tars Tarkas the story which Sola had told me that night upon the sea bottom during the march to Thark.

He said but little, but the great muscles of his face worked in passion and in agony at recollection of the horrors which had been heaped upon the only thing he had ever loved in all his cold, cruel, terrible existence.

He no longer demurred when I suggested that we go before Tal Hajus, only saying that he would like to speak to Sarkoja first. At his request I accompanied him to her quarters, and the look of venomous hatred she cast upon me was almost adequate recompense for any future misfortunes this accidental return to Thark might bring me.

"Sarkoja," said Tars Tarkas, "forty years ago you were instrumental in bringing about the torture and death of a woman named Gozava. I have just discovered that the warrior who loved that woman has learned of your part in the transaction. He may not kill you, Sarkoja, it is not our custom, but there is nothing to prevent him tying one end of a strap about your neck and the other end to a wild thoat, merely to test your fitness to survive and help perpetuate our race. Having heard that he would do this on the morrow, I thought it only right to warn you, for I am a just man. The river Iss is but a short pilgrimage, Sarkoja. Come, John Carter."

The next morning Sarkoja was gone, nor was she ever seen after.

In silence we hastened to the jeddak's palace, where we were immediately admitted to his presence; in fact, he could scarcely wait to see me and was standing erect upon his platform glowering at the entrance as I came in.

"Strap him to that pillar," he shrieked. "We shall see who it is dares strike the mighty Tal Hajus. Heat the irons; with my own hands I shall burn the eyes from his head that he may not pollute my person with his vile gaze."

"Chieftains of Thark," I cried, turning to the assembled council and ignoring Tal Hajus, "I have been a chief among you, and today I have fought for Thark shoulder to shoulder with her greatest warrior. You owe me, at least, a hearing. I have won that much today. You claim to be just people—"

"Silence," roared Tal Hajus. "Gag the creature and bind him as I command."

"Justice, Tal Hajus," exclaimed Lorquas Ptomel. "Who are you to set aside the customs of ages among the Tharks."

"Yes, justice!" echoed a dozen voices, and so, while Tal Hajus fumed and frothed, I continued.

"You are a brave people and you love bravery, but where was your mighty jeddak during the fighting today? I did not see him in the thick of battle; he was not there. He rends defenseless women and little children in his lair, but how recently has one of you seen him fight with men? Why, even I, a midget beside him, felled him with a single blow of my fist. Is it of such that the Tharks fashion their jeddaks? There stands beside me now a great Thark, a mighty warrior and a noble man. Chieftains, how sounds, Tars Tarkas, Jeddak of Thark?"

A roar of deep-toned applause greeted this suggestion.

"It but remains for this council to command, and Tal Hajus must prove his fitness to rule. Were he a brave man he would invite Tars Tarkas to combat, for he does not love him, but Tal Hajus is afraid; Tal Hajus, your jeddak, is a coward. With my bare hands I could kill him, and he knows it."

After I ceased there was tense silence, as all eyes were riveted upon Tal Hajus. He did not speak or move, but the blotchy green of his countenance turned livid, and the froth froze upon his lips.

"Tal Hajus," said Lorquas Ptomel in a cold, hard voice, "never in my long life have I seen a jeddak of the Tharks so humiliated. There could be but one answer to this arraignment. We wait it." And still Tal Hajus stood as though petrified.

"Chieftains," continued Lorquas Ptomel, "shall the jeddak, Tal Hajus, prove his fitness to rule over Tars Tarkas?"

There were twenty chieftains about the rostrum, and twenty swords flashed high in assent.

There was no alternative. That decree was final, and so Tal Hajus drew his long-sword and advanced to meet Tars Tarkas.

The combat was soon over, and, with his foot upon the neck of the dead monster, Tars Tarkas became jeddak among the Tharks.

His first act was to make me a full-fledged chieftain with the rank I had won by my combats the first few weeks of my captivity among them.

Seeing the favorable disposition of the warriors toward Tars Tarkas, as well as toward me, I grasped the opportunity to enlist them in my cause against Zodanga. I told Tars Tarkas the story of my adventures, and in a few words had explained to him the thought I had in mind.

"John Carter has made a proposal," he said, addressing the council, "which meets with my sanction. I shall put it to you briefly. Dejah Thoris, the Princess of Helium, who was our prisoner, is now held by the jeddak of Zodanga, whose son she must wed to save her country from devastation at the hands of the Zodangan forces.

"John Carter suggests that we rescue her and return her to Helium. The loot of Zodanga would be magnificent, and I have often thought that had we an alliance with the people of Helium we could obtain sufficient assurance of sustenance to permit us to increase the size and frequency of our hatchings, and thus become unquestionably supreme among the green men of all Barsoom. What say you?"

It was a chance to fight, an opportunity to loot, and they rose to the bait as a speckled trout to a fly.

For Tharks they were wildly enthusiastic, and before another half hour had passed twenty mounted messengers were speeding across dead sea bottoms to call the hordes together for the expedition.

In three days we were on the march toward Zodanga, one hundred thousand strong, as Tars Tarkas had been able to enlist the services of three smaller hordes on the promise of the great loot of Zodanga.

At the head of the column I rode beside the great Thark while at the heels of my mount trotted my beloved Woola.

We traveled entirely by night, timing our marches so that we camped during the day at deserted cities where, even to the beasts, we were all kept indoors during the daylight hours. On the march Tars Tarkas, through his remarkable ability and statesmanship, enlisted fifty thousand more warriors from various hordes, so that, ten days after we set out we halted at midnight outside the great walled city of Zodanga, one hundred and fifty thousand strong.

The fighting strength and efficiency of this horde of ferocious green monsters was equivalent to ten times their number of red men. Never in the history of Barsoom, Tars Tarkas told me, had such a force of green warriors marched to battle together. It was a monstrous task to keep even a semblance of harmony among them, and it was a marvel to me that he got them to the city without a mighty battle among themselves.

But as we neared Zodanga their personal quarrels were submerged by their greater hatred for the red men, and especially for the Zodangans, who had for years waged a ruthless campaign of extermination against the green men, directing special attention toward despoiling their incubators.

Now that we were before Zodanga the task of obtaining entry to the city devolved upon me, and directing Tars Tarkas to hold his forces in two divisions out of earshot of the city, with each division opposite a large gateway, I took twenty dismounted warriors and approached one of the small gates that pierced the walls at short intervals. These gates have no regular guard, but are covered by sentries, who patrol the avenue that encircles the city just within the walls as our metropolitan police patrol their beats.

The walls of Zodanga are seventy-five feet in height and fifty feet thick. They are built of enormous blocks of carborundum, and the task of entering the city seemed, to my escort of green warriors, an impossibility. The fellows who had been detailed to accompany me were of one of the smaller hordes, and therefore did not know me.

Placing three of them with their faces to the wall and arms locked, I commanded two more to mount to their shoulders, and a sixth I ordered to climb upon the shoulders of the upper two. The head of the topmost warrior towered over forty feet from the ground.

In this way, with ten warriors, I built a series of three steps from the ground to the shoulders of the topmost man. Then starting from a short distance behind them I ran swiftly up from one tier to the next, and with a final bound from the broad shoulders of the highest I clutched the top of the great wall and quietly drew myself to its broad expanse. After me I dragged six lengths of leather from an equal number of my warriors. These lengths we had previously fastened together, and passing one end to the topmost warrior I lowered the other end cautiously over the opposite side of the wall toward the avenue below. No one was in sight, so, lowering myself to the end of my leather strap, I dropped the remaining thirty feet to the pavement below.

I had learned from Kantos Kan the secret of opening these gates, and in another moment my twenty great fighting men stood within the doomed city of Zodanga.

I found to my delight that I had entered at the lower boundary of the enormous palace grounds. The building itself showed in the distance a blaze of glorious light, and on the instant I determined to lead a detachment of warriors directly within the palace itself, while the balance of the great horde was attacking the barracks of the soldiery.

Dispatching one of my men to Tars Tarkas for a detail of fifty Tharks, with word of my intentions, I ordered ten warriors to capture and open one of the great gates while with the nine remaining I took the other. We were to do our work quietly, no shots were to be fired and no general advance made until I had reached the palace with my fifty Tharks. Our plans worked to perfection. The two sentries we met were dispatched to their fathers upon the banks of the lost sea of Korus, and the guards at both gates followed them in silence.

CHAPTER TWENTY-FIVE
THE LOOTING OF ZODANGA

A S THE GREAT GATE WHERE I STOOD swung open my fifty Tharks, headed by Tars Tarkas himself, rode in upon their mighty thoats. I led them to the palace walls, which I negotiated easily without assistance. Once inside, however, the gate gave me considerable trouble, but I finally was rewarded by seeing it swing upon its huge hinges, and soon my fierce escort was riding across the gardens of the jeddak of Zodanga.

As we approached the palace I could see through the great windows of the first floor into the brilliantly illuminated audience chamber of Than Kosis. The immense hall was crowded with nobles and their women, as though some important function was in progress. There was not a guard in sight without the palace, due, I presume, to the fact that the city and palace walls were considered impregnable, and so I came close and peered within.

At one end of the chamber, upon massive golden thrones encrusted with diamonds, sat Than Kosis and his consort, surrounded by officers and dignitaries of state. Before them stretched a broad aisle lined on either side with soldiery, and as I looked there entered this aisle at the far end of the hall, the head of a procession which advanced to the foot of the throne.

First there marched four officers of the jeddak's Guard bearing a huge salver on which reposed, upon a cushion of scarlet silk, a great golden chain with a collar and padlock at each end. Directly behind these officers came four others carrying a similar salver which supported the magnificent ornaments of a prince and princess of the reigning house of Zodanga.

At the foot of the throne these two parties separated and halted, facing each other at opposite sides of the aisle. Then came more dignitaries, and the officers of the palace and of the army, and finally two figures entirely muffled in scarlet silk, so that not a feature of either was discernible. These two stopped at the foot of the throne, facing Than Kosis. When the balance of the procession had entered and assumed their stations Than Kosis addressed the couple standing before him. I could not hear his words, but presently two officers advanced and removed the scarlet robe from one of the figures, and I saw that Kantos Kan had failed in his mission, for it was Sab Than, Prince of Zodanga, who stood revealed before me.

Than Kosis now took a set of the ornaments from one of the salvers and placed one of the collars of gold about his son's neck, springing the padlock fast. After a few more words addressed to Sab Than he turned to the other figure, from which the officers now removed the enshrouding silks, disclosing to my now comprehending view Dejah Thoris, Princess of Helium.

The object of the ceremony was clear to me; in another moment Dejah Thoris would be joined forever to the Prince of Zodanga. It was an impressive and beautiful ceremony, I presume, but to me it seemed the most fiendish sight I had ever witnessed, and as the ornaments were adjusted upon her beautiful figure and her collar of gold swung open in the hands of Than Kosis I raised my long-sword above my head, and, with the heavy hilt, I shattered the glass of the great window and sprang into the midst of the astonished assemblage. With a bound I was on the steps of the platform beside Than Kosis, and as he stood riveted with surprise I brought my long-sword down upon the golden chain that would have bound Dejah Thoris to another.

In an instant all was confusion; a thousand drawn swords menaced me from every quarter, and Sab Than sprang upon me with a jeweled dagger he had drawn from his nuptial ornaments. I could have killed him as easily as I might a fly, but the age-old custom of Barsoom stayed my hand, and grasping his wrist as the dagger flew toward my heart I held him as though in a vise and with my long-sword pointed to the far end of the hall.

"Zodanga has fallen," I cried. "Look!"

All eyes turned in the direction I had indicated, and there, forging through the portals of the entranceway rode Tars Tarkas and his fifty warriors on their great thoats.

A cry of alarm and amazement broke from the assemblage, but no word of fear, and in a moment the soldiers and nobles of Zodanga were hurling themselves upon the advancing Tharks.

Thrusting Sab Than headlong from the platform, I drew Dejah Thoris to my side. Behind the throne was a narrow doorway and in this Than Kosis now stood facing me, with drawn long-sword. In an instant we were engaged, and I found no mean antagonist.

As we circled upon the broad platform I saw Sab Than rushing up the steps to aid his father, but, as he raised his hand to strike, Dejah Thoris sprang before him and then my sword found the spot that made Sab Than jeddak of Zodanga. As his father rolled dead upon the floor the new jeddak tore himself free from Dejah Thoris' grasp, and again we faced each other. He was soon joined by a quartet of officers, and, with my back against a golden throne, I fought once again for Dejah Thoris. I was hard pressed to defend myself and yet not strike down Sab Than and, with him, my last chance to win the woman I loved. My blade was swinging with the rapidity of lightning as I sought to parry the thrusts and cuts of my opponents. Two I had disarmed, and one was down, when several more rushed to the aid of their new ruler, and to avenge the death of the old.

As they advanced there were cries of "The woman! The woman! Strike her down; it is her plot. Kill her! Kill her!"

Calling to Dejah Thoris to get behind me I worked my way toward the little doorway back of the throne, but the officers realized my intentions, and three of them sprang in behind me and blocked my chances for gaining a position where I could have defended Dejah Thoris against an army of swordsmen.

The Tharks were having their hands full in the center of the room, and I began to realize that nothing short of a miracle could save Dejah Thoris and myself, when I saw Tars Tarkas surging through the crowd of pygmies that swarmed about him. With one swing of his mighty long-sword he laid a dozen corpses at his feet, and so he hewed a pathway before him until in another moment he stood upon the platform beside me, dealing death and destruction right and left.

The bravery of the Zodangans was awe-inspiring, not one attempted to escape, and when the fighting ceased it was because only Tharks remained alive in the great hall, other than Dejah Thoris and myself.

Sab Than lay dead beside his father, and the corpses of the flower of Zodangan nobility and chivalry covered the floor of the bloody shambles.

My first thought when the battle was over was for Kantos Kan, and leaving Dejah Thoris in charge of Tars Tarkas I took a dozen warriors and hastened to the dungeons beneath the palace. The jailers had all left to join the fighters in the throne room, so we searched the labyrinthine prison without opposition.

I called Kantos Kan's name aloud in each new corridor and compartment, and finally I was rewarded by hearing a faint response. Guided by the sound, we soon found him helpless in a dark recess.

He was overjoyed at seeing me, and to know the meaning of the fight, faint echoes of which had reached his prison cell. He told me that the air patrol had captured him before he reached the high tower of the palace, so that he had not even seen Sab Than.

We discovered that it would be futile to attempt to cut away the bars and chains which held him prisoner, so, at his suggestion I returned to search the bodies on the floor above for keys to open the padlocks of his cell and of his chains.

Fortunately among the first I examined I found his jailer, and soon we had Kantos Kan with us in the throne room.

The sounds of heavy firing, mingled with shouts and cries, came to us from the city's streets, and Tars Tarkas hastened away to direct the fighting without. Kantos Kan accompanied him to act as guide, the green warriors commencing a thorough search of the palace for other Zodangans and for loot, and Dejah Thoris and I were left alone.

She had sunk into one of the golden thrones, and as I turned to her she greeted me with a wan smile.

"Was there ever such a man!" she exclaimed. "I know that Barsoom has never before seen your like. Can it be that all Earth men are as you?

Alone, a stranger, hunted, threatened, persecuted, you have done in a few short months what in all the past ages of Barsoom no man has ever done: joined together the wild hordes of the sea bottoms and brought them to fight as allies of a red Martian people."

"The answer is easy, Dejah Thoris," I replied smiling. "It was not I who did it, it was love, love for Dejah Thoris, a power that would work greater miracles than this you have seen."

A pretty flush overspread her face and she answered,

"You may say that now, John Carter, and I may listen, for I am free."

"And more still I have to say, ere it is again too late," I returned. "I have done many strange things in my life, many things that wiser men would not have dared, but never in my wildest fancies have I dreamed of winning a Dejah Thoris for myself—for never had I dreamed that in all the universe dwelt such a woman as the Princess of Helium. That you are a princess does not abash me, but that you are you is enough to make me doubt my sanity as I ask you, my princess, to be mine."

"He does not need to be abashed who so well knew the answer to his plea before the plea were made," she replied, rising and placing her dear hands upon my shoulders, and so I took her in my arms and kissed her.

And thus in the midst of a city of wild conflict, filled with the alarms of war; with death and destruction reaping their terrible harvest around her, did Dejah Thoris, Princess of Helium, true daughter of Mars, the God of War, promise herself in marriage to John Carter, Gentleman of Virginia.

CHAPTER TWENTY-SIX
THROUGH CARNAGE TO JOY

SOMETIME LATER TARS TARKAS and Kantos Kan returned to report that Zodanga had been completely reduced. Her forces were entirely destroyed or captured, and no further resistance was to be expected from within. Several battleships had escaped, but there were thousands of war and merchant vessels under guard of Thark warriors.

The lesser hordes had commenced looting and quarreling among themselves, so it was decided that we collect what warriors we could, man as many vessels as possible with Zodangan prisoners and make for Helium without further loss of time.

Five hours later we sailed from the roofs of the dock buildings with a fleet of two hundred and fifty battleships, carrying nearly one hundred thousand green warriors, followed by a fleet of transports with our thoats.

Behind us we left the stricken city in the fierce and brutal clutches of some forty thousand green warriors of the lesser hordes. They were looting, murdering, and fighting amongst themselves. In a hundred places they had applied the torch, and columns of dense smoke were rising above the city as though to blot out from the eye of heaven the horrid sights beneath.

In the middle of the afternoon we sighted the scarlet and yellow towers of Helium, and a short time later a great fleet of Zodangan battleships rose from the camps of the besiegers without the city, and advanced to meet us.

The banners of Helium had been strung from stem to stem of each of our mighty craft, but the Zodangans did not need this sign to realize that we were enemies, for our green Martian warriors had opened fire upon them almost as they left the ground. With their uncanny marksmanship they raked the oncoming fleet with volley after volley.

The twin cities of Helium, perceiving that we were friends, sent out hundreds of vessels to aid us, and then began the first real air battle I had ever witnessed.

The vessels carrying our green warriors were kept circling above the contending fleets of Helium and Zodanga, since their batteries were useless in the hands of the Tharks who, having no navy, have no skill in naval gunnery. Their small-arm fire, however, was most effective, and the final outcome of the engagement was strongly influenced, if not wholly determined, by their presence.

At first the two forces circled at the same altitude, pouring broadside after broadside into each other. Presently a great hole was torn in the hull of one of the immense battle craft from the Zodangan camp; with a lurch she turned completely over, the little figures of her crew plunging, turning and twisting toward the ground a thousand feet below; then with sickening velocity she tore after them, almost completely burying herself in the soft loam of the ancient sea bottom.

A wild cry of exultation arose from the Heliumite squadron, and with redoubled ferocity they fell upon the Zodangan fleet. By a pretty maneuver two of the vessels of Helium gained a position above their adversaries, from which they poured upon them from their keel bomb batteries a perfect torrent of exploding bombs.

Then, one by one, the battleships of Helium succeeded in rising above the Zodangans, and in a short time a number of the beleaguering battleships were drifting hopeless wrecks toward the high scarlet tower of greater Helium. Several others attempted to escape, but they were soon surrounded by thousands of tiny individual fliers, and above each hung a monster battleship of Helium ready to drop boarding parties upon their decks.

Within but little more than an hour from the moment the victorious Zodangan squadron had risen to meet us from the camp of the besiegers the battle was over, and the remaining vessels of the conquered Zodangans were headed toward the cities of Helium under prize crews.

There was an extremely pathetic side to the surrender of these mighty fliers, the result of an age-old custom which demanded that surrender should be signalized by the voluntary plunging to earth of the commander of the vanquished vessel. One after another the brave fellows, holding their colors high above their heads, leaped from the towering bows of their mighty craft to an awful death.

Not until the commander of the entire fleet took the fearful plunge, thus indicating the surrender of the remaining vessels, did the fighting cease, and the useless sacrifice of brave men come to an end.

We now signaled the flagship of Helium's navy to approach, and when she was within hailing distance I called out that we had the Princess Dejah Thoris on board, and that we wished to transfer her to the flagship that she might be taken immediately to the city.

As the full import of my announcement bore in upon them a great cry arose from the decks of the flagship, and a moment later the colors of the Princess of Helium broke from a hundred points upon her upper works. When the other vessels of the squadron caught the meaning of the signals flashed them they took up the wild acclaim and unfurled her colors in the gleaming sunlight.

The flagship bore down upon us, and as she swung gracefully to and touched our side a dozen officers sprang upon our decks. As their astonished gaze fell upon the hundreds of green warriors, who now came forth from the fighting shelters, they stopped aghast, but at sight of Kantos Kan, who advanced to meet them, they came forward, crowding about him.

Dejah Thoris and I then advanced, and they had no eyes for other than her. She received them gracefully, calling each by name, for they were men high in the esteem and service of her grandfather, and she knew them well.

"Lay your hands upon the shoulder of John Carter," she said to them, turning toward me, "the man to whom Helium owes her princess as well as her victory today."

They were very courteous to me and said many kind and complimentary things, but what seemed to impress them most was that I had won the aid of the fierce Tharks in my campaign for the liberation of Dejah Thoris, and the relief of Helium.

"You owe your thanks more to another man than to me," I said, "and here he is; meet one of Barsoom's greatest soldiers and statesmen, Tars Tarkas, Jeddak of Thark."

With the same polished courtesy that had marked their manner toward me they extended their greetings to the great Thark, nor, to my surprise, was he much behind them in ease of bearing or in courtly speech. Though not a garrulous race, the Tharks are extremely formal, and their ways lend themselves amazingly to dignified and courtly manners.

Dejah Thoris went aboard the flagship, and was much put out that I would not follow, but, as I explained to her, the battle was but partly won; we still had the land forces of the besieging Zodangans to account for, and I would not leave Tars Tarkas until that had been accomplished.

The commander of the naval forces of Helium promised to arrange to have the armies of Helium attack from the city in conjunction with our land attack, and so the vessels separated and Dejah Thoris was borne in triumph back to the court of her grandfather, Tardos Mors, Jeddak of Helium.

In the distance lay our fleet of transports, with the thoats of the green warriors, where they had remained during the battle. Without landing stages it was to be a difficult matter to unload these beasts upon the open plain, but there was nothing else for it, and so we put out for a point about ten miles from the city and began the task.

It was necessary to lower the animals to the ground in slings and this work occupied the remainder of the day and half the night. Twice we were attacked by parties of Zodangan cavalry; but with little loss, however, and after darkness shut down they withdrew.

As soon as the last thoat was unloaded Tars Tarkas gave the command to advance, and in three parties we crept upon the Zodangan camp from the north, the south and the east.

About a mile from the main camp we encountered their outposts and, as had been prearranged, accepted this as the signal to charge. With wild, ferocious cries and amidst the nasty squealing of battle-enraged thoats we bore down upon the Zodangans.

We did not catch them napping, but found a well-entrenched battle line confronting us. Time after time we were repulsed until, toward noon, I began to fear for the result of the battle.

The Zodangans numbered nearly a million fighting men, gathered from pole to pole, wherever stretched their ribbonlike waterways, while pitted against them were less than a hundred thousand green warriors. The forces from Helium had not arrived, nor could we receive any word from them.

Just at noon we heard heavy firing all along the line between the Zodangans and the cities, and we knew then that our much-needed reinforcements had come.

Again Tars Tarkas ordered the charge, and once more the mighty thoats bore their terrible riders against the ramparts of the enemy. At the same moment the battle line of Helium surged over the opposite breastworks of the Zodangans and in another moment they were being crushed as between two millstones. Nobly they fought, but in vain.

The plain before the city became a veritable shambles ere the last Zodangan surrendered, but finally the carnage ceased, the prisoners were marched back to Helium, and we entered the greater city's gates, a huge triumphal procession of conquering heroes.

The broad avenues were lined with women and children, among which were the few men whose duties necessitated that they remain within the city during the battle. We were greeted with an endless round of applause and showered with ornaments of gold, platinum, silver, and precious jewels. The city had gone mad with joy.

My fierce Tharks caused the wildest excitement and enthusiasm. Never before had an armed body of green warriors entered the gates of Helium, and that they came now as friends and allies filled the red men with rejoicing.

That my poor services to Dejah Thoris had become known to the Heliumites was evidenced by the loud crying of my name, and by the loads of ornaments that were fastened upon me and my huge thoat as we passed up the avenues to the palace, for even in the face of the ferocious appearance of Woola the populace pressed close about me.

As we approached this magnificent pile we were met by a party of officers who greeted us warmly and requested that Tars Tarkas and his jeds with the jeddaks and jeds of his wild allies, together with myself, dismount and accompany them to receive from Tardos Mors an expression of his gratitude for our services.

At the top of the great steps leading up to the main portals of the palace stood the royal party, and as we reached the lower steps one of their number descended to meet us. He was an almost perfect specimen of manhood; tall, straight as an arrow, superbly muscled and with the carriage and bearing of a ruler of men. I did not need to be told that he was Tardos Mors, Jeddak of Helium.

The first member of our party he met was Tars Tarkas and his first words sealed forever the new friendship between the races.

"That Tardos Mors," he said, earnestly, "may meet the greatest living warrior of Barsoom is a priceless honor, but that he may lay his hand on the shoulder of a friend and ally is a far greater boon."

"Jeddak of Helium," returned Tars Tarkas, "it has remained for a man of another world to teach the green warriors of Barsoom the meaning of friendship; to him we owe the fact that the hordes of Thark can understand you; that they can appreciate and reciprocate the sentiments so graciously expressed."

Tardos Mors then greeted each of the green jeddaks and jeds, and to each spoke words of friendship and appreciation.

As he approached me he laid both hands upon my shoulders.

"Welcome, my son," he said; "that you are granted, gladly, and without one word of opposition, the most precious jewel in all Helium, yes, on all Barsoom, is sufficient earnest of my esteem."

We were then presented to Mors Kajak, Jed of lesser Helium, and father of Dejah Thoris. He had followed close behind Tardos Mors and seemed even more affected by the meeting than had his father.

He tried a dozen times to express his gratitude to me, but his voice choked with emotion and he could not speak, and yet he had, as I was to later learn, a reputation for ferocity and fearlessness as a fighter that was remarkable even upon warlike Barsoom. In common with all Helium he worshipped his daughter, nor could he think of what she had escaped without deep emotion.

CHAPTER TWENTY-SEVEN
FROM JOY TO DEATH

FOR TEN DAYS THE HORDES OF THARK and their wild allies were feasted and entertained, and, then, loaded with costly presents and escorted by ten thousand soldiers of Helium commanded by Mors Kajak, they started on the return journey to their own lands. The jed of lesser Helium with a small party of nobles accompanied them all the way to Thark to cement more closely the new bonds of peace and friendship.

Sola also accompanied Tars Tarkas, her father, who before all his chieftains had acknowledged her as his daughter.

Three weeks later, Mors Kajak and his officers, accompanied by Tars Tarkas and Sola, returned upon a battleship that had been dispatched to Thark to fetch them in time for the ceremony which made Dejah Thoris and John Carter one.

For nine years I served in the councils and fought in the armies of Helium as a prince of the house of Tardos Mors. The people seemed never to tire of heaping honors upon me, and no day passed that did not bring some new proof of their love for my princess, the incomparable Dejah Thoris.

In a golden incubator upon the roof of our palace lay a snow-white egg. For nearly five years ten soldiers of the jeddak's Guard had constantly stood over it, and not a day passed when I was in the city that Dejah Thoris and I did not stand hand in hand before our little shrine planning for the future, when the delicate shell should break.

Vivid in my memory is the picture of the last night as we sat there talking in low tones of the strange romance which had woven our lives together and of this wonder which was coming to augment our happiness and fulfill our hopes.

In the distance we saw the bright white light of an approaching airship, but we attached no special significance to so common a sight. Like a bolt of lightning it raced toward Helium until its very speed bespoke the unusual.

Flashing the signals which proclaimed it a dispatch bearer for the jeddak, it circled impatiently awaiting the tardy patrol boat which must convoy it to the palace docks.

Ten minutes after it touched at the palace a message called me to the council chamber, which I found filling with the members of that body.

On the raised platform of the throne was Tardos Mors, pacing back and forth with tense-drawn face. When all were in their seats he turned toward us.

"This morning," he said, "word reached the several governments of Barsoom that the keeper of the atmosphere plant had made no wireless report for two days, nor had almost ceaseless calls upon him from a score of capitals elicited a sign of response.

"The ambassadors of the other nations asked us to take the matter in hand and hasten the assistant keeper to the plant. All day a thousand cruisers have been searching for him until, just now one of them returns bearing his dead body, which was found in the pits beneath his house horribly mutilated by some assassin.

"I do not need to tell you what this means to Barsoom. It would take months to penetrate those mighty walls, in fact the work has already commenced, and there would be little to fear were the engine of the pumping plant to run as it should and as they all have for hundreds of years; but the worst, we fear, has happened. The instruments show a rapidly decreasing air pressure on all parts of Barsoom—the engine has stopped.

"My gentlemen," he concluded, "we have at best three days to live."

There was absolute silence for several minutes, and then a young noble arose, and with his drawn sword held high above his head addressed Tardos Mors.

"The men of Helium have prided themselves that they have ever shown Barsoom how a nation of red men should live, now is our opportunity to show them how they should die. Let us go about our duties as though a thousand useful years still lay before us."

The chamber rang with applause and as there was nothing better to do than to allay the fears of the people by our example we went our ways with smiles upon our faces and sorrow gnawing at our hearts.

When I returned to my palace I found that the rumor already had reached Dejah Thoris, so I told her all that I had heard.

"We have been very happy, John Carter," she said, "and I thank whatever fate overtakes us that it permits us to die together."

The next two days brought no noticeable change in the supply of air, but on the morning of the third day breathing became difficult at the higher altitudes of the rooftops. The avenues and plazas of Helium were filled with people. All business had ceased. For the most part the people looked bravely into the face of their unalterable doom. Here and there, however, men and women gave way to quiet grief.

Toward the middle of the day many of the weaker commenced to succumb and within an hour the people of Barsoom were sinking by thousands into the unconsciousness which precedes death by asphyxiation.

Dejah Thoris and I with the other members of the royal family had collected in a sunken garden within an inner courtyard of the palace. We conversed in low tones, when we conversed at all, as the awe of the grim shadow of death crept over us. Even Woola seemed to feel the weight of the impending calamity, for he pressed close to Dejah Thoris and to me, whining pitifully.

The little incubator had been brought from the roof of our palace at the request of Dejah Thoris and she sat gazing longingly upon the unknown little life that now she would never know.

As it was becoming perceptibly difficult to breathe Tardos Mors arose, saying,

"Let us bid each other farewell. The days of the greatness of Barsoom are over. Tomorrow's sun will look down upon a dead world which through all eternity must go swinging through the heavens peopled not even by memories. It is the end."

He stooped and kissed the women of his family, and laid his strong hand upon the shoulders of the men.

As I turned sadly from him my eyes fell upon Dejah Thoris. Her head was drooping upon her breast, to all appearances she was lifeless. With a cry I sprang to her and raised her in my arms.

Her eyes opened and looked into mine.

"Kiss me, John Carter," she murmured. "I love you! I love you! It is cruel that we must be torn apart who were just starting upon a life of love and happiness."

As I pressed her dear lips to mine the old feeling of unconquerable power and authority rose in me. The fighting blood of Virginia sprang to life in my veins.

"It shall not be, my princess," I cried. "There is, there must be some way, and John Carter, who has fought his way through a strange world for love of you, will find it."

And with my words there crept above the threshold of my conscious mind a series of nine long forgotten sounds. Like a flash of lightning in the darkness their full purport dawned upon me—the key to the three great doors of the atmosphere plant!

Turning suddenly toward Tardos Mors as I still clasped my dying love to my breast I cried,

"A flier, Jeddak! Quick! Order your swiftest flier to the palace top. I can save Barsoom yet."

He did not wait to question, but in an instant a guard was racing to the nearest dock and though the air was thin and almost gone at the rooftop they managed to launch the fastest one-man, air-scout machine that the skill of Barsoom had ever produced.

Kissing Dejah Thoris a dozen times and commanding Woola, who would have followed me, to remain and guard her, I bounded with my old agility and strength to the high ramparts of the palace, and in another moment I was headed toward the goal of the hopes of all Barsoom.

I had to fly low to get sufficient air to breathe, but I took a straight course across an old sea bottom and so had to rise only a few feet above the ground.

I traveled with awful velocity for my errand was a race against time with death. The face of Dejah Thoris hung always before me. As I turned for a last look as I left the palace garden I had seen her stagger and sink upon the ground beside the little incubator. That she had dropped into the last coma which would end in death, if the air supply remained unreplenished, I well knew, and so, throwing caution to the winds, I flung overboard everything but the engine and compass, even to my ornaments, and lying on my belly along the deck with one hand on the steering wheel and the other pushing the speed lever to its last notch I split the thin air of dying Mars with the speed of a meteor.

An hour before dark the great walls of the atmosphere plant loomed suddenly before me, and with a sickening thud I plunged to the ground before the small door which was withholding the spark of life from the inhabitants of an entire planet.

Beside the door a great crew of men had been laboring to pierce the wall, but they had scarcely scratched the flintlike surface, and now most of them lay in the last sleep from which not even air would awaken them.

Conditions seemed much worse here than at Helium, and it was with difficulty that I breathed at all. There were a few men still conscious, and to one of these I spoke.

"If I can open these doors is there a man who can start the engines?" I asked.

"I can," he replied, "if you open quickly. I can last but a few moments more. But it is useless, they are both dead and no one else upon Barsoom knew the secret of these awful locks. For three days men crazed with fear have surged about this portal in vain attempts to solve its mystery."

I had no time to talk, I was becoming very weak and it was with difficulty that I controlled my mind at all.

But, with a final effort, as I sank weakly to my knees I hurled the nine thought waves at that awful thing before me. The Martian had crawled to my side and with staring eyes fixed on the single panel before us we waited in the silence of death.

Slowly the mighty door receded before us. I attempted to rise and follow it but I was too weak.

"After it," I cried to my companion, "and if you reach the pump room turn loose all the pumps. It is the only chance Barsoom has to exist tomorrow!"

From where I lay I opened the second door, and then the third, and as I saw the hope of Barsoom crawling weakly on hands and knees through the last doorway I sank unconscious upon the ground.

CHAPTER TWENTY-EIGHT
AT THE ARIZONA CAVE

I T WAS DARK WHEN I OPENED MY EYES AGAIN. Strange, stiff garments were upon my body; garments that cracked and powdered away from me as I rose to a sitting posture.

I felt myself over from head to foot and from head to foot I was clothed, though when I fell unconscious at the little doorway I had been naked. Before me was a small patch of moonlit sky which showed through a ragged aperture.

As my hands passed over my body they came in contact with pockets and in one of these a small parcel of matches wrapped in oiled paper. One of these matches I struck, and its dim flame lighted up what appeared to be a huge cave, toward the back of which I discovered a strange, still figure huddled over a tiny bench. As I approached it I saw that it was the dead and mummified remains of a little old woman with long black hair, and the thing it leaned over was a small charcoal burner upon which rested a round copper vessel containing a small quantity of greenish powder.

Behind her, depending from the roof upon rawhide thongs, and stretching entirely across the cave, was a row of human skeletons. From the thong which held them stretched another to the dead hand of the little old woman; as I touched the cord the skeletons swung to the motion with a noise as of the rustling of dry leaves.

It was a most grotesque and horrid tableau and I hastened out into the fresh air; glad to escape from so gruesome a place.

The sight that met my eyes as I stepped out upon a small ledge which ran before the entrance of the cave filled me with consternation.

A new heaven and a new landscape met my gaze. The silvered mountains in the distance, the almost stationary moon hanging in the sky, the cacti-studded valley below me were not of Mars. I could scarce believe my eyes, but the truth slowly forced itself upon me—I was looking upon Arizona from the same ledge from which ten years before I had gazed with longing upon Mars.

Burying my head in my arms I turned, broken, and sorrowful, down the trail from the cave.

Above me shone the red eye of Mars holding her awful secret, forty-eight million miles away.

Did the Martian reach the pump room? Did the vitalizing air reach the people of that distant planet in time to save them? Was my Dejah Thoris alive, or did her beautiful body lie cold in death beside the tiny golden incubator in the sunken garden of the inner courtyard of the palace of Tardos Mors, the jeddak of Helium?

For ten years I have waited and prayed for an answer to my questions. For ten years I have waited and prayed to be taken back to the world of my lost love. I would rather lie dead beside her there than live on Earth all those millions of terrible miles from her.

The old mine, which I found untouched, has made me fabulously wealthy; but what care I for wealth!

As I sit here tonight in my little study overlooking the Hudson, just twenty years have elapsed since I first opened my eyes upon Mars.

I can see her shining in the sky through the little window by my desk, and tonight she seems calling to me again as she has not called before since that long dead night, and I think I can see, across that awful abyss of space, a beautiful black-haired woman standing in the garden of a palace, and at her side is a little boy who puts his arm around her as she points into the sky toward the planet Earth, while at their feet is a huge and hideous creature with a heart of gold.

I believe that they are waiting there for me, and something tells me that I shall soon know.

*The new prisoner was
astride a No-van warrior...*

CONTENTS

PROLOGUE
THE MESSAGE FROM MARS

I MET HIM IN THE BLUE ROOM of the Transoceanic Liner *Harding* the night of Mars Day—June 10, 1967. I had been wandering about the city for several hours prior to the sailing of the flier watching the celebration, dropping in at various places that I might see as much as possible of scenes that doubtless will never again be paralleled—a world gone mad with joy. There was only one vacant chair in the Blue Room and that at a small table at which he was already seated alone. I asked his permission and he graciously invited me to join him, rising as he did so, his face lighting with a smile that compelled my liking from the first.

I had thought that Victory Day, which we had celebrated two months before, could never be eclipsed in point of mad national enthusiasm, but the announcement that had been made this day appeared to have had even a greater effect upon the minds and imaginations of the people.

The more than half-century of war that had continued almost uninterruptedly since 1914 had at last terminated, and practically for the first time since the activities of the human race were preserved for posterity in any enduring form no civilized, or even semicivilized, nation maintained a battle line upon any portion of the globe. War was at an end—definitely and forever. Arms and ammunition were being dumped into the five oceans; the vast armadas of the air were being scrapped or converted into carriers for purposes of peace and commerce.

The peoples of all nations had celebrated—victors and vanquished alike—for they were tired of war. At least they thought that they were tired of war; but were they? What else did they know? Only the oldest of men could recall even a semblance of world peace, the others knew nothing but war. Men had been born and lived their lives and died with their grandchildren clustered about them—all with the alarms of war ringing constantly in their ears. Perchance the little area of their activities was never actually encroached upon by the ironshod hoof of battle; but always somewhere war endured, now receding like the salt tide only to return again; until there arose that great tidal wave of human emotion in 1959

169

that swept the entire world for eight bloody years, and receding, left peace upon a spent and devastated world.

Two months had passed—two months during which the world appeared to stand still, to mark time, to hold its breath. What now? We have peace, but what shall we do with it? The leaders of thought and of action are trained for but one condition—war. The reaction brought despondency—our nerves, accustomed to the constant stimulus of excitement, cried out against the monotony of peace, and yet no one wanted war again. We did not know what we wanted.

And then came the announcement that I think saved a world from madness, for it directed our minds along a new line to the contemplation of a fact far more engrossing than prosaic wars and equally as stimulating to the imagination and the nerves—intelligible communication had at last been established with Mars!

Generations of wars had done their part to stimulate scientific research to the end that we might kill one another more expeditiously, that we might transport our youth more quickly to their shallow graves in alien soil, that we might transmit more secretly and with greater celerity our orders to slay our fellow men. And always, generation after generation, there had been those few who could detach their minds from the contemplation of massacre and looking forward to a happier era concentrate their talents and their energies upon the utilization of scientific achievement for the betterment of mankind and the rebuilding of civilization.

Among these was that much ridiculed but devoted coterie who had clung tenaciously to the idea that communication could be established with Mars. The hope that had been growing for a hundred years had never been permitted to die, but had been transmitted from teacher to pupil with ever-growing enthusiasm, while the people scoffed as, a hundred years before, we are told, they scoffed at the experimenters with *flying machines*, as they chose to call them.

About 1940 had come the first reward of long years of toil and hope, following the perfection of an instrument which accurately indicated the direction and distance of the focus of any radio-activity with which it might be attuned. For several years prior to this all the more highly sensitive receiving instruments had recorded a series of three dots and three dashes which began at precise intervals of twenty-four hours and thirty-seven minutes and continued for approximately fifteen minutes.

The new instrument indicated conclusively that these signals, if they were signals, originated always at the same distance from the Earth and in the same direction as the point in the universe occupied by the planet Mars.

It was five years later before a sending apparatus was evolved that bade fair to transmit its waves from Earth to Mars. At first their own message was repeated—three dots and three dashes. Although the usual interval of time had not elapsed since we had received their daily signal, ours was immediately answered. Then we sent a message consisting of five dots and two dashes, alternating. Immediately they replied with five dots and two dashes and we knew beyond peradventure of a doubt that we were in communication with the Red Planet, but it required twenty-two years of unremitting effort, with the most brilliant intellects of two worlds concentrated upon it, to evolve and perfect an intelligible system of intercommunication between the two planets.

Today, this tenth of June, 1967, there was published broadcast to the world the first message from Mars. It was dated Helium, Barsoom, and merely extended greetings to a sister world and wished us well. But it was the beginning.

The Blue Room of *The Harding* was, I presume, but typical of every other gathering place in the civilized world. Men and women were eating, drinking, laughing, singing and talking. The flier was racing through the air at an altitude of little over a thousand feet. Its engines, motivated wirelessly from power plants thousands of miles distant, drove it noiselessly and swiftly along its overnight pathway between Chicago and Paris.

I had of course crossed many times, but this instance was unique because of the epoch-making occasion which the passengers were celebrating, and so I sat at the table longer than usual, watching my fellow diners, with, I imagine, a slightly indulgent smile upon my lips, since—I mention it in no spirit of egotism—it had been my high privilege to assist in the consummation of a hundred years of effort that had borne fruit that day. I looked around at my fellow diners and then back to my table companion.

He was a fine-looking chap, lean and bronzed—one need not have noted the Air Corps overseas service uniform, the Admiral's stars and anchors or the wound stripes to have guessed that he was a fighting man; he looked it, every inch of him, and there were a full seventy-two inches.

We talked a little—about the great victory and the message from Mars, of course, and though he often smiled I noticed an occasional shadow of sadness in his eyes and once, after a particularly mad outburst of pandemonium on the part of the celebrators, he shook his head, remarking: "Poor devils!" and then: "It is just as well—let them enjoy life while they may. I envy them their ignorance."

"What do you mean?" I asked.

He flushed a little and then smiled. "Was I speaking aloud?" he asked.

I repeated what he had said and he looked steadily at me for a long minute before he spoke again. "Oh, what's the use!" he exclaimed, almost petulantly; "you wouldn't understand and of course you wouldn't believe. I do not understand it myself; but I have to believe because I know—I know from personal observation. God! if you could have seen what I have seen."

"Tell me," I begged; but he shook his head dubiously.

"Do you realize that there is no such thing as Time?" he asked suddenly— "That man has invented Time to suit the limitations of his finite mind, just as he has named another thing, that he can neither explain nor understand. Space?"

"I have heard of such a theory," I replied; "but I neither believe nor disbelieve—I simply do not know."

I thought I had him started and so I waited as I have read in fiction stories is the proper way to entice a strange narrative from its possessor. He was looking beyond me and I imagined that the expression of his eyes denoted that he was witnessing again the thrilling scenes of the past. I must have been wrong, though—in fact I was quite sure of it when he next spoke.

"If that girl isn't careful," he said, "the thing will upset and give her a nasty fall—she is much too near the edge."

I turned to see a richly dressed and much disheveled young lady busily dancing on a tabletop while her friends and the surrounding diners cheered her lustily.

My companion arose. "I have enjoyed your company immensely," he said, "and I hope to meet you again. I am going to look for a place to sleep now—they could not give me a stateroom—I don't seem to be able to get enough sleep since they sent me back." He smiled.

"Miss the gas shells and radio bombs, I suppose," I remarked.

"Yes," he replied, "just as a convalescent misses smallpox."

"I have a room with two beds," I said. "At the last minute my secretary was taken ill. I'll be glad to have you share the room with me."

He thanked me and accepted my hospitality for the night—the following morning we would be in Paris.

As we wound our way among the tables filled with laughing, joyous diners, my companion paused beside that at which sat the young woman who had previously attracted his attention. Their eyes met and into hers came a look of puzzlement and half-recognition. He smiled frankly in her face, nodded and passed on.

"You know her, then?" I asked.

"I shall—in two hundred years," was his enigmatical reply.

We found my room, and there we had a bottle of wine and some little cakes and a quiet smoke and became much better acquainted.

It was he who first reverted to the subject of our conversation in the Blue Room.

"I am going to tell you," he said, "what I have never told another; but on the condition that if you retell it you are not to use my name. I have several years of this life ahead of me and I do not care to be pointed out as a lunatic. First let me say that I do not try to explain anything, except that I do not believe prevision to be a proper explanation. I have actually *lived* the experiences I shall tell you of, and that girl we saw dancing on the table tonight lived them with me; but she does not know it. If you care to, you can keep in mind the theory that there is no such thing as Time—just keep it in mind—you cannot understand it, or at least I cannot. Here goes."

CHAPTER ONE
THE FLIGHT OF *THE BARSOOM*

I HAD INTENDED TELLING YOU my story of the days of the twenty-second century, but it seems best, if you are to understand it, to tell first the story of my great-great-grandfather who was born in the year 2000."

I must have looked up at him quizzically, for he smiled and shook his head as one who is puzzled to find an explanation suited to the mental capacity of his auditor.

"My great-great-grandfather was, in reality, the great-great-grandson of my previous incarnation which commenced in 1896. I married in 1916, at the age of twenty. My son Julian was born in 1917. I never saw him. I was killed in France in 1918—on Armistice Day.

"I was again reincarnated in my son's son in 1937. I am thirty years of age. My son was born in 1970—that is the son of my 1937 incarnation—and his son, Julian 5th, in whom I again returned to Earth, in the year 2000. I see you are confused, but please remember my injunction that you are to try to keep in mind the theory that there is no such thing as Time. It is now the year 1967 yet I recall distinctly every event of my life that occurred in four incarnations—the last that I recall being that which had its origin in the year 2100. Whether I actually skipped three generations that time or through some caprice of Fate I am merely unable to visualize an intervening incarnation, I do not know.

"My theory of the matter is that I differ only from my fellows in that I can recall the events of many incarnations, while they can recall none of theirs other than a few important episodes of that particular one they are experiencing; but perhaps I am wrong. It is of no importance. I will tell you the story of Julian 5th who was born in the year 2000, and then, if we have time and you yet are interested, I will tell you of the torments during the harrowing days of the twenty-second century, following the birth of Julian 9th in 2100."

I will try to tell the story in his own words in so far as I can recall them, but for various reasons, not the least of which is that I am lazy, I shall omit superfluous quotation marks—that is, with your permission, of course.

My name is Julian. I am called Julian 5th. I come of an illustrious family—my great-great-grandfather, Julian 1st, a major at twenty-two, was killed in France early in The Great War. My great-grandfather, Julian 2nd, was killed in battle in Turkey in 1938. My grandfather, Julian 3rd, fought continuously from his sixteenth year until peace was declared in his thirtieth year. He died in 1992 and during the last twenty-five years of his life was an Admiral of the Air, being transferred at the close of the war to command of the International Peace Fleet, which patrolled and policed the world. He also was killed in line of duty, as was my father who succeeded him in the service.

At sixteen I graduated from the Air School and was detailed to the International Peace Fleet, being the fifth generation of my line to wear the uniform of my country. That was in 2016, and I recall that it was a matter of pride to me that it rounded out the full century since Julian 1st graduated from West Point, and that during that one hundred years no adult male of my line had ever owned or worn civilian clothes.

Of course there were no more wars, but there still was fighting. We had the pirates of the air to contend with and occasionally some of the uncivilized tribes of Russia, Africa and central Asia required the attention of a punitive expedition. However, life seemed tame and monotonous to us when we read of the heroic deeds of our ancestors from 1914 to 1967, yet none of us wanted war. It had been too well schooled into us that we must not think of war, and the International Peace Fleet so effectively prevented all preparation for war that we all knew there could never be another. There wasn't a firearm in the world other than those with which we were armed, and a few of ancient design that were kept as heirlooms, or in museums, or that were owned by savage tribes who could procure no ammunition for them, since we permitted none to be manufactured. There was not a gas shell nor a radio bomb, nor any engine to discharge or project one; and there wasn't a big gun of any caliber in the world. I veritably believed that a thousand men equipped with the various engines of destruction that had reached their highest efficiency at the close of the war in 1967 could have conquered the world; but there were not a thousand men so armed—there never could be a thousand men so equipped anywhere upon the face of the Earth. The International Peace Fleet was equipped and manned to prevent just such a calamity.

But it seems that Providence never intended that the world should be without calamities. If man prevented those of possible internal origin there still remained undreamed of external sources over which he had no control. It was one of these which was to prove our undoing. Its seed was sown thirty-three years before I was born, upon that historic day, June 10th, 1967, that Earth received her first message from Mars, since which the two planets have remained in constant friendly communication, carrying on a commerce of reciprocal enlightenment. In some branches of the arts and sciences the Martians, or Barsoomians, as they call themselves, were far in advance of us, while in others we had progressed more rapidly than they. Knowledge was thus freely exchanged to the advantage of both worlds. We learned of their history and customs and they of ours, though they had for ages already known much more of us than we of them. Martian news held always a prominent place in our daily papers from the first.

They helped us most, perhaps, in the fields of medicine and aeronautics, giving us in one, the marvelous healing lotions of Barsoom and in the other, knowledge of the Eighth Ray, which is more generally known on Earth as the Barsoomian Ray, which is now stored in the buoyancy tanks of every air craft and has made obsolete those ancient types of plane that depended upon momentum to keep them afloat.

That we ever were able to communicate intelligibly with them is due to the presence upon Mars of that deathless Virginian, John Carter, whose miraculous transportation to Mars occurred March 4th, 1866, as every school child of the twenty-first century knows. Had not the little band of Martian scientists, who sought so long to communicate with Earth, mistakenly formed themselves into a secret organization for political purposes, messages might have been exchanged between the two planets nearly half a century before they were, and it was not until they finally called upon John Carter that the present interplanetary code was evolved.

Almost from the first the subject which engrossed us all the most was the possibility of an actual exchange of visits between Earth Men and Barsoomians. Each planet hoped to be the first to achieve this, yet neither withheld any information that would aid the other in the consummation of the great fact. It was a generous and friendly rivalry which about the time of my graduation from the Air School seemed, in theory at least, to be almost ripe for successful consummation by one or the other. We had the Eighth Ray, the motors, the oxygenating devices, the insulating pro-cesses—everything to insure the safe and certain transit of a specially designed air craft to Mars, were Mars the only other inhabitant of space. But it was not and it was the other planets and the Sun that we feared.

In 2015 Mars had dispatched a ship for Earth with a crew of five men provisioned for ten years. It was hoped that with good luck the trip might be made in something less than five years, as the craft had developed an actual trial speed of one thousand miles per hour. At the time of my graduation the ship was already off its course almost a million miles and generally conceded to be hopelessly lost. Its crew, maintaining constant radio communication with both Earth and Mars, still hoped for success, but the best informed upon both worlds had given them up.

We had had a ship about ready at the time of the sailing of the Martians, but the government at Washington had forbidden the venture when it became apparent that the Barsoomian ship was doomed—a wise decision, since our vessel was no better equipped than theirs. Nearly ten years elapsed before anything further was accomplished in the direction of assuring any greater hope of success for another interplanetary venture into space, and this was directly due to the discovery made by a former classmate of mine, Lieutenant Commander Orthis, one of the most brilliant men I have ever known, and at the same time one of the most unscrupulous, and, to me at least, the most obnoxious.

We had entered the Air School together—he from New York and I from Illinois—and almost from the first day we had seemed to discover a mutual antagonism that, upon his part at least, must have been considerably strengthened by numerous unfortunate occurrences during our four years beneath the same roof. In the first place he was not popular with either the cadets, the instructors, or the officers of the school, while I was most fortunate in this respect. In those various fields of athletics in which he considered himself particularly expert, it was always I, unfortunately, who excelled him and kept him from major honors. In the classroom he outshone us all—even the instructors were amazed at the brilliancy of his intellect—and yet as we passed from grade to grade I often topped him in the final examinations. I ranked him always as a cadet officer, and upon graduation I took a higher grade among the new ensigns than he—a rank that had many years before been discontinued, but which had recently been revived.

From then on I saw little of him, his services confining him principally to land service, while mine kept me almost constantly on the air in all parts of the world. Occasionally I heard of him—usually something unsavory; he had married a nice girl and abandoned her—there had been talk of an investigation of his accounts—and the last that there was a rumor that he was affiliated with a secret order that sought to overthrow the government. Some things I might believe of Orthis, but not this.

And during these nine years since graduation, as we had drifted apart in interests, so had the breach between us been widened by constantly increasing difference in rank. He was a Lieutenant Commander and I a Captain, when in 2024 he announced the discovery and isolation of the Eighth Solar Ray, and within two months those of the Moon, Mercury, Venus and Jupiter. The Eighth Barsoomian and the Eighth Earthly Rays had already been isolated, and upon Earth the latter erroneously called by the name of the former.

Orthis' discoveries were hailed upon two planets as the key to actual travel between the Earth and Barsoom, since by means of these several rays the attraction of the Sun and the planets, with the exception of Saturn, Uranus and Neptune, could be definitely overcome and a ship steer a direct and unimpeded course through space to Mars. The effect of the pull of the three farther planets was considered negligible, owing to their great distance from both Mars and Earth.

Orthis wanted to equip a ship and start at once, but again government intervened and forbade what it considered an unnecessary risk. Instead Orthis was ordered to design a small radio-operated flier, which would carry no one aboard, and which it was believed could be automatically operated for at least half the distance between the two planets. After his designs were completed, you may imagine his chagrin, and mine as well, when I was detailed to supervise construction, yet I will say that Orthis hid his natural emotions well and gave me perfect cooperation in the work we were compelled to undertake together, and which was as distasteful to me as to him. On my part I made it as easy for him as I could, working with him rather than over him.

It required but a short time to complete the experimental ship and during this time I had an opportunity to get a still better insight into the marvelous intellectual ability of Orthis, though I never saw into his mind or heart.

It was late in 2024 that the ship was launched upon its strange voyage, and almost immediately, upon my recommendation, work was started upon the perfection of the larger ship that had been in course of construction in 2015 at the time that the loss of the Martian ship had discouraged our government in making any further attempt until the then seemingly insurmountable obstacles should have been overcome. Orthis was again my assistant, and with the means at our disposal it was a matter of less than eight months before *The Barsoom*, as she was christened, was completely overhauled and thoroughly equipped for the interplanetary voyage. The various eighth rays that would assist us in overcoming the pull of the Sun, Mercury, Venus, Earth, Mars and Jupiter were stored in carefully constructed and well protected tanks within the hull, and there was a smaller tank at the bow containing the Eighth Lunar Ray, which would permit us to pass safely within the zone of the moon's influence without danger of being attracted to her barren surface.

Messages from the original Martian ship had been received from time to time and with diminishing strength for nearly five years after it had left Mars. Its commander in his heroic fight against the pull of the Sun had managed to fall within the grip of Jupiter and was, when last heard from far out in the great void between that planet and Mars. During the past four years the fate of the ship could be naught but conjecture—all that we could be certain of was that its unfortunate crew would never again return to Barsoom.

Our own experimental ship had been speeding upon its lonely way now for eight months, and so accurate had Orthis' scientific deductions proven that the most delicate instrument could detect no slightest deviation from its prescribed course. It was then that Orthis began to importune the government to permit him to set out with the new craft that was now completed. The authorities held out, however, until the latter part of 2025 when, the experimental ship having been out a year and still showing no deviation from its course, they felt reasonably assured that the success of the venture was certain and that no useless risk of human life would be involved.

The Barsoom required five men properly to handle it, and as had been the custom through many centuries when an undertaking of more than usual risk was to be attempted, volunteers were called for, with the result that fully half the personnel of the International Peace Fleet begged to be permitted to form the crew of five.

The government finally selected their men from the great number of volunteers, with the result that once more was I the innocent cause of disappointment and chagrin to Orthis, as I was placed in command, with Orthis, two lieutenants and an ensign completing the roster.

The Barsoom was larger than the craft dispatched by the Martians, with the result that we were able to carry supplies for fifteen years. We were equipped with more powerful motors which would permit us to maintain an average speed of over twelve hundred miles an hour, carrying in addition an engine recently developed by Orthis which generated sufficient power from light to propel the craft at half speed in the event that our other engine should break down. None of us was married, Orthis' abandoned wife having recently died. Our estates were taken under trusteeship by the government. Our farewells were made at an elaborate ball at the White House on December 24, 2025, and on Christmas day we rose from the landing stage at which *The Barsoom* had been moored, and amid the blare of bands and the shouting of thousands of our fellow country-men we arose majestically into the blue.

I shall not bore you with dry, technical descriptions of our motors and equipment. Suffice it to say that the former were of three types—those which propelled the ship through the air and those which propelled it through ether, the latter of course represented our most important equip-ment, and consisted of powerful multiple-exhaust separators which isolated the true Barsoomian Eighth Ray in great quantities, and, by exhausting it rapidly earthward, propelled the vessel toward Mars. These separators were so designed that, with equal facility, they could isolate the Earthly Eighth Ray which would be necessary for our return voyage. The auxiliary engine, which I mentioned previously and which was Orthis' latest invention, could be easily adjusted to isolate the eighth ray of any planet or satellite or of the Sun itself, thus insuring us motive power in any part of the universe by the simple expedient of generating and exhausting the eighth ray of the nearest heavenly body. A fourth type of generator drew oxygen from the ether, while another emanated insulating rays which insured us a uniform temperature and external pressure at all times, their action being analogous to that of the atmosphere surrounding the Earth. Science had, therefore, permitted us to construct a little world, which moved at will through space—a little world inhabited by five souls.

Had it not been for Orthis' presence I could have looked forward to a reasonably pleasurable voyage, for West and Jay were extremely likeable fellows and sufficiently mature to be companionable, while young Norton, the ensign, though but seventeen years of age, endeared himself to all of us from the very start of the voyage by his pleasant manners, his consid-eration and his willingness in the performance of his duties. There were three staterooms aboard *The Barsoom*, one of which I occupied alone, while West and Orthis had the second and Jay and Norton the third. West and Jay were lieutenants and had been classmates at the air school. They would of course have preferred to room together, but could not unless I com-manded it or Orthis requested it. Not wishing to give Orthis any grounds for offense I hesitated to make the change, while Orthis, never having thought a considerate thought or done a considerate deed in his life, could not, of course, have been expected to suggest it. We all messed together, West, Jay and Norton taking turns at preparing the meals. Only in the actual operation of the ship were the lines of rank drawn strictly. Otherwise we associated as equals, nor would any other arrangement have been endurable upon such an undertaking, which required that we five be practically imprisoned together upon a small ship for a period of not less than five years. We had books and writing materials and games, and we were, of course, in constant radio communication with both Earth and Mars, receiving continuously the latest news from both planets. We listened to opera and oratory and heard the music of two worlds, so that we were not lacking for entertainment. There was always a certain constraint in Orthis' manner toward me, yet I must give him credit for behaving outwardly admirably. Unlike the others we never exchanged pleasantries with one another, nor could I, knowing as I did that Orthis hated me, and feeling for him personally the contempt that I felt because of his character. Intellectually he commanded my highest admiration, and upon intellectual grounds we met without constraint or reserve, and many were the profitable discussions we had during the first days of what was to prove a very brief voyage.

It was about the second day that I noticed with some surprise that Orthis was exhibiting a friendly interest in Norton. It had never been Orthis' way to make friends, but I saw that he and Norton were much together and that each seemed to derive a great deal of pleasure from the society of the other. Orthis was a good talker. He knew his profession thoroughly, and was an inventor and scientist of high distinction. Norton, though but a boy, was himself the possessor of a fine mind. He had been honor-man in his graduating class, heading the list of ensigns for that year, and I could not help but notice that he was drinking in every word along scientific lines that Orthis vouchsafed.

We had been out about six days when Orthis came to me and suggested, that inasmuch as West and Jay had been classmates and chums that they be permitted to room together and that he had spoken to Norton who had said that he would be agreeable to the change and would occupy West's bunk in Orthis' stateroom. I was very glad of this for it now meant that my subordinates would be paired off in the most agreeable manner, and as long as they were contented, I knew that the voyage from that standpoint at least would be more successful. I was, of course, a trifle sorry to see a fine boy like Norton brought under the influence of Orthis, yet I felt that what little danger might result would be offset by the influence of West and Jay and myself or counterbalanced by the liberal education which five years' constant companionship with Orthis would be to any man with whom Orthis would discuss freely the subjects of which he was master.

We were beginning to feel the influence of the Moon rather strongly. At the rate we were traveling we would pass closest to it upon the twelfth day, or about the 6th of January, 2026.

Our course would bring us within about twenty thousand miles of the Moon, and as we neared it I believe that the sight of it was the most impressive thing that human eye had ever gazed upon before. To the naked eye it loomed large and magnificent in the heavens, appearing over ten times the size that it does to terrestrial observers, while our powerful glasses brought its weird surface to such startling proximity that one felt that he might reach out and touch the torn rocks of its tortured mountains.

This nearer view enabled us to discover the truth or falsity of the theory that has been long held by some scientists that there is a form of vegetation upon the surface of the Moon. Our eyes were first attracted by what appeared to be movement upon the surface of some of the valleys and in the deeper ravines of the mountains. Norton exclaimed that there were creatures there, moving about, but closer observation revealed the fact of the existence of a weird fungus-like vegetation which grew so rapidly that we could clearly discern the phenomena. From the several days' observation which we had at close range we came to the conclusion that the entire life span of this vegetation is encompassed in a single sidereal month. From the spore it developed in the short period of a trifle over twenty-seven days into a mighty plant that is sometimes hundreds of feet in height. The branches are angular and grotesque, the leaves broad and thick, and in the plants which we discerned the seven primary colors were distinctly represented. As each portion of the Moon passed slowly into shadow the vegetation first drooped, then wilted, then crumbled to the ground, apparently disintegrating almost immediately into a fine, dustlike powder—at least in so far as our glasses revealed, it quite disappeared entirely. The movement which we discerned was purely that of rapid growth, as there is no wind upon the surface of the Moon. Both Jay and Orthis were positive that they discerned some form of animal life, either insect or reptilian. These I did not myself see, though I did perceive many of the broad, flat leaves which seemed to have been partially eaten, which certainly strengthened the theory that there is other than vegetable life upon our satellite.

I presume that one of the greatest thrills that we experienced in this adventure, that was to prove a veritable Pandora's box of thrills, was when we commenced to creep past the edge of the Moon and our eyes beheld for the first time that which no other human eyes had ever rested upon— portions of that two-fifths of the Moon's surface which is invisible from the Earth.

We had looked with awe upon Mare Crisium and Lacus Somniorum, Sinius Roris, Oceanus Procellarum and the four great mountain ranges. We had viewed at close range the volcanoes of Opollonius, Secchi, Borda, Tycho and their mates, but all these paled into insignificance as there unrolled before us the panorama of the vast unknown.

I cannot say that it differed materially from that portion of the Moon that is visible to us—it was merely the glamour of mystery which had surrounded it since the beginning of time that lent to it its thrill for us. Here we observed other great mountain ranges and wide undulating plains, towering volcanoes and mighty craters and the same vegetation with which we were now become familiar.

We were two days past the Moon when our first trouble developed. Among our stores were one hundred and twenty quarts of spirits per man, enough to allow us each a liberal two ounces per day for a period of five years. Each night, before dinner, we had drunk to the President in a cocktail which contained a single ounce of spirits, the idea being to conserve our supply in the event of our journey being unduly protracted as well as to have enough in the event that it became desirable fittingly to celebrate any particular occasion.

Toward the third meal hour of the thirteenth day of the voyage Orthis entered the messroom noticeably under the influence of liquor.

History narrates that under the regime of prohibition drunkenness was common and that it grew to such proportions as to become a national menace, but with the repeal of the Prohibition Act, nearly a hundred years ago, the habit of drinking to excess abated, so that it became a matter of disgrace for any man to show his liquor, and in the service it was considered as reprehensible as cowardice in action. There was therefore but one thing for me to do. I ordered Orthis to his quarters.

He was drunker than I had thought him, and he turned upon me like a tiger.

"You damned cur," he cried. "All my life you have stolen everything from me; the fruits of all my efforts you have garnered by chicanery and trickery, and even now, were we to reach Mars, it is you who would be lauded as the hero—not I whose labor and intellect have made possible this achievement. But by God we will not reach Mars. Not again shall you profit by my efforts. You have gone too far this time, and now you dare to order me about like a dog and an inferior—I, whose brains have made you what you are."

I held my temper, for I saw that the man was unaccountable for his words. "Go to your quarters, Orthis," I repeated my command. "I will talk with you again in the morning."

West and Jay and Norton were present. They seemed momentarily paralyzed by the man's condition and gross insubordination. Norton, however, was the first to recover. Jumping quickly to Orthis' side he laid his hand upon his arm. "Come, sir," he said, and to my surprise Orthis accompanied him quietly to their stateroom.

During the voyage we had continued the fallacy of night and day, gauging them merely by our chronometers, since we moved always through utter darkness, surrounded only by a tiny nebula of light, produced by the Sun's rays impinging upon the radiation from our insulating generator. Before breakfast, therefore, on the following morning I sent for Orthis to come to my stateroom. He entered with a truculent swagger, and his first words indicated that if he had not continued drinking, he had at least been moved to no regrets for his unwarranted attack of the previous evening.

"Well," he said, "what in hell are you going to do about it?"

"I cannot understand your attitude, Orthis," I told him. "I have never intentionally injured you. When orders from government threw us together I was as much chagrined as you. Association with you is as distasteful to me as it is to you. I merely did as you did—obeyed orders. I have no desire to rob you of anything, but that is not the question now. You have been guilty of gross insubordination and of drunkenness. I can prevent a repetition of the latter by confiscating your liquor and keeping it from you during the balance of the voyage, and an apology from you will atone for the former. I shall give you twenty-four hours to reach a decision. If you do not see fit to avail yourself of my clemency, Orthis, you will travel to Mars and back again in irons. Your decision now and your behavior during the balance of the voyage will decide your fate upon our return to Earth. And I tell you, Orthis, that if I possibly can do so I shall use the authority which is mine upon this expedition and expunge from the log the record of your transgressions last night and this morning. Now go to your quarters; your meals will be served there for twenty-four hours and at the end of that time I shall receive your decision. Meanwhile your liquor will be taken from you."

He gave me an ugly look, turned upon his heel and left my stateroom.

Norton was on watch that night. We were two days past the Moon. West, Jay and I were asleep in our staterooms, when suddenly Norton entered mine and shook me violently by the shoulder.

"My God, Captain," he cried, "come quick. Commander Orthis is destroying the engines."

I leaped to my feet and followed Norton amidships to the engine room, calling to West and Jay as I passed their stateroom. Through the bull's-eye in the engine room door, which he had locked, we could see Orthis working over the auxiliary generator which was to have proven our salvation in an emergency, since by means of it we could overcome the pull of any planet into the sphere of whose influence we might be carried. I breathed a sigh of relief as my eyes noted that the main battery of engines was functioning properly, since, as a matter of fact, we had not expected to have to rely at all upon the auxiliary generator, having stored sufficient quantities of the Eighth Ray of the various heavenly bodies by which we might be influenced, to carry us safely throughout the entire extent of the long voyage. West and Jay had joined us by this time, and I now called to Orthis, commanding him to open the door. He did something more to the generator and then arose, crossed the engine room directly to the door, unbolted it and threw the door open. His hair was disheveled, his face drawn, his eyes shining with a peculiar light, but withal his expression denoted a drunken elation that I did not at the moment understand.

"What have you been doing here, Orthis?" I demanded. "You are under arrest, and supposed to be in your quarters."

"You'll see what I've been doing," he replied truculently, "and it's done—it's done—it can't ever be undone. I've seen to that."

I grabbed him roughly by the shoulder. "What do you mean? Tell me what you have done, or by God I will kill you with my own hands," for I knew, not only from his words but from his expression, that he had accomplished something which he considered very terrible.

The man was a coward and he quailed under my grasp. "You wouldn't dare to kill me," he cried, "and it don't make any difference, for we'll all be dead in a few hours. Go and look at your damned compass."

CHAPTER TWO
THE HEART OF THE MOON

NORTON, WHOSE WATCH IT WAS, had already hurried toward the pilot room where were located the controls and the various instruments. This room, which was just forward of the engine room, was in effect a circular conning-tower which projected about twelve inches above the upper hull. The entire circumference of this twelve-inch superstructure was set with small ports of thick crystal glass.

As I turned to follow Norton I spoke to West. "Mr. West," I said, "you and Mr. Jay will place Lieutenant Commander Orthis in irons immediately. If he resists, kill him."

As I hurried after Norton I heard a volley of oaths from Orthis and a burst of almost maniacal laughter. When I reached the pilothouse I found Norton working very quietly with the controls. There was nothing hysterical in his movements, but his face was absolutely ashen.

"What is wrong, Mr. Norton?" I asked. But as I looked at the compass simultaneously I read my answer there before he spoke. We were moving at right angles to our proper course.

"We are falling toward the Moon, sir," he said, "and she does not respond to her control."

"Shut down the engines," I ordered, "they are only accelerating our fall."

"Aye, aye, sir," he replied.

"The Lunar Eighth Ray tank is of sufficient capacity to keep us off the Moon," I said. "If it has not been tampered with, we should be in no danger of falling to the Moon's surface."

"If it has not been tampered with, sir; yes, sir, that is what I have been thinking."

"But the gauge here shows it full to capacity," I reminded him.

"I know, sir," he replied, "but if it were full to capacity, we should not be falling so rapidly."

Immediately I fell to examining the gauge, almost at once discovering that it had been tampered with and the needle set permanently to indicate a maximum supply. I turned to my companion.

"Mr. Norton," I said, "please go forward and investigate the Lunar Eighth Ray tank, and report back to me immediately."

The young man saluted and departed. As he approached the tank it was necessary for him to crawl through a very restricted place beneath the deck.

In about five minutes Norton returned. He was not so pale as he had been, but he looked very haggard.

"Well?" I inquired as he halted before me.

"The exterior intake valve has been opened, sir," he said, "the rays were escaping into space. I have closed it, sir."

The valve to which he referred was used only when the ship was in dry dock, for the purpose of refilling the buoyancy tank, and, because it was so seldom used and as a further precaution against accident, the valve was placed in an inaccessible part of the hull where there was absolutely no likelihood of its being accidentally opened.

Norton glanced at the instrument. "We are not falling quite so rapidly now," he said.

"Yes," I replied, "I had noted that, and I have also been able to adjust the Lunar Eighth Ray gauge—it shows that we have about half the original pressure."

"Not enough to keep us from going aground," he commented.

"No, not here, where there is no atmosphere. If the Moon had an atmosphere we could at least keep off the surface if we wished to. As it is, however, I imagine that we will be able to make a safe landing, though, of course that will do us little good. You understand, I suppose, Mr. Norton, that this is practically the end."

He nodded. "It will be a sad blow to the inhabitants of two worlds," he remarked, his entire forgetfulness of self indicating the true nobility of his character.

"It is a sad report to broadcast," I remarked, "but it must be done, and at once. You will, please, send the following message to the Secretary of Peace:

"U. S. S. *The Barsoom*, January 6, 2026, about twenty thousand miles off the Moon. Lieutenant Commander Orthis, while under the influence of liquor, has destroyed auxiliary engine and opened exterior intake valve Lunar Eighth Ray buoyancy tank. Ship sinking rapidly. Will keep you—"

Norton, who had seated himself at the radio desk, leaped suddenly to his feet and turned toward me. "My God, sir," he cried, "he has destroyed the radio outfit also. We can neither send nor receive."

A careful examination revealed the fact that Orthis had so cleverly and completely destroyed the instruments that there was no hope of repairing them. I turned to Norton.

"We are not only dead, Norton, but we are buried, as well."

I smiled as I spoke and he answered me with a smile that betokened his utter fearlessness of death.

"I have but one regret, sir," he said, "and that is that the world will never know that our failure was not due to any weakness of our machinery, ship or equipment."

"That is, indeed, too bad," I replied, "for it will retard transportation between the two worlds possibly a hundred years—maybe forever."

I called to West and Jay who by this time had placed Orthis in irons and confined him to his stateroom. When they came I told them what had happened, and they took it as coolly as did Norton. Nor was I surprised, for these were fine types selected from the best of that splendid organization which officered the International Peace Fleet.

Together we immediately made a careful inspection of the ship, which revealed no further damage than that which we had already discovered, but which was sufficient as we well knew, to preclude any possibility of our escaping from the pull of the Moon.

"You gentlemen realize our position as well as I," I told them. "Could we repair the auxiliary generator we might isolate the Lunar Eighth Ray, refill our tank, and resume our voyage. But the diabolical cleverness with which Lieutenant Commander Orthis has wrecked the machine renders this impossible. We might fight away from the surface of the Moon for a considerable period, but in the end it would avail us nothing. It is my plan, therefore, to make a landing. In so far as the actual lunar conditions are concerned, we are confronted only by a mass of theories, many of which are conflicting. It will, therefore, be at least a matter of consuming interest to us to make a landing upon this dead world where we may observe it closely, but there is also the possibility, remote, I grant you, that we may discover conditions there which may in some manner alleviate our position. At least we can be no worse off. To live for fifteen years cooped in the hull of this dead ship is unthinkable. I may speak only for myself, but to me it would be highly preferable to die immediately than to live on thus, knowing that there was no hope of rescue. Had Orthis not destroyed the radio outfit we could have communicated with Earth and another ship been outfitted and sent to our rescue inside a year. But now we cannot tell them, and they will never know our fate. The emergency that has arisen has, however, so altered conditions that I do not feel warranted in taking this step without consulting you gentlemen. It is a matter now largely of the duration of our lives. I cannot proceed upon the mission upon which I have been dispatched, nor can I return to Earth. I wish, therefore, that you would express yourselves freely concerning the plan which I have outlined."

West, who was the senior among them, was naturally the one to reply first. He told me that he was content to go wherever I led, and Jay and Norton in turn signified a similar willingness to abide by whatever decision I might reach. They also assured me that they were as keen to explore the surface of the Moon at close range as I, and that they could think of no better way of spending the remainder of their lives than in the acquisition of new experiences and the observation of new scenes.

"Very well, Mr. Norton," I said, "you will set your course directly toward the Moon."

Aided by lunar gravity our descent was rapid.

As we plunged through space at a terrific speed, the satellite seemed to be leaping madly toward us, and at the end of fifteen hours I gave orders to slack off and brought the ship almost to a stop about nine thousand feet above the summit of the higher lunar peaks. Never before had I gazed upon a more awe-inspiring scene than that presented by those terrific peaks towering five miles above the broad valleys at their feet. Sheer cliffs of three and four thousand feet were nothing uncommon, and all was rendered weirdly beautiful by the variegated colors of the rocks and the strange prismatic hues of the rapidly growing vegetation upon the valley floors. From our lofty elevation above the peaks we could see many craters of various dimensions, some of which were huge chasms, three and four miles in diameter. As we descended slowly we drifted directly over one of these abysses, into the impenetrable depths of which we sought to strain our eyesight. Some of us believed that we detected a faint luminosity far below, but of that we could not be certain. Jay thought it might be the reflected light from the molten interior. I was confident that had this been the case there would have been a considerable rise of temperature as we passed low across the mouth of the crater.

At this altitude we made an interesting discovery. There is an atmosphere surrounding the Moon. It is extremely tenuous, but yet it was recorded by our barometer at an altitude of about fifteen hundred feet above the highest peak we crossed. Doubtless in the valleys and deep ravines, where the vegetation thrived, it is denser, but that I do not know, since we never landed upon the surface of the Moon. As the ship drifted we presently noted that it was taking a circular course paralleling the rim of the huge volcanic crater above which we were descending. I immediately gave orders to alter our course since, as we were descending constantly, we should presently be below the rim of the crater and, being unable to rise, be hopelessly lost in its huge maw.

It was my plan to drift slowly over one of the larger valleys as we descended, and make a landing amidst the vegetation which we perceived growing in riotous profusion and movement beneath us. But when West, whose watch it now was, attempted to alter the course of the ship, he found that it did not respond. Instead it continued to move slowly in a great circle around the inside rim of the crater. At the moment of this discovery we were not much more than five hundred feet above the summit of the volcano, and we were constantly, though slowly, dropping. West looked up at us, smiled, and shook his head.

"It is no use, sir," he said, addressing me. "It is about all over, sir, and there won't even be any shouting. We seem to be caught in what one might call a lunar whirlpool, for you will have noticed, sir, that our circles are constantly growing smaller."

"Our speed does not seem to be increasing," I remarked, "as would follow were we approaching the vortex of a true whirlpool."

"I think I can explain it, sir," said Norton. "It is merely due to the action of the Lunar Eighth Ray which still remains in the forward buoyancy tank. Its natural tendency is to push itself away from the Moon, which, as far as we are concerned, is represented by the rim of this enormous crater. As each portion of the surface repels us in its turn we are pushed gently along in a lessening circle, because, as we drop nearer the summit of the peak the greater the reaction of the Eighth Lunar Ray. If I am not mistaken in my theory our circle will cease to narrow after we have dropped beneath the rim of the crater."

"I guess you are right, Norton," I said. "At least it is a far more tenable theory than that we are being sucked into the vortex of an enormous whirlpool. There is scarcely enough atmosphere for that, it seems to me."

As we dropped slowly below the rim of the crater the tenability of Norton's theory became more and more apparent, for presently, though our speed increased slightly, the diameter of our circular course remained constant, and, at a little greater depth, our speed as well. We were descending now at the rate of a little over ten miles an hour, the barometer recording a constantly increasing atmospheric pressure, though nothing approximating that necessary to the support of life upon Earth. The temperature rose slightly, but not alarmingly. From a range of twenty-five or thirty below zero, immediately after we had entered the shadow of the crater's interior, it rose gradually to zero at a point some one hundred and twenty-five miles below the summit of the giant extinct volcano that had engulfed us.

During the next ten miles our speed diminished rapidly, until we suddenly realized that we were no longer falling, but that our motion had been reversed and we were rising. Up we went for approximately eight miles, when suddenly we began to fall again. Again we fell, but this time for only six miles, when our motion was reversed and we rose again a distance of about four miles. This seesawing was continued until we finally came to rest at about what we estimated was a distance of some one hundred and thirty miles below the summit of the crater. It was quite dark, and we had only our instruments to tell us of what was happening to the ship, the interior of which was, of course, brilliantly illuminated and comfortably warm.

Now below us, and now above us, for the ship had rolled completely over each time we had passed the point at which we came finally to rest, we had noted the luminosity that Norton had first observed from above the mouth of the crater. Each of us had been doing considerable thinking, and at last young Norton could contain himself no longer.

"I beg your pardon, sir," he said deferentially, "but won't you tell us what you think of it; what your theory is as to where we are and why we hang here in midair, and why the ship rolled over every time we passed this point?"

"I can only account for it," I replied, "upon a single and rather preposterous hypothesis, which is that the Moon is a hollow sphere, with a solid crust some two hundred and fifty miles in thickness. Gravity is preventing us from rising above the point where we now are, while centrifugal force keeps us from falling."

The others nodded. They too had been forced to accept the same apparently ridiculous theory, since there was none other that could explain our predicament. Norton had walked across the room to read the barometer which he had rather neglected while the ship had been performing her eccentric antics far below the surface of the Moon. I saw his brows knit as he glanced at it, and then I saw him studying it carefully, as though to assure himself that he had made no mistake in the reading. Then he turned toward us.

"There must be something wrong with this instrument, sir," he said. "It is registering pressure equivalent to that at the Earth's surface."

I walked over and looked at the instrument. It certainly was registering the pressure that Norton had read, nor did there seem to be anything wrong with the instrument.

"There is a way to find out," I said. "We can shut down the insulating generator and open an air cock momentarily. It won't take five seconds to determine whether the barometer is correct or not." It was, of course, in some respects a risky proceeding, but with West at the generator, Jay at the air cock and Norton at the pump I knew that we would be reasonably safe, even if there proved to be no atmosphere without. The only danger lay in the chance that we were hanging in a poisonous gas of the same density as the earthly atmosphere, but as there was no particular incentive to live in the situation in which we were, we each felt that no matter what chance we might take it would make little difference in the eventual outcome of our expedition.

I tell you that it was a very tense moment as the three men took their posts to await my word of command. If we had indeed discovered a true atmosphere beneath the surface of the Moon, what more might we not discover? If it were an atmosphere, we could propel the ship in it, and we could, if nothing more, go out on deck to breathe fresh air. It was arranged that at my word of command West was to shut off the generator, Jay to open the air cock, and Norton to start the pump. If fresh air failed to enter through the tube Jay was to give the signal, whereupon Norton would reverse the pump, West start the generator, and immediately Jay would close the air cock again.

As Jay was the only man who was to take a greater chance than the others, I walked over and stood beside him, placing my nostrils as close to the air cock as his. Then I gave the word of command. Everything worked perfectly and an instant later a rush of fresh, cold air was pouring into the hull of *The Barsoom*. West and Norton had been watching the effects upon our faces closely, so that they knew almost as soon as we did that the result of our test had been satisfactory. We were all smiles, though just why we were so happy I am sure none of us could have told. Possibly it was just because we had found a condition that was identical with an earthly condition, and though we might never see our world again we could at least breathe air similar to hers.

I had them start the motors again then, and presently we were moving in a great spiral upward toward the interior of the Moon. Our progress was very slow, but as we rose the temperature rose slowly, too, while the barometer showed a very slightly decreasing atmospheric pressure. The luminosity, now above us, increased as we ascended, until finally the sides of the great well through which we were passing became slightly illuminated.

All this time Orthis had remained in irons in his stateroom. I had given instructions that he was to be furnished food and water, but no one was to speak to him, and I had taken Norton into my stateroom with me. Knowing Orthis to be a drunkard, a traitor and a potential murderer I had no sympathy whatsoever for him. I had determined to court-martial him and did not intend to spend the few remaining hours or years of my life cooped up in a small ship with him, and I knew that the verdict of any court, whether composed of the remaining crew of *The Barsoom* or appointed by the Judge Advocate General of the Navy, could result in but one thing, and that was death for Orthis. I had left the matter, however, until we were not pressed with other matters of greater importance, and so he still lived, though he shared neither in our fears, our hopes, nor our joys.

About twenty-six hours after we entered the mouth of the crater at the surface of the Moon we suddenly emerged from its opposite end to look upon a scene that was as marvelous and weird, by comparison with the landscape upon the surface of the Moon, as the latter was in comparison with that of our own Earth. A soft, diffused light revealed to us in turn mountains, valleys and sea, the details of which were more slowly encompassed by our minds. The mountains were as rugged as those upon the surface of the satellite, and appeared equally as lofty. They were, however, clothed with verdure almost to their summits, at least a few that were within our range of vision. And there were forests, too—strange forests, of strange trees, so unearthly in appearance as to suggest the weird phantasmagoria of a dream.

We did not rise much above five hundred feet from the opening of the well through which we had come from outer space when I descried an excellent landing place and determined to descend. This was readily accomplished, and we made a safe landing close to a large forest and near the bank of a small stream. Then we opened the forward hatch and stepped out upon the deck of *The Barsoom*, the first Earth Men to breathe the air of Luna. It was, according to Earth time, eleven A.M., January 8, 2026.

I think that the first thing which engaged our interest and attention was the strange, and then, to us, unaccountable luminosity which pervaded the interior of the Moon. Above us were banks of fleecy clouds, the undersurfaces of which appeared to be lighted from beneath, while, through breaks in the cloud banks we could discern a luminous firmament beyond, though nowhere was there any suggestion of a central incandescent orb radiating light and heat as does our sun. The clouds themselves cast no shadows upon the ground, nor, in fact, were there any well-defined shadows even directly beneath the hull of the ship or surrounding the forest trees which grew close at hand. The shadows were vague and nebulous, blending off into nothingness at their edges. We ourselves cast no more shadows upon the deck of *The Barsoom* than would have been true upon a cloudy day on Earth. Yet the general illumination surrounding us approximated that of a very slightly hazy Earth day. This peculiar lunar light interested us profoundly, but it was some time before we discovered the true explanation of its origin. It was of two kinds, emanating from widely different sources, the chief of which was due to the considerable radium content of the internal lunar soil, and principally of the rock forming the loftier mountain ranges, the radium being so combined as to diffuse a gentle perpetual light which pervaded the entire interior of the Moon.

The secondary source was sunlight, which penetrated to the interior of the Moon through the hundreds of thousands of huge craters penetrating the lunar crust. It was this sunlight which carried heat to the inner world, maintaining a constant temperature of about eighty degrees Fahrenheit.

Centrifugal force, in combination with the gravity of the Moon's crust, confined the internal lunar atmosphere to a blanket which we estimated at about fifty miles in thickness over the inner surface of this buried world. This atmosphere rarefies rapidly as one ascends the higher peaks, with the result that these are constantly covered with perpetual snow and ice, sending great glaciers down mighty gorges toward the central seas. It is this condition which has probably prevented the atmosphere, confined as it is within an almost solid sphere, from becoming superheated, through the unthinkable ages that this condition must have existed. The Earth seasons are reflected but slightly in the Moon, there being but a few degrees difference between summer and winter. There are, however, periodic windstorms, which recur with greater or less regularity once each sidereal month, due, I imagine, to the unequal distribution of crater openings through the crust of the Moon, a fact which must produce an unequal absorption of heat at various times and in certain localities. The natural circulation of the lunar atmosphere, affected as it is by the constantly changing volume and direction of the Sun's rays, as well as the great range of temperature between the valleys and the ice-clad mountain peaks, produces frequent storms of greater or less violence. High winds are accompanied by violent rains upon the lower levels and blinding snowstorms among the barren heights above the vegetation line. Rains which fall from low-hanging clouds are warm and pleasant; those which come from high clouds are cold and disagreeable, yet however violent or protracted the storm, the illumination remains practically constant—there are never any dark, lowering days within the Moon, nor is there any night.

CHAPTER THREE
HUMAN QUADRUPEDS

O F COURSE WE DID NOT REACH all these conclusions in a few moments, but I have given them here merely as the outcome of our deductions following a considerable experience within the Moon. Several miles from the ship rose foothills which climbed picturesquely toward the cloudy heights of the loftier mountains behind them, and as we looked in the direction of these latter, and then out across the forest, there was appreciable to us a strangeness that at first we could not explain, but which we later discovered was due to the fact that there was no horizon, the distance that one could see being dependent solely upon one's power of vision. The general effect was of being in the bottom of a tremendous bowl, with sides so high that one might not see the top.

The ground about us was covered with rank vegetation of pale hues— lavenders, violets, pinks and yellows predominating. Pink grasses which became distinctly flesh-color at maturity grew in abundance, and the stalks of most of the flowering plants were of this same peculiar hue. The flowers themselves were often of highly complex form, of pale and delicate shades, of great size and rare beauty. There were low shrubs that bore a berrylike fruit, and many of the trees of the forest carried fruit of considerable size and of a variety of forms and colors. Norton and Jay were debating the possible edibility of some of these, but I gave orders that no one was to taste them until we had had an opportunity to learn by analysis or otherwise those varieties that were nonpoisonous.

There was aboard *The Barsoom* a small laboratory equipped especially for the purpose of analyzing the vegetable and mineral products of Mars according to earthly standards, as well as other means of conducting research work upon our sister planet. As we had sufficient food aboard for a period of fifteen years, there was no immediate necessity for eating any of the lunar fruit, but I was anxious to ascertain the chemical properties of the water since the manufacture of this necessity was slow, laborious and expensive. I therefore instructed West to take a sample from the stream and subject it to laboratory tests, and the others I ordered below for sleep.

They were rather more keen to set out upon a tour of exploration, nor could I blame them, but as none of us had slept for rather better than forty-eight hours I considered it of importance that we recuperate our vital forces against whatever contingency might confront us in this unknown world. Here were air, water and vegetation—the three prime requisites for the support of animal life—and so I judged it only reasonable to assume that animal life existed within the Moon. If it did exist, it might be in some highly predatory form, against which it would tax our resources to the utmost to defend ourselves. I insisted, therefore, upon each of us obtaining his full quota of sleep before venturing from the safety of *The Barsoom*.

We already had seen evidences of life of a low order, both reptile and insect, or perhaps it would be better to describe the latter as flying reptiles, as they later proved to be—toad-like creatures with the wings of bats, that flitted among the fleshy boughs of the forest, emitting plaintive cries. Upon the ground near the ship we had seen but a single creature, though the moving grasses had assured us that there were others there aplenty. The thing that we had seen had been plainly visible to us all and may be best described as a five-foot snake with four frog-like legs, and a flat head with a single eye in the center of the forehead. Its legs were very short, and as it moved along the ground it both wriggled like a true snake and scrambled with its four short legs. We watched it to the edge of the river and saw it dive in and disappear beneath the surface.

"Silly looking beggar," remarked Jay, "and devilish unearthly."

"I don't know about that," I returned. "He possessed nothing visible to us that we are not familiar with on Earth. Possibly he was assembled after a slightly different plan from any Earth creature; but aside from that he is familiar to us, even to his amphibious habits. And these flying-toads, too; what of them? I see nothing particularly remarkable about them. We have just as strange forms on Earth, though nothing precisely like these. Mars, too, has forms of animal and vegetable life peculiar to herself, yet nothing the existence of which would be impossible upon Earth, and she has, as well, human forms almost identical with our own. You see what I am trying to suggest?"

"Yes, sir," replied Jay; "that there may be human life similar to our own within the Moon."

"I see no reason to be surprised should we discover human beings here," I said; "nor would I be surprised to find a reasoning creature of some widely divergent form. I would be surprised, however, were we to find no form analogous to the human race of Earth."

"That is, a dominant race with well-developed reasoning faculties?" asked Norton.

"Yes, and it is because of this possibility that we must have sleep and keep ourselves fit, since we may not know the disposition of these creatures, provided they exist, nor the reception that they will accord us. And so, Mr. Norton, if you will get a receptacle and fetch some water from the stream we will leave Mr. West on watch to make his analysis and the rest of us will turn in."

Norton went below and returned with a glass jar in which to carry the water and the balance of us lined the rail with our service revolvers ready in the event of an emergency as he went over the side. None of us had walked more than a few steps since coming on deck after our landing. I had noticed a slightly peculiar sensation of buoyancy, but in view of the numerous other distractions had given it no consideration. As Norton reached the bottom of the ladder and set foot on lunar soil I called to him to make haste. Just in front of him was a low bush and beyond it lay the river, about thirty feet distant. In response to my command he gave a slight leap to clear the bush and, to our amazement as well as to his own consternation, rose fully eighteen feet into the air, cleared a space of fully thirty-five feet and lit in the river.

"Come!" I said to the others, wishing them to follow me to Norton's aid, and sprang for the rail; but I was too impetuous. I never touched the rail, but cleared it by many feet, sailed over the intervening strip of land, and disappeared beneath the icy waters of the lunar river. How deep it was I do not know; but at least it was over my head. I found myself in a sluggish, yet powerful current, the water seeming to move much as a heavy oil moves to the gravity of Earth. As I came to the surface I saw Norton swimming strongly for the bank and a second later Jay emerged not far from me. I glanced quickly around for West, whom I immediately perceived was still on the deck of *The Barsoom*, where, of course, it was his duty to remain, since it was his watch.

The moment that I realized that my companions were all safe I could not repress a smile, and then Norton and Jay commenced to laugh, and we were still laughing when we pulled ourselves from the stream a short distance below the ship.

"Get your sample, Norton?" I asked.

"I still have the container, sir," he replied, and indeed he had clung to it throughout his surprising adventure, as Jay and I, fortunately, had clung to our revolvers. Norton removed the cap from the bottle and dipped the latter into the stream. Then he looked up at me and smiled.

"I think we have beaten Mr. West to it, sir," he said. "It seems like very good water, sir, and when I struck it I was so surprised that I must have swallowed at least a quart."

"I tested a bit of it myself," I replied. "As far as we three are concerned, Mr. West's analysis will not interest us if he discovers that lunar water contains poisonous matter, but for his own protection we will let him proceed with his investigation."

"It is strange, sir," remarked Jay, "that none of us thought of the natural effects of the lesser gravity of the Moon. We have discussed the matter upon many occasions, as you will recall, yet when we faced the actual condition we gave it no consideration whatsoever."

"I am glad," remarked Norton, "that I did not attempt to jump the river—I should have been going yet. Probably landed on the top of some mountain."

As we approached the ship I saw West awaiting us with a most serious and dignified mien; but when he saw that we were all laughing he joined us, telling us after we reached the deck, that he had never witnessed a more surprising or ludicrous sight in his life.

We went below then and after closing and securing the hatch, three of us repaired to our bunks, while West with the sample of lunar water went to the laboratory. I was very tired and slept soundly for some ten hours, for it was the middle of Norton's watch before I awoke.

The only important entry upon the log since I had turned in was West's report of the results of his analysis of the water, which showed that it was not only perfectly safe for drinking purposes but unusually pure, with an extremely low saline content.

I had been up about a half an hour when West came to me, saying that Orthis requested permission to speak to me. Twenty-four hours before, I had been fairly well determined to bring Orthis to trial and execute him immediately, but that had been when I had felt that we were all hopelessly doomed to death on his account. Now, however, with a habitable world beneath our feet, surrounded by conditions almost identical with those which existed upon Earth, our future looked less dark, and because of this I found myself in a quandary as to what course of action to pursue in the matter of Orthis' punishment. That he deserved death there was no question, but when men have faced death so closely and escaped, temporarily at least, I believe that they must look upon life as a most sacred thing and be less inclined to deny life to others. Be that as it may, the fact remains that having sent for Orthis in compliance with his request I received him in a mood of less stern and uncompromising justice than would have been the case twenty-four hours previous. When he had been brought to my stateroom and stood before me, I asked him what he wished to say to me. He was entirely sober now and bore himself with a certain dignity that was not untinged with humility.

"I do not know what has occurred since I was put in irons, as you have instructed the others not to speak to me or answer my questions. I know, of course, however, that the ship is at rest and that pure air is circulating through it, and I have heard the hatch raised and footsteps upon the upper deck. From the time that has elapsed since I was placed under arrest I know that the only planet upon which we have had time to make a landing is the Moon, and so I may guess that we are upon the surface of the Moon. I have had ample time to reflect upon my actions. That I was intoxicated is, of course, no valid excuse, and yet it is the only excuse that I have to offer. I beg, sir, that you will accept the assurance of my sincere regret of the unforgivable things that I have done, and that you will permit me to live and atone for my wrongdoings, for if we are indeed upon the surface of the Moon it may be that we can ill spare a single member of our small party. I throw myself, sir, entirely upon your mercy, but beg that you will give me another chance."

Realizing my natural antipathy for the man and wishing most sincerely not to be influenced against him because of it, I let his plea influence me against my better judgment with the result that I promised him that I would give the matter careful consideration, discuss it with the others, and be influenced largely by their decision. I had him returned to his stateroom then and sent for the other members of the party. With what fidelity my memory permitted I repeated to them in Orthis' own words his request for mercy.

"And now, gentlemen," I said, "I would like to have your opinions in the matter. It is of as much moment to you as to me, and under the peculiar circumstances in which we are placed, I prefer in so far as possible to defer wherever I can to the judgment of the majority. Whatever my final action, the responsibility will be mine. I do not seek to divide that, and it may be that I shall act contrary to the wishes of the majority in some matters, but in this one I really wish to abide by your desires because of the personal antagonism that has existed between Lieutenant Commander Orthis and myself since boyhood."

I knew that none of these men liked Orthis, yet I knew, too, that they would approach the matter in a spirit of justice tempered by mercy, and so I was not at all surprised when one after another they assured me that they would be glad if I would give the man another opportunity.

Again I sent for Orthis, and after explaining to him that inasmuch as he had given me his word to commit no disloyal act in the future I should place him on parole, his eventual fate depending entirely upon his own conduct; then had his irons removed and told him that he was to return to duty. He seemed most grateful and assured us that we would never have cause to regret our decision. Would to God that instead of freeing him I had drawn my revolver and shot him through the heart!

We were all pretty well rested up by this time, and I undertook to do a little exploring in the vicinity of the ship, going out for a few hours each day with a single companion, leaving the other three upon the ship. I never went far afield at first, confining myself to an area some five miles in diameter between the crater and the river. Upon both sides of the latter, below where the ship had landed, was a considerable extent of forest. I ventured into this upon several occasions and once, just about time for us to return to the ship, I came upon a well-marked trail in the dust of which were the imprints of three-toed feet. Each day I set the extreme limit of time that I would absent myself from the ship with instructions that two of those remaining aboard should set out in search of me and my companion, should we be absent over the specified number of hours. Therefore, I was unable to follow the trail the day upon which I discovered it, since we had scarcely more than enough time to make a brief examination of the tracks if we were to reach the ship within the limit I had allowed.

It chanced that Norton was with me that day and in his quiet way was much excited by our discovery. We were both positive that the tracks had been made by a four-footed animal, something that weighed between two hundred and fifty and three hundred pounds. How recently it had been used we could scarcely estimate, but the trail itself gave every indication of being a very old one. I was sorry that we had no time to pursue the animal which had made the tracks but determined that upon the following day I should do so. We reached the ship and told the others what we had discovered. They were much interested and many and varied were the conjectures as to the nature of the animals whose tracks we had seen.

After Orthis had been released from arrest Norton had asked permission to return to the former's stateroom. I had granted his request and the two had been very much together ever since. I could not understand Norton's apparent friendship for this man, and it almost made me doubt the young ensign. One day I was to learn the secret of this intimacy, but at the time I must confess that it puzzled me considerably and bothered me not a little, for I had taken a great liking to Norton and disliked to see him so much in the company of a man of Orthis' character.

Each of the men had now accompanied me on my short excursions of exploration with the exception of Orthis. Inasmuch as his parole had fully reinstated him among us in theory at least, I could not very well discriminate against him and leave him alone of all the others aboard ship as I pursued my investigations of the surrounding country.

The day following our discovery of the trail, I accordingly invited him to accompany me, and we set out early, each armed with a revolver and a rifle. I advised West, who automatically took command of the ship during my absence, that we might be gone considerably longer than usual and that he was to feel no apprehension and send out no relief party unless we should be gone a full twenty-four hours, as I wished to follow up the spoor we had discovered, learn where the trail led and have a look at the animal that had made it.

I led the way directly to the spot at which we had found the trail, about four miles downriver from the ship and apparently in the heart of dense forest.

The flying-toads darted from tree to tree about us, uttering their weird and plaintive cries, while upon several occasions, as in the past, we saw four-legged snakes such as we had seen upon the day of our landing. Neither the toads nor the snakes bothered us, seeming only to wish to avoid us.

Just before we came upon the trail, both Orthis and I thought we heard the sound of footsteps ahead of us—something similar to that made by a galloping animal—and when we came upon the trail a moment later it was apparent to both of us that dust was hanging in the air and slowly settling on the vegetation nearby. Something, therefore, had passed over the trail but a minute or two before we arrived. A brief examination of the spoor revealed the fact that it had been made by a three-toed animal whose direction of travel was to our right and toward the river, at this point some half mile from us.

I could not help but feel considerable inward excitement, and I was sorry that one of the others had not been with me, for I never felt perfectly at ease with Orthis. I had done considerable hunting in various parts of the world where wild game still exists but I had never experienced such a thrill as I did at the moment that I undertook to stalk this unknown beast upon an unknown trail in an unknown world. Where the trail would lead me, what I should find upon it, I never knew from one step to another, and the lure of it because of that was tremendous. The fact that there were almost nine million square miles of this world for me to explore, and that no Earth Man had ever before set foot upon an inch of it, helped a great deal to compensate for the fact that I knew I could never return to my own Earth again.

The trail led to the edge of the river which at this point was very wide and shallow. Upon the opposite shore, I could see the trail again directly opposite and I knew therefore that this was a ford. Without hesitating, I stepped into the river, and as I did so I glanced to my left to see stretching before me as far as my eye could reach a vast expanse of water. Here then I had stumbled upon the mouth of the river and, beyond, a lunar sea.

The land upon the opposite side of the river was rolling and grass-covered, but in so far as I could see, almost treeless. As I turned my eyes from the sea back toward the opposite shore, I saw that which caused me to halt in my tracks, cock my rifle and issue a cautious warning to Orthis for silence, for there before us upon a knoll stood a small horselike animal.

It would have been a long shot, possibly five hundred yards, and I should have preferred to have come closer but there was no chance to do that now, for we were in the middle of the river in plain view of the animal which stood there watching us intently. I had scarcely raised my rifle, however, ere it wheeled and disappeared over the edge of the knoll upon which it had been standing.

"What did it look like to you, Orthis?" I asked my companion.

"It was a good ways off," he replied, "and I only just got my binoculars on it as it disappeared, but I could have sworn that it wore a harness of some sort. It was about the size of a small pony, I should say, but it didn't have a pony's head."

"It appeared tailless to me," I remarked.

"I saw no tail," said Orthis, "nor any ears or horns. It was a devilish funny looking thing. I don't understand it. There was something about it—" he paused. "My God, sir, there was something about it that looked human."

"It gave me that same impression, too, Orthis, and I doubt if I should have fired had I been able to cover it, for just at the instant that I threw my rifle to my shoulder I felt that same strange impression that you mention. There was something human about the thing."

As we talked, we had been moving on across the ford which we found an excellent one, the water at no time coming to our waists while the current was scarcely appreciable. Finally, we stepped out on the opposite shore and a moment later, far to the left, we caught another glimpse of the creature that we had previously seen. It stood upon a distant knoll, evidently watching us.

Orthis and I raised our binoculars to our eyes almost simultaneously and for a full minute we examined the thing as it stood there, neither of us speaking, and then we dropped our glasses and looked at each other.

"What do you make of it, sir?" he asked.

I shook my head. "I don't know what to make of it, Orthis," I replied; "but I should swear that I was looking straight into a human face, and yet the body was that of a quadruped."

"There can be no doubt of it, sir," he replied, "and this time one could see the harness and the clothing quite plainly. It appears to have some sort of a weapon hanging at its left side. Did you notice it, sir?"

"Yes, I noticed it, but I don't understand it."

A moment longer we stood watching the creature until it turned and galloped off, disappearing behind the knoll on which it had stood. We decided to follow the trail which led in a southerly direction, feeling reasonably assured that we were more likely to come in contact with the creature or others similar to it upon the trail than off of it. We had gone but a short distance when the trail approached the river again, which puzzled me at the time somewhat, as we had gone apparently directly away from the river since we had left the ford, but after we had gone some mile and a half, we found the explanation, since we came again to another ford while on beyond we saw the river emptying into the sea and realized that we had crossed an island lying in the mouth of the river.

I was hesitating as to whether to make the crossing and continue along the trail or to go back and search the island for the strange creature we had discovered. I rather hoped to capture it, but since I had finally descried its human face, I had given up all intention of shooting it unless I found that it would be necessary to do so in self-defense. As I stood there, rather undecided, our attention was attracted back to the island by a slight noise, and as we looked in the direction of the disturbance, we saw five of the creatures eyeing us from high land a quarter of a mile away. When they saw that they were discovered they galloped boldly toward us. They had come a short distance only, when they stopped again upon a high knoll, and then one of them raised his face toward the sky and emitted a series of piercing howls. Then they came on again toward us nor did they pause until they were within fifty feet of us, when they came to a sudden halt.

CHAPTER FOUR
IN THE HANDS OF THE VA-GAS

OUR FIRST VIEW OF THE CREATURES proved beyond a question of a doubt that they were in effect human quadrupeds. The faces were very broad, much broader than any human faces that I have ever seen, but their profiles were singularly like those of the ancient North American Indians. Their bodies were covered with a garment with short legs that ended above the knees, and which was ornamented about the collar and also about the bottom of each leg with a rather fanciful geometric design. About the barrel of each was a surcingle and connected with it by a backstrap was something analogous to a breeching in Earth horse harness. Where the breeching straps crossed on either side, was a small circular ornament, and there was a strap resembling a trace leading from this forward to the collar, passing beneath a quite large, circular ornament, which appeared to be supported by the surcingle. Smaller straps, running from these two ornaments upon the left side, supported a sheath in which was carried what appeared to be a knife of some description. And upon the right side a short spear was carried in a boot, similarly suspended from the two ornaments, much as the carbine of our ancient Earth cavalry was carried. The spear, which was about six feet long, was of peculiar design, having a slender, well-shaped head, from the base of which a crescent-shaped arm curved backward from one side, while upon the side opposite the crescent was a short, sharp point at right angles to the median line of the weapon.

For a moment we stood there eyeing each other, and from their appearance I judged that they were as much interested in us as we were in them. I noticed that they kept looking beyond us, across the river toward the mainland. Presently, I turned for a glance in the same direction, and far away beyond a thin forest I saw a cloud of dust which seemed to be moving rapidly toward us. I called Orthis' attention to it.

"Reinforcements," I said. "That is what that fellow was calling for when he screamed. I think we had better try conclusions with the five before any more arrive. We will try to make friends first, but if we are unsuccessful we must fight our way back toward the ship at once."

Accordingly, I stepped forward toward the five with a smile upon my lips and my hand outstretched. I knew of no other way in which to carry to them an assurance of our friendliness. At the same time, I spoke a few words in English in a pleasant and conciliatory tone. Although I knew that my words would be meaningless to them, I hoped that they would catch their intent from my inflection.

Immediately upon my advance, one of the creatures turned and spoke to another, indicating to us for the first time that they possessed a spoken language. Then he turned and addressed me in a tongue that was, of course, utterly meaningless to me; but if he had misinterpreted my action, I could not misunderstand that which accompanied his words, for he reared up on his hind feet and simultaneously drew his spear and a wicked-looking, short-bladed sword or dagger, his companions at the same time following his example, until I found myself confronted by an array of weapons backed by scowling, malignant faces. Their leader uttered a single word which I interpreted as meaning halt, and so I halted.

I pointed to Orthis and to myself, and then to the trail along which we had come, and then back in the direction of the ship. I was attempting to tell them that we wished to go back whence we had come. Then I turned to Orthis.

"Draw your revolver," I said, "and follow me. If they interfere we shall have to shoot them. We must get out of this before the others arrive."

As we turned to retrace our steps along the trail, the five dropped upon all fours, still holding their weapons in their forepaws, and galloped quickly to a position blocking our way.

"Stand aside," I yelled, and fired my pistol above their heads. From their actions, I judged that they had never before heard the report of a firearm, for they stood an instant in evident surprise, and then wheeled and galloped off for about a hundred yards, where they turned and halted again, facing us. They were still directly across our trail, and Orthis and I moved forward determinedly toward them. They were talking among themselves, and at the same time watching us closely.

When we had arrived at a few yards from them, I again threatened them with my pistol, but they stood their ground, evidently reassured by the fact that the thing that I held in my hand, though it made a loud noise, inflicted no injury. I did not want to shoot one of them if I could possibly avoid it, so I kept on toward them, hoping that they would make way for us; but instead they reared again upon their hind feet and threatened us with their weapons.

Just how formidable their weapons were, I could not, of course, determine; but I conjectured that if they were at all adept in its use, their spear might be a very formidable thing indeed. I was within a few feet of them now, and their attitude was more warlike than ever, convincing me that they had no intention of permitting us to pass peacefully.

Their features, which I could now see distinctly, were hard, fierce, and cruel in the extreme. Their leader seemed to be addressing me, but, of course, I could not understand him; but when, at last, standing there upon his hind feet, with evidently as much ease as I stood upon my two legs, he carried his spear back in a particularly menacing movement, I realized that I must act and act quickly.

I think the fellow was just on the point of launching his spear at me, when I fired. The bullet struck him square between the eyes, and he dropped like a log, without a sound. Instantly, the others wheeled again and galloped away, this time evincing speed that was almost appalling, clearing spaces of a hundred feet in a single bound, even though handicapped, as they must have been, by the weapons which they clutched in their forepaws.

A glance behind me showed the dust cloud rapidly approaching the river, upon the mainland, and calling to Orthis to follow me, I ran rapidly along the trail which led back in the direction of the ship.

The four Moon creatures retreated for about half a mile, and then halted and faced us. They were still directly in our line of retreat, and there they stood for a moment, evidently discussing their plans. We were nearing them rapidly, for we had discovered that we, too, could show remarkable speed, when retarded by gravity only one-sixth of that of Earth. To clear forty feet at a jump was nothing, our greatest difficulty lying in a tendency to leap to too great heights, which naturally resulted in cutting down our horizontal distance. As we neared the four, who had taken their stand upon the summit of a knoll, I heard a great splashing in the river behind us, and turning, saw that their reinforcements were crossing the ford, and would soon be upon us. There appeared to be fully a hundred of them, and our case looked hopeless indeed, unless we could manage to pass the four ahead of us, and reach the comparative safety of the forest beyond the first ford.

"Commence firing, Orthis," I said. "Shoot to kill. Take the two at the left as your targets, and I'll fire at the two at the right. We had better halt and take careful aim, as we cannot afford to waste ammunition."

We came to a stop about twenty-five yards from the foremost creature, which is a long pistol shot; but they were standing still upon the crest of a knoll, distinctly outlined against the sky, and were such a size as to present a most excellent target. Our shots rang out simultaneously. The creature at the left, at which Orthis had aimed, leaped high into the air, and fell to the ground, where it lay kicking convulsively. The one at the right uttered a piercing shriek, clutched at its breast, and dropped dead. Then Orthis and I charged the remaining two, while behind us we heard loud weird cries and the pounding of galloping feet. The two before us did not retreat this time, but came to meet us, and again we halted and fired. This time they were so close that we could not miss them, and the last of our original lunar foemen lay dead before us.

We ran then, ran as neither of us had imagined human beings ever could run. I know that I covered over fifty feet in many a leap, but by comparison with the speed of the things behind us, we might have been standing still. They fairly flew over the lavender sward, indicating that those, which we had first seen, had at no time extended themselves in an effort to escape us. I venture to say that some of them leaped fully three hundred feet at a time, and now, at every bound, they emitted fierce and terrible yells, which I assumed to be their war cry, intended to intimidate us.

"It's no use, Orthis," I said to my companion. "We might as well make our stand here and fight it out. We cannot reach the ford. They are too fast for us."

We stopped then, and faced them, and when they saw we were going to make a stand, they circled and halted about a hundred yards distant, entirely surrounding us. We had killed five of their fellows, and I knew we could hope for no quarter. We were evidently confronted by a race of fierce and warlike creatures, the appearance of which, at least, gave no indication of the finer characteristics that are so much revered among humankind upon Earth. After a good look at one of them, I could not imagine the creature harboring even the slightest conception of the word mercy, and I knew that if we ever escaped that fierce cordon, it would be by fighting our way through it.

"Come," I said to Orthis, "straight through for the ford," and turning again in that direction, I started blazing away with my pistol as I walked slowly along the trail. Orthis was at my side, and he, too, fired as rapidly as I. Each time our weapons spoke, a Moon Man fell. And now, they commenced to circle us at a run, much as the Indians of the western plains circled the parked wagon trains of our long-gone ancestors in North America. They hurled spears at us, but I think the sound of our revolvers and the effect of the shots had to some measure unnerved them, for their aim was poor and we were not, at any time, seriously menaced.

As we advanced slowly, firing, we made many hits, but I was horrified to see that every time one of the creatures fell, the nearest of his companions leaped upon him and cut his throat from ear to ear. Some of them had only to fall to be dispatched by his fellows. A bullet from Orthis' weapon shattered the hind leg of one of them, bringing him to the ground. It was, of course, not a fatal wound, but the creature had scarcely gone down, when the nearest to him sprang forward, and finished him. And thus we walked slowly toward the ford, and I commenced to have hope that we might reach it and make our escape. If our antagonists had been less fearless, I should have been certain of it, but they seemed almost indifferent to their danger, evidently counting upon their speed to give them immunity from our bullets. I can assure you that they presented most difficult targets, moving as they did in great leaps and bounds. It was probably more their number than our accuracy that permitted us the hits we made.

We were almost at the ford when the circle suddenly broke, and then formed a straight line parallel to us, the leader swinging his spear about his head, grasping the handle at its extreme end. The weapon moved at great speed, in an almost horizontal plane. I was wondering at the purpose of his action, when I saw that three or four of those directly in the rear of him had commenced to swing their spears in a similar manner. There was something strangely menacing about it that filled me with alarm. I fired at the leader and missed, and at the report of my pistol, a half dozen of them let go of their swift whirling spears, and an instant later, I realized the purpose of their strange maneuver; for the heavy weapons shot toward us, butts first, with the speed of lightning, the crescent-like hooks catching us around a leg, an arm and the neck, hurling us backward to the ground, and each time we essayed to rise, we were struck again, until we finally lay there, bruised and half stunned, and wholly at the mercy of our antagonists, who galloped forward quickly, stripping our weapons from us. Those who had hurled their spears at us recovered them, and then they all gathered about, examining us, and jabbering among themselves.

Presently, the leader spoke to me, prodding me with the sharp point of his spear. I took it that he wanted me to arise, and I tried to do so, but I was pretty much all in and fell back each time I essayed to obey. Then he spoke to two of his followers, who lifted me and laid me across the back of a third. There I was fastened in a most uncomfortable position by means of leather straps which were taken from various parts of the harnesses of several of the creatures. Orthis was similarly lashed to another of them, whereupon they moved slowly back in the direction from which they had come, stopping, as they went, to collect the bodies of their dead, which were strapped to the backs of others of their companions. The fellow upon whom I rode had several well-defined gaits, one of which, a square trot, was the acme of torture for me, since I was bruised and hurt and had been placed across him face down, upon my belly; but inasmuch as this gait must have been hard, too, upon him, while thus saddled with a burden, he used it but little, for which I was tremendously thankful. When he changed to a single-foot, which, fortunately for me, he often did, I was much less uncomfortable.

As we crossed the ford toward the mainland, it was with difficulty that I kept from being drowned, since my head dragged in the water for a considerable distance and I was mighty glad when we came out again on shore. The thing that bore me was consistently inconsiderate of me, bumping me against others, and against the bodies of their slain that were strapped to the backs of his fellows. He was apparently quite tireless, as were the others, and we often moved for what seemed many miles at a fast run. Of course, my lunar weight was equivalent to only about thirty pounds on Earth while our captors seemed fully as well-muscled as a small earthly horse, and as we later learned, were capable of carrying heavy burdens.

How long we were on the march, I do not know, for where it is always daylight and there is no sun nor other means of measuring time, one may only guess at its duration, the result being influenced considerably by one's mental and physical sensations during the period. Judged by these considerations, then, we might have been on the trail for many hours, for I was not only most uncomfortable in body, but in mind as well. However that may be, I know only that it was a terrible journey; that we crossed rivers twice after reaching the mainland, and came at last to our destination, amid low hills, where there was a level, parklike space, dotted with weird trees. Here the straps were loosened, and we were dumped upon the ground, more dead than alive, and immediately surrounded by great numbers of creatures who were identical with those who had captured us.

When I was finally able to sit up and look about, I saw that we were at the threshold of a camp or village, consisting of a number of rectangular huts, with high-peaked roofs, thatched or rather shingled, with the broad, round leaves of the trees that grew about.

We saw now for the first time the females and the young. The former were similar to the males, except that they were of lighter build, and they were far more numerous. They had udders, with from four to six teats, and many of them were followed by numerous progeny, several that I saw having as high as six young in a litter. The young were naked, but the females wore a garment similar to that worn by the males, except that it was less ornate, as was their harness and other trappings. From the way the women and children rushed upon us as we were unloaded in camp, I felt that they were going to tear us to pieces, and I really believe they would have had not our captors prevented. Evidently the word was passed that we were not to be injured, for after the first rush they contented themselves with examining us, and sometimes feeling of us or our clothing, the while they discussed us, but with the bodies of those who were slain, it was different, for when they discovered these where they had been unloaded upon the ground, they fell upon them and commenced to devour them, the warriors joining them in the gruesome and terrible feast. Orthis and I understood now that they had cut the throats of their fellows to let the blood, in anticipation of the repast to come.

As we came to understand them and the conditions under which they lived, many things concerning them were explained. For example, at least two-thirds of the young that are born are males, and yet there are only about one-sixth as many adult males, as there are females. They are naturally carnivorous, but with the exception of one other creature upon which they prey, there is no animal in that part of the interior lunar world with which I am familiar, that they may eat with safety. The flying-toad and the walking snake and the other reptilia are poisonous, and they dare not eat them. The time had been, I later learned, possibly, however, ages before, when many other animals roamed the surface of the inner Moon, but all had become extinct except our captors and another creature, of which we, at the time of our capture, knew nothing, and these two preyed upon one another, while the species which was represented by those into whose hands we had fallen, raided the tribes and villages of their own kind for food, and ate their own dead, as we had already seen. As it was the females to whom they must look for the production of animal food, they did not kill these of their own species and never ate the body of one. Enemy women of their own kind, whom they captured, they brought to their villages, each warrior adding to his herd the individuals that he captured. As only the males are warriors, and as no one will eat the flesh of a female, the mortality among the males is, accordingly, extremely high, accounting for the vastly greater number of adult females. The latter are very well treated, as the position of a male in a community is dependent largely upon the size of his herd.

The principal mortality among the females results from three causes— raids by the other flesh-eating species which inhabit the inner lunar world, quarrels arising from jealousy among themselves, and death while bringing forth their young, especially during lean seasons when their warriors have been defeated in battle and have been unable to furnish them with flesh.

These creatures eat fruit and herbs and nuts as well as meat, but they do not thrive well upon these things exclusively. Their existence, therefore, is dependent upon the valor and ferocity of their males whose lives are spent in making raids and forays against neighboring tribes and in defending their own villages against invaders.

As Orthis and I sat watching the disgusting orgy of cannibalism about us, the leader of the party that had captured us came toward us from the center of the village, and speaking a single word, which I later learned meant come, he prodded us with his spearpoint until finally we staggered to our feet. Repeating the word, then, he started back into the village.

"I guess he wants us to follow him, Orthis," I said. And so we fell in behind the creature, which was evidently what he desired, for he nodded his head, and stepped on in the direction that he had taken, which led toward a very large hut—by far the largest in the village.

In the side of the hut presented to us there seemed to be but a single opening, a large door covered by heavy hanging, which our conductor thrust aside as we entered the interior with him. We found ourselves in a large room, without any other opening whatsoever, save the doorway through which we had entered, and over which the hanging had again been drawn, yet the interior was quite light, though not so much so as outside, but there were no means for artificial lighting apparent. The walls were covered with weapons and with the skulls and other bones of creatures similar to our captors, though Orthis and I both noticed a few skulls much narrower than the others and which, from their appearance, might have been the human skulls of Earth Men, though in discussing it later, we came to the conclusion that they were the skulls of the females and the young of the species, whose faces are not so wide as the adult male.

Lying upon a bed of grasses at the opposite side of the room was a large male whose skin was of so much deeper lavender hue than the others that we had seen, as to almost suggest a purple. The face, though badly disfigured by scars, and grim and ferocious in the extreme, was an intelligent one, and the instant that I looked into those eyes, I knew that we were in the presence of a leader. Nor was I wrong, for this was the chief or king of the tribe into whose clutches Fate had thrown us.

A few words passed between the two, and then the chief arose and came toward us. He examined us very critically, our clothing seeming to interest him tremendously. He tried to talk with us, evidently asking us questions, and seemed very much disgusted when it became apparent to him that we could not understand him, nor he us, for Orthis and I spoke to one another several times, and once or twice addressed him. He gave some instructions to the fellow who had brought us, and we were taken out again, and to another hut, to which there was presently brought a portion of the carcass of one of the creatures we had killed before we were captured. I could not eat any of it, however, and neither could Orthis; and after a while, by signs and gestures, we made them understand that we wished some other kind of food, with the result that a little later, they brought us fruit and vegetables, which were more palatable and, as we were to discover later, sufficiently nutritious to carry us along and maintain our strength.

I had become thirsty, and by simulating drinking, I finally succeeded in making plain to them my desire in that direction, with the result that they led us out to a little stream which ran through the village, and there we quenched our thirst.

We were still very weak and sore from the manhandling we had received, but we were both delighted to discover that we were not seriously injured, nor were any of our bones broken.

CHAPTER FIVE
A LUNAR STORM

SHORTLY AFTER WE ARRIVED at the village, they took away our watches, our pocketknives, and everything that we possessed of a similar nature, and which they considered as curiosities. The chief wore Orthis' wristwatch above one forepaw and mine above the other, but as he did not know how to wind them, nor the purpose for which they were intended, they did him or us no good. The result was, however, that it was now entirely impossible for us to measure time in any way, and I do not know, even to this day, how long we were in this strange village. We ate when we were hungry, and slept when we were tired. It was always daylight; and it seemed that there were always raiding parties going out or returning, so that flesh was plentiful, and we became rather reconciled to our fate, in so far as the immediate danger of being eaten was concerned, but why they kept us alive, as we had slain so many of their fellows, I could not understand.

It must have been immediately after we arrived that they made an attempt to teach us their language. Two females were detailed for this duty. We were given unlimited freedom within certain bounds, which were well indicated by the several sentries which constantly watched from the summit of hills surrounding the village. Past these we could not go, nor do I know that we had any particular desire to do so, since we realized only too well that there would be little chance of our regaining the ship should we escape the village, inasmuch as we had not the remotest idea in what direction it lay.

Our one hope lay in learning their language, and then utilizing our knowledge in acquiring some definite information as to the surrounding country and the location of *The Barsoom*.

It did not seem to take us very long to learn their tongue, though, of course, I realize that it may really have been months. Almost before we knew it, we were conversing freely with our captors. When I say freely, it is possible that I exaggerate a trifle, for though we could understand them fairly well, it was with difficulty that we made ourselves understood, yet we managed it some way, handicapped as we were by the peculiarities of the most remarkable language of which I have any knowledge.

It is a very difficult language to speak, and as a written language, would be practically impossible. For example, there is their word *gu-e-ho*, for which Orthis and I discovered twenty-seven separate and distinct meanings, and that there are others I have little or no doubt. Their speech is more aptly described as song, the meaning of each syllable being governed by the note in which it is sung. They speak in five notes, which we may describe as A, B, C, D and E. *Gu* sung in A means something radically different from *gu* sung in E, and again if *gu*, is sung in A, followed by *e* in G, it means something other than if *gu* had been sung in D followed by *e* in A.

Fortunately for us, there are no words of over three syllables, and most of them consist of only one or two, or we should have been entirely lost. The resulting speech, however, is extremely beautiful, and Orthis used to say that if he closed his eyes, he could imagine himself living constantly in grand opera.

The chief's name, as we learned, was Ga-va-go; the name of the tribe or village was No-vans, while the race to which they belonged was known as Va-gas.

When I felt that I had mastered the language sufficiently well to make myself at least partially understood, I asked to speak to Ga-va-go, and shortly thereafter, I was taken to him.

"You have learned our speech?" he asked.

I nodded in the affirmative. "I have," I said, "and I have come to ask why we are held captives and what you intend to do with us. We did not come to seek a quarrel with you. We wish only to be friends, and to be allowed to go our way in peace."

"What manner of creature are you," he asked, "and where do you come from?"

I asked him if he had ever heard of the Sun or the stars or the other planets or any worlds outside his own, and he replied that he had not, and that there were no such things.

"But there are, Ga-va-go," I said, "and I and my companion are from another world, far, far outside your own. An accident brought us here. Give us back our weapons, and let us go."

He shook his head negatively.

"Where you come from, do you eat one another?" he asked.

"No," I replied, "we do not."

"Why?" he asked, and I saw his eyes narrow as he awaited my reply.

Was it mental telepathy or just luck that put the right answer in my mouth, for somehow, intuitively, I seemed to grasp what was in the creature's mind.

"Our flesh is poison," I said, "those who eat it die."

He looked at me then for a long time, with an expression upon his face which I could not interpret. It may have been that he doubted my word, or again, it may have been that my reply confirmed his suspicion, I do not know; but presently he asked me another question.

"Are there many like you in the land where you live?"

"Millions upon millions," I replied.

"And what do they eat?"

"They eat fruits and vegetables and the flesh of animals," I answered.

"What animals?" he asked.

"I have seen no animals here like them," I replied, "but there are many kinds unlike us, so that we do not have to eat flesh of our own race."

"Then you have all the flesh that you want?"

"All that we can eat," I replied. "We raise these animals for their flesh."

"Where is your country?" he demanded. "Take me to it."

I smiled. "I cannot take you to it," I said. "It is upon another world."

It was quite evident that he did not believe me, for he scowled at me ferociously.

"Do you wish to die?" he demanded.

I told him that I had no such longing.

"Then you will lead me to your country," he said, "where there is plenty of flesh for everyone. You may think about it until I send for you again. Go!" And thus he dismissed me. Then he sent for Orthis, but what Orthis told him, I never knew exactly, for he would not tell me, and as our relations, even in our captivity, were far from friendly, I did not urge him to any confidences. I had occasion to notice, however, that from that time Ga-va-go indicated a marked preference for Orthis, and the latter was often called to his hut.

I was momentarily expecting to be summoned in to Ga-va-go's presence, and learn my fate, when he discovered that I could not lead him to my country, where flesh was so plentiful. But at about this time we broke camp, and in the press of other matters, he evidently neglected to take any further immediate action in my case, or at least, so I thought, until I later had reason to suspect that he felt that he need no longer depend upon me to lead him to this land of milk and honey.

The Va-gas are a nomadic race, moving hither and thither, either as they are pressed by some foes, or till their victories have frightened away the other tribes from their vicinity, in either of which events, they march in search of fresh territory. The move that we made now was necessitated by the fact that all the other tribes nearby had fled before the ferocity of the No-vans, whose repeated and successful raids had depleted the villages of their neighbors and filled them with terror.

The breaking of camp was a wonderfully simple operation. All their few belongings, consisting of extra clothing, trappings, weapons, and their treasured skulls and bones of victims, were strapped to the backs of the women. Orthis and I each bestrode a warrior detailed by Ga-va-go for the purpose of transporting us, and we filed out of the village, leaving the huts behind.

Ga-va-go, with a half-dozen warriors, galloped far ahead. Then came a strong detachment of warriors, with the women folks behind them, another detachment of warriors following in the rear of the women and children, while others rode upon either flank. A mile or so in the rear, came three warriors, and there were two or three scattered far out on either flank. Thus we moved, thoroughly protected against surprise, regulating our speed by that of the point with which Ga-va-go traveled.

Because of the women and the children, we moved more slowly than warriors do when on the march alone, when they seldom, if ever, travel slower than a trot, and more generally, at a fast gallop. We moved along a well-worn trail, passing several deserted villages, from which the prey of the No-vans had fled. We crossed many rivers, for the lunar world is well watered. We skirted several lakes, and at one point of high ground, I saw, far at our left, the waters of what appeared to be a great ocean.

There was never a time when Orthis and I were not plentifully supplied with food, for there is an abundance of it growing throughout all the territory we crossed, but the No-vans had been without flesh for several days and were, in consequence, mad with hunger, as the fruits and vegetables which they ate seemed not to satisfy them at all.

We were moving along at a brisk trot when, without warning, we were struck by a sudden gust of wind that swept, cold and refreshing, down from some icy mountain fastness. The effect upon the No-vans was electrical. I would not have had to understand their language to realize that they were terrified. They looked apprehensively about and increased their speed as though endeavoring to overtake Ga-va-go, who was now far ahead with the point. A moment later a dash of rain struck us, and then it was every man for himself and the devil take the hindmost, as they broke into a wild stampede to place themselves close to their chief. Their hysterical flight was like the terrorized rush of wild cattle. They jostled and tripped one another, and stumbled and fell and were trampled upon, in their haste to escape.

Old Ga-va-go had stopped with his point, and was waiting for us. Those who accompanied him seemed equally terrified with the rest, but evidently they did not dare run until Ga-va-go gave the word. I think, however, that they all felt safer when they were close to him, for they had a great deal of confidence in him, yet they were still pretty badly frightened, and it would not have taken much to have set them off again into another rout. Ga-va-go waited until the last of the rearguard straggled in, and then he set off directly toward the mountains, the entire tribe moving in a compact mass, though they might have fallen easy prey to an ambush or any sudden attack. They knew, however, what I half guessed, that knowing that their enemies were as terrified of the storm as they, there was little danger of their being attacked—none whatever, in fact.

We came at last to a hillside covered with great trees which offered some protection from both the wind and the rain, which had now arisen to the proportion of a hurricane.

As we came to a halt, I slipped from the back of the warrior who had been carrying me, and found myself beside one of the women who had taught Orthis and me the language of the Va-gas.

"Why is everyone so terrified?" I asked her.

"It is Zo-al," she whispered, fearfully. "He is angry."

"Who is Zo-al?" I asked.

She looked at me in wide-eyed astonishment. "Who is Zo-al!" she repeated. "They told me that you said that you came from another world, and I can well believe it, when you ask, who is Zo-al?"

"Well, who is he?" I insisted.

"He is a great beast," she whispered. "He is everywhere. He lives in all the great holes in the ground, and when he is angry, he comes forth and makes the water fall and the air run away. We know that there is no water up there," and she pointed toward the sky. "But when Zo-al is angry, he makes water fall from where there is no water, so mighty is Zo-al, and he makes the air to run away so that the trees fall before it as it rushes past, and huts are knocked flat or carried high above the ground. And then, O terror of terrors, he makes a great noise, before which mighty warriors fall upon the ground and cover up their ears. We have angered Zo-al, and he is punishing us, and I do not dare to ask him not to send the big noise."

It was at that instant that there broke upon my ears the most terrific detonation that I have ever heard. So terrific was it that I thought my eardrums had burst, and simultaneously, a great ball of fire seemed to come rolling down from the mountain heights above us.

The woman, covering her ears, shuddered, and when she saw the ball of fire, she voiced a piercing shriek.

"The light that devours!" she cried. "When that comes too, it is the end, for then is Zo-al mad with rage."

The ground shook to the terrifying noise, and though the ball of fire did not pass close to us, still could I feel the heat of it even as it went by at a distance, leaving a trail of blackened and smoking vegetation in its rear. What flames there were, the torrential rain extinguished almost immediately. It must have traveled about ten miles, down toward the sea, across rolling hills and level valleys, when suddenly it burst, the explosion being followed by a report infinitely louder than that which I had first heard. An earthquake could scarce have agitated the ground more terrifyingly than did this peal of lunar thunder.

I had witnessed my first lunar electrical storm, and I did not wonder that the inhabitants of this strange world were terrified by it. They attribute these storms, as they do all their troubles, to Zo-al, a great beast, which is supposed to dwell in the depth of the lunar craters, the lower ends of which open into the interior lunar world. As we cowered there among the trees, I wondered if they were not afraid that the wind would blow the forest down and crush them, and I asked the woman who stood beside me.

"Yes," she said, "that often happens, but more often does it happen that if one is caught in a clearing, the air that runs away picks him up and carries him along to drop him from a great height upon the hard ground. The trees bend before they break, and those who watch are warned, and they escape destruction if they are quick. When the wind that runs seizes one, there is no escape."

"It seems to me," I said, "that it would have been safer if Ga-va-go had led us into one of those sheltered ravines," and I indicated a gorge in the hillside at our right.

"No," she said, "Ga-va-go is wise. He led us to the safest spot. We are sheltered from the air that runs away, and perhaps a little from the light that devours, nor can the waters that drown, reach us here, for presently they will fill that ravine full."

Nor was she wrong. Rushing down from the hillside, the water poured in torrents into the ravine, and presently, though it must have been twenty or thirty feet deep, it was filled almost to overflowing. Whoever had sought refuge there, would have been drowned and washed away to the big ocean far below. It was evident that Ga-va-go had not been actuated solely by blind terror, though I came to know that he must have felt terror, for these terrible electrical storms alone can engender it in the breasts of these fearless and ferocious people.

The storm must have lasted for a considerable time; how long, of course, I do not know, but some idea of its duration may be gained by the fact that I became hungry and ate of the fruit of the trees, which sheltered us, at least six times, and slept twice. We were soaked to the skin and very cold, for the rain evidently came from a great altitude. During the entire storm, the No-vans scarcely moved from their positions beneath the trees, with their backs toward the storm, where they stood with lowered heads like cattle. We experienced twelve detonations of the ground-shaking thunder, and witnessed six manifestations of the light that devours. Trees had fallen all about us, and as far as we could see, the grasses lay flat and matted upon the ground. They told me that storms of the severity of this were infrequent, though rain and wind, accompanied

by electrical manifestations, might be expected at any season of the year—I
use that expression from habit, for one can scarcely say that there are any
well-marked seasonal changes within the Moon that could indicate corresponding divisions of time as upon the Earth. From what I was able to
gather from observation and from questioning the Va-gas, lunar vegetation
reproduces itself entirely independent of any seasonal restrictions, the
frequency and temperature of the rains having, seemingly, the greatest
influence in the matter. A period of drought and cold rains retards growth
and germination, while frequent warm rains have an opposite effect, the
result being that you find vegetation of the same variety in all stages of
development, growing side by side—blossoms upon one tree, fruit upon
another, and the dry seedpods upon a third. Not even, therefore, by the
growth of plant life, might one measure time within the Moon, and the
period of gestation among the Va-gas is similarly irregular, being affected
by the physical condition of the female as well as by climatic conditions,
I imagine. When the tribe is well-fed, and the weather warm, the warriors
victorious, and the minds of the women at peace, they bring forth their
young in an incredibly short period. On the other hand, a period of cold,
or of hunger, and of long marches, following defeat, induces an opposite
result. It seems to me that the females nurse their young for a very short
period of time, for they grow rapidly, and as soon as their molars are
through, and they can commence eating meat, they are weaned. They are
devilish little rascals, their youthful exuberance finding its outlet in acts
of fiendish cruelty. As they are not strong enough to inflict their tortures
on adults they perpetrate them upon one another, with the result that
the weaker are often killed, after they are weaned and have left the protection of their savage mothers. Of course, they tried to play some of their
fiendish tricks on Orthis and myself, but after we had knocked a few of
them down, they left us severely alone.

During the storm, they huddled, shivering and cold, against the adults.
Possibly I should be ashamed to say it, but I felt no pity for them, and
rather prayed that they would all be chilled to death, so hateful and
wantonly cruel were they. As they become adults, they are less wanton in
their atrocities, though no less cruel, their energies, however, being intel-
ligently directed upon the two vital interests of their lives—procuring
flesh and women.

Shortly after the rain ceased, the wind began to abate, and as I was cold, cramped and uncomfortable, I walked out into the open, in search of exercise that would stimulate my circulation and warm me again. As I walked briskly to and fro, looking here and there at the evidences of the recent storm, my glance chanced to rise toward the sky, and there I saw what appeared at first to be a huge bird, a few hundred feet above the forest in which we had sought shelter. It was flapping its great wings weakly and seemed to be almost upon the verge of exhaustion, and though I could see that it was attempting to fly back in the direction of the mountains, the force of the wind was steadily carrying it in the direction of the lowlands and the sea. Presently it would be directly above me, and as it drew nearer, I knit my brows in puzzlement, for except for its wings, and what appeared to be a large hump upon its back, its form bore a striking resemblance to that of a human being.

Some of the No-vans evidently saw me looking upwards thus interestedly, and prompted by curiosity, joined me. When they saw the creature flying weakly overhead, they set up a great noise, until presently all the tribe had run into the open and were looking up at the thing above us.

The wind was lessening rapidly, but it still was strong enough to carry the creature gently toward us, and at the same time I perceived that whatever it was, it was falling slowly to the ground, or more correctly, sinking slowly.

"What is it?" I asked of the warrior standing beside me.

"It is a U-ga," he replied. "Now shall we eat."

I had seen no birds in the lunar world, and as I knew they would not eat the flying reptiles, I guessed that this must be some species of bird life, but as it dropped closer, I became more and more convinced that it was a winged human being, or at least a winged creature with human form.

As it fluttered toward the ground, the No-vans ran along to meet it, waiting for it to fall within reach. As they did so, Ga-va-go called to them to bring the creature to him alive and unharmed.

I was about a hundred yards from the spot, when the poor thing finally fell into their clutches. They dragged it to the ground roughly, and a moment later I was horrified to see them tear its wings from it and the hump from its back. There was a great deal of grumbling at Ga-va-go's order, as following the storm and their long fast, the tribe was ravenously hungry.

"Flesh, flesh!" they growled. "We are hungry. Give us flesh!" But Ga-va-go paid no attention to them, standing to one side beneath a tree, awaiting the prisoner that they were bringing toward him.

CHAPTER SIX
AN EXODUS AND A BATTLE

ORTHIS, WHO WAS BECOMING the almost constant companion of the chief, was standing beside the latter, while I was twenty-five or thirty yards away, and directly between Ga-va-go and the warriors who were approaching with the prisoner, who would of necessity have to pass close beside me. I remained where I was, therefore, in order to get a better look at it, which was rather difficult because it was almost entirely surrounded by No-vans. However as they came opposite me, there was a little break momentarily in the ranks, and I had my first opportunity, though brief, for a closer observation of the captive; and my comprehension was almost staggered by what my eyes revealed to me, for there before me, was as perfectly formed a human female as I had ever seen. By earthly standards, she appeared a girl of about eighteen, with hair of glossy blackness, that suggested more the raven's wing than aught else and a skin of almost marble whiteness, slightly tinged with a creamy shade. Only in the color of her skin, did she differ from earthly women in appearance, except that she seemed far more beautiful than they. Such perfection of features seemed almost unbelievable. Had I seen her first posed motionless, I could have sworn that she was chiseled from marble, yet there was nothing cold about her appearance. She fairly radiated life and feeling. If my first impression had been startling, it was nothing to the effect that was produced when she turned her eyes full upon me. Her black brows were two thin, penciled arches, beneath which were dark wells of light, vying in blackness with her raven hair. On either cheek was just the faintest suggestion of a deeper cream, and to think that these hideous creatures saw in that form divine only flesh to eat! I shuddered at the thought and then my eyes met hers and I saw an expression of incredulity and surprise registered in those liquid orbs. She half-turned her head as she was dragged past, that she might have a further look at me, for doubtless she was as surprised to see a creature like me as I was to see her.

Involuntarily I started forward. Whether there was an appeal for succor in those eyes I do not know, but at least they aroused within me instantly, that natural instinct of a human male to protect the weak. And so

223

it was that I was a little behind her and to her right, when she was halted before Ga-va-go.

The savage Va-gas' chieftain eyed her coldly, while from all sides there arose cries of "Give us flesh! Give us flesh! We are hungry!" to which Ga-va-go paid not the slightest attention.

"From whence come you, U-ga?" he demanded.

Her head was high, and she eyed him with cold dignity as she replied, "From Laythe."

The No-van raised his brows. "Ah," he breathed, "from Laythe. The flesh of the women from Laythe is good," and he licked his thin lips.

The girl narrowed her eyes, and tilted her chin a bit higher. "Rympth!" she ejaculated, disgustedly.

As rympth is the name of the four-legged snake of Va-nah, the inner lunar world, and considered the lowest and most disgusting of created things, she could not well have applied a more opprobrious epithet to the No-van chieftain, but if it had been her intent to affront him, his expression gave no indication that she had succeeded.

"Your name?" he asked.

"Nah-ee-lah," she replied.

"Nah-ee-lah," he repeated, "Ah, you are the daughter of Sagroth, Jemadar of Laythe."

She nodded in indifferent affirmation, as though aught he might say was a matter of perfect indifference to her.

"What do you expect us to do with you?" asked Ga-va-go, a question which suggested a cat playing with a mouse before destroying it.

"What can I expect of the Va-gas, other than that they will kill me and eat me?" she replied.

A roar of savage assent arose from the creatures surrounding her. Ga-va-go flashed a quick look of anger and displeasure at his people.

"Do not be too sure of that," he snapped. "This be little more than a meal for Ga-va-go alone. It would but whet the appetite of the tribe."

"There are two more," suggested a bold warrior, close beside me, pointing at me and at Orthis.

"Silence!" roared Ga-va-go. "Since when did you become chief of the No-vans?"

"We can starve without a chief," muttered the warrior who had spoken, and from two or three about him arose grumblings of assent.

Swift, at that, Ga-va-go reared upon his hind feet, and in the same motion, drew and hurled his spear, the sharp point penetrating the breast of the malcontent, piercing his heart. As the creature fell, the warrior closest to him slit his throat, while another withdrew Ga-va-go's spear from the corpse, and returned it to the chief.

"Divide the carcass among you," commanded the chief, "and whosoever thinks that there is not enough, let him speak as that one spoke, and there shall be more flesh to eat."

Thus did Ga-va-go, chief of the No-vans, hold the obedience of his savage tribesmen. There was no more muttering then, but I saw several cast hungry eyes at me—hungry, angry eyes that boded me no good.

In what seemed an incredibly short space of time, the carcass of the slain warrior had been divided and devoured, and once again we set out upon the march, in search of new fields to conquer, and fresh flesh to eat.

Now Ga-va-go sent scouts far in advance of the point, for we were entering territory which he had not invaded for a long time, a truth which was evidenced by the fact that there were only about twenty warriors in the tribe, besides Ga-va-go, who were at all familiar with the territory. Naturally quarrelsome and disagreeable, the No-vans were far from pleasant companions upon that memorable march, since they had not recovered from the fright and discomforts of the storm and, in addition, were ravenously hungry. I imagine that none, other than Ga-va-go, could have held them. What his purpose was in preserving the three prisoners, that would have made such excellent food for the tribe, I did not know. However, we were not slain, though I judged the fellow who carried me, would much sooner have eaten me, and to vent his spite upon me he trotted as much as he could, and I can assure you that he had the most devilishly execrable trot I ever sat. I felt that he was rather running the thing into the ground, for he had an easy rack, which would have made it much more comfortable for both of us, and inasmuch as I knew that I was safe as long as I was under Ga-va-go's protection, I made up my mind to teach the fellow a lesson, which I finally did, although almost as much to my discomfort as his, by making no effort to ease myself upon his back so that at every step I rose high and came down hard upon him, sitting as far back as possible so as to pound his kidneys painfully. It made him very angry and he threatened me with all kinds of things if I didn't desist, but I only answered by suggesting that he take an easier gait, which at last he was forced to do.

Orthis was riding ahead with Ga-va-go, who as usual led the point, while the new prisoner astride a No-van warrior was with the main body, as was I.

Once the warriors that we bestrode paced side by side, and I saw the girl eyeing me questioningly. She seemed much interested in the remnants of my uniform, which must have differed greatly from any clothing she had seen in her own world. It seemed that she spoke and understood the same language that Ga-va-go used, and so at last I made bold to address her.

"It is unfortunate," I said, "that you have fallen into the hands of these creatures. I wish that I might be of service to you, but I also am a prisoner."

She acknowledged my speech with a slight inclination of her head, and at first I thought that she was not going to reply, but finally looking me full in the face she asked, "What are you?"

"I am one of the inhabitants of the planet Earth."

"Where is that, and what is planet?" she asked, for I had had to use the Earth word, since there is no word of similar meaning in the language of the Va-gas.

"You know, of course," I said, "that space outside of Va-nah is filled with other worlds. The closest to Va-nah is Earth, which is many, many times larger than your world. It is from Earth that I come."

She shook her head. "I do not understand," she said. She closed her eyes, and waved her hands with a gesture that might have included the universe. "All, all, is rock," she said, "except here in the center of everything, in this space we call Va-nah. All else is rock."

I suppressed a smile at the vast egotism of Va-nah, but yet how little different is it from many worldings, who conceive that the entire cosmos exists solely for the inhabitants of Earth. I even know men in our own enlightened twenty-first century, who insist that Mars is not inhabited and that the messages that are purported to come from our sister planet, are either the evidences of a great world hoax, or the voice of the devil luring people from belief in the true God.

"Did you ever see my like in Va-nah?" I asked her.

"No," she replied, "I never did, but I have not been to every part of Va-nah. Va-nah is a very great world, and there are many corners of it of which I know nothing."

"I am not of Va-nah," I told her again, "I am from another world far, far away"; and then I tried to explain something of the universe to her—of the Sun and the planets and their satellites, but I saw that it was as far beyond her as are the conceptions of eternity and space beyond the finite mind of Earth Men. She simply couldn't get it, that was all. To her, everything was solid rock that we know as space. She thought for a long time, though, and then she said, "Ah, perhaps after all there may be other worlds than Va-nah. The great Hoos, those vast holes that lead into the eternal rock, may open into other worlds like Va-nah. I have heard that theory discussed, but no one in Va-nah believes it. It is true, then!" she exclaimed brightly, "and you come from another world like Va-nah. You came through one of the Hoos, did you not?"

"Yes, I came through one of the Hoos," I replied—the word means hole in the Va-gas tongue—"but I did not come from a world like Va-nah. Here you live upon the inside of a hollow sphere. We Earth Men live upon the outside of a similar though much larger sphere."

"But what holds it up?" she cried, laughing. It was the first time that she had laughed, and it was a very contagious laugh, and altogether delightful. Although I knew that it would probably be useless, I tried to explain the whole thing to her, commencing with the nebular hypothesis, and winding up with the relations that exist between the Moon and the Earth. If I didn't accomplish anything else, I at least gave her something to distract her mind from her grave predicament, and to amuse her temporarily, for she laughed often at some of my statements. I had never seen so gay and vivacious a creature, nor one so entirely beautiful as she. The single, sleeveless, tunic-like garment that she wore, fell scarcely to her knees and as she bestrode the No-van warrior, it often flew back until her thighs, even, were exposed. Her figure was divinely perfect, its graceful contours being rather accentuated than hidden by the diaphanous material of her dainty covering; but when she laughed, she exposed two rows of even white teeth that would be the envy of the most beautiful of Earth Maids.

"Suppose," she said, "that I should take a handful of gravel and throw it up in the air. According to your theory the smaller would all commence to revolve about the larger and they would go flying thus wildly around in the air forever, but that is not what would happen. If I threw a handful of gravel into the air it would fall immediately to the ground again, and if the worlds you tell me of were cast thus into the air, they too would fall, just as the gravel falls."

It was useless, but I had known that from the beginning. What would be more interesting would be to question her, and that I had wished to do for some time, but she always put me off with a pretty gesture and a shake of her head, insisting that I answer some of her questions instead, but this time I insisted.

"Tell me, please," I asked, "how you came to the spot where you were captured, how you flew, and what became of your wings, and why, when they tore them from you, it did not injure you?"

She laughed at that quite merrily.

"The wings do not grow upon us," she explained, "we make them and fasten them upon our arms."

"Then you can support yourself in the air with wings fastened to your arms?" I demanded, incredulously.

"Oh, no," she said, "the wings we use simply for propelling ourselves through the air. In a bag, upon our backs, we carry a gas that is lighter than air. It is this gas which supports us, and we carry it in such quantities as to maintain a perfect equilibrium, so that we may float at any altitude, or with our wings rise or fall gently; but as I hovered over Laythe, came the air that runs, and seizing me with its strong arms bore me off across the surface of Va-nah. Futilely I fought against it until I was spent and weak, and then it dropped me into the clutches of the Va-gas, for the gas in my bag had become depleted. It was not intended to carry me aloft for any great length of time." She had used a word which, when I questioned her, she explained so that I understood that it meant time, and I asked her what she meant by it and how she could measure it, since I had seen no indication of the Va-gas having any conception of a measurable aspect of duration.

Nah-ee-lah explained to me that the Va-gas, who were a lower order, had no means of measuring time, but that the U-ga, the race to which she belonged, had always been able to compute time through their observation of the fact that during certain periods the bottoms of the Hoos, or craters, were illuminated, and for another period they were dark, and so they took as a unit of measure the total period from the beginning of this light in a certain crater to its beginning again, and this they called a *ula*, which corresponds with a sidereal month. By mechanical means they divide this into a hundred parts, called *ola*, the duration of each of which is about six hours and thirty-two minutes Earth time. Ten ulas make a *keld*, which one might call the lunar year of about two hundred and seventy-two days Earth time.

I asked her many questions and took great pleasure in her answers, for she was a bright, intelligent girl, and although I saw many evidences of regal dignity about her, yet her manner toward me was most natural and unaffected, and I could not help but feel that she occupied a position of importance among her own people.

Our conversation was suddenly interrupted, however, by a messenger from the point, who came racing back at tremendous speed, carrying word from Ga-va-go that the scouts were signaling that they had discovered a large village, and that the warriors were to prepare to fight.

Immediately we moved up rapidly to Ga-va-go, and then we all advanced toward the scout who could be seen upon a knoll far ahead. We were cautioned to silence, and as we moved at a brisk canter over the soft, pale lavender vegetation of the inner Moon, the feet of the Va-gas giving forth no sound, the picture presented to my earthly eyes was weird and mysterious in the extreme.

When we reached the scout, we learned that the village was situated just beyond a low ridge not far distant, so Ga-va-go gave orders that the women, the children, and the three prisoners should remain under a small guard where we were until they had topped the ridge, when we were to advance to a position where we might overlook the village, and if the battle was against the No-vans we could retreat to a point which he indicated to the warriors left to guard us. This was to be the rendezvous, for following defeat the Va-gas warriors scatter in all directions, thus preventing any considerable body of them being attacked and destroyed by a larger body of the pursuing enemy.

As we stood there upon the knoll, watching Ga-va-go and his savage warriors galloping swiftly toward the distant ridge, I could not but wonder that the inhabitants of the village which they were about to attack had not placed sentinels along the ridge to prevent just such a surprise as this, but when I questioned one of the warriors who had been left to guard us, he said that not all the Va-gas tribes were accustomed to posting sentinels when they felt themselves reasonably safe from attack. It had always been Ga-va-go's custom, however, and to it they attributed his supremacy among the other Va-gas tribes over a large territory.

"After a tribe has made a few successful raids and returned victorious, they are filled with pride," the warrior explained to me, "and presently they begin to think that no one dares to attack them and then they grow careless, and little by little the custom of posting sentinels drops into disuse. The very fact that they have no sentinels indicates that they are a large, powerful and successful tribe. We shall feed well for a long time."

The very idea of the thought that was passing through his mind, was repellent in the extreme, and I fairly shuddered when I contemplated the callousness with which this creature spoke of the coming orgy, in which he hoped to devour flesh of his own kind.

Presently we saw our force disappear beyond the ridge, and then we too, advanced, and as we moved forward there came suddenly to us, from the distance the fierce and savage war cry of the No-vans and a moment later it was answered by another no less terrible, rising from the village beyond the ridge. Our guards hastened us then, to greater speed, until, at a full run, we mounted the steep slope of the ridge and halted upon its crest.

Below us lay a broad valley, and in the center a long, beautiful lake, the opposite shore of which was clothed in forest while that nearest us was open and parklike, dotted here and there with beautiful trees, and in this open space we descried a large village.

The ferocity of the scene below us was almost indescribable. The No-vans warriors were circling the village at a rapid run, attempting to keep the enemy in a compact mass within, where it would present a better target for their spears. Already the ground was dotted with corpses. There were no wounded, for whenever one fell the nearest to him whether friend or foe cut his throat, since the victors would devour them all without partiality. The females and the young had taken refuge in the huts, from the doorways of which they watched the progress of the battle. The defenders attempted repeatedly to break through the circling No-vans. The warrior with whom I had been talking told me that if they were successful the females and the young would follow them through the break scattering in all directions, while their warriors attempted to encircle the No-vans. It was almost immediately evident that the advantage lay with the force that succeeded in placing this swift-moving circle about its enemy, and keeping the enemy within it until they had been dispatched, for those in the racing circle presented a poor target, while the compact mass of warriors milling in the center could scarce be missed.

Following several unsuccessful attempts to break through the ring of savage foemen the defenders suddenly formed another smaller ring within, and moving in the opposite direction to the No-vans, raced in a rapid circle. No longer did they cast spears at the enemy, but contented themselves with leaping and bounding at a rapid gait. At first it seemed to me that they had lost their heads with terror, but at last I realized that they were executing a strategic maneuver which demonstrated both cunning and high discipline. In the earlier stages of the battle each side had depended for its weapons upon those hurled by the opposing force, but now the defenders hurled no weapons, and it became apparent that the No-vans would soon no longer have spears to cast at them. The defenders were also lessening their casualties by moving in a rapid circle in a direction opposite to that taken by the attackers, but it must have required high courage and considerable discipline to achieve this result since it is difficult in the extreme to compel men to present themselves continuously as living targets for a foe while they themselves are permitted to inflict no injury upon the enemy.

Ga-va-go apparently was familiar with the ruse, for suddenly he gave a loud cry which was evidently a command. Instantaneously, his entire force wheeled in their tracks and raced in the opposite direction paralleling the defenders of the village, and immediately thereafter cast their remaining spears at comparatively easy targets.

The defenders, who were of the tribe called Lu-thans, wheeled instantly to reverse the direction of their flight. Those wounded in the sudden onslaught stumbled and fell, tripping and impeding the others, with the result that for an instant they were a tangled mass, without order or formation. Then it was that Ga-va-go and his No-vans leaped in upon them with their short, wicked sword-daggers. At once the battle resolved itself into a ferocious and bloody hand-to-hand conflict, in which daggers and teeth and three-toed paws each did their share to inflict injury upon an antagonist. In their efforts to escape a blow, or to place themselves in an advantageous position, many of the combatants leaped high into the air, sometimes between thirty and forty feet. Their shrieks and howls were continuous and piercing. Corpses lay piled so thick as to impede the movements of the warriors, and the ground was slippery with blood, yet on and on they fought, until it seemed that not a single one would be left alive.

"It is almost over," remarked the warrior at my side. "See, there are two or three No-vans now attacking each Lu-than."

It was true, and I saw that the battle could last but a short time. As a matter of fact it ended almost immediately, the remaining Lu-thans suddenly attempting to break away and scatter in different directions. Some of them succeeded in escaping, possibly twenty but I am sure that there were not more than that, and the rest fell.

Ga-va-go and his warriors did not pursue the few who had escaped, evidently considering that it was not worth the effort, since there were not enough of them to menace the village, and there was already plenty of meat lying fresh and warm upon the ground.

We were summoned now, and as we filed down into the village, great was the rejoicing of our females and young.

Guards were placed over the women and children of the defeated Lu-thans, and then at a signal from Ga-va-go, the No-vans fell upon the spoils of war. It was a revolting spectacle, as mothers devoured their sons, and wives, their husbands. I do not care to dwell upon it.

When the victors had eaten their fill, the prisoners were brought forth under heavy guard, and divided by the Va-gas between the surviving No-vans warriors. There was no favoritism shown in the distribution of the prisoners, except that Ga-va-go was given first choice, and received also those that remained after as nearly equal a distribution as possible had been made. I had expected that the male children would be killed, but they were not, being inducted into the tribe upon an equal footing with those that had been born into it.

Being capable of no sentiments of either affection or loyalty, it is immaterial to these creatures to what tribe they belong, but once inducted into a tribe, the instinct of self-preservation holds them to it, since they would be immediately slain by the members of any other tribe.

I learned shortly after this engagement that Ga-va-go had lost fully half his warriors, and that this was one of the most important battles that the tribe had ever fought. The spoils, however, had been rich, for they had taken over ten thousand women and fully fifty thousand young, and great quantities of weapons, harness, and apparel.

The flesh that they could not eat was wrapped up and buried, and I was told that it would remain in excellent condition almost indefinitely.

CHAPTER SEVEN
THE MOON MAID ESCAPES

A FTER OCCUPYING THE NEW VILLAGE, Orthis and I were separated, he being assigned a hut close to Ga-va-go, while I was placed in another section of the village. If I could have been said to have been on good terms with any of the terrible creatures of the tribe, it was with the woman who had taught me the language of the Va-gas, and it was from her that I learned why Orthis was treated with such marked distinction by Ga-va-go, whom, it seemed, he had promised to lead to the land of our origin, where, he had assured the savage chieftain, he would find flesh in abundance.

Nah-ee-lah was confined in still another part of the village, and I only saw her occasionally, for it was evident that Ga-va-go wished to keep the prisoners separated. Upon one occasion when I met her at the shore of the lake I asked her why it was that they had not slain and eaten her, and she told me that when Ga-va-go had discovered her identity, and that her father was a Jemadar, a ruler of a great city, he had sent messengers with an offer to return Nah-ee-lah for a ransom of one hundred young women of the city of Laythe.

"Do you think your father will send the ransom?" I asked.

"I do not know," she replied. "I do not see how they are going to get a message to him, for ordinarily, my race kills the Va-gas on sight. They may succeed, however, but even so, it is possible that my father will not send the ransom. I would not wish him to. The daughters of my father's people are as dear to them, as am I to him. It would be wrong to give a hundred of the daughters of Laythe in return for one, even though she be the daughter of the Jemadar."

We had drunk, and were returning toward our huts when, wishing to prolong our conversation and to be with this pleasant companion while I might, I suggested that we walk farther into the woods and gather fruit. Nah-ee-lah signified her willingness, and together we strolled out of the village into the denser woods at its rear, where we found a particularly delicious fruit growing in abundance. I gathered some and offered it to her, but she refused, thanking me, saying that she had but just eaten.

"Do they bring the fruit to you," I asked, "or do you have to come and gather it yourself?"

"What fruit I eat I gather," she replied, "but they bring me flesh. It is of that which I have just eaten, and so I do not care for fruit now."

"Flesh!" I exclaimed. "What kind of flesh?"

"The flesh of the Va-gas, of course," she replied. "What other flesh might a U-ga eat?"

I fear that I ill-concealed my surprise and disgust at the thought that the beautiful Nah-ee-lah ate of the flesh of the Va-gas.

"You, too, eat of the flesh of these creatures?" I demanded.

"Why not?" she asked. "You eat flesh, do you not, in your own country. You have told me that you raise beasts solely for their flesh."

"Yes," I replied, "that is true, but we eat only the flesh of lower orders; we do not eat the flesh of humans."

"You mean that you do not eat the flesh of your own species," she said.

"Yes," I replied, "that is what I mean."

"Neither do I," she said. "The Va-gas are not of the same species as the U-ga. They are a lower order, just as are the creatures whose flesh you eat in your own country. You have told me of beef, and of mutton, and of pork, which you have described as creatures that run about on four legs, like the Va-gas. What is the difference, then, between the eating of the flesh of pork and beef or mutton, and the eating of Va-gas, who are low creatures also?"

"But they have human faces!" I cried, "and a spoken language."

"You had better learn to eat them," she said, "otherwise you will eat no flesh in Va-nah."

The more I thought about it the more reason I saw in her point of view. She was right. She was no more transgressing any natural law in eating the flesh of the Va-gas than do we, eating the flesh of cattle. To her the Va-gas were less than cattle. They were dangerous and hated enemies. The more I analyzed the thing, the more it seemed to me that we humans of the Earth were more surely transgressing a natural law by devouring our domestic animals, many of which we learned to love, than were the U-ga of Va-nah in devouring the flesh of their four-footed foes, the Va-gas. Upon our earthly farms we raise calves and sheep and little pigs, and oftentimes we become greatly attached to individuals and they to us. We gain their confidence, and they have implicit trust in us, and yet, when they are of the right age, we slay and devour them. Presently it did not seem either wrong or unnatural that Nah-ee-lah should eat the flesh of the Va-gas, but as for myself, I could never do it, nor ever did.

I reverted again to the matter of her ransom. "If it is not paid," I asked, "what will become of you?"

"The Va-gas will eat me," she said simply.

She asked me many questions about my world and its customs, and answered many that I asked her. She was much interested when she learned that our men had but a single wife, for the U-ga, like the Va-gas, have many. She thought that would be very nice, for in Laythe, she said, most of the trouble arose from a man's women quarreling among themselves.

"And you have but one wife, then?" she asked.

"I have none," I replied, "I am not married."

"Why?" she asked.

"I have never fallen in love with anyone," I replied.

"You have no children then? How terrible!" she said.

"Why?" I asked.

"Why?" she repeated. "Because if you die without leaving children, that is the end of you."

"It is the end of me anyway, is it not?" I inquired.

"If we leave children, it is not the end of us," she replied. "We live again in our children's children, maybe many generations later, but at least we have a chance to live again, unless all our children die childless. It is because of this that the U-ga men have so many wives, for the more children they have, the greater assurance that they will live again. I was to have been married just about the time that the air that runs carried me away from Laythe, but now," she sighed, "I shall never have children, and so I shall be dead forever. I am sorry, for I like to live, and I was very anxious to keep on living forever."

Having myself some well-defined convictions upon reincarnation, I was interested in what she said, so I questioned her further, asking her what made her believe she would live again in her posterity, if she had any.

"Because I have lived in the past," she replied. "Is not that sufficient proof that I will live in the future? Do we not, all of us, recall having lived in the past, and therefore, is it not safe for us all to assume that we shall live again?"

"How do you know that you have lived in the past?" I asked.

She looked at me quizzically. "What is my memory given to me for?" she demanded.

"You mean that you can remember past incarnations?" I asked.

"Certainly," she replied. "'Way back in the beginning, ages ago, incarnations far removed are but vague and hazy, and doubtless prior to those are others which I cannot recall at all, but the more recent ones are quite distinct in my memory."

"Have you always been about what you are now?" I asked.

"I have always been a female," she replied, "but not always a princess, nor have I always been of Laythe. I have been slave, commoner, and princess and queen in the past. Sometimes my lives have been happy, and sometimes they have not, but there was always happiness in the thought that I should live again, and in the hope for a great number of happy existences in the future."

We had left the forest, and were returning to the village to our huts when, near the large hut occupied by Ga-va-go, we came suddenly upon Orthis. At the sight of us together he scowled.

"If I were you," he said to me, "I would not associate with her too much. It may arouse the displeasure of Ga-va-go."

It was the first time that Orthis had spoken to me since we had occupied this village. I did not like his tone or his manner.

"You will please to mind your own business, Orthis," I said to him, and continued on with Nah-ee-lah. I saw the man's eyes narrow malignantly, and then he turned, and entered the hut of Ga-va-go, the chief of the No-vans.

Every time I went to the river, I had to pass in the vicinity of Nah-ee-lah's hut. It was a little out of my way, but I always made the slight detour in the hope of meeting her, though I had never entered her hut nor called for her, since she had never invited me and realizing her position, I did not wish to intrude. I was of course ignorant of the social customs of her people, and feared offending her accidentally.

It chanced that the next time that I walked down to the lake shore, following our stroll in the woods, I made my usual detour that I might pass by the hut of Nah-ee-lah. As I came near I heard voices, one of which

I recognized as that of Nah-ee-lah, and the other, a man's voice. The girl's tones were angry and imperious.

"Leave my presence, creature!" were the first words that I could distinguish, and then the man's voice.

"Come," he said, ingratiatingly. "Let us be friends. Come to my hut, and you will be safe, for Ga-va-go is my friend." The voice was the voice of Orthis.

"Go!" she ordered him again. "I would as soon lie with Ga-va-go as with you."

"Know then," cried Orthis, angrily, "that you will go, whether you wish it or not, for Ga-va-go has given you to me. Come!" and then he must have seized her, for I heard her cry out, "How dare you lay hands upon me, Nah-ee-lah, princess of Laythe!"

I was close beside the entrance to the hut now, and I did not wait to hear any more, but thrusting the hanging aside entered. There they were, in the center of the single room, Orthis struggling to drag the girl toward the opening while she resisted and struck at him. Orthis' back was toward me and he did not know that there was another in the hut until I had stepped up behind him and grasping him roughly by the shoulder, had jerked him from the girl and swung him about facing me.

"You cad," I said; "get out of here before I kick you out, and don't ever let me hear of you molesting this girl again."

His eyes narrowed, and he looked at me with an ugly light in them. "Since boyhood, you have cheated me out of all that I wished. You ruined my life on Earth, but now, conditions are reversed. The tables are turned. Believe me, then, when I tell you that if you interfere with me you sign your own death warrant. It is only by my favor that you live at all. If I gave the word Ga-va-go would destroy you at once. Go then to your hut and stop your meddling in the affairs of others—a habit that you developed in a most flagrant degree on Earth, but which will avail you nothing here within the Moon. The woman is mine. Ga-va-go has given her to me. Even if her father should fail to send the ransom her life shall be spared as long as I desire her. Your interference then can only result in your death, and do her no good, for provided you are successful in keeping me from her, you would be but condemning her to death in the event that her father does not send the ransom, and Ga-va-go has told me that there is little likelihood of that, since it is scarcely possible that his messengers will be able to deliver Ga-va-go's demands to Sagroth."

"You have heard him," I said, turning to the girl. "What are your wishes in the matter. Perhaps he speaks the truth."

"I have no doubt but that he speaks the truth," she replied, "but know, strangers, that the honor of a princess of Laythe is dearer than her life."

"Very well, Orthis," I said to the man. "You have heard her. Now get out."

He was almost white with anger, and for a moment I thought that he was going to attack me, but he was ever a coward, and contenting himself with giving me a venomous look, he walked from the hut without another word.

I turned to Nah-ee-lah, after the hanging had dropped behind Orthis. "It is too bad," I said, "that with all your suffering at the hands of the Va-gas, you should also be annoyed by one who is practically of your own species."

"Your kindness more than compensates," she replied graciously. "You are a brave man, and I am afraid that you are going to suffer for your protection of me. This man is powerful. He has made wonderful promises to Ga-va-go. He is going to teach him how to use the strange weapons that you brought from your own world. The woman who brings me my meat told me of all this, and that the tribe is much excited by the promises that your friend has made to Ga-va-go. He will teach them to make the weapons, such as you slew their warriors with, so that they will be invincible, and may go abroad in Va-nah slaying all who oppose them and even raiding the cities of the U-ga. He has told them that he will lead them to the strange thing which brought you from your world to Va-nah, and that there they will find other weapons, like those that you carried, and having the noise which they make, and the things with which they kill. All these he says they may have, and that later he will build other things, such as brought you from your world to Va-nah, and he will take Ga-va-go and all the No-vans to what you call Earth."

"If there is any man in the universe who might do it, it is he," I replied, "but there is little likelihood that he can do it. He is merely deceiving Ga-va-go in the hope of prolonging his own life, against the possibility that an opportunity to escape will develop, in which event he will return to our ship and our friends. He is a bad man though, Nah-ee-lah, and you must be careful of him. There is a vacant hut near yours, and I will come and live in it. There is no use in asking Ga-va-go, for if he is friendly with Orthis, he will not permit me to make the change. If you ever need me, call 'Julian' as loud as you can, and I will come."

"You are very good," she said. "You are like the better men of Laythe, the high nobles of the court of the Jemadar, Sagroth, my father. They too are honorable men, to whom a woman may look for protection, but there are no others in all Va-nah since the Kalkars arose thousands of kelds ago, and destroyed the power of the nobles and the Jemadars, and all the civilization that was Va-nah's. Only in Laythe, have we preserved a semblance of the old order. I wish I might take you to Laythe, for there you would be safe and happy. You are a brave man. It is strange that you are not married."

I was upon the point of making some reply, when the hangings at the doorway parted, and a No-van warrior entered. Behind him were three others. They were walking erect, with drawn spears.

"Here he is," said the leader, and then, addressing me, "Come!"

"Why?" I asked. "What do you want of me?"

"Is it for you to question," he demanded, "when Ga-va-go commands?"

"He has sent for me?" I asked.

"Come!" repeated the leader, and an instant later they had hooked their spears about my arms and neck and none too gently they dragged me from the hut. I had something of a presentiment that this was to be the end. At the doorway I half turned to glance back at the girl. She was standing wide-eyed and tense, watching them drag me away.

"Good-bye—Julian," she said. "We shall never meet again for there is none to carry our souls to a new incarnation."

"We are not dead yet," I called back, "and remember if you need me call me," and then the hanging dropped behind us, and she was shut off from my vision.

They did not take me to my own hut, but to another, not far distant from Nah-ee-lah's, and there they bound my hands and feet with strips of leather and threw me upon the ground. Afterward they left me, dropping the hanging before the entrance. I did not think that they would eat me, for Orthis had joined with me in explaining to Ga-va-go and the others that our flesh was poisonous, and though they may have questioned the veracity of our statements, nevertheless I was quite sure that they would not risk the chance of our having told the truth.

The Va-gas obtain their leather by curing the hides of their dead. The better portions they use for their trappings and harness. The other portions they cut into thin strips, which they use in lieu of rope. Most of this is very strong, but some of it is not, especially that which is improperly cured.

The warriors who had been sent to seize me had scarcely left the hut before I commenced working with my bonds in an attempt to loosen or break them. I exerted all my strength in the effort, until I became sure that those which held my hands were stretching. The effort, however, was very tiring, and I had to stop often and rest. I do not know how long I worked at them, but it must have been a very long time before I became convinced that however much they gave they were not going to break. Just what I intended to do with my freedom I do not know, since there was little or no chance that I might escape from the village. Perpetual daylight has its disadvantages, and this was one of them, that there was no concealing nocturnal darkness during which I might sneak away from the village unseen.

As I lay resting after my exertions, I suddenly became aware of a strange, moaning sound from without, and then the hut shook, and I realized that another storm had come. Soon after I heard the beat of rain drops on the roof, and then a staggering, deafening peal of lunar thunder. As the storm waxed in violence, I could imagine the terror of the No-vans, nor even in my plight could I resist the desire to smile at their discomfiture. I knew that they must all be hiding in their huts, and again I renewed my efforts to break the bonds at my wrists, but all to no avail; and then suddenly, above the moaning of the wind and the beating of the rain, there came distinctly to my ears in a clear, full voice, a single word: "Julian!"

"Nah-ee-lah," I thought. "She needs me. What are they doing to her?" There flashed quickly before my mental vision a dozen scenes, in each of which I saw the divine figure of the Moon Maid, the victim of some fiendish brutality. Now she was being devoured by Ga-va-go; now some of the females were tearing her to pieces, and again the warriors were piercing that beautiful skin with their cruel spears; or it was Orthis, come to claim Ga-va-go's gift. It was this last thought, I think, which turned me almost mad, giving to my muscles the strength of a dozen men. I have always been accounted a powerful man, but in the instant that that sweet voice came across the storm to find me, and my imagination pictured her in the clutches of Orthis, something within moved me to Herculean efforts far transcending aught that I had previously achieved. As though they had been cotton twine now, the leather bonds at my wrists snapped asunder, and an instant later those at my ankles were torn away, and I was upon my feet. I sprang to the door and into the open, where I found myself in a maelstrom of wind and rain. In two bounds I had cleared the space between the hut in which I had been confined and that occupied by Nah-ee-lah, had torn the hanging aside, and had sprung into the interior; and there I beheld the materialization of my last vision—there was Orthis, one arm about the slender body of the girl pinning her arms close to her side, while his other hand was at her throat, choking her and pressing her slowly backward across his knees toward the ground.

He was facing the door this time, and saw me enter, and as he realized who it was, he hurled the girl roughly from him and rose to meet me. For once in his life he seemed to know no fear, and I think that what with his passion for the girl, and the hatred he felt for me, and the rage that my interference must have engendered, he was momentarily insane, for he suddenly leaped upon me like a madman, and for an instant I came near going down beneath his blows—but only for an instant, and then I caught him heavily upon the chin with my left fist, and again, full in the face with my right, and though he was a splendid boxer, he was helpless in my hands. Neither of us had a weapon, or one of us certainly would have been killed in short order. As it was I tried to kill him with my bare fists, and at last, when he had fallen for the dozenth time, and I had picked him up and held him upon his feet and struck him repeatedly again and again, he no longer moved I was sure that he was dead, and it was with a feeling of relief and of satisfaction in a duty well performed that I looked down upon his lifeless body. Then I turned to Nah-ee-lah.

"Come," I said, "there has been given to us this chance for escape. Never again may such a fortuitous combination of circumstances arise. The Va-gas will be hiding in their huts, crouching in terror of the storm. I do not know whither we may fly, but wherever it be, we can be in no greater danger than we are here."

She shuddered a little at the thought of going out into the terrors of the storm. Though not so fearful of it as the ignorant Va-gas, she still feared the wrath of the elements, as do all the inhabitants of Va-nah, but she did not hesitate, and as I stretched out a hand, she placed one of hers within it, and together we stepped out into the swirling rain and wind.

CHAPTER EIGHT
INTO THE MOUTH OF THE CRATER

NAH-EE-LAH AND I passed through the village of the No-vans undetected, since the people of Ga-va-go were cowering in their huts, terror-stricken by the storm. The girl led me immediately to high ground and upward along a barren ridge toward the high mountains in the distance. I could see that she was afraid though she tried to hide it from me, putting on a brave front that I was sure she was far from feeling. My respect for her increased, as I have always respected courage, and I believe that it requires the highest courage to do that which fills one with fear. The man who performs heroic acts without fear is less brave than he who overcomes his cowardice.

Realizing her fear I retained her hand in mine, that the contact might impart to her a little of the confidence that I felt, now that I was temporarily at least out of the clutches of the Va-gas.

We had reached the ridge above the village when the thought that we were weaponless and without means of protection overwhelmed me. I had been in so much of a hurry to escape the village that I had overlooked this very vital consideration. I spoke to Nah-ee-lah about it, telling her that I had best return to the village and make an effort to regain possession of my own weapons and ammunition. She tried to dissuade me, telling me that such an attempt was foredoomed to failure and prophesying that I would be recaptured.

"But we cannot cross this savage world of yours, Nah-ee-lah, without means of protection," I urged. "We do not know at what minute some fierce creature may confront us—think how helpless we shall be without weapons with which to defend ourselves."

"There are only the Va-gas," she said, "to fear in this part of Va-nah. We know no other dangerous beast, except the tor-ho. They are seldom seen. Against the Va-gas your weapons would be useless, as you already have discovered. The risk of meeting a tor-ho is infinitely less than that which you will incur if you attempt to enter Ga-va-go's hut to secure your weapons. You simply could not do it and escape, for doubtless the dwelling of the Chief is crowded with warriors."

I was compelled, finally, to admit the wisdom of her reasoning and to forego an attempt to secure my rifle and pistol, though I can assure you that I felt lost without them, especially when thus venturing forth into a new world so strange to me as Va-nah, and so savage. As a matter of fact, from what I gleaned from Nah-ee-lah, there was but a single spot upon the entire inner lunar world where she and I could hope to be even reasonably free from danger, and that was her native city of Laythe. Even there I should have enemies, she told me, for her race is ever suspicious of strangers; but the friendship of the princess would be my protection, she assured me with a friendly pressure of the hand.

The rain and wind must have persisted for a considerable time, for when it was finally over and we looked back through a clear atmosphere we found that a low range of mountains lay between us and the distant sea. We had crossed these and were upon a plateau at the foot of the higher peaks. The sea looked very far away indeed, and we could not even guess at the location of the No-vans village from which we had escaped.

"Do you think they will pursue us?" I asked her.

"Yes," she said; "they will try to find us, but it will be like looking for a raindrop in the ocean. They are creatures of the lowlands—I am of the mountains. Down there," and she pointed into the valley, "they might find me easily, but in my own mountains—no."

"We are near Laythe?" I asked.

"I do not know. Laythe is hard to find—it is well hidden. It is for this reason that it exists at all. Its founders were pursued by the Kalkars, and had they not found an almost inaccessible spot they would have been discovered and slain long before they could have constructed an impregnable city."

She led me then straight into the mighty mountains of the Moon, past the mouths of huge craters that reached through the lunar crust to the surface of the satellite, along the edges of yawning chasms that dropped three, four, yes, sometimes five miles, sheer into frightful gorges, and then out upon vast plateaus, but ever upward toward the higher peaks that seemed to topple above us in the distance. The craters, as a rule, lay in the deep gorges, but some we found upon the plateaus, and even a few opened into the summits of mountain peaks as do those upon the outer surface of planets. Those in the low places were, I believe, the openings through which the original molten lunar core was vomited forth by the surface volcanoes upon the outer crust.

Nah-ee-lah told me that the secret entrance to Laythe lay just below the lip of one of these craters, and it was this she sought. To me the quest seemed hopeless, for as far as the eye could reach lay naught but an indescribable jumble of jagged peaks, terrific gorges and bottomless craters. Yet always the girl seemed to find a way among or about them—instinctively, apparently, she found trails and footholds where there were no trails and where a chamois might have been hard put to it to find secure footing.

In these higher altitudes we found a vegetation that differed materially from that which grew in the lowlands. Edible fruits and berries were, however, still sufficiently plentiful to keep us reasonably well supplied with food. When we were tired we usually managed to find a cave in which we could rest in comparative security, and when it was possible to do so Nah-ee-lah always insisted upon barricading the entrance with rocks, since there was always the danger, she told me, of our being attacked by tor-hos. These bloodthirsty creatures while rare, were nevertheless very much to be feared, since not only were they voracious meat eaters and of such a savage disposition that they attacked nearly everything they saw in wanton ferocity, but even a minor wound inflicted by their fangs or talons often proved fatal, because of the fact that their principal diet was the poisonous flesh of the rympth and the flying-toad. I tried to get Nah-ee-lah to describe the creature to me, but inasmuch as there was no creature with which we were both familiar that she might compare it with, I learned little more from her than that it stood between eighteen inches and two feet in height, had long, sharp fangs, four legs and was hairless.

As an aid to climbing, as well as to give me some means of protection, I broke a stout and rather heavy branch from one of the mountain trees, the wood of which was harder than any that I had seen growing in the lowlands. To roam a strange and savage world armed only with a wooden stick seemed to me the height of rashness, but there was no alternative until the time arrived when I might find the materials with which to fashion more formidable weapons. I had in mind a bow and arrows and was constantly on the lookout for wood which I considered adapted to the former, and I also determined to forego my cane for a spear whenever the material for the making of one came to hand. I had little time, however, for such things, as it seemed that when we were not sleeping we were constantly upon the move, Nah-ee-lah becoming more and more impatient to find her native city as the chances for so doing lessened—and it seemed to me that they were constantly lessening. While I was quite sure that she had no more idea where Laythe lay than I, yet we stumbled on and on and on, through the most stupendous mountain ranges that the mind of man can conceive, nor ever, apparently, did Nah-ee-lah discover a single familiar landmark upon which to hang a shred of hope that eventually we might come upon Laythe.

I never saw such a sanguine and hopeful person as Nah-ee-lah. It was her constant belief that Laythe lay just beyond the next mountain, in spite of the fact that she was invariably mistaken—which seemed never to lessen the exuberance of her enthusiasm for the next guess—which I knew beforehand was going to be a wrong guess.

Once just after we had rounded the shoulder of a mountain we came upon a little strip of level land clinging to the side of a mighty peak. I was in the lead—a position which I tried always to take when it was not absolutely necessary for Nah-ee-lah to go ahead in order to find a trail. As I came around the shoulder of the mountain, and in full sight of the little level area, I was positive that I saw a slight movement among some bushes at my right about halfway along one side of the little plain.

As we came abreast of the spot, upon which I kept my eye, there broke upon our ears the most hideous scream that I have ever heard, and simultaneously there leaped from the concealment of the bushes a creature about the size of a North American mountain lion, though quite evidently a reptile and probably a tor-ho, as such it proved to be. There was something about the head and face which suggested the cat family to me, yet there was really no resemblance between it and any of the earthly felines. It came at me with those terrible curved fangs bared and bristling and as it came it emitted the most terrifying sounds—I have called them screams, because that word more nearly describes them than any other, and yet they were a combination of shrieks and moans—the most blood-curdling that I have ever heard.

Nah-ee-lah grasped my arm. "Run!" she cried, "run." But I shook her loose and stood my ground. I wanted to run, that I will admit, but where to? The creature was covering the ground at tremendous speed and our only avenue of escape was the narrow trail over which we had just come, which clung precariously to the side of a perpendicular cliff. And so I stood there waiting, my feeble stick grasped in both hands. Just what I expected to do with it I scarcely knew until the tor-ho was upon me. Then I swung for its head as a batter swings for a pitched ball. I struck it square upon the nose—a terrific blow that not only stopped it, but felled it. I could hear the bones crushing beneath the impact of my crude weapon and I thought that I had done for the thing with that single blow, but I did not know the tremendous vitality of the creature. Almost instantly it was up and at me again, and again I struck it, this time upon the side of the head, and again I heard bones crush and again it fell heavily to the ground.

What appeared to be cold blood was oozing slowly from its wounded face as it came at me for the third time, its eyes glaring hideously, its broken jaws agape to seize me, while its shrieks and moans rose to a perfect frenzy of rage and pain. It reared up and struck at me with its talons now, but I met it again with my bludgeon and this time I broke a foreleg.

How long I fought that awful thing I cannot even guess. Time and time again it charged me furiously and each time, though often by but a miracle of fortune, I managed to keep it from closing, and each blow that I delivered crushed and maimed it a little more, until at last it was nothing but a bleeding wreck of pulp, still trying to crawl toward me upon its broken legs and seize me and drag me down with its broken, toothless jaws. Even then it was with the greatest difficulty that I killed it, that I might put it out of its misery.

Rather exhausted, I turned to look for Nah-ee-lah, and much to my surprise, I found her standing directly behind me.

"I thought you had run away," I said.

"No," she said, "you did not run and so I did not, but I never thought that you would be able to kill it."

"You thought that it would kill me, then?" I asked.

"Certainly," she replied. "Even now I cannot understand how you were able to overcome a tor-ho with that pitiful little stick of wood."

"But if you thought I was going to be killed," I insisted, "why was it that you did not seek safety in flight?"

"If you had been killed I should not have cared to live," she said simply.

I did not exactly understand her attitude and scarcely knew what reply to make.

"It was very foolish of you," I said at last, rather blunderingly, "and if we are attacked again you must run and save yourself."

She looked at me for a moment with a peculiar expression upon her face which I could not interpret and then turned and resumed her way in the direction in which we had been traveling when our journey had been interrupted by the tor-ho. She did not say anything, but I felt that I had offended her and I was sorry. I did not want her falling in love with me, though, and according to earthly standards, her statement that she would rather die than live without me might naturally have been interpreted as a confession of love. The more I thought of it, however, as we moved along in silence, the more possible it seemed to me that her standards might differ widely from mine and that I was only proving myself to be an egotistical ass in assuming that Nah-ee-lah loved me. I wished that I might explain matters to her, but it is one of those things that is rather difficult to explain, and I realized that it might be made much worse if I attempted to do so.

We had been such good friends and our fellowship had been so perfect that the apparently strained silence which existed between us was most depressing. Nah-ee-lah had always been a talkative little person and always gay and cheerful, even under the most trying conditions.

I was rather tired out after my encounter with the tor-ho and should have liked to stop for a rest, but I did not suggest it, neither did Nah-ee-lah, and so we continued on our seemingly interminable way, though, almost exhausted as I was, I dropped some little distance behind my beautiful guide.

She was quite out of sight ahead of me upon the winding trail when suddenly I heard her calling my name aloud. I answered her as, simultaneously, I broke into a run, for I did not know but what she might be in danger, though her voice did not sound at all like it. She was only a short distance ahead and when I came in sight of her I saw her standing at the edge of a mighty crater. She was facing me and she was smiling.

"Oh, Julian," she cried, "I have found it. I am home and we are safe at last."

"I am glad, Nah-ee-lah," I said. "I have been much worried on account of the dangers to which you have been constantly subjected, as well as because of a growing fear that you would never be able to find Laythe."

"Oh, my!" she exclaimed, "I knew that I would find it. If I had to hunt through every mountain range in Va-nah I would have found it."

"You are quite sure that this is the crater where lies the entrance to Laythe?" I asked her.

"There is no doubt of it, Julian," she replied, and she pointed downward over the lip of the crater toward a narrow ledge which lay some twenty feet below and upon which I saw what appeared to be the mouth of a cave opening into the crater.

"But, how are we going to reach it?" I asked.

"It may be difficult," she replied, "but we will find a way."

"I hope so, Nah-ee-lah," I said, "but without a rope or wings I do not see how we are going to accomplish it."

"In the mouth of the tunnel," explained Nah-ee-lah, "there are long poles, each of which has a hook at one end. Ages ago there were no other means of ingress or egress to the city and those who came out to hunt or for any other purpose came through this long tunnel from the city, and from the ledge below they raised their poles and placed the hooked ends over the rim of the crater, after which it was a simple matter to clamber up or down the poles as they wished; but it has been long since these tunnels were used by the people of Va-nah, who had no further need of them after the perfection of the flying wings which you saw me using when I was captured by the Va-gas."

"If they used poles, so may we," I said, "since there are plenty of young trees growing close to the rim of the crater. The only difficulty will be in felling one of them.

"We can do that," said Nah-ee-lah, "if we can find some sharp fragments of stone. It will be slow work, but it can be done," and she started immediately to hunt for a fragment with a cutting edge. I joined her in the search and it was not long before we had discovered several pieces of obsidian with rather sharp edges. We then started to work upon a young tree about four inches in diameter that grew almost straight for a height of some thirty feet.

Cutting the tree down with our bits of lava glass was tedious work, but finally it was accomplished, and we were both much elated when the tree toppled and fell to the ground. Cutting away the branches occupied almost as long a time, but that, too, was finally accomplished. The next problem which confronted us was that of making the top of the pole secure enough to hold while we descended to the ledge before the mouth of the tunnel. We had no rope and nothing with which to fashion one, other than my garments, which I was loath to destroy, inasmuch as in these higher altitudes it was often cold. Presently, however, I hit upon a plan which, if Nah-ee-lah's muscles and my nerves withstood the strain it put upon them, bade fair to assure the success of our undertaking. I lowered the larger end of the pole over the side of the crater until the butt rested upon the ledge before the mouth of the tunnel. Then I turned to Nah-ee-lah.

"Lie down flat at full length, Nah-ee-lah," I directed her, "and hold this pole securely with both hands. You will only have to keep it from toppling to the sides or outward, and to that, I think, your strength is equal. While you hold it, I will descend to the mouth of the tunnel and raise one of the regular hooked poles which you say should be deposited there. If they are not, I believe that I can hold our own pole securely from below while you descend." She looked over into the vast abyss below and shuddered. "I can hold it at the top," she said, "if the bottom does not slip from the ledge."

"That is a chance that I shall have to take," I replied, "but I will descend very carefully and I think there will be little danger upon that score."

I could see, upon a more careful examination of the ledge below, that there was some danger of an accident such as she suggested.

Nah-ee-lah took her position as I had directed and lay grasping the pole securely in both hands at the rim of the crater, which was absolutely perpendicular at this point, and I prepared to make the perilous descent.

I can assure you that my sensations were far from pleasurable as I looked over into that awful abyss. The crater itself was some four or five miles in diameter, and, as I had every reason to suspect, extended fully two hundred and fifty miles through the lunar crust to the surface of the Moon. It was one of the most impressive moments of my life as I clung balancing upon the edge of that huge orifice, gazing into the silent, mysterious depths below. And then I seized the pole very gently and lowered myself over the edge.

"Courage, Julian!" whispered Nah-ee-lah; "I shall hold very tight."

"I shall be quite safe, Nah-ee-lah," I assured her. "I must be safe, for if I am not, how are you to reach the ledge and Laythe?"

As I descended very slowly I tried not to think at all, but to exclude from my mind every consideration of the appalling depths beneath me. I could not have been more than two feet from the ledge when the very thing that we both tried so hard to guard against transpired—a splintered fragment of the pole's butt crumpled beneath my weight and that slight jar was just sufficient to start the base of my precarious ladder sliding toward the edge of the narrow projection upon which I had rested it, and beyond which lay eternity. Above me I heard a slight scream and then the pole slipped from the ledge and I felt myself falling.

It was over in an instant. My feet struck the ledge and I threw myself within the mouth of the tunnel. And then, above me, I heard Nah-ee-lah's voice crying in agonized tones:

"Julian! Julian! I am falling!"

Instantly I sprang to my feet and peered upward from the mouth of the tunnel upon a sight that froze my blood, so horrifying did it seem, for there above me, still clinging to the pole, hung Nah-ee-lah, her body, with the exception of her legs, completely over the edge of the crater. Just as I looked up she dropped the pole and although I made a grab for it I missed it and it fell past me into the maw of the crater.

"Julian! Julian! You are safe!" she cried; "I am glad of that. It terrified me so when I thought you were falling and I tried my best to hold the pole, but your weight dragged me over the edge of the crater. Good-bye, Julian, I cannot hold on much longer."

"You must, Nah-ee-lah!" I cried; "do not forget the hooked poles that you told me of. I will find one and have you down in no time." And even as I spoke I turned and dove into the tunnel; but my heart stood still at the thought that the poles might not be there. My first glance revealed only the bare rock of walls and floor and ceiling and no hooked poles in sight. I sprang quickly farther into the tunnel which turned abruptly a few yards ahead of me and just around the bend my eyes were gladdened by the sight of a dozen or more of the poles which Nah-ee-lah had described. Seizing one of them, I ran quickly back to the entrance. I was almost afraid to look up, but as I did so I was rewarded by the sight of Nah-ee-lah's face smiling down at me—she could smile even in the face of death, could Nah-ee-lah.

"Just a moment more, Nah-ee-lah!" I cried to her, as I raised the pole and caught the hook upon the crater's rim. There were small protuberances on either side of the pole for its entire length, which made climbing it comparatively simple.

"Make haste, Julian!" she cried, "I am slipping."

It wasn't necessary for her to tell me to make haste. I think that I never did anything more quickly in my life than I climbed that pole, but I reached her not an instant too soon, for even as my arm slipped about her, her hold upon the ledge above gave way, and she came down head foremost upon me. I had no difficulty in catching her and supporting her weight. My only fear was that the hook above might not sustain the added weight under the strain of her falling body. But it held, and I blessed the artisan who had made it thus strong.

A moment later I had descended to the mouth of the tunnel and drawn Nah-ee-lah into the safety of its interior. My arm was still around her and hers about me as she stood there sobbing upon my breast. She was utterly relaxed and her supple body felt so helpless against me that there was suddenly aroused within me a feeling such as I had never experienced before—a rather indescribable feeling, yet one which induced, seemingly, an irresistible and ridiculous desire to go forth and slay whole armies of men in protection of this little Moon Maid. It must have been a sudden mental reversion to some ancient type of crusading ancestor of the Middle Ages—some knight in armor from whose loins I had sprung, transmitting to me his own flamboyant, yet none the less admirable, chivalry. The feeling rather surprised me, for I have always considered myself more or less practical and hardheaded. But more sober thought finally convinced me that it was but a nervous reaction from the thrilling moments through which we had both just passed, coupled with her entire helplessness and dependence upon me. Be that as it may, I disengaged her arms from about my neck as gently and as quickly as I could and lowered her carefully to the floor of the tunnel, so that she sat with her back leaning against one of the walls.

"You are very brave, Julian," she said, "and very strong."

"I am afraid I am not very brave," I told her. "I am almost weak from fright even now—I was so afraid that I would not reach you in time, Nah-ee-lah."

"It is the brave man who is afraid after the danger is past," she said. "He has no time to think of fear until after the happening is all over. You may have been afraid for me, Julian, but you could not have been afraid for yourself, or otherwise you would not have taken the risk of catching me as I fell. Even now I cannot understand how you were able to hold me."

"Perhaps," I reminded her, "I am stronger than the men of Va-nah, for my earthly muscles are accustomed to overcoming a gravity six times as great as that upon your world. Had this same accident happened upon Earth I might not have been able to hold you when you fell."

CHAPTER NINE
THE FIGHT WITH THE KALKARS

THE TUNNEL IN WHICH I FOUND MYSELF and along which Nah-ee-lah led me toward the city of Laythe was remarkable in several particulars. It was largely of natural origin, seemingly consisting of a series of caves which may have been formed by bubbles in the cooling lava of the original molten flow and which had later been connected by man to form a continuous subterranean corridor. The caves themselves were usually more or less spherical in shape and the debris from the connecting passageways had been utilized to fill the bottoms of them to the level of the main floor of the passageway. The general trend of the tunnel was upward from the point at which we had entered it, and there was a constant draught of air rushing along it in the same direction in which we were moving, assuring me that it was undoubtedly well ventilated for its full length. The walls and ceiling were coated with a substance of which radium was evidently one of the ingredients, since even after we had lost sight of the entrance the passageway was well illuminated. We had been moving along in silence for quite a little distance when I finally addressed Nah-ee-lah.

"It must seem good," I said, "to travel again this familiar tunnel of your native city. I know how happy I should be were I thus approaching my own birthplace."

"I am glad to be returning to Laythe," she said, "for many reasons, but for one I am sorry, and as for this passageway it is scarcely more familiar to me than to you, since I have traversed it but once before in my life and that when I was a little girl and came here with my father and his court upon the occasion of his periodical inspection of the passageway, which is now practically never used."

"If you are not familiar with the tunnel," I asked, "are you sure that there is no danger of our going astray at some fork or branch?"

"There is but the one passageway," she replied, "which leads from the crater to Laythe."

"And how long is the tunnel?" I asked. "Will we soon enter the city?"

"No," she replied, "it is a great distance from the crater to Laythe."

We had covered some little distance at this time, possibly five or six miles,

252

and she had scarcely ceased speaking when a turn in the passageway led us into a cave of larger proportions than any through which we had previously passed and from the opposite side of which two passageways diverged.

"I thought there were no branches," I remarked.

"I do not understand it," she said. "There is no branch from the tunnel of Laythe."

"Could it be possible that we are in the wrong tunnel?" I asked, "and that this does not lead to Laythe?"

"A moment before I should have been sure that we were in the right tunnel," she replied, "but now, Julian, I do not know, for never had I heard of any branch of our own tunnel."

We had crossed the cave and were standing between the openings of the two divergent passageways.

"Which one shall we take?" I asked, but again she shook her head.

"I do not know," she replied.

"Listen!" I cautioned her. "What was that?" For I was sure that I had heard a sound issuing from one of the tunnels.

We stood peering into an aperture which revealed about a hundred yards of the passageway before an abrupt turn hid the continuation of it from our view. We could hear what now resolved itself into the faint sound of voices approaching us along the corridor, and then quite suddenly the figure of a man appeared around the corner of the turn. Nah-ee-lah leaped to one side out of sight, drawing me with her.

"A Kalkar!" she whispered. "Oh, Julian, if they find us we are lost."

"If there is only one of them I can take care of him," I said.

"There will be more than one," she replied; "there will be many."

"Then, let us return the way we came and make our way to the top of the crater's rim before they discover us. We can throw their hooked poles into the crater, including the one which we use to ascend from the mouth of the tunnel, thus effectually preventing any pursuit."

"We cannot cross this room again to the tunnel upon the opposite side without being apprehended," she replied. "Our only hope is in hiding in this other tunnel until they have passed and trusting to chance that we meet no one within it."

"Come, then," I said. "I dislike the idea of flying like a scared rabbit, but neither would there be any great wisdom in facing armed men without a single weapon of defense."

Even as we had whispered thus briefly together, we found the voices from the other tunnel had increased and I thought that I noted a tone of excitement in them, though the speakers were still too far away for us to understand their words. We moved swiftly up the branch tunnel, Nah-ee-lah in the lead, and after passing the first turn we both felt comparatively safe, for Nah-ee-lah was sure that the men who had interrupted our journey were a party of hunters on their way to the outer world by means of the crater through which we had entered the tunnel and that they would not come up the branch in which we were hiding. Thus believing, we halted after we were safely out of sight and hearing of the large cave we had just left.

"That man was a Kalkar," said Nah-ee-lah, "which means that we are in the wrong tunnel and that we must retrace our steps and continue our search for Laythe upon the surface of the ground." Her voice sounded tired and listless, as though hope had suddenly deserted her brave heart. We were standing shoulder to shoulder in the narrow corridor and I could not resist the impulse to place an arm about her and comfort her.

"Do not despair, Nah-ee-lah," I begged her; "we are no worse off than we have been and much better off than before we escaped the Va-gas of Ga-va-go. Then do you not recall that you mentioned one drawback to your return to Laythe—that you might be as well off here as there? What was the reason, Nah-ee-lah?"

"Ko-tah wants me in marriage," she replied. "Ko-tah is very powerful. He expects one day to be Jemadar of Laythe. This he cannot be while I live unless he marries me."

"Do you wish to marry him?" I asked.

"No," she said; "not now. Before—" she hesitated—"before I left Laythe I did not care so very much; but now I know that I cannot wed with Ko-tah."

"And your father," I continued, "what of him—will he insist that you marry Ko-tah?"

"He cannot do otherwise," replied Nah-ee-lah, "for Ko-tah is very powerful. If my father refuses to permit me to marry him Ko-tah may overthrow him, and when my father is dead, should I still refuse to marry Ko-tah he may slay me, also, and then become Jemadar easily, for the blood of Jemadars flows in his veins."

"It appears to me, Nah-ee-lah, that you will be about as badly off at home as anywhere else in Va-nah. It is too bad that I cannot take you to my own Earth, where you would be quite safe, and I am sure, happy."

"I wish that you might, Julian," she replied simply.

I was about to reply when she placed slim fingers upon my lips. "Hush, Julian!" she whispered, "they are following us up this corridor. Come quickly, we must escape before they overtake us," and so saying, she turned and ran quickly along the corridor which led neither of us knew whither.

But we were soon to find out, for we had gone but a short distance when we came to the tunnel's end in a large circular chamber, at one end of which was a rostrum upon which were a massive, elaborately carved desk and a chair of similar design. Below the rostrum were arranged other chairs in rows, with a broad aisle down the center. The furniture, though of peculiar design and elaborately carved with strange figures of unearthly beasts and reptiles, was not, for all of that, markedly dissimilar to articles of the same purpose fabricated upon Earth. The chairs had four legs, high backs and broad arms, seeming to have been designed equally for durability, service, and comfort.

I glanced quickly around the apartment, as we first entered, only taking in the details later, but I saw that there was no other opening than the one through which we had entered.

"We will have to wait here, Nah-ee-lah," I said. "Perhaps, though, all will be well—the Kalkars may prove friendly."

She shook her head negatively. "No," she said, "they will not be friendly."

"What will they do to us?" I asked.

"They will make slaves of us," she replied, "and we shall spend the balance of our lives working almost continuously until we drop with fatigue under the cruelest of taskmasters, for the Kalkars hate us of Laythe and will hesitate at nothing that will humiliate or injure us."

She had scarcely ceased speaking when there appeared in the entrance of the cave the figure of a man about my own height dressed in a tunic similar to Nah-ee-lah's but evidently made of leather. He carried a knife slung in a scabbard depending from a shoulder belt, and in his right hand he grasped a slender lance. His eyes were close set upon either side of a prominent, hooked nose. They were watery, fishy, blue eyes, and the hair growing profusely above his low forehead was flaxen in color. His physique was admirable, except for a noticeable stoop. His feet were very large and his gait awkward when he moved. Behind him I could see the heads and shoulders of others. They stood there grinning at us for a moment, most malevolently, it seemed to me, and then they entered the cave—a full dozen of them. There were several types, with eyes and hair of different colors, the former ranging from blue to brown, the latter from light blond to almost black.

As they emerged from the mouth of the tunnel they spread out and advanced slowly toward us. We were cornered like rats in a trap. How I longed for the feel of my automatic at my hip! I envied them their slender spears and their daggers. If I could have but these I might have a chance at least to take Nah-ee-lah out of their clutches and save her from the hideous fate of slavery among the Kalkars, for I had guessed what such slavery would mean to her from the little that she had told me, and I had guessed, too, that she would rather die than submit to it. For my own part, life held little for me; I had long since definitely given up any hope of ever returning to my own world, or of finding the ship and being reunited with West and Jay and Norton. There came upon me at that moment, however, a sense of appreciation of the fact that since we had left the village of the No-vans I had been far from unhappy, nor could I attribute this to aught else than the companionship of Nah-ee-lah—a realization that convinced me that I should be utterly miserable were she to be taken from me now. Was I to submit supinely then, to capture and slavery for myself and worse than death for Nah-ee-lah, with the assurance of consequent separation from her? No. I held up my hand as a signal for the advancing Kalkars to halt.

"Stop!" I commanded. "Before you advance farther I wish to know your intentions toward us. We entered this tunnel, mistaking it for that which led to the city of my companion. Permit us to depart in peace and all will be well."

"All will be well, anyway," replied the leader of the Kalkars. "You are a strange creature, such as I have never before seen in Va-nah. Of you we know nothing except that you are not of the Kalkars, and therefore an enemy of the Kalkars, but this other is from Laythe."

"You will not permit us to go in peace, then?" I demanded.

He laughed sneeringly. "Nor in any other way," he said.

I had been standing in the aisle, with my hand upon one of the chairs near the rostrum and now I turned to Nah-ee-lah who was standing close beside me.

"Come," I said to her, "follow me; stay close behind me."

Several of the Kalkars were coming down the main aisle toward us, and as I turned toward them from speaking to Nah-ee-lah, I raised the chair which my hand had been resting upon, and swinging it quickly around my head hurled it full in the face of the leader. As he went down Nah-ee-lah and I ran forward, gaining a little toward the opening of the tunnel, and then without pausing I hurled another chair and a third and a fourth, in rapid succession. The Kalkars tried to bring us down with their lances, but they were so busy dodging chairs that they could not cast their weapons accurately, and even those few which might otherwise have struck us were warded off by my rather remarkable engines of defense.

There had been four Kalkars advancing toward us down the center aisle. The balance of the party had divided, half of it circling the cave to the left and the other half to the right, with the evident intention of coming up the center aisle from behind us. This maneuver had started just before I commenced hurling chairs at the four directly in front of us, and now when those who had intended to take us from the rear discovered that we were likely to make our way through to the tunnel's entrance, some of them sprang toward us along the passageways between the chairs, which necessitated my turning and devoting a moment's attention to them. One huge fellow was in the lead, coming across the backs of the chairs leaping from seat to seat; and being the closest to me, he was naturally my first target. The chairs were rather heavy and the one that I let drive at him caught him full in the chest with an impact that brought a howl from him and toppled him over across the backs of the chairs behind him, where he hung limp and motionless. Then I turned my attention again to those before us, all of whom had fallen before my massive ammunition. Three of them lay still, but one of them had scrambled to his feet and was in the very act of casting his lance as I looked. I stopped the weapon with a chair and as the fellow went down I caught a glimpse of Nah-ee-lah from the corners of my eyes as she snatched the lance from the first Kalkar who had fallen and hurled it at someone behind me. I heard a scream of rage and pain and then I turned in time to see another of the Kalkars fall almost at my feet, the lance embedded in his heart.

The way before us was temporarily open, while the Kalkars behind us had paused, momentarily, at least, in evident consternation at the havoc I wrought with these unseemly weapons against which they had no defense.

"Get two knives and two lances from those who have fallen," I cried to Nah-ee-lah, "while I hold these others back."

She did as I bade, and slowly we backed toward the mouth of the tunnel. My chairs had accounted for half our enemies when at last we stood in the opening, each armed with a lance and a knife.

"Now, run, Nah-ee-lah, as you never ran before," I whispered to my companion. "I can hold them off until you have reached the mouth of the tunnel and clambered to the rim of the crater. If I am lucky, I will follow you."

"I will not leave you, Julian," she replied, "we will go together or not at all."

"But you must, Nah-ee-lah," I insisted, "it is for you that I have been fighting them. What difference can it make in my fate where I am when in Va-nah—all here are my enemies."

She laid her hand gently upon my arm. "I will not leave you, Julian," she repeated, "and that is final."

The Kalkars within the room were now advancing toward us menacingly.

"Halt!" I cried to them, "you see what fate your companions have met, because you would not let us go in peace. That is all we ask. I am armed now and it will be death to any who follow us."

They paused and I saw them whispering together as Nah-ee-lah and I backed along the corridor, a turn in which soon shut them from our view. Then we wheeled and ran like deer along the winding passageway. I did not feel very safe from capture at any time, but at least I breathed a sigh of relief after we had passed the chamber from which the Kalkars had run us into the *cul-de-sac*, and we had seen no sign of any other of their kind. We heard no sound of pursuit, but that in itself meant nothing, since the Kalkars are shod with soft leather sandals, the material for which, like all their other leather trappings, is made of the skins of Va-gas and of the prisoners from Laythe.

As we came to the pile of hooked poles which marked the last turn before the entrance of the tunnel I breathed an inward sigh of relief. Stooping, I gathered them all in my arms, and then we ran on to the opening into the crater, where I cast all but one of the poles into the abyss. That which I retained I hooked over the lip of the crater and then, turning to Nah-ee-lah, I bade her ascend.

"You should have saved two of the poles," she said, "and then we could have ascended together; but I will make haste and you can follow me immediately, for we do not know but that they are pursuing us. I cannot imagine that they will let us escape thus easily."

Even as she spoke I heard the soft patter of sandal-shod feet up the corridor.

"Make haste, Nah-ee-lah," I cried; "they come!"

Climbing a pole is slow work at best, but when one is suspended over the brink of a bottomless chasm and is none too sure of the security of the hook that is holding the pole above, one must needs move cautiously. Yet, even so, Nah-ee-lah scrambled upward so rapidly as to fill me with apprehension for her safety. Nor were my fears entirely groundless, for, standing in the mouth of the tunnel, where I could keep one eye upon Nah-ee-lah and the other toward the turn around which my pursuers would presently come in view, I saw the girl's hands grasp the rim of the crater at the very instant that the hook came loose and the pole dropped past me into the abyss. I might have caught it as it fell, but my whole mind was fixed upon Nah-ee-lah and her grave danger. Would she be able to draw herself upward, or would she fall? I saw her straining frantically to raise her body above the edge of the volcano, and then from up the corridor behind me came an exultant cry and I turned to face a brawny Kalkar who was racing toward me.

CHAPTER TEN
THE KALKAR CITY

NOW INDEED, DID I HAVE A REASON to curse the stupidity that had permitted me to cast into the abyss all of the hooked poles save one, since even this one was now lost to me and I was utterly without means of escape from the tunnel.

As the fellow approached me at a rapid run I hurled my lance, but being unaccustomed to the weapon, I missed, and then he was upon me, dropping his own lance as he leaped for me, for it was evidently his desire to take me alive and unharmed. I thought that I was going to have him now, for I believed that I was more than a match for him, but there are tricks in every method of attack and this lunar warrior was evidently well schooled in his own methods of offense. He scarcely seemed to touch me, and yet he managed to trip me and push me simultaneously so that I fell heavily backward to the ground and turning a little sideways as I fell, I must have struck my head against the side of the tunnel, for that is the last that I remember until I regained consciousness in the very cave that Nah-ee-lah and I had reached when we saw the first of the Kalkars. I was surrounded by a party of eight of the Kalkars, two of whom were half carrying, half dragging me. I learned later that in the fight before the rostrum I had killed four of their number.

The fellow who had captured me was in very good humor, doubtless because of his success, and when he discovered that I had regained consciousness he started to converse with me.

"You thought that you could escape from Gapth, did you?" he cried, "but never; you might escape from the others, but not from me—no, not from Gapth."

"I did the principal thing that I desired to do," I replied, wishing to learn if Nah-ee-lah had escaped.

"What is that?" demanded Gapth.

"I succeeded in accomplishing the escape of my companion," I replied.

He made a wry face at that. "If Gapth had been there a moment earlier she would not have escaped, either," he said, and by that I knew that she had escaped, unless she had fallen back into the crater; and I was amply repaid for my own capture if it had won freedom for Nah-ee-lah.

"Although I did not escape this time," I said, "I shall next time."

He laughed a nasty laugh. "There will be no next time," he said, "for we are taking you to the city, and once there, there is no escape, for this is the only avenue by which you can reach the outer world and once within the city you never can retrace your steps to the mouth of the tunnel."

I was not so sure of that, myself, for my sense of direction and that of location are very well developed within me. The degree of perfection attained in orientation by many officers of the International Peace Fleet has been described as almost miraculous, and even among such as these my ability in this line was a matter of comment. I was glad, therefore, that the fellow had warned me, since now I should be particularly upon the watch for each slightest scrap of information that would fix in my memory whatever route I might be led over. From the cave in which I regained consciousness there was but a single route to the mouth of the tunnel, but from here on into the city I must watch every turn and fork and crossing and draw upon the tablets of my memory an accurate and detailed map of the entire route.

"We do not even have to confine our prisoners," continued Gapth, "after we have so marked them that their ownership may always be determined."

"How do you mark them?" I asked.

"With heated irons we make the mark of the owner here," and he touched my forehead just above my eyes.

"Pleasant," I thought to myself, and then aloud: "Shall I belong to you?"

"I do not know," he replied, "but you will belong to whomever The Twentyfour allot you."

We moved on after we left the cave for a considerable period of time in silence. I was busy making mental notes of every salient feature that might be useful to me in retracing my steps, but I found nothing other than a winding and gently ascending corridor, without crossings or branches, until we reached the foot of a long flight of stone steps at the summit of which we emerged into a large chamber in the walls of which there must have been at least a dozen doorways, where, to my great disappointment, I was immediately blindfolded. They whirled me around then, but evidently it was done perfunctorily, since it was exactly one full turn and I was halted in my tracks facing precisely in the same direction that I had been before. This I was positive of, for our powers of orientation are often tested in this way in the air service. Then they marched me straight forward across the room through a doorway directly opposite that at which I had entered the chamber. I could tell when we left the larger chamber and entered the corridor from the different sound which our footsteps made. We advanced along this corridor ninety-seven paces, when we turned abruptly to the right and at the end of thirty-three paces emerged into another chamber, as I could easily tell again from the sound of our footsteps the instant we crossed the threshold. They led me about this chamber a couple of times with the evident intention of bewildering me, but in this they did not succeed, for when they turned again into a corridor I knew that it was the same corridor from which I had just emerged and that I was retracing my steps. This time they took me back thirty-three paces and then turned abruptly to the right. I could not but smile to myself when I realized that we were now continuing directly along the same corridor as that which we had entered immediately after they had first blindfolded me, their little excursion through the short corridor into the second chamber having been but a ruse to bewilder me. A moment later, at the foot of a flight of steps they removed the blind, evidently satisfied that there was now no chance of my being able to retrace my steps and find the main tunnel leading to the crater, while, as a matter of fact, I could easily have retraced every foot of it blindfolded.

From here on we climbed interminable stairways, passed through numerous corridors and chambers, all of which were illuminated by the radium-bearing substance which coated their walls and ceilings, and then we emerged suddenly upon a terrace into the open air, and I obtained my first view of a lunar city. It was built around a crater, and the buildings were terraced back from the rim, the terraces being generally devoted to the raising of garden truck and the principal fruit-bearing trees and shrubs. The city extended upward several hundred feet, the houses, as I learned later, being built one upon another, the great majority of them, therefore, being without windows looking upon the outer world.

I was led along the terrace for a short distance, and during this brief opportunity for observation I deduced that the cultivated terraces lay upon the roofs of the tier of buildings next below. To my right I could see the terraced steps extending downward to the rim of the crater. Nearly all the terraces were covered with vegetation, and in numerous places I saw what appeared to be Va-gas feeding upon the plants, and this I later learned was the fact, and that the Kalkars, when they are able to capture members of the race of Va-gas, keep them in captivity and breed them as we breed cattle, for their flesh. It is necessary, to some extent, to change the diet of the Va-gas almost exclusively to vegetation, though this diet is supplemented by the flesh of the Kalkars, and their Laythean slaves who die, the Va-gas thus being compelled to serve the double purpose of producing flesh for the Kalkars and acting as their scavengers as well.

Upon my left were the faces of buildings, uniformly two stories in height, with an occasional slender tower rising fifteen, twenty or sometimes as high as thirty feet from the terraced roofs above. It was into one of these buildings that my captors led me after we had proceeded a short distance along the terrace, and I found myself in a large apartment in which were a number of male Kalkars, and at a desk facing the entrance a large, entirely

263

bald man who appeared to be of considerable age. To this person I was led by Gapth, who narrated my capture and the escape of Nah-ee-lah.

The fellow before whom I had been brought questioned me briefly. He made no comment when I told him that I was from another world, but he examined my garments rather carefully and then after a moment turned to Gapth.

"We will hold him for questioning by The Twentyfour," he said. "If he is not of Va-nah he is neither Kalkar nor Laythean, and consequently, he must be flesh of a lower order and therefore may be eaten." He paused a moment and fell to examining a large book which seemed to be filled with plans upon which strange hieroglyphics appeared. He turned over several leaves, and finally coming evidently to the page he sought, he ran a forefinger slowly over it until it came to rest near the center of the plat. "You may confine him here," he said to Gapth, "in chamber eight of the twenty-fourth section, at the seventh elevation, and you will produce him upon orders from The Twentyfour when next they meet," and then to me: "It is impossible for you to escape from the city, but if you attempt it, it may be difficult for us to find you again immediately and when we do you will be tortured to death as an example to other slaves. Go!"

I went; following Gapth and the others who had conducted me to the presence of this creature. They led me back into the very corridor from which we had emerged upon the terrace and then straight into the heart of that amazing pile for fully half a mile, where they shoved me roughly into an apartment at the right of the corridor with the admonition that I stay there until I was wanted.

I found myself in a dimly lighted, rectangular room, the air of which was very poor, and at the first glance I discovered that I was not alone, for upon a bench against the opposite wall sat a man. He looked up as I entered and I saw that his features were very fine and that he had black hair like Nah-ee-lah. He looked at me for a moment with a puzzled expression in his eyes and then he addressed me.

"You, too, are a slave?" he asked.

"I am not a slave," I replied, "I am a prisoner."

"It is all the same," he said; "but from whence come you? I have never seen your like before in Va-nah."

"I do not come from Va-nah," I replied, and then I briefly explained my origin and how I came to be in his world. He did not understand me,

I am sure, for though he seemed to be, and really was, highly intelligent, he could not conceive of any condition concerning which he had had no experience and in this way he did not differ materially from intelligent and highly educated Earth Men.

"And you," I asked, at length—"you are not a Kalkar? From whence come you?"

"I am from Laythe," he replied. "I fell outside the city and was captured by one of their hunting parties."

"Why all this enmity," I asked, "between the men of Laythe and the Kalkars—who are the Kalkars, anyway?"

"You are not of Va-nah," he said, "that I can see, or you would not ask these questions. The Kalkars derive their name from a corruption of a word meaning The Thinkers. Ages ago we were one race, a prosperous people living at peace with all the world of Va-nah. The Va-gas we bred for flesh, as we do today within our own city of Laythe and as the Kalkars do within their city. Our cities, towns and villages covered the slopes of the mountains and stretched downward to the sea. No corner of the three oceans but knew our ships, and our cities were joined together by a network of routes along which passed electrically driven trains"—he did not use the word trains, but an expression which might be liberally translated as ships of the land—"while other great carriers flew through the air. Our means of communication between distant points were simplified by science through the use of electrical energy, with the result that those who lived in one part of Va-nah could talk with those who lived in any other part of Va-nah, though it were to the remotest ends of the world. There were ten great divisions, each ruled by its Jemadar, and each division vied with all the others in the service which it rendered to its people. There were those who held high positions and those who held low; there were those who were rich and those who were poor, but the favors of the state were distributed equally among them, and the children of the poor had the same opportunities for education as the children of the rich, and there it was that our troubles first started. There is a saying among us that 'no learning is better than a little,' and I can well believe this true when I consider the history of my world, where, as the masses became a little educated, there developed among them a small coterie that commenced to find fault with everyone who had achieved greater learning or greater power than they. Finally, they organized themselves into a secret society called

The Thinkers, but known more accurately to the rest of Va-nah as those who thought that they thought. It is a long story, for it covers a great period of time, but the result was that, slowly at first, and later rapidly. The Thinkers, who did more talking than thinking, filled the people with dissatisfaction, until at last they arose and took over the government and commerce of the entire world. The Jemadars were overthrown and the ruling class driven from power, the majority of them being murdered, though some managed to escape, and it was these, my ancestors, who founded the city of Laythe. It is believed that there are other similar cities in remote parts of Va-nah inhabited by the descendants of the Jemadar and noble classes, but Laythe is the only one of which we have knowledge. The Thinkers would not work, and the result was that both government and commerce fell into rapid decay. They not only had neither the training nor the intelligence to develop new things, but they could not carry out the old that had been developed for them. The arts and sciences languished and died with commerce and government, and Va-nah fell back into barbarism. The Va-gas saw their chance and threw off the yoke that had held them through countless ages. As the Kalkars had driven the noble class into the lofty mountains, so the Va-gas drove the Kalkars. Practically every vestige of the ancient culture and commercial advancement of Va-nah has been wiped from the face of the world. The Laytheans have held their own for many centuries, but their numbers have not increased.

"Many generations elapsed before the Laytheans found sanctuary in the city of Laythe, and during that period they, too, lost all touch with the science and advancement and the culture of the past. Nor was there any way in which to rebuild what the Kalkars had torn down, since they had destroyed every written record and every book in every library in Va-nah. And so occupied are both races in eking out a precarious existence that there is little likelihood that there will ever again be any advancement made along these lines—it is beyond the intellectual powers of the Kalkars, and the Laytheans are too weak numerically to accomplish aught."

"It does look hopeless," I said, "almost as hopeless as our situation. There is no escape, I imagine, from this Kalkar city, is there?"

"No," he said, "none whatever. There is only one avenue and we are so confused when we are brought into the city that it would be impossible for us to find our way out again through this labyrinth of corridors and chambers."

"And if we did win our way to the outer world we would be as bad off, I presume, for we could never find Laythe, and sooner or later would be recaptured by the Kalkars or taken by the Va-gas. Am I not right?"

"No," he said, "you are not right. If I could reach the rim of the crater beyond this city I could find my way to Laythe. I know the way well, for I am one of Ko-tah's hunters and am thoroughly familiar with the country for great distances in all directions from Laythe."

So this was one of Ko-tah's men. I was glad, indeed, that I had not mentioned Nah-ee-lah or told him of her possible escape, or of my acquaintance with her.

"And who is Ko-tah?" I asked, feigning ignorance.

"Ko-tah is the most powerful noble of Laythe," he replied, "some day he will be Jemadar, for now that Nah-ee-lah, the Princess, is dead, and Sagroth, the Jemadar, grows old, it will not be long before there is a change."

"And if the Princess should return to Laythe," I asked, "would Ko-tah still become Jemadar then, upon the death of Sagroth?"

"He would become Jemadar in any event," replied my companion, "for had the Princess not been carried off by the air that runs away, Ko-tah would have married her, unless she refused, in which event she might have died—people do die, you know."

"You feel no loyalty, then," I asked, "for your old Jemadar, Sagroth, or for his daughter, the Princess?"

"On the contrary, I feel every loyalty toward them, but like many others, I am afraid of Ko-tah, for he is very powerful and we know that sooner or later he will become ruler of Laythe. That is why so many of the high nobles have attached themselves to him—it is not through love of Ko-tah, but through fear that he recruits his ranks."

"But the Princess!" I exclaimed, "would the nobles not rally to her defense?"

"What would be the use?" he asked. "We of Laythe do but exist in the narrow confines of our prison city. There is no great future to which we may look forward in this life, but future incarnations may hold for us a brighter prospect. It is no cruelty, then, to kill those who exist now under the chaotic reign of anarchy which has reduced Va-nah to a wilderness."

I partially caught his rather hopeless point of view and realized that the fellow was not bad or disloyal at heart, but like all his race, reduced to a state of hopelessness that was the result of ages of retrogression to which they could see no end.

"I can find the way to the mouth of the tunnel where it opens into the crater," I told him. "But how can we reach it unarmed through a city populated with our enemies who would slay us on sight?"

"There are never very many people in the chambers or corridors far removed from the outer terraces, and if we were branded upon the forehead, as accepted slaves are, and your apparel was not so noticeable, we might possibly reach the tunnel without weapons."

"Yes," I said, "my clothes are a handicap. They would immediately call attention to us; yet, it is worth risking, for I know that I can find my way back to the crater and I should rather die than remain a slave of the Kalkars."

The truth of the matter was that I was not prompted so much by abhorrence of the fate that seemed in store for me, as by a desire to learn if Nah-ee-lah had escaped. I was constantly haunted by the horrid fear that her hold upon the rim of the crater had given and that she had fallen into the abyss below. Gapth had thought that she had escaped, but I knew that she might have fallen without either of us having seen her, since the pole up which she had clambered had been fastened a little beyond the opening of the tunnel, so that, had her hold become loosened, she would not have fallen directly past the aperture. The more I thought of it, the more anxious I became to reach Laythe and institute a search for her.

While we were still discussing our chances of escape, two slaves brought us food in the shape of raw vegetables and fruit. I scanned them carefully for weapons, but they had none, a circumstance to which they may owe their lives. I could have used their garments, had they been other than slaves, but I had hit upon a bolder plan than this and must wait patiently for a favorable opportunity to put it into practice.

After eating I became sleepy and was about to stretch out upon the floor of our prison when my companion, whose name was Moh-goh, told me that there was a sleeping apartment adjoining the room in which we were, that had been set apart for us.

The doorway leading to the sleeping chamber was covered by heavy hangings, and as I parted them and stepped into the adjoining chamber, I found myself in almost total darkness, the walls and ceiling of this room not having been treated with the illuminating coating used in the corridors and apartments which they wished to maintain in a lighted condition. I later learned that all their sleeping apartments were thus naturally dark. In one corner of the room was a pile of dried vegetation which I discovered must answer the purpose of mattress and covering, should I require any. However, I was not so particular, as I had been accustomed to only the roughest of fare since I had left my luxurious stateroom aboard *The Barsoom*. How long I slept I do not know, but I was awakened by Moh-goh calling me. He was leaning over me, shaking me by the shoulder.

"You are wanted," he whispered. "They have come to take us before The Twentyfour."

"Tell them to go to the devil," I said, for I was very sleepy and only half awake. Of course, he did not know what devil meant, but evidently he judged from my tone that my reply was disrespectful to the Kalkars.

"Do not anger them," he said, "it will only make your fate the harder. When The Twentyfour command, all must obey."

"Who are The Twentyfour?" I demanded.

"They compose the committee that rules this Kalkar city."

I was thoroughly awakened now and rose to my feet, following him into the adjoining chamber, where I saw two Kalkar warriors standing impatiently awaiting us. As I saw them a phrase leaped to my brain and kept repeating itself: "There are but two, there are but two."

They were across the room from us, standing by the entrance, and Moh-goh was close to me.

"There are but two," I whispered to him in a low voice, "you take one and I will take the other. Do you dare?"

"I will take the one at the right," he replied, and together we advanced across the room slowly toward the unsuspecting warriors. The moment that we were in reach of them we leaped for them simultaneously. I did not see how Moh-goh attacked his man, for I was busy with my own, though it took me but an instant to settle him, for I struck him a single terrific blow upon the chin and as he fell I leaped upon him, wresting his dagger from its scabbard and plunging it into his heart before he could regain his senses from the stunning impact of my fist. Then I turned to assist Moh-goh, only to discover that he needed no assistance, but was already arising from the body of his antagonist, whose throat was cut from ear to ear with his own weapon.

"Quick!" I cried to Moh-goh, "drag them into the sleeping apartment before we are discovered"; and a moment later we had deposited the two corpses in the dimly lighted apartment adjoining.

"We will leave the city as Kalkar warriors," I said, commencing to strip the accoutrements and garments from the man I had slain.

Moh-goh grinned. "Not a bad idea," he said. "If you can find the route to the crater it is possible that we may yet escape."

It took us but a few moments to effect the change, and after we had hidden the bodies beneath the vegetation that had served us as a bed and stepped out into the other chamber, where we could have a good look at one another, we realized that if we were not too closely scrutinized we might pass safely through the corridors beneath the Kalkar city, for the Kalkars are a mongrel breed, comprising many divergent types. My complexion, which differed outrageously from that of either the Kalkars or the Laytheans, constituted our greatest danger, but we must take the chance, and at least we were armed.

"Lead the way," said Moh-goh, "and if you can find the crater I can assure you that I can find Laythe."

"Very good," I said, "come," and stepping into the corridor I moved off confidently in the direction that I knew I should find the passageways and stairs along which I had been conducted from the crater tunnel. I was as confident of success as though I were traversing the most familiar precinct of my native city.

We traveled a considerable distance without meeting anyone, and at last reached the chamber in which I had been blindfolded. As we entered it I saw fully a score of Kalkars lolling upon benches or lying upon vegetation that was piled upon the floor. They looked up as we entered, and at the same time Moh-goh stepped in front of me.

"Who are you and where are you going?" demanded one of the Kalkars.

"By order of The Twentyfour," said Moh-goh, and stepped into the room. Instantly I realized that he did not know in which direction to go, and that by his hesitancy all might be lost.

"Straight ahead, straight across the room," I whispered to him, and he stepped out briskly in the direction of the entrance to the tunnel. Fortunately for us, the chamber was not brilliantly lighted, and the Kalkars were at the far end of it; otherwise they must certainly have discovered my deception, at least, since any sort of close inspection would have revealed the fact that I was not of Va-nah. However, they did not halt us, though I was sure that I saw one of them eyeing me suspiciously, and I venture to say that I took the last twenty steps without drawing a breath.

It was quickly over, however, and we had entered the tunnel which now led without further confusing ramifications directly to the crater.

"We were fortunate," I said to Moh-goh.

"That we were," he replied.

In silence, then, that we might listen for pursuit, or for the sound of Kalkars ahead of us, we hastened rapidly along the descending passageway toward the mouth of the tunnel where it opened into the crater; and at last, as we rounded the last turn and I saw the light of day ahead of me, I breathed a deep sigh of relief, though almost simultaneously my happiness turned to despair at the sudden recollection that there were no hooked poles here to assist us to the summit of the crater wall. What were we to do?

"Moh-goh," I said, turning to my companion as we halted at the end of the tunnel, "there are no poles with which to ascend. I had forgotten it, but in order to prevent the Kalkars from ascending after me, I threw all but one into the abyss, and that one slipped from the rim and was lost also, just as my pursuers were about to seize me."

I had not told Moh-goh that I had had a companion, since it would be difficult to answer any questions he might propound on the subject without revealing the identity of Nah-ee-lah.

"Oh, we can overcome that," replied my companion. "We have these two spears, which are extremely stout, and inasmuch as we shall have plenty of time, we can easily arrange them in some way that will permit us to ascend to the summit of the crater. It is very fortunate that we were not pursued."

The Kalkar's spears had a miniature crescent-shaped hook at the base of their point similar to the larger ones effected by the Va-gas. Moh-goh thought that we could fasten the two spears securely together and then catch the small hook of the upper one upon the rim of the crater, testing its hold thoroughly before either of us attempted to ascend. Beneath his tunic he wore a rope coiled around his waist which he explained to me was a customary part of the equipment of all Laytheans. It was his idea to tie one end of this around the waist of whichever of us ascended first, the other going as far back into the tunnel as possible and bracing himself, so that in the event that the climber fell, he would be saved from death, though I figured that he would get a rather nasty shaking up and some bad bruises, under the best of circumstances.

I volunteered to go first and began fastening one end of the rope securely about my waist while Moh-goh made the two spears fast together with a short length that he had cut from the other end. He worked rapidly, with deft, nimble fingers, and seemed to know pretty well what he was doing. In the event that I reached the summit in safety, I was to pull up the spears and then haul Moh-goh up by the rope.

Having fastened the rope to my satisfaction, I stood as far out upon the ledge before the entrance to the tunnel as I safely could, and with my back toward the crater looked up at the rim twenty feet above me, in a vain attempt to select from below, if possible, a reasonably secure point upon which to hook the spear. As I stood thus upon the edge of eternity, steadying myself with one hand against the tunnel wall, there came down to me from out of the tunnel a noise which I could not mistake. Moh-goh heard it, too, and looked at me, with a rueful shake of his head and a shrug of his shoulders.

"Everything is against us, Earth Man," he said, for this was the name he had given me when I told him what my world was called.

CHAPTER ELEVEN
LAYTHE

THE PURSUERS WERE NOT YET in sight, but I knew from the nearness of the sound of approaching footsteps that it would be impossible to complete the splicing of the spears, to find a secure place for the hook above, and for me to scramble upward to the rim of the crater and haul Moh-goh after me before they should be upon us. Our position looked almost hopeless. I could think of no avenue of escape, and yet I tried, and as I stood there with bent head, my eyes cast upon the floor of the tunnel, they fell upon the neatly coiled rope lying at my feet, one end of which was fastened securely about my waist. Instantly there flashed into my mind a mad inspiration. I glanced up at the overhanging rim above me. Could I do it? There was a chance—the lesser gravity of the Moon placed the thing within the realm of possibility, and yet by all earthly standards it was impossible. I did not wait, I could not wait, for had I given the matter any thought I doubt that I would have had the nerve to attempt it. Behind me lay a cavern opening into the depths of space, into which I should be dashed if my mad plan failed; but, what of it? Better death than slavery. I stooped low, then, and concentrating every faculty upon absolute coordination of mind and muscles, I leaped straight upward with all the strength of my legs.

And in that instant during which my life hung in the balance, of what did I think? Of home, of Earth, of the friends of my childhood? No—of a pale and lovely face, with great, dark eyes and a perfect forehead, surmounted by a wealth of raven hair. It was the image of Nah-ee-lah, the Moon Maid, that I would have carried with me into eternity, had I died that instant.

But, I did not die. My leap carried me above the rim of the crater, where I lunged forward and fell sprawling, my arms and upper body upon the surface of the ground. Instantly I turned about and lying upon my belly, seized the rope in both hands.

"Quick, Moh-goh!" I cried to my companion below; "make the rope fast about you, keep hold of the spears and I will drag you up!"

"Pull away," he answered me instantly, "I have no time to make the rope fast about me. They are almost upon me, pull away and be quick about it."

I did as he bade, and a moment later his hands grasped the rim of the crater and with my assistance he gained the top, dragging the spears after him. For a moment he stood there in silence looking at me with a most peculiar expression upon his face; then he shook his head.

"I do not understand, yet," he said, "how you did it, but it was very wonderful."

"I scarcely expected to accomplish it in safety, myself," I replied, "but anything is better than slavery."

From below us came the voices of the Kalkars in angry altercation. Moh-goh picked up a fragment of rock, and leaning over the edge of the crater, threw it down among them. "I got one," he said, turning to me with a laugh, "he tumbled off into nothing; they hate that. They believe that there is no reincarnation for those who fall into a crater."

"Do you think that they will try to follow us?" I asked.

"No," he said, "they will be afraid to use their hooked poles here for a long time, lest we should be in the neighborhood and shove them off into the crater. I will drop another rock down if any of them are in sight and then we will go upon our way. I do not fear them here in the hills, anyway.

There is always plenty of broken stone upon the level places, and we of Laythe are trained to use it most effectively—almost as far as I can throw, I can score a hit."

The Kalkars had withdrawn into the tunnel, so Moh-goh lost his opportunity to dispatch another, and presently turned away from the crater and set out into the mountains, I following close behind.

I can assure you that I felt much better, now that I was armed with a spear and a knife, and as we walked I practiced casting stones, at Moh-goh's suggestion and under his instruction, until I became rather proficient in the art.

I shall not weary you with a narration of our journey to Laythe. How long it took, I do not know. It may have consumed a day, a week, or a month, for time seemed quite a meaningless term in Va-nah, but at length, after clambering laboriously from the bottom of a deep gorge, we stood upon the edge of a rolling plateau, and at some little distance beheld what at first appeared to be a cone-shaped mountain, rising fully a mile into the air above the surface of the plateau.

"There," cried Moh-goh, "is Laythe! The crater where lies the entrance to the tunnel leading to the city is beyond it."

As we approached the city, the base of which we must skirt in order to reach the crater beyond, I was able to obtain a better idea of the dimensions and methods of construction of this great interior lunar city, the base of which was roughly circular and about six miles in diameter, ranging from a few hundred to a thousand feet above the level of the plateau. The base of the city appeared to be the outer wall of an ancient extinct volcano, the entire summit of which had been blown off during some terrific eruption of a bygone age. Upon this base the ancient Laytheans had commenced the construction of their city, the houses of which rose one upon another as did those of the Kalkar city from which we had just escaped. The great age of Laythe was attested by the tremendous height to which these superimposed buildings had arisen, the loftiest wall of Laythe now rising fully a mile above the floor of the plateau. Narrow terraces encircled the periphery of the towering city, and as we approached more closely I saw doors and windows opening upon the terraces and figures moving to and fro, the whole resembling closely an enormous hive of bees. When we had reached a point near the base of the city, I saw that we had been discovered, for directly above us there were people at various points who were unquestionably looking down at us and commenting upon us.

"They have seen us from above," I said to Moh-goh, "why don't you hail them?"

"They take us for Kalkars," he replied. "It is easier for us to enter the city by way of the tunnel, where I shall have no difficulty in establishing my identity."

"If they think we are Kalkars," I said, "will they not attack us?"

"No," he replied, "Kalkars often pass Laythe. If they do not try to enter the city, we do not molest them."

"Your people fear them, then?" I asked.

"It practically amounts to that," he replied. "They greatly outnumber us, perhaps a thousand to one, and as they are without justice, mercy or honor we try not to antagonize them unnecessarily."

We came at length to the mouth of the crater, and here Moh-goh looped his rope about the base of a small tree growing close to the rim and slipped down to the opening of the tunnel directly beneath. I followed his example, and when I was beside him Moh-goh pulled the rope in, coiled it about his waist, and we set off along the passageway leading toward Laythe.

After my long series of adventures with unfriendly people in Va-nah, I had somewhat the sensation of one returning home after a long absence, for Moh-goh had assured me that the people of Laythe would receive me well and that I should be treated as a friend. He even assured me that he would procure for me a good berth in the service of Ko-tah. My greatest regret now was for Nah-ee-lah, and that she was not my companion, instead of Moh-goh. I was quite sure that she was lost, for had she escaped, falling back into the crater outside the Kalkar city, I doubted that she could successfully have found her way to Laythe. My heart had been heavy since we had been separated, and I had come to realize that the friendship of this little Moon Maid had meant a great deal more to me than I had thought. I could scarcely think of her now without a lump coming into my throat, for it seemed cruel, indeed, that one so young and lovely should have met so untimely an end.

The distance between the crater and the city of Laythe is not great, and presently we came directly out upon the lower terrace within the city. This terrace is at the very rim of the crater around which Laythe is built. And here we ran directly into the arms of a force of about fifty warriors.

Moh-goh emerged from the tunnel with his spear grasped in both hands high above his head, the point toward the rear, and I likewise, since he had cautioned me to do so. So surprised were the warriors to see any creatures emerge from this tunnel, which had been so long disused, that we were likely to have been slain before they realized that we had come before them with the signal of peace.

The guard that is maintained at the inner opening of the tunnel is considered by the Laytheans as more or less of an honorary assignment, the duties of which are performed perfunctorily.

"What do you here, Kalkars?" exclaimed the commander of the guard.

"We are not Kalkars," replied my companion. "I am Moh-goh the Paladar, and this be my friend. Can it be that you, Ko-vo the Kamadar, do not know me?"

"Ah!" cried the commander of the guard, "it is, indeed, Moh-goh the Paladar. You have been given up as lost."

"I was lost, indeed, had it not been for this, my friend," replied Moh-goh, nodding his head in my direction. "I was captured by the Kalkars and incarcerated in City No. 337."

"You escaped from a Kalkar city?" exclaimed Ko-vo, in evident incredulity. "That is impossible. It never has been accomplished."

"But we did accomplish it," replied Moh-goh, "thanks to my friend here," and then he narrated briefly to Ko-vo the details of our escape.

"It scarce seems possible," commented the Laythean, when Moh-goh had completed his narrative, "and what may be the name of your friend, Moh-goh, and from what country did you say he came?"

"He calls himself Ju-lan-fit," replied Moh-goh, for that was as near as he could come to the pronunciation of my name. And so it was that as Ju-lan-fit I was known to the Laytheans as long as I remained among them. They thought that fifth, which they pronounced "fit," was a title similar to one of those which always followed the name of its possessor in Laythe, as Sagroth the Jemadar, or Emperor; Ko-vo the Kamadar, a title which corresponds closely to that of the English Duke; and Moh-goh the Paladar, or Count. And so, to humor them, I told them that it meant the same as their Javadar, or Prince. I was thereafter called sometimes Ju-lan-fit, and sometimes Ju-lan Javadar, as the spirit moved him who addressed me.

At Moh-goh's suggestion, Ko-vo the Kamadar detailed a number of his men to accompany us to Moh-goh's dwelling, lest we have difficulty in passing through the city in our Kalkar garb.

As we had stood talking with Ko-vo, my eyes had been taking in the interior sights of this lunar city. The crater about which Laythe is built appeared to be between three and four miles in width, the buildings facing it and rising terrace upon terrace to a height of a mile at least, were much more elaborate of architecture and far richer in carving than those of the Kalkar City No. 337. The terraces were broad and well cultivated, and as we ascended toward Moh-goh's dwelling I saw that much pains had been taken to elaborately landscape many of them, there being pools and rivulets and waterfalls in numerous places. As in the Kalkar city, there were Va-gas fattening for food in little groups upon various terraces. They were sleek and fat and appeared contented, and I learned later that they were perfectly satisfied with their lot, having no more conception of the purpose for which they were bred or the fate that awaited them than have the beef cattle of Earth.

The U-ga of Laythe have induced this mental state in their Va-gas herds by a process of careful selection covering a period of ages, possibly, during which time they have conscientiously selected for breeding purposes the most stupid and unimaginative members of their herds.

At Moh-goh's dwelling we were warmly greeted by the members of his family—his father, mother and two sisters—all of whom, like the other Laytheans I had seen, were of striking appearance. The men were straight and handsome, the women physically perfect and of great beauty.

I could see in the affectionate greetings which they exchanged an indication of a family life and ties similar to those which are most common upon Earth, while their gracious and hospitable reception of me marked them as people of highly refined sensibilities. First of all they must hear Moh-goh's story, and then, after having congratulated us and praised us, they set about preparing baths and fresh apparel for us, in which they were assisted by a corps of servants, descendants, I was told, of the faithful servitors who had remained loyal to the noble classes and accompanied them in their exile.

We rested for a short time after our baths, and then Moh-goh announced that he must go before Ko-tah, to whom it was necessary that he report, and that he would take me with him. I was appareled now in raiment befitting my supposed rank and carried the weapons of a Laythean gentleman—a short lance, or javelin, a dagger and a sword, but with my relatively darker skin and my blond hair, I could never hope to be aught than an object of remark in any Laythean company. Owing to the color of my hair, some of them thought that I was a Kalkar, but upon this score my complexion set them right.

Ko-tah's dwelling was, indeed, princely, stretching along a broad terrace for fully a quarter of a mile, with its two stories and its numerous towers and minarets. The entire face of the building was elaborately and beautifully carved, the decorations in their entirety recording pictographically the salient features of the lives of Ko-tah's ancestors.

Armed nobles stood on either side of the massive entrance way, and long before we reached this lunar prince I realized that possibly he was more difficult to approach than one of earthly origin, but at last we were ushered into his presence, and Moh-goh, with the utmost deference, presented me to Ko-tah the Javadar. Having assumed a princely title and princely raiment, I chose to assume princely prerogatives as well, believing that my position among the Laytheans would be better assured and all my interests furthered if they thought me of royal blood, and so I acknowledged my introduction to Ko-tah as though we were equals and that he was being presented to me upon the same footing that I was being presented to him.

I found him, like all his fellows, a handsome man, but with a slightly sinister expression which I did not like. Possibly I was prejudiced against him from what Nah-ee-lah had told me, but be that as it may, I conceived a dislike and distrust for him the moment that I laid eyes upon him, and I think, too, that he must have sensed my attitude, for, though he was outwardly gracious and courteous, I believe that Ko-tah the Javadar never liked me.

It is true that he insisted upon allotting me quarters within his palace and that he gave me service high among his followers, but I was at that time a novelty among them, and Ko-tah was not alone among the royalty who would have been glad to have entertained me and showered favors upon me, precisely as do Earth Men when a titled stranger, or famous man from another land, comes to their country.

Although I did not care for him, I was not loath to accept his hospitality, since I felt that because of my friendship for Nah-ee-lah I owed all my loyalty to Sagroth the Jemadar, and if by placing myself in the camp of the enemy I might serve the father of Nah-ee-lah, I was justified in so doing.

I found myself in a rather peculiar position in the palace of Ko-tah, since I was supposed to know little or nothing of internal condition in Laythe, and yet had learned from both Nah-ee-lah and Moh-goh a great deal concerning the intrigues and politics of this lunar city. For example, I was not supposed to know of the existence of Nah-ee-lah. Not even did Moh-goh know that I had heard of her; and so until her name was mentioned, I could ask no questions concerning her, though I was anxious indeed, to discover if by any miracle of chance, she had returned in safety to Laythe, or if aught had been learned concerning her fate.

Ko-tah held me in conversation for a considerable period of time, asking many questions concerning Earth and my voyage from that planet to the Moon. I knew that he was skeptical, and yet he was a man of such intelligence as to realize that there must be something in the Universe beyond his understanding or his knowledge. His eyes told him that I was not a native of Va-nah, and his ears must have corroborated the testimony of his eyes, for try as I would, I never was able to master the Va-nahan language so that I could pass for a native.

At the close of our interview Ko-tah announced that Moh-goh would also remain in quarters in the palace, suggesting that if it was agreeable to me, my companion should share my apartments with me.

"Nothing would give me greater pleasure, Ko-tah the Javadar," I said, "than to have my good friend, Moh-goh the Paladar, always with me."

"Excellent!" exclaimed Ko-tah. "You must both be fatigued. Go, therefore, to your apartments and rest. Presently I will repair to the palace of the Jemadar with my court, and you will be notified in sufficient time to prepare yourselves to accompany me."

The audience was at an end, and we were led by nobles of Ko-tah's palace to our apartments, which lay upon the second floor in pleasant rooms overlooking the terraces down to the brink of the great, yawning crater below.

Until I threw myself upon the soft mattress that served as a bed for me, I had not realized how physically exhausted I had been. Scarcely had I permitted myself to relax in the luxurious ease which precedes sleep ere I was plunged into profound slumber, which must have endured for a considerable time, since when I awoke I was completely refreshed. Moh-goh was already up and in the bath, a marble affair fed by a continuous supply of icy water which originated among the ice-clad peaks of the higher mountains behind Laythe. The bather had no soap, but used rough fiber gloves with which he rubbed the surface of his skin until it glowed. These baths rather took one's breath away, but amply repaid for the shock by the sensation of exhilaration and well-being which resulted from them.

In addition to private baths in each dwelling, each terrace supported a public bath, in which men, women and children disported themselves, recalling to my mind the ancient Roman baths which earthly history records.

The baths of the Jemadar which I was later to see in the palace of Sagroth were marvels of beauty and luxury. Here, when the Emperor entertains, his guests amuse themselves by swimming and diving, which, from what I have been able to judge, are the national sports of the Laytheans. The Kalkars care less for the water, while the Va-gas only enter it through necessity.

I followed Moh-goh in the bath, in which my first sensation was that I was freezing to death. While we were dressing a messenger from Ko-tah summoned us to his presence, with instructions that we were to be prepared to accompany him to the palace of Sagroth the Jemadar.

CHAPTER TWELVE
KO-TAH THREATENS THE PRINCESS

THE PALACE OF THE EMPEROR STANDS, a magnificent pile, upon the loftiest terrace of Laythe, extending completely around the enormous crater. There are but three avenues leading to it from the terraces below—three magnificent stairways, each of which may be closed by enormous gates of stone, apparently wrought from huge slabs and intricately chiseled into marvelous designs, so that at a distance they present the appearance of magnificent lacework. Each gate is guarded by a company of fifty warriors, their tunics bearing the imperial design in a large circle over the left breast.

The ceremony of our entrance to the imperial terrace was most gorgeous and impressive. Huge drums and trumpets blared forth a challenge as we reached the foot of the stairway which we were to ascend to the palace.

High dignitaries in gorgeous trappings came down the steps to meet us, as if to formally examine the credentials of Ko-tah and give official sanction to his entrance. We were then conducted through the gateway across a broad terrace beautifully landscaped and ornamented by statuary that was most evidently the work of finished artists. These works of art comprised both life size and heroic figures of individuals and groups, and represented for the most part historic or legendary figures and events of the remote past, though there were also likenesses of all the rulers of Laythe, up to and including Sagroth the present Jemadar.

Upon entering the palace we were led to a banquet hall, where we were served with food, evidently purely in accordance with ancient court ceremonial, since there was little to eat and the guests barely tasted of that which was presented to them. This ceremony consumed but a few minutes of Earth time, following which we were conducted through spacious hallways to the throne room of the Jemadar, an apartment of great beauty and considerable size. Its decorations and lines were simple, almost to severity, yet suggesting regal dignity and magnificence. Upon a dais at the far end of the room were three thrones, that in the center being occupied by a man whom I knew at once to be Sagroth, while upon either side sat a woman.

Ko-tah advanced and made his obeisance before his ruler, and after the exchange of a few words between them Ko-tah returned and conducted me to the foot of Sagroth's throne.

I had been instructed that it was in accordance with court etiquette that I keep my eyes upon the ground until I had been presented and Sagroth had spoken to me, and that then I should be introduced to the Jemadav, or Empress, when I might raise my eyes to her, also, and afterward to the occupant of the third throne when I should be formally presented to her.

Sagroth spoke most graciously to me, and as I raised my eyes I saw before me a man of great size and evident strength of character. He was by far the most regal appearing individual my eyes had ever rested upon, while his low, well-modulated, yet powerful voice accentuated the majesty of his mien. It was he who presented me to his Jemadav, whom I discovered to be a creature fully as regal in appearance as her imperial mate, and although doubtless well past middle age, still possessing remarkable beauty, in which was to be plainly noted Nah-ee-lah's resemblance to her mother.

Again I lowered my eyes as Sagroth presented me to the occupant of the third throne.

"Ju-lan the Javadar," he repeated the formal words of the presentation, "raise your eyes to the daughter of Laythe, Nah-ee-lah the Nonovar."

As my eyes, filled doubtless with surprise and incredulity, shot to the face of Nah-ee-lah, I was almost upon the verge of an exclamation of the joy and happiness which I felt in seeing her again and in knowing that she was safely returned to her parents and her city once more. But as my eyes met hers the exuberance of my spirit was as effectually and quickly checked by her cold glance and haughty mien as if I had received a blow in the face.

There was no hint of recognition in Nah-ee-lah's expression. She nodded coldly in acknowledgment of the presentation and then let her eyes pass above my head toward the opposite end of the throne room. My pride was hurt, and I was angry, but I would not let her see how badly I was hurt. I have always prided myself upon my control, and so I know that then I hid my emotion and turned once more to Sagroth, as though I had received from his daughter the Nonovar precisely the favor that I had a right to expect. If the Jemadar had noticed aught peculiar in either Nah-ee-lah's manner or mine, he gave no hint of it. He spoke again graciously to me and then dismissed me, with the remark that we should meet again later.

Having withdrawn from the throne room, Ko-tah informed me that following the audience I should have an opportunity to meet Sagroth less formally, since he had commanded that I remain in the palace as his guest during the meal which followed.

"It is a mark of distinction," said Ko-tah, "but remember, Ju-lan the Javadar, that you have accepted the friendship of Ko-tah and are his ally."

"Do not embroil me in the political intrigues of Laythe," I replied. "I am a stranger, with no interest in the internal affairs of your country, for the reason that I have no knowledge of them."

"One is either a friend or an enemy," replied Ko-tah.

"I am not sufficiently well acquainted to be accounted either," I told him; "nor shall I choose my friends in Laythe until I am better acquainted, nor shall another choose them for me."

"You are a stranger here," said Ko-tah. "I speak in your best interests, only. If you would succeed here; aye, if you would live, even, you must choose quickly and you must choose correctly. I, Ko-tah the Javadar, have spoken."

"I choose my own friends," I replied, "according to the dictates of my honor and my heart. I, Ju-lan the Javadar, have spoken."

He bowed low in acquiescence, and when he again raised his eyes to mine I was almost positive from the expression in them that his consideration of me was marked more by respect than resentment.

"We shall see," was all that he said, and withdrew, leaving me to the kindly attention of some of the gentlemen of Sagroth's court who had been standing at a respectful distance out of earshot of Ko-tah and myself. These men chatted pleasantly with me for some time until I was bidden to join Sagroth in another part of the palace.

I found myself now with a man who had evidently thrown off the restraint of a formal audience, though without in the slightest degree relinquishing either his dignity or his majesty. He spoke more freely and his manner was more democratic. He asked me to be seated, nor would he himself sit until I had, a point of Laythean court etiquette which made a vast impression on me, since it indicated that the first gentleman of the city must also be the first in courtesy. He put question after question to me concerning my own world and the means by which I had been transported to Va-nah.

"There are fragmentary, extremely fragmentary, legends handed down from extreme antiquity which suggest that our remote ancestors had some knowledge concerning the other worlds of which you speak," he said, "but these have been considered always the veriest of myths. Can it be possible that, after all, they are based upon truth?"

"The remarkable part of them," I suggested, "is that they exist at all, since it is difficult to understand how any knowledge of the outer Universe could ever reach to the buried depths of Va-nah."

"No, not by any means," he said, "if what you tell me is the truth, for our legends bear out the theory that Va-nah is located in the center of an enormous globe and that our earliest progenitors lived upon the outer surface of this globe, being forced at last by some condition which the legends do not even suggest, to find their way into this inner world."

I shook my head. It did not seem possible.

"And, yet," he said, noting the doubt that my expression evidently betrayed, "you yourself claim to have reached Va-nah from a great world far removed from our globe which you call the Moon. If you reached us from another world, is it then so difficult to believe that those who preceded us reached Va-nah from the outer crust of this Moon? It is almost an historic certainty," he continued, "that our ancestors possessed great ships which navigated the air. As you entered Va-nah by means of a similar conveyance, may not they have done likewise?"

I had to admit that it was within the range of possibilities, and in so doing, to avow that the Moon Men of antiquity had been millions of years in advance of their brethren of the Earth.

But, after all, was it such a difficult conclusion to reach when one considers the fact that the Moon being smaller, must have cooled more rapidly than Earth, and therefore, provided that it had an atmosphere, have been habitable to man ages before man could have lived upon our own planet?

We talked pleasantly upon many subjects for some time, and then, at last, Sagroth arose.

"We will join the others at the tables now," he said, and as he led the way from the apartment in which we had been conversing alone, stone doors opened before us as by magic, indicating that the Jemadar of Laythe was not only well served, but well protected, or possibly well spied upon.

After we emerged from the private audience, guards accompanied us, some preceding the Jemadar and some following, and thus we moved in semistate through several corridors and apartments until we came out upon a balcony upon the second floor of the palace overlooking the terraces and the crater.

Here, along the rail of the balcony, were numerous small tables, each seating two, all but two of the tables being occupied by royal and noble retainers and their women. As the Jemadar entered, these all arose, facing him respectfully, and simultaneously through another entrance, came the Jemadav and Nah-ee-lah.

They stood just within the room, waiting until Sagroth and I crossed to them. While we were doing so, Sagroth very courteously explained the procedure I was to follow.

"You will place yourself upon the Nonovar's left," he concluded, "and conduct her to her table precisely as I conduct the Jemadav."

Nah-ee-lah's head was high as I approached her and she vouchsafed me only the merest inclination of it in response to my respectful salutation.

In silence we followed Sagroth and his Empress to the tables reserved for us. The balance of the company remained standing until, at a signal from Sagroth, we all took our seats. It was necessary for me to watch the others closely, as I knew nothing concerning the social customs of Laythe, but when I saw that conversation had become general I glanced at Nah-ee-lah.

"The Princess of Laythe so soon forgets her friends?" I asked.

"The Princess of Laythe never forgets her friends," she replied.

"I know nothing of your customs here," I said, "but in my world even royalty may greet their friends with cordiality and seeming pleasure."

"And here, too," she retorted.

I saw that something was amiss, that she seemed to be angry with me, but the cause I could not imagine. Perhaps she thought I had deserted her at the entrance to the tunnel leading to the Kalkar city. But no, she must have guessed the truth. What then, could be the cause of her cold aloofness, who, the last that I had seen of her, had been warm with friendship?

"I wonder," I said, trying a new tack, "if you were as surprised to see me alive as I you. I had given you up for lost, Nah-ee-lah, and I had grieved more than I can tell you. When I saw you in the audience chamber I could scarce repress myself, but when I saw that you did not wish to recognize me, I could only respect your desires."

She made no reply, but turned and looked out the window across the terraces and the crater to the opposite side of Laythe. She was ice, who had been almost fire. No longer was she little Nah-ee-lah, the companion of my hardships and dangers. No longer was she friend and confidante, but a cold and haughty Princess, who evidently looked upon me with disfavor. Her attitude outraged all the sacred tenets of friendship, and I was angered.

"Princess," I said, "if it is customary for Laytheans thus to cast aside the sacred bonds of friendship, I should do as well to be among the Va-gas or the Kalkars."

"The way to either is open," she replied haughtily. "You are not a prisoner in Laythe."

Thereafter conversation languished and expired, as far at least, as Nah-ee-lah and I were concerned, and I was more than relieved when the unpleasant function was concluded.

Two young nobles took me in charge, following the meal; as it seemed that I was to remain as a guest in the palace for awhile, and as I expressed a desire to see as much of the imperial residence as I might be permitted to, they graciously conducted me upon a tour of inspection. We went out upon the outer terraces which overlooked the valleys and the mountains, and never in my life have I looked upon a landscape more majestic or inspiring. The crater of Laythe, situated upon a broad plateau entirely surrounded by lofty mountains, titanic peaks that would dwarf our Alps into insignificance and reduce the Himalayas to foothills, lowered far into the distance upon the upper side, the ice-clad summits of those more distant seemed to veritably topple above us, while a thousand feet below us the pinks and lavenders of the weird lunar vegetation lay like a soft carpet upon the gently undulating surface of the plateau.

But my guides seemed less interested in the scenery than in me. They plied me with questions continually, until I was more anxious to be rid of them than aught else that I could think of. They asked me a little concerning my own world and what I thought of Laythe, and if I found the Princess Nah-ee-lah charming, and my opinion of the Emperor Sagroth. My answers must have been satisfactory, for presently they came very close to me and one of them whispered:

"You need not fear to speak in our presence. We, too, are friends and followers of Ko-tah."

"The Devil!" I thought. "They are bound to embroil me in their petty intrigues. What do I care for Sagroth or Ko-tah or"—and then my thoughts reverted to Nah-ee-lah. She had treated me cruelly. Her cold aloofness and her almost studied contempt had wounded me, yet I could not say to myself that Nah-ee-lah was nothing to me. She had been my friend and I had been hers, and I should remain her friend to my dying day. Perhaps, then, if these people were bound to draw me into their political disputes, I might turn their confidences into profit for Nah-ee-lah. I had never told them that I was a creature of Ko-tah's, for I was not, nor had I ever told Ko-tah that I was an enemy to Sagroth; in fact, I had led him to believe the very opposite. And so I gave these two an evasive answer which might have meant anything, and they chose to interpret it as meaning that I was one of them. Well, what could I do? It was not my fault if they insisted upon deceiving themselves, and Nah-ee-lah might yet need the friendship that she had scorned.

"Has Sagroth no loyal followers, then," I asked, "that you are all so sure of the success of the *coup d'état* that Ko-tah plans?"

"Ah, you know about it then!" cried one of them. "You are in the confidence of the Javadar."

I let them think that I was. It could do no harm, at least.

"Did he tell you when it was to happen?" asked the other.

"Perhaps, already I have said too much," I replied. "The confidences of Ko-tah are not to be lightly spread about."

"You are right," said the last speaker. "It is well to be discreet, but let us assure you, Ju-lan the Javadar, that we are equally in the confidence and favor of Ko-tah with any of those who serve him; otherwise, he would not have entrusted us with a portion of the work which must be done within the very palace of the Jemadar."

"Have you many accomplices here?" I asked.

"Many," he replied, "outside of the Jemadar's guards. They remain loyal to Sagroth. It is one of the traditions of the organization, and they will die for him, to a man and," he added with a shrug, "they shall die, never fear. When the time arrives and the signal is given, each member of the guard will be set upon by two of Ko-tah's faithful followers."

I do not know how long I remained in the City of Laythe. Time passed rapidly, and I was very happy after I returned to the dwelling of Moh-goh. I swam and dived with them and their friends in the baths upon our terrace, and also in those of Ko-tah. I learned to use the flying wings that I had first seen upon Nah-ee-lah the day that she fell exhausted into the clutches of the Va-gas, and many were the lofty and delightful excursions we took into the higher mountains of the Moon, when Moh-goh or his friends organized pleasure parties for the purpose. Constantly surrounded by people of culture and refinement, by brave men and beautiful women, my time was so filled with pleasurable activities that I made no effort to gauge it. I felt that I was to spend the balance of my life here, and I might as well get from it all the pleasure that Laythe could afford.

I did not see Nah-ee-lah during all this time, and though I still heard a great deal concerning the conspiracy against Sagroth, I presently came to attach but little importance to what I did hear, after I learned that the conspiracy had been on foot for over thirteen kelds, or approximately about ten earthly years, and seemed, according to my informers, no nearer consummation than it ever had been in the past.

Time does not trouble these people much, and I was told that it might be twenty kelds before Ko-tah took action, though on the other hand, he might strike within the next ola.

There was an occurrence during this period which aroused my curiosity, but concerning which Moh-goh was extremely reticent. Upon one of the occasions that I was a visitor in Ko-tah's palace, I was passing through a little used corridor in going from one chamber to another, when just ahead of me a door opened and a man stepped out in front of me. When he heard my footsteps behind him he turned and looked at me, and then stepped quickly back into the apartment he had just left and closed the door hurriedly behind him. There would have been nothing particularly remarkable in that, had it not been for the fact that the man was not a Laythean, but unquestionably a Kalkar.

Believing that I had discovered an enemy in the very heart of Laythe, I leaped forward, and throwing open the door, followed into the apartment into which the man had disappeared. To my astonishment, I found myself confronted by six men, three of whom were Kalkars, while the other three were Laytheans, and among the latter I instantly recognized Ko-tah, himself. He flushed angrily as he saw me, but before he could speak I bowed and explained my action.

"I crave your pardon, Javadar," I said. "I thought that I saw an enemy of Laythe in the heart of your palace, and that by apprehending him I should serve you best"; and I started to withdraw from the chamber.

"Wait," he said. "You did right, but lest you misunderstand their presence here, I may tell you that these three are prisoners."

"I realized that at once when I saw you, Javadar," I replied, though I knew perfectly that he had lied to me; and then I backed from the room, closing the door after me.

I spoke to Moh-goh about it the next time that I saw him.

"You saw nothing, my friend," he said. "Remember that—you saw nothing."

"If you mean that it is none of my business, Moh-goh," I replied, "I perfectly agree with you, and you may rest assured that I shall not meddle in affairs that do not concern me."

However, I did considerable thinking upon the matter, and possibly I went out of my way a little more than one should who is attending strictly to his own business, that I might keep a little in touch with the course of the conspiracy, for no matter what I had said to Moh-goh, no matter how

I attempted to convince myself that it did not interest me, the truth remained that anything that affected in any way the fate of Nah-ee-lah transcended in interest any event which might transpire within Va-nah, in so far as I was concerned.

The unobtrusive espionage which I practiced bore fruit, to the extent that it permitted me to know that on at least three other occasions delegations of Kalkars visited Ko-tah.

The fact that this ancient palace of the Prince of Laythe was a never-ending source of interest to me aided me in my self-imposed task of spying upon the conspirators, for the retainers of Ko-tah were quite accustomed to see me in out-of-the-way corridors and passages, oftentimes far from the inhabited portions of the building.

Upon the occasion of one of these tours I had descended to a lower terrace, along an ancient stone stairway which wound spirally downward and had discovered a dimly lighted room in which were stored a number of ancient works of art, I was quietly examining these, when I heard voices in an adjoining chamber.

"Upon no other conditions will he assist you, Javadar," said the speaker, whose voice I first heard.

"His demands are outrageous," replied a second speaker. "I refuse to consider them. Laythe is impregnable. He can never take it." The voice was that of Ko-tah.

"You do not know him, Laythean," replied the other. "He has given us engines of destruction with which we can destroy any city in Va-nah. He will give you Laythe. Is that not enough?"

"But he will be Jemadar of Jemadars and rule us all!" exclaimed Ko-tah. "The Jemadar of Laythe can be subservient to none."

"If you do not accede he will take Laythe in spite of you and reduce you to the status of a slave."

"Enough, Kalkar!" cried Ko-tah, his voice trembling with rage. "Be gone! Tell your master that Ko-tah refuses his base demands."

"You will regret it, Laythean," replied the Kalkar, "for you do not know what this creature has brought from another world in knowledge of war and the science of destruction of human life."

"I do not fear him," snapped Ko-tah, "my swords are many, my spearmen are well trained. Be gone, and do not return until your master is ready to sue with Ko-tah for an alliance."

I heard receding footsteps then, and following that, a silence which I thought indicated that all had left the chamber, but presently I heard Ko-tah's voice again.

"What think you of it?" he asked. And then I heard the voice of a third man, evidently a Laythean, replying:

"I think that if there is any truth in the fellow's assertions, we may not too quickly bring about the fall of Sagroth and place you upon the throne of Laythe, for only thus may we stand united against a common outside enemy."

"You are right," replied the Javadar. "Gather our forces. We shall strike within the ola."

I wanted to hear more, but they passed out of the chamber then, and their voices became only a subdued murmur which quickly trailed off into silence. What should I do? Within six hours Ko-tah would strike at the power of Sagroth, and I well knew what that would mean to Nah-ee-lah; either marriage with the new Jemadar, or death, and I guessed that the proud Princess would choose the latter in preference to Ko-tah.

CHAPTER THIRTEEN
KO-TAH IS KILLED

AS RAPIDLY AS I COULD I made my way from the palace of Ko-tah, and upward, terrace by terrace, toward the palace of the Jemadar. I had never presented myself at Sagroth's palace since Nah-ee-lah had so grievously offended me. I did not even know the customary procedure to follow to gain an audience with the Emperor, but nevertheless I came boldly to the carven gates and demanded to speak with the officer in command of the guards. When he came I told him that I desired to speak either with Sagroth or the Princess Nah-ee-lah at once, upon a matter of the most urgent importance.

"Wait," he said, "and I will take your message to the Jemadar."

He was gone for what seemed to me a very long time, but at last he returned, saying that Sagroth would see me at once, and I was conducted through the gates and into the palace toward the small audience chamber in which Sagroth had once received me so graciously. As I was ushered into the room I found myself facing both Sagroth and Nah-ee-lah.

The attitude of the Jemadar seemed apparently judicial, but that of the Princess was openly hostile.

"What are you doing here, traitor?" she demanded, without waiting for Sagroth to speak, and at the same instant a door upon the opposite side of the room burst open and three warriors leaped into the apartment with bared swords. They wore the livery of Ko-tah, and I knew instantly the purpose for which they had come. Drawing my own sword, I leaped forward.

"I have come to defend the life of the Jemadar and his Princess," I cried, as I sprang between them and the advancing three.

"What means this?" demanded Sagroth. "How dare you enter the presence of your Jemadar with drawn sword?"

"They are the assassins of Ko-tah come to slay you!" I cried. "Defend yourself, Sagroth of Laythe!" And with that, I tried to engage the three until help arrived.

I am no novice with the sword. The art of fencing has been one of my chief diversions since my cadet days in the Air School, and I did not fear the Laytheans, though I knew that, even were they but mediocre swordsmen, I could not for long withstand the assaults of three at once. But upon this point I need not have concerned myself, for no sooner had I spoken than Sagroth's sword leaped from its scabbard, and placing himself at my side, he fought nobly and well in defense of his life and his honor.

One of our antagonists merely tried to engage me while the other two assassinated the Jemadar. And so, seeing that he was playing me, and that I could do with him about as I pleased if I did not push him too hard, I drove him back a few steps until I was close at the side of one of those who engaged Sagroth. Then before any could know my intention, I wheeled and lunged my sword through the heart of one of those who opposed the father of Nah-ee-lah. So quickly had I disengaged my former antagonist, so swift my lunge, that I had recovered and was ready to meet the renewed assaults of the first who had engaged me almost before he realized what had happened.

It was man against man, now, and the odds were even. I had no opportunity to watch Sagroth, but from the ring of steel on steel, I knew that the two were bitterly engaged. My own man kept me well occupied. He was a magnificent swordsman, but he was only fighting for his life; I was fighting for more—for my life and for my honor, too, since after the word "traitor" that Nah-ee-lah had hurled at me, I had felt that I must redeem myself in her eyes. I did not give any thought at all to the question as to just why I should care what Nah-ee-lah the Moon Maid thought of me, but something within me reacted mightily to the contempt that she had put into that single word.

I could catch an occasional glimpse of her standing there behind the massive desk at which her father had sat upon the first occasion of my coming to this chamber. She stood there very tense, her wide eyes fixed upon me in evident incredulity.

I had almost worn my man down and we were fighting now so that I was facing Nah-ee-lah, with my back toward the doorway through which the three assassins had entered. Sagroth must have been more than holding his own, too, for I could see his opponent slowly falling back before the older man's assaults. And then there broke above the clang of steel a girl's voice—Nah-ee-lah's—raised in accents of fear.

"Julian, beware! Behind you! Behind you!"

At the instant of her warning the eyes of my antagonist left mine, which, for his own good, they never should have done, and passed in a quick glance over my shoulder at something or someone behind me. His lack of concentration cost him his life. I saw my opening the instant that it was made, and with a quick lunge I passed my blade through his heart. Whipping it out again, I wheeled to face a dozen men springing into the chamber. They paid no attention to me, but leaped toward Sagroth, and before I could prevent he went down with half a dozen blades through his body.

Upon the opposite side of the desk from us was another doorway directly behind Nah-ee-lah, and in the instant that she saw Sagroth fall, she called to me in a low voice: "Come, Julian, quick! Or we, too, are lost."

Realizing that the Jemadar was dead and that it would be folly to remain and attempt to fight this whole roomful of warriors, I leaped the desk and followed Nah-ee-lah through the doorway beyond. There was a cry, then, from someone within the room, to stop us, but Nah-ee-lah wheeled and slammed the door in their faces as they rushed forward, fastened it upon our side and then turned to me.

"Julian," she said, "how can you ever forgive me? You who have risked your life for the Jemadar, my father, in spite of the contemptible treatment that in my ignorance I have accorded you?"

"I could have explained," I said, "but you would not let me. Appearances were against me, and so I cannot blame you for thinking as you did."

"It was wicked of me not to listen to you, Julian, but I thought that Ko-tah had won you over, as he has won over even some of the staunchest friends of Sagroth."

"You might have known, Nah-ee-lah, that, even could I have been disloyal to your father, I never could have been disloyal to his daughter."

"I did not know," she said. "How could I?"

There suddenly came over me a great desire to take her in my arms and cover those lovely lips with kisses. I could not tell why this ridiculous obsession had seized upon me, nor why, of a sudden, I became afraid of little Nah-ee-lah, the Moon Maid. I must have looked very foolish indeed, standing there looking at her, and suddenly I realized how fatuous I must appear, and so I shook myself and laughed.

"Come, Nah-ee-lah," I said, "we must not remain here. Where can I take you, that you will be safe?"

"Upon the outer terrace there may be some of the loyal guards," she replied, "but if Ko-tah has already taken the palace, flight will be useless."

"From what I know of the conspiracy, it will be useless," I replied, "for the service of Sagroth and his palace is rotten with the spies and retainers of the Javadar."

"I feared as much," she said. "The very men who came to assassinate Sagroth wore the imperial livery less than an ola since."

"Are there none, then, loyal to you?" I asked her.

"The Jemadar's guard is always loyal," she said, "but they number scarce a thousand men."

"How may we summon them?" I asked.

"Let us go to the outer terraces and if there are any of them there we can congregate the balance, or as many of them as Ko-tah has left alive."

"Come, then," I said, "let us hasten;" and together, hand in hand, we ran along the corridors of the Jemadar's palace to the outer terraces of the highest tier of Laythe. There we found a hundred men, and when we had told them of what had happened within the palace they drew their swords and, surrounding Nah-ee-lah, they shouted:

"To the death for Nah-ee-lah, Jemadav of Laythe!"

They wanted to remain there and protect her, but I told them that there would be nothing gained by that, that sooner or later they would be overwhelmed by far greater numbers, and the cause of Nah-ee-lah lost.

"Send a dozen men," I said to their commander, "to rally all of the loyal guards that remain alive. Tell them to come to the throne room, ready to lay down their lives for the new Jemadav, and then let the dozen continue on out into the city, rallying the people to the protection of Nah-ee-lah. As for us, we will accompany her immediately to the throne room, and there, place her upon the throne and proclaim her ruler of Laythe. A hundred men may hold the throne room for a long time, if we reach it before Ko-tah reaches it with his forces."

The officer looked at Nah-ee-lah questioningly.

"Your command, Jemadav?" he inquired.

"We will follow the plan of Ju-lan the Javadar," she replied.

Immediately a dozen warriors were dispatched to rally the Imperial Guard and arouse the loyal citizens of the city to the protection of their new Jemadav, while the balance of us conducted Nah-ee-lah by a short course toward the throne room.

As we entered the great chamber at one end, Ko-tah and a handful of warriors came in at the other, but we had the advantage, in that we entered through a doorway directly behind the throne and upon the dais.

"Throw your men upon the main entrance," I called to the officer of the guard, "and hold it until reinforcements come"; and then, as the hundred raced the length of the throne room toward the surprised and enraged Ko-tah, I led Nah-ee-lah to the central throne and seated her upon it. Then stepping forward, I raised my hand for silence.

"The Jemadar Sagroth is dead!" I cried. "Behold Nah-ee-lah, the Jemadav of Laythe!"

"Stop!" cried Ko-tah, "she may share the throne with me, but she may not possess it alone."

"Take that traitor!" I called to the loyal guard, and they rushed forward, evidently glad to do my bidding. But Ko-tah did not wait to be taken. He was accompanied by only a handful of men, and when he saw that the guard really intended to seize him and realized that he would be given short shift at the hands of Nah-ee-lah and myself, he turned and fled. But I knew he would come back, and come back he did, though not until after the majority of the Jemadav's guard had gathered within the throne room.

He came with a great concourse of warriors, and the fighting was furious, but he might have brought a million men against our thousand and not immediately have overcome us, since only a limited number could fight at one time in the entrance way to the throne room. Already the corpses lay stacked as high as a man's head, yet no single member of Ko-tah's forces had crossed the threshold.

How long the fight was waged I do not know, but it must have been for a considerable time, since I know that our men fought in relays and rested many times, and that food was brought from other parts of the palace to the doorway behind the throne, and there were times when Ko-tah's forces withdrew and rested and recuperated, but always they came back in greater number, and eventually I realized we must be worn down by the persistence of their repeated attacks.

And then there arose slowly a deep-toned sound, at first we could not interpret. It rose and fell in increasing volume, until finally we knew that it was the sound of human voices, the voices of a great mob—of a mighty concourse of people and that it was sweeping toward us slowly and resistlessly.

Closer and closer it approached the palace as it rose, terrace upon terrace, toward the lofty pinnacle of Laythe. The fighting at the entrance to the throne room had almost ceased. Both sides were worn down almost to utter exhaustion, and now we but stood upon our arms upon either side of the wall of corpses that lay between us, our attention centered upon the sound of the growling multitude that was sweeping slowly upward toward us.

"They come," cried one of Nah-ee-lah's nobles, "to acclaim the new Jemadav and to tear the minions of Ko-tah the traitor to pieces!"

He spoke in a loud voice that was easily audible to Ko-tah and his retainers in the corridor without.

"They come to drag the spawn of Sagroth from the throne!" cried one of Ko-tah's followers. And then from the throne came the sweet, clear voice of Nah-ee-lah:

"Let the people's will be done," she said, and thus we stood, awaiting the verdict of the populace. Nor had we long to wait, for presently we realized that they had reached the palace terrace and entered the building itself. We could hear the shouting horde moving through the corridors and chambers, and finally the muffled bellowing resolved itself into articulate words:

"Sagroth is no more! Rule, Ko-tah, Jemadar of Laythe!"

I turned in consternation toward Nah-ee-lah. "What does it mean?" I cried. "Have the people turned against you?"

"Ko-tah's minions have done their work well during these many kelds," said the commander of the Jemadav's guard, who stood upon the upper steps of the dais, just below the throne. "They have spread lies and sedition among the people which not even Sagroth's just and kindly reign could overcome."

"Let the will of the people be done," repeated Nah-ee-lah.

"It is the will of fools betrayed by a scoundrel," cried the commander of the guard. "While there beats a single heart beneath the tunic of a guardsman of the Jemadav, we shall fight for Nah-ee-lah, Empress of Laythe."

Ko-tah's forces, now augmented by the rabble, were pushing their way over the corpses and into the throne room, so that we were forced to join the defenders, that we might hold them off while life remained to any of us. When the commander of the guard saw me fighting at his side he asked me to return to Nah-ee-lah.

"We must not leave the Jemadav alone," he said. "Return and remain at her side, Ju-lan the Javadar, and when the last of us has fallen, drive your dagger into her heart." I shuddered and turned back toward Nah-ee-lah. The very thought of plunging my dagger into that tender bosom fairly nauseated me. There must be some other way, and yet, what other means of escape could there be for Nah-ee-lah, who preferred death to the dishonor of surrender to Ko-tah, the murderer of her father? As I reached Nah-ee-lah's side, and turned again to face the entrance to the throne room, I saw that the warriors of Ko-tah were being pushed into the chamber by the mob behind them and that our defenders were being overwhelmed by the great number of their antagonists. Ko-tah, with a half dozen warriors, had been carried forward, practically without volition, by the press of numbers in their rear, and even now, with none to intercept him, was running rapidly up the broad center aisle toward the throne. Some of those in the entranceway saw him, and as he reached the foot of the steps leading to the dais, a snarling cry arose:

"Ko-tah the Jemadar!"

With bared sword, the fellow leaped toward me where I stood alone between Nah-ee-lah and her enemies.

"Surrender, Julian!" she cried. "It is futile to oppose them. You are not of Laythe. Neither duty nor honor impose upon you the necessity of offering your life for one of us. Spare him, Ko-tah!" she cried to the advancing

Javadar, "and I will bow to the will of the people and relinquish the throne to you."

"Ko-tah the traitor shall never sit upon the throne of Nah-ee-lah!" I exclaimed, and leaping forward, I engaged the Prince of Laythe.

His warriors were close behind him, and it behooved me to work fast, and so I fought as I had never guessed that it lay within me to fight, and at the instant that the rabble broke through the remaining defenders and poured into the throne room of the Jemadars of Laythe, I slipped my point into the heart of Ko-tah. With a single piercing shriek, he threw his hands above his head and toppled backward down the steps to lie dead at the foot of the throne he had betrayed.

For an instant the silence of death reigned in the great chamber. Friend and foe stood alike in the momentary paralysis of shocked surprise.

That tense, breathless silence had endured for but a moment, when it was shattered by a terrific detonation. We felt the palace tremble and rock. The assembled mob looked wildly about, their eyes filled with fear and questioning. But before they could voice a question, another thunderous report burst upon our startled ears, and then from the city below the palace there arose the shrieks and screams of terrified people. Again the palace trembled, and a great crack opened in one of the walls of the throne room. The people saw it, and in an instant their anger against the dynasty of Sagroth was swallowed in the mortal terror which they felt for their own safety. With shrieks and screams they turned and bolted for the doorway. The weaker were knocked down and trampled upon. They fought with fists and swords and daggers, in their mad efforts to escape the crumbling building. They tore the clothing from one another, as each sought to drag back his fellow, that he might gain further in the race for the outer world.

And as the rabble fought, Nah-ee-lah and I stood before the throne of Laythe, watching them, while below us the few remaining members of the Jemadar's guard stood viewing in silent contempt the terror of the people.

Explosion after explosion followed one another in rapid succession. The people had fled. The palace was empty, except for that handful of us faithful ones who remained within the throne room.

"Let us go," I said to Nah-ee-lah, "and discover the origin of these sounds, and the extent of the damage that is being done."

"Come," she said, "here is a short corridor to the inner terrace, where we may look down upon the entire city of Laythe." And then, turning to the commander of the guard she said: "Proceed, please, to the palace gates, and secure them against the return of our enemies, if they have by this time all fled from the palace grounds."

The officer bowed, and followed by the few heroic survivors of the Jemadar's guard, he left by another corridor for the palace gates, while I followed Nah-ee-lah up a stairway that led to the roof of the palace.

Coming out upon the upper terrace, we made our way quickly to the edge overlooking the city and the crater. Below us a shrieking multitude ran hither and thither from terrace to terrace, while, now here and now there, terrific explosions occurred that shattered age-old structures and carried debris high into the air. Many terraces showed great gaps and tumbled ruins where other explosions had occurred and smoke and flames were rising from a dozen portions of the city.

But an instant it took me to realize that the explosions were caused by something that was being dropped into the city from above, and as I looked up I saw a missile describing an arc above the palace, past which it hurtled to a terrace far below, and at once I realized that the missile had originated outside the city. Turning quickly, I ran across the terrace to the outer side which overlooked the plateau upon which the city stood. I could not repress an exclamation of astonishment at the sight that greeted my eyes, for the surface of the plateau was alive with warriors. Nah-ee-lah had followed me and was standing at my elbow. "The Kalkars," she said. "They have come again to reduce Laythe. It has been long since they attempted it, many generations ago, but what is it, Julian, that causes the great noise and the destruction and the fires within Laythe?"

"It is this which fills me with surprise," I said, "and not the presence of the Kalkar warriors. Look! Nah-ee-lah," and I pointed to a knoll lying at the verge of the plateau, where, unless my eyes deceived me badly, there was mounted a mortar which was hurling shells into the city of Laythe. "And there, and there," I continued, pointing to other similar engines of destruction mounted at intervals. "The city is surrounded with them, Nah-ee-lah. Have your people any knowledge of such engines of warfare or of high explosives?" I demanded.

"Only in our legends are such things mentioned," she replied. "It has been ages since the inhabitants of Va-nah lost the art of manufacturing such things."

As we stood there talking, one of the Jemadar's guards emerged from the palace and approached us.

"Nah-ee-lah, Jemadav," he cried, "there is one here who craves audience with you and who says that if you listen to him you may save your city from destruction."

"Fetch him," replied Nah-ee-lah. "We will receive him here."

We had but a moment to wait when the guardsman returned with one of Ko-tah's captains.

"Nah-ee-lah, Jemadav," he cried, when she had given him permission to speak, "I come to you with a message from one who is Jemadar of Jemadars, ruler of all Va-nah. If you would save your city and your people, listen well."

The girl's eyes narrowed. "You are speaking to your Jemadav, fellow," she said. "Be careful, not only of your words, but of your tone."

"I come but to save you," replied the man sullenly. "The Kalkars have discovered a great leader, and they have joined together from many cities to overthrow Laythe. My master does not wish to destroy this ancient city, and there is but one simple condition upon which he will spare it."

"Name your condition," said Nah-ee-lah.

"If you will wed him, he will make Laythe the capital of Va-nah, and you shall rule with him as Jemadav of Jemadavs."

Nah-ee-lah's lips curled in scorn. "And who is the presumptuous Kalkar that dares aspire to the hand of Nah-ee-lah?" she demanded.

"He is no Kalkar, Jemadav," replied the messenger. "He is one from another world, who says that he knows you well and that he has loved you long."

"His name," snapped Nah-ee-lah impatiently.

"He is called Or-tis, Jemadar of Jemadars."

Nah-ee-lah turned toward me with elevated brows and a smile of comprehension upon her face.

"Or-tis," she repeated.

"Now, I understand, my Jemadav," I said, "and I am commencing to have some slight conception of the time that must have elapsed since I first landed within Va-nah, for even since our escape from the Va-gas Orthis has had time to discover the Kalkars and ingratiate himself among them, to conspire with them for the overthrow of Laythe, and to manufacture explosives and shells and the guns which are reducing Laythe this moment.

Even had I not heard the name, I might have guessed that it was Orthis, for it is all so like him—ingrate, traitor, cur."

"Go back to your master," she said to the messenger, "and tell him that Nah-ee-lah, Jemadav of Laythe, would as leave mate with Ga-va-go the Va-gas as with him, and that Laythe will be happier destroyed and her people wiped from the face of Va-nah than ruled by such a beast. I have spoken. Go."

The fellow turned and left us, being accompanied from Nah-ee-lah's presence by the guardsman who had fetched him, and whom Nah-ee-lah commanded to return as soon as he had conducted the other outside the palace gates. Then the girl turned to me:

"O, Julian, what shall I do? How may I combat these terrible forces that you have brought to Va-nah from another world?"

I shook my head. "We, too, could manufacture both guns and ammunition to combat him, but now we have not the time, since Laythe will be reduced to a mass of ruins before we could even make a start. There is but one way, Nah-ee-lah, and that is to send your people—every fighting man that you can gather, and the women, too, if they can bear arms, out upon the plateau in an effort to overwhelm the Kalkars and destroy the guns."

She stood and thought for a long time, and presently the officer of the guard returned and halted before her, awaiting her commands. Slowly she raised her head and looked at him.

"Go into the city," she said, "and gather every Laythean who can carry a sword, a dagger, or a lance. Tell them to assemble on the inner terraces below the castle, and that I, Nah-ee-lah their Jemadav, will address them. The fate of Laythe rests with you. Go."

CHAPTER FOURTEEN
BACK TO *THE BARSOOM*

T HE CITY WAS ALREADY IN FLAMES in many places, and though the people fought valiantly to extinguish them, it seemed to me that they but spread the more rapidly with each succeeding minute. And then, as suddenly as it had commenced, the bombardment ceased. Nah-ee-lah and I crossed over to the outer edge of the terrace to see if we could note any new movement by the enemy, nor did we have long to wait. We saw a hundred ladders raised as if by magic toward the lowest terrace, which rose but a bare two hundred feet above the base of the city. The men who carried the ladders were not visible to us when they came close to the base of the wall, but I guessed from the distant glimpses that I caught of the ladders as they were rushed forward by running men that here, again, Orthis' earthly knowledge and experience had come to the assistance of the Kalkars, for I was sure that only some form of extension ladder could be successfully used to reach even the lowest terrace.

When I saw their intention I ran quickly down into the palace and out upon the terrace before the gates, where the remainder of the guard were stationed, and there I told them what was happening and urged them to hasten the people to the lowest terrace to repulse the enemy before they had secured a foothold upon the city. Then I returned to Nah-ee-lah, and together we watched the outcome of the struggle, but almost from the first I realized that Laythe was doomed, for before any of her defenders could reach the spot, fully a thousand Kalkars had clambered to the terrace, and there they held their own while other thousands ascended in safety to the city.

We saw the defenders rush forth to attack them, and for a moment, so impetuous was their charge, I thought that I had been wrong and that the Kalkars might yet be driven from Laythe. Fighting upon the lower outer terrace far beneath us was a surging mass of shouting warriors. The Kalkars were falling back before the impetuous onslaught of the Laytheans.

"They have not the blood in their veins," whispered Nah-ee-lah, clinging tightly to my arm. "One noble is worth ten of them. Watch them. Already are they fleeing."

And so it seemed, and the rout of the Kalkars appeared almost assured, as score upon score of them were hurled over the edge of the terrace, to fall mangled and bleeding upon the ground hundreds of feet below.

But suddenly a new force seemed to be injected into the strife. I saw a stream of Kalkars emerging above the edge of the lower terrace—new men clambering up the ladders from the plateau below, and as they came they shouted something which I could not understand, but the other Kalkars seemed to take heart and made once more the semblance of a stand against the noble Laytheans, and I saw one, the leader of the new-comers, force his way into the battling throng. And then I saw him raise his hand above his head and hurl something into the midst of the compact ranks of the Laytheans.

Instantly there was a terrific explosion and a great, bloody gap lay upon the terrace where an instant before a hundred of the flower of the fighting men of Laythe had been so gloriously defending their city and their honor.

"Grenades," I exclaimed. "Hand grenades!"

"What is it, Julian? What is it that they are doing down there?" cried Nah-ee-lah. "They are murdering my people."

"Yes, Nah-ee-lah, they are murdering your people, and well may Va-nah curse the day that Earth Men set foot upon your world."

"I do not understand, Julian," she said.

"This is the work of Orthis," I said, "who has brought from Earth the knowledge of diabolical engines of destruction. He first shelled the city with what must have been nothing more than crude mortars, for it is impossible that he has had the time to construct the machinery to build any but the simplest of guns. Now his troops are hurling hand grenades among your men. There is no chance, Nah-ee-lah, for the Laytheans to successfully pit their primitive weapons against the modern agents of destruction which Orthis has brought to bear against them. Laythe must surrender or be destroyed."

Nah-ee-lah laid her head upon my shoulder and wept softly. "Julian," she said at last, "this is the end, then. Take me to the Jemadav, my mother, please, and then you must go and make your peace with your fellow Earth Man. It is not right that you, a stranger, who have done so much for me, should fall with me and Laythe."

"The only peace I can make with Orthis, Nah-ee-lah," I replied, "is the peace of death. Orthis and I may not live together again in the same world."

She was crying very softly, sobbing upon my shoulder, and I put my arm about her in an effort to quiet her.

"I have brought you only suffering and danger, and now death, Julian," she said, "when you deserve naught but happiness and peace."

I suddenly felt very strange and my heart behaved wretchedly, so that when I attempted to speak it pounded so that I could say nothing and my knees shook beneath me. What had come over me? Could it be possible that already Orthis had loosed his poison gas? Then, at last, I managed to gather myself together.

"Nah-ee-lah," I said, "I do not fear death if you must die, and I do not seek happiness except with you."

She looked up suddenly, her great, tear-dimmed eyes wide and gazing deep into mine.

"You mean—Julian? You mean—?"

"I mean, Nah-ee-lah, that I love you," I replied, though I must have stumbled through the words in a most ridiculous manner, so frightened was I.

"Ah, Julian," she sighed, and put her arms about my neck.

"And you, Nah-ee-lah!" I exclaimed incredulously, as I crushed her to me, "can it be that you return my love?"

"I have loved you always," she replied. "From the very first, almost—way back when we were prisoners together in the No-vans' village. You Earth Men must be very blind, my Julian. A Laythean would have known it at once, for it seemed to me that upon a dozen occasions I almost avowed my love openly to you."

"Alas, Nah-ee-lah! I must have been very blind, for I had not guessed until this minute that you loved me."

"Now," she said, "I do not care what happens. We have one another, and if we die together, doubtless we shall live together in a new incarnation."

"I hope so," I said, "but I should much rather be sure of it and live together in this."

"And I, too, Julian, but that is impossible."

We were walking now through the corridors of the palace toward the chamber occupied by her mother, but we did not find her there and Nah-ee-lah became apprehensive as to her safety. Hurriedly we searched through other chambers of the palace, until at last we came to the little audience chamber in which Sagroth had been slain, and as we threw open the door I saw a sight that I tried to hide from Nah-ee-lah's eyes as I drew her around in an effort to force her back into the corridor. Possibly she guessed what impelled my action, for she shook her head and murmured: "No, Julian; whatever it is I must see it." And then she pushed her way gently past me, and we stood together upon the threshold, looking at the harrowing sight which the interior of the room displayed.

There were the bodies of the assassins Sagroth and I had slain, and the dead Jemadar, too, precisely as he had fallen, while across his breast lay the body of Nah-ee-lah's mother, a dagger self-thrust through her heart.

For just a moment Nah-ee-lah stood there looking at them in silence, as though in prayer, and then she turned wearily away and left the chamber, closing the door behind her. We walked on in silence for some time, ascending the stairway back to the upper terrace. Upon the inner side, the flames were spreading throughout the city, roaring like a mighty furnace and vomiting up great clouds of smoke, for though the Laythean terraces are supported by tremendous arches of masonry, yet there is much wood used in the interior construction of the buildings, while the hangings and the furniture are all inflammable.

"We had no chance to save the city," said Nah-ee-lah, with a sigh. "Our people, called from their normal duties by the false Ko-tah, were leaderless. The firefighters, instead of being at their posts, were seeking the life of their Jemadar. Unhappy day! Unhappy day!"

"You think they could have stopped the fire?" I asked.

"The little ponds, the rivulets, the waterfalls, the great public baths and the tiny lakes that you see upon every terrace were all built with fire protection in mind. It is easy to divert their waters and flood any tier of buildings. Had my people been at their posts, this, at least, could not have happened."

As we stood watching the flames we suddenly saw people emerging in great numbers upon several of the lower terraces. They were evidently in terrified flight, and then others appeared upon terraces above them— Kalkars who hurled hand grenades amongst the Laytheans beneath them. Men, women, and children ran hither and thither, shrieking and crying and seeking for shelter, but from the buildings behind them, rushing them outward upon the terraces, came other Kalkars with hand grenades. The fires hemmed the people of Laythe upon either side and the Kalkars attacked them from the rear and from above. The weaker fell and were trodden to death, and I saw scores fall upon their own lances or drive daggers into the hearts of their loved ones.

The massacre spread rapidly around the circumference of the city and the Kalkars drove the people from the upper terraces downward between the raging fires which were increasing until the mouth of the great crater was filled with roaring flames and smoke. In the occasional gaps we could catch glimpses of the holocaust beneath us.

A sudden current of air rising from the crater lifted the smoke pall high for a moment, revealing the entire circumference of the crater, the edge of which was crowded with Laytheans. And then I saw a warrior from the opposite side leap upon the surrounding wall that bordered the lower terrace at the edge of the yawning crater. He turned and called aloud some message to his fellows, and then wheeling, threw his arms above his head and leaped outward into the yawning, bottomless abyss. Instantly the others seemed to be inoculated with the infection of his mad act. A dozen men leaped to the wall and dove head foremost into the crater. The thing spread slowly at first, and then with the rapidity of a prairie fire, it ran around the entire circle of the city. Women hurled their children in and then leaped after them. The multitude fought one with another for a place upon the wall from which they might cast themselves to death. It was a terrible—an awe-inspiring sight.

Nah-ee-lah covered her eyes with her hands. "My poor people!" she cried. "My poor people!" And far below her, by the thousands now, they were hurling themselves into eternity, while above them the screaming Kalkars hurled hand grenades among them and drove the remaining inhabitants of Laythe, terrace by terrace, down toward the crater's rim.

Nah-ee-lah turned away. "Come, Julian," she said, "I cannot look, I cannot look." And together we walked across the terrace to the outer side of the city.

Almost directly beneath us upon the next terrace was a palace gate and as we reached a point where we could see it, I was horrified to see that the Kalkars had made their way up the outer terraces to the very palace walls. The Jemadar's guard was standing there ready to defend the palace against the invaders. The great stone gates would have held indefinitely against spears and swords, but even the guardsmen must have guessed that their doom was already sealed and that these gates, that had stood for ages, an ample protection to the Jemadars of Laythe, were about to fall, as the Kalkars halted fifty yards away, and from their ranks a single individual stepped forth a few paces.

As my eyes alighted upon him I seized Nah-ee-lah's arm, "Orthis!" I cried. "It is Orthis." At the same instant the man's eyes rose above the gates and fell upon us. A nasty leer curled his lips as he recognized us.

"I come to claim my bride," he cried, in a voice that reached us easily, "and to balance my account with you, at last," and he pointed a finger at me.

In his right hand he held a large, cylindrical object, and as he ceased speaking he hurled it at the gates precisely as a baseball pitcher pitches a swift ball.

The missile struck squarely at the bottom of the gates. There was a terrific explosion, and the great stone portals crumbled, shattered into a thousand fragments. The last defense of the Empress of Laythe had fallen, and with it there went down in bloody death at least half the remaining members of her loyal guard.

Instantly the Kalkars rushed forward, hurling hand grenades among the survivors of the guard.

Nah-ee-lah turned toward me and put her arms about my neck.

"Kiss me once more, Julian," she said, "and then the dagger."

"Never, never, Nah-ee-lah!" I cried. "I cannot do it."

"But I can!" she exclaimed, and drew her own from its sheath at her hip.

I seized her wrist. "Not that, Nah-ee-lah!" I cried. "There must be some other way." And then there came to me a mad inspiration. "The wings!" I cried. "Where are they kept? The last of your people have been destroyed. Duty no longer holds you here. Let us escape, even if it is only to frustrate Orthis' plans and deny him the satisfaction of witnessing our death."

"But, where can we go?" she asked.

"We may at least choose our own manner of death," I replied, "far from Laythe and far from the eyes of an enemy who would gloat over our undoing."

"You are right, Julian. We still have a little time, for I doubt if Orthis or his Kalkars can quickly find the stairway leading to this terrace." And then she led me quickly to one of the many towers that rise above the palace. Entering it, we ascended a spiral staircase to a large chamber at the summit of the tower. Here were kept the imperial wings. I fastened Nah-ee-lah's to her and she helped me with mine, and then from the pinnacle of the tower we arose above the burning city of Laythe and flew rapidly toward the distant lowlands and the sea. It was in my mind to search out, if possible, the location of *The Barsoom*, for I still entertained the mad hope that my companions yet lived—if I did, why not they?

The heat above the city was almost unendurable and the smoke suffocating, yet we passed through it, so that almost immediately we were hidden from the view of that portion of the palace from which we had arisen, with the result that when Orthis and his Kalkars finally found their way to the upper terrace, as I have no doubt they did, we had disappeared—whither they could not know.

We flew and drifted with the wind across the mountainous country toward the plains and the sea, it being my intention upon reaching the latter to follow the coastline until I came to a river marked by an island at its mouth. From that point I knew that I could reach the spot where *The Barsoom* had landed.

Our long flight must have covered a considerable period of time, since it was necessary for us to alight and rest many times and to search for food. We met, fortunately, with no mishaps, and upon the several occasions when we were discovered by roving bands of Va-gas we were able to soar far aloft and escape them easily. We came at length, however, to the sea, the coast of which I followed to the left, but though we passed the mouths of many rivers, I discovered none that precisely answered the description of that which I sought.

It was borne in upon me at last that our quest was futile, but where we were to find a haven of safety neither of us could guess. The gas in our bags was losing its buoyancy and we had no means wherewith to replenish it. It would still maintain us for a short time, but how long neither of us knew, other than that it had not nearly the buoyancy that it originally possessed.

Off the coast we had seen islands almost continuously and I suggested to Nah-ee-lah that we try to discover one upon which grew the fruits and nuts and vegetables necessary for our subsistence, and where we might also have a constant supply of fresh water.

I discovered that Nah-ee-lah knew little about these islands, practically nothing in fact, not even as to whether they were inhabited; but we determined to explore one, and to this end we selected an island of considerable extent that lay about ten miles offshore. We reached it without difficulty and circled slowly above it, scrutinizing its entire area carefully. About half of it was quite hilly, but the balance was rolling and comparatively level. We discovered three streams and two small lakes upon it, and an almost riotous profusion of vegetable growth, but nowhere did we discern the slightest indication that it was inhabited. And so at last, feeling secure, we made our landing upon the plain, close to the beach.

It was a beautiful spot, a veritable Garden of Eden, where we two might have passed the remainder of our lives in peace and security, for though we later explored it carefully, we found not the slightest evidence that it had ever known the foot of man.

Together we built a snug shelter against the storms. Together we hunted for food, and during our long periods of idleness we lay upon the soft sward beside the beach, and to pass the time away, I taught Nah-ee-lah my own language.

It was a lazy, indolent, happy life that we spent upon this enchanted isle, and yet, though we were happy in our love, each of us felt the futility of our existence, where our lives must be spent in useless idleness.

We had, however, given up definitely hope for any other form of existence. And thus we were lying one time, as was our wont after eating, stretched in luxurious ease upon our backs on the soft lunar grasses, I with my eyes closed, when Nah-ee-lah suddenly grasped me by the arm.

"Julian," she cried, "what is it? Look!"

I opened my eyes, to find her sitting up and gazing into the sky toward the mainland, a slim forefinger indicating the direction of the object that had attracted her attention and aroused her surprised interest.

As my eyes rested upon the thing her pointing finger indicated, I leaped to my feet with an exclamation of incredulity, for there, sailing parallel with the coast at an altitude of not more than a thousand feet, was a ship, the lines of which I knew as I had known my mother's face. It was *The Barsoom*.

Grasping Nah-ee-lah by the arm, I dragged her to her feet. "Come, quick, Nah-ee-lah!" I cried, and urged her rapidly toward our hut, where we had stored the wings and the gas bags which we had never thought to use again, yet protected carefully, though why we knew not.

There was still gas in the bags—enough to support us in the air, with the assistance of our wings, but to fly thus for long distances would have been most fatiguing, and there was even a question as to whether we could cross the ten miles of sea that lay between us and the mainland; yet I was determined to attempt it. Hastily we donned the wings and bags, and rising together, flapped slowly in the direction of the mainland.

The Barsoom was cruising slowly along a line that would cross ours before we could reach the shore, but I hoped that they would sight us and investigate.

We flew as rapidly as I dared, for I could take no chances upon exhausting Nah-ee-lah, knowing that it would be absolutely impossible for me to support her weight and my own, with our depleted gas bags. There was no way in which I could signal to *The Barsoom*. We must simply fly toward her. That was the best that we could do, and finally, try though we would, I realized that we should be too late to intercept her and that unless they saw us and changed their course, we should not come close enough to hail them. To see my friends passing so near, and yet to be unable to apprise them of my presence filled me with melancholy. Not one of the many vicissitudes and dangers through which I had passed since I left Earth depressed me more than the sight of *The Barsoom* forging slowly past us without speaking. I saw her change her course then and move inland still further from us, and I could not but dwell upon our unhappy condition, since now we might never again be able to reach the safety of our island, there being even a question as to whether the gas bags would support us to the mainland.

They did, however, and there we alighted and rested, while *The Barsoom* sailed out of sight toward the mountains.

"I shall not give it up, Nah-ee-lah," I cried. "I am going to follow *The Barsoom* until we find it, or until we die in the attempt. I doubt if we ever can reach the island again, but we can make short flights here on land, and by so doing, we may overtake my ship and my companions."

After resting for a short time, we arose again, and when we were above the trees I saw *The Barsoom* far in the distance, and again it was circling, this time toward the left, so we altered our course and flew after it. But presently we realized that it was making a great circle and hope renewed within our breasts, giving us the strength to fly on and on, though we were forced to come down often for brief rests. As we neared the ship we saw that the circles were growing smaller, but it was not until we were within about three miles of her that I realized that she was circling the mouth of a great crater, the walls of which rose several hundred feet above the surrounding country. We had been forced to land again to rest, when there flashed upon my mind a sudden realization of the purpose of the maneuvers of *The Barsoom*—she was investigating the crater, preparatory to an attempt to pass through it into outer space and seek to return to Earth again.

As this thought impinged upon my brain, a wave of almost hopeless horror overwhelmed me as I thought of being definitely left forever by my companions and that by but a few brief minutes Nah-ee-lah was to be robbed of life and happiness and peace, for at that instant the hull of *The Barsoom* dropped beneath the rim of the crater and disappeared from our view.

Rising quickly with Nah-ee-lah, I flew as rapidly as my tired muscles and exhausted gas bag would permit toward the rim of the crater. In my heart of hearts I knew that I should be too late, for once they had decided to make the attempt, the ship would drop like a plummet into the depths, and by the time I reached the mouth of the abyss it would be lost to my view forever.

And yet I struggled on, my lungs almost bursting from the exertion of my mad efforts toward speed. Nah-ee-lah trailed far behind, for if either of us could reach *The Barsoom* in time we should both be saved, and I could fly faster than Nah-ee-lah; otherwise, I should never have separated myself from her by so much as a hundred yards.

Though my lungs were pumping like bellows, I venture to say that my heart stood still for several seconds before I topped the crater's rim.

At the same instant that I expected the last vestige of my hopes to be dashed to pieces irrevocably and forever, I crossed the rim and beheld *The Barsoom* not twenty feet below me, just over the edge of the abyss, and upon her deck stood West and Jay and Norton.

As I came into view directly above them, West whipped out his revolver and leveled it at me, but the instant that his finger pressed the trigger Norton sprang forward and struck his hand aside.

"My God, sir!" I heard the boy cry, "it is the Captain." And then they all recognized me, and an instant later I almost collapsed as I fell to the deck of my beloved ship.

My first thought was of Nah-ee-lah, and at my direction *The Barsoom* rose swiftly and moved to meet her.

"Great Scott!" cried my guest, leaping to his feet and looking out of the stateroom window, "I had no idea that I had kept you up all night. Here we are in Paris already."

"But the rest of your story," I cried. "You have not finished it, I know. Last night, as you were watching them celebrating in the Blue Room, you made a remark which led me to believe that some terrible calamity threatened the world."

"It does," he said, "and that was what I meant to tell you about, but this story of the third incarnation of which I am conscious was necessary to an understanding of how the great catastrophe overwhelmed the people of the Earth."

"But, did you reach Earth again?" I demanded.

"Yes," he said, "in the year 2036. I had been ten years within Va-nah, but did not know whether it was ten months or a century until we landed upon Earth."

He smiled then. "You notice that I still say I. It is sometimes difficult for me to recall which incarnation I am in. Perhaps it will be clearer to you if I say Julian 5th returned to Earth in 2036, and in the same year his son, Julian 6th, was born to his wife, Nah-ee-lah the Moon Maid."

"But how could he return to Earth in the disabled *Barsoom*?"

"Ah," he said, "that raises a point that was of great interest to Julian 5th. After he regained *The Barsoom*, naturally one of the first questions he asked was as to the condition of the ship and their intentions, and when he learned that they had, in reality, been intending to pass through the crater toward the Earth he questioned them further and discovered that it was the young ensign, Norton, who had repaired the engine, having been able to do it by information that he had gleaned from Orthis, after winning the latter's friendship. Thus was explained the intimacy between the two, which Julian 5th had so deplored, but which he now saw that young Norton had encouraged for a patriotic purpose."

"We are docked now and I must be going. Thank you for your hospitality and for your generous interest," and he held out his hand toward me.

"But the story of Julian 9th," I insisted, "am I never to hear that?"

"If we meet again, yes," he promised, with a smile.

"I shall hold you to it," I told him.

"If we meet again," he repeated, and departed, closing the stateroom door after him.

PIRATES OF VENUS

"We can wait no longer," I said, and then to the angan, *"Take the janjong and fly to the ship. She is closer now; you can make it; you must make it!"*

Contents

CHAPTER ONE
CARSON NAPIER

F A FEMALE FIGURE IN A WHITE SHROUD enters your bedchamber at midnight on the thirteenth day of this month, answer this letter; otherwise, do not."

Having read this far in the letter, I was about to consign it to the wastebasket, where all my crank letters go; but for some reason I read on, "If she speaks to you, please remember her words and repeat them to me when you write." I might have read on to the end; but at this juncture the telephone bell rang, and I dropped the letter into one of the baskets on my desk. It chanced to be the "out" basket; and had events followed their ordinary course, this would have been the last of the letter and the incident in so far as I was concerned, for from the "out" basket the letter went to the files.

It was Jason Gridley on the telephone. He seemed excited and asked me to come to his laboratory at once. As Jason is seldom excited about anything, I hastened to accede to his request and satisfy my curiosity. Jumping into my roadster, I soon covered the few blocks that separate us, to learn that Jason had good grounds for excitement. He had just received a radio message from the inner world, from Pellucidar.

On the eve of the departure of the great dirigible, O-220, from the Earth's core, following the successful termination of that historic expedition, Jason had determined to remain and search for von Horst, the only missing member of the party; but Tarzan, David Innes, and Captain Zuppner had persuaded him of the folly of such an undertaking, inasmuch as David had promised to dispatch an expedition of his own native Pellucidarian warriors to locate the young German lieutenant if he still lived and it were possible to discover any clue to his whereabouts.

Notwithstanding this, and though he had returned to the outer world with the ship, Jason had always been harassed by a sense of responsibility for the fate of von Horst, a young man who had been most popular with all the members of the expedition; and had insisted time and time again that he regretted having left Pellucidar until he had exhausted every means within his power of rescuing von Horst or learned definitely that he was dead.

Jason waved me to a chair and offered me a cigarette. "I've just had a message from Abner Perry," he announced, "the first for months."

"It must have been interesting," I commented, "to excite *you*."

"It was," he admitted. "A rumor has reached Sari that von Horst has been found."

Now as this pertains to a subject entirely foreign to the present volume, I might mention that I have alluded to it only for the purpose of explaining two facts which, while not vital, have some slight bearing on the remarkable sequence of events which followed. First, it caused me to forget the letter I just mentioned, and, second, it fixed the date in my mind—the tenth.

My principal reason for mentioning the first fact is to stress the thought that the matter of the letter, so quickly and absolutely forgotten, had no opportunity to impress itself upon my mind and therefore could not, at least objectively, influence my consideration of ensuing events. The letter was gone from my mind within five minutes of its reading as completely as though it had never been received.

The next three days were exceedingly busy ones for me, and when I retired on the night of the thirteenth my mind was so filled with the annoying details of a real estate transaction that was going wrong, that it was some time before I could sleep. I can truthfully affirm that my last thoughts were of trust deeds, receivers in equity, and deficiency judgments.

What awoke me, I do not know. I sat up with a start just in time to see a female figure, swathed in what appeared to be a white winding sheet, enter my room through the door. You will note that I say door rather than doorway, for such was the fact; the door was closed. It was a clear, moonlit night; the various homely objects in my room were plainly discernible, especially the ghostly figure now hovering near the foot of my bed.

I am not subject to hallucinations, I had never seen a ghost, I had never wished to, and I was totally ignorant of the ethics governing such a situation. Even had the lady not been so obviously supernatural, I should yet have been at a loss as to how to receive her at this hour in the intimacy of my bedchamber, for no strange lady had ever before invaded its privacy, and I am of Puritan stock.

"It is midnight of the thirteenth," she said, in a low, musical voice.

"So it is," I agreed, and then I recalled the letter that I had received on the tenth.

"He left Guadalupe today," she continued; "he will wait in Guaymas for your letter."

That was all. She crossed the room and passed out of it, not through the window which was quite convenient, but through the solid wall. I sat there for a full minute, staring at the spot where I had last seen her and endeavoring to convince myself that I was dreaming, but I was not dreaming; I was wide awake. In fact I was so wide awake that it was fully an hour before I had successfully wooed Morpheus, as the Victorian writers so neatly expressed it, ignoring the fact that his sex must have made it rather embarrassing for gentlemen writers.

I reached my office a little earlier than usual the following morning, and it is needless to say that the first thing that I did was to search for that letter which I had received on the tenth. I could recall neither the name of the writer nor the point of origin of the letter, but my secretary recalled the latter, the letter having been sufficiently out of the ordinary to attract his attention.

"It was from somewhere in Mexico," he said, and as letters of this nature are filed by states and countries, there was now no difficulty in locating it.

You may rest assured that this time I read the letter carefully. It was dated the third and postmarked Guaymas. Guaymas is a seaport in Sonora, on the Gulf of California.

Here is the letter:

My dear Sir:

Being engaged in a venture of great scientific importance, I find it necessary to solicit the assistance (not financial) of someone psychologically harmonious, who is at the same time of sufficient intelligence and culture to appreciate the vast possibilities of my project.

Why I have addressed you I shall be glad to explain in the happy event that a personal interview seems desirable. This can only be ascertained by a test which I shall now explain.

If a female figure in a white shroud enters your bedchamber at midnight on the thirteenth day of this month, answer this letter;

otherwise, do not. If she speaks to you, please remember her words and repeat them to me when you write.

Assuring you of my appreciation of your earnest consideration of this letter, which I realize is rather unusual, and begging that you hold its contents in strictest confidence until future events shall have warranted its publication, I am, Sir,

Very respectfully yours,
Carson Napier.

"It looks to me like another nut," commented Rothmund.

"So it did to me on the tenth," I agreed; "but today is the fourteenth, and now it looks like another story."

"What has the fourteenth got to do with it?" he demanded.

"Yesterday was the thirteenth," I reminded him.

"You don't mean to tell me—" he started, skeptically.

"That is just what I do mean to tell you," I interrupted. "The lady came, I saw, she conquered."

Ralph looked worried. "Don't forget what your nurse told you after your last operation," he reminded me.

"Which nurse? I had nine, and no two of them told me the same things."

"Jerry. She said that narcotics often affected a patient's mind for months afterward." His tone was solicitous.

"Well, at least Jerry admitted that I had a mind, which some of the others didn't. Anyway, it didn't affect my eyesight; I saw what I saw. Please take a letter to Mr. Napier."

A few days later I received a telegram from Napier dated Guaymas.

"letter received stop thanks stop shall call on you tomorrow," it read.

"He must be flying," I commented.

"Or coming in a white shroud," suggested Ralph. "I think I'll phone Captain Hodson to send a squad car around here; sometimes these nuts are dangerous." He was still skeptical.

I must admit that we both awaited the arrival of Carson Napier with equal interest. I think Ralph expected to see a wild-eyed maniac. I could not visualize the man at all.

About eleven o'clock the following morning Ralph came into my study. "Mr. Napier is here," he said.

"Does his hair grow straight out from his scalp, and do the whites of his eyes show all around the irises?" I inquired, smiling.

"No," replied Ralph, returning the smile; "he is a very fine-looking man, but," he added, "I still think he's a nut."

"Ask him to come in," and a moment later Ralph ushered in an exceptionally handsome man whom I judged to be somewhere between twenty-five and thirty years old, though he might have been even younger.

He came forward with extended hand as I rose to greet him, a smile lighting his face; and after the usual exchange of banalities he came directly to the point of his visit.

"To get the whole picture clearly before you," he commenced, "I shall have to tell you something about myself. My father was a British army officer, my mother an American girl from Virginia. I was born in India while my father was stationed there, and brought up under the tutorage of an old Hindu who was much attached to my father and mother. This Chand Kabi was something of a mystic, and he taught me many things that are not in the curriculums of schools for boys under ten. Among them was telepathy, which he had cultivated to such a degree that he could converse with one in psychological harmony with himself quite as easily at great distances as when face to face. Not only that, but he could project mental images to great distances, so that the recipient of his thought waves could see what Chand Kabi was seeing, or whatever else Chand Kabi wished him to see. These things he taught me."

"And it was thus you caused me to see my midnight visitor on the thirteenth?" I inquired.

He nodded. "That test was necessary in order to ascertain if we were in psychological harmony. Your letter, quoting the exact words that I had caused the apparition to appear to speak, convinced me that I had at last found the person for whom I have been searching for some time.

"But to get on with my story. I hope I am not boring you, but I feel that it is absolutely necessary that you should have full knowledge of my antecedents and background in order that you may decide whether I am worthy of your confidence and assistance, or not." I assured him that I was far from being bored, and he proceeded.

"I was not quite eleven when my father died and my mother brought me to America. We went to Virginia first and lived there for three years with my mother's grandfather, Judge John Carson, with whose name and reputation you are doubtless familiar, as who is not?

"After the grand old man died, mother and I came to California, where I attended public schools and later entered a small college at Claremont, which is noted for its high scholastic standing and the superior personnel of both its faculty and student body.

"Shortly after my graduation the third and greatest tragedy of my life occurred—my mother died. I was absolutely stunned by this blow. Life seemed to hold no further interest for me. I did not care to live, yet I would not take my own life. As an alternative I embarked upon a life of recklessness. With a certain goal in mind, I learned to fly. I changed my name and became a stunt man in pictures.

"I did not have to work. Through my mother I had inherited a considerable fortune from my great-grandfather, John Carson; so great a fortune that only a spendthrift could squander the income. I mention this only because the venture I am undertaking requires considerable capital, and I wish you to know that I am amply able to finance it without help.

"Not only did life in Hollywood bore me, but here in Southern California were too many reminders of the loved one I had lost. I determined to travel, and I did. I flew all over the world. In Germany I became interested in rocket cars and financed several. Here my idea was born. There was nothing original about it except that I intended to carry it to a definite conclusion. I would travel by rocket to another planet.

"My studies had convinced me that of all the planets Mars alone offered presumptive evidence of habitability for creatures similar to ourselves. I was at the same time convinced that if I succeeded in reaching Mars the probability of my being able to return to Earth was remote. Feeling that I must have some reason for embarking upon such a venture, other than selfishness, I determined to seek out someone with whom I could communicate in the event that I succeeded. Subsequently it occurred to me that this might also afford the means for launching a second expedition, equipped to make the return journey, for I had no doubt but that there would be many adventurous spirits ready to undertake such an excursion once I had proved it feasible.

"For over a year I have been engaged in the construction of a gigantic rocket on Guadalupe Island, off the west coast of Lower California.

The Mexican government has given me every assistance, and today everything is complete to the last detail. I am ready to start at any moment."

As he ceased speaking, he suddenly faded from view. The chair in which he had been sitting was empty. There was no one in the room but myself. I was stunned, almost terrified. I recalled what Rothmund had said about the effect of the narcotics upon my mentality. I also recalled that insane people seldom realize that they are insane. Was *I* insane! Cold sweat broke out upon my forehead and the backs of my hands. I reached toward the buzzer to summon Ralph. There is no question but that Ralph is sane. If he had seen Carson Napier and shown him into my study—what a relief that would be!

But before my finger touched the button Ralph entered the room. There was a puzzled expression on his face. "Mr. Napier is back again," he said, and then he added, "I didn't know he had left. I just heard him talking to you."

I breathed a sigh of relief as I wiped the perspiration from my face and hands; if I was crazy, so was Ralph. "Bring him in," I said, "and this time you stay here."

When Napier entered there was a questioning look in his eyes. "Do you fully grasp the situation as far as I have explained it?" he asked, as though he had not been out of the room at all.

"Yes, but—" I started.

"Wait, please," he requested. "I know what you are going to say, but let me apologize first and explain. I have not been here before. That was my final test. If you are confident that you saw me and talked to me and can recall what I said to you as I sat outside in my car, then you and I can communicate just as freely and easily when I am on Mars."

"But," interjected Rothmund, "you *were* here. Didn't I shake hands with you when you came in, and talk to you?"

"You thought you did," replied Napier.

"Who's loony now?" I inquired inelegantly, but to this day Rothmund insists that we played a trick on him.

"How do you know he's here now, then?" he asked.

"I don't," I admitted.

"I am, this time," laughed Napier. "Let's see; how far had I gotten?"

"You were saying that you were all ready to start, had your rocket set up on Guadalupe Island," I reminded him.

"Right! I see you got it all. Now, as briefly as possible, I'll outline what I hope you will find it possible to do for me. I have come to you for several reasons, the more important of which are your interest in Mars, your profession (the results of my experiment must be recorded by an experienced writer), and your reputation for integrity—I have taken the liberty of investigating you most thoroughly. I wish you to record and publish the messages you receive from me and to administer my estate during my absence."

"I shall be glad to do the former, but I hesitate to accept the responsibility of the latter assignment," I demurred.

"I have already arranged a trust that will give you ample protection," he replied in a manner that precluded further argument. I saw that he was a young man who brooked no obstacles; in fact I think he never admitted the existence of an obstacle. "As for your remuneration," he continued, "you may name your own figure."

I waved a deprecatory hand. "It will be a pleasure," I assured him.

"It may take a great deal of your time," interjected Ralph, "and your time is valuable."

"Precisely," agreed Napier. "Mr. Rothmund and I will, with your permission, arrange the financial details later."

"That suits me perfectly," I said, for I detest business and everything connected with it.

"Now, to get back to the more important and far more interesting phases of our discussion; what is your reaction to the plan as a whole?"

"Mars is a long way from Earth," I suggested; "Venus is nine or ten million miles closer, and a million miles are a million miles."

"Yes, and I would prefer going to Venus," he replied. "Enveloped in clouds, its surface forever invisible to man, it presents a mystery that intrigues the imagination; but recent astronomical research suggests conditions there inimical to the support of any such life as we know on Earth. It has been thought by some that, held in the grip of the Sun since the era of her pristine fluidity, she always presents the same face to him, as does the Moon to Earth. If such is the case, the extreme heat of one hemisphere and the extreme cold of the other would preclude life.

"Even if the suggestion of Sir James Jeans is borne out by fact, each of her days and nights is several times as long as ours on Earth, these long nights having a temperature of thirteen degrees below zero, Fahrenheit, and the long days a correspondingly high temperature."

"Yet even so, life might have adapted itself to such conditions," I contended; "man exists in equatorial heat and arctic cold."

"But not without oxygen," said Napier. "St. John has estimated that the amount of oxygen above the cloud envelope that surrounds Venus is less than one tenth of one per cent of the terrestrial amount. After all, we have to bow to the superior judgment of such men as Sir James Jeans, who says, 'The evidence, for what it is worth, goes to suggest that Venus, the only planet in the solar system outside Mars and the Earth on which life could possibly exist, possesses no vegetation and no oxygen for higher forms of life to breathe,' which definitely limits my planetary exploration to Mars."

We discussed his plans during the remainder of the day and well into the night, and early the following morning he left for Guadalupe Island in his Sikorsky amphibian. I have not seen him since, at least in person, yet, through the marvelous medium of telepathy, I have communicated with him continually and seen him amid strange, unearthly surroundings that have been graphically photographed upon the retina of my mind's eye. Thus I am the medium through which the remarkable adventures of Carson Napier are being recorded on Earth; but I am only that, like a typewriter or a dictaphone—the story that follows is his.

CHAPTER TWO
OFF FOR MARS

A S I SET MY SHIP DOWN in the sheltered cove along the shore of desolate Guadalupe a trifle over four hours after I left Tarzana, the little Mexican steamer I had chartered to transport my men, materials, and supplies from the mainland rode peacefully at anchor in the tiny harbor, while on the shore, waiting to welcome me, were grouped the laborers, mechanics, and assistants who had worked with such wholehearted loyalty for long months in preparation for this day. Towering head and shoulders above the others loomed Jimmy Welsh, the only American among them.

I taxied in close to shore and moored the ship to a buoy, while the men launched a dory and rowed out to get me. I had been absent less than a week, most of which had been spent in Guaymas awaiting the expected letter from Tarzana, but so exuberantly did they greet me, one might have thought me a long-lost brother returned from the dead, so dreary and desolate and isolated is Guadalupe to those who must remain upon her lonely shores for even a brief interval between contacts with the mainland.

Perhaps the warmth of their greeting may have been enhanced by a desire to conceal their true feelings. We had been together constantly for months, warm friendships had sprung up between us, and tonight we were to separate with little likelihood that they and I should ever meet again. This was to be my last day on Earth; after today I should be as dead to them as though three feet of earth covered my inanimate corpse.

It is possible that my own sentiments colored my interpretation of theirs, for I am frank to confess that I had been apprehending this last moment as the most difficult of the whole adventure. I have come in contact with the peoples of many countries, but I recall none with more lovable qualities than Mexicans who have not been contaminated by too close contact with the intolerance and commercialism of Americans. And then there was Jimmy Welsh! It was going to be like parting with a brother when I said good-bye to him. For months he had been begging to go with me; and I knew that he would continue to beg up to the last minute, but I could not risk a single life unnecessarily.

We all piled into the trucks that we had used to transport supplies and materials from the shore to the camp, which lay inland a few miles, and bumped over our makeshift road to the little tableland where the giant torpedo lay upon its mile long track.

"Everything is ready," said Jimmy. "We polished off the last details this morning. Every roller on the track has been inspected by at least a dozen men, we towed the old crate back and forth over the full length of the track three times with the truck, and then repacked all the rollers with grease. Three of us have checked over every item of equipment and supplies individually; we've done about everything but fire the rockets; and now we're ready to go—you *are* going to take me along, aren't you, Car?"

I shook my head. "Please don't, Jimmy," I begged; "I have a perfect right to gamble with my own life, but not with yours; so forget it. But I am going to do something for you," I added, "just as a token of my appreciation of the help you've given me and all that sort of rot. I'm going to give you my ship to remember me by."

He was grateful, of course, but still he could not hide his disappointment in not being allowed to accompany me, which was evidenced by an invidious comparison he drew between the ceiling of the Sikorsky and that of the old crate, as he had affectionately dubbed the great torpedolike rocket that was to bear me out into space in a few hours.

"A thirty-five-million-mile ceiling," he mourned dolefully; "think of it! Mars for a ceiling!"

"And may I hit the ceiling!" I exclaimed, fervently.

The laying of the track upon which the torpedo was to take off had been the subject of a year of calculation and consultation. The day of departure had been planned far ahead and the exact point at which Mars would rise above the eastern horizon on that night calculated, as well as the time; then it was necessary to make allowances for the rotation of the Earth and the attraction of the nearer heavenly bodies. The track was then laid in accordance with these calculations. It was constructed with a very slight drop in the first three-quarters of a mile and then rose gradually at an angle of two and one-half degrees from horizontal.

A speed of four and one-half miles per second at the takeoff would be sufficient to neutralize gravity; to overcome it, I must attain a speed of 6.93 miles per second. To allow a sufficient factor of safety I had powered the torpedo to attain a speed of seven miles per second at the end of the runway, which I purposed stepping up to ten miles per second while passing through the Earth's atmosphere. What my speed would be through space was problematical, but I based all my calculations on the theory that it would not deviate much from the speed at which I left the Earth's atmosphere, until I came within the influence of the gravitational pull of Mars.

The exact instant at which to make the start had also caused me considerable anxiety. I had calculated it again and again, but there were so many factors to be taken into consideration that I had found it expedient to have my figures checked and rechecked by a well-known physicist and an equally prominent astronomer. Their deductions tallied perfectly with mine—the torpedo must start upon its journey toward Mars sometime before the red planet rose above the eastern horizon. The trajectory would be along a constantly flattening arc, influenced considerably at first by the Earth's gravitational pull, which would decrease inversely as the square of the distance attained. As the torpedo left the Earth's surface on a curved tangent, its departure must be so nicely timed that when it eventually escaped the pull of the Earth its nose would be directed toward Mars.

On paper, these figures appeared most convincing; but, as the moment approached for my departure, I must confess to a sudden realization that they were based wholly upon theory, and I was struck with the utter folly of my mad venture.

For a moment I was aghast. The enormous torpedo, with its sixty tons, lying there at the end of its mile long track, loomed above me, the semblance of a gargantuan coffin—my coffin, in which I was presently to be dashed to Earth, or to the bottom of the Pacific, or cast out into space to wander there to the end of time. I was afraid. I admit it, but it was not so much the fear of death as the effect of the sudden realization of the stupendousness of the cosmic forces against which I had pitted my puny powers that temporarily unnerved me.

Then Jimmy spoke to me. "Let's have a last look at things inside the old crate before you shove off," he suggested, and my nervousness and my apprehensions vanished beneath the spell of his quiet tones and his matter-of-fact manner. I was myself again.

Together we inspected the cabin, where are located the controls, a wide and comfortable berth, a table, a chair, writing materials, and a well-stocked bookshelf. Behind the cabin is a small galley and just behind the galley a storeroom containing canned and dehydrated foods sufficient to last me a year. Back of this is a small battery room containing storage batteries for lighting, heating, and cooking, a dynamo, and a gas engine. The extreme stern compartment is filled with rockets and the intricate mechanical device by which they are fed to the firing chambers by means of the controls in the cabin. Forward of the main cabin is a large compartment in which are located the water and oxygen tanks, as well as a quantity of odds and ends necessary either to my safety or comfort.

Everything, it is needless to say, is fastened securely against the sudden and terrific stress that must accompany the takeoff. Once out in space, I anticipate no sense of motion, but the start is going to be rather jarring. To absorb, as much as possible, the shock of the takeoff, the rocket consists of two torpedoes, a smaller torpedo within a larger one, the former considerably shorter than the latter and consisting of several sections, each one comprising one of the compartments I have described. Between the inner and outer shells and between each two compartments is installed a system of ingenious hydraulic shock absorbers designed to more or less gradually overcome the inertia of the inner torpedo during the takeoff. I trust that it functions properly.

In addition to these precautions against disaster at the start, the chair in which I shall sit before the controls is not only heavily overstuffed but is secured to a track or framework that is equipped with shock absorbers. Furthermore, there are means whereby I may strap myself securely into the chair before taking off.

I have neglected nothing essential to my safety, upon which depends the success of my project.

Following our final inspection of the interior, Jimmy and I clambered to the top of the torpedo for a last inspection of the parachutes, which I hope will sufficiently retard the speed of the rocket after it enters the atmosphere of Mars to permit me to bail out with my own parachute in time to make a safe landing. The main parachutes are in a series of compartments running the full length of the top of the torpedo. To explain them more clearly, I may say that they are a continuous series of batteries of parachutes, each battery consisting of a number of parachutes of increasing diameter from the uppermost, which is the smallest. Each battery is in an individual compartment, and each compartment is covered by a separate hatch that can be opened at the will of the operator by controls in the cabin. Each parachute is anchored to the torpedo by a separate cable. I expect about one-half of them to be torn loose while checking the speed of the torpedo sufficiently to permit the others to hold and further retard it to a point where I may safely open the doors and jump with my own parachute and oxygen tank.

The moment for departure was approaching. Jimmy and I had descended to the ground and the most difficult ordeal now faced me—that of saying good-bye to these loyal friends and coworkers. We did not say much, we were too filled with emotion, and there was not a dry eye among us. Without exception none of the laborers could understand why the nose of the torpedo was not pointed straight up in the air if my intended destination were Mars. Nothing could convince them that I would not shoot out a short distance and make a graceful nosedive into the Pacific— that is, if I started at all, which many of them doubted.

There was a handclasp all around, and then I mounted the ladder leaning against the side of the torpedo and entered it. As I closed the door of the outer shell, I saw my friends piling into the trucks and pulling away, for I had given orders that no one should be within a mile of the rocket when I took off, fearing, as I did, the effect upon them of the terrific explosions that must accompany the takeoff. Securing the outer door with its great vaultlike bolts, I closed the inner door and fastened it; then I took my seat before the controls and buckled the straps that held me to the chair.

I glanced at my watch. It lacked nine minutes of the zero hour. In nine minutes I should be on my way out into the great void, or in nine minutes I should be dead. If all did not go well, the disaster would follow within a fraction of a split second after I touched the first firing control.

Seven minutes! My throat felt dry and parched; I wanted a drink of water, but there was no time.

Four minutes! Thirty-five million miles are a lot of miles, yet I planned on spanning them in between forty and forty-five days.

Two minutes! I inspected the oxygen gauge and opened the valve a trifle wider.

One minute! I thought of my mother and wondered if she were way out there somewhere waiting for me.

Thirty seconds! My hand was on the control. Fifteen seconds! Ten, five, four, three, two—one!

I turned the pointer! There was a muffled roar. The torpedo leaped forward. I was off!

I knew that the takeoff was a success. I glanced through the port at my side at the instant that the torpedo started, but so terrific was its initial speed that I saw only a confused blur as the landscape rushed past. I was thrilled and delighted by the ease and perfection with which the takeoff had been accomplished, and I must admit that I was not a little surprised by the almost negligible effects that were noticeable in the cabin. I had had the sensation as of a giant hand pressing me suddenly back against the upholstery of my chair, but that had passed almost at once, and now there was no sensation different from that which one might experience sitting in an easy chair in a comfortable drawing room on terra firma.

There was no sensation of motion after the first few seconds that were required to pass through the Earth's atmosphere, and now that I had done all that lay within my power to do, I could only leave the rest to momentum, gravitation, and fate. Releasing the straps that held me to the chair, I moved about the cabin to look through the various ports, of which there were several in the sides, keel, and top of the torpedo.

Space was a black void dotted with countless points of light. The Earth I could not see, for it lay directly astern; far ahead was Mars. All seemed well. I switched on the electric lights, and seating myself at the table, made the first entries in the log; then I checked over various computations of time and distances.

My calculations suggested that in about three hours from the takeoff the torpedo would be moving almost directly toward Mars; and from time to time I took observations through the wide-angle telescopic periscope that is mounted flush with the upper surface of the torpedo's shell, but the results were not entirely reassuring. In two hours Mars was dead ahead—the arc of the trajectory was not flattening as it should. I became apprehensive. What was wrong? Where had our careful computations erred?

I left the periscope and gazed down through the main keel port. Below and ahead was the Moon, a gorgeous spectacle as viewed through the clear void of space from a distance some seventy-two thousand miles less than I had ever seen it before and with no earthly atmosphere to reduce visibility. Tycho, Plato, and Copernicus stood out in bold relief upon the brazen disc of the great satellite, deepening by contrast the shadows of Mare Serenitatis and Mare Tranquillitatis. The rugged peaks of the Apennine and the Altai lay revealed as distinctly as I had ever seen them through the largest telescope. I was thrilled, but I was distinctly worried, too.

Three hours later I was less than fifty-nine thousand miles from the Moon; where its aspect had been gorgeous before, it now beggared description, but my apprehension had cause to increase in proportion; I might say, as the square of its increasing gorgeousness. Through the periscope I had watched the arc of my trajectory pass through the plane of Mars and drop below it. I knew quite definitely then that I could never reach my goal. I tried not to think of the fate that lay ahead of me; but, instead, sought to discover the error that had wrought this disaster.

For an hour I checked over various calculations, but could discover nothing that might shed light on the cause of my predicament; then I switched off the lights and looked down through the keel port to have a closer view of the Moon. It was not there! Stepping to the port side of the cabin, I looked through one of the heavy circular glasses out into the void of space. For an instant I was horror stricken; apparently just off the port bow loomed an enormous world. It was the Moon, less than twenty-three thousand miles away, and I was hurtling toward it at the rate of thirty-six thousand miles an hour!

I leaped to the periscope, and in the next few seconds I accomplished some lightning mental calculating that must constitute an all-time record. I watched the deflection of our course in the direction of the Moon, following it across the lens of the periscope, I computed the distance to the Moon and the speed of the torpedo, and I came to the conclusion that I had better than a fighting chance of missing the great orb. I had little fear of anything but a direct hit, since our speed was so great that the attraction of the Moon could not hold us if we missed her even by a matter of feet; but it was quite evident that it had affected our flight, and with this realization came the answer to the question that had been puzzling me.

To my mind flashed the printer's story of the first perfect book. It had been said that no book had ever before been published containing not a single error. A great publishing house undertook to publish such a book. The galley proofs were read and reread by a dozen different experts, the page proofs received the same careful scrutiny. At last the masterpiece was ready for the press—errorless! It was printed and bound and sent out to the public, and then it was discovered that the title had been misspelled on the title page. With all our careful calculation, with all our checking and rechecking, we had overlooked the obvious; we had not taken the Moon into consideration at all.

Explain it if you can; I cannot. It was just one of those things, as people say when a good team loses to a poor one; it was a *break*, and a bad one. How bad it was I did not even try to conjecture at the time; I just sat at the periscope watching the Moon racing toward us. As we neared it, it presented the most gorgeous spectacle that I have ever witnessed. Each mountain peak and crater stood out in vivid detail. Even the great height of summits over twenty-five thousand feet appeared distinguishable to me, though imagination must have played a major part in the illusion, since I was looking down upon them from above.

Suddenly I realized that the great sphere was passing rapidly from the field of the periscope, and I breathed a sigh of relief—we were not going to score a clean hit, we were going to pass by.

I returned then to the porthole. The Moon lay just ahead and a little to the left. It was no longer a great sphere; it was a world that filled my whole range of vision. Against its black horizon I saw titanic peaks; below me huge craters yawned. I stood with God on high and looked down upon a dead world.

Our transit of the Moon required a little less than four minutes; I timed it carefully that I might check our speed. How close we came I may only guess; perhaps five thousand feet above the tallest peaks, but it was close enough. The pull of the Moon's gravitation had definitely altered our course, but owing to our speed we had eluded her clutches. Now we were racing away from her, but to what?

The nearest star, Alpha Centauri, is twenty-five and a half million million miles from Earth. Write that on your typewriter—25,500,000,000,000 miles. But why trifle with short distances like this? There was little likelihood that I should visit Alpha Centauri with all the wide range of space at my command and many more interesting places to go. I knew that I had ample room in which to wander, since science has calculated the diameter of space to be eighty-four thousand million light years, which, when one reflects that light travels at the rate of one hundred eighty-six thousand miles a second, should satisfy the wanderlust of the most inveterate roamer.

However, I was not greatly concerned with any of these distances, as I had food and water for only a year, during which time the torpedo might travel slightly more than three hundred fifteen million miles. Even if it reached our near neighbor, Alpha Centauri, I should not then be greatly interested in the event, as I should have been dead for over eighty thousand years. Such is the immensity of the universe!

During the next twenty-four hours the course of the torpedo nearly paralleled the Moon's orbit around the Earth. Not only had the pull of the Moon deflected its course, but now it seemed evident that the Earth had seized us and that we were doomed to race through eternity around her, a tiny, second satellite. But I did not wish to be a moon, certainly not an insignificant moon that in all probability might not be picked up by even the largest telescope.

The next month was the most trying of my life. It seems the height of egotism even to mention my life in the face of the stupendous cosmic forces that engulfed it; but it was the only life I had and I was fond of it, and the more imminent seemed the moment when it should be snuffed out, the better I liked it.

At the end of the second day it was quite apparent that we had eluded the grip of the Earth. I cannot say that I was elated at the discovery. My plan to visit Mars was ruined. I should have been glad to return to Earth. If I could have landed safely on Mars, I certainly could have landed safely on Earth. But there was another reason why I should have been glad to have returned to Earth, a reason that loomed, large and terrible, ahead—the Sun. We were heading straight for the Sun now. Once in the grip of that mighty power, nothing could affect our destiny; we were doomed. For three months I must await the inevitable end, before plunging into that fiery furnace. Furnace is an inadequate word by which to suggest the Sun's heat, which is reputedly from thirty to sixty million degrees at the center, a fact which should not have concerned me greatly, since I did not anticipate reaching the center.

The days dragged on, or, I should say, the long night—there were no days, other than the record that I kept of the passing hours. I read a great deal. I made no entries in the log. Why write something that was presently to be plunged into the Sun and consumed? I experimented in the galley, attempting fancy cooking. I ate a great deal; it helped to pass the time away, and I enjoyed my meals.

On the thirtieth day I was scanning space ahead when I saw a gorgeous, shimmering crescent far to the right of our course; but I must confess that I was not greatly interested in sights of any sort. In sixty days I should be in the Sun. Long before that, however, the increasing heat would have destroyed me. The end was approaching rapidly.

CHAPTER THREE
RUSHING TOWARD VENUS

THE PSYCHOLOGICAL EFFECTS OF AN EXPERIENCE such as that through which I had been passing must be considerable, and even though they could be neither weighed nor measured, I was yet conscious of changes that had taken place in me because of them. For thirty days I had been racing alone through space toward absolute annihilation, toward an end that would probably not leave a single nucleus of the atoms that compose me an electron to carry on with, I had experienced the ultimate in solitude, and the result had been to deaden my sensibilities; doubtless a wise provision of nature.

Even the realization that the splendid crescent, looming enormously off the starboard bow of the torpedo, was Venus failed to excite me greatly. What if I were to approach Venus more closely than any other human being of all time! It meant nothing. Were I to see God, himself, even that would mean nothing. It became apparent that the value of what we see is measurable only by the size of our prospective audience. Whatever I saw, who might never have an audience, was without value.

Nevertheless, more to pass away the time than because I was particularly interested in the subject, I began to make some rough calculations. These indicated that I was about eight hundred sixty-five thousand miles from the orbit of Venus and that I should cross it in about twenty-four hours. I could not, however, compute my present distance from the planet accurately. I only knew that it appeared very close. When I say close, I mean relatively. The Earth was some twenty-five million miles away, the Sun about sixty-eight million, so that an object as large as Venus, at a distance of one or two million miles, appeared close.

As Venus travels in her orbit at the rate of nearly twenty-two miles per second, or over one million six hundred thousand miles in a terrestrial day, it appeared evident to me that she would cross my path sometime within the next twenty-four hours.

It occurred to me that, passing closely, as was unavoidable, she might deflect the course of the torpedo and save me from the Sun; but I knew this to be a vain hope. Undoubtedly, the path of the torpedo would be bent, but the Sun would not relinquish his prey. With these thoughts, my apathy returned, and I lost interest in Venus.

Selecting a book, I lay down on my bed to read. The interior of the cabin was brightly illuminated. I am extravagant with electricity. I have the means of generating it for eleven more months; but I shall not need it after a few weeks, so why should I be parsimonious?

I read for a few hours, but as reading in bed always makes me sleepy, I eventually succumbed. When I awoke, I lay for a few minutes in luxurious ease. I might be racing toward extinction at the rate of thirty-six thousand miles an hour, but I, myself, was unhurried. I recalled the beautiful spectacle that Venus had presented when I had last observed her and decided to have another look at her. Stretching languorously, I arose and stepped to one of the starboard portholes.

The picture framed by the casing of that circular opening was gorgeous beyond description. Apparently less than half as far away as before, and twice as large, loomed the mass of Venus outlined by an aureole of light where the Sun, behind her, illuminated her cloudy envelope and lighted to burning brilliance a thin crescent along the edge nearest me.

I looked at my watch. Twelve hours had passed since I first discovered the planet, and now, at last, I became excited. Venus was apparently half as far away as it had been twelve hours ago, and I knew that the torpedo had covered half the distance that had separated us from her orbit at that time. A collision was possible, it even seemed within the range of probability that I should be dashed to the surface of this inhospitable, lifeless world.

Well, what of it? Am I not already doomed? What difference can it make to me if the end comes a few weeks sooner than I had anticipated? Yet I was excited. I cannot say that I felt fear. I have no fear of death—that left me when my mother died; but now that the great adventure loomed so close I was overwhelmed by contemplation of it and the great wonder that it induced. What would follow?

The long hours dragged on. It seemed incredible to me, accustomed though I am to thinking in units of terrific speed, that the torpedo and Venus were racing toward the same point in her orbit at such inconceivable velocities, the one at the rate of thirty-six thousand miles per hour, the other at over sixty-seven thousand.

It was now becoming difficult to view the planet through the side port, as she moved steadily closer and closer to our path. I went to the periscope—she was gliding majestically within its range. I knew that at that moment the torpedo was less than thirty-six thousand miles, less than an hour, from the path of the planet's orbit, and there could be no doubt now but that she had already seized us in her grasp. We were destined to make a clean hit. Even under the circumstances I could not restrain a smile at the thought of the marksmanship that this fact revealed. I had aimed at Mars and was about to hit Venus; unquestionably the all-time cosmic record for poor shots.

Even though I did not shrink from death, even though the world's best astronomers have assured us that Venus must be unfitted to support human life, that where her surface is not unutterably hot it is unutterably cold, even though she be oxygenless, as they aver, yet the urge to live that is born with each of us compelled me to make the same preparations to land that I should have had I successfully reached my original goal, Mars.

Slipping into a fleece-lined suit of coveralls, I donned goggles and a fleece-lined helmet; then I adjusted the oxygen tank that was designed to hang in front of me, lest it foul the parachute, and which can be automatically jettisoned in the event that I reach an atmosphere that will support life, for it would be an awkward and dangerous appendage to be cumbered with while landing. Finally, I adjusted my chute.

I glanced at my watch. If my calculations have been correct, we should strike in about fifteen minutes. Once more I returned to the periscope.

The sight that met my eyes was awe inspiring. We were plunging toward a billowing mass of black clouds. It was like chaos on the dawn of creation. The gravitation of the planet had seized us. The floor of the cabin was no longer beneath me—I was standing on the forward bulkhead now; but this condition I had anticipated when I designed the torpedo. We were diving nose on toward the planet. In space there had been neither up nor down, but now there was a very definite down.

From where I stood I could reach the controls, and beside me was the door in the side of the torpedo. I released three batteries of parachutes and opened the door in the wall of the inner torpedo. There was a noticeable jar, as though the parachutes had opened and temporarily checked the speed of the torpedo. This must mean that I had entered an atmosphere of some description and that there was not a second to waste.

With a single movement of a lever I loosed the remaining parachutes; then I turned to the outer door. Its bolts were controlled by a large wheel set in the center of the door and were geared to open quickly and with ease. I adjusted the mouthpiece of the oxygen line across my lips and quickly spun the wheel.

Simultaneously the door flew open and the air pressure within the torpedo shot me out into space. My right hand grasped the rip cord of my chute; but I waited. I looked about for the torpedo. It was racing almost parallel with me, all its parachutes distended above it. Just an instant's glimpse I had of it, and then it dove into the cloud mass and was lost to view; but what a weirdly magnificent spectacle it had presented in that brief instant!

Safe now from any danger of fouling with the torpedo, I jerked the rip cord of my parachute just as the clouds swallowed me. Through my fleece-lined suit I felt the bitter cold; like a dash of ice water the cold clouds slapped me in the face; then, to my relief, the chute opened, and I fell more slowly.

Down, down, down I dropped. I could not even guess the duration, nor the distance. It was very dark and very wet, like sinking into the depths of the ocean without feeling the pressure of the water. My thoughts during those long moments were such as to baffle description. Perhaps the oxygen made me a little drunk; I do not know. I felt exhilarated and intensely eager to solve the great mystery beneath me. The thought that I was about to die did not concern me so much as what I might see before I died. I was about to land on Venus—the first human being in all the world to see the face of the veiled planet.

Suddenly I emerged into a cloudless space; but far below me were what appeared in the darkness to be more clouds, recalling to my mind the often advanced theory of the two cloud envelopes of Venus. As I descended, the temperature rose gradually, but it was still cold.

As I entered the second cloud bank, there was a very noticeable rise in temperature the farther I fell. I shut off the oxygen supply and tried breathing through my nose. By inhaling deeply I discovered that I could take in sufficient oxygen to support life, and an astronomical theory was shattered. Hope flared within me like a beacon on a fog-hid landing field.

As I floated gently downward, I presently became aware of a faint luminosity far below. What could it be? There were many obvious reasons why it could not be sunlight; sunlight would not come from below, and, furthermore, it was night on this hemisphere of the planet. Naturally many weird conjectures raced through my mind. I wondered if this could be the light from an incandescent world, but immediately discarded that explanation as erroneous, knowing that the heat from an incandescent world would long since have consumed me. Then it occurred to me that it might be refracted light from that portion of the cloud envelope illuminated by the Sun, yet if such were the case, it seemed obvious that the clouds about me should be luminous, which they were not.

There seemed only one practical solution. It was the solution that an Earth man would naturally arrive at. Being what I am, a highly civilized creature from a world already far advanced by science and invention, I attributed the source of this light to these twin forces of superior intelligence. I could only account for that faint glow by attributing it to the reflection upon the underside of the cloud mass of artificial light produced by intelligent creatures upon the surface of this world toward which I was slowly settling.

I wondered what these beings would be like, and if my excitement grew as I anticipated the wonders that were soon to be revealed to my eyes, I believe that it was a pardonable excitement, under the circumstances. Upon the threshold of such an adventure who would not have been moved to excitement by contemplation of the experiences awaiting him?

Now I removed the mouthpiece of the oxygen tube entirely and found that I could breathe easily. The light beneath me was increasing gradually. About me I thought I saw vague, dark shapes among the cloud masses. Shadows, perhaps, but of what? I detached the oxygen tank and let it fall. I distinctly heard it strike something an instant after I had released it. Then a shadow loomed darkly beneath me, and an instant later my feet struck something that gave beneath them.

I dropped into a mass of foliage and grasped wildly for support. A moment later I began to fall more rapidly and guessed what had happened; the parachute had been uptilted by contact with the foliage. I clutched at leaves and branches, fruitlessly, and then I was brought to a sudden stop; evidently the chute had fouled something. I hoped that it would hold until I found a secure resting place.

As I groped about in the dark, my hand finally located a sturdy branch, and a moment later I was astride it, my back to the bole of a large tree— another theory gone the ignoble path of countless predecessors; it was evident that there was vegetation on Venus. At least there was one tree; I could vouch for that, as I was sitting in it, and doubtless the black shadows I had passed were other, taller trees.

Having found secure lodgment, I divested myself of my parachute after salvaging some of its ropes and the straps from the harness, which I thought I might find helpful in descending the tree. Starting at the top of a tree, in darkness and among clouds, one may not be positive what the tree is like nearer the ground. I also removed my goggles. Then I commenced to descend. The girth of the tree was enormous, but the branches grew suf-ficiently close together to permit me to find safe footing.

I did not know how far I had fallen through the second cloud stratum before I lodged in the tree nor how far I had descended the tree, but all together it must have been close to two thousand feet; yet I was still in the clouds. Could the entire atmosphere of Venus be forever fog laden? I hoped not, for it was a dreary prospect.

The light from below had increased a little as I descended, but not much; it was still dark about me. I continued to descend. It was tiresome work and not without danger, this climbing down an unfamiliar tree in a fog, at night, toward an unknown world. But I could not remain where I was, and there was nothing above to entice me upward; so I continued to descend.

What a strange trick fate had played me. I had wanted to visit Venus, but had discarded the idea when assured by my astronomer friends that the planet could not support either animal or vegetable life. I had started for Mars, and now, fully ten days before I had hoped to reach the red planet, I was on Venus, breathing perfectly good air among the branches of a tree that evidently dwarfed the giant sequoias.

The illumination was increasing rapidly now, the clouds were thinning; through breaks I caught glimpses far below, glimpses of what appeared to be an endless vista of foliage, softly moonlit—but Venus had no moon. In that, insofar as the seeming moonlight was concerned, I could fully concur with the astronomers. This illumination came from no moon, unless Venus' satellite lay beneath her inner envelope of clouds, which was preposterous.

A moment later I emerged entirely from the cloud bank, but though I searched in all directions, I saw nothing but foliage, above, around, below me, yet I could see far down into that abyss of leaves. In the soft light I could not determine the color of the foliage, but I was sure that it was not green; it was some light, delicate shade of another color.

I had descended another thousand feet since I had emerged from the clouds, and I was pretty well exhausted (the month of inactivity and overeating had softened me), when I saw just below me what appeared to be a causeway leading from the tree I was descending to another adjacent. I also discovered that from just below where I clung the limbs had been cut away from the tree to a point below the causeway. Here were two startling and unequivocal evidences of the presence of intelligent beings. Venus was inhabited! But by what? What strange, arboreal creatures built causeways high among these giant trees? Were they a species of monkey-man? Were they of a high or low order of intelligence? How would they receive me?

At this juncture in my vain speculations I was startled by a noise above me. Something was moving in the branches overhead. The sound was coming nearer, and it seemed to me that it was being made by something of considerable size and weight, but perhaps, I realized, that conjecture was the child of my imagination. However, I felt most uncomfortable. I was unarmed. I have never carried weapons. My friends had urged a perfect arsenal upon me before I embarked upon my adventure, but I had argued that if I arrived on Mars unarmed it would be *prima facie* evidence of my friendly intentions, and even if my reception were warlike, I should be no worse off, since I could not hope, single-handed, to conquer a world, no matter how well armed I were.

Suddenly, above me, to the crashing of some heavy body through the foliage were added hideous screams and snarls; and in the terrifying dissonance I recognized the presence of more than a single creature. Was I being pursued by all the fearsome denizens of this Venusian forest?

Perhaps my nerves were slightly unstrung; and who may blame them if they were, after what I had passed through so recently and during the long, preceding month? They were not entirely shattered, however, and I could still appreciate the fact that night noises often multiply themselves in a most disconcerting way. I have heard coyotes yapping and screaming around my camp on Arizona nights when, but for the actual knowledge that there were but one or two of them, I could have sworn that there were a hundred, had I trusted only to my sense of hearing.

But in this instance I was quite positive that the voices of more than a single beast were mingling to produce the horrid din that, together with the sound of their passage, was definitely and unquestionably drawing rapidly nearer me. Of course I did not know that the owners of those awesome voices were pursuing me, though a still, small voice within seemed to be assuring me that such was the fact.

I wished that I might reach the causeway below me (I should feel better standing squarely on two feet), but it was too far to drop and there were no more friendly branches to give me support; then I thought of the ropes I had salvaged from the abandoned parachute. Quickly uncoiling them from about my waist, I looped one of them over the branch upon which I sat, grasped both strands firmly in my hands, and prepared to swing from my porch. Suddenly the screams and snarling growls ceased; and then, close above me now, I heard the noise of something descending toward me and saw the branches shaking to its weight.

Lowering my body from the branch, I swung downward and slid the fifteen or more feet to the causeway, and as I alighted the silence of the great forest was again shattered by a hideous scream just above my head. Looking up quickly, I saw a creature launching itself toward me and just beyond it a snarling face of utter hideousness. I caught but the briefest glimpse of it—just enough to see that it was a face, with eyes and a mouth—then it was withdrawn amidst the foliage.

Perhaps I only sensed that hideous vision subconsciously at the time, for the whole scene was but a flash upon the retina of my eye, and the other beast was in midair above me at the instant; but it remained indelibly impressed upon my memory, and I was to recall it upon a later day under circumstances so harrowing that the mind of mortal Earth man may scarce conceive them.

As I leaped back to avoid the creature springing upon me, I still clung to one strand of the rope down which I had lowered myself to the causeway. My grasp upon the rope was unconscious and purely mechanical; it was in my hand, and my fist was clenched; and as I leaped away, I dragged the rope with me. A fortuitous circumstance, no doubt, but a most fortunate one.

The creature missed me, alighting on all fours a few feet from me, and there it crouched, apparently slightly bewildered, and, fortunately for me, it did not immediately charge, giving me the opportunity to collect my wits and back slowly away, at the same time mechanically coiling the rope in my right hand. The little, simple things one does in moments of stress or excitement often seem entirely beyond reason and incapable of explanation; but I have thought that they may be dictated by a subconscious mind reacting to the urge of self-preservation. Possibly they are not always well directed and may as often fail to be of service as not, but then it may be possible that subconscious minds are no less fallible than the objective mind, which is wrong far more often than it is right. I cannot but seek for some explanation of the urge that caused me to retain that rope, since, all unknown to me, it was to be the slender thread upon which my life was to hang.

Silence had again descended upon the weird scene. Since the final scream of the hideous creature that had retreated into the foliage after this thing had leaped for me, there had been no sound. The creature that crouched facing me seemed slightly bewildered. I am positive now that it had not been pursuing me, but that it itself had been the object of pursuit by the other beast that had retreated.

In the dim half-light of the Venusian night I saw confronting me a creature that might be conjured only in the half-delirium of some horrid nightmare. It was about as large as a full-grown puma, and stood upon four handlike feet that suggested that it might be almost wholly arboreal. The front legs were much longer than the hind, suggesting, in this respect, the hyena; but here the similarity ceased, for the creature's furry pelt was striped longitudinally with alternate bands of red and yellow, and its hideous head bore no resemblance to any earthly animal. No external ears were visible, and in the low forehead was a single large, round eye at the end of a thick antenna about four inches long. The jaws were powerful and armed with long, sharp fangs, while from either side of the neck projected a powerful chela. Never have I seen a creature so fearsomely armed for offense as was this nameless beast of another world. With those powerful crablike pincers it could easily have held an opponent far stronger than a man and dragged it to those terrible jaws.

For a time it eyed me with that single, terrifying eye that moved to and fro at the end of its antenna, and all the time its chelae were waving slowly, opening and closing. In that brief moment of delay I looked about me, and the first thing that I discovered was that I stood directly in front of an opening cut in the bole of the tree; an opening about three feet wide and over six feet high. But the most remarkable thing about it was that it was closed by a door; not a solid door, but one suggesting a massive wooden grill.

As I stood contemplating it and wondering what to do, I thought that I saw something moving behind it. Then a voice spoke to me out of the darkness beyond the door. It sounded like a human voice, though it spoke in a language that I could not understand. The tones were peremptory. I could almost imagine that it said, "Who are you, and what do you want here in the middle of the night?"

"I am a stranger," I said. "I come in peace and friendship."

Of course I knew that whatever it was behind that door, it could not understand me; but I hoped that my tone would assure it of my peaceful designs. There was a moment's silence and then I heard other voices. Evidently the situation was being discussed; then I saw that the creature facing me upon the causeway was creeping toward me, and I turned my attention from the doorway to the beast.

I had no weapons, nothing but a length of futile rope; but I knew that

I must do something. I could not stand there supinely and let the creature seize and devour me without striking a blow in my own defense. I uncoiled a portion of the rope and, more in despair than with any hope that I could accomplish anything of a defensive nature, flicked the end of it in the face of the advancing beast. You have seen a boy snap a wet towel at a companion; perhaps you have been flicked in that way, and if you have, you know that it hurts.

Of course I did not expect to overcome my adversary by any such means as this; to be truthful, I did not know what I did expect to accomplish. Perhaps I just felt that I must do something, and this was the only thing that occurred to me. The result merely demonstrated the efficiency of that single eye and the quickness of the chelae. I snapped that rope as a ringmaster snaps a whip; but though the rope end traveled with great speed and the act must have been unexpected, the creature caught the rope in one of its chelae before it reached its face. Then it hung on and sought to drag me toward those frightful jaws.

I learned many a trick of roping from a cowboy friend of my motion picture days, and one of these I now put into use in an endeavor to entangle the crablike chelae. Suddenly giving the rope sufficient slack, I threw a half hitch around the chela that gripped it, immediately following it with a second, whereupon the creature commenced to pull desperately away. I think it was motivated solely by an instinctive urge to pull toward its jaws anything that was held in its chelae; but for how long it would continue to pull away before it decided to change its tactics and charge me, I could not even guess; and so I acted upon a sudden inspiration and hurriedly made fast the end of the rope that I held to one of the stout posts that supported the handrail of the causeway; then, of a sudden, the thing charged me, roaring furiously.

I turned and ran, hoping that I could get out of the reach of those terrible chelae before the creature was stopped by the rope; and this I but barely managed to do. I breathed a sigh of relief as I saw the great body flipped completely over on its back as the rope tautened, but the hideous scream of rage that followed left me cold. Nor was my relief of any great duration, for as soon as the creature had scrambled to its feet, it seized the rope in its other chela and severed it as neatly as one might with a pair of monstrous tinner's snips; and then it was after me again, but this time it did not creep.

It seemed evident that my stay upon Venus was to be brief, when suddenly the door in the tree swung open and three men leaped to the causeway just behind the charging terror that was swiftly driving down upon me. The leading man hurled a short, heavy spear that sank deep into the back of my infuriated pursuer. Instantly the creature stopped in its tracks and wheeled about to face these new and more dangerous tormentors; and as he did so two more spears, hurled by the companions of the first man, drove into his chest, and with a last frightful scream, the thing dropped in its tracks, dead.

Then the leading man came toward me. In the subdued light of the forest he appeared no different from an Earth man. He held the point of a straight, sharp sword pointed at my vitals. Close behind him were the other two men, each with a drawn sword.

The first man spoke to me in a stern, commanding voice, but I shook my head to indicate that I could not understand; then he pressed the point of his weapon against my coveralls, opposite the pit of my stomach, and jabbed. I backed away. He advanced and jabbed at me again, and again I backed along the causeway. Now the other two men advanced and the three of them fell to examining me, meanwhile talking among themselves.

I could see them better now. They were about my own height and in every detail of their visible anatomy they appeared identical with terrestrial human beings, nor was a great deal left to my imagination—the men were almost naked. They wore loincloths and little else other than the belts that supported the scabbards of their swords. Their skins appeared to be much darker than mine, and their faces were smooth and handsome.

Several times one or another of them addressed me and I always replied, but neither understood what the other said. Finally, after a lengthy discussion, one of them reentered the opening in the tree and a moment later I saw the interior of a chamber, just within the doorway, illuminated; then one of the two remaining men motioned me forward and pointed toward the doorway.

Understanding that he wished me to enter, I stepped forward, and, as I passed them, they kept their sword points against my body—they were taking no chances with me. The other man awaited me in the center of a large room hewn from the interior of the great tree. Beyond him were other doorways leading from this room, doubtless into other apartments. There were chairs and a table in the room; the walls were carved and painted; there was a large rug upon the floor; from a small vessel depending from the center of the ceiling a soft light illuminated the interior as brightly as might sunlight flooding through an open window, but there was no glare.

The other men had entered and closed the door, which they fastened by a device that was not apparent to me at the time; then one of them pointed to a chair and motioned me to be seated. Under the bright light they examined me intently, and I them. My clothing appeared to puzzle them most; they examined and discussed its material, texture, and weave, if I could judge correctly by their gestures and inflections.

Finding the heat unendurable in my fleece-lined coveralls, I removed them and my leather coat and polo shirt. Each newly revealed article aroused their curiosity and comment. My light skin and blond hair also received their speculative attention.

Presently one of them left the chamber, and while he was absent another removed the various articles that had lain upon the table. These consisted of what I took to be books bound in wooden and in leather covers, several ornaments, and a dagger in a beautifully wrought sheath.

When the man who had left the room returned, he brought food and drink which he placed upon the table; and by signs the three indicated that I might eat. There were fruits and nuts in highly polished, carved wooden bowls; there was something I took to be bread, on a golden platter; and there was honey in a silver jug. A tall, slender goblet contained a whitish liquid that resembled milk. This last receptacle was a delicate, translucent ceramic of an exquisite blue shade. These things and the appointments of the room bespoke culture, refinement, and good taste, making the savage apparel of their owners appear incongruous.

The fruits and nuts were unlike any with which I was familiar, both in appearance and flavor; the bread was coarse but delicious; and the honey, if such it were, suggested candied violets to the taste. The milk (I can find no other earthly word to describe it) was strong and almost pungent, yet far from unpleasant. I imagined at the time that one might grow to be quite fond of it.

The table utensils were similar to those with which we are familiar in civilized portions of the Earth; there were hollowed instruments with which to dip or scoop, sharp ones with which to cut, and others with tines with which to impale. There was also a handled pusher, which I recommend to earthly hostesses. All these were of metal.

While I ate, the three men conversed earnestly, one or another of them occasionally offering me more food. They seemed hospitable and courteous, and I felt that if they were typical of the inhabitants of Venus I should find my life here a pleasant one. That it would not be a bed of roses, however, was attested by the weapons that the men constantly wore; one does not carry a sword and a dagger about with him unless he expects to have occasion to use them, except on dress parade.

When I had finished my meal, two of the men escorted me from the room by a rear doorway, up a flight of circular stairs, and ushered me into a small chamber. The stairway and corridor were illuminated by a small lamp similar to that which hung in the room where I had eaten, and light from this lamp shone through the heavy wooden grating of the door, into the room where I was now locked and where my captors left me to my own devices.

Upon the floor was a soft mattress over which were spread coverings of a silky texture. It being very warm, I removed all of my clothing except my undershorts and lay down to sleep. I was tired after my arduous descent of the giant tree and dozed almost immediately. I should have been asleep at once had I not been suddenly startled to wakefulness by a repetition of that hideous scream with which the beast that had pursued me through the tree had announced its rage and chagrin when I had eluded it.

However, it was not long before I fell asleep, my dozing mind filled with a chaos of fragmentary recollections of my stupendous adventure.

CHAPTER FOUR
TO THE HOUSE OF THE KING

WHEN I AWOKE, it was quite light in the room, and through a window I saw the foliage of trees, lavender and heliotrope and violet in the light of a new day. I arose and went to the window. I saw no sign of sunlight, yet a brightness equivalent to sunlight pervaded everything. The air was warm and sultry. Below me I could see sections of various causeways extending from tree to tree. On some of these I caught glimpses of people. All the men were naked, except for loincloths, nor did I wonder at their scant apparel, in the light of my experience of the temperatures on Venus. There were both men and women; and all the men were armed with swords and daggers, while the women carried daggers only. All those whom I saw seemed to be of the same age; there were neither children nor old people among them. All appeared comely.

From my barred window I sought a glimpse of the ground, but as far down as I could see there was only the amazing foliage of the trees, lavender, heliotrope, and violet. And what trees! From my window I could see several enormous boles fully two hundred feet in diameter. I had thought the tree I descended a giant, but compared with these, it was only a sapling.

As I stood contemplating the scene before me, there was a noise at the door behind me. Turning, I saw one of my captors entering the room. He greeted me with a few words, which I could not understand, and a pleasant smile, that I could. I returned his smile and said, "Good morning!"

He beckoned to me to follow him from the room, but I made signs indicating that I wished to don my clothes first. I knew I should be hot and uncomfortable in them; I was aware that no one I had seen here wore any clothing, yet so powerful are the inhibitions of custom and habit that I shrank from doing the sensible thing and wearing only my undershorts.

At first, when he realized what I wished to do, he motioned me to leave my clothes where they were and come with him as I was; but eventually he gave in with another of his pleasant smiles. He was a man of fine physique, a little shorter than I; by daylight, I could see that his skin was about that shade of brown that a heavy suntan imparts to people of my own race; his eyes were dark brown, his hair black. His appearance formed a marked contrast to my light skin, blue eyes, and blond hair.

When I had dressed, I followed him downstairs to a room adjoining the one I had first entered the previous night. Here the man's two companions and two women were seated at a table on which were a number of vessels containing food. As I entered the room the women's eyes were turned upon me curiously; the men smiled and greeted me as had their fellow, and one of them motioned me to a chair. The women appraised me frankly but without boldness, and it was evident that they were discussing me freely between themselves and with the men. They were both uncommonly good-looking, their skins being a shade lighter than those of the men, while their eyes and hair were of about the same color as those of their male companions. Each wore a single garment of a silken material similar to that of which my bed cover had been made and in the form of a long sash, which was wrapped tightly around the body below the armpits, confining the breasts. From this point it was carried halfway around the body downward to the waist, where it circled the body again, the loose end then passing between the legs from behind and up through the sash in front, after the manner of a G-string, the remainder falling in front to the knees.

In addition to these garments, which were beautifully embroidered in colors, the women wore girdles from which depended pocket pouches and sheathed daggers, and both were plentifully adorned with ornaments such as rings, bracelets, and hair ornaments. I could recognize gold and silver among the various materials of which these things were fabricated, and there were others that might have been ivory and coral; but what impressed me most was the exquisite workmanship they displayed, and I imagined that they were valued more for this than for the intrinsic worth of the materials that composed them. That this conjecture might be in accordance with fact was borne out by the presence among their ornaments of several of the finest workmanship, obviously carved from ordinary bone.

On the table was bread different from that which I had had the night before, a dish that I thought might be eggs and meat baked together, several which I could not recognize either by appearance or taste, and the familiar milk and honey that I had encountered before. The foods varied widely in range of flavor, so that it would have been a difficult palate indeed that would not have found something to its liking.

During the meal they engaged in serious discussion, and I was certain from their glances and gestures that I was the subject of their debate. The two girls enlivened the meal by attempting to carry on a conversation with me, which appeared to afford them a great deal of merriment, nor could I help joining in their laughter, so infectious was it. Finally one of them hit upon the happy idea of teaching me their language. She pointed to herself and said, "Zuro," and to the other girl and said, "Alzo"; then the men became interested, and I soon learned that the name of him who seemed to be the head of the house, the man who had first challenged me the preceding night, was Duran, the other two Olthar and Kamlot.

But before I had mastered more than these few words and the names of some of the foods on the table, breakfast was over and the three men had conducted me from the house. As we proceeded along the causeway that passed in front of the house of Duran, the interest and curiosity of those we passed were instantly challenged as their eyes fell upon me; and it was at once evident to me that I was a type either entirely unknown on Venus or at least rare, for my blue eyes and blond hair caused quite as much comment as my clothing, as I could tell by their gestures and the direction of their gaze.

We were often stopped by curious friends of my captors, or hosts (I was not sure yet in which category they fell); but none offered me either harm or insult, and if I were the object of their curious scrutiny, so were they of mine. While no two of them were identical in appearance, they were all handsome and all apparently of about the same age. I saw no old people and no children.

Presently we approached a tree of such enormous diameter that I could scarcely believe the testimony of my eyes when I saw it. It was fully five hundred feet in diameter. Stripped of branches for a hundred feet above and below the causeway, its surface was dotted with windows and doors and encircled by wide balconies or verandas. Before a large and elaborately carved doorway was a group of armed men before whom we halted while Duran addressed one of their number.

I thought at the time that he called this man Tofar, and such I learned later was his name. He wore a necklace from which depended a metal disc bearing a hieroglyphic in relief; otherwise he was not accoutered differently from his companions. As he and Duran conversed, he appraised me carefully from head to feet. Presently he and Duran passed through the doorway into the interior of the tree, while the others continued to examine me and question Kamlot and Olthar.

While I waited there, I embraced the opportunity to study the elaborate carvings that surrounded the portal, forming a frame fully five feet wide. The motif appeared historical, and I could easily imagine that the various scenes depicted important events in the life of a dynasty or a nation. The workmanship was exquisite, and it required no stretch of the imagination to believe that each delicately carved face was the portrait of some dead or living celebrity. There was nothing grotesque in the delineation of the various figures, as is so often the case in work of a similar character on Earth, and only the borders that framed the whole and separated contiguous plaques were conventional.

I was still engrossed by these beautiful examples of the wood carver's art when Duran and Tofar returned and motioned Olthar and Kamlot and me to follow them into the interior of the great tree. We passed through several large chambers and along wide corridors, all carved from the wood of the living tree, to the head of a splendid stairway, which we descended to another level. The chambers near the periphery of the tree received their light through windows, while the interior chambers and corridors were illuminated by lamps similar to those I had already seen in the house of Duran.

Near the foot of the stairway we had descended we entered a spacious chamber, before the doorway to which stood two men armed with spears and swords, and before us, across the chamber, we saw a man seated at a table near a large window. Just inside the doorway we halted, my companions standing in respectful silence until the man at the table looked up and spoke to them; then they crossed the room, taking me with them, and halted before the table, upon the opposite side of which the man sat facing us.

He spoke pleasantly to my companions, calling each by name, and when they replied they addressed him as Jong. He was a fine-looking man with a strong face and a commanding presence. His attire was similar to that worn by all the other male Venusians I had seen, differing only in that he wore about his head a fillet that supported a circular metal disc in the center of his forehead. He appeared much interested in me and watched me intently while listening to Duran, who, I had no doubt, was narrating the story of my strange and sudden appearance the night before.

When Duran had concluded, the man called Jong addressed me. His manner was serious, his tones kindly. Out of courtesy, I replied, though I knew that he could understand me no better than I had understood him. He smiled and shook his head; then he fell into a discussion with the others. Finally he struck a metal gong that stood near him on the table; then he arose and came around the table to where I stood. He examined my clothing carefully, feeling its texture and apparently discussing the materials and the weave with the others. Then he examined the skin of my hands and face, felt of my hair, and made me open my mouth that he might examine my teeth. I was reminded of the horse market and the slave block. "Perhaps," I thought, "the latter is more apropos."

A man entered now whom I took to be a servant and, receiving instructions from the man called Jong, departed again, while I continued to be the object of minute investigation. My beard, which was now some twenty-four hours old, elicited considerable comment. It is not a beautiful beard at any age, being sparse and reddish, for which reason I am careful to shave daily when I have the necessary utensils.

I cannot say that I enjoyed this intimate appraisal, but the manner in which it was conducted was so entirely free from any suggestion of intentional rudeness or discourtesy, and my position here was so delicate that my better judgment prevented me from openly resenting the familiarities of the man called Jong. It is well that I did not.

Presently a man entered through a doorway at my right. I assumed that he had been summoned by the servant recently dispatched. As he came forward, I saw that he was much like the others; a handsome man of about thirty. There are those who declaim against monotony; but for me there can never be any monotony of beauty, not even if the beautiful things were all identical, which the Venusians I had so far seen were not. All were beautiful, but each in his own way.

The man called Jong spoke to the newcomer rapidly for about five minutes, evidently narrating all that they knew about me and giving instructions. When he had finished, the other motioned me to follow him; and a few moments later I found myself in another room on the same level. It had three large windows and was furnished with several desks, tables, and chairs. Most of the available wall space was taken up by shelves on which reposed what I could only assume to be books—thousands of them.

The ensuing three weeks were as delightful and interesting as any that I have ever experienced. During this time, Danus, in whose charge I had been placed, taught me the Venusian language and told me much concerning the planet, the people among whom I had fallen, and their history. I found the language easy to master, but I shall not at this time attempt to describe it fully. The alphabet consists of twenty-four characters, five of which represent vowel sounds, and these are the only vowel sounds that the Venusian vocal cords seem able to articulate. The characters of the alphabet all have the same value, there being no capital letters. Their system of punctuation differs from ours and is more practical; for example, before you start to read a sentence you know whether it is exclamatory, interrogative, a reply to an interrogation, or a simple statement. Characters having values similar to the comma and semicolon are used much as we use these two; they have no colon; their character that functions as does our period follows each sentence, their question mark and exclamation point preceding the sentences the nature of which they determine.

A peculiarity of their language that renders it easy to master is the absence of irregular verbs; the verb root is never altered for voice, mode, tense, number, or person, distinctions that are achieved by the use of several simple, auxiliary words.

While I was learning to speak the language of my hosts, I also learned to read and write it, and I spent many enjoyable hours delving into the large library of which Danus is the curator while my tutor was absent attending to his other duties, which are numerous. He is chief physician and surgeon of his country, physician and surgeon to the king, and head of a college of medicine and surgery.

One of the first questions that Danus had asked me when I had acquired a working knowledge of his language was where I came from, but when I told him I had come from another world more than twenty-six million miles from his familiar Amtor, which is the name by which the Venusians know their world, he shook his head skeptically.

"There is no life beyond Amtor," he said. "How can there be life where all is fire?"

"What is your theory of the—" I started, but I had to stop. There is no Amtorian word for universe, neither is there any for sun, moon, star, or planet. The gorgeous heavens that we see are never seen by the inhabitants of Venus, obscured as they perpetually are by the two great cloud envelopes that surround the planet. I started over again. "What do you believe surrounds Amtor?" I asked.

He stepped to a shelf and returned with a large volume, which he opened at a beautifully executed map of Amtor. It showed three concentric circles. Between the two inner circles lay a circular belt designated as Trabol, which means warm country. Here the boundaries of seas, continents, and islands were traced to the edges of the two circles that bounded it, in some places crossing these boundaries as though marking the spots at which venturesome explorers had dared the perils of an unknown and inhospitable land.

"This is Trabol," explained Danus, placing a finger upon that portion of the map I have briefly described. "It entirely surrounds Strabol, which lies in the center of Amtor. Strabol is extremely hot, its land is covered with enormous forests and dense undergrowth, and is peopled by huge land animals, reptiles, and birds, its warm seas swarm with monsters of the deep. No man has ventured far into Strabol and lived to return.

"Beyond Trabol," he continued, placing his finger on the outer band designated as Karbol (Cold Country), "lies Karbol. Here it is as cold as Strabol is hot. There are strange animals there too, and adventurers have returned with tales of fierce human beings clothed in fur. But it is an inhospitable land into which there is no occasion to venture and which few dare penetrate far for fear of being precipitated over the rim into the molten sea."

"Over what rim?" I asked.

He looked at me in astonishment. "I can well believe that you come from another world when you ask me such questions as you do," he remarked. "Do you mean to tell me that you know nothing of the physical structure of Amtor?"

"I know nothing of your theory concerning it," I replied.

"It is not a theory; it is a fact," he corrected me gently. "In no other way may the various phenomena of nature be explained. Amtor is a huge disc with an upturned rim, like a great saucer; it floats upon a sea of molten metal and rock, a fact that is incontrovertibly proved by the gushing forth of this liquid mass occasionally from the summits of mountains, when a hole has been burned in the bottom of Amtor. Karbol, the cold country, is a wise provision of nature that tempers the terrific heat that must constantly surge about the outer rim of Amtor.

"Above Amtor, and entirely surrounding her above the molten sea, is a chaos of fire and flame. From this our clouds protect us. Occasionally there have occurred rifts in the clouds, and at such times the heat from the fires above, when the rifts occurred in the daytime, has been so intense as to wither vegetation and destroy life, while the light that shone through was of blinding intensity. When these rifts occurred at night there was no heat, but we saw the sparks from the fire shining above us."

I tried to explain the spherical shape of the planets and that Karbol was only the colder country surrounding one of Amtor's poles, while Strabol, the hot country, lay in the equatorial region; that Trabol was merely one of two temperate zones, the other one being beyond the equatorial region, which was a band around the middle of a globe and not, as he supposed, a circular area in the center of a disc. He listened to me politely, but only smiled and shook his head when I had finished.

At first I could not comprehend that a man of such evident intelligence, education, and culture should cling to such a belief as his, but when I stopped to consider the fact that neither he nor any of his progenitors had ever seen the heavens, I began to realize that there could not be much foundation for any other theory, and even theories must have foundations. I also realized, even more than I had before, something of what astronomy has meant to the human race of Earth in the advancement of science and civilization. Could there have been such advancement had the heavens been perpetually hidden from our view? I wonder.

But I did not give up. I drew his attention to the fact that if his theory were correct, the boundary between Trabol and Strabol (the temperate and the equatorial zones) should be much shorter than that separating Trabol from Karbol, the polar region, as was shown on the map, but could not have been proved by actual survey; while my theory would require that the exact opposite be true, which was easily demonstrable and must have been demonstrated if surveys had ever been made, which I judged from the markings on the map to be the case.

He admitted that surveys had been made and that they had shown the apparent discrepancy that I had pointed out, but he explained this ingeniously by a purely Amtorian theory of the relativity of distance, which he proceeded to elucidate.

"A degree is one thousandth part of the circumference of a circle," he commenced. (This is the Amtorian degree, her savants not having had the advantage of a visible sun to suggest another division of the circumference of a circle as did the Babylonians, who hit upon three hundred sixty as being close enough.) "And no matter what the length of the circumference, it measures just one thousand degrees. The circle which separates Strabol from Trabol is necessarily one thousand degrees in length. You will admit that?"

"Certainly," I replied.

"Very good! Then, will you admit that the circle which separates Trabol from Karbol measures exactly one thousand degrees?"

I nodded my assent.

"Things which equal the same thing equal each other, do they not? Therefore, the inner and outer boundaries of Trabol are of equal length, and this is true because of the truth of the theory of relativity of distance. The degree is our unit of linear measure. It would be ridiculous to say that the farther one was removed from the center of Amtor the longer the unit of distance became; it only appears to become longer; in relation to the circumference of the circle and in relation to the distance from the center of Amtor it is precisely the same.

"I know," he admitted, "that on the map it does not appear to be the same, nor do actual surveys indicate that it is the same; but it must be the same, for if it were not, it is obvious that Amtor would be larger around the closer one approached the center and smallest of all at the perimeter, which is so obviously ridiculous as to require no refutation.

"This seeming discrepancy caused the ancients considerable perturbation until about three thousand years ago, when Klufar, the great scientist, expounded the theory of relativity of distance and demonstrated that the real and apparent measurements of distance could be reconciled by multiplying each by the square root of minus one."

I saw that argument was useless and said no more; there is no use arguing with a man who can multiply anything by the square root of minus one.

CHAPTER FIVE
THE GIRL IN THE GARDEN

FOR SOME TIME I HAD BEEN AWARE that I was in the house of Mintep, the king, and that the country was called Vepaja. Jong, which I had originally thought to be his name, was his title; it is Amtorian for king. I learned that Duran was of the house of Zar and that Olthar and Kamlot were his sons; Zuro, one of the women I had met there, was attached to Duran; the other, Alzo, was attached to Olthar; Kamlot had no woman. I use the word attached partially because it is a reasonably close translation of the Amtorian word for the connection and partially because no other word seems exactly to explain the relationship between these men and women.

They were not married, because the institution of marriage is unknown here. One could not say that they belonged to the men, because they were in no sense slaves or servants, nor had they been acquired by purchase or feat of arms. They had come willingly, following a courtship, and they were free to depart whenever they chose, just as the men were free to depart and seek other connections; but, as I was to learn later, these connections are seldom broken, while infidelity is as rare here as it is prevalent on Earth.

Each day I took exercise on the broad veranda that encircled the tree at the level upon which my apartment was located; at least, I assumed that it encircled the tree, but I did not know, as that portion assigned to me was but a hundred feet long, a fifteenth part of the circumference of the great tree. At each end of my little segment was a fence. The section adjoining mine on the right appeared to be a garden, as it was a mass of flowers and shrubbery growing in soil that must have been brought up from that distant surface of the planet that I had as yet neither set foot upon nor seen. The section on my left extended in front of the quarters of several young officers attached to the household of the king. I call them young because Danus told me they were young, but they appear to be about the same age as all the other Amtorians I have seen. They were pleasant fellows, and after I learned to speak their language we occasionally had friendly chats together.

But in the section at my right I had never seen a human being; and then one day, when Danus was absent and I was walking alone, I saw a girl among the flowers there. She did not see me; and I only caught the briefest glimpse of her, but there was something about her that made me want to see her again, and thereafter I rather neglected the young officers on my left.

Though I haunted the end of my veranda next the garden for several days, I did not again see the girl during all that time. The place seemed utterly deserted until one day I saw the figure of a man among the shrubbery. He was moving with great caution, creeping stealthily; and presently, behind him, I saw another and another, until I had counted five of them all together.

They were similar to the Vepajans, yet there was a difference. They appeared coarser, more brutal, than any of the men I had as yet seen; and in other ways they were dissimilar to Danus, Duran, Kamlot, and my other Venusian acquaintances. There was something menacing and sinister, too, in their silent, stealthy movements.

I wondered what they were doing there; and then I thought of the girl, and for some reason the conclusion was forced upon me that the presence of these men here had something to do with her, and that it boded her harm. Just in what way I could not even surmise, knowing so little of the people among whom fate had thrown me; but the impression was quite definite, and it excited me. Perhaps it rather overcame my better judgment, too, if my next act is any index to the matter.

Without thought of the consequences and in total ignorance of the identity of the men or the purpose for which they were in the garden, I vaulted the low fence and followed them. I made no noise. They had not seen me originally because I had been hidden from their view by a larger shrub that grew close to the fence that separated the garden from my veranda. It was through the foliage of this shrub that I had observed them, myself unobserved.

Moving cautiously but swiftly, I soon overtook the hindmost man and saw that the five were moving toward an open doorway beyond which, in a richly furnished apartment, I saw the girl who had aroused my curiosity and whose beautiful face had led me into this mad adventure. Almost simultaneously, the girl glanced up and saw the leading man at the doorway. She screamed, and then I knew that I had not come in vain.

Instantly I leaped upon the man in front of me, and as I did so I gave a great shout, hoping by that means to distract the attention of the other four from the girl to me, and in that I was wholly successful. The other four turned instantly. I had taken my man so completely by surprise that I was able to snatch his sword from its scabbard before he could recover his wits; and as he drew his dagger and struck at me, I ran his own blade through his heart; then the others were upon me.

Their faces were contorted by rage, and I could see that they would give me no quarter.

The narrow spaces between the shrubbery reduced the advantage which four men would ordinarily have had over a single antagonist, for they could attack me only singly; but I knew what the outcome must eventually be if help did not reach me, and as my only goal was to keep the men from the girl, I backed slowly toward the fence and my own veranda as I saw that all four of the men were following me.

My shout and the girl's scream had attracted attention; and presently I heard men running in the apartment in which I had seen the girl, and her voice directing them toward the garden. I hoped they would come before the fellows had backed me against the wall, where I was confident that I must go down in defeat beneath four swords wielded by men more accustomed to them than I. I thanked the good fortune, however, that had led me to take up fencing seriously in Germany, for it was helping me now, though I could not long hold out against these men with the Venusian sword which was a new weapon to me.

I had reached the fence at last and was fighting with my back toward it. The fellow facing me was cutting viciously at me. I could hear the men coming from the apartment. Could I hold out? Then my opponent swung a terrific cut at my head, and, instead of parrying it, I leaped to one side and simultaneously stepped in and cut at him. His own swing had carried him off balance, and, of course, his guard was down. My blade cut deep into his neck, severing his jugular. From behind him another man was rushing upon me.

Relief was coming. The girl was safe. I could accomplish no more by remaining there and being cut to pieces, a fate I had only narrowly averted in the past few seconds. I hurled my sword, point first, at the oncoming Venusian; and as it tore into his breast I turned and vaulted the fence into my own veranda.

Then, as I looked back, I saw a dozen Vepajan warriors overwhelm the two remaining intruders, butchering them like cattle. There was no shouting and no sound other than the brief clash of swords as the two sought desperately but futilely to defend themselves. The Vepajans spoke no word. They seemed shocked and terrified, though their terror had most certainly not been the result of any fear of their late antagonists. There was something else which I did not understand, something mysterious in their manner, their silence, and their actions immediately following the encounter.

Quickly they seized the bodies of the five strange warriors that had been killed and, carrying them to the outer garden wall, hurled them over into that bottomless abyss of the forest the terrific depths of which my eyes had never been able to plumb. Then, in equal silence, they departed from the garden by the same path by which they had entered it.

I realized that they had not seen me, and I knew that the girl had not. I wondered a little how they accounted for the deaths of the three men I had disposed of, but I never learned. The whole affair was a mystery to me and was only explained long after in the light of ensuing events.

I thought that Danus might mention it and thus give me an opportunity to question him; but he never did, and something kept me from broaching the subject to him, modesty perhaps. In other respects, however, my curiosity concerning these people was insatiable; and I fear that I bored Danus to the verge of distraction with my incessant questioning, but I excused myself on the plea that I could only learn the language by speaking it and hearing it spoken; and Danus, that most delightful of men, insisted that it was not only a pleasure to inform me but his duty as well, the jong having requested him to inform me fully concerning the life, customs, and history of the Vepajans.

One of the many things that puzzled me was why such an intelligent and cultured people should be living in trees, apparently without servants or slaves and with no intercourse, as far as I had been able to discover, with other peoples; so one evening I asked him.

"It is a long story," replied Danus; "much of it you will find in the histories here upon my shelves, but I can give you a brief outline that will at least answer your question.

"Hundreds of years ago the kings of Vepaja ruled a great country. It was not this forest island where you now find us, but a broad empire that embraced a thousand islands and extended from Strabol to Karbol; it included broad land masses and great oceans; it was graced by mighty cities and boasted a wealth and commerce unsurpassed through all the centuries before or since.

"The people of Vepaja in those days were numbered in the millions; there were millions of merchants and millions of wage earners and millions of slaves, and there was a smaller class of brain workers. This class included the learned professions of science, medicine, and law, of letters and the creative arts. The military leaders were selected from all classes. Over all was the hereditary jong.

"The lines between the classes were neither definitely nor strictly drawn; a slave might become a free man, a free man might become anything he chose within the limits of his ability, short of jong. In social intercourse the four principal classes did not intermingle with each other, due to the fact that members of one class had little in common with members of the other classes and not through any feeling of superiority or inferiority. When a member of a lower class had won by virtue of culture, learning, or genius to a position in a higher class, he was received upon an equal footing, and no thought was given to his antecedents.

"Vepaja was prosperous and happy, yet there were malcontents.

These were the lazy and incompetent. Many of them were of the criminal class. They were envious of those who had won to positions which they were not mentally equipped to attain. Over a long period of time they were responsible for minor discord and dissension, but the people either paid no attention to them or laughed them down. Then they found a leader. He was a laborer named Thor, a man with a criminal record.

"This man founded a secret order known as Thorists and preached a gospel of class hatred called Thorism. By means of lying propaganda he gained a large following, and as all his energies were directed against a single class, he had all the vast millions of the other three classes to draw from, though naturally he found few converts among the merchants and employers which also included the agrarian class.

"The sole end of the Thorist leaders was personal power and aggrandizement; their aims were wholly selfish, yet, because they worked solely among the ignorant masses, they had little difficulty in deceiving their dupes, who finally rose under their false leaders in a bloody revolution that sounded the doom of the civilization and advancement of a world.

"Their purpose was the absolute destruction of the cultured class. Those of the other classes who opposed them were to be subjugated or destroyed; the jong and his family were to be killed. These things accomplished, the people would enjoy absolute freedom; there would be no masters, no taxes, no laws.

"They succeeded in killing most of us and a large proportion of the merchant class; then the people discovered what the agitators already knew, that someone must rule, and the leaders of Thorism were ready to take over the reins of government. The people had exchanged the beneficent rule of an experienced and cultured class for that of greedy incompetents and theorists.

"Now they are all reduced to virtual slavery. An army of spies watches over them, and an army of warriors keeps them from turning against their masters; they are miserable, helpless, and hopeless.

"Those of us who escaped with our jong sought out this distant, uninhabited island. Here we constructed tree cities, such as this, far above the ground, from which they cannot be seen. We brought our culture with us and little else; but our wants are few, and we are happy. We would not return to the old system if we might. We have learned our lesson, that a people divided amongst themselves cannot be happy. Where there are even slight class distinctions there are envy and jealousy. Here there are none; we are all of the same class. We have no servants; whatever there is to do we do better than servants ever did it. Even those who serve the jong are not servants in the sense that they are menials, for their positions are considered posts of honor, and the greatest among us take turns in filling them."

"But I still do not understand why you choose to live in trees, far above the ground," I said.

"For years the Thorists hunted us down to kill us," he explained, "and we were forced to live in hidden, inaccessible places; this type of city was the solution of our problem. The Thorists still hunt us; and there are still occasional raids, but now they are for a very different purpose. Instead of wishing to kill us, they now wish to capture as many of us as they can.

"Having killed or driven away the brains of the nation, their civilization has deteriorated, disease is making frightful inroads upon them which they are unable to check, old age has reappeared and is taking its toll; so they seek to capture the brains and the skill and the knowledge which they have been unable to produce and which we alone possess."

"Old age is reappearing! What do you mean?" I asked.

"Have you not noticed that there are no signs of old age among us?" he inquired.

"Yes, of course," I replied, "nor any children. I have often meant to ask you for an explanation."

"These are not natural phenomena," he assured me; "they are the crowning achievements of medical science. A thousand years ago the serum of longevity was perfected. It is injected every two years and not only provides immunity from all diseases but insures the complete restoration of all wasted tissue.

"But even in good there is evil. As none grew old and none died, except those who met with violent deaths, we were faced with the grave dangers of overpopulation. To combat this, birth control became obligatory. Children are permitted now only in sufficient numbers to replace actual losses in population. If a member of a house is killed, a woman of that house is permitted to bear a child, if she can; but after generations of childlessness there is a constantly decreasing number of women who are capable of bearing children. This situation we have met by anticipating it.

"Statistics compiled over a period of a thousand years indicate the average death rate expectancy per thousand people; they have also demonstrated that only fifty per cent of our women are capable of bearing children; therefore, fifty per cent of the required children are permitted yearly to those who wish them, in the order in which their applications are filed."

"I have not seen a child since I arrived in Amtor," I told him.

"There are children here," he replied, "but, of course, not many."

"And no old people," I mused. "Could you administer that serum to me, Danus?"

He smiled. "With Mintep's permission, which I imagine will not be difficult to obtain. Come," he added, "I'll take some blood tests now to determine the type and attenuation of serum best adapted to your requirements." He motioned me into his laboratory.

When he had completed the tests, which he accomplished with ease and rapidity, he was shocked by the variety and nature of malignant bacteria they revealed.

"You are a menace to the continued existence of human life on Amtor," he exclaimed with a laugh.

"I am considered a very healthy man in my own world," I assured him.

"How old are you?" he asked.

"Twenty-seven."

"You would not be so healthy two hundred years from now if all those bacteria were permitted to have their way with you."

"How old might I live to be if they were eradicated?" I asked.

He shrugged. "We do not know. The serum was perfected a thousand years ago. There are people among us today who were of the first to receive injections. I am over five hundred years old; Mintep is seven hundred. We believe that, barring accidents, we shall live forever; but, of course, we do not know. Theoretically, we should."

He was called away at this juncture; and I went out on the veranda to take my exercise, of which I have found that I require a great deal, having always been athletically inclined. Swimming, boxing, and wrestling had strengthened and developed my muscles since I had returned to America with my mother when I was eleven, and I became interested in fencing while I was traveling in Europe after she died. During my college days I was amateur middleweight boxer of California, and I captured several medals for distance swimming; so the enforced inactivity of the past two months had galled me considerably. Toward the end of my college days I had grown into the heavyweight class, but that had been due to an increase of healthy bone and sinew; now I was at least twenty pounds heavier and that twenty pounds was all fat.

On my one hundred feet of veranda I did the best I could to reduce. I ran miles, I shadow boxed, I skipped rope, and I spent hours with the old seventeen setting-up exercises of drill regulations. Today I was shadow boxing near the right end of my veranda when I suddenly discovered the girl in the garden observing me. As our eyes met I halted in my tracks and smiled at her. A frightened look came into her eyes, and she turned and fled. I wondered why.

Puzzled, I walked slowly back toward my apartment, my exercises forgotten. This time I had seen the girl's full face, looked her squarely in the eyes, and I had been absolutely dumfounded by her beauty. Every man and woman I had seen since I had come to Venus had been beautiful; I had come to expect that. But I had not expected to see in this or any other world such indescribable perfection of coloring and features, combined with character and intelligence, as that which I had just seen in the garden beyond my little fence. But why had she run away when I smiled?

Possibly she had run away merely because she had been discovered watching me for, after all, human nature is about the same everywhere. Even twenty-six million miles from Earth there are human beings like ourselves and a girl, with quite human curiosity, who runs away when she is discovered. I wondered if she resembled earthly girls in other respects, but she seemed too beautiful to be just like anything on Earth or in heaven. Was she young or old? Suppose she were seven hundred years old!

I went to my apartment and prepared to bathe and change my loincloth; I had long since adopted the apparel of Amtor. As I glanced in a mirror that hangs in my bathroom I suddenly understood why the girl may have looked frightened and run away—my beard! It was nearly a month old now and might easily have frightened anyone who had never before seen a beard.

When Danus returned I asked him what I could do about it. He stepped into another room and returned with a bottle of salve.

"Rub this into the roots of the hair on your face," he directed, "but be careful not to get it on your eyebrows, lashes, or the hair on your head. Leave it there a minute and then wash your face."

I stepped into my bathroom and opened the jar; its contents looked like vaseline and smelled like the devil, but I rubbed it into the roots of my beard as Danus had directed. When I washed my face a moment later my beard came off, leaving my face smooth and hairless. I hurried back to the room where I had left Danus.

"You are quite handsome after all," he remarked. "Do all the people of this fabulous world of which you have told me have hair growing on their faces?"

"Nearly all," I replied, "but in my country the majority of men keep it shaved off."

"I should think the women would be the ones to shave," he commented. "A woman with hair on her face would be quite repulsive to an Amtorian."

"But our women do not have hair on their faces," I assured him.

"And the men do! A fabulous world indeed."

"But if Amtorians do not grow beards, what was the need of this salve that you gave me?" I asked.

"It was perfected as an aid to surgery," he explained. "In treating scalp wounds and in craniectomies it is necessary to remove the hair from about the wound. This unguent serves the purpose better than shaving and also retards the growth of new hair for a longer time."

"But the hair will grow out again?" I asked.

"Yes, if you do not apply the unguent too frequently," he replied.

"How frequently?" I demanded.

"Use it every day for six days and the hair will never again grow on your face. We used to use it on the heads of confirmed criminals. Whenever one saw a bald-headed man or a man wearing a wig he watched his valuables."

"In my country when one sees a bald-headed man," I said, "he watches his girls. And that reminds me; I have seen a beautiful girl in a garden just to the right of us here. Who is she?"

"She is one whom you are not supposed to see," he replied. "Were I you, I should not again mention the fact that you have seen her. Did she see you?"

"She saw me," I replied.

"What did she do?" His tone was serious.

"She appeared frightened and ran."

"Perhaps you had best keep away from that end of the veranda," he suggested.

There was that in his manner which precluded questions, and I did not pursue the subject further. Here was a mystery, the first suggestion of mystery that I had encountered in the life of Vepaja, and naturally it piqued my curiosity. Why should I not look at the girl? I had looked at other women without incurring displeasure. Was it only this particular girl upon whom I must not look, or were there other girls equally sacrosanct? It occurred to me that she might be a priestess of some holy order, but I was forced to discard that theory because of my belief that these people had no religion, at least none that I could discover in my talks with Danus. I had attempted to describe some of our earthly religious beliefs to him, but he simply could not perceive either their purpose or meaning any more than he could visualize the solar system of the universe.

Having once seen the girl, I was anxious to see her again; and now that the thing was proscribed, I was infinitely more desirous than ever to look upon her divine loveliness and to speak with her. I had not promised Danus that I would heed his suggestions, for I was determined to ignore them should the opportunity arise.

I was commencing to tire of the virtual imprisonment that had been my lot ever since my advent upon Amtor, for even a kindly jailer and a benign prison regime are not satisfactory substitutes for freedom. I had asked Danus what my status was and what they planned for me in the future, but he had evaded a more direct answer by saying that I was the guest of Mintep, the jong, and that my future would be a matter of discussion when Mintep granted me an audience.

Suddenly now I felt more than before the restrictions of my situation, and they galled me.

I had committed no crime. I was a peaceful visitor to Vepaja. I had neither the desire nor the power to harm anyone. These considerations decided me. I determined to force the issue.

A few minutes ago I had been contented with my lot, willing to wait the pleasure of my hosts; now I was discontented. What had induced this sudden change? Could it be the mysterious alchemy of personality that had transmuted the lead of lethargy to the gold of ambitious desire? Had the aura of a vision of feminine loveliness thus instantly reversed my outlook upon life?

I turned toward Danus. "You have been very kind to me," I said, "and my days here have been happy, but I am of a race of people who desire freedom above all things. As I have explained to you, I am here through no intentional fault of my own; but I am here, and being here I expect the same treatment that would be accorded you were you to visit my country under similar circumstances."

"And what treatment would that be?" he asked.

"The right to life, liberty, and the pursuit of happiness—freedom," I explained. I did not think it necessary to mention chambers of commerce dinners, Rotary and Kiwanis luncheons, triumphal parades and ticker tape, keys to cities, press representatives and photographers, nor news reel cameramen, the price that he would undoubtedly have had to pay for life, liberty, and the pursuit of happiness.

"But, my dear friend, one would think from your words that you are a prisoner here!" he exclaimed.

"I am, Danus," I replied, "and none knows it better than you."

He shrugged. "I am sorry that you feel that way about it, Carson."

"How much longer is it going to last?" I demanded.

"The jong is the jong," he replied. "He will send for you in his own time; until then, let us continue the friendly relations that have marked our association up to now."

"I hope they will never be changed, Danus," I told him, "but you may tell Mintep, if you will, that I cannot accept his hospitality much longer; if he does not send for me soon, I shall leave on my own accord."

"Do not attempt that, my friend," he warned me.

"And why not?"

"You would not live to take a dozen steps from the apartments that have been assigned you," he assured me seriously.

"Who would stop me?"

"There are warriors posted in the corridors," he explained; "they have their orders from the jong."

"And yet I am not a prisoner!" I exclaimed with a bitter laugh.

"I am sorry that you raised the question," he said, "as otherwise you might never have known."

Here indeed was the iron hand in the velvet glove. I hoped it was not wielded by a wolf in sheep's clothing. My position was not an enviable one. Even had I the means to escape, there was no place that I could go. But I did not want to leave Vepaja—I had seen the girl in the garden.

CHAPTER SIX
GATHERING TAREL

WEEK PASSED, a week during which I permanently discarded my reddish whiskers and received an injection of the longevity serum. The latter event suggested that possibly Mintep would eventually liberate me, for why bestow immortality upon a potential enemy who is one's prisoner; but then I knew that the serum did not confer absolute immortality—Mintep could have me destroyed if he wished, by which thought was suggested the possibility that the serum had been administered for the purpose of lulling me into a sense of security which I did not, in reality, enjoy. I was becoming suspicious.

While Danus was injecting the serum, I asked him if there were many doctors in Vepaja. "Not so many in proportion to the population as there were a thousand years ago," he replied.

"All the people are now trained in the care of their bodies and taught the essentials of health and longevity. Even without the serums we use to maintain resistance to disease constantly in the human body, our people would live to great ages. Sanitation, diet, and exercise can accomplish wonders by themselves.

"But we must have some doctors. Their numbers are limited now to about one to each five thousand citizens, and in addition to administering the serum, the doctors attend those who are injured by the accidents of daily life, in the hunt, and in duels and war.

"Formerly there were many more doctors than could eke out an honest living, but now there are various agencies that restrict their numbers. Not only is there a law restricting these, but the ten years of study required, the long apprenticeship thereafter, and the difficult examinations that must be passed have all tended to reduce the numbers who seek to follow this profession; but another factor probably achieved more than all else to rapidly reduce the great number of doctors that threatened the continuance of human life on Amtor in the past.

"This was a regulation that compelled every physician and surgeon to file a complete history of each of his cases with the chief medical officer of his district. From diagnosis to complete recovery or death, each detail of the handling of each case had to be recorded and placed on record for the public to consult. When a citizen requires the services of a physician or surgeon now, he may easily determine those who have been successful and those who have not. Fortunately, today there are few of the latter. The law has proved a good one."

This was interesting, for I had had experience with physicians and surgeons on Earth. "How many doctors survived the operation of this new law?" I asked.

"About two percent," he replied.

"There must have been a larger proportion of good doctors on Amtor than on Earth," I commented.

Time hung heavily upon my hands. I read a great deal, but an active young man cannot satisfy all his varied life interests with books alone. And then there was the garden at my right. I had been advised to avoid that end of my veranda, but I did not, at least not when Danus was absent. When he was away I haunted that end of the veranda, but it seemed deserted.

And then one day I caught a glimpse of her; she was watching me from behind a flowering shrub.

I was close to the fence that separated my runway from her garden; it was not a high fence, perhaps slightly under five feet. She did not run this time, but stood looking straight at me, possibly thinking that I could not see her because of the intervening foliage. I could not see her plainly enough, that is true; and, God, how I wanted to see her!

What is that inexplicable, subtle attraction that some woman holds for every man? For some men there is only one woman in the world who exercises this influence upon him, or perhaps if there are more, the others do not cross his path; for other men there are several; for some none. For me there was this girl of an alien race, upon an alien planet. Perhaps there were others, but if there were, I had never met them. In all my life before I had never been moved by such an irresistible urge. What I did, I did upon the strength of an impulse as uncontrollable as a law of nature; perhaps it was a law of nature that motivated me. I vaulted the fence.

Before the girl could escape me, I stood before her. There were consternation and horror in her eyes. I thought that she was afraid of me.

"Do not be afraid," I said; "I have not come to harm you, only to speak to you."

She drew herself up proudly. "I am not afraid of you," she said; "I—," she hesitated and then started over. "If you are seen here you will be destroyed. Go back to your quarters at once and never dare such a rash act again."

I thrilled to the thought that the fear that I had seen so clearly reflected in her eyes was for my safety. "How may I see you?" I asked.

"You may never see me," she replied.

"But I have seen you, and I intend seeing you again. I am going to see a lot of you, or die in the attempt."

"Either you do not know what you are doing or you are mad," she said and turned her back on me as she started to walk away.

I seized her arm. "Wait," I begged.

She wheeled on me like a tigress and slapped my face, and then she whipped the dagger from the scabbard at her girdle. "How dare you," she cried, "lay a hand upon me! I should kill you."

"Why don't you?" I asked.

"I loathe you," she said, and it sounded as though she meant it.

"I love you," I replied, and I knew that I spoke the truth.

At that declaration her eyes did indeed reflect horror. She wheeled then so quickly that I could not stop her and was gone. I stood for a moment, debating whether I should follow her or not, and then a modicum of reason intervened to save me from such an asininity. An instant later I had vaulted the fence again. I did not know whether anyone had seen me or not, and I did not care.

When Danus returned a short time later, he told me that Mintep had sent him for me. I wondered if the summons was in any way related to my adventure in the garden at the right, but I did not inquire. If it were, I should know in due time. The attitude of Danus was unchanged, but that no longer reassured me. I was beginning to suspect that the Amtorians were masters of dissimulation.

Two young officers from the quarters adjoining mine accompanied us to the chamber where the jong was to question me. Whether or not they were acting as an escort to prevent my escape I could not tell. They chatted pleasantly with me during the short walk along the corridor and up the staircase to the level above; but then the guards usually chat pleasantly with the condemned man, if he feels like chatting. They accompanied me into the room where the jong sat. This time he was not alone; there were a number of men gathered about him, and among these I recognized Duran, Olthar, and Kamlot. For some reason the assemblage reminded me of a grand jury, and I could not help but wonder if they were going to return a true bill.

I bowed to the jong, who greeted me quite pleasantly enough, and smiled and nodded to the three men in whose home I had spent my first night on Venus. Mintep looked me over in silence for a moment or two; when he had seen me before I had been dressed in my earthly clothes, now I was garbed (or ungarbed) like a Vepajan.

"Your skin is not as light in color as I thought it," he commented.

"Exposure to light on the veranda has darkened it," I replied. I could not say sunlight, because they have no word for sun, of the existence of which they do not dream. However, such was the case, the ultraviolet rays of sunlight having penetrated the cloud envelopes surrounding the planet and tanned my body quite as effectively as would exposure to the direct rays of the sun have done.

"You have been quite happy here, I trust," he said.

"I have been treated with kindness and consideration," I replied, "and have been quite as happy as any prisoner could reasonably be expected to be."

The shadow of a smile touched his lips. "You are candid," he commented.

"Candor is a characteristic of the country from which I come," I replied.

"However, I do not like the word prisoner," he said.

"Neither do I, jong, but I like the truth. I have been a prisoner, and I have been awaiting this opportunity to ask you why I am a prisoner and to demand my freedom."

He raised his eyebrows; then he smiled quite openly. "I think that I am going to like you," he said; "you are honest and you are courageous, or I am no judge of men."

I inclined my head in acknowledgment of the compliment. I had not expected that he would receive my blunt demand in a spirit of such generous understanding; but I was not entirely relieved, for experience had taught me that these people could be very suave while being most uncompromising.

"There are some things that I wish to tell you and some questions that I wish to ask you," he continued. "We are still beset by our enemies, who yet send occasional raiding parties against us, who upon numerous occasions have sought to introduce their spies among us. We have three things that they require if they are not to suffer extinction: scientific knowledge, and the brains and experience to apply it. Therefore they go to any lengths to abduct our men, whom they purpose holding in slavery and forcing to apply the knowledge that they themselves do not have. They also abduct our women in the hope of breeding children of greater mentality than those which are now born to them.

"The story that you told of crossing millions of miles of space from another world is, of course, preposterous and naturally aroused our suspicions. We saw in you another Thorist spy, cleverly disguised. For this reason you have been under the careful and intelligent observation of Danus for many days. He reports that there is no doubt but that you were totally ignorant of the Amtorian language when you came among us, and as this is the only language spoken by any of the known races of the world, we have come to the conclusion that your story may be, in part, true. The fact that your skin, hair, and eyes differ in color from those of any known race is further substantiation of this conclusion. Therefore, we are willing to admit that you are not a Thorist, but the questions remain: who are you, and from whence came you?"

"I have told only the truth," I replied; "I have nothing to add other than to suggest that you carefully consider the fact that the cloud masses surrounding Amtor completely obscure your view and therefore your knowledge of what lies beyond."

He shook his head. "Let us not discuss it; it is useless to attempt to overthrow the accumulated scientific research and knowledge of thousands of years. We are willing to accept you as of another race, perhaps, as was suggested by the clothing you wore upon your arrival, from cold and dreary Karbol. You are free to come and go as you please. If you remain, you must abide by the laws and customs of Vepaja, and you must become self-supporting. What can you do?"

"I doubt that I can compete with Vepajans at their own trades or professions," I admitted, "but I can learn something if I am given time."

"Perhaps we can find someone who will undertake your training," said the jong, "and in the meantime you may remain in my house, assisting Danus."

"We will take him into our house and train him," spoke up Duran, "if he cares to help us collect tarel and hunt."

Tarel is the strong, silky fiber from which their cloth and cordage are made. I imagined that collecting it would be tame and monotonous work, but the idea of hunting appealed to me. In no event, however, could I ignore Duran's well-meant invitation, as I did not wish to offend him, and, furthermore, anything would be acceptable that would provide the means whereby I might become self-supporting. I therefore accepted his offer, and, the audience being concluded, I bid good-bye to Danus, who invited me to visit him often, and withdrew with Duran, Olthar, and Kamlot.

As no mention had been made of the subject, I concluded that no one had witnessed my encounter with the girl in the garden, who was still uppermost in my thoughts and the principal cause of my regret that I was to leave the house of the jong.

Once more I was established in the house of Duran, but this time in a larger and more comfortable room. Kamlot took charge of me. He was the younger of the brothers, a quiet, reserved man with the muscular development of a trained athlete. After he had shown me my room, he took me to another apartment, a miniature armory, in which were many spears, swords, daggers, bows, shields, and almost countless arrows. Before a window was a long bench with racks in which were tools of various descriptions; above the bench were shelves upon which were stacked the raw materials for the manufacture of bows, arrows, and spear shafts. Near the bench were a forge and anvil, and there were sheets and rods and ingots of metal stored nearby.

"Have you ever used a sword?" he asked as he selected one for me.

"Yes, but for exercise only," I replied; "in my country we have perfected weapons that render a sword useless in combat."

He asked me about these weapons and was much interested in my description of earthly firearms. "We have a similar weapon on Amtor," he said. "We of Vepaja do not possess them, because the sole supply of the material with which they are charged lies in the heart of the Thorist country. When the weapons are made they are charged with an element that emits a ray of extremely short wavelength that is destructive of animal tissue, but the element only emits these rays when exposed to the radiation of another rare element. There are several metals that are impervious to these rays. Those shields that you see hanging on the walls, the ones that are metal covered, are ample protection from them. A small shutter of similar metal is used in the weapon to separate the two elements; when this shutter is raised and one element is exposed to the emanations of the other, the destructive R-ray is released and passes along the bore of the weapon toward the target at which the latter has been aimed.

"My people invented and perfected this weapon," he added ruefully, "and now it has been turned against us; but we get along very well with what we have, as long as we remain in our trees.

"In addition to a sword and dagger, you will need a bow, arrows, and a spear," and as he enumerated them he selected the various articles for me, the last of which was really a short, heavy javelin. A swiveled ring was attached to the end of the shaft of this weapon, and attached to the ring was a long, slender cord with a hand loop at its extremity. This cord, which was no heavier than ordinary wrapping twine, Kamlot coiled in a peculiar way and tucked into a small opening in the side of the shaft.

"What is the purpose of that cord?" I asked, examining the weapon.

"We hunt high in the trees," he replied, "and if it were not for the cord we should lose many spears."

"But that cord is not heavy enough for that, is it?" I asked.

"It is of tarel," he replied, "and could support the weight of ten men. You will learn much of the properties and value of tarel before you have been with us long. Tomorrow we shall go out together and gather some. It has been rather scarce of late."

At the evening meal that day I met Zuro and Alzo again, and they were most gracious to me. In the evening they all joined in teaching me the favorite Vepajan game, tork, which is played with pieces that are much like those used in mah jong and bears a startling resemblance to poker.

I slept well that night in my new quarters and when daylight broke I arose, for Kamlot had warned me that we should start early upon our expedition. I cannot say that I looked forward with any considerable degree of enthusiasm to spending the day gathering tarel. The climate of Vepaja is warm and sultry, and I pictured the adventure as being about as monotonous and disagreeable as picking cotton in Imperial Valley.

After a light breakfast, which I helped Kamlot prepare, he told me to get my weapons. "You should always wear your sword and dagger," he added.

"Even in the house?" I asked.

"Always, wherever you are," he replied. "It is not only a custom, but it is the law. We never know when we may be called upon to defend ourselves, our houses, or our jong."

"Those are all that I need bring, I suppose," I remarked as I was leaving the room.

"Bring your spear, of course; we are going to gather tarel," he replied.

Why I should need a spear to gather tarel I could not imagine; but I brought all the weapons that he had mentioned, and when I returned he handed me a bag with a strap that went around my neck to support it at my back.

"Is this for the tarel?" I asked.

He replied that it was.

"You do not expect to gather much," I remarked.

"We may not get any," he replied. "If we get a bagful between us we may do some tall boasting when we return."

I said no more, thinking it best to learn by experience rather than to be continually revealing my lamentable ignorance. If tarel were as scarce as his statement suggested, I should not have much picking to do, and that suited me perfectly. I am not lazy, but I like work that keeps my mind on the alert.

When we were both ready, Kamlot led the way upstairs, a procedure which mystified me, but did not tempt me into asking any more questions. We passed the two upper levels of the house and entered a dark, spiral staircase that led still farther upward into the tree. We ascended this for about fifteen feet, when Kamlot halted and I heard him fumbling with something above me.

Presently the shaft was bathed with light, which I saw came through a small circular opening that had been closed with a stout door. Through this opening Kamlot crawled, and I followed him, to find myself on a limb of the tree. My companion closed and locked the door, using a small key. I now saw that the door was covered on the outside with bark, so that when it was closed it would have been difficult for anyone to have detected it.

With almost monkeylike agility, Kamlot ascended, while I, resembling anything but a monkey in this respect, followed, thankful for the lesser gravitational pull of Venus, however little less than that of Earth it might be, for I am not naturally arboreal.

After ascending about a hundred feet, Kamlot crossed to an adjacent tree, the branches of which interlocked with those of the one we had been ascending, and again the upward climb commenced. Occasionally the

Vepajan stopped to listen as we passed from tree to tree or clambered to higher levels. After we had traveled for an hour or more, he stopped again and waited until I had overtaken him. A finger on his lips enjoined me to silence.

"Tarel," he whispered, pointing through the foliage in the direction of an adjacent tree.

I wondered why he had to whisper it, as my eyes followed the direction of his index finger. Twenty feet away I saw what appeared to be a huge spider web, partially concealed by the intervening foliage.

"Be ready with your spear," whispered Kamlot. "Put your hand through the loop. Follow me, but not too closely; you may need room to cast your spear. Do you see him?"

"No," I admitted. I saw nothing but the suggestion of a spider web; what else I was supposed to see I did not know.

"Neither do I, but he may be hiding. Look up occasionally so that he can't take you by surprise from above."

This was more exciting than picking cotton in Imperial Valley, though as yet I did not know just what there was to be excited about. Kamlot did not appear excited; he was very cool, but he was cautious. Slowly he crept toward the great web, his javelin ready in his hand; and I followed. When we were in full sight of it we saw that it was empty. Kamlot drew his dagger.

"Start cutting it away," he said. "Cut close to the branches and follow the web around; I will cut in the other direction until we meet. Be careful that you do not get enmeshed in it, especially if he happens to return."

"Can't we go around it?" I asked.

Kamlot looked puzzled. "Why should we go around it?" he demanded, a little shortly I thought.

"To get the tarel," I replied.

"What do you suppose this is?" he demanded.

"A spider's web."

"It is tarel."

I subsided. I had thought that the tarel he pointed at was beyond the web, although I had seen nothing; but then of course I had not known what tarel was or what it looked like. We had been cutting away for a few minutes when I heard a noise in a tree near us. Kamlot heard it at the same time.

"He is coming," he said. "Be ready!" He slipped his dagger into its sheath and grasped his spear. I followed his example.

The sound stopped, but I could see nothing through the foliage. Presently there was a rustling among the foliage, and a face appeared some fifteen yards from us. It was a hideous face—the face of a spider tremendously enlarged. When the thing saw that we had discovered it, it emitted the most frightful scream I had ever heard save once before. Then I recognized them—the voice and the face. It had been a creature such as this that had pursued my pursuer the night that I had dropped to the causeway in front of the house of Duran.

"Be ready," cautioned Kamlot; "he will charge."

The words had scarcely crossed the lips of the Vepajan when the hideous creature rushed toward us. Its body and legs were covered with long, black hair, and there was a yellow spot the size of a saucer above each eye. It screamed horribly as it came, as though to paralyze us with terror.

Kamlot's spear hand flew back and forward, and the heavy javelin, rushing to meet the maddened creature, buried itself deeply in the repulsive carcass; but it did not stop the charge. The creature was making straight for Kamlot as I hurled my javelin, which struck it in the side; but even this did not stop it, and to my horror I saw it seize my companion as he fell back upon the great limb upon which he had stood, with the spider on top of him.

The footing was secure enough for Kamlot and the spider, for they were both accustomed to it, but to me it seemed very precarious. Of course the tree limbs were enormous and often the branches were laced together, yet I felt anything but secure. However, I had no time to think of that now. If not already dead, Kamlot was being killed. Drawing my sword, I leaped to the side of the huge arachnid and struck viciously at its head, whereupon it abandoned Kamlot and turned upon me; but it was badly wounded now and moved with difficulty.

As I struck at that hideous face, I was horrified to see that Kamlot lay as though dead. He did not move. But I had only time for that single brief glance. If I were not careful I, too, should soon be dead. The thing confronting me seemed endowed with unsapable vitality. It was oozing sticky blood from several wounds, at least two of which I thought should have been almost instantly lethal; yet still it struggled to reach me with the powerful claws that terminated its forelegs, that it might draw me to those hideous jaws.

The Vepajan blade is a keen, two-edged affair, a little wider and thicker near the point than at the haft, and, while not well balanced to my way of thinking, is a deadly cutting weapon. I found it so in this my first experience with it, for as a great claw reached out to seize me I severed it with a single blow. At this the creature screamed more horribly than ever, and with its last remaining vitality sprang upon me as you have seen spiders spring upon their prey. I cut at it again as I stepped back; and then thrust my point directly into that hideous visage, as the weight of the creature overbore me and I went down beneath it.

As it crashed upon me, my body toppled from the great branch upon which I had been standing, and I felt myself falling. Fortunately, the interlacing, smaller branches gave me some support; I caught at them and checked my fall, bringing up upon a broad, flat limb ten or fifteen feet below. I had clung to my sword, and being unhurt, clambered back as quickly as I could to save Kamlot from further attack, but he needed no protection—the great targo, as the creature is called, was dead.

Dead also was Kamlot; I could find no pulse nor detect any beating of the heart. My own sank within my breast. I had lost a friend, I who had so few here, and I was as utterly lost as one may be. I knew that I could not retrace our steps to the Vepajan city, even though my life depended upon my ability to do so, as it doubtless did. I could descend, but whether I was still over the city or not I did not know; I doubted it.

So this was gathering tarel; this was the occupation that I had feared would bore me with its monotony!

CHAPTER SEVEN
BY KAMLOT'S GRAVE

HAVING SET OUT TO GATHER TAREL, I finished the work that Kamlot and I had nearly completed when the targo attacked us; if I succeeded in finding the city, I should at least bring something to show for our efforts. But what about Kamlot? The idea of leaving the body here was repugnant to me. Even in the brief association I had had with the man I had come to like him and to look upon him as my friend. His people had befriended me; the least that I could do would be to take his body back to them. I realized, of course, that that was going to be something of a job, but it must be done. Fortunately, I am extraordinarily muscular, and then, too, the gravitational pull of Venus favored me more than would that of Earth, giving me an advantage of over twenty pounds in the dead weight I should have to carry and even a little better than that in the amount of my own live weight, for I am heavier than Kamlot.

With less difficulty than I had anticipated I succeeded in getting Kamlot's body onto my back and trussed there with the cord attached to his javelin. I had previously strapped his weapons to him with strands of the tarel that half filled my bag, for, being unfamiliar with all the customs of the country, I did not know precisely what would be expected of me in an emergency of this nature, and preferred to be on the safe side.

The experiences of the next ten or twelve hours are a nightmare that I should like to forget. Contact with the dead and naked body of my companion was sufficiently gruesome, but the sense of utter bewilderment and futility in this strange world was even more depressing. As the hours passed, during which I constantly descended, except for brief rests, the weight of the corpse seemed to increase. In life Kamlot would have weighed about one hundred eighty pounds on Earth, nearly one hundred sixty on Venus, but by the time darkness enveloped the gloomy forest I could have sworn that he weighed a ton.

So fatigued was I that I had to move very slowly, testing each new hand- and foothold before trusting my tired muscles to support the burden they were carrying, for a weak hold or a misstep would have plunged me into eternity. Death was ever at my elbow.

It seemed to me that I descended thousands of feet and yet I had seen no sign of the city. Several times I heard creatures moving through the trees at a distance, and twice I heard the hideous scream of a targo. Should one of these monstrous spiders attack me—well, I tried not to think about that. Instead I tried to occupy my mind with recollections of my earthly friends; I visualized my childhood days in India as I studied under old Chand Kabi, I thought of dear old Jimmy Welsh, and I recalled a bevy of girls I had liked and with some of whom I had almost been serious. These recalled the gorgeous girl in the garden of the jong, and the visions of the others faded into oblivion. Who was she? What strange interdiction had forbidden her to see or to speak with me? She had said that she loathed me, but she had heard me tell her that I loved her. That sounded rather silly now that I gave it thought. How could I love a girl the first instant that I laid eyes upon her, a girl concerning whom I knew absolutely nothing, neither her age nor her name? It was preposterous, yet I knew that it was true. I loved the nameless beauty of the little garden.

Perhaps my preoccupation with these thoughts made me careless; I do not know, but my mind was filled with them when my foot slipped a little after night had fallen. I grasped for support, but the combined weights of myself and the corpse tore my hands loose, and with my dead companion I plunged downward into the darkness. I felt Death's cold breath upon my cheek.

We did not fall far, being brought up suddenly by something soft that gave to our combined weights, then bounced up again, vibrating like a safety net such as we have all seen used by aerial performers. In the faint but all-pervading light of the Amtorian night I could see what I had already guessed—I had fallen into the web of one of Amtor's ferocious spiders!

I tried to crawl to an edge where I might seize hold of a branch and drag myself free, but each move but entangled me the more. The situation was horrible enough, but a moment later it became infinitely worse, as, glancing about me, I saw at the far edge of the web the huge, repulsive body of a targo.

I drew my sword and hacked at the entangling meshes of the web as the fierce arachnid crept slowly toward me. I recall wondering if a fly entangled in a spider's web suffered the hopelessness and the mental anguish that seized me as I realized the futility of my puny efforts to escape this lethal trap and the ferocious monster advancing to devour me. But at least I had some advantages that no fly enjoys. I had my sword and a reasoning brain; I was not so entirely helpless as the poor fly.

The targo crept closer and closer. It uttered no sound. I presume that it was satisfied that I could not escape and saw no reason why it should seek to paralyze me with fright. From a distance of about ten feet it charged, moving with incredible swiftness upon its eight hairy legs. I met it with the point of my sword.

There was no skill in my thrust; it was just pure luck that my point penetrated the creature's tiny brain. When it collapsed lifeless beside me, I could scarcely believe the testimony of my eyes. I was saved!

Instantly I fell to work severing the strands of tarel that enmeshed me, and in four or five minutes I was free and had lowered myself to a branch below. My heart was still pounding rapidly and I was weak from exhaustion. For a quarter of an hour I remained resting; then I continued the seemingly endless descent out of this hideous forest.

What other dangers confronted me I could not guess. I knew that there were other creatures in this gigantic wood; those powerful webs, capable of sustaining the weight of an ox, had not been built for man alone. During the preceding day I had caught occasional glimpses of huge birds, which might themselves, if carnivorous, prove as deadly menaces as the targo; but it was not them that I feared now, but the nocturnal prowlers that haunt every forest by night.

Down and down I descended, feeling that each next moment must witness the final collapse of my endurance. The encounter with the targo had taken terrific toll of my great strength, already sapped by the arduous experiences of the day, yet I could not stop, I dared not. Yet how much longer could I drive exhausted nature on toward the brink of utter collapse?

I had about reached the end of my endurance when my feet struck solid ground. At first I could not believe the truth, but glancing down and about me I saw that I had indeed reached the floor of the forest; after a month on Venus I had at last placed foot upon her surface. I could see little or nothing—just the enormous boles of great trees in whatever direction I looked. Beneath my feet lay a thick matting of fallen leaves, turned white in death.

I cut the cords that bound the corpse of Kamlot to my back and lowered my poor comrade to the ground; then I threw myself down beside him and was asleep almost immediately.

When I awoke, it was daylight again. I looked about me, but could see nothing but the counterpane of whitened leaves spread between the boles of trees of such gargantuan girth that I almost hesitate to suggest the size of some of them, lest I discredit the veracity of this entire story of my experiences on Venus. But indeed they must needs be huge to support their extraordinary height, for many of them towered over six thousand feet above the surface of the ground, their lofty pinnacles enshrouded forever in the eternal fog of the inner cloud envelope.

To suggest an idea of the size of some of these monsters of the forest,

I may say that I walked around the bole of one, counting over a thousand paces in the circuit, which gives, roughly, a diameter of a thousand feet, and there were many such. A tree ten feet in diameter appeared a frail and slender sapling—and there can be no vegetation upon Venus!

What little knowledge of physics I had and a very slight acquaintance with botany argued that trees of such height could not exist, but there must be some special, adaptive forces operating on Venus that permit the seemingly impossible. I have attempted to figure it out in terms of earthly conditions, and I have arrived at some conclusions that suggest possible explanations for the phenomenon. If vertical osmosis is affected by gravity, then the lesser gravity of Venus would favor the growth of taller trees, and the fact that their tops are forever in the clouds would permit them to build up an ample supply of carbohydrates from the abundant water vapor, provided there was the requisite amount of carbon dioxide in the atmosphere of Venus to promote this photosynthetic process.

I must admit, however, that at the time I was not greatly interested in these intriguing speculations; I had to think about myself and poor Kamlot. What was I to do with the corpse of my friend? I had done my best to return him to his people, and failed. I doubted now that I could ever find his people. There remained but a single alternative; I must bury him.

This decided, I started to scrape away the leaves beside him, that I might reach the ground beneath and dig a grave. There were about a foot of leaves and leaf mold and below that a soft, rich soil which I loosened easily with the point of my spear and scooped out with my hands. It did not take me long to excavate a nice grave; it was six feet long, two feet wide, and three feet deep. I gathered some freshly fallen leaves and carpeted its bottom with them, and then I gathered some more to place around and over Kamlot after I had lowered him to his final resting place.

While I worked I tried to recall the service for the dead; I wanted Kamlot to have as decent and orderly a burial as I could contrive.

I wondered what God would think about it, but I had no doubt but that he would receive this first Amtorian soul to be launched into the unknown with a Christian burial and welcome him with open arms.

As I stooped and put my arms about the corpse to lower it into the grave, I was astounded to discover that it was quite warm. This put an entirely new aspect on the matter. A man dead for eighteen hours should be cold. Could it be that Kamlot was not dead? I pressed an ear to his chest; faintly I heard the beating of his heart. Never before had I experienced such an access of relief and joy. I felt as one reborn to new youth, to new hopes, to new aspirations. I had not realized until that instant the depth of my loneliness.

But why was Kamlot not dead? and how was I to resuscitate him? I felt that I should understand the former before I attempted the latter. I examined the wound again. There were two deep gashes on his chest just below the presternum. They had bled but little, and they were discolored, as I now noticed, by a greenish tint. It was this, meaningless though it may be, that suggested an explanation of Kamlot's condition.

Something about that greenish tint suggested poison to my mind, and at once I recalled that there were varieties of spiders that paralyzed their victims by injecting a poison into them that preserved them in a state of suspended animation until they were ready to devour them. The targo had paralyzed Kamlot!

My first thought was to stimulate circulation and respiration, and to this end I alternately massaged his body and applied the first aid measures adapted to the resuscitation of the drowned. Which of these accomplished the result I do not know (perhaps each helped a little), but at any rate I was rewarded after a long period of effort with evidences of returning animation. Kamlot sighed and his eyelids fluttered. After another considerable period, during which I nearly exhausted myself, he opened his eyes and looked at me.

At first his gaze was expressionless and I thought that perhaps his mind had been affected by the poison; then a puzzled, questioning look entered his eyes and eventually recognition. I was witnessing a resurrection.

"What happened?" he asked in a whisper, and then, "Oh, yes, I recall; the targo got me." He sat up, with my assistance, and looked around. "Where are we?" he demanded.

"On the ground," I replied, "but where on the ground I do not know."

"You saved me from the targo," he said. "Did you kill it? But you must have, or you never could have gotten me away from it. Tell me about it."

Briefly, I told him. "I tried to get you back to the city, but I became lost and missed it. I have no idea where it lies."

"What is this?" he asked, glancing at the excavation beside him.

"Your grave," I replied. "I thought that you were dead."

"And you carried a corpse half a day and half a night! But why?"

"I do not know all the customs of your people," I replied; "but your family has been kind to me, and the least that I could do was to bring your body back to them, nor could I leave a friend up there to be devoured by birds and beasts."

"I shall not forget," he said quietly. He tried to rise then, but I had to assist him. "I shall be all right presently," he assured me, "after I have exercised a little. The effects of the targo's poison wear off in about twenty-four hours even without treatment. What you have done for me has helped to dissipate them sooner, and a little exercise will quickly eradicate the last vestiges of them." He stood looking about as though in an effort to orient himself, and as he did so his eyes fell upon his weapons, which I had intended burying with him and which lay on the ground beside the grave. "You even brought these!" he exclaimed. "You are a jong among friends!"

After he had buckled his sword belt about his hips, he picked up his spear, and together we walked through the forest, searching for some sign that would indicate that we had reached a point beneath the city, Kamlot having explained that trees along the important trails leading to the location of the city were marked in an inconspicuous and secret manner, as were certain trees leading upward to the hanging city.

"We come to the surface of Amtor but seldom," he said, "though occasionally trading parties descend and go to the coast to meet vessels from the few nations with which we carry on a surreptitious commerce. The curse of Thorism has spread far, however, and there are few nations of which we have knowledge that are not subject to its cruel and selfish domination. Once in a while we descend to hunt the basto for its hide and flesh."

"What is a basto?" I inquired.

"It is a large, omnivorous animal with powerful jaws armed with four great fangs in addition to its other teeth. On its head grow two heavy horns. At the shoulder it is as tall as a tall man. I have killed them that weighed thirty-six hundred tob."

A tob is the Amtorian unit of weight, and is the equivalent of one third of an English pound; all weights are computed in tobs or decimals thereof, as they use the decimal system exclusively in their tables of weights and measures. It seems to me much more practical than the confusing earthly collection of grains, grams, ounces, pounds, tons, and the other designations in common use among the various nations of our planet.

From Kamlot's description I visualized the basto as an enormous boar with horns, or a buffalo with the jaws and teeth of a carnivore, and judged that its twelve hundred pounds of weight would render it a most formidable beast. I asked him with what weapons they hunted the animal.

"Some prefer arrows, others spears," he explained, "and it is always handy to have a low branched tree nearby," he added with a grin.

"They are bellicose?" I asked.

"Very. When a basto appears upon the scene, man is as often the hunted as the hunter, but we are not hunting bastos now. What I should most like to find is a sign that would tell me where we are."

We moved on through the forest, searching for the tiny road signs of the Vepajans, which Kamlot had described to me as well as explaining the location in which they are always placed. The sign consists of a long, sharp nail with a flat head bearing a number in relief. These nails are driven into trees at a uniform height from the ground. They are difficult to find, but it is necessary to have them so, lest the enemies of the Vepajans find and remove them, or utilize them in their search for the cities of the latter.

The method of the application of these signs to the requirements of the Vepajans is clever. They would really be of little value to any but a Vepajan as guideposts, yet each nail tells a remarkable story to the initiated; briefly it tells him precisely where he is on the island that comprises the kingdom of Mintep, the jong. Each nail is placed in position by a surveying party and its exact location is indicated on a map of the island, together with the number on the head of the nail. Before a Vepajan is permitted to descend to the ground alone, or to lead others there, he must memorize the location of every sign nail in Vepaja. Kamlot had done so. He told me that if we could find but a single nail he would immediately know the direction of and distance to those on either side of it, our exact position upon the island, and the location of the city; but he admitted that we might wander a long time before we discovered a single nail.

The forest was monotonously changeless. There were trees of several species, some with branches that trailed the ground, others bare of branches for hundreds of feet from their bases. There were boles as smooth as glass and as straight as a ship's mast, without a single branch as far up as the eye could see. Kamlot told me that the foliage of these grew in a single enormous tuft far up among the clouds.

I asked him if he had ever been up there, and he said he had climbed, he believed, to the top of the tallest tree, but that he had nearly frozen to death in the attempt. "We get our water supply from these trees," he remarked. "They drink in the water vapor among the clouds and carry it down to their roots. They are unlike any other tree. A central, porous core carries the water from the clouds to the roots, from whence it rises again in the form of sap that carries the tree's food upward from the ground. By tapping one of these trees anywhere you may obtain a copious supply of clear, cool water—a fortunate provision of—"

"Something is coming, Kamlot," I interrupted. "Do you hear it?"

He listened intently for a moment. "Yes," he replied. "We had better take to a tree, at least until we see what it is."

As he climbed into the branches of a nearby tree, I followed him; and there we waited. Distinctly I could hear something moving through the forest as it approached us. The soft carpet of leaves beneath its feet gave forth but little sound—just a rustling of the dry leaves. Nearer and nearer it came, apparently moving leisurely; then, suddenly, its great head came into view from behind the bole of a tree a short distance from us.

"A basto," whispered Kamlot, but from his previous description of the beast I had already guessed its identity.

It looked like a basto, only more so. From the eyes up its head resembled that of an American bison, with the same short, powerful horns. Its poll and forehead were covered with thick, curly hair, its eyes were small and red-rimmed. Its hide was blue and of about the same texture as that of an elephant, with sparsely growing hairs except upon the head and at the tip of the tail. It stood highest at the shoulders and sloped rapidly to its rump. Its front legs were short and stocky and ended in broad, three-toed feet; its hind legs were longer and the hind feet smaller, a difference necessitated by the fact that the forelegs and feet carried fully three-quarters of the beast's weight. Its muzzle was similar to that of a boar, except that it was broader, and carried heavy, curved tusks.

"Here comes our next meal," remarked Kamlot in an ordinary tone of voice. The basto stopped and looked about as he heard my companion's voice. "They are mighty good eating," added Kamlot, "and we have not eaten for a long while. There is nothing like a basto steak grilled over a wood fire."

My mouth commenced to water. "Come on," I said, and started to climb down from the tree, my spear ready in my hand.

"Come back!" called Kamlot. "You don't know what you are doing."

The basto had located us and was advancing, uttering a sound that would have put to shame the best efforts of a full-grown lion. I do not know whether to describe it as a bellow or a roar. It started with a series of grunts and then rose in volume until it shook the ground.

"He seems to be angry," I remarked; "but if we are going to eat him we must kill him first, and how are we to kill him if we remain in the tree?"

"I am not going to remain in the tree," replied Kamlot, "but you are. You know nothing about hunting these beasts, and you would probably not only get yourself killed but me into the bargain. You stay where you are. I will attend to the basto."

This plan did not suit me at all, but I was forced to admit Kamlot's superior knowledge of things Amtorian and his greater experience and defer to his wishes; but nevertheless I held myself ready to go to his assistance should occasion require.

To my surprise, he dropped his spear to the ground and carried in its stead a slender leafy branch which he cut from the tree before descending to engage the bellowing basto. He did not come down to the floor of the forest directly in front of the beast, but made his way part way around the tree before descending, after asking me to keep the basto's attention diverted, which I did by shouting and shaking a branch of the tree.

Presently, to my horror, I saw Kamlot out in the open a dozen paces in rear of the animal, armed only with his sword and the leafy branch which he carried in his left hand. His spear lay on the ground not far from the enraged beast and his position appeared utterly hopeless should the basto discover him before he could reach the safety of another tree. Realizing this, I redoubled my efforts to engage the creature's attention, until Kamlot shouted to me to desist.

I thought that he must have gone crazy and should not have heeded him had not his voice attracted the attention of the basto and frustrated any attempt that I might have made to keep the beast's eyes upon me. The instant that Kamlot called to me the great head turned ponderously in his direction and the savage eyes discovered him. The creature wheeled and stood for a moment eyeing the rash but puny man-thing; then it trotted toward him.

I waited no longer but dropped to the ground with the intention of attacking the thing from the rear. What happened thereafter happened so quickly that it was over almost in the time it takes to tell it. As I started in pursuit, I saw the mighty basto lower its head and charge straight for my companion, who stood there motionless with his puny sword and the leafy branch grasped one in either hand. Suddenly, at the very instant that I thought the creature was about to impale him on those mighty horns, he waved the leaf covered branch in its face and leaped lightly to one side, simultaneously driving the keen point of his blade downward from a point in front of the left shoulder until the steel was buried to the hilt in the great carcass.

The basto stopped, its four legs spread wide; for an instant it swayed, and then it crashed to the ground at the feet of Kamlot. A shout of admiration was on my lips when I chanced to glance upward. What attracted my attention I do not know, perhaps the warning of that inaudible voice which we sometimes call a sixth sense. What I saw drove the basto and the feat of Kamlot from my thoughts.

"My God!" I cried in English, and then in Amtorian, "Look, Kamlot! What are those?"

CHAPTER EIGHT
ON BOARD THE *SOFAL*

HOVERING JUST ABOVE US, I saw what at first appeared to be five enormous birds; but which I soon recognized, despite my incredulity, as winged men. They were armed with swords and daggers, and each carried a long rope at the end of which dangled a wire noose.

"Voo klangan!" shouted Kamlot. (The birdmen!)

Even as he spoke a couple of wire nooses settled around each of us. We struggled to free ourselves, striking at the snares with our swords, but our blades made no impression upon the wires, and the ropes to which they were attached were beyond our reach. As we battled futilely to disengage ourselves, the klangan settled to the ground, each pair upon opposite sides of the victim they had snared. Thus they held us so that we were helpless, as two cowboys hold a roped steer, while the fifth angan approached us with drawn sword and disarmed us. (Perhaps I should explain that angan is singular, klangan plural, plurals of Amtorian words being formed by prefixing *kloo* to words commencing with a consonant and *kl* to those commencing with a vowel.)

Our capture had been accomplished so quickly and so deftly that it was over, with little or no effort on the part of the birdmen, before I had had time to recover from the astonishment that their weird appearance induced. I now recalled having heard Danus speak of *voo klangan* upon one or two occasions, but I had thought that he referred to poultry breeders or something of that sort. How little could I have dreamed of the reality!

"I guess we are in for it," remarked Kamlot gloomily.

"What will they do with us?" I inquired.

"Ask them," he replied.

"Who are you?" demanded one of our captors.

For some reason I was astonished to hear him speak, although I do not know why anything should have astonished me now. "I am a stranger from another world," I told him. "My friend and I have no quarrel with you. Let us go."

"You are wasting your breath," Kamlot advised me.

"Yes, he is wasting his breath," agreed the angan. "You are Vepajans, and we have orders to bring Vepajans to the ship. You do not look like a Vepajan," he added, surveying me from head to feet, "but the other does."

"Anyway, you are not a Thorist, and therefore you must be an enemy," interjected another.

They removed the nooses from about us and tied ropes around our necks and other ropes about our bodies beneath our arms; then two klangan seized the ropes attached to Kamlot and two more those attached to me, and, spreading their wings, rose into the air, carrying us with them. Our weight was supported by the ropes beneath our arms, but the other ropes were a constant suggestion to us of what might happen if we did not behave ourselves.

As they flew, winding their way among the trees, our bodies were suspended but a few feet above the ground, for the forest lanes were often low ceiled by overhanging branches. The klangan talked a great deal among themselves, shouting to one another and laughing and singing, seemingly well satisfied with themselves and their exploit. Their voices were soft and mellow, and their songs were vaguely reminiscent of religious spirituals.

As Kamlot was carried in front of me, I had an opportunity to observe the physical characteristics of these strange creatures into whose hands we had fallen. They had low, receding foreheads, huge, beaklike noses, and undershot jaws; their eyes were small and close set, their ears flat and slightly pointed. Their chests were large and shaped like those of birds, and their arms were very long, ending in long-fingered, heavy-nailed hands. The lower part of the torso was small, the hips narrow, the legs very short and stocky, ending in three-toed feet equipped with long, curved talons. Feathers grew upon their heads instead of hair. When they were excited, as when they attacked us, these feathers stand erect, but ordinarily they lie flat. They are all alike; commencing near the root they are marked with a band of white, next comes a band of black, then another of white, and the tip is red. Similar feathers also grow at the lower extremity of the torso in front, and there is another, quite large bunch just above the buttocks—a gorgeous tail which they open into a huge pompon when they wish to show off.

Their wings, which consist of a very thin membrane supported on a light framework, are similar in shape to those of a bat and do not appear adequate to the support of the apparent weight of the creatures' bodies, but I was to learn later that this apparent weight is deceptive, since their bones, like the bones of true birds, are hollow.

The creatures carried us a considerable distance, though how far I do not know. We were in the air fully eight hours; and, where the forest permitted, they flew quite rapidly. They seemed utterly tireless, though Kamlot and I were all but exhausted long before they reached their destination. The ropes beneath our arms cut into our flesh, and this contributed to our exhaustion as did our efforts to relieve the agony by seizing the ropes above us and supporting the weight of our bodies with our hands.

But, as all things must, this hideous journey ended at last. Suddenly we broke from the forest and winged out across a magnificent landlocked harbor, and for the first time I looked upon the waters of a Venusian sea. Between two points that formed the harbor's entrance I could see it stretching away as far as the eye could reach—mysterious, intriguing, provocative. What strange lands and stranger people lay off there beyond the beyond? Would I ever know?

Suddenly now my attention and my thoughts were attracted to something in the left foreground that I had not before noticed; a ship lay at anchor on the quiet waters of the harbor and just beyond it a second ship. Toward one of them our captors were winging. As we approached the nearer and smaller, I saw a craft that differed but little in the lines of its hull from earthly ships. It had a very high bow, its prow was sharp and sloped forward in a scimitarlike curve; the ship was long and narrow of beam. It looked as though it might have been built for speed. But what was its motive power? It had no masts, sails, stacks, nor funnels. Aft were two oval houses—a smaller one resting upon the top of a larger; on top of the upper house was an oval tower surmounted by a small crow's nest. There were doors and windows in the two houses and the tower. As we came closer, I could see a number of open hatches in the deck and people standing on the walkways that surrounded the tower and the upper house and also upon the main deck. They were watching our approach.

As our captors deposited us upon the deck, we were immediately surrounded by a horde of jabbering men. A man whom I took to be an officer ordered the ropes removed from us, and while this was being done he questioned the klangan who had brought us.

All the men that I saw were similar in color and physique to the Vepajans, but their countenances were heavy and unintelligent; very few of them were good-looking, and only one or two might have been called handsome. I saw evidences of age among them and of disease—the first I had seen on Amtor.

After the ropes had been removed, the officer ordered us to follow him, after detailing four villainous-looking fellows to guard us, and conducted us aft and up to the tower that surmounted the smaller house. Here he left us outside the tower, which he entered.

The four men guarding us eyed us with surly disfavor. "Vepajans, eh!" sneered one. "Think you're better than ordinary men, don't you? But you'll find out you ain't, not in The Free Land of Thora; there everybody's equal. I don't see no good in bringing your kind into the country anyway. If I had my way you'd get a dose of this," and he tapped a weapon that hung in a holster at his belt.

The weapon, or the grip of it, suggested a pistol of some kind, and I supposed that it was one of those curious firearms discharging deadly rays, that Kamlot had described to me. I was about to ask the fellow to let me see it when the officer emerged from the tower and ordered the guard to bring us in.

We were escorted into a room in which sat a scowling man with a most unprepossessing countenance. There was a sneer on his face as he appraised us, the sneer of the inferior man for his superior, that tries to hide but only reveals the inferiority complex that prompts it. I knew that I was not going to like him.

"Two more klooganfal!" he exclaimed. (A ganfal is a criminal.) "Two more of the beasts that tried to grind down the workers; but you didn't succeed, did you? Now we are the masters. You'll find that out even before we reach Thora. Is either of you a doctor?"

Kamlot shook his head. "Not I," he said. The fellow, whom I took to be the captain of the ship, eyed me closely. "You are no Vepajan," he said. "What are you, anyway? No one ever saw a man with yellow hair and blue eyes before."

"As far as you are concerned," I replied, "I am a Vepajan. I have never been in any other country in Amtor."

"What do you mean by saying as far as I am concerned?" he demanded.

"Because it doesn't make any difference what you think about it," I snapped. I did not like the fellow, and when I do not like people I have difficulty in hiding the fact. In this case I did not try to hide it.

He flushed and half rose from his chair. "It doesn't, eh?" he cried.

"Sit down," I advised him. "You're here under orders to bring back Vepajans. Nobody cares what you think about them, but you'll get into trouble if you don't bring them back." Diplomacy would have curbed my tongue, but I am not particularly diplomatic, especially when I am angry, and now I was both angry and disgusted, for there had been something in the attitude of all these people toward us that bespoke ignorant prejudice and bitterness. Furthermore, I surmised from scraps of information I had picked up from Danus, as well as from the remarks of the sailor who had announced that he would like to kill us, that I was not far wrong in my assumption that the officer I had thus addressed would be exceeding his authority if he harmed us. However, I realized that I was taking chances, and awaited with interest the effect of my words.

The fellow took them like a whipped cur and subsided after a single weakly blustering, "We'll see about that." He turned to a book that lay open before him. "What is your name?" he asked, nodding in Kamlot's direction. Even his nod was obnoxious.

"Kamlot of Zar," replied my companion.

"What is your profession?"

"Hunter and wood carver."

"You are a Vepajan?"

"Yes."

"From what city of Vepaja?"

"From Kooaad," replied Kamlot.

"And you?" demanded the officer, addressing me.

"I am Carson of Napier," I replied, using the Amtorian form; "I am a Vepajan from Kooaad."

"What is your profession?"

"I am an *aviator*," I replied, using the English word and English pronunciation.

"A what?" he demanded. "I never heard of such a thing." He tried to write the word in his book and then he tried to pronounce it, but he could do neither, as the Amtorians have no equivalents for many of our vowel sounds and seem unable even to pronounce them. Had I written the word for him in Amtorian he would have pronounced it *ah-vy-ah-tore*, as they cannot form the long *a* and short *o* sounds, and their *i* is always long.

Finally, to cover his ignorance, he wrote something in his book, but what it was I did not know; then he looked up at me again. "Are you a doctor?"

"Yes," I replied, and as the officer made the notation in his book, I glanced at Kamlot out of the corner of an eye and winked.

"Take them away," the man now directed, "and be careful of this one," he added, indicating me; "he is a doctor."

We were taken to the main deck and led forward to the accompaniment of jeers and jibes from the sailors congregated on the deck. I saw the klangan strutting around, their tail feathers erect. When they saw us, they pointed at Kamlot, and I heard them telling some of the sailors that he was the one who had slain the basto with a single sword thrust, a feat which appeared to force their admiration, as well it might have.

We were escorted to an open hatch and ordered below into a dark, poorly ventilated hole, where we found several other prisoners. Some of them were Thorans undergoing punishment for infractions of discipline; others were Vepajan captives like ourselves, and among the latter was one who recognized Kamlot and hailed him as we descended into their midst.

"Jodades, Kamlot!" he cried, voicing the Amtorian greeting "luck-to-you."

"Ra jodades," replied Kamlot; "what ill fortune brings Honan here?"

"'Ill fortune' does not describe it," replied Honan; "catastrophe would be a better word. The klangan were seeking women as well as men; they saw Duare" (pronounced Doo-ah´-ree) "and pursued her; as I sought to protect her they captured me."

"Your sacrifice was not in vain," said Kamlot; "had you died in the performance of such a duty it would not have been in vain."

"But it was in vain; that is the catastrophe."

"What do you mean?" demanded Kamlot.

"I mean that they got her," replied Honan dejectedly.

"They captured Duare!" exclaimed Kamlot in tones of horror. "By the life of the jong, it cannot be."

"I wish it were not," said Honan.

"Where is she? on this ship?" demanded Kamlot.

"No; they took her to the other, the larger one."

Kamlot appeared crushed, and I could only attribute his dejection to the hopelessness of a lover who has irretrievably lost his beloved. Our association had not been either sufficiently close nor long to promote confidences, and so I was not surprised that I had never heard him mention the girl, Duare, and, naturally, under the circumstances, I could not question him concerning her. I therefore respected his grief and his silence, and left him to his own sad thoughts.

Shortly after dawn the following morning the ship got under way. I wished that I might have been on deck to view the fascinating sights of this strange world, and my precarious situation as a prisoner of the hated Thorists engendered less regret than the fact that I, the first Earth man to sail the seas of Venus, was doomed to be cooped up in a stuffy hole below deck where I could see nothing. But if I had feared being kept below for the duration of the voyage, I was soon disillusioned, for shortly after the ship got underway we were all ordered on deck and set to scrubbing and polishing.

As we came up from below, the ship was just passing between the two headlands that formed the entrance to the harbor, in the wake of the larger vessel; and I obtained an excellent view of the adjacent land, the shore that we were leaving, and the wide expanse of ocean stretching away to the horizon.

The headlands were rocky promontories clothed with verdure of delicate hues and supporting comparatively few trees, which were of a smaller variety than the giants upon the mainland. These latter presented a truly awe-in-spiring spectacle from the open sea to the eyes of an Earth man, their mighty boles rearing their weirdly colored foliage straight up for five thousand feet, where they were lost to view among the clouds. But I was not permitted to gaze for long upon the wonders of the scene. I had not been ordered above for the purpose of satisfying the aesthetic longings of my soul.

Kamlot and I were set to cleaning and polishing guns. There were a number of these on either side of the deck, one at the stern, and two on the tower deck. I was surprised when I saw them, for there had been no sign of armament when I came on board the preceding day; but I was not long in discovering the explanation—the guns were mounted on disappearing carriages, and when lowered, a sliding hatch, flush with the deck, concealed them.

The barrels of these pieces were about eight inches in diameter, while the bore was scarcely larger than my little finger; the sights were ingenious and complicated, but there was no breech block in evidence nor any opening into a breech, unless there was one hidden beneath a hoop that encircled the breech, to which it was heavily bolted. The only thing that I could discover that might have been a firing device projected from the rear of the breech and resembled the rotating crank that is used to revolve the breech block in some types of earthly guns.

The barrels of the guns were about fifteen feet long and of the same diameter from breech to muzzle. When in action they can be extended beyond the rail of the ship about two thirds of their length, thus affording a wider horizontal range and more deck room, which would be of value on a ship such as that on which I was a captive, which was of narrow beam.

"What do these guns fire?" I asked Kamlot, who was working at my side.

"T-rays," he replied.

"Do those differ materially from the R-rays you described when you were telling me about the small arms used by the Thorans?"

"The R-ray destroys only animal tissue," he replied, "while there is nothing that the T-ray may not dissipate. It is a most dangerous ray to work with because even the material of the gun barrel itself is not wholly impervious to it, and the only reason that it can be used at all is that its greatest force is expended along the line of least resistance, which in this case naturally is the bore of the gun. But eventually it destroys the gun itself."

"How is it fired?" I asked.

He touched the crank at the end of the breech. "By turning this, a shutter is raised that permits radiations from element 93 to impinge on the charge, which consists of element 97, thus releasing the deadly T-ray."

"Why couldn't we turn this gun about and rake the ship above deck," I suggested, "thus wiping out the Thorans and giving us our freedom?"

He pointed to a small, irregular hole in the end of the crank shaft. "Because we haven't the key that fits this," he replied.

"Who has the key?"

"The officers have keys to the guns they command," he replied. "In the captain's cabin are keys to all the guns, and he carries a master key that will unlock any of them. At least that was the system in the ancient Vepajan navy, and it is doubtless the same today in the Thoran navy."

"I wish we could get hold of the master key," I said.

"So do I," he agreed, "but that is impossible."

"Nothing is impossible," I retorted.

He made no answer, and I did not pursue the subject, but I certainly gave it a lot of thought.

As I worked, I noted the easy, noiseless propulsion of the ship and asked Kamlot what drove it. His explanation was long and rather technical; suffice it to say that the very useful element 93 (vik-ro) is here again employed upon a substance called lor, which contains a considerable proportion of the element yor-san (105). The action of vik-ro upon yor-san results in absolute annihilation of the lor, releasing all its energy. When you consider that there is eighteen thousand million times as much energy liberated by the annihilation of a ton of coal than by its combustion you will appreciate the inherent possibilities of this marvelous Venusian scientific discovery. Fuel for the life of the ship could be carried in a pint jar.

I noticed as the day progressed that we cruised parallel to a coastline, after crossing one stretch of ocean where no land was in sight, and thereafter for several days I noted the same fact—land was almost always in sight. This suggested that the land area of Venus might be much greater in proportion to its seas; but I had no opportunity to satisfy my curiosity on that point, and of course I took no stock in the maps that Danus had shown me, since the Amtorians' conception of the shape of their world precluded the existence of any dependable maps.

Kamlot and I had been separated, he having been detailed to duty in the ship's galley, which was located in the forward part of the main deck house aft. I struck up a friendship with Honan; but we did not work together, and at night we were usually so tired that we conversed but little before falling asleep on the hard floor of our prison. One night, however, the sorrow of Kamlot having been brought to my mind by my own regretful recollections of the nameless girl of the garden, I asked Honan who Duare was.

"She is the hope of Vepaja," he replied, "perhaps the hope of a world."

CHAPTER NINE
SOLDIERS OF LIBERTY

ONSTANT ASSOCIATION BREEDS a certain *camaraderie* even between enemies. As the days passed, the hatred and contempt which the common sailors appeared to have harbored for us when we first came aboard the ship were replaced by an almost friendly familiarity, as though they had discovered that we were not half bad fellows after all; and, for my part, I found much to like in these simple though ignorant men. That they were the dupes of unscrupulous leaders is about the worst that may be said of them. Most of them were kindly and generous; but their ignorance made them gullible, and their emotions were easily aroused by specious arguments that would have made no impression upon intelligent minds.

Naturally, I became better acquainted with my fellow prisoners than with my guards, and our relations were soon established upon a friendly basis. They were greatly impressed by my blond hair and blue eyes which elicited inquiries as to my genesis. As I answered their questions truthfully, they became deeply interested in my story, and every evening after the day's work was completed I was besieged for tales of the mysterious, far distant world from which I came. Unlike the highly intelligent Vepajans, they believed all that I told them, with the result that I was soon a hero in their eyes; I should have been a god had they had any conception of deities of any description.

In turn, I questioned them; and discovered, with no surprise, that they were not at all contented with their lots. The former free men among them had long since come to the realization that they had exchanged this freedom, and their status of wage earners, for slavery to the state, that could no longer be hidden by a nominal equality.

Among the prisoners were three to whom I was particularly attracted by certain individual characteristics in each. There was Gamfor, for instance, a huge, hulking fellow who had been a farmer in the old days under the jongs. He was unusually intelligent, and although he had taken part in the revolution, he was now bitter in his denunciation of the Thorists, though this he was careful to whisper to me in secrecy.

Another was Kiron, the soldier, a clean-limbed, handsome, athletic fellow who had served in the army of the jong, but mutinied with the others at the time of the revolution. He was being disciplined now for insubordination to an officer who had been a petty government clerk before his promotion.

The third had been a slave. His name was Zog. What he lacked in intelligence he made up in strength and good nature. He had killed an officer who had struck him and was being taken back to Thora for trial and execution. Zog was proud of the fact that he was a free man, though he admitted that the edge was taken off his enthusiasm by the fact that everyone else was free and the realization that he had enjoyed more freedom as a slave than he did now as a freeman.

"Then," he explained, "I had one master; now I have as many masters as there are government officials, spies, and soldiers, none of whom cares anything about me, while my old master was kind to me and looked after my welfare."

"Would you like to be really free?" I asked him, for a plan had been slowly forming in my mind.

But to my surprise he said, "No, I should rather be a slave."

"But you'd like to choose your own master, wouldn't you?" I demanded.

"Certainly," he replied, "if I could find someone who would be kind to me and protect me from the Thorists."

"And if you could escape from them now, you would like to do so?"

"Of course! But what do you mean? I cannot escape from them."

"Not without help," I agreed, "but if others would join you, would you make the attempt?"

"Why not? They are taking me back to Thora to kill me. I could be no worse off, no matter what I did. But why do you ask all these questions?"

"If we could get enough to join us, there is no reason why we should not be free," I told him. "When you are free, you may remain free or choose a master to your liking." I watched closely for his reaction.

"You mean another revolution?" he asked. "It would fail. Others have tried, but they have always failed."

"Not a revolution," I assured him, "just a break for liberty."

"But how could we do it?"

"It would not be difficult for a few men to take this ship," I suggested. "The discipline is poor, the night watches consist of too few men; they are so sure of themselves that they would be taken completely by surprise."

Zog's eyes lighted. "If we were successful, many of the crew would join us," he said. "Few of them are happy; nearly all of them hate their officers. I think the prisoners would join us almost to a man, but you must be careful of spies—they are everywhere. That is the greatest danger you would have to face. There can be no doubt but there is at least one spy among us prisoners."

"How about Gamfor," I asked; "is he all right?"

"You can depend upon Gamfor," Zog assured me. "He does not say much, but in his eyes I can read his hatred of them."

"And Kiron?"

"Just the man!" exclaimed Zog. "He despises them, and he does not care who knows it; that is the reason he is a prisoner. This is not his first offense, and it is rumored that he will be executed for high treason."

"But I thought that he only talked back to an officer and refused to obey him," I said.

"That is high treason—if they wish to get rid of a man," explained Zog. "You can depend on Kiron. Do you wish me to speak to him about the matter?"

"No," I told him. "I will speak to him and to Gamfor; then if anything goes wrong before we are ready to strike, if a spy gets wind of our plot, you will not be implicated."

"I do not care about that," he exclaimed. "They can kill me for but one thing, and it makes no difference which thing it is they kill me for."

"Nevertheless, I shall speak to them, and if they will join us, we can then decide together how to approach others."

Zog and I had been working together scrubbing the deck at the time, and it was not until night that I had an opportunity to speak with Gamfor and Kiron. Both were enthusiastic about the plan, but neither thought that there was much likelihood that it would succeed. However, each assured me of his support; and then we found Zog, and the four of us discussed details throughout half the night. We had withdrawn to a far corner of the room in which we were confined and spoke in low whispers with our heads close together.

The next few days were spent in approaching recruits—a very ticklish business, since they all assured me that it was almost a foregone conclusion that there was a spy among us. Each man had to be sounded out by devious means, and it had been decided that this work should be left to Gamfor and Kiron. I was eliminated because of my lack of knowledge concerning the hopes, ambitions, and the grievances of these people, or their psychology; Zog was eliminated because the work required a much higher standard of intelligence than he possessed.

Gamfor warned Kiron not to divulge our plan to any prisoner who too openly avowed his hatred of the Thorists. "This is a timeworn trick that all spies adopt to lull the suspicions of those they suspect of harboring treasonable thoughts, and to tempt them into avowing their apostasy. Select men whom you know to have a real grievance, and who are moody and silent," he counselled.

I was a little concerned about our ability to navigate the ship in the event that we succeeded in capturing her, and I discussed this matter with both Gamfor and Kiron. What I learned from them was illuminating, if not particularly helpful.

The Amtorians have developed a compass similar to ours. According to Kiron, it points always toward the center of Amtor—that is, toward the center of the mythical circular area called Strabol, or Hot Country. This statement assured me that I was in the southern hemisphere of the planet, the needle of the compass, of course, pointing north toward the north magnetic pole. Having no sun, moon, nor stars, their navigation is all done by dead reckoning; but they have developed instruments of extreme delicacy that locate land at great distances, accurately indicating this distance and the direction; others that determine speed, mileage, and drift, as well as a depth gauge wherewith they may record soundings anywhere within a radius of a mile from the ship.

All of their instruments for measuring distances utilize the radioactivity of the nuclei of various elements to accomplish their ends. The gamma ray, for which they have, of course, another name, being uninfluenced by the most powerful magnetic forces, is naturally the ideal medium for their purposes. It moves in a straight line and at uniform speed until it meets an obstruction, where, even though it may not be deflected, it is retarded, the instrument recording such retardation and the distance at which it occurs. The sounding device utilizes the same principle. The instrument records the distance from the ship at which the ray encounters the resistance of the ocean's bottom; by constructing a right triangle with this distance representing the hypotenuse it is simple to compute both the depth of the ocean and the distance from the ship at which bottom was found, for they have a triangle of which one side and all three angles are known.

Owing to their extremely faulty maps, however, the value of these instruments has been greatly reduced, for no matter what course they lay, other than due north, if they move in a straight line they are always approaching the antarctic regions. They may know that land is ahead and its distance, but they are never sure what land it is, except where the journey is a short and familiar one. For this reason they cruise within sight of land wherever that is practical, with the result that journeys that might otherwise be short are greatly protracted. Another result is that the radius of Amtorian maritime exploration has been greatly circumscribed; so much so that I believe there are enormous areas in the south temperate zone that have never been discovered by the Vepajans or the Thorists, while the very existence of the northern hemisphere is even unguessed by them. On the maps that Danus showed me considerable areas contained nothing but the single word *joram*, ocean.

However, notwithstanding all this (and possibly because of it), I was confident that we could manage to navigate the ship quite as satisfactorily as her present officers, and in this Kiron agreed.

"At least we know the general direction of Thora," he argued; "so all we have to do is sail in the other direction."

As our plans matured, the feasibility of the undertaking appeared more and more certain. We had recruited twenty prisoners, five of whom were Vepajans, and this little band we organized into a secret order with passwords, which were changed daily, signs, and a grip, the last reminiscent of my fraternity days in college. We also adopted a name. We called ourselves Soldiers of Liberty. I was chosen *vookor*, or captain. Gamfor,

Kiron, Zog, and Honan were my principal lieutenants, though I told them that Kamlot would be second in command if we were successful in taking the ship.

Our plan of action was worked out in detail; each man knew exactly what was expected of him. Certain men were to overpower the watch, others were to go to the officers' quarters and secure their weapons and keys; then we would confront the crew and offer those who chose an opportunity to join us. The others—well, there I was confronted with a problem. Almost to a man the Soldiers of Liberty wanted to destroy all those who would not join us, and really there seemed no alternative; but I still hoped that I could work out a more humane disposition of them.

There was one man among the prisoners of whom we were all suspicious. He had an evil face, but that was not his sole claim upon our suspicions—he was too loud in his denunciation of Thorism. We watched him carefully, avoiding him whenever we could, and each member of the band was warned to be careful when talking to him. It was evident to Gamfor first that this fellow, whose name was Anoos, was suspicious. He persisted in seeking out various members of our group and engaging them in conversation which he always led around to the subject of Thorism and his hatred of it, and he constantly questioned each of us about the others, always insinuating that he feared certain ones were spies. But of course we had expected something of this sort, and we felt that we had guarded against it. The fellow might be as suspicious of us as he wished; so long as he had no evidence against us I did not see how he could harm us.

One day Kiron came to me evidently laboring under suppressed excitement. It was at the end of the day, and our food had just been issued to us for the evening meal—dried fish and a hard, dark-colored bread made of coarse meal.

"I have news, Carson," he whispered.

"Let us go off in a corner and eat," I suggested, and we strolled away together, laughing and talking of the day's events in our normal voices. As we seated ourselves upon the floor to eat our poor food, Zog joined us.

"Sit close to us, Zog," directed Kiron; "I have something to say that no one but a Soldier of Liberty may hear."

He did not say Soldier of Liberty, but "kung, kung, kung," which are the Amtorian initials of the order's title. Kung is the name of the Amtorian character that represents the *k* sound in our language, and when I first translated the initials I was compelled to frown at the similarity they bore to those of a reviled and discredited secret order in the United States of America.

"While I am talking," Kiron admonished us, "you must laugh often, as though I were telling a humorous tale; then, perhaps, no one will suspect that I am not.

"Today I was working in the ship's armory, cleaning pistols," he commenced. "The soldier who guarded me is an old friend of mine; we served together in the army of the jong. He is as a brother to me. For either the other would die. We talked of old times under the banners of the jong and compared those days with these, especially we compared the officers of the old regime with those of the present. Like me and like every old soldier, he hates his officers; so we had a pleasant time together.

"Finally he said to me, quite suddenly, 'What is this I hear of a conspiracy among the prisoners?'

"That almost took me off my feet; but I showed no emotion, for there are times when one must not trust even a brother. 'What have you heard?' I asked.

"'I overheard one of the officers speaking to another,' he told me. 'He said that a man named Anoos had reported the matter to the captain, and that the captain had told Anoos to get the names of all the prisoners whom he knew to be involved in the conspiracy and to learn their plans if he possibly could.'

"'And what did Anoos say?' I asked my friend.

"'He said that if the captain would give him a bottle of wine he believed that he could get one of the conspirators drunk and worm the story from him. So the captain gave him a bottle of wine. That was today.'

"My friend looked at me very closely, and then he said, 'Kiron, we are more than brothers. If I can help you, you have but to ask.'

"I knew this, and knowing how close to discovery we already were, I decided to confide in him and enlist his aid; so I told him. I hope you do not feel that I did wrong, Carson."

"By no means," I assured him. "We have been forced to tell others of our plans whom we knew and trusted less well than you know and trust your friend. What did he say when you had told him?"

"He said that he would help us, and that when we struck he would join us. He promised, too, that many others of the soldiers would do likewise; but the most important thing he did was to give me a key to the armory."

"Good!" I exclaimed. "There is no reason now why we should not strike at once."

"Tonight?" asked Zog eagerly.

"Tonight!" I replied. "Pass the word to Gamfor and Honan, and you four to the other Soldiers of Liberty."

We all laughed heartily, as though someone had told a most amusing story, and then Kiron and Zog left me, to acquaint Gamfor and Honan with our plan.

But upon Venus as upon Earth, the best laid plans of mice and men "gang aft a-gley," which is slang for haywire. Every night since we had sailed from the harbor of Vepaja the hatch had been left off our ill-smelling prison to afford us ventilation, a single member of the watch patrolling near to see that none of us came out; but tonight the hatch was closed.

"This," growled Kiron, "is the result of Anoos' work."

"We shall have to strike by daylight," I whispered, "but we cannot pass the word tonight. It is so dark down here that we should certainly be overheard by someone outside our own number if we attempted it."

"Tomorrow then," said Kiron.

I was a long time getting to sleep that night, for my mind was troubled by fears for our entire plan. It was obvious now that the captain was suspicious, and that while he might not know anything of the details of what we purposed, he did know that something was in the air, and he was taking no chances.

During the night, as I lay awake trying to plan for the morrow, I heard someone prowling around the room, and now and again a whisper.

I could only wonder who it was and try to guess what he was about. I recalled the bottle of wine that Anoos was supposed to have, and it occurred to me that he might be giving a party, but the voices were too subdued to bear out that theory. Finally I heard a muffled cry, a noise that sounded like a brief scuffle, and then silence again fell upon the chamber.

"Someone had a bad dream," I thought and fell asleep.

Morning came at last, and the hatch was removed, letting a little light in to dissipate the gloom of our prison. A sailor lowered a basket containing the food for our meager breakfast. We gathered about it and each took his share, and moved away to eat it, when suddenly there was a cry from the far side of the room.

"Look what's here!" the man shouted. "Anoos has been murdered!"

CHAPTER TEN
MUTINY

YES, ANOOS HAD BEEN MURDERED, and there was a great hue and cry, much more of a hue and cry, it seemed to me, than the death of an ordinary prisoner should have aroused. Officers and soldiers swarmed in our quarters. They found Anoos stretched out on his back, a bottle of wine at his side. His throat was discolored where powerful fingers had crushed it. Anoos had been choked to death.

Soon they herded us on deck, where we were searched for weapons following an order from the captain of the ship, who had come forward to conduct an investigation. He was angry and excited and, I believe, somewhat frightened. One by one, he questioned us. When it was my turn to be questioned, I did not tell him what I had heard during the night; I told him that I had slept all night on the far side of the room from where Anoos' body was discovered.

"Were you acquainted with the dead man?" he asked.

"No more so than with any of the other prisoners," I replied.

"But you are very well acquainted with some of them," he said rather pointedly, I thought. "Have you ever spoken with the man?"

"Yes, he has talked to me on several occasions."

"About what?" demanded the captain.

"Principally about his grievances against the Thorists."

"But he was a Thorist," exclaimed the captain.

I knew that he was trying to pump me to discover if I harbored any suspicions concerning the actual status of Anoos, but he was not clever enough to succeed. "I certainly would never had suspected it from his conversation," I replied. "If he were a Thorist, he must have been a traitor to his country, for he continually sought to enlist my interest in a plan to seize the ship and murder all her officers. I think he approached others, also." I spoke in a tone loud enough to be heard by all, for I wanted the Soldiers of Liberty to take the cue from me.

If enough of us told the same story it might convince the officers that Anoos' tale of a conspiracy was hatched in his own brain and worked up by his own efforts in an attempt to reap commendation and reward from his superiors, a trick by no means foreign to the ethics of spies.

"Did he succeed in persuading any of the prisoners to join him?" asked the captain.

"I think not; they all laughed at him."

"Have you any idea who murdered him?"

"Probably some patriot who resented his treason," I lied glibly.

As he questioned the other men along similar lines, I was pleased to discover that nearly every one of the Soldiers of Liberty had been approached by the perfidious Anoos, whose traitorous overtures they had virtuously repulsed. Zog said that he had never talked with the man, which, to the best of my knowledge, was the truth.

When the captain finished his investigation, he was farther from the truth than when he commenced it, for I am certain that he went aft convinced that there had been no truth in the tales that Anoos had carried to him.

I had been considerably worried at the time we were being searched, for fear that the key to the armory would be discovered on Kiron, but it had not been, and later he told me that he had hidden it in his hair the night before as a precaution against just such an eventuality as had occurred.

The Amtorian day consists of 26 hours, 56 minutes, 4 seconds of Earth time, which the Amtorians divide into twenty equal periods called *te*, which, for clarity, I shall translate into its nearest earthly equivalent, hour, although it contains 80.895 Earth minutes. On shipboard, the hours are sounded by a trumpeter, there being a distinguishing bar of music for each hour of the day. The first hour, or one o'clock, corresponds to mean sunrise. It is then that the prisoners are awakened and given food; forty minutes later they start work, which continues until the tenth hour, with a short recess for food in the middle of the day. Occasionally we were allowed to quit work at the ninth and even the eighth hour, according to the caprices of our masters.

On this day the Soldiers of Liberty congregated during the midday rest period, and, my mind being definitely determined on immediate action, I passed the word around that we would strike during the afternoon at the moment the trumpeter sounded the seventh hour. As many of us as were working aft near the armory were to make a dash for it with Kiron, who would unlock it in the event that it were locked. The remainder were to attack the soldiers nearest them with anything that they could use as weapons, or with their bare hands if they had no weapons, and take the soldiers' pistols and swords from them. Five of us were to account for the officers. Half of our number was to constantly shout our battle cry, "For liberty!" The other half was instructed to urge the remaining prisoners and the soldiers to join us.

It was a mad scheme and one in which only desperate men could have found hope.

The seventh hour was chosen because at that time the officers were nearly all congregated in the wardroom, where a light meal and wine were served them daily. We should have preferred launching our plan at night, but we feared a continuation of the practice of locking us below deck would prevent, and our experience with Anoos had taught us that we might expect the whole conspiracy to be divulged by another spy at any time; therefore we dared not wait.

I must confess to a feeling of increasing excitement as the hour approached. As, from time to time, I glanced at the other members of our little band, I thought that I could note signs of nervousness in some of them, while others worked on as placidly as though nothing unusual was about to occur. Zog was one of these. He was working near me. He never glanced toward the tower deck from which the trumpeter would presently sound the fateful notes, though it was with difficulty that I kept my eyes from it at all. No one would have thought that Zog was planning to attack the soldier lolling near him, nor have imagined that the night before he had murdered a man. He was humming a tune, as he polished the barrel of the big gun on which he was working.

Gamfor and, fortunately, Kiron were working aft, scrubbing the deck, and I saw that Kiron kept scrubbing closer and closer to the door of the armory. How I wished for Kamlot as the crucial moment approached! He could have done so much to insure the success of our *coup*, and yet he did not even know that such a stroke was contemplated, much less that it was so soon to be launched.

As I glanced about, I met Zog's gaze. Very solemnly he closed his left eye. At last he had given a sign that he was alert and ready. It was a little thing, but it put new heart into me. For some reason, during the past half hour I had felt very much alone.

The time was approaching the zero hour. I moved closer to my guard, so that I stood directly in front of him with my back toward him. I knew precisely what I was going to do, and I knew that it would be successful. Little did the man behind me dream that in a minute, or perhaps a few seconds, he would be lying senseless on the deck, or that the man he guarded would be carrying his sword, his dagger, and his pistol as the last notes of the seventh hour floated sweetly out across the calm waters of this Amtorian sea.

My back was now toward the deck houses. I could not see the trumpeter when he emerged from the tower to sound the hour, but I knew that it could not be long now before he stepped out onto the tower deck. Yet when the first note sounded I was as startled as though I had expected it never to sound. I presume it was the reaction after the long period of nervous tension.

My nervousness, however, was all mental; it did not affect my physical reactions to the needs of the moment. As the first note came softly down to my awaiting ears, I pivoted on a heel and swung my right for the chin of my unsuspecting guard. It was one of those blows that is often described as a haymaker, and it made hay. The fellow dropped in his tracks. As I stooped to recover his arms, pandemonium broke loose upon the deck. There were shrieks and groans and curses, and above all rose the war cry of the Soldiers of Liberty—my band had struck, and it had struck hard.

For the first time now, I heard the weird staccato hiss of Amtorian firearms. You have heard an X-ray machine in operation? It was like that, but louder and more sinister. I had wrenched the sword and pistol from the scabbard and holster of my fallen guard, not taking the time to remove his belt. Now I faced the scene for which I had so long waited. I saw the powerful Zog wrest the weapons from a soldier, and then lift the man's body above his head and cast it overboard. Evidently Zog had no time for proselyting.

At the door to the armory a battle was being waged; men were trying to enter, and soldiers were shooting them down. I ran in that direction. A soldier leaped in front of me, and I heard the hiss of the death rays that must have passed close to my body, as he tried to stop me. He must have been either nervous or a very poor shot, for he missed me. I turned my own weapon upon him and pressed the lever. The man slumped to the deck with a hole in his chest, and I ran on.

The fight at the door of the armory was hand to hand with swords, daggers, and fists, for by now the members of the two factions were so intermingled that none dared use a firearm for fear of injuring a comrade. Into this melee I leaped. Tucking the pistol into the band of my G-string, I ran my sword through a great brute who was about to knife Honan; then I grabbed another by the hair and dragged him from the door, shouting to Honan to finish him—it took too long to run a sword into a man and then pull it out again. What I wanted was to get into the armory to Kiron's side and help him.

All the time I could hear my men shouting, "For liberty!" or urging the soldiers to join us—as far as I had been able to judge, all the prisoners had already done so. Now another soldier barred my way. His back was toward me, and I was about to seize him and hurl him back to Honan and the others who were fighting at his side, when I saw him slip his dagger into the heart of a soldier in front of him and, as he did so, cry, "For liberty!" Here was one convert at least. I did not know it then, but at that time there were already many such.

When I finally got into the armory, I found Kiron issuing arms as fast as he could pass them out. Many of the mutineers were crawling through the windows of the room to get weapons, and to each of these Kiron passed several swords and pistols, directing the men to distribute them on deck.

Seeing that all was right here, I gathered a handful of men and started up the companionway to the upper decks, from which the officers were firing down upon the mutineers and, I may say, upon their own men as well. In fact, it was this heartless and stupid procedure that swung many of the soldiers to our side. Almost the first man I saw as I leaped to the level of the second deck was Kamlot. He had a sword in one hand and a pistol in the other, and he was firing rapidly at a group of officers who were evidently attempting to reach the main deck to take command of the loyal soldiers there.

You may be assured that it did my heart good to see my friend again, and as I ran to his side and opened fire on the officers, he flashed me a quick smile of recognition.

Three of the five officers opposing us had fallen, and now the remaining two turned and fled up the companionway to the top deck. Behind us were twenty or more mutineers eager to reach the highest deck, where all the surviving officers had now taken refuge, and I could see more mutineers crowding up the companionway from the main deck to join their fellows. Kamlot and I led the way to the next deck, but at the head of the companionway the surging mob of howling, cursing mutineers brushed past us to hurl themselves upon the officers.

The men were absolutely out of control, and as there were but few of my original little band of Soldiers of Liberty among them, the majority of them knew no leader, with the result that it was every man for himself. I wished to protect the officers, and it had been my intention to do so; but I was helpless to avert the bloody orgy that ensued with a resulting loss of life entirely disproportionate to the needs of the occasion.

The officers, fighting for their lives with their backs against a wall, took heavy toll of the mutineers, but they were eventually overwhelmed by superior numbers. Each of the common soldiers and sailors appeared to have a special grudge to settle either with some individual officer or with them all as a class and for the time all were transformed into maniacal furies, as time and again they charged the last fortress of authority, the oval tower on the upper deck.

Each officer that fell, either killed or wounded, was hurled over the rail to the deck below, where willing hands cast the body to the main deck from which, in turn, it was thrown into the sea. And then, at last, the mutineers gained access to the tower, from which they dragged the remaining officers, butchering them on the upper deck or hurling them to their shrieking fellows below.

The captain was the last to be dragged out.

They had found him hiding in a cupboard in his cabin. At sight of him arose such a scream of hate and rage as I hope never to hear again. Kamlot and I were standing at one side, helpless witnesses of this holocaust of hate. We saw them literally tear the captain to pieces and cast him into the sea.

With the death of the captain the battle was over, the ship was ours. My plan had succeeded, but the thought suddenly assailed me that I had created a terrible power that it might be beyond me to control. I touched Kamlot on the arm. "Follow me," I directed and started for the main deck.

"Who is at the bottom of this?" asked Kamlot as we forced our way among the excited mutineers.

"The mutiny was my plan, but not the massacre," I replied. "Now we must attempt to restore order out of chaos."

"If we can," he remarked dubiously.

As I made my way toward the main deck, I collected as many of the original band of Soldiers of Liberty as we passed, and when I finally reached my destination, I gathered most of them about me. Among the mutineers I had discovered the trumpeter who had unknowingly sounded the signal for the outbreak, and him I caused to sound the call that should assemble all hands on the main deck. Whether or not the notes of the trumpet would be obeyed, I did not know, but so strong is the habit of discipline among trained men that immediately the call sounded the men began to pour onto the deck from all parts of the vessel.

I mounted the breech of one of the guns, and, surrounded by my faithful band, I announced that the Soldiers of Liberty had taken over the ship, that those who wished to accompany us must obey the vookor of the band; the others would be put ashore.

"Who is vookor?" demanded a soldier whom I recognized as one of those who had been most violent in the attack upon the officers.

"I am," I replied.

"The vookor should be one of us," he growled.

"Carson planned the mutiny and carried it to success," shouted Kiron. "Carson is vookor."

From the throats of all my original band and from a hundred new recruits rose a cheer of approval, but there were many who remained silent or spoke in grumbling undertones to those nearest them. Among these was Kodj, the soldier who had objected to my leadership, and I saw that already a faction was gathering about him.

"It is necessary," I said, "that all men return at once to their duties, for the ship must be handled, no matter who commands. If there is any question about leadership, that can be settled later. In the meantime, I am in command; Kamlot, Gamfor, Kiron, Zog, and Honan are my lieutenants; with me, they will officer the ship. All weapons must be turned over immediately to Kiron at the armory, except those carried by men regularly detailed by him for guard duty."

"No one is going to disarm me," blustered Kodj. "I have as much right to carry weapons as anyone. We are all free men now. I take orders from no one."

Zog, who had edged closer to him as he spoke, seized him by the throat with one of his huge hands and with the other tore the belt from about his hips. "You take orders from the new vookor or you go overboard," he growled, as he released the man and handed his weapons to Kiron.

For a moment there was silence, and there was a tenseness in the situation that boded ill; then someone laughed and cried, "No one is going to disarm me," mimicking Kodj. That brought a general laugh, and I knew that for the time being the danger was over. Kiron, sensing that the moment was ripe, ordered the men to come to the armory and turn in their weapons, and the remainder of the original band herded them aft in his wake.

It was an hour before even a semblance of order or routine had been reestablished. Kamlot, Gamfor, and I were gathered in the chart room in the tower. Our consort was hull down below the horizon, and we were discussing the means that should be adopted to capture her without bloodshed and rescue Duare and the other Vepajan prisoners aboard her. The idea had been in my mind from the very inception of the plan to seize our own ship, and it had been the first subject that Kamlot had broached after we had succeeded in quieting the men and restoring order; but Gamfor was frankly dubious concerning the feasibility of the project.

"The men are not interested in the welfare of Vepajans," he reminded us, "and they may resent the idea of endangering their lives and risking their newfound liberty in a venture that means nothing whatever to them."

"How do you feel about it, personally?" I asked him.

"I am under your orders," he replied; "I will do anything that you command, but I am only one—you have two hundred whose wishes you must consult."

"I shall consult only my officers," I replied; "to the others, I shall issue orders."

"That is the only way," said Kamlot in a tone of relief.

"Inform the other officers that we shall attack the *Sovong* at daybreak," I instructed them.

"But we dare not fire on her," protested Kamlot, "lest we endanger the life of Duare."

"I intend boarding her," I replied. "There will be no one but the watch on deck at that hour. On two other occasions the ships have been brought close together on a calm sea; so our approach will arouse no suspicion. The boarding party will consist of a hundred men who will remain concealed until the command to board is given when the ships are alongside one another. At that hour in the morning the sea is usually calm; if it is not calm tomorrow morning we shall have to postpone the attack until another morning.

"Issue strict orders that there is to be no slaughter; no one is to be killed who does not resist. We shall remove all of the *Sovong*'s small arms and the bulk of her provisions, as well as the Vepajan prisoners, to the *Sofal*."

"And then what do you propose doing?" asked Gamfor.

"I am coming to that," I replied, "but first I wish to ascertain the temper of the men aboard the *Sofal*. You and Kamlot will inform the other officers of my plans insofar as I have explained them; then assemble the original members of the Soldiers of Liberty and explain my intentions to them. When this has been done, instruct them to disseminate the information among the remainder of the ship's company, reporting to you the names of all those who do not receive the plan with favor. These we shall leave aboard the *Sovong* with any others who may elect to transfer to her. At the eleventh hour muster the men on the main deck. At that time I will explain my plans in detail."

After Kamlot and Gamfor had departed to carry out my orders, I returned to the chart room. The *Sofal*, moving ahead at increased speed, was slowly overhauling the *Sovong*, though not at a rate that might suggest pursuit. I was certain that the *Sovong* knew nothing of what had transpired upon her sister ship, for the Amtorians are unacquainted with wireless communication, and there had been no time for the officers of the *Sofal* to signal their fellows aboard the *Sovong*, so suddenly had the mutiny broken and so quickly had it been carried to a conclusion.

As the eleventh hour approached, I noticed little groups of men congregated in different parts of the ship, evidently discussing the information that the Soldiers of Liberty had spread among them. One group, larger than the others, was being violently harangued by a loudmouthed orator whom I recognized as Kodj. It had been apparent from the first that the fellow was a troublemaker. Just how much influence he had, I did not know; but I felt that whatever it was, it would be used against me. I hoped to be rid of him after we had taken the *Sovong*.

The men congregated rapidly as the trumpeter sounded the hour, and I came down the companionway to address them. I stood just above them, on one of the lower steps, where I could overlook them and be seen by all.

Most of them were quiet and appeared attentive. There was one small group muttering and whispering—Kodj was its center.

"At daybreak we shall board and take the *Sovong*," I commenced. "You will receive your orders from your immediate officers, but I wish to emphasize one in particular—there is to be no unnecessary killing. After we have taken the ship we shall transfer to the *Sofal* such provisions, weapons, and prisoners as we wish to take with us. At this time, also, we shall transfer from the *Sofal* to the *Sovong* all of you who do not wish to remain on this ship under my command, as well as those whom I do not care to take with me," and as I said this, I looked straight at Kodj and the malcontents surrounding him.

"I shall explain what I have in mind for the future, so that each of you may be able to determine between now and daybreak whether he cares to become a member of my company. Those who do will be required to obey orders; but they will share in the profits of the cruise, if there are profits. The purposes of the expedition are twofold: To prey on Thorist shipping and to explore the unknown portions of Amtor after we have returned the Vepajan prisoners to their own country.

"There will be excitement and adventure; there will be danger, too; and I want no cowards along, nor any troublemakers. There should be profits, for I am assured that richly laden Thorist ships constantly ply the known seas of Amtor; and I am informed that we can always find a ready market for such spoils of war as fall into our hands—and war it shall be, with the Soldiers of Liberty fighting the oppression and tyranny of Thorism.

"Return to your quarters now, and be prepared to give a good account of yourselves at daybreak."

CHAPTER ELEVEN
DUARE

I GOT LITTLE SLEEP THAT NIGHT. My officers were constantly coming to me with reports. From these I learned, what was of the greatest importance to me, the temper of the crew. None was averse to taking the *Sovong*, but there was a divergence of opinion as to what we should do thereafter. A few wanted to be landed on Thoran soil, so that they could make their way back to their homes; the majority was enthusiastic about plundering merchant ships; the idea of exploring the unknown waters of Amtor filled most of them with fear; some were averse to restoring the Vepajan prisoners to their own country; and there was an active and extremely vocal minority that insisted that the command of the vessel should be placed in the hands of Thorans. In this I could see the hand of Kodj even before they told me that the suggestion had come from the coterie that formed his following.

"But there are fully a hundred," said Gamfor, "upon whose loyalty you may depend. These have accepted you as their leader, and they will follow you and obey your commands."

"Arm these," I directed, "and place all others below deck until after we have taken the *Sovong*. How about the klangan? They took no part in the mutiny. Are they for us or against us?"

Kiron laughed. "They received no orders one way or the other," he explained. "They have no initiative. Unless they are motivated by such primitive instincts as hunger, love, or hate, they do nothing without orders from a superior."

"And they don't care who their master is," interjected Zog. "They serve loyally enough until their master dies, or sells them, or gives them away, or is overthrown; then they transfer the same loyalty to a new master."

"They have been told that you are their new master," said Kamlot, "and they will obey you." As there were only five of the birdmen aboard the *Sofal*, I had not been greatly exercised about their stand; but I was glad to learn that they would not be antagonistic.

At the twentieth hour I ordered the hundred upon whom we could depend assembled and held in the lower deck house, the others having all been confined below earlier in the night, in the accomplishment of which a second mutiny was averted only by the fact that all the men had been previously disarmed except the loyal Soldiers of Liberty.

All during the night we had been gradually gaining upon the unsuspecting *Sovong* until now we were scarcely a hundred yards astern of her, slightly aport. Across our starboard bow I could see her looming darkly in the mysterious nocturnal glow of the moonless Amtorian night, her lanterns white and colored points of light, her watch dimly visible upon her decks.

Closer and closer the *Sofal* crept toward her prey. A Soldier of Liberty, who had once been an officer in the Thoran navy, was at the wheel; no one was on deck but the members of the watch; in the lower deck house a hundred men were huddled waiting for the command to board; I stood beside Honan in the chart room (he was to command the *Sofal* while I led the boarding party), my eyes upon the strange Amtorian chronometer. I spoke a word to him and he moved a lever. The *Sofal* crept a little closer to the *Sovong*. Then Honan whispered an order to the helmsman and we closed in upon our prey.

I hastened down the companionway to the main deck and gave the signal to Kamlot standing in the doorway of the deck house. The two ships were close now and almost abreast. The sea was calm; only a gentle swell raised and lowered the softly gliding ships. Now we were so close that a man could step across the intervening space from the deck of one ship to that of the other.

The officer of the watch aboard the *Sovong* hailed us. "What are you about?" he demanded. "Sheer off, there!"

For answer I ran across the deck of the *Sofal* and leaped aboard the other ship, a hundred silent men following in my wake. There was no shouting and little noise—only the shuffling of sandaled feet and the subdued clank of arms.

Behind us the grappling hooks were thrown over the rail of the *Sovong*. Every man had been instructed as to the part he was to play.

Leaving Kamlot in command on the main deck, I ran to the tower deck with a dozen men, while Kiron led a score of fighting men to the second deck where most of the officers were quartered.

Before the officer of the watch could gather his scattered wits, I had him covered with a pistol. "Keep quiet," I whispered, "and you will not be harmed." My plan was to take as many of them as possible before a general alarm could be sounded and thus minimize the necessity for bloodshed; therefore, the need for silence. I turned him over to one of my men after disarming him; and then I sought the captain, while two of my detachment attended to the helmsman.

I found the officer for whom I sought reaching for his weapons. He had been awakened by the unavoidable noise of the boarding party, and, suspecting that something was amiss, had seized his weapons as he arose and uncovered the lights in his cabin.

I was upon him as he raised his pistol, and struck it from his hand before he could fire; but he stepped back with his sword on guard, and thus we stood facing one another for a moment.

"Surrender," I told him, "and you will not be harmed."

"Who are you?" he demanded, "and where did you come from?"

"I was a prisoner on board the *Sofal*," I replied, "but now I command her. If you wish to avoid bloodshed, come out on deck with me and give the command to surrender."

"And then what?" he demanded. "Why have you boarded us if not to kill?"

"To take off provisions, weapons, and the Vepajan prisoners," I explained.

Suddenly the hissing staccato of pistol fire came up to us from the deck below.

"I thought there was to be no killing!" he snapped.

"If you want to stop it, get out there and give the command to surrender," I replied.

"I don't believe you," he cried. "It's a trick," and he came at me with his sword.

I did not wish to shoot him down in cold blood, and so I met his attack with my own blade. The advantage was on his side in the matter of skill, for I had not yet fully accustomed myself to the use of the Amtorian sword; but I had an advantage in strength and reach and in some tricks of German swordplay that I had learned while I was in Germany.

The Amtorian sword is primarily a cutting weapon, its weight near the tip making it particularly effective for this method of attack, though it lessens its effectiveness in parrying thrusts, rendering it a rather sluggish defensive weapon. I therefore found myself facing a savage cutting attack against which I had difficulty in defending myself. The officer was an active man and skillful with the sword. Being experienced, it did not take him long to discover that I was a novice, with the result that he pressed his advantage viciously, so that I soon regretted my magnanimity in not resorting to my pistol before the encounter began; but it was too late now—the fellow kept me so busy that I had no opportunity to draw the weapon.

He forced me back and around the room until he stood between me and the doorway, and then, having me where no chance for escape remained, he set to work to finish me with dispatch. The duel, as far as I was concerned, was fought wholly on the defensive. So swift and persistent was his attack that I could only defend myself, and not once in the first two minutes of the encounter did I aim a single blow at him.

I wondered what had become of the men who had accompanied me; but pride would not permit me to call upon them for help, nor did I learn until later that it would have availed me nothing, since they were having all that they could attend to in repelling the attack of several officers who had run up from below immediately behind them.

The teeth of my antagonist were bared in a grim and ferocious smile, as he battered relentlessly at my guard, as though he already sensed victory and was gloating in anticipation. The clanging of steel on steel now drowned all sounds from beyond the four walls of the cabin where we fought; I could not tell if fighting were continuing in other parts of the ship, nor, if it were, whether it were going in our favor or against us. I realized that I *must* know these things, that I was responsible for whatever took place aboard the *Sovong*, and that I must get out of that cabin and lead my men either in victory or defeat.

Such thoughts made my position even more impossible than as though only my life were at stake and drove me to attempt heroic measures for releasing myself from my predicament and my peril. I must destroy my adversary, and I must do so at once!

He had me now with my back almost against the wall. Already his point had touched me upon the cheek once and twice upon the body, and though the wounds were but scratches, I was covered with blood. Now he leaped upon me in a frenzy of determination to have done with me instantly, but this time I did not fall back. I parried his cut, so that his sword passed to the right of my body which was now close to his; and then I drew back my point, and, before he could recover himself, drove it through his heart.

As he sagged to the floor, I jerked my sword from his body and ran from his cabin. The entire episode had required but a few minutes, though it had seemed much longer to me, yet in that brief time much had occurred on the decks and in the cabins of the *Sovong*. The upper decks were cleared of living enemies; one of my own men was at the wheel, another at the controls; there was still fighting on the main deck where some of the *Sovong*'s officers were making a desperate last stand with a handful of their men. But by the time I reached the scene of the battle, it was over; the officers, assured by Kamlot that their lives would be spared, had surrendered—the *Sovong* was ours. The *Sofal* had taken her first prize!

As I sprang into the midst of the excited warriors on the main deck,

I must have presented a sorry spectacle, bleeding, as I was, from my three wounds; but my men greeted me with loud cheers. I learned later that my absence from the fighting on the main deck had been noticed and had made a poor impression on my men, but when they saw me return bearing the scars of combat, my place in their esteem was secured. Those three little scratches proved of great value to me, but they were as nothing in comparison with the psychological effect produced by the wholly disproportionate amount of blood they had spilled upon my naked hide.

We now quickly rounded up our prisoners and disarmed them. Kamlot took a detachment of men and released the Vepajan captives whom he transferred at once to the *Sofal*. They were nearly all women, but I did not see them as they were taken from the ship, being engaged with other matters. I could imagine, though, the joy in the hearts of Kamlot and Duare at this reunion, which the latter at least had probably never even dared to hope for.

Rapidly we transferred all of the small arms of the *Sovong* to the *Sofal*, leaving only sufficient to equip the officers of the ill-starred vessel. This work was entrusted to Kiron and was carried out by our own men, while Gamfor, with a contingent of our new-made prisoners, carried all of the *Sovong*'s surplus provisions aboard our own ship. This done, I ordered all the *Sovong*'s guns thrown overboard—by that much at least I would cripple the power of Thora. The last act in this drama of the sea was to march our one hundred imprisoned malcontents from the *Sofal* to the *Sovong* and present them to the latter's new commander with my compliments. He did not seem greatly pleased, however, nor could I blame him. Neither were the prisoners pleased. Many of them begged me to take them back aboard the *Sofal*; but I already had more men than I felt were needed to navigate and defend the ship; and each of the prisoners had been reported as having expressed disapproval of some part or all of our plan; so that I, who must have absolute loyalty and cooperation, considered them valueless to me.

Kodj, strange to say, was the most persistent. He almost went on his knees as he pleaded with me to permit him to remain with the *Sofal*, and he promised me such loyalty as man had never known before; but I had had enough of Kodj and told him so. Then, when he found that I could not be moved, he turned upon me, swearing by all his ancestors that he would get even with me yet, even though it took a thousand years.

Returning to the deck of the *Sofal*, I ordered the grappling hooks cast off; and presently the two ships were under way again, the *Sovong* proceeding toward the Thoran port that was her destination, the *Sofal* back toward Vepaja. Now, for the first time, I had opportunity to inquire into our losses and found that we had suffered four killed and twenty-one wounded, the casualties among the crew of the *Sovong* having been much higher.

For the greater part of the remainder of the day I was busy with my officers organizing the personnel of the *Sofal* and systematizing the activities of this new and unfamiliar venture, in which work Kiron and Gamfor were of inestimable value; and it was not until late in the afternoon that I had an opportunity to inquire into the welfare of the rescued Vepajan captives. When I asked Kamlot about them, he said that they were none the worse for their captivity aboard the *Sovong*.

"You see, these raiding parties have orders to bring the women to Thora unharmed and in good condition," he explained. "They are destined for more important persons than ships' officers, and that is their safeguard."

"However, Duare said that notwithstanding this, the captain made advances to her. I wish I might have known it while I was still aboard the *Sovong*, that I might have killed him for his presumption." Kamlot's tone was bitter and he showed signs of unusual excitement.

"Let your mind rest at ease," I begged him; "Duare has been avenged."

"What do you mean?"

"I killed the captain myself," I explained.

He clapped a hand upon my shoulder, his eyes alight with pleasure. "Again you have won the undying gratitude of Vepaja," he cried. "I wish that it might have been my good fortune to have killed the beast and thus wiped out the insult upon Vepaja, but if I could not be the one, then I am glad that it was you, Carson, rather than another."

I thought that he took the matter rather seriously and was placing too much importance upon the action of the *Sovong*'s captain, since it had resulted in no harm to the girl; but then, of course, I realized that love plays strange tricks upon a man's mental processes, so that an affront to a mistress might be magnified to the proportions of a national calamity.

"Well, it is all over now," I said, "and your sweetheart has been returned to you safe and sound."

At that he looked horrified. "My sweetheart!" he exclaimed. "In the name of the ancestors of all the jongs! Do you mean to tell me that you do not know who Duare is?"

"I thought of course that she was the girl you loved," I confessed. "Who is she?"

"Of course I love her," he explained; "all Vepaja loves her—she is the virgin daughter of a Vepajan jong!"

Had he been announcing the presence of a goddess on shipboard, his tone could have been no more reverential and awed. I endeavored to appear more impressed than I was, lest I offend him.

"Had she been the woman of your choice," I said, "I should have been even more pleased to have had a part in her rescue than had she been the daughter of a dozen jongs."

"That is nice of you," he replied, "but do not let other Vepajans hear you say such things. You have told me of the divinities of that strange world from which you come; the persons of the jong and his children are similarly sacred to us."

"Then, of course, they shall be sacred to me," I assured him.

"By the way, I have word for you that should please you—a Vepajan would consider it a high honor. Duare desires to see you, that she may thank you personally. It is irregular, of course; but then circumstances have rendered strict adherence to the etiquette and customs of our country impracticable, if not impossible. Several hundred men already have looked upon her, many have spoken to her, and nearly all of them were enemies; so it can do no harm if she sees and speaks with her defenders and her friends."

I did not understand what he was driving at, but I assented to what he had said and told him that I would pay my respects to the princess before the day was over.

I was very busy; and, if the truth must be told, I was not particularly excited about visiting the princess. In fact, I rather dreaded it, for I am not particularly keen about fawning and kowtowing to royalty or anything else; but I decided that out of respect for Kamlot's feelings I must get the thing over as soon as possible, and after he had left to attend to some duty, I made my way to the quarters allotted to Duare on the second deck.

The Amtorians do not knock on a door—they whistle. It is rather an improvement, I think, upon our custom. One has one's own distinctive whistle. Some of them are quite elaborate airs. One soon learns to recognize the signals of one's friends. A knock merely informs you that someone wishes to enter; a whistle tells you the same thing and also reveals the identity of your caller.

My signal, which is very simple, consists of two short low notes followed by a higher longer note; and as I stood before the door of Duare and sounded this, my mind was not upon the princess within but upon another girl far away in the tree city of Kooaad, in Vepaja. She was often in my mind—the girl whom I had glimpsed but twice, to whom I had spoken but once and that time to avow a love that had enveloped me as completely, spontaneously, and irrevocably as would death upon some future day.

In response to my signal a soft, feminine voice bade me enter. I stepped into the room and faced Duare. At sight of me her eyes went wide and a quick flush mounted her cheeks. "You!" she exclaimed.

I was equally dumfounded—she was the girl from the garden of the jong!

CHAPTER TWELVE
"A SHIP!"

WHAT A STRANGE *CONTRETEMPS*! Its suddenness left me temporarily speechless; the embarrassment of Duare was only too obvious. Yet it was that unusual paradox, a happy *contretemps*—for me at least.

I advanced toward her, and there must have been a great deal more in my eyes than I realized, for she shrank back, flushing even more deeply than before.

"Don't touch me!" she whispered. "Don't dare!"

"Have I ever harmed you?" I asked.

That question seemed to bring her confidence. She shook her head. "No," she admitted, "you never have—physically. I sent for you to thank you for the service you have already rendered me; but I did not know it was *you*. I did not know that the Carson they spoke of was the man who—" She stopped there and looked at me appealingly.

"The man who told you in the garden of the jong that he loved you," I prompted her.

"Don't!" she cried. "Can it be that you do not realize the offensiveness, the criminality of such a declaration?"

"Is it a crime to love you?" I asked.

"It is a crime to tell me so," she replied with something of haughtiness.

"Then I am a confirmed criminal," I replied, "for I cannot help telling you that I love you, whenever I see you."

"If that is the case, you must not see me again, for you must never again speak those words to me," she said decisively. "Because of the service you have rendered me, I forgive you your past offenses; but do not repeat them."

"What if I can't help it?" I inquired.

"You must help it," she stated seriously; "it is a matter of life and death to you."

Her words puzzled me. "I do not understand what you mean," I admitted.

"Kamlot, Honan, any of the Vepajans aboard this ship would kill you if they knew," she replied. "The jong, my father, would have you destroyed upon our return to Vepaja—it would all depend upon whom I told first."

I came a little closer to her and looked straight into her eyes. "You would never tell," I whispered.

"Why not? What makes you think that?" she demanded, but her voice quavered a little.

"Because you want me to love you," I challenged her.

She stamped her foot angrily. "You are beyond reason or forbearance or decency!" she exclaimed. "Leave my cabin at once; I do not wish ever to see you again."

Her bosom was heaving, her beautiful eyes were flashing, she was very close to me, and an impulse seized me to take her in my arms. I wanted to crush her body to mine, I wanted to cover her lips with kisses; but more than all else I wanted her love, and so I restrained myself, for fear that I might go too far and lose the chance to win the love that I felt was hovering just below the threshold of her consciousness. I do not know why I was so sure of that, but I was. I could not have brought myself to force my attentions upon a woman to whom they were repugnant, but from the first moment that I had seen this girl watching me from the garden in Vepaja, I had been impressed by an inner consciousness of her interest in me, her more than simple interest. It was just one of those things that are the children of old Chand Kabi's training, a training that has made me infinitely more intuitive than a woman.

"I am sorry that you are sending me away into virtual exile," I said. "I do not feel that I deserve that, but of course the standards of your world are not the standards of mine. There, a woman is not dishonored by the love of a man, or by its avowal, unless she is already married to another," and then of a sudden a thought occurred to me that should have occurred before. "Do you already belong to some man?" I demanded, chilled by the thought.

"Of course not!" she snapped. "I am not yet nineteen." I wondered that it had never before occurred to me that the girl in the garden of the jong might be already married.

I did not know what that had to do with it, but I was glad to learn that she was not seven hundred years old. I had often wondered about her age, though after all it could have made no difference, since on Venus, if anywhere in the universe, people are really no older than they look—I mean, as far as their attractiveness is concerned.

"Are you going?" she demanded, "or shall I have to call one of the Vepajans and tell them that you have affronted me?"

"And have me killed?" I asked. "No, you cannot make me believe that you would ever do that."

"Then *I* shall leave," she stated, "and remember that you are never to see me or speak to me again."

With that parting and far from cheering ultimatum she quit the room, going into another of her suite. That appeared to end the interview; I could not very well follow her, and so I turned and made my way disconsolately to the captain's cabin in the tower.

As I thought the matter over, it became obvious to me that I not only had not made much progress in my suit, but that there was little likelihood that I ever should. There seemed to be some insuperable barrier between us, though what it was I could not imagine. I could not believe that she was entirely indifferent to me; but perhaps that was just a reflection of my egotism, for I had to admit that she had certainly made it plain enough both by words and acts that she wished to have nothing to do with me. I was unquestionably *persona non grata*.

Notwithstanding all this, or maybe because of it, I realized that this second and longer interview had but served to raise my passion to still greater heat, leaving me in a fine state of despair. Her near presence on board the *Sofal* was constantly provocative, while her interdiction of any relations between us only tended to make me more anxious to be with her. I was most unhappy, and the monotony of the now uneventful voyage back toward Vepaja offered no means of distraction. I wished that we might sight another vessel, for any ship that we sighted would be an enemy ship. We were outlaws, we of the *Sofal*—pirates, buccaneers, privateers. I rather leaned toward the last and most polite definition of our status. Of course we had not as yet been commissioned by Mintep to raid shipping for Vepaja, but we were striking at Vepaja's enemies, and so I felt that we had some claim upon the dubious respectability of privateerism. However, either of the other two titles would not have greatly depressed me. Buccaneer has a devil-may-care ring to it that appeals to my fancy; it has a trifle more *haut ton* than pirate.

There is much in a name. I had liked the name of the *Sofal* from the first. Perhaps it was the psychology of that name that suggested the career upon which I was now launched. It means killer. The verb meaning kill is *fal*. The prefix *so* has the same value as the suffix *er* in English; so *sofal* means killer. *Vong* is the Amtorian word for defend; therefore, *Sovong*, the name of our first prize, means defender; but the *Sovong* had not lived up to her name.

I was still meditating on names in an effort to forget Duare, when Kamlot joined me, and I decided to take the opportunity to ask him some questions concerning certain Amtorian customs that regulated the social intercourse between men and maids. He opened a way to the subject by asking me if I had seen Duare since she sent for me.

"I saw her," I replied, "but I do not understand her attitude, which suggested that it was almost a crime for me to look at her."

"It would be under ordinary circumstances," he told me, "but of course, as I explained to you before, what she and we have passed through has temporarily at least minimized the importance of certain time-honored Vepajan laws and customs.

"Vepajan girls attain their majority at the age of twenty; prior to that they may not form a union with a man. The custom, which has almost the force of a law, places even greater restrictions upon the daughters of a jong. They may not even see or speak to any man other than their blood relatives and a few well-chosen retainers until after they have reached their twentieth birthday. Should they transgress, it would mean disgrace for them and death for the man."

"What a fool law!" I ejaculated, but I realized at last how heinous my transgression must have appeared in the eyes of Duare.

Kamlot shrugged. "It may be a fool law," he said, "but it is still the law; and in the case of Duare its enforcement means much to Vepaja, for she is the hope of Vepaja."

I had heard that title conferred upon her before, but it was meaningless to me. "Just what do you mean by saying that she is the hope of Vepaja?" I asked.

"She is Mintep's only child. He has never had a son, though a hundred women have sought to bear him one. The life of the dynasty ends if Duare bears no son; and if she is to bear a son, then it is essential that the father of that son be one fitted to be the father of a jong."

"Have they selected the father of her children yet?" I asked.

"Of course not," replied Kamlot. "The matter will not even be broached until after Duare has passed her twentieth birthday."

"And she is not even nineteen yet," I remarked with a sigh.

"No," agreed Kamlot, eyeing me closely, "but you act as though that fact were of importance to you."

"It is," I admitted.

"What do you mean?" he demanded.

"I intend to marry Duare!"

Kamlot leaped to his feet and whipped out his sword. It was the first time that I had ever seen him show marked excitement. I thought he was going to kill me on the spot.

"Defend yourself!" he cried. "I cannot kill you until you draw."

"Just why do you wish to kill me at all?" I demanded. "Have you gone crazy?"

The point of Kamlot's sword dropped slowly toward the floor. "I do not wish to kill you," he said rather sadly, all the nervous excitement gone from his manner. "You are my friend, you have saved my life—no, I would rather die myself than kill you, but the thing you have just said demands it."

I shrugged my shoulders; the thing was inexplicable to me. "What did I say that demands death?" I demanded.

"That you intend to marry Duare."

"In my world," I told him, "men are killed for saying that they do *not* intend marrying some girl." I had been sitting at the desk in my cabin at the time that Kamlot had threatened me, and I had not arisen; now I stood up and faced him. "You had better kill me, Kamlot," I said, "for I spoke the truth."

He hesitated for a moment, standing there looking at me; then he returned his sword to its scabbard. "I cannot," he said huskily. "May my ancestors forgive me! I cannot kill my friend.

"Perhaps," he added, seeking some extenuating circumstance, "you should not be held accountable to customs of which you had no knowledge. I often forget that you are of another world than ours. But tell me, now that I have made myself a party to your crime by excusing it, what leads you to believe that you will marry Duare? I can incriminate myself no more by listening to you further."

"I intend to marry her, because I know that I love her and believe that she already half loves me."

At this Kamlot appeared shocked and horrified again. "That is impossible," he cried. "She never saw you before; she cannot dream what is in your heart or your mad brain."

"On the contrary, she has seen me before; and she knows quite well what is in my 'mad brain,'" I assured him. "I told her in Kooaad; I told her again today."

"And she listened?"

"She was shocked," I admitted, "but she listened; then she upbraided me and ordered me from her presence."

Kamlot breathed a sigh of relief. "At least *she* has not gone mad. I cannot understand on what you base your belief that she may return your love."

"Her eyes betrayed her; and, what may be more convincing, she did not expose my perfidy and thus send me to my death."

He pondered that and shook his head. "It is all madness," he said; "I can make nothing of it. You say that you talked with her in Kooaad, but that would have been impossible. But if you had ever even seen her before, why did you show so little interest in her fate when you knew that she was a prisoner aboard the *Sovong*? Why did you say that you thought that she was my sweetheart?"

"I did not know until a few minutes ago," I explained, "that the girl I saw and talked with in the garden at Kooaad was Duare, the daughter of the jong."

A few days later I was again talking with Kamlot in my cabin when we were interrupted by a whistle at the door; and when I had bade him do so, one of the Vepajan prisoners that we had rescued from the *Sovong* entered. He was not from Kooaad but from another city of Vepaja, and therefore none of the other Vepajans aboard knew anything concerning him. His name was Vilor, and he appeared to be a decent sort of fellow, though rather inclined to taciturnity. He had manifested considerable interest in the klangan and was with them often, but had explained this idiosyncrasy on the grounds that he was a scholar and wished to study the birdmen, specimens of which he had never before seen.

"I have come," he explained in response to my inquiry, "to ask you to appoint me an officer. I should like to join your company and share in the work and responsibilities of the expedition."

"We are well officered now," I explained, "and have all the men we need. Furthermore," I added frankly, "I do not know you well enough to be sure of your qualifications. By the time we reach Vepaja, we shall be better acquainted; and if I need you then, I will tell you."

"Well, I should like to do something," he insisted. "May I guard the janjong until we reach Vepaja?"

He referred to Duare, whose title, compounded of the two words daughter and king, is synonymous to princess. I thought that I noticed just a trace of excitement in his voice as he made the request.

"She is well guarded now," I explained.

"But I should like to do it," he insisted. "It would be a service of love and loyalty for my jong. I could stand the night guard; no one likes that detail ordinarily."

"It will not be necessary," I said shortly; "the guard is already sufficient."

"She is in the after cabins of the second deck house, is she not?" he asked.

I told him that she was.

"And she has a special guard?"

"A man is always before her door at night," I assured him.

"Only one?" he demanded, as though he thought the guard insufficient.

"In addition to the regular watch, we consider one man enough; she has no enemies aboard the *Sofal*." These people were certainly solicitous of the welfare and safety of their royalty, I thought; and, it seemed to me, unnecessarily so. But finally Vilor gave up and departed, after begging me to give his request further thought.

"He seems even more concerned about the welfare of Duare than you," I remarked to Kamlot after Vilor had gone.

"Yes, I noticed that," replied my lieutenant thoughtfully.

"There is no one more concerned about her than I," I said, "but I cannot see that any further precautions are necessary."

"Nor I," agreed Kamlot; "she is quite well protected now."

We had dropped Vilor from our minds and were discussing other matters, when we heard the voice of the lookout in the crow's nest shouting, "Voo notar!" ("A ship!") Running to the tower deck, we got the bearings of the stranger as the lookout announced them the second time, and, sure enough, almost directly abeam on the starboard side we discerned the superstructure of a ship on the horizon.

For some reason which I do not clearly understand, the visibility on Venus is usually exceptionally good. Low fogs and haze are rare, notwithstanding the humidity of the atmosphere. This condition may be due to the mysterious radiation from that strange element in the planet's structure which illuminates her moonless nights; I do not know.

At any rate, we could see a ship, and almost immediately all was excitement aboard the *Sofal*. Here was another prize, and the men were eager to be at her. As we changed our course and headed for our victim, a cheer rose from the men on deck. Weapons were issued, the bow gun and the two tower guns were elevated to firing positions. The *Sofal* forged ahead at full speed.

As we approached our quarry, we saw that it was a ship of about the same size as the *Sofal* and bearing the insignia of Thora. Closer inspection revealed it to be an armed merchantman.

I now ordered all but the gunners into the lower deck house, as I planned on boarding this vessel as I had the *Sovong* and did not wish her to see our deck filled with armed men before we came alongside. As before, explicit orders were issued; every man knew what was expected of him; all were cautioned against needless killing. If I were to be a pirate, I was going to be as humane a pirate as possible. I would not spill blood needlessly.

I had questioned Kiron, Gamfor, and many another Thoran in my company relative to the customs and practices of Thoran ships of war until

I felt reasonably familiar with them. I knew for instance that a warship might search a merchantman. It was upon this that I based my hope of getting our grappling hooks over the side of our victim before he could suspect our true design.

When we were within hailing distance of the ship, I directed Kiron to order her to shut down her engines, as we wished to board and search her; and right then we ran into our first obstacle. It came in the form of a pennant suddenly hoisted at the bow of our intended victim. It meant nothing to me, but it did to Kiron and the other Thorans aboard the *Sofal*.

"We'll not board her so easily after all," said Kiron. "She has an ongyan on board, and that exempts her from search. It probably also indicates that she carries a larger complement of soldiers than a merchantman ordinarily does."

"Whose friend?" I asked, "Yours?" for ongyan means great friend, in the sense of eminent or exalted.

Kiron smiled. "It is a title. There are a hundred klongyan in the oligarchy; one of them is aboard that ship. They are great friends unquestionably, great friends of themselves; they rule Thora more tyrannically than any jong and for themselves alone."

"How will the men feel about attacking a ship bearing so exalted a personage?" I inquired.

"They will fight among themselves to be the first aboard and to run a sword through him."

"They must not kill him," I replied. "I have a better plan."

"They will be hard to control once they are in the thick of a fight," Kiron assured me; "I have yet to see the officer who can do it. In the old days, in the days of the jongs, there were order and discipline; but not now."

"There will be aboard the *Sofal*," I averred. "Come with me; I am going to speak to the men."

Together we entered the lower deck house where the majority of the ship's company was massed, waiting for the command to attack. There were nearly a hundred rough and burly fighting men, nearly all of whom were ignorant and brutal. We had been together as commander and crew for too short a time for me to gauge their sentiments toward me; but I realized that there must be no question in any mind as to who was captain of the ship, no matter what they thought of me.

Kiron had called them to attention as we entered, and now every eye was on me as I started to speak. "We are about to take another ship," I began, "on board which is one whom Kiron tells me you will want to kill. He is an ongyan. I have come here to tell you that he must not be killed." Growls of disapproval greeted this statement, but, ignoring them, I continued, "I have come here to tell you something else, because I have been informed that no officer can control you after you enter battle. There are reasons why it will be better for us to hold this man prisoner than to kill him, but these have nothing to do with the question; what you must understand is that my orders and the orders of your other officers must be obeyed.

"We are embarked upon an enterprise that can succeed only if discipline be enforced. I expect the enterprise to succeed. I will enforce discipline. Insubordination or disobedience will be punishable by death. That is all."

As I left the room, I left behind me nearly a hundred silent men. There was nothing to indicate what their reaction had been. Purposely, I took Kiron out with me; I wanted the men to have an opportunity to discuss the matter among themselves without interference by an officer. I knew that I had no real authority over them, and that eventually they must decide for themselves whether they would obey me; the sooner that decision was reached the better for all of us.

Amtorian ships employ only the most primitive means of intercommunication. There is a crude and cumbersome hand signaling system in which flags are employed; then there is a standardized system of trumpet calls which covers a fairly wide range of conventional messages, but the most satisfactory medium and the one most used is the human voice.

Since our quarry had displayed the pennant of the ongyan, we had held a course parallel to hers and a little distance astern. On her main deck a company of armed men was congregated. She mounted four guns, which had been elevated into firing position. She was ready, but I think that as yet she suspected nothing wrong in our intentions.

Now I gave orders that caused the *Sofal* to close in upon the other ship, and as the distance between them lessened I saw indications of increasing excitement on the decks of our intended victim.

"What are you about?" shouted an officer from her tower deck. "Stand off there! There is an ongyan aboard us."

As no reply was made him, and as the *Sofal* continued to draw nearer, his excitement waxed. He gesticulated rapidly as he conversed with a fat man standing at his side; then he screamed, "Stand off! or someone will suffer for this"; but the *Sofal* only moved steadily closer. "Stand off, or I'll fire!" shouted the captain.

For answer I caused all our starboard guns to be elevated into firing position. I knew he would not dare fire now, for a single broadside from the *Sofal* would have sunk him in less than a minute, a contingency which I wished to avoid as much as he.

"What do you want of us?" he demanded.

"We want to board you," I replied, "without bloodshed if possible."

"This is revolution! This is treason!" shouted the fat man at the captain's side. "I order you to stand off and leave us alone. I am the ongyan, Moosko," and then to the soldiers on the main deck he screamed, "Repel them! Kill any man who sets foot upon that deck!"

Chapter Thirteen
Catastrophe

A T THE SAME MOMENT THAT THE ONGYAN, Moosko, ordered his soldiers to repel any attempt to board his ship, her captain ordered full speed ahead and threw her helm to starboard. She veered away from us and leaped ahead in an effort to escape. Of course I could have sunk her, but her loot would have been of no value to me at the bottom of the sea; instead I directed the trumpeter at my side to sound full speed ahead to the officer in the tower, and the chase was on.

The *Yan*, whose name was now discernible across her stern, was much faster than Kiron had led me to believe; but the *Sofal* was exceptionally speedy, and it soon became obvious to all that the other ship could not escape her. Slowly we regained the distance that we had lost in the first, unexpected spurt of the *Yan*; slowly but surely we were closing up on her.

Then the captain of the *Yan* did just what I should have done had I been in his place; he kept the *Sofal* always directly astern of him and opened fire on us with his after tower gun and with a gun similarly placed in the stern on the lower deck. The maneuver was tactically faultless, since it greatly reduced the number of guns that we could bring into play without changing our course, and was the only one that might offer him any hope of escape.

There was something eerie in the sound of that first heavy Amtorian gun that I had heard. I saw nothing, neither smoke nor flame; there was only a loud staccato roar more reminiscent of machine gun fire than of any other sound. At first there was no other effect; then I saw a piece of our starboard rail go and two of my men fall to the deck.

By this time our bow gun was in action. We were in the swell of the *Yan*'s wake, which made accurate firing difficult. The two ships were racing ahead at full speed; the prow of the *Sofal* was throwing white water and spume far to either side; the sea in the wake of the *Yan* was boiling, and a heavy swell that we were quartering kept the ships rolling. The thrill of the chase and of battle was in our blood, and above all was the venomous rattle of the big guns.

I ran to the bow to direct the fire of the gun there, and a moment later we had the satisfaction of seeing the crew of one of the *Yan*'s guns crumple to the deck man by man, as our gunner got his sights on them and mowed them down.

The *Sofal* was gaining rapidly upon the *Yan*, and our guns were concentrating on the tower gun and the tower of the enemy. The ongyan had long since disappeared from the upper deck, having doubtlessly sought safety in a less exposed part of the ship, and in fact there were only two men left alive upon the tower deck where he had stood beside the captain; these were two of the crew of the gun that was giving us most trouble.

I did not understand at the time why the guns of neither ship were more effective. I knew that the T-ray was supposedly highly destructive, and so I could not understand why neither ship had been demolished or sunk; but that was because I had not yet learned that all the vital parts of the ships were protected by a thin armor of the same metal of which the large guns were composed, the only substance at all impervious to the T-ray. Had this not been true, our fire would have long since put the *Yan* out of commission, as our T-rays, directed upon her after tower gun, would have passed on through the tower, killing the men at the controls and destroying the controls themselves. Eventually this would have happened, but it would have been necessary first to have destroyed the protective armor of the tower.

At last we succeeded in silencing the remaining gun, but if we were to draw up alongside the *Yan* we must expose ourselves to the fire of other guns located on her main deck and the forward end of the tower. We had already suffered some losses, and I knew that we must certainly expect a great many more if we put ourselves in range of those other guns; but there seemed no other alternative than to abandon the chase entirely, and that I had no mind to do.

Giving orders to draw up along her port side, I directed the fire of the bow gun along her rail where it would rake her port guns one by one as we moved up on her, and gave orders that each of our starboard guns in succession should open fire similarly as they came within range of the *Yan*'s guns. Thus we kept a steady and continuous fire streaming upon the unhappy craft as we drew alongside her and closed up the distance between us.

We had suffered a number of casualties, but our losses were nothing compared to those of the *Yan*, whose decks were now strewn with dead and dying men. Her plight was hopeless, and her commander must at last have realized it, for now he gave the signal of surrender and stopped his engines. A few minutes later we were alongside and our boarding party had clambered over her rail.

As Kamlot and I stood watching these men who were being led by Kiron to take possession of the prize and bring certain prisoners aboard the *Sofal*, I could not but speculate upon what their answer was to be to my challenge for leadership. I knew that their freedom from the constant menace of their tyrannical masters was so new to them that they might well be expected to commit excesses, and I dreaded the result, for I had determined to make an example of any men who disobeyed me, though I fell in the attempt. I saw the majority of them spread over the deck under the command of the great Zog, while Kiron led a smaller detachment to the upper decks in search of the captain and the ongyan.

Fully five minutes must have elapsed before I saw my lieutenant emerge from the tower of the *Yan* with his two prisoners. He conducted them down the companionway and across the main deck toward the *Sofal*, while a hundred members of my pirate band watched them in silence. Not a hand was raised against them as they passed.

Kamlot breathed a sigh of relief as the two men clambered over the rail of the *Sofal* and approached us. "I think that our lives hung in the balance then, quite as much as theirs," he said, and I agreed with him, for if my men had started killing aboard the *Yan* in defiance of my orders, they would have had to kill me and those loyal to me to protect their own lives.

The ongyan was still blustering when they were halted in front of me, but the captain was awed. There was something about the whole incident that mystified him, and when he got close enough to me to see the color of my hair and eyes, I could see that he was dumfounded.

"This is an outrage," shouted Moosko, the ongyan. "I will see that every last man of you is destroyed for this." He was trembling, and purple with rage.

"See that he does not speak again unless he is spoken to," I instructed Kiron, and then I turned to the captain. "As soon as we have taken what we wish from your ship," I told him, "you will be free to continue your voyage. I am sorry that you did not see fit to obey me when I ordered you to stop for boarding; it would have saved many lives. The next time you are ordered to lay to by the *Sofal*, do so; and when you return to your own country, advise other shipmasters that the *Sofal* is abroad and that she is to be obeyed."

"Do you mind telling me," he asked, "who you are and under what flag you sail?"

"For the moment I am a Vepajan," I replied, "but we sail under our own flag. No country is responsible for what we do, nor are we responsible to any country."

Pressing the crew of the *Yan* into service, Kamlot, Kiron, Gamfor, and Zog had all her weapons, such of her provisions as we wished, and the most valuable and least bulky portion of her cargo transferred to the *Sofal* before dark. We then threw her guns overboard and let her proceed upon her way.

Moosko I retained as a hostage in the event that we should ever need one; he was being held under guard on the main deck until I could determine just what to do with him. The Vepajan women captives we had rescued from the *Sovong*, together with our own officers who were also quartered on the second deck, left me no vacant cabin in which to put Moosko, and I did not wish to confine him below deck in the hole reserved for common prisoners.

I chanced to mention the matter to Kamlot in the presence of Vilor, when the latter immediately suggested that he would share his own small cabin with Moosko and be responsible for him. As this seemed an easy solution of the problem, I ordered Moosko turned over to Vilor, who took him at once to his cabin.

The pursuit of the *Yan* had taken us off our course, and now, as we headed once more toward Vepaja, a dark land mass was dimly visible to starboard. I could not but wonder what mysteries lay beyond that shadowy coastline, what strange beasts and men inhabited that *terra incognita* that stretched away into Strabol and the unexplored equatorial regions of Venus. To partially satisfy my curiosity, I went to the chart room, and after determining our position as accurately as I could by dead reckoning, I discovered that we were off the shore of Noobol. I remembered having heard Danus mention this country, but I could not recall what he had told me about it.

Lured by imaginings, I went out onto the tower deck and stood alone, looking out across the faintly illuminated nocturnal waters of Amtor toward mysterious Noobol. The wind had risen to almost the proportions of a gale, the first that I had encountered since my coming to the Shepherd's Star; heavy seas were commencing to run, but I had every confidence in the ship and in the ability of my officers to navigate her under any circumstances; so I was not perturbed by the increasing violence of the storm. It occurred to me though that the women aboard might be frightened, and my thoughts, which were seldom absent from her for long, returned to Duare. Perhaps she was frightened!

Even no excuse is a good excuse to the man who wishes to see the object of his infatuation; but now I prided myself that I had a real reason for seeing her and one that she herself must appreciate, since it was prompted by solicitude for her welfare. And so I went down the companionway to the second deck with the intention of whistling before the door of Duare; but as I had to pass directly by Vilor's cabin, I thought that I would take the opportunity to look in on my prisoner.

There was a moment's silence following my signal, and then Vilor bade me enter. As I stepped into the cabin, I was surprised to see an angan sitting there with Moosko and Vilor. Vilor's embarrassment was obvious; Moosko appeared ill at ease and the birdman frightened. That they were disconcerted did not surprise me, for it is not customary for members of the superior race to fraternize with klangan socially. But if they were embarrassed, I was not. I was more inclined to be angry. The position of the Vepajans aboard the *Sofal* was a delicate one. We were few in numbers, and our ascendency depended wholly upon the respect we engendered and maintained in the minds of the Thorans, who constituted the majority of our company, and who looked up to the Vepajans as their superiors despite the efforts of their leaders to convince them of the equality of all men.

"Your quarters are forward," I said to the angan; "you do not belong here."

"It is not his fault," said Vilor, as the birdman rose to leave the cabin. "Moosko, strange as it may seem, had never seen an angan; and I fetched this fellow here merely to satisfy his curiosity. I am sorry if I did wrong."

"Of course," I said, "that puts a slightly different aspect on the matter, but I think it will be better if the prisoner inspects the klangan on deck where they belong. He has my permission to do so tomorrow."

The angan departed, I exchanged a few more words with Vilor, and then I left him with his prisoner and turned toward the after cabin where Duare was quartered, the episode that had just occurred fading from my mind almost immediately, to be replaced by far more pleasant thoughts.

There was a light in Duare's cabin as I whistled before her door, wondering if she would invite me in or ignore my presence. For a time there was no response to my signal, and I had about determined that she would not see me, when I heard her soft, low voice inviting me to enter.

"You are persistent," she said, but there was less anger in her voice than when last she had spoken to me.

"I came to ask if the storm has frightened you and to assure you that there is no danger."

"I am not afraid," she replied. "Was that all that you wished to say?"

It sounded very much like a dismissal. "No," I assured her, "nor did I come solely for the purpose of saying it."

She raised her eyebrows. "What else could you have to say to me—that you have not already said?"

"Perhaps I wished to repeat," I suggested.

"You must not!" she cried.

I came closer to her. "Look at me, Duare; look me in the eyes and tell me that you do not like to hear me tell you that I love you!"

Her eyes fell. "I must not listen!" she whispered and rose as though to leave the room.

I was mad with love for her; her near presence sent the hot blood boiling through my veins; I seized her in my arms and drew her to me; before she could prevent it, I covered her lips with mine. Then she partially tore away from me, and I saw a dagger gleaming in her hand.

"You are right," I said. "Strike! I have done an unforgivable thing. My only excuse is my great love for you; it swept away reason and honor."

Her dagger hand dropped to her side. "I cannot," she sobbed, and, turning, fled from the room.

I went back to my own cabin, cursing myself for a beast and a cad. I could not understand how it had been possible for me to have committed such an unpardonable act. I reviled myself, and at the same time the memory of that soft body crushed against mine and those perfect lips against my lips suffused me with a warm glow of contentment that seemed far removed from repentance.

I lay awake for a long time after I went to bed, thinking of Duare, recalling all that had ever passed between us. I found a hidden meaning in her cry, "I must not listen!" I rejoiced in the facts that once she had refused to consign me to death at the hands of others and that again she had refused to kill me herself. Her "I cannot" rang in my ears almost like an avowal of love. My better judgment told that I was quite mad, but I found joy in hugging my madness to me.

The storm increased to such terrific fury during the night that the screeching of the wind and the wild plunging of the *Sofal* awakened me just before dawn. Arising immediately, I went on deck, where the wind almost carried me away. Great waves lifted the *Sofal* on high, only to plunge her the next moment into watery abysses. The ship was pitching violently; occasionally a huge wave broke across her bow and flooded the main deck; across her starboard quarter loomed a great land mass that seemed perilously close. The situation appeared fraught with danger.

I entered the control room and found both Honan and Gamfor with the helmsman. They were worried because of our proximity to land. Should either the engines or the steering device fail, we must inevitably be driven ashore. I told them to remain where they were, and then I went down to the second deck house to arouse Kiron, Kamlot, and Zog.

As I turned aft from the foot of the companionway on the second deck, I noticed that the door of Vilor's cabin was swinging open and closing again with each roll of the vessel; but I gave the matter no particular thought at the time and passed on to awaken my other lieutenants.

Having done so, I kept on to Duare's cabin, fearing that, if awake, she might be frightened by the rolling of the ship and the shrieking of the wind. To my surprise, I found her door swinging on its hinges.

Something, I do not know what, aroused my suspicion that all was not right far more definitely than the rather unimportant fact that the door to her outer cabin was unlatched. Stepping quickly inside, I uncovered the light and glanced quickly about the room. There was nothing amiss except, perhaps, the fact that the door to the inner cabin where she slept was also open and swinging on its hinges. I was sure that no one could be sleeping in there while both those doors were swinging and banging. It was possible, of course, that Duare was too frightened to get up and close them.

I stepped to the inner doorway and called her name aloud. There was no reply. I called again, louder; again, silence was my only answer. Now I was definitely perturbed. Stepping into the room, I uncovered the light and looked at the bed. It was empty—Duare was not there! But in the far corner of the cabin lay the body of the man who had stood guard outside her door.

Throwing conventions overboard, I hastened to each of the adjoining cabins where the rest of the Vepajan women were quartered. All were there except Duare. They had not seen her; they did not know where she was. Frantic from apprehension, I ran back to Kamlot's cabin and acquainted him with my tragic discovery. He was stunned.

"She must be on board," he cried. "Where else can she be?"

"I know she *must* be," I replied, "but something tells me she is not. We must search the ship at once—from stem to stern."

Zog and Kiron were emerging from their cabins as I came from Kamlot's. I told them of my discovery and ordered the search commenced; then I hailed a member of the watch and sent him to the crow's nest to question the lookout. I wanted to know whether he had seen anything unusual transpiring on the ship during his watch, for from his lofty perch he could overlook the entire vessel.

"Muster every man," I told Kamlot; "account for every human being on board; search every inch of the ship."

As the men left to obey my instructions, I recalled the coincidence of the two cabin doors swinging wide—Duare's and Vilor's. I could not imagine what relation either fact had to the other, but I was investigating everything, whether it was of a suspicious nature or not; so I ran quickly to Vilor's cabin, and the moment that I uncovered the light I saw that both Vilor and Moosko were missing. But where were they? No man could have left the *Sofal* in that storm and lived, even could he have launched a boat, which would have been impossible of accomplishment, even in fair weather, without detection.

Coming from Vilor's cabin, I summoned a sailor and dispatched him to inform Kamlot that Vilor and Moosko were missing from their cabin and direct him to send them to me as soon as he located them; then I returned to the quarters of the Vepajan women for the purpose of questioning them more carefully.

I was puzzled by the disappearance of Moosko and Vilor, which, taken in conjunction with the absence of Duare from her cabin, constituted a mystery of major proportions; and I was trying to discover some link of circumstance that might point a connection between the two occurrences, when I suddenly recalled Vilor's insistence that he be permitted to guard Duare. Here was the first, faint suggestion of a connecting link. However, it seemed to lead nowhere. These three people had disappeared from their cabins, yet reason assured me that they would be found in a short time, since it was impossible for them to leave the ship, unless—

It was that little word "unless" that terrified me most of all. Since I had discovered that Duare was not in her cabin, a numbing fear had assailed me that, considering herself dishonored by my avowal of love, she had hurled herself overboard. Of what value now the fact that I constantly upbraided myself for my lack of consideration and control? Of what weight my vain regrets?

Yet now I saw a tiny ray of hope. If the absence of Vilor and Moosko from their cabin and Duare from hers were more than a coincidence, then it were safe to assume that they were together and ridiculous to believe that all three had leaped overboard.

With these conflicting fears and hopes whirling through my brain, I came to the quarters of the Vepajan women, which I was about to enter when the sailor I had sent to question the lookout in the crow's nest came running toward me in a state of evident excitement.

"Well," I demanded, as, breathless, he halted before me, "what did the lookout have to say?"

"Nothing, my captain," replied the man, his speech retarded by excitement and exertion.

"Nothing! and why not?" I snapped.

"The lookout is dead, my captain," gasped the sailor.

"Dead!"

"Murdered."

"How?" I asked.

"A sword had been run through his body—from behind, I think. He lay upon his face."

"Go at once and inform Kamlot; tell him to replace the lookout and investigate his death, then to report to me."

Shaken by this ominous news, I entered the quarters of the women. They were huddled together in one cabin, pale and frightened, but outwardly calm.

"Have you found Duare?" one of them asked immediately.

"No," I replied, "but I have discovered another mystery—the ongyan, Moosko, is missing and with him the Vepajan, Vilor."

"Vepajan!" exclaimed Byea, the woman who had questioned me concerning Duare. "Vilor is no Vepajan."

"What do you mean?" I demanded. "If he is not a Vepajan, what is he?"

"He is a Thoran spy," she replied. "He was sent to Vepaja long ago to steal the secret of the longevity serum, and when we were captured the klangan took him, also, by mistake. We learned this, little by little, aboard the *Sovong*."

"But why was I not informed when he was brought aboard?" I demanded.

"We supposed that everyone knew it," explained Byea, "and thought that Vilor was transferred to the *Sofal* as a prisoner."

Another link in the chain of accumulating evidence! Yet I was as far as ever from knowing where either end of the chain lay.

Chapter Fourteen
Storm

AFTER QUESTIONING THE WOMEN, I went to the main deck, too impatient to await the reports of my lieutenants in the tower where I belonged. I found that they had searched the ship and were just coming to me with their report. None of those previously discovered missing had been found, but the search had revealed another astounding fact—the five klangan also were missing!

Searching certain portions of the ship had been rather dangerous work, as she was rolling heavily, and the deck was still occasionally swept by the larger seas; but it had been accomplished without mishap, and the men were now congregated in a large room in the main deck house. Kamlot, Gamfor, Kiron, Zog, and I had also entered this same room, where we were discussing the whole mysterious affair. Honan was in the control room of the tower.

I told them that I had just discovered that Vilor was not Vepajan but a Thoran spy, and had reminded Kamlot of the man's request that he be allowed to guard the janjong. "I learned something else from Byea while I was questioning the women," I added. "During their captivity aboard the *Sovong*, Vilor persisted in annoying Duare with his attentions; he was infatuated with her."

"I think that gives us the last bit of evidence we need to enable us to reconstruct the hitherto seemingly inexplicable happenings of the past night," said Gamfor. "Vilor wished to possess Duare; Moosko wished to escape from captivity. The former had fraternized with the klangan and made friends of them; that was known to everyone aboard the *Sofal*. Moosko was an ongyan; during all their lives, doubtless, the klangan have looked upon the klongyan as the fountain heads of supreme authority. They would believe his promises, and they would obey his commands.

"Doubtless Vilor and Moosko worked out the details of the plot together. They dispatched an angan to kill the lookout, lest their movements arouse suspicion and be reported before they could carry their plan to a successful conclusion. The lookout disposed of, the other klangan congregated in Vilor's cabin; then Vilor, probably accompanied by Moosko, went to the cabin of Duare, where they killed the guard and seized her in her sleep, silenced her with a gag, and carried her to the gangway outside, where the klangan were waiting.

"A gale was blowing, it is true, but it was blowing toward land which lay but a short distance to starboard; and the klangan are powerful fliers.

"There you have what I believe to be a true picture of what happened aboard the *Sofal* while we slept."

"And you believe that the klangan carried these three people to the shores of Noobol?" I asked.

"I think there can be no question but that such is the fact," replied Gamfor.

"I quite agree with him," interjected Kamlot.

"Then there is but one thing to do," I announced. "We must turn back and land a searching party on Noobol."

"No boat could live in this sea," objected Kiron.

"The storm will not last forever," I reminded him. "We shall lie off the shore until it abates. I am going up to the tower; I wish you men would remain here and question the crew; it is possible that there may be someone among them who has overheard something that will cast new light on the subject. The klangan are great talkers, and they may have dropped some remark that will suggest the ultimate destination Vilor and Moosko had in mind."

As I stepped out onto the main deck, the *Sofal* rose upon the crest of a great wave and then plunged nose downward into the watery abyss beyond, tilting the deck forward at an angle of almost forty-five degrees. The wet and slippery boards beneath my feet gave them no hold, and I slid helplessly forward almost fifty feet before I could check my descent. Then the ship buried her nose in a mountainous wave and a great wall of water swept the deck from stem to stern, picking me up and whirling me helplessly upon its crest.

For a moment I was submerged, and then a vagary of the Titan that had seized me brought my head above the water, and I saw the *Sofal* rolling and pitching fifty feet away.

Even in the immensity of interstellar space I had never felt more helpless nor more hopeless than I did at that moment on the storm-lashed sea of an unknown world, surrounded by darkness and chaos and what terrible creatures of this mysterious deep I could not even guess. I was lost! Even if my comrades knew of the disaster that had overwhelmed me, they were helpless to give me aid. No boat could live in that sea, as Kiron had truly reminded us, and no swimmer could breast the terrific onslaught of those racing, wind-driven mountains of water that might no longer be described by so puny a word as wave.

Hopeless! I should not have said that; I am never without hope. If I could not swim against the sea, perhaps I might swim with it; and at no great distance lay land. I am an experienced distance swimmer and a powerful man. If any man could survive in such a sea, I knew that I could; but if I could not, I was determined that I should at least have the satisfaction of dying fighting.

I was hampered by no clothes, as one could scarcely dignify the Amtorian loincloth with the name of clothing; my only impediment was my weapons; and these I hesitated to discard, knowing that my chances for survival on that unfriendly shore would be slight were I unarmed. Neither the belt, nor the pistol, nor the dagger inconvenienced me, and their weight was negligible; but the sword was a different matter. If you have never tried swimming with a sword dangling from your middle, do not attempt it in a heavy sea. You might think that it would hang straight down and not get in the way, but mine did not. The great waves hurled me about mercilessly, twisting and turning me; and now my sword was buffeting me in some tender spot, and now it was getting between my legs, and once, when a wave turned me completely over, it came down on top of me and struck me on the head; yet I would not discard it.

After the first few minutes of battling with the sea, I concluded that I was in no immediate danger of being drowned. I could keep my head above the waves often enough and long enough to insure sufficient air for my lungs; and, the water being warm, I was in no danger of being chilled to exhaustion, as so often occurs when men are thrown into cold seas. Therefore, as closely as I could anticipate any contingency in this unfamiliar world, there remained but two major and immediate threats against my life. The first lay in the possibility of attack by some ferocious monster of the Amtorian deeps; the second, and by far the more serious, the storm-lashed shore upon which I must presently attempt to make a safe landing.

This in itself should have been sufficient to dishearten me, for I had seen seas breaking upon too many shores to lightly ignore the menace of

STORM 445

those incalculable tons of hurtling waters pounding, crashing, crushing, tearing their way even into the rocky heart of the eternal hills.

I swam slowly in the direction of the shore, which, fortunately for me, was in the direction that the storm was carrying me. I had no mind to sap my strength by unnecessarily overexerting myself; and so, as I took it easily, content to keep afloat as I moved slowly shoreward, daylight came; and as each succeeding wave lifted me to its summit, I saw the shore with increasing clearness. It lay about a mile from me, and its aspect was most forbidding. Huge combers were breaking upon a rocky coastline, throwing boiling fountains of white spume high in air; above the howling of the tempest, the thunder of the surf rolled menacingly across that mile of angry sea to warn me that death lay waiting to embrace me at the threshold of safety.

I was in a quandary. Death lay all about me; it remained but for me to choose the place and manner of the assignation; I could drown where I was, or I could permit myself to be dashed to pieces on the rocks. Neither eventuality aroused any considerable enthusiasm in my breast. As a mistress, death seemed sadly lacking in many essentials. Therefore, I decided not to die.

Thoughts may be, as has been said, things; but they are not everything. No matter how favorably I thought of living, I knew that I must also do something about it. My present situation offered me no chance of salvation; the shore alone could give me life; so I struck out for the shore. As I drew nearer it, many things, some of them quite irrelevant, passed through my mind; but some were relevant, among them the Burial Service. It was not a nice time to think of this, but then we cannot always control our thoughts; however, "In the midst of life we are in death" seemed wholly appropriate to my situation. By twisting it a bit, I achieved something that contained the germ of hope—in the midst of death there is life. Perhaps—

The tall waves, lifting me high, afforded me for brief instants vantage points from which I could view the death ahead in the midst of which I sought for life. The shoreline was becoming, at closer range, something more than an unbroken line of jagged rocks and white water; but details were yet lacking, for each time I was allowed but a brief glimpse before being dropped once more to the bottom of a watery chasm.

My own efforts, coupled with the fury of the gale driving me shoreward, brought me rapidly to the point where I should presently be seized by the infuriated seas and hurled upon the bombarded rocks that reared their jagged heads bleakly above the swirling waters of each receding comber.

A great wave lifted me upon its crest and carried me forward—the end had come! With the speed of a race horse it swept me toward my doom; a welter of spume engulfed my head; I was twisted and turned as a cork in a whirlpool; yet I struggled to lift my mouth above the surface for an occasional gasp of air; I fought to live for a brief moment longer, that I might not be dead when I was dashed by the merciless sea against the merciless rocks—thus dominating is the urge to live.

I was carried on; moments seemed an eternity! Where were the rocks? I almost yearned for them now to end the bitterness of my futile struggle. I thought of my mother and of Duare. I even contemplated, with something akin to philosophic calm, the strangeness of my end. In that other world that I had left forever no creature would ever have knowledge of my fate. Thus spoke the eternal egotism of man, who, even in death, desires an audience.

Now I caught a brief glimpse of rocks. They were upon my left! when they should have been in front of me. It was incomprehensible. The wave tore on, carrying me with it; and still I lived, and there was only water against my naked flesh.

Now the fury of the sea abated. I rose to the crest of a diminishing comber to look with astonishment upon the comparatively still waters of an inlet. I had been carried through the rocky gateway of a landlocked cove, and before me I saw a sandy crescent beach. I had escaped the black fingers of death; I had been the beneficiary of a miracle!

The sea gave me a final fillip that rolled me high upon the sands to mingle with the wrack and flotsam she had discarded. I stood up and looked about me. A more devout man would have given thanks, but I felt that as yet I had little for which to give thanks. My life had been spared temporarily, but Duare was still in peril.

The cove into which I had been swept was formed by the mouth of a canyon that ran inland between low hills, the sides and summits of which were dotted with small trees. Nowhere did I see any such giants as grow in Vepaja; but perhaps, I mused, what I see here are not trees on Venus but only underbrush. However, I shall call them trees, since many of them were from fifty to eighty feet in height.

A little river tumbled down the canyon's bottom to empty into the cove; pale violet grass, starred with blue and purple flowers, bordered it and clothed the hills. There were trees with red boles, smooth and glossy as lacquer. There were trees with azure boles. Whipping in the gale was the same weird foliage of heliotrope and lavender and violet that had rendered the forests of Vepaja so unearthly to my eyes. But beautiful and unusual as was the scene, it could not claim my undivided attention. A strange freak of fate had thrown me upon this shore to which, I had reason to believe, Duare must undoubtedly have been carried; and now my only thought was to take advantage of this fortunate circumstance and attempt to find and succor her.

I could only assume that in the event her abductors had brought her to this shore their landing must have been made farther along the coast to my right, which was the direction from which the *Sofal* had been moving. With only this slight and unsatisfactory clue, I started immediately to scale the side of the canyon and commence my search.

At the summit I paused a moment to survey the surrounding country and get my bearings. Before me stretched a rolling tableland, tree-dotted and lush with grass, and beyond that, inland, rose a range of mountains, vague and mysterious along the distant horizon. My course lay to the east, along the coast (I shall use the earthly references to points of compass); the mountains were northward, toward the equator. I am assuming of course that I am in the southern hemisphere of the planet. The sea was south of me. I glanced in that direction, looking for the *Sofal*; there she was, far out and moving toward the east. Evidently my orders were being carried out, and the *Sofal* was lying offshore waiting for calm weather that would permit a landing.

Now I turned my steps toward the east. At each elevation I stopped and scanned the tableland in all directions, searching for some sign of those I sought. I saw signs of life, but not of human life. Herbivorous animals grazed in large numbers upon the flower-starred violet plain. Many that were close enough to be seen plainly appeared similar in form to earthly animals, but there was none exactly like anything I had ever seen on Earth. Their extreme wariness and the suggestion of speed and agility in their conformations suggested that they had enemies; the wariness, that among these enemies was man; the speed and agility, that swift and ferocious carnivores preyed upon them.

These observations served to warn me that I must be constantly on the alert for similar dangers that might threaten me, and I was glad that the tableland was well supplied with trees growing at convenient intervals. I had not forgotten the ferocious basto that Kamlot and I had encountered in Vepaja, and, though I had seen nothing quite so formidable as yet among the nearer beasts, there were some creatures grazing at a considerable distance from me whose lines suggested a too great similarity to those bisonlike omnivores to insure ease of mind.

I moved rather rapidly, as I was beset by fears for Duare's safety and felt that if I did not come upon some clue this first day my search might prove fruitless. The klangan, I believed, must have alighted near the coast, where they would have remained at least until daylight, and my hope was that they might have tarried longer. If they had winged away immediately, my chances of locating them were slight; and now my only hope lay in the slender possibility that I might come across them before they took up their flight for the day.

The tableland was cut by gullies and ravines running down to the sea. Nearly all of these carried streams varying in size from tiny rivulets to those which might he dignified by the appellation of river, but none that I encountered offered any serious obstacle to my advance, though upon one or two occasions I was forced to swim the deeper channels. If these rivers were inhabited by dangerous reptiles, I saw nothing of them, though I admit that they were constantly on my mind as I made my way from bank to bank.

Once, upon the tableland, I saw a large, catlike creature at a distance, apparently stalking a herd of what appeared to be a species of antelope; but either it did not see me or was more interested in its natural prey, for although I was in plain sight, it paid no attention to me.

Shortly thereafter I dropped into a small gully, and when I had regained the higher ground upon the opposite side the beast was no longer in sight; but even had it been, it would have been driven from my thoughts by faint sounds that came to me out of the distance far ahead. There were what sounded like the shouts of men and the unmistakable hum of Amtorian pistol fire.

Though I searched diligently with my eyes to the far horizon, I could see no sign of the authors of these noises; but it was enough for me to know that there were human beings ahead and that there was fighting there. Being only human, I naturally pictured the woman I loved in the

center of overwhelming dangers, even though my better judgment told
me that the encounter reverberating in the distance might have no connection with her or her abductors.

Reason aside, however, I broke into a run; and as I advanced the sounds
waxed louder. They led me finally to the rim of a considerable canyon, the
bottom of which formed a level valley of entrancing loveliness, through
which wound a river far larger than any I had yet encountered.

But neither the beauty of the valley nor the magnitude of the river held
my attention for but an instant. Down there upon the floor of that nameless canyon was a scene that gripped my undivided interest and left me
cold with apprehension. Partially protected by an outcropping of rock at
the river's edge, six figures crouched or lay. Five of them were klangan, the
sixth a woman. It was Duare!

Facing them, hiding behind trees and rocks, were a dozen hairy, manlike
creatures hurling rocks from slings at the beleaguered six or loosing crude
arrows from still cruder bows. The savages and the klangan were hurling
taunts and insults at one another, as well as missiles; it was these sounds
that I had heard from a distance blending with the staccato hum of the
klangan's pistols.

Three of the klangan lay motionless upon the turf behind their barrier,
apparently dead. The remaining klangan and Duare crouched with pistols
in their hands, defending their position and their lives. The savages cast
their stone missiles directly at the three whenever one of them showed any
part of his body above the rocky breastwork, but the arrows they discharged
into the air so that they fell behind the barrier.

Scattered about among the trees and behind rocks were the bodies of
fully a dozen hairy savages who had fallen before the fire of the klangan,
but, while Duare's defenders had taken heavy toll of the enemy, the outcome
of the unequal battle could have been only the total destruction of the
klangan and Duare had it lasted much longer.

The details which have taken long in the telling I took in at a single
glance, nor did I waste precious time in pondering the best course of
action. At any moment one of those crude arrows might pierce the girl I
loved; and so my first thought was to divert the attention of the savages,
and perhaps their fire, from their intended victims to me.

I was slightly behind their position, which gave me an advantage, as
also did the fact that I was above them. Yelling like a wild man, I leaped

down the steep side of the canyon, firing my pistol as I charged. Instantly the scene below me changed. The savages, taken partially from the rear and unexpectedly menaced by a new enemy, leaped to their feet in momentary bewilderment; and simultaneously the two remaining klangan, recognizing me and realizing that succor was at hand, sprang from the shelter of their barrier and ran forward to complete the demoralization of the savages.

Together we shot down six of the enemy before the rest finally turned and fled, but they were not routed before one of the klangan was struck full between the eyes by a jagged bit of rock. I saw him fall, and when we were no longer menaced by a foe I went to him, thinking that he was only stunned; but at that time I had no conception of the force with which these primitive, apelike men cast the missiles from their slings. The fellow's skull was crushed, and a portion of the missile had punctured his brain. He was quite dead when I reached him.

Then I hastened to Duare. She was standing with a pistol in her hand, tired and disheveled, but otherwise apparently little worse for the harrowing experiences through which she had passed. I think that she was glad to see me, for she certainly must have preferred me to the hairy apemen from which I had been instrumental in rescuing her; yet a trace of fear was reflected in her eyes, as though she were not quite sure of the nature of the treatment she might expect from me. To my shame, her fears were justified by my past behavior; but I was determined that she should never again have cause to complain of me. I would win her confidence and trust, hoping that love might follow in their wake.

There was no light of welcome in her eyes as I approached her, and that hurt me more than I can express. Her countenance reflected more a pathetic resignation to whatever new trials my presence might portend.

"You have not been harmed?" I asked. "You are all right?"

"Quite," she replied. Her eyes passed beyond me, searching the summit of the canyon wall down which I had charged upon the savages. "Where are the others?" she asked in puzzled and slightly troubled tones.

"What others?" I inquired.

"Those who came with you from the *Sofal* to search for me."

"There were no others; I am quite alone."

Her countenance assumed an even deeper gloom at this announcement. "Why did you come alone?" she asked fearfully.

"To be honest with you, it was through no fault of my own that I came at all at this time," I explained. "After we missed you from the *Sofal*, I gave orders to stand by off the coast until the storm abated and we could land a searching party. Immediately thereafter I was swept overboard, a most fortunate circumstance as it turned out; and naturally when I found myself safely ashore my first thought was of you. I was searching for you when I heard the shouts of the savages and the sound of pistol fire."

"You came in time to save me from them," she said, "but for what? What are you going to do with me now?"

"I am going to take you to the coast as quickly as possible," I replied, "and there we will signal the *Sofal*. She will send a boat to take us off."

Duare appeared slightly relieved at this recital of my plans. "You will win the undying gratitude of the jong, my father, if you return me to Vepaja unharmed," she said.

"To have served his daughter shall be reward enough for me," I replied, "even though I succeed in winning not even her gratitude."

"That you already have for what you have just done at the risk of your life," she assured me, and there was more graciousness in her voice than before.

"What became of Vilor and Moosko?" I asked.

Her lip curled in scorn. "When the kloonobargan attacked us, they fled."

"Where did they go?" I asked.

"They swam the river and ran away in that direction." She pointed toward the east.

"Why did the klangan not desert you also?"

"They were told to protect me. They know little else than to obey their superiors, and, too, they like to fight. Having little intelligence and no imagination, they are splendid fighters."

"I cannot understand why they did not fly away from danger and take you with them when they saw that defeat was certain. That would have insured the safety of all."

"By the time they were assured of that, it was too late," she explained. "They could not have risen from behind our protection without being destroyed by the missiles of the kloonobargan."

This word, by way of parenthesis, is an interesting example of the derivation of an Amtorian substantive. Broadly, it means savages; literally, it means hairy men. In the singular, it is nobargan. *Gan* is man; *bar* is hair. *No* is a contraction of *not* (with), and is used as a prefix with the same value that the suffix *y* has in English; therefore *nobar* means hairy, *nobargan*, hairy man. The prefix *kloo* forms the plural, and we have *kloonobargan* (hairy men), savages.

After determining that the four klangan were dead, Duare, the remaining angan, and I started down the river toward the ocean. On the way Duare told me what had occurred on board the *Sofal* the preceding night, and I discovered that it had been almost precisely as Gamfor had pictured it.

"What was their object in taking you with them?" I asked.

"Vilor wanted me," she replied.

"And Moosko merely wished to escape?"

"Yes. He thought that he would be killed when the ship reached Vepaja."

"How did they expect to survive in a wild country like this?" I asked. "Did they know where they were?"

"They said that they thought that the country was Noobol," she replied, "but they were not positive. The Thorans have agents in Noobol who are fomenting discord in an attempt to overthrow the government. There are several of these in a city on the coast, and it was Moosko's intention to search for this city, where he was certain that he would find friends who would be able to arrange transportation for himself, Vilor, and me to Thora."

We walked on in silence for some time. I was just ahead of Duare, and the angan brought up the rear. He was crestfallen and dejected. His head and tail feathers drooped. The klangan are ordinarily so vociferous that this preternatural silence attracted my attention, and, thinking that he might have been injured in the fight, I questioned him.

"I was not wounded, my captain," he replied.

"Then what is the matter with you? Are you sad because of the deaths of your comrades?"

"It is not that," he replied; "there are plenty more where they came from. It is because of my own death that I am sad."

"But you are not dead!"

"I shall be soon," he averred.

"What makes you think so?" I demanded.

"When I return to the ship, they will kill me for what I did last night.

If I do not return, I shall be killed here. No one could live alone for long in such a country as this."

"If you serve me well and obey me, you will not be killed if we succeed in reaching the *Sofal* again," I assured him.

At that he brightened perceptibly. "I shall serve you well and obey you, my captain," he promised, and presently he was smiling and singing again as though he had not a single care in the world and there was no such thing as death.

On several occasions, when I had glanced back at my companions, I had discovered Duare's eyes upon me, and in each instance she had turned them away quickly, as though I had surprised and embarrassed her in some questionable act. I had spoken to her only when necessary, for I had determined to atone for my previous conduct by maintaining a purely official attitude toward her that would reassure her and give her no cause for apprehension as to my intentions.

This was a difficult role for me to play while I yearned to take her into my arms and tell her again of the great love that was consuming me; but I had succeeded so far in controlling myself and saw no reason to believe that I should not be able to continue to do so, at least as long as Duare continued to give me no encouragement. The very idea that she might give me encouragement caused me to smile in spite of myself.

Presently, much to my surprise, she said, "You are very quiet. What is the matter?"

It was the first time that Duare had ever opened a conversation with me or given me any reason to believe that I existed for her as a personality; I might have been a clod of earth or a piece of furniture, for all the interest she had seemed to take in me since those two occasions upon which I had surprised her as she watched me from the concealing foliage of her garden.

"There is nothing the matter with me," I assured her. "I am only concerned with your welfare and the necessity for getting you back to the *Sofal* as quickly as possible."

"You do not talk any more," she complained. "Formerly, when I saw you, you used to talk a great deal."

"Probably altogether too much," I admitted, "but you see, now I am trying not to annoy you."

Her eyes fell to the ground. "It would not annoy me," she said almost inaudibly, but now that I was invited to do the very thing that I had been longing to do, I became dumb; I could think of nothing to say. "You see," she continued in her normal voice, "conditions are very different now from any that I have ever before encountered. The rules and restrictions under which I have lived among my own people cannot, I now realize, be expected to apply to situations so unusual or to people and places so foreign to those whose lives they were intended to govern.

"I have been thinking a great deal about many things—and you. I commenced to think these strange thoughts after I saw you the first time in the garden at Kooaad. I have thought that perhaps it might be nice to talk to other men than those I am permitted to see in the house of my father, the jong. I became tired of talking to these same men and to my women, but custom had made a slave and a coward of me. I did not dare do the things I most wished to do. I always wanted to talk to you, and now for the brief time before we shall be again aboard the *Sofal*, where I must again be governed by the laws of Vepaja, I am going to be free; I am going to do what I wish; I am going to talk to you."

This naive declaration revealed a new Duare, one in the presence of whom it was going to be most difficult to maintain an austere Platonicism; yet I continued to steel myself to the carrying out of my resolve.

"Why do you not talk to me?" she demanded when I made no immediate comment on her confession.

"I do not know what to talk about," I admitted, "unless I talk about the one thing that is uppermost in my mind."

She was silent for a moment, her brows knit in thought, and then she asked with seeming innocence, "What is that?"

"Love," I said, looking into her eyes.

Her lids dropped and her lips trembled. "No!" she exclaimed. "We must not talk of that; it is wrong; it is wicked."

"Is love wicked on Amtor?" I asked.

"No, no; I do not mean that," she hastened to deny; "but it is wrong to speak to me of love until after I am twenty."

"May I then, Duare?" I asked.

She shook her head, a little sadly I thought. "No, not even then," she answered. "You may never speak to me of love, without sinning, nor may I listen without sinning, for I am the daughter of a jong."

"Perhaps it would be safer were we not to talk at all," I said glumly.

"Oh, yes, let us talk," she begged. "Tell me about the strange world you are supposed to come from."

To amuse her, I did as she requested; and walking beside her I devoured her with my eyes until at last we came to the ocean. Far out I saw the *Sofal*, and now came the necessity for devising a scheme by which we might signal her.

On either side of the canyon, through which the river emptied into the ocean, were lofty cliffs. That on the west side, and nearer us, was the higher, and to this I made my way, accompanied by Duare and the angan. The ascent was steep, and most of the way I found it, or made it, necessary to assist Duare, so that often I had my arm about her as I half carried her upward.

At first I feared that she might object to this close contact; but she did not, and in some places where it was quite level and she needed no help, though I still kept my arm about her, she did not draw away nor seem to resent the familiarity.

At the summit of the cliff I hastily gathered dead wood and leaves with the assistance of the angan, and presently we had a signal fire sending a smoke column into the air. The wind had abated, and the smoke rose far above the cliff before it was dissipated. I was positive that it would be seen aboard the *Sofal*, but whether it would be correctly interpreted, I could not know.

A high sea was still running that would have precluded the landing of a small boat, but we had the angan, and if the *Sofal* were to draw in more closely to shore, he could easily transport us to her deck one at a time. However, I hesitated to risk Duare in the attempt while the ship was at its present considerable distance from shore, as what wind there was would have been directly in the face of the angan.

From the summit of this cliff we could overlook the cliff on the east side of the canyon, and presently the angan called my attention to something in that direction. "Men are coming," he said.

I saw them immediately, but they were still too far away for me to be able to identify them, though even at a distance I was sure that they were not of the same race as the savages which had attacked Duare and the klangan.

Now indeed it became imperative that we attract the attention of the *Sofal* immediately, and to that end I built two more fires at intervals from the first, so that it might be obvious to anyone aboard the ship that this was in fact a signal rather than an accidental fire or a campfire.

Whether or not the *Sofal* had seen our signal, it was evident that the party of men approaching must have; and I could not but believe that, attracted by it, they were coming to investigate. Constantly they were drawing nearer, and as the minutes passed we saw that they were armed men of the same race as the Vepajans.

They were still some distance away when we saw the *Sofal* change her course and point her bow toward shore. Our signal had been seen, and our comrades were coming to investigate; but would they be in time? For us it was a thrilling race. The wind had sprung up again and the sea was rising once more. I asked the angan if he could breast the gale, for I had determined to send Duare off at once if I received a favorable reply.

"I could alone," he said, "but I doubt that I could if I were carrying another."

We watched the *Sofal* plunging and wallowing in the rising sea as it forged steadily closer, and we watched the men drawing near with equal certainty. There was no doubt in my mind as to which would reach us first; my only hope now was that the *Sofal* could lessen the distance in the meantime sufficiently so that it would be safe for the angan to attempt to carry Duare to her.

Now the men had reached the summit of the cliff on the opposite side of the canyon, and here they halted and observed us while carrying on a discussion of some nature.

"Vilor is with them!" exclaimed Duare suddenly.

"And Moosko," I added. "I see them both now."

"What shall we do?" cried Duare. "Oh, they must not get me again!"

"They shall not," I promised her.

Down the canyon side they came now. We watched them swim the river and cross to the foot of the cliff where we were standing. We watched the *Sofal* creeping slowly shoreward. I went to the edge of the cliff and looked down upon the ascending men. They were halfway up now. Then I returned to Duare and the angan.

"We can wait no longer," I said, and then to the angan, "Take the janjong and fly to the ship. She is closer now; you can make it; you *must* make it!"

He started to obey, but Duare drew away from him. "I will not go," she said quietly. "I will not leave you here alone!"

For those words I would gladly have laid down my life. Here again was still another Duare. I had expected nothing like this, for I did not feel that she owed me any such loyalty. It was not as though she had loved me; one might expect such self-sacrifice on the part of a woman for the man she loves. I was swept completely from my feet, but only for an instant. The enemy, if such it were, must by now be almost to the summit of the cliff, in a moment they would be upon us, and even as the thought touched my mind, I saw the first of them running toward us.

"Take her!" I cried to the angan. "There is no time to waste now."

He reached for her, but she attempted to elude him; and then I caught her, and as I touched her, all my good resolutions were swept away, as I felt her in my arms. I pressed her to me for an instant; I kissed her, and then I gave her over to the birdman.

"Hurry!" I cried. "They come!"

Spreading his powerful wings, he rose from the ground, while Duare stretched her hands toward me. "Do not send me away from you, Carson! Do not send me away! I love you!"

But it was too late; I would not have called her back could I have done so, for the armed men were upon me.

Thus I went into captivity in the land of Noobol, an adventure that is no part of this story; but I went with the knowledge that the woman I loved, loved me, and I was happy.

EDGAR RICE BURROUGHS: MASTER OF ADVENTURE

The creator of the immortal characters Tarzan of the Apes and John Carter of Mars, EDGAR RICE BURROUGHS is one of the world's most popular authors. Mr. Burroughs' timeless tales of heroes and heroines transport readers from the jungles of Africa and the dead sea bottoms of Barsoom to the miles-high forests of Amtor and the savage inner world of Pellucidar, and even to alien civilizations beyond the farthest star. Mr. Burroughs' books are estimated to have sold hundreds of millions of copies, and they have spawned 60 films and 250 television episodes.

About Edgar Rice Burroughs, Inc.

Founded in 1923 by Edgar Rice Burroughs, one of the first authors to incorporate himself, EDGAR RICE BURROUGHS, INC., holds numerous trademarks and the rights to all literary works of the author still protected by copyright, including stories of Tarzan of the Apes and John Carter of Mars. The company oversees authorized adaptations of his literary works in film, television, radio, publishing, theatrical stage productions, licensing, and merchandising. Edgar Rice Burroughs, Inc., continues to manage and license the vast archive of Mr. Burroughs' literary works, fictional characters, and corresponding artworks that has grown for over a century. The company is still owned by the Burroughs family and remains headquartered in Tarzana, California, the town named after the Tarzana Ranch Mr. Burroughs purchased there in 1919 that led to the town's future development.

In 2015, under the leadership of President James Sullos, the company relaunched its publishing division, which was founded by Mr. Burroughs in 1931. With the publication of new authorized editions of Mr. Burroughs' works and brand-new novels and stories by today's talented authors, the company continues its long tradition of bringing tales of wonder and imagination featuring the Master of Adventure's many iconic characters and exotic worlds to an eager reading public.

Visit **EdgarRiceBurroughs.com** for more information.

EDGAR RICE BURROUGHS AUTHORIZED LIBRARY™

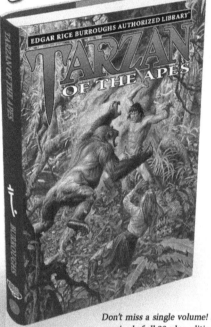

COLLECT EVERY VOLUME!

For the first time ever, the Edgar Rice Burroughs Authorized Library presents the complete literary works of the Master of Adventure in handsome uniform editions. Published by the company founded by Burroughs himself in 1923, each volume of the Authorized Library is packed with extras and rarities not to be found in any other edition. From cover art and frontispieces by legendary artist Joe Jusko to forewords and afterwords by today's authorities and luminaries to a treasure trove of bonus materials mined from the company's extensive archives in Tarzana, California, the Edgar Rice Burroughs Authorized Library will take you on a journey of wonder and imagination you will never forget.

Don't miss a single volume! Sign up for email updates at ERBurroughs.com to keep apprised of all 80-plus editions of the Authorized Library as they become available.

TARZAN OF THE APES · THE RETURN OF TARZAN · THE BEASTS OF TARZAN · THE SON OF TARZAN · TARZAN AND THE JEWELS OF OPAR · JUNGLE TALES OF TARZAN · TARZAN THE UNTAMED · TARZAN THE TERRIBLE · TARZAN AND THE GOLDEN LION · TARZAN AND THE ANT MEN · TARZAN, LORD OF THE JUNGLE · TARZAN AND THE LOST EMPIRE · TARZAN AT THE EARTH'S CORE · TARZAN THE INVINCIBLE · TARZAN TRIUMPHANT · TARZAN AND THE CITY OF GOLD · TARZAN AND THE LION MEN · TARZAN AND THE LEOPARD MEN · TARZAN'S QUEST · TARZAN THE MAGNIFICENT · TARZAN AND THE FORBIDDEN CITY · TARZAN AND THE FOREIGN LEGION · TARZAN AND THE MADMAN

BURROUGHS

1 2 3 4 5 6 7 8 9 10 11 12 13 14 15 16 17 18 19 20 21 22 23

THE JOURNEY BEGINS AT ERBURROUGHS.COM

THE FIRST COMIC BOOK ADVENTURES EVER PUBLISHED BY EDGAR RICE BURROUGHS, INC.!

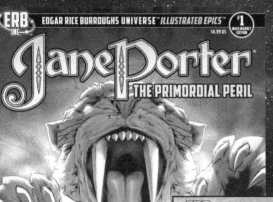

JANE PORTER®: THE PRIMORDIAL PERIL

32-PAGE, FULL-COLOR COMIC BOOK

WRITTEN BY
MIKE WOLFER

ART BY
ROY ALLAN MARTINEZ

JANE PORTER® AND THE CITY OF FIRE

74-PAGE, FULL-COLOR GRAPHIC NOVEL

WRITTEN BY
MIKE WOLFER

ART BY
MIRIANA PUGLIA

EDGAR RICE BURROUGHS UNIVERSE™ ILLUSTRATED EPICS™

ERB INC.

AVAILABLE EXCLUSIVELY FROM ERBURROUGHS.COM

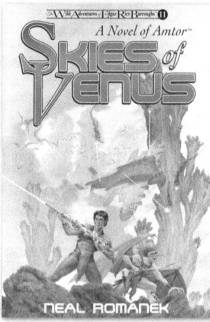

Edgar Rice Burroughs, Inc.

A whole universe of ERB collectibles, including books, T-shirts, DVDs, statues, puzzles, playing cards, dust jackets, art prints, and MORE!

Your one-stop destination for all things ERB!

VISIT US ONLINE AT ERBURROUGHS.COM

Printed in the USA
CPSIA information can be obtained
at www.ICGtesting.com
LVHW090711030724
784134LV00004B/17/J